THE
SKYBOUND
SEA

THE AEONS' GATE BOOK THREE

SAM SYKES

an imprint of **Prometheus Books**
Amherst, NY

Published 2012 by Pyr®, an imprint of Prometheus Books

Cover illustration copyright © Paul Young
Cover design by Grace M. Conti-Zilsberger

Inquiries should be addressed to
Pyr
59 John Glenn Drive
Amherst, New York 14228–2119
VOICE: 716–691–0133
FAX: 716–691–0137
WWW.PYRSF.COM

16 15 14 13 12   5 4 3 2 1

Library of Congress Cataloging-in-Publication Data

Sykes, Sam.
    The skybound sea / by Sam Sykes.
        p. cm. — (The Aeons' Gate ; bk. 3)
    ISBN 978–1–61614–676–4 (pbk.)
    ISBN 978–1–61614–677–1 (ebook)
    1. Human-alien encounters. 2. Extraterrestrial beings—Fiction. I. Title.

PS3619.Y545S59 2012
813'.6—dc23
                                                                    2012018454

Printed in the United States of America

ACKNOWLEDGMENTS

The end of a trilogy comes with a lot of feelings. If you can simultaneously eat a slice of pizza while hitting your pinky finger as hard as you can with a hammer, you'll have a pretty good grasp of what they are. And like the two books that have come before it, none of this would have happened without a few key people.

Most notably, my editors, Simon Spanton and Lou Anders, were of amazing help in getting this produced. As was my agent, Danny Baror, who was probably the most important part. And no slouch at all were my gurus: Matt "Skunk Ape" Hayduke, John "Hot Mess" Henes, and Carl Emmanuel "The Dangling Participle" Cohen.

But most importantly, I'd like to thank you, the reader. If you've been with me this far, I can guarantee everything is only going to get more intense from here. But it's far too late to back out now.

You and me, baby. We're going down this road.

Together.

ACT ONE

THE BEAST'S
MANY NAMES

PROLOGUE

The Aeons' Gate
Island of Teji
The Beginning of Fall

No matter what god he believes in, a man is not entitled to much in life.

The Gods gave him breath. Then they gave him needs. Then they stopped giving. Society affords him only a few extra luxuries: the desire for gold and the demand to spend it.

And the choices he has for himself are even more limited. If he lives well, he gets to choose to die. If he doesn't, he gets to choose to kill. And the men who kill are small men with small pleasures.

The Gods have no love for those who don't kill in Their name. Society loathes a man who doesn't fight under a banner. A small man doesn't get to choose who or how or when or why he kills.

But sometimes he gets lucky.

And then he gets to sit behind Gevrauch's desk and see what the Bookkeeper sees. He sees how they die.

I've never considered myself a lucky man until now.

I've made poor choices.

I chose to accept the job posed to me: to guard the priest that guarded the book that opens heaven and hell. I chose to follow the book when it was stolen by those who would use it to open the latter.

I chose to kill for this book.

I am an adventurer, after all. No god, no banner.

And for the Gods and for society, I killed to retrieve the book and keep the Undergates closed that the misbegotten servants of the Gods, the Aeons, might be kept shut tight in the bowels of the earth.

Most of what happened next was out of my hands.

We retrieved the tome from the demons from a floating tomb and set out to return to civilization and claim our reward. I suppose I could be blamed for thinking that things would be somehow simpler with a manuscript used to open up hell in my possession.

But that's beside the point.

We were shipwrecked upon a graveyard masquerading as an island. Teji: the battlefield where Aeons rebelled against heaven, where the seas rose to swallow the world, and where mortals fought to preserve the dominion of the Gods. Teji was born in death, killed in battle, and we found more of both there.

The island became a new battlefront, one that raged among three armies. All of which had equally strong desires to kill us. Some men are just popular.

The Abysmyths, the aforementioned demons, came searching for the tome, hoping to use it to return their hell-bound mother to an earth she could drown alive.

They—and we—found the netherlings instead. No one knows where they came from or what they are beyond four major qualities they share: they are led by a sadist calling himself Sheraptus, they are mostly women, they are purple, and they want everyone, demon and mortal, dead.

It might seem a bit gratuitous to add a race of tattooed, bloodthirsty lizardmen to the mix, but like I said, out of my hands. And they added themselves to a growing list of people eager to kill over this book.

Anyone reading this might be sensing a pattern developing.

And still, we escaped them all. We found sanctuary with the natives of Teji: the Owauku and the Gonwa. More lizardmen, though these ones at least had a king. I suppose that made them more trustworthy than the ones that wanted to chop off our heads. We were welcomed with open arms. We were feasted, celebrated. I was offered an opportunity, a decision. I took it.

I gave up.

The tome had been lost in the shipwreck. I chose to let it stay lost. I chose to turn around, return empty-handed but for a sword I dearly wanted to put away. I wanted to be a man who didn't have to kill. I wanted to be a man who had a life.

A life with my companions.

Former companions, excuse me.

I made my choice. I was denied. And we were betrayed.

Togu, their king, had his reasons for handing us over to the netherlings, bound and helpless. Those are irrelevant. His reasons for finding the tome and delivering it to them are likewise meaningless. What matters is that they came for us, led by Sheraptus, and took the tome. He took the women. He left the rest of us to die.

We didn't.

He had taken Asper, though. He had taken Kataria. At the time, I couldn't bear that thought. At the time, I couldn't let that happen. I should have. I know that now.

But then, I made another choice.

We came to rescue them. Bralston, an agent of the Venarium that had been tracking Sheraptus, aided us with an impromptu arrival. And together, we fought.

When the netherlings came, I killed them. When the demons came after them, I killed them. I fought to save my companions. I fought to save Kataria. I fought to protect them, protect our new life together.

I chose again.

I was betrayed again.

They abandoned me. To the netherlings' blades and the demons' claws, they abandoned me. *Gariath leapt overboard. Denaos took Asper away. Dreadaeleon fled with Bralston.*

Kataria looked into my eyes as I was about to die.

Kataria turned away.

I survived. Because of something inside me, something I used to be afraid of, I survived. The Shen, the demons, the netherlings, my own companions . . . I survived them all. I will continue to do so.

And I will be the only one left.

On Teji, I found something. Ice that spoke. Ice that had a memory. It talked to me of betrayals and liars and killers. And I listened.

That thing inside me. I can hear it clearly now. It tells me the truth. Tells me how we will survive. I wonder why I never listened to it before. But now it makes so much sense. Now I know.

Everyone must die.

Starting with my betrayers.

Denaos and Asper are at odds with each other. That's never been anything to note since they returned from Sheraptus's ship and their obnoxious quarrels became silent ones. She does not pray. He does not stop drinking.

Dreadaeleon does, though. He looks to them with envy, as though he resents not being a part of that frigid silence. When he is not doing that, he wallows in self-pity. He keeps company with Bralston. I have heard him pleading with the agent, begging him for petty things that I don't care about.

We thought Gariath lost to us in the shipwreck. He is the one that caused it, after all, the one who had always been eager to die. When we found him alive, I thought it a sign that we were meant to return to a normal life. But now he speaks of the Shen, our enemies, in almost reverent tones. Fitting. Obvious. Clear.

And Kataria . . .

Maybe it's my fault. Maybe I wanted too much. Maybe I wanted it badly enough to overlook the fact that she was a shict and I was a race she was sworn to slaughter. Maybe.

But she betrayed me. Like the others. She has to die. First. Slowly.

. . . or so I think.

It gets hard to think sometimes. It's hard to remember what that night was like. I never asked her why she abandoned me. I never asked her why she was speaking with a greenshict, those killers of men.

She has her reasons . . . right?

But are they good? If I asked her, maybe she'd tell me. Maybe we could still do this.

Sometimes, I think about it.

Then the voice starts screaming.

9

The Shen took the tome and fled to their island home of Jaga. We follow them there. The demons will, too, and the netherlings. I'll kill them all.

This is what we were meant to do.

This is why we live.

We kill.

They die.

Our choice.

Our plan is to go to Jaga. Our plan is to find the tome, to keep it out of the hands of the Shen and everyone else. The island is far away. The way is treacherous. That doesn't matter.

The traitors are coming with me.

I'm going to bury them there.

ONE

MANKIND

He awoke from the nightmares and said it.

"Hanth."

He rose, slipped a dirty and threadbare robe over his body and wore nothing else. He stared at his hands, mortal soft and human frail.

"Hanth."

He left a small hovel, one of many. He walked with a person, one of many, down to the harbor. Carried over their heads, passed along by his hands, he watched a corpse slide from their grasp, into the bay, and disappear under the depths. A short prayer. A short funeral.

One of many.

"Hanth."

His name was Hanth.

He knew this after only three repetitions.

Three days ago, it took twenty times for him to remember that he was Hanth. Two days ago, it took eleven times to remember that he was not the Mouth. And today, after three repetitions, he remembered everything.

He remembered his father now, sailor and drunk. He remembered his mother, gone when he learned to walk. He remembered the promise he made to the child and wife he didn't know, that Hanth would be there.

He met his wife and child. He kept his promise. Those memories were the ones that hurt, filled him with pain exquisite, like needles driven into flesh thought numb. Exciting. Excruciating.

And they never ended there. The needle slid deeper. He remembered the days when he lost them both. He remembered the day he begged deaf gods and their greedy servants to save his child. He remembered cursing them, cursing the name that could do nothing for them.

He threw away that name.

He heard Ulbecetonth speak to him in the darkness.

He became the Mouth.

"Hanth."

That was his name now. The memories would not go. He didn't want them to go. Mother Deep meant nothing.

So, too, did her commands. So, too, did the fealty he once swore to her.

He remembered that, too. The sound of a beating heart would not let him forget.

In the distance, so far away as to have come from another life, he could hear it. Its beat was singular and steady; a foot tapping impatiently. He turned and looked to the lonely temple at the edge of Port Yonder, the decrepit church standing upon a sandy cliff. The people left it there for the goddess they honored.

The people knew nothing. They did not know what the wars had left imprisoned in that temple.

And as long as he lived, they never would.

He had once agreed to make them know. He had agreed to bring Daga-Mer back. The Mouth had agreed to that.

He was Hanth.

Daga-Mer would wait forever.

He turned his back on the Father now, as he had turned his back on his former life, and turned his attentions to the harbor.

Another body. Another splash.

One of many since the longfaces attacked.

What they had come for, no one knew. Even though the Mouth had once been their enemy, Hanth knew nothing of their motives, why they had come to Yonder, why they had slaughtered countless people, why they burned the city, why they had attacked the temple and done nothing more than shattered a statue and left.

He knew only that they *had* done these things. The bodies, indiscriminately butchered, lay as evidence amongst half the city that was now reduced to ashen skeletons.

His concerns were no longer for them, but for the dead and for the people who carried them, bodies in one hand and sacrifices in the other as they moved in slow lines to the harbor.

One procession bowed their heads for a moment, then turned away and left. Another came to take their place at the edge of the docks. Another would follow them. By nightfall, the first procession would be back.

"Not going to join in?"

He turned, saw the girl with the bushy black hair and the broad grin against her dusky skin that had not diminished in the slightest, even if her hands were darkened with dried blood and she reeked of death and ashes.

"Kasla."

He never had to repeat her name.

She glanced past his shoulder to the funerary processions. "Is it that you're choosing to stand away from them or did they choose for you?" Upon his perplexed look, she sighed. "They don't speak well of you, Hanth. After all you've done for us, after you helped distribute food and organize the arrangements, they still don't trust you."

He said nothing. He didn't blame them. He didn't care.

"Might be because of your skin," she said, holding her arm out and comparing it to his. "No one's going to believe you once lived here when you look like a pimple on someone's tanned ass."

"It's not that," he replied.

She sighed. "No, it's not. You don't pray with them, Hanth. They want to appreciate you. They want to see you as someone sent from Zamanthras, to guide them."

He stared at her, unmoved.

"And that's kind of hard to do when you spit on Her name," Kasla sighed. "Couldn't you just humor them?"

"I could," he said.

"Then why don't you?"

He regarded her with more coldness than he intended and spoke.

"Because they would hold their child's lifeless body in their hands and beg for Zamanthras to bring her back," he said, "and when no one would deign to step from heaven to do anything, they would know me a liar. People can hate me if they want. I will do what the Gods can't and help them anyway."

It was harder to turn away from her than it was to turn away from anything, from everything else. It was harder to hear the pain in her voice than it was to hear the heartbeat of a demon.

"Then how," she asked softly, "will you ever call this city home?"

He closed his eyes, sighed. She was angry. She was disappointed in him. He used to know how to handle this.

He looked, instead, to the distant warehouse, the largest building seated not far away from the temple. It, too, was a prison, though of a more common nature. It held a captive of flesh and blood behind a heavy door. Its prisoner's heart beat with a sound that could not reach Hanth's ears.

"Rashodd," he said the name. "He did not try to escape?"

"He didn't, no. Algi watches his cell now." He could sense the question before she asked it. "How did you know his name?"

"He's a Cragsman," Hanth replied, evading it less than skillfully. "A shallow intellect and all the savagery and cunning of a bear. If we've two more men to spare, then put them both on watch with Algi."

"That's difficult," she said. "Everyone not busy with the dead are busy with the dying. We've still got the sick to think about."

Hanth had been avoiding the problem and the ill alike, never once coming close to the run-down building that had been used to house them. He could handle the dead. He could quell unrest. He could not handle illness.

Not without remembering his daughter.

And yet, it was a problem to handle, one whose origins were not even agreed upon. Plague and bad fish were blamed at first, but the disease lingered. More began to speak of poison, delivered from the hands of shicts ever dedicated to ending humanity. Whispers, rumors; both likely wrong, but requiring attention.

One more problem that he would have to face, along with the dead, along with dwindling resources, along with the prisoner Rashodd, along with Daga-Mer, along with the fact that he had once entered this city with the intent of ending it. He would tell them and they would hate him, someday.

Kasla . . .

He would never tell her.

She would never hate him.

He cast his gaze skyward. Clouds roiled, darkened. Thunder rumbled, echoed. A lone seagull circled overhead, soundless against the churning skies.

"Rain?" Kasla asked.

"Water," he replied. *One problem alleviated, at least.*

Yet the promise of more water did not cause him the relief it should have, not so long as his eyes remained fixed upon the seagull.

"That's odd," she said, following his gaze. "It's flying in such tight circles. I've never seen a gull move so . . ."

Unnaturally, he thought, dread rising in his craw. *Gulls don't.*

His fears mounted with every moment, every silent flutter of feathers, even before he could behold the thing fully. He swallowed hard as it came down, flapping its wings as it plopped upon two yellow feet and ruffled its feathers, turning two vast eyes upon him.

He heard Kasla gasp as she stared into its face. He had no breath left for such a thing.

"What in the name of . . ." Words and Gods failed her. "What *is* it?"

He did not tell her. He had hoped to never tell her.

But the Omen stared back at him.

From feet to neck, it was a squat gull. Past that, it was a nightmare: a withered face, sagging flesh, and hooked nose disguising female features that barely qualified as such. Its teeth, little yellow needles, chattered as it stared at them both with tremendous white orbs, a gaze too vast to be capable of focusing on anything.

It was not the monstrosity's gaze that caused his blood to freeze, not when it tilted its head back, opened its mouth, and spoke.

"*He's loose*," a man's voice, barely a notch above a boy's, and terrified, echoed in its jaws. "*Sweet Mother, he's loose! Get back! Get back in your cell! Someone! ANYONE! HELP!*"

"That's . . . that's Algi's voice," Kasla gasped, eyes wide and trembling. "How is . . . what's going—"

"*Zamanthras help me, Zamanthras help me,*" Algi's voice echoed through the Omen's mouth. "*Please don't . . . no, you don't have to do this. Please! Don't! PLEASE!*"

"Hanth . . . what . . ." Kasla's voice brimmed with confusion and sorrow as her eyes brimmed with tears.

"In oblivion, salvation," a dozen voices answered her. "In obedience, salvation. In acceptance, salvation. In defiance . . ."

He looked up. Seated across the roof of a building like a choir, a dozen sets of vast eyes stared back, a dozen jaws of yellow needles chattered in unison and, as one dreadful voice, spoke.

"*Damnation.*"

"What are they, Hanth?" Kasla was crying. "What *are* they?"

"Hide," he told her, taking steps backward. "Run. Get everyone as far away from here as you can."

"There are boats, we could—"

"Stay on dry land! Stay out of the water! Tell them to leave the dead and the sick."

"What? We can't just leave them here to—"

No finish to the plea. No beginning to an answer. He was running.

People cast scowls at his back, shouted at him as he rudely shoved through their processions, cursed his blasphemies. That was easy to ignore. Kasla called after him, begged him to come back. That was not.

They could despise him. He would still save them. He would try.

Thunder clashed overhead, an echoing boom that shook his bones. He glanced up. The clouds swirled swiftly as if stirred in a cauldron. At their center, a dark eye of darker calm formed.

Directly over the temple. It followed the heartbeat.

"*He wears the storm as a crown.*"

He charged through the city streets, toward the warehouse turned into a prison. He would have prayed that its charge was still there. He would have prayed that the Omen was nothing more than a sick joke from a spiteful beast. He would have, if he thought any god still had ears for him.

He rounded a corner and the warehouse loomed before him. Its doors had been shattered. Algi, young and scrawny, stood against the doorframe, his legs dangling beneath him as his own spear pinned him to the wood through his chest. Algi's eyes, wide and white, were staring at Hanth with the same fear Hanth knew would be reflected a hundred times over if he didn't act fast.

A thick drop of rain fell upon his brow. It trickled down, sickly and hot, sticky and odorous to dangle in front of his eye. Red.

"The skies bleed for him."

He was sprinting now, heart pounding in his chest as he made for the temple. The trail was marked, through streets and over sands, by immense footprints painted in blood.

Hanth could barely remember fear, but it was coming back swiftly. Overhead, thunder roared, lightning painted the skies a brilliant white for a moment. And for a moment, in shadows, he saw them, a hundred wings flapping, a hundred gazes turned to the city.

And its people.

He ran faster.

The temple doors were smashed open, the bar that had held them fast lay shattered on the ground. Darkness loomed within, the loneliness that only came from a god neglected. He charged in.

The temple was dark inside, darker than it was the last time he had been here. Dominating the center was the pool twenty men across. The waters were calm, placid, not a ripple to them.

Despite the thunderous heartbeat pulsing from beneath them.

Hanth stared at the water, wincing. The beating heart was almost unbearable here, an agony to listen to as its pulse quickened, blood raced with anticipation. Yet he forced himself to stare at it.

"Their jealous waters hold him prisoner."

And then, to the tower of tattooed flesh and graying hair that stood at its edge.

"They call you Hanth, now, do they?"

Rashodd's smile would have been repellent even if not for the hideous scarring of his face. Still, his half-missing nose, the crimson scab where an ear had once been, and his wiry beard certainly didn't make him any more pleasant to look upon.

"When last I saw you, they called you the Mouth of Ulbecetonth and I called you ally." He gestured to his face. "And this is what came of that."

Still, Hanth found it easier to overlook both the Cragsman's imposing musculature and his disfigurement when he spied the man's great arm extended over the pool, a hand missing three fingers precariously clutching a dark vial containing darker liquid.

The only remaining mortal memory of the demon queen herself, the only thing capable of penetrating the smothering waters and calling Daga-Mer to a world that had long since forgotten him.

And as Hanth's ears filled with the thunder of a heart beating, he knew he was not the only one to recognize it.

"I hid that for a reason."

Hanth's words and his tentative step forward were both halted by the precarious tremble of Rashodd's maimed hand.

"I found it," the Cragsman replied. "For a different one."

"Why?"

"Can you truly be so dull, sir?" Rashodd asked. "That I am here suggests that I am charged with doing that which you cannot." His eye twitched, his smile grew hysterical at the edge. "I've heard Her voice, Mouth. I've heard Her song. And it was beautiful."

"I am here, too, Rashodd," Hanth said, recalling delicateness. "I heard her song. I heard her voice." He stepped forward, remembering caution. "And because I am here, I tell you that whatever she has promised you is nothing. Whatever she offers is meaningless, whatever she demands is too much."

"You forsook Her," Rashodd whispered, watching him evenly. His hand stood mercifully still, the vial clenched in his fingers. "You turned your back on all that was promised to you. The Prophet told me."

"The Prophet is her lie," Hanth said, taking another step forward. "They tell you only what you wish to hear. They can't offer you what you truly wish."

"They offered me everything," Rashodd said, his eyes going to the floor. "My face . . . my fingers . . ." He brushed a mutilated hand against a scarred visage. "And the man who did this to me." His gaze snapped up with such suddenness to make Hanth pause midstep. "And you . . . they told me they offered you much more."

"They offered me nothing I wanted," Hanth replied.

"They offered you a release from pain," Rashodd whispered, "so much pain."

"Pain that I need. Pain that I need to be my daughter's father, pain that I need to exist."

The Cragsman's scarred face twitched, his head shook. It was as though he heard Hanth's voice through one ear and was assaulted by another, inaudible voice through the scab that had once been the other.

"Need pain . . . to exist," Rashodd muttered. "But that doesn't . . . what could that—"

Hanth recognized the indecision, the torment upon the man's mutilated features. He had felt it enough times to recognize that whatever other unheard voice was speaking to Rashodd louder and more convincingly.

So when Rashodd's eyes drifted to the floor, Hanth's drifted to the vial, and he made ready to leap.

"Hanth."

He froze when Rashodd looked up. He felt his blood go cold at the tears brimming in the man's eyes. Tears belonged on people who flinched and felt pain and knew sin. Hanth knew enough of the Cragsman's deeds to know that tears on him were a mockery.

"You've suffered so much," Rashodd whispered.

"And I would prevent more," Hanth said, his eyes never leaving the vial.

"I suppose I've been terribly selfish, haven't I?" The Cragsman chuckled lightly. "I thought She could give me everything I wanted, everything I needed."

"I once thought the same, too."

"You did."

The gaze he fixed upon Hanth was bright, hopeful, and horrifying.

"And that's why I have to do this."

Fingers twitched.

"For both of us."

And Hanth screamed.

It was a formless noise, impossible of conveying anything beyond the very immediate sense that something had gone very wrong. It was long. It was loud. It, along with his lunge, were completely incapable of stopping the vial from falling out of Rashodd's maimed fingers.

Into the waters, where it landed without a ripple.

Hanth hit the floor, his hand still outstretched, his mouth still open. He could not see Rashodd, focused only on the air that the vial had once occupied. He could not hear Rashodd, focused only on the sound of a heartbeat steadily growing fainter.

The time between each fading beat stretched into an agonized eternity, until finally, it stopped altogether—and Hanth's with it.

It began, first, as a pinprick: a faint crimson barely visible amidst the darkness of the water. Hanth could only stare, watching it grow with each breath he took, watching it grow with each rising sound of the beating heart. Soon, it was the size of a fist, then a head, then a man.

When the hellish red glow consumed the field entirely, the water began to churn. The red became consumed, devoured by a black shadow that rose from beneath. A shape colossal rose swiftly to the surface, split it apart.

A great hand, webbed and black and tall as a man, burst from the water and set itself down upon the water's edge, stone rent beneath its long claws.

Rashodd was saying something, laughing, crying maybe. Hanth didn't hear it. Hanth didn't hear him scream when he disappeared beneath another black claw. The heartbeat was thunder, the groan that came from below was the sound of ships breaking, tides flowing, earth drowning.

Daga-Mer was free. The sky wailed and shed tears.

And through the storm, sea, and stone, Hanth could hear but one thing. He heard Kasla's scream. And at that, he was on his feet.

"*I prayed for a better way, Hanth.*" There was a macabre tranquility in Rashodd's voice as the Cragsman called from the deep. "*Heaven gave no answer.*"

No time for Rashodd. No time for Daga-Mer or the ominous creak of the temple's roof or the thunderous roar of water as another arm pulled free of the pool.

The sky bled. Thunder roared. The world ended around him. But he could still save a small part of it.

He prayed he could.

He sprinted out of the temple doors into Yonder's streets. Hell greeted him.

Their songs were wretched to hear, their plump bodies sitting in rows innumerable upon the roofs of houses. Their gazes, bright and bulbous and countless like stars, were turned upon the city streets. The Omens sang.

"Salvation comes," they lilted in dire unison. "Shackles rust. Fires cease to burn. The blind shall still hear and the deaf shall still see. She comes for you. Rejoice!"

Their chants chased fat globs of red falling from the sky even while a tide of wailing terror rose up from the throngs of people choking the streets below.

The chaos was not yet terrible enough to blind him to the sight of his former followers, those he had led as the Mouth. The frogmen slinked through the crowd in thick veins of white, hairless skin. Eyes black as the storm overhead and as pitiless, they waded through the crowds, knives aloft and webbed hands grabbing.

There was wailing. There was shrieking. There was begging and pleading and prayers to gods that couldn't hear them over the thunder. The Omens sang and the frogmen gurgled and the blood continued to fall from the sky. Hanth could but cry out and hope to be heard.

"*Kasla!*"

The roof of the temple cracked behind him. A howl, centuries old and leagues deep, rang out from a hollow heart. Hanth threw himself into the crowd.

"*Kasla!*"

At every turn was he met with flesh and fear: the people whom had to be shoved past, the frogmen that had to be knocked over. The former clung to him and begged him for help, accused him for bringing this down upon them. The latter would take them, webbed hands sliding into mouths, groping throats, hauling them into the dark, their screams drowning.

And he ignored them all.

"*Kasla!*"

She would never hear him. He clung to her name to block out the terror. He clung to her name to remind himself of who had to walk away from this when the city was dead and its people sang songs in the deep.

He spied a gap in the crowd, an exposed mouth of an alley. He seized the opportunity, slipping through the chaos and into the darkness without knowing where he was going. Stopping was not an option. If he stopped, he would think and he would know the odds of finding Kasla alive.

But he had to think. Not long, not hard, just enough to consider.

Sound was smothered in the gloom, but the terror was as thick as the red on the streets. He could but hear his own breath and those screams so desperate as to reach the dark.

"Kasla?" he called out.

"Here . . ." a voice answered.

Hers? A woman's, certainly . . . wasn't it? He followed it, regardless. He could not afford to think what else it might be.

"Come on, then," the voice spoke again. A woman's, certainly. "It's safe out here. I promise." He strained to hear it, so soft and weak. "Yes, I know it can be scary. But I'll take care of you, all right?"

"Kasla?"

"Yes," she whispered back. "Yes, I'm sure. Yes, I'm *really* sure. Remember the promise I made you when your father left?"

What was she talking about?

"I promised you I'd never let anything hurt you like that again. I haven't, have I?"

He rounded the corner and saw the sea lapping at the streets. The wall here had decayed and crumbled away, the alley ending where the ocean began. He saw the woman who was not Kasla, kneeling with her hands extended, her face painted with blood, her tears shining.

Lightning flashed soundlessly overhead.

And he saw the creature looming over her.

It rose on a pillar of coiled gray flesh, a macabre flower that blossomed into an emaciated torso, withered breasts dangling from visible ribs. A spindly neck gave way to a bloated head and black, void-like eyes. A fleshy stalk dangled from its brow, the tip of it pulsating with a blue light that would have been pleasant had it not illuminated so clearly the woman.

"*Thisisthewaytherightwaytheonlyway . . .*"

The whispers rose from a pair of womanly lips, twitching delicately within a pair of skeletal, fishlike jaws. They were meant for the woman. It was Hanth's curse that he could hear them, too.

"*Somuchsufferingsomuchpainandwhocomestohelpyouwhowhowho . . .*"

"So much pain," the woman sobbed. "Why would Zamanthras let him be born into such a world?"

"*Noonewilltellyounooneanswersnogodslistennoonecaresnooneevercares . . .*"

"I hear a voice. I hear Her."

"No," Hanth whispered, taking a tentative step forward.

"*MotherDeepknowsyourpainfeelsyourpainknowsyourpromise . . .*"

"I promised . . ." the woman said to the darkness.

"*Keephimsafeneverlethimfeelpaineverythingissafedownbelowendlessblueaworldofendlessblueforyouandyourchild . . .*"

"Child," he said.

He caught sight of the boy, crawling out from under his hiding place. He ran to his mother's blood-covered arms.

"That's right," she said through the tears. "Come to me, darling. We'll end this all together." She collected him up in her arms, stroked his sticky hair and laid a kiss upon his forehead. "Father's down there. You'll see."

She turned toward the ocean.

"Everything we've ever wanted . . . is down below."

"*NO!*"

He screamed. It was lost in the storm.

So, too, was the sound of two bodies, large and small, striking the water and slipping beneath the waves, leaving nothing more than ripples.

The creature turned to him. The blue light illuminated the frown of one of its mouths, the perverse joy of the other.

"*Couldhavesavedthemcouldhavestoppedthiscouldhavegonemucheasier . . .*" It whispered to him and only to him. "*Yourfaultyourfaultyourfault . . .*"

The beast lowered itself to the ground, hauled itself to the edge of the water on two thin limbs.

"*BetrayedHerabandonedHerforsookHerafterallShepromised . . .*"

It looked at him. He saw his horror reflected in its obsidian eyes. It spoke, without whispers. And he heard its true voice, thick and choking.

"But She will not abandon you, Mouth."

He saw the creature disappearing only in glimpses: a gray tail slipped beneath the water, azure light winked out in the gloom.

And he was left with but ripples.

His back buckled, struck with the sudden despair that only now had caught up with him. Realization upon horrifying realization was heaped upon him and he fell to his knees.

Hanth would die here.

Daga-Mer had risen. The faithful ran rampant throughout Yonder, a tide of flesh and song that would drown the world. Ulbecetonth would speak to that world and find ears ready to listen, ready to believe that everything they wanted lay beneath the sea. His family was dead.

Kasla was gone.

He remembered despair clearly.

"No . . ."

Denial, too.

He clambered to his feet. Hanth would die soon, but not yet.

Where? Where could she have gone? She had said something, hadn't she? Before he left, she had said . . . what was it? Something about them, not leaving *them*. Who were they?

The sick. The wounded. She would have tried to find them. Because she was the person he would run through hell to find.

He slipped through the alleys, found himself back on the streets. The tides of panic had relented, the people vanished. Those who hadn't been hauled away lay trampled in the streets.

He could not help them now. He walked slowly, wary of any of frogmen that might lurk in the shadows. It only took a few steps to realize the folly of that particular plan. If any frogmen came for him, they would be aware of him long before he was of them.

The Omens, lining the rooftops in rows of unblinking eyes, would see to that.

"Denial is a sin," they chanted, their voices echoing each other down the line. "The faithful deny nothing. The penitent denies heaven. The heathen denies everything."

Empty words to those who knew the Omens. Risen from the congealed hatred that followed demons and the faithful alike, they were merely parasites feeding and regurgitating the angst and woe their demonic hosts sowed in quantity. Without anything resembling a genuine thought, they could say nothing he could care to hear.

"She's going to die, Mouth."

Or so he thought.

He looked, wide-eyed, up at the dozens of chattering mouths, all chanting a different thing at him.

"She's going to die."

"You're going to watch it."

"She's going to suffer, Mouth."

"Sacrifices must be made."

"Promises must be kept."

"You could have stopped this."

And he was running again, as much to escape as to find Kasla. Their voices welled like tides behind him.

"Why do you deny Mother Deep?"

"You could have saved her."

"This is how it must be, Mouth."

"Mother Deep won't deny you."

"She's going to cry out, Mouth."

"All because of you."

Ignore them, he told himself. *They're nothing. You find her. You find her and everything will be fine. You're going to die. They're going to kill you for what you've done. But she'll live and everything will be fine.*

It was the kind of logic that could only make sense to the kind of man who ran through hell.

He carried that logic with him as he would a holy symbol as he found the decrepit building. He carried that logic with him through the door and into it.

Before they had taken to housing the wounded here, it had been a warehouse: decaying, decrepit, stagnant. When it was filled with the sick and the dying, it had been no cheerier. The air had hung thick with ragged breaths, gasps brimming with poison, groans of agony.

But it was only when Hanth found the room still and soundless that he despaired.

In long lines, the sick lay upon cots against the wall, motionless in the dark. No more moaning. No more pain. Lightning flashed, briefly illuminating faces that had been twisted earlier that morning. A sheen, glistening like gossamer, lay over faces that were now tranquil with a peace they would have never known before.

His eyelid twitched. He caught the stirring of shadows.

"Hanth?"

And he saw Kasla. Standing between the rows of beds, she stared into a darkness that grew into an abyss at the end of the room, like blood congealing in the dead. He laid a hand upon her and felt the tremble of her body.

"We have to go," he said firmly.

"The city . . ."

"It's not ours anymore." He tugged on her shoulder. "Kasla, come."

"I can't, Hanth." Her voice was choked. "It won't let me."

He didn't have to ask. He stared into the shadows. He saw it, too.

There was movement: faint, barely noticeable. He would have missed it entirely if he didn't know what lurked in that darkness. Even if he couldn't see the great, fishlike head, he knew it turned to face him. Even if he couldn't see the wide, white eyes, he knew they watched him.

But the teeth he could see. There was no darkness deep enough.

"Child," its voice was the gurgling cries of drowning men. "You return to us."

It was instinct that drove Hanth to step protectively in front of Kasla, old instinct he strove to forget once. Logic certainly didn't have anything to do with it; he knew what lurked in that shadow.

"And where are your tears?" the Abysmyth asked. "Where is your joy for the impending salvation?" It swept its vast eyes to the dead people lining the walls. "Ah. The scent of death may linger. It should not trouble you. They are free from the torments their gods saw fit to deliver to them."

The demon moved. A long arm, jointed in four places, extended from the shadows. Viscous gossamer ooze dripped from its webbed talons.

"They were cured," it said, "of many things at once."

"Keep them," Hanth said. "Keep the dead. Keep the living. The girl and I will leave."

"Leave?" The Abysmyth's head swung back and forth contemplatively. "To what, child? Do you think me so compassionless as to you let you run to a deaf and lightless eternity? To cast you from bliss?"

"I will keep my burdens."

"What does a lamb know of burden? What does it know beyond its pasture? There is more to life. Mother will show you."

It shifted. It rose. A painfully emaciated body, a skeleton wrapped in ebon skin, rose up. Its head scraped the ceiling. Its eyes were vast and vacant as they looked down upon Hanth.

"Mother will not abandon any of her children."

He heard a scream die in Kasla's throat and leak out of her mouth as a breathless gasp. Hanth met the demon's gaze.

"Ulbecetonth is gone," he said flatly. "And she's gone for a reason."

He began to step backward, forcing Kasla to move with him toward the door.

"She can have her endless blue. You and the rest of your faithful can join her. One hell's as good as another."

The demon merely stared. Its eyes were dead, unreadable. Hanth held his breath as he continued to back away with Kasla.

"You don't belong here," he said, "and neither does your bitch of a mother."

The moment the demon lunged forward, he suspected he might have gone too far.

A great black fist emerged from the darkness and smashed upon the floor in a splintering crater. The demon's head followed, a great fish skull, skin black as the shadows from which it came. It trembled to show the fury its dead eyes could not.

"*You're wrong!*" it gurgled. "We belong here! We *do!* It was you who drove us out! You who rejected us!" It pulled the rest of its body out of the shadows, tall and thin and quaking. "We offer you *everything* and you deny us still! Call us monsters, call us beasts, call Mother a . . . a . . ."

Its voice became a formless roar as it burst out of the shadows, sprinting forward on long, skeletal legs. Hanth seized Kasla's hand. Without a word, he hauled her toward the door, as fast as fear would carry them.

"*You don't even care!*" it bellowed after them. "*You don't even care! Look at what you're doing! You'll ruin everything!*"

They burst out the door, fled down the wet, sticky streets. The Abysmyth's voice chased them.

"*He comes! You'll see! You'll see we're right!*"

The roads were thick with stale fear and moisture. The heavens roiled and bled like a living thing. The city was bereft of humanity, but not life.

The frogmen came out in tides, pouring out of every alley mouth, leaping off of every roof, bursting from every doorway. Hanth swept his eyes about for escape and wherever they settled another emerged. They ran from reaching hands and needle-filled mouths.

Every egress was blocked by pale, hairless flesh. Every movement monitored and met with a shrieking chorus from the Omens flying overhead. Every word he tried to shout to her was lost in the whispers that rose from the waters beyond and sank into his skull.

"*Can'tfleecan'tfleecan'tflee . . .*"

"*Nogodsnoprayersnoblasphemynothingnothingnothing . . .*"

"*Hecomeshecomeshecomes . . .*"

And then, all noise from nature and demon alike, went silent before the sound.

A heartbeat. Like thunder.

A great tremor shook the city, sent them falling to their knees. There was the sound of rock dying and water wailing and skies screaming. Hanth tried to rise, tried to pull her up, tried to tell her she would survive, tried not to look to the temple.

25

He failed.

Cracks veined the domed roof, growing wider and wider until they shattered completely. Fragments of stone burst and fell as hail. A shadow blacker than night arose to kiss the bleeding heavens. The creature turned; a pulsating red light at the center of its chest beat slowly.

Water peeled from its titanic body, mingling with the red rain. With each tremor of its heart, roads of glowing red were mapped across its black flesh. It groaned, long and loud, as it rested its titanic claws upon the shattered rim of the temple's roof. Its head lolled, eyes burned, jaws gaped open wide.

Daga-Mer, alive and free, turned to heaven.

And howled.

TWO

IN THE GRISTLE

Beneath Lenk's feet, a world turned slowly. Not his world.

That world was back on dry land, back where the dawn was rising and people still slept in dread of the moment they would have to open their eyes. That world was full of traitors and fire and people who walked around pretending he had no reason to kill them.

That world was where he had slept for the last two nights with the sound of a voice in his head, a voice that whispered plots and told him he had no choice but to kill those people. That world was where he had fallen asleep last night.

He suspected he might be dreaming, still.

That would explain why he was standing on the water like it were dry land.

That world swirled beneath him. He had watched it all night. When he should have been dreaming of flames and betrayal and his hands wrapped around a slender throat beneath wide green eyes, when he should have been hearing something whisper in his head, something telling him those eyes would see nothing.

He had been staring at fish.

Beneath his feet, they stirred as the morning returned color to that world. Coral rose in bright and vivid stains. A fish came out, something drab and gray with bulging eyes and clumsy fins. If it were possible to waddle underwater, it would have done so, clumsily navigating over the coral that seemed all the bleaker for its presence.

It drew too close to a shadowy nook within the coral. A serpentine eel shot out, eyes glassy even as it rent the fish with narrow jaws. It gobbled up what it could before slinking back into its lair, leaving a few white chunks to drift up to the surface and bump against the soles of Lenk's boots.

In an instant, he had seen hope, betrayal, and death. Fitting.

"How do you figure?" something responded to his thoughts.

A voice rose up from the water, something cold and distant. He didn't blink; voices in his head were nothing new. This was not the cold and distant voice he knew, though. This was less of a cold blade sunk into his skull and more like a clammy hand on his shoulder.

"As near as I understand," he said, "every day for a fish begins with them rising out of the water to go scavenge for food."

"*Is that hope or necessity?*"

"Little difference."

"*Agreed. Continue.*"

"Thus, to go out when one expects to find food and instead finding death . . ."

"*Betrayal?*"

"That was my thinking."

"*Counterpoint.*"

"Go ahead."

"*If one could even argue a fish is aware enough of its own existence to feel hope, one might think it wouldn't feel a great deal of hope by going into a world infested by things that are much bigger and nastier than itself with the slim chance of finding enough food to avoid dying of starvation and instead dying of eels.*"

"That's betrayal."

"*That's nature.*"

"I disagree."

"*Go right ahead.*"

"I would, but . . ." He rubbed his temples. "Kataria usually tells me about these things. I'm sure if I talked it over with her—" That thought was cut off by a frigid, wordless whisper. "Look, what's your point?"

"*Hope is circumstantial. Betrayal, too.*"

He stared down into the water, blinked once.

"I'm insane."

"*You think you are.*"

"I'm having a conversation with a body of water." He furrowed his brow contemplatively. "For the . . . fifth time, I think?" He looked thoughtful. "Though this is only the fourth time it's talked back, so I've got that going, at least."

"*It's only insanity if the water isn't telling you anything. Is this not a productive conversation for you?*"

"To be honest?"

"*Please.*"

"Even if I could get past the whole 'standing *on* the ocean talking *to* the ocean' . . . thing," he said, "I've had enough conversations with voices rising from nowhere to know that this probably won't end well. So just tell me to kill, make some ominous musings, and I'll be on my way to kill my friends."

"Friends?"

"Former friends, sorry."

"Former?"

"Is that how I sound when I repeat everything? The others were right, that is annoying."

"There's no hate in your voice when you speak of them. You don't sound like a man who wants to kill his friends, former or no."

He didn't listen to himself often, but he was certain he had spoken with conviction last night before he went to sleep. The conversation with another voice in his head—the one cold and clear as the night—had seemed so certain. They went over their plans together, again and again: find Jaga, find the tome, kill everyone in their way, kill the people who had betrayed them.

Betrayed them . . . or betrayed him? It was harder to remember now what they had spoken of last night. But his *had* been a voice full of certainty, full of justice and hatred and nightmare logic.

Unless that hadn't been his voice.

A chill crept up his spine, became a frigid hand at the base of his skull. It gripped with icy fingers, sending a spike of pain through his body that did not relent until he shut his eyes tightly.

And when he opened them again, the world was on fire.

He was back on a ship full of fire and of enemies that lay dead on the deck, except for the one that held him by the throat and pressed a knife down into his shoulder. He was back in his world and he was going to die.

And she was there. Short and slender, her green eyes wild and feathers in her hair. There was a bow in her hands and a hand around his throat and a blade in his shoulder and an arrow on the string and blood. Blood and fire. Everywhere. And she did nothing.

He was going to die and she was going to do nothing.

That wasn't how it ended. He hadn't died back then. Someone else knew that, but not him and not in this world. In this world, something else happened. He ignored the hand around his throat and the knife in his shoulder. He got to his feet and she was watching and she was screaming and her throat was in his hands and it felt like ice. And he started to squeeze.

That hadn't happened, either.

He opened his eyes. That world was gone. The water was back and talking to him.

"*Ah,*" it said, "*I see.*"

"You don't," he replied. "You don't have eyes. You don't have a face."

"I can fix that."

The water stirred underneath. There was someone looking at him from the floor of the sea. A woman, not a pretty one. Her face was hard angles and her hair was white. Her chin was too sharp and her cheekbones were too hard. Her eyes were too blue.

But it was a face.

"*Better now?*"

"You're all the way down there," he said. "How do I—"

And suddenly, he did. The water gave out beneath him and he was floating down, upside down. He could breathe. That wasn't too alarming; this *was* the fifth time. That which should not be possible was only impressive when it was not possible. When it was not impossible, then it was not possible to be impressed.

He came to a halt, bobbing in the water as he looked into her face. She was smiling at him with a face that shouldn't ever smile. Their eyes met and they stared. He asked, finally.

"So," he said, "am I dreaming, insane, or dead?"

"Oh, Lenk," she said, "you know you never have to choose."

He had memorized the length of one knucklebone.

He used that to count down his hands. Three knucklebones across, six knucklebones down. Eighteen knucklebones, in total; possibly a few extra accounting for inaccuracy of the thumbs. If he counted the back of his hands, double that. His hands were as wide and long as thirty-six knucklebones in total.

He had dainty hands. That bothered him.

But all Dreadaeleon could think about as he stared at his dainty, disappointing hands was how much paper would be made out of his skin when he was dead.

It didn't take long for the trembling to set in, the surge of electricity coursing beneath his skin. Three breaths before blue sparks began to dance across his fingertips. Three breaths today. It had been six breaths yesterday.

Getting worse, he thought. *Can't be too much longer now. How much do you figure? A month? Two? How does the Decay work, again? It begins with the flaming urine, ends with the trembles? Or was it something else? Reversal of internal and external organs? Probably. Dead with your rectum in your mouth. That'd be just your luck, old man. Still, better that you'll be leaving soon so she doesn't have to see you—*

"Well?"

"What?" he blurted out suddenly at the sound of the woman's voice. He grabbed his hand by the wrist and forced it out of sight.

Asper looked at him flatly. She pointed to the corpse on the table.

"I know *she* can wait forever, but I can't." She gestured with her chin. "Are you ready for this?"

He glanced down at his lap and took stock of his tools. Charcoal, parchment; he nodded.

"Are you?"

She glanced down at her table and took stock of her tools. Cloth, water, scalpel, bonesaw, crank-drill, needle, a knife that once made a man soil himself in fear; he blanched as she nodded.

"And how about you?" He followed her gaze up to the wall of the hut, to the dark man in a dark coat.

Bralston hadn't moved from that spot—arms crossed over his broad chest, brows furrowed, completely silent—in half an hour. He didn't seem to think Asper's inquiry worthy of breaking that record over. His sole movement was a brief nod and twitch of the lips.

"Proceed."

Clearly less than enthused with the command, she nonetheless looked to Dreadaeleon. "Here we go, then. Note the subject." She looked down at the corpse. "What do we call this, anyway?"

It was female. It was also naked. Beyond that, the creature was rather hard to classify. It had two legs, two hands, all knotted with thick muscle under purple skin. Its three-fingered hands, broad as a man's, were clenched tight in rigor. Its face was hardly feminine, far too long and clenched like its fists. Its eyes, without pupil or iris, had refused to close in death.

"A netherling," Dreadaeleon said. "That's what they call themselves."

"Yeah, but necropsy subjects are usually categorized by their scholarly names in old Talanic," she said. "This is . . ." She gestured helplessly over the corpse. "New."

"True, they haven't really been discovered yet, have they?" Dreadaeleon tapped the charcoal to his chin, quirking a brow. "Except by us. We could call it something slightly more scholarly." He stared down at his paper thoughtfully. "How do you say 'head-stomping bloodthirsty she-beast' in old Talanic?"

"The subject shall be known as 'Heretic,'" Bralston said simply. "The Venarium will make proper notation when I deliver the report."

She fixed him with an unyielding stare. "Others interested in medicine might want to know what we discover."

Dreadaeleon cringed preemptively. As a Librarian of the Venarium, Bralston was the penultimate secretive station to an organization whose standard reply to requests for the sharing of information typically fell under a category marked "crimes against humanity *and* nature." And as a much meagerer member of the same organization, Dreadaeleon could but wince at Bralston's impending reaction.

He felt more foolish than surprised when Bralston merely sighed.

"Netherling will do for the moment," he said.

He was still surprised, though he suspected he ought not be. Bralston, curt to the point of insult, seemed to have a patience for Asper that Dreadaeleon found deeply confusing.

And unnerving, he thought as he noted the smile Bralston cast toward her.

"Proceed," he said gently. "Please."

Dreadaeleon took a bit more pleasure than he suspected he should have in Asper's lack of a returned smile. She didn't smile much at all lately, not since that night on the ship. She barely said anything, either. Only after the necropsy was requested did she even deign to say two words to him.

Another thing he took pleasure in. Another thing to be ashamed of. Later, though.

"Fine," she said, turning back to the corpse. "Netherling." She took up the scalpel between two fingers. "Incision one."

Amongst the various descriptors she used for necropsy, "easy" wasn't one of them. The scalpel did not so much bite seamlessly into the netherling's cold flesh as chew through it, the incision requiring both hands and more than a little sawing to cut open. When it was finally done, her brow glistened along with the innards.

"First note," she grunted, setting the scalpel aside, "she's made out of jerked meat."

"Subject displays remarkable resilience of flesh," Dreadaeleon muttered, scribbling.

"Now what the hell was wrong with what I said?" Asper snapped.

He blinked. "It . . . uh . . ."

"Oh, good. Write that down instead." She glowered at him for a moment before turning it to the opened corpse. "There's so much muscle here." Her incisions were less than precise as she cut through the sinew. "Organs appear intact and normal, if slightly enlarged." She prodded about the creature's innards with the scalpel. "No sign of rotting. Intestine is shorter than that of a human's."

"Carnivorous," Bralston observed. "All of this suggests a predatory bent."

"Possibly," Asper said, nodding sagely, "that conclusion *would* be supported by their teeth and the fact that they've tried to *kill us several times already.* Of course they're predatory, you half-wit."

Dreadaeleon swallowed hard, looking wide-eyed to the Librarian. Bralston's face remained a dark, expressionless mask. He nodded as easy as he might have if she had asked if he had wanted tea. Preferable to a gesture that preceded incineration, but the boy couldn't help but be baffled at his superior's seeming obliviousness to the priestess's attitude.

"Continue, then," he said.

Asper, too, seemed taken aback by this. Though her disbelief lasted only as long as it took her to pick up the bonesaw.

"Her ribcage is . . . thick," she said, applying the serrated edge to the bone. After three grinding saws, she took the tool in both hands. "*Really* thick. This is like cutting metal."

"It can't be that hard," Dreadaeleon said. "I've seen Gariath break their bones before."

"Really?" Asper said without looking up. "A hulking, four-hundred pound monstrosity can break metal? I feel as though your intellect may be wasted on simply taking notes."

At that, Dreadaeleon did more than merely cringe. "Look, I don't know what I did to upset you, but—"

"Continue, please," Bralston interrupted. His words were directed at Asper, though his glare he affixed to Dreadaeleon.

"But I—" the boy began to protest.

"*Continue.*"

"Fine," the word was muttered both by Asper and Dreadaeleon at the same time.

It took a few more moments of sickening sawing sounds before Asper finally removed the bonesaw, more than a few teeth broken off its blade. Dreadaeleon did not consider himself a squeamish man; having cooked people alive with his hands and a word tended to preclude such a thing. Yet there was something about this necropsy, of the many he had witnessed, that made him uneasy.

The priestess's hands were soaked and glistening a dark red. She hadn't requested any gloves and snapped at him when he had suggested it. She used only a damp cloth to clean up, and barely at that. When she mopped her brow, red stains were left behind and she continued, heedless, as she plucked up the pliers.

Of course, he thought, perhaps it weren't the operation that made him cringe so much as the operator. He had never seen her like this, never heard her like this. Her pendant, the phoenix of her patron god Talanas, was missing from her throat; a rare sight grown more common of late.

What happened to you on that ship?

And he might have asked, if he weren't silenced by the deafening crack of a ribcage being split apart.

"Huh," she said, brows lofting in curiosity. "That's interesting." She reached inside, prodding something within the corpse with her scalpel.

"What is it?" Bralston said.

33

"This thing has two hearts."

Dreadaeleon's face screwed up. "That's impossible."

"You're right, I'm lying about that." She rolled her eyes. "Come up and see for yourself."

It was more a dare than anything else, if her tone was any indication, and Dreadaeleon half considered not taking it. But he rejected that; he couldn't back down in front of her. Perhaps she was challenging him, personally. Perhaps whatever plagued her now, he could fix. She knew that, and he knew that he couldn't do that if he backed down.

So he rose and he walked over to the corpse and he instantly regretted doing so.

The dead netherling met his gaze, her white eyes still filled with hate so long after being dragged lifeless out of the ocean. He swallowed hard as he looked down to the creature's open ribcage. Amidst the mass of thick veins and—Asper hadn't been lying—muscle everywhere, he saw the organs: a large, fist-shaped muscle and a smaller, less developed one hanging beside it.

"So . . ." He furrowed his brow, trying to force himself not to look away. "What does that mean?"

"It could be one of many possibilities," Bralston suggested. "Perhaps it was something specific needed for wherever they come from. Past necropsies of creatures from harsh environments have revealed special adaptations."

"Perhaps," Asper said, "or perhaps she's just a mass of ugly muscle and hate so big that she needed a second heart, like I assumed in the beginning."

"Funny," Dreadaeleon said.

"What is?" she asked.

"I don't know, I would have thought you'd enjoy this." He looked up at her and saw her blank expression. He coughed, offering a weak smile. "I mean, you always showed an interest in physiology. It's something that your church teaches you, right? When we were beginning, when we first met up with Lenk, he would always have us, you and I that is, cut up whatever animal we killed to see if we could get anything edible. Remember?"

She stared at him flatly.

"A necessity of being adventurers out of work, of course," he said, "but you and I would always spend time investigating the carcass, detailing everything. It was our thing, you know? We were the ones that cut it up. We were the ones that catalogued it. If our findings before didn't get us noticed, I'm sure this—" he gestured to the netherling, "—would. So . . ." He shrugged. "I guess maybe I just thought of this as old times. Better times."

When he looked back at her, her expression was no longer blank. Something stirred behind her gaze. He felt his pulse race.

Steady, old man, he cautioned himself. *She might break down any moment now. She's going to break down and fall weeping into your arms and you'll hold her tightly and find out what plagues her. I hope Bralston knows to leave the room. Any moment now. What is that in her eyes, anyway? Better know so you can be prepared. Sorrow? Pain? Desire?*

"You," she whispered harshly, "stupid little *roach.*"

Possibly not desire.

"What?" he asked.

"*Those* were your better times for us? Up to my elbows in fat and blood while you scribbled away notes on livers and kidneys? *That's* what you think of when you think of us?"

"I was just—"

"You were just being freakish and weird, as usual," she snarled. "Is there *anything* about you that *doesn't* make one's skin crawl?"

He reeled as if struck. He hadn't quite expected that. Nor did he really expect to say what he said next.

"Yes," he said calmly, "I've been told my ability to keep silent around the ignorant and mentally deficient is quite admirable."

"I find that hard to believe, as I've never actually seen you be silent."

"No? Well, let me refresh your memory." His voice was sharp and cold, like a blade. "Whenever you've prayed to deities that don't exist, whenever you've blamed something on the will of your gods that *you* could have helped, whenever you've prattled on about heavens and morals and all this other garbage you don't actually believe for any reason other than to convince your toddler-with-fever-delirium-equivalent brain that you're in *any* way superior to *any* of the people you choose to share company with," he spat the last words, "I've. Said. *Nothing.*"

And so, too, did she say nothing.

No threats. No retorts. No tears. She turned around, calmly walked past Bralston and left the hut, hands smeared with blood, brow smeared with blood, leaving a room full of silence.

Bralston stared at the door before looking back to Dreadaeleon.

"You disappoint me, concomitant," he said simply.

"*Good,*" Dreadaeleon spat back. "I'll start a running tally. By the end of the day, I hope to have *everyone* dumber than me loathing me. I'll throw a party to celebrate it."

"One might call your intelligence into question, acting the way you do."

"One might, if one were a lack-witted imbecile. You saw the way she was talking to me, talking to *you.*"

"I did."

"And you said nothing."

"Possibly because my experience with women extends past necropsies," Bralston said smoothly. "Concomitant, your ire is understandable, but not an excuse for losing your temper. A member of the Venarium is, above all else, in control of his abilities and himself."

Dreadaeleon flashed a black, humorless smile at the man. "You are just hilarious."

"And why is that?"

Dreadaeleon replied by holding up his hand. Three breaths. The tremors set in. Bralston nodded. Dreadaeleon did not relent, even when the tremors became worse and the electric sparks began building on his fingers. Bralston glared at him.

"That's enough."

"No, it isn't."

The tremor encompassed his entire arm, electricity crackling and spitting before loosing itself in an erratic web of lightning that raked against the wall of the hut where Bralston had once been. The Librarian, having sidestepped neatly, regarded the wall smoldering with flames. He drew in a sharp breath and exhaled, a white cloud of frost smothering the flames beneath it.

When he looked back up, Dreadaeleon was holding his arm to his chest and gritting his teeth.

"The Decay is getting worse," he said, "at a far more advanced rate than has ever been documented. I *can't* control *anything* about me, least of all my abilities."

"Hence our departure to Cier'Djaal," Bralston replied. "Once we can get you to the Venarium, we can—"

"Do not say cure me."

"I was not going to. There is no cure for the Decay."

"Don't say help me."

"There is little help for it."

"Then why are we going?" Dreadaeleon demanded. "*Why* am I going there for any reason but to die so you can harvest my bones to be made into merroskrit?"

"As you say, you're advancing at a progressed rate. Beyond the harvesting, we could learn from—"

"Let *me* learn from it, instead!" Dreadaeleon all but screamed. "Let *me* try to figure out how this works."

"There is no 'how this works' to the Decay, concomitant."

"This isn't any normal Decay. I felt it strongly days ago, when we were first shipwrecked on Teji. But that night when we swept into Sheraptus's ship, I was . . . the power . . ." His eyes lit up at the memory. "When I was there to save Asper, when I . . . when I *felt* what I did, I could control it. I could do more than control it. My theory holds weight, Librarian. Magic is as much a part of us as emotion, why wouldn't emotions affect our magic?"

"Concomitant . . ." Bralston said with a sigh.

"And with these days? With all the tension between my companions and I?" He shook his arm at Bralston. "With what just happened? It only adds *more* weight to my theory! Emotions affect magic and I can—"

"You can do *nothing* but your duty," Bralston snapped suddenly. His eyes burned against his dark skin. "Your companions are *adventurers*, concomitant: criminals on their best day. *You* are a member of the Venarium. You have no obligations to them beyond what I, as your senior, say you do. And *I* say you are going to *die*, very soon and very painfully.

"And I will *not* watch you languish in their—" he thrust a finger toward the door, "—company. I will not watch you die with no one but criminal scum to look on helplessly as they wait for the last breath to leave you before they can rifle your body and feed it to the sharks." He inhaled deeply, regaining some composure. "Coarse as it may seem, this is protocol for a reason, Dreadaeleon. Whatever else the Venarium might do once the Decay claims your body, we are your people. We know how to take care of you in your final days."

Dreadaeleon said nothing, staring down at his arm. It began to tremble once more. He focused to keep it down.

"When do we leave, then?"

"By the end of today," Bralston replied. "As soon as I conclude business on the island."

"With whom? The Venarium has no sway out in the Reaching Isles."

"The Venarium holds sway anywhere there is a heretic. Even if Sheraptus is gone, we are duty-bound to make certain that none of his taint remains."

"Lenk agrees with you," Dreadaeleon said, sighing. "That's why he's had Denaos on interrogation duty."

"Denaos . . ." Bralston whispered the name more softly than he would whisper death's. "Where is he conducting this . . . interrogation?"

"In another hut at the edge of the village," Dreadaeleon replied. "But he doesn't want to be—"

He looked up. Bralston was gone. And he was alone.

37

THREE

THE ETIQUETTE
OF BLOODSHED

It always seemed to begin with fire.

As it had begun in Steadbrook, that village he once called home that no one had ever heard of and no one ever would. Fire had been there, where it had all begun. Fire was still there, years later, every time Lenk closed his eyes.

It licked at him now as it consumed the barns and houses around him, as it sampled the slow-roasted dead before giving away all pretenses of being civilized and messily devoured skin, cloth, and wood in great red gulps. It belched, cackled at its own crudeness, and reached out to him with sputtering hands. The fire wanted him to join them; in feast or in frolic, it didn't matter.

Lenk was concerned with the dead.

He walked among them, saw faces staring up at him. Man. Woman. Old man's beard charred black and skin crackling. Through smoke-covered mirrors, they looked like him. He didn't remember their names.

He looked up, found that the night sky had moved too fast and the earth was hurrying to keep up. He was far away from Steadbrook now, that world left on another earth smoldered black. Wood was under his feet now, smoldering with the same fire that razed the mast overhead. A ship. A memory.

A different kind of fire.

This one didn't care about him. This fire ate in resentful silence, consuming sail and wood and dying in the water rising up beneath him. Again, Lenk paid no attention. He was again concerned with the faces, the faces that meant something to him.

The faces of the traitors.

Denaos, dark-eyed; Asper, sullen; Dreadaeleon, arrogant; Gariath, inhuman. They loomed out of the fire at him. They didn't ask him if he was hot. He was rather cold, in fact, as cold as the sword that had appeared in his hand. They didn't ask him about that, either. They turned away, one by one. They showed their necks to him.

And he cut them down, one by one, until one face remained.

Kataria.

Green-eyed.

Full of treason.

She didn't show him her neck. He couldn't very well cut her head off when she was looking right at him. His eyes stared into her.

Blue eyes.

Full of hate.

It was his eyes she stared into. It wasn't his hands that wrapped themselves around her throat. It wasn't his voice that said this was right. It wasn't his blood that flowed into his fingers, caused his bones to shiver as they strained to warm themselves in her throat.

But these were his eyes, her eyes. As the world burned down around them and sank into a callous sea, their eyes were full of each other.

He shut his eyes. When he opened them again, he was far below the sea. A fish, bloated and spiny and glassy-eyed stared at him, fins wafting gently as it bobbed up and down in front of him.

"So, anyway," he said, "that's basically how it all happened."

The fish reared back, seeming to take umbrage at his breaking of the tranquil silence. It turned indignantly and sped away, disappearing into the curtains of life emerging from the reef.

"Rude."

"Well, what did you expect?"

He turned and the woman was seated upon a sphere of wrinkled coral. Her head was tilted toward him.

"I am talking and breathing while several feet underwater."

"You don't seem surprised by that," she said.

"This sort of thing happens to me a lot." He tapped his brow. "The voices in my head tend to change things. It didn't seem all that unreasonable that they might make me talk with a fish." He looked at her intently. "You should know all this, shouldn't you?"

"Why would I?"

"Can't you read my thoughts?"

"Not exactly."

"All the other ones have been able to."

"I'm not a voice in your head," she replied.

Amongst everything else in . . . whatever this was, that was the most believable. Her voice came from the water, in the cold current that existed solely between them. It swirled around him, through him, everywhere but within him.

"What are you, then?" he asked.

"I am just like you."

"Not *just* like me."

"Well, no, obviously. I don't want to murder *my* friends."

"You said you couldn't—"

"I didn't, you showed me." She leapt off the coral, scattering a school of red fish as she landed neatly. A cloud of sand rose, drifted away on a current that would not touch her. "And before that, you told me."

"When?"

"When you cried out," she said, turning to walk away. "I've been hearing you for a while now. There aren't a lot of voices anymore, so I hear the few that scream pretty clearly."

As she walked farther away, the sea became intolerably warm. The cold current followed her and so did he. He didn't see when she stopped beside the craggy coral, and he had to skid to a halt. She didn't even look up at him as she peered into a black hole within the coral.

"Voices?"

"Two of them," she said, reaching into the black hole. "Always two of them. One in pain, one always crying out, one weeping bitterly and always saying 'no, no, no.' That is the voice I follow. That is the one that's faint."

She winced as a tremor ran along her arm. She withdrew it and the eel that had clamped its jaws onto her fingers. It writhed angrily as she brought her hand about its slender neck and brought it up to her face to stare into its white eyes.

"And the other?" Lenk asked.

"Always louder, always cold and black. It doesn't speak to me so much as speak to mine, speak to the cold inside of me."

He stared at her, the question forming on his tongue, even though he already knew the answer. He had to ask. He had to hear her say it.

"What does it tell you to do?" he asked.

She looked at him. Her fingers clenched. The snapping sound was short. The eel hung limply in her hands, its tail curled up, up, seeking the sun as she clenched its lifeless body.

41

"To kill," she said simply.

Their eyes met each other, peering deeper than eyes had a right to. It was as if each one sought to pry open the other's head and peer inside and see what each one's frigid voice was muttering to them.

He could feel the cold creeping up his spine. He knew what his was telling him.

"So," he said softly, reaching for a sword that wasn't there, "you're here to—"

"Kill you?" Her smile was not warm. "No." She released the eel and let it drift away. "It's not in my nature."

He rubbed his head. "I don't mean to be rude, but this is about the time I start losing patience with the other voices in my head, too, so could you kindly tell me why you *are* here?"

"Because, Lenk, you're about to kill yourself."

"The thought had occurred. I'm just worried that hell will be much worse than . . ." He gestured around the reef. "You know, *this.*"

"What makes you so sure there's a hell?"

"Because I've seen what comes out of it."

"Demons aren't made in hell. They're made *by* hell." She leveled a finger at him. "The kind of hell that you're going through."

"I don't—"

"*You do.*" She spoke cold, sharp, with enough force to send the fish swirling into hiding. Color died, leaving grim, gray corals and endless blue. "You hear it every time you think you're alone, you see it every time you close your eyes. You feel it in your blood, you feel it sharing your body. It never talks loud enough for others to hear, but it deafens you, and if they could hear what it says, you know they'd cry out like you do.

"Kill. *Kill,*" she hissed. "You obey. Just to make it stop. But no matter how much your sword drinks, it will never be enough." She narrowed her eyes at him. "If you kill them, Lenk, if you kill *her,* it still won't be enough."

Her voice echoed through water, through his blood. She wasn't just talking to him. Something else had heard her.

And it tried to numb him, reaching out to cool his blood and turn his bones to ice. It only made the chill of her voice all the more keen, made the warmth of the ocean grow ever more intolerable. He wanted to cry out, he wanted to collapse, he wanted to let go and see if the current could carry him far enough that he might drift forever.

Those were not things he could do. Not anymore. So he inclined his head, just enough to avoid her gaze, and whispered.

"Yeah. That makes sense."

"Then you know?" she asked. "Do you know how to fight it? That you *have* to fight it?"

Her voice was hard, but falsely so, something that had been brittle to begin with and hammered with a mallet in an awkward grip. Not hard enough to squelch the hope in her voice. She asked not for his sake alone.

He hated to answer.

"I'm not afraid of it, anymore."

He tilted his head back up, turning his gaze skyward. The sun was distant, a shimmering blur on a surface so far away as to be mythical.

"I used to be," he said. "But it says so many things. I tried ignoring it and I felt fear. I tried arguing and I felt pain. But now, I'm not afraid. I don't hurt. I'm numb."

"If you can safely ignore it, then is there a problem? If you don't feel the need to kill—"

"I do." He spoke with a casualness that unnerved himself. "The voice, when it speaks, tells me about how they abandoned me, how they betrayed me. It tells me they have to die for us to be safe. I try to ignore it . . . but it's hard."

"You said you were numb, that you weren't afraid."

"It's not the voice that scares me." He met her gaze now. He smiled faintly. "It's that I'm beginning to agree with it."

Denaos looked at himself in the blade. No scars, still. More wrinkles than there used to be. A pair of ugly bags under eyes that he chose not to look at, but no scars.

He had that, at least.

Appearance was one point of pride amongst many for him. There were other things he had hoped he would be remembered for: his taste in wine, an ear for song, and a way with women that sat firmly between the realms of poetry and witchcraft.

And killing, his conscience piped up. *Don't forget killing.*

And killing. He was not bad at it.

Still, he thought as he surveyed himself, if none of those could be his legacy, looks would have to suffice.

And yet, as he saw the man in the blade, he wondered if perhaps he might have to discount that, too. His was a face used to masks: sharp, perceptive eyes over a malleable mouth ready to smile, frown, or spit curses as needed, all set within firm, square features.

Those eyes were sunken now, dark seeds buried in dark soil, hidden under long hair poorly kempt. His features were caked with stubble, grime, a dried glistening of liquid he hadn't bothered to clean away. And his mouth twitched, not quite sure what it was supposed to do.

Fitting. He didn't know who this mask was supposed to portray.

Looks, then, were not to be what he was remembered for. His eyes drifted to the far side of the table, to the bottle long drained. His preferences in alcohol, too, had broadened to "anything short of embalming fluid, providing nothing else is at hand; past that, it's all fine."

He would not be remembered as a handsome man, then. Nor a man of liquids or songs. What else was left?

The glistening of steel answered. He looked at the blade, its edge everything he wasn't: sharpened, honed, precise. An example, three fingers long and with a polished wooden hilt and a taste for blood.

Killing, then.

"Are we doing this or what?" a growling voice asked.

That, he thought, *and a way with women.*

He tilted the knife slightly. She was still there. He had hoped she wouldn't be, though that might have been hard, given that she was bound to the chair. Still, less hard considering what she was.

Indeed, it was difficult to see how Semnein Xhai was still held by the rawhide bonds. They might have bit into her purple flesh, they might have been tied tightly by hands that were used to tying. Her arm might have been twisted and ruined, thanks to Asper. But that purple flesh was thick over thicker muscle, and his hands were shakier these days.

She stared at him in the blade, her eyes white and without pupils. Her hair hung about her in greasy white strands, framing a face that was sharp and long as the knife.

And looking oddly impatient, he thought. Odder still, given that she knew full well what he could do with this. The scar on her collarbone attested to that. The fresh cut beneath her ribcage, shallow and hesitant, gave a less enthusiastic review.

He had been wearing a different mask that day, that of a man who had a better legacy than him, a man who was less good at killing. But he would do better today. He had people counting on him to find out information. That was a slightly better legacy.

Still killing, though, his conscience said. *Or did you think you were going to let her go after she told you what you wanted to know? Pardon, if she tells you.*

Not now, he replied. *People are counting on me.*

Right, right. Terribly sorry. Shall we?

His face changed in the blade. His mask came back on. Dark eyes hard, jaw set tightly, twitching mouth stilled for now. Hands steadied themselves. He smiled into the blade: knife-cruel, knife-long.

Let's.

He held up the knife and regarded her through the reflection of its steel. Glass was fickle. Steel had a hard time lying. He knew what he was doing. He knew this should have been easier than it was.

One look into her long, purple face reminded him why it wasn't. No fear in her reflection. Fear would have been easy to use. Contempt, too, would have been nice. Lust would have been passable, if weird. But what was on her was something hard as the rest of her, something impatient and unimpressed.

That was hard to work with. That hadn't gotten any easier.

Not impossible, though.

"And?" she grunted. "Any more questions today?"

"No," he replied, voice as soft as the sunlight filtering through the reed walls. "I want to tell fairy tales today."

No reply. No confusion or derision. She was listening.

She was also fifteen paces behind him.

"Old ones, good ones," he whispered. "I want to tell the stories that mothers make crying children silent with. Handsome princes—" he paused, turned the blade, stared into his own eyes, "—ugly witches—" he ran his finger along the blade, felt it gently lick his flesh, "—pretty, pale princesses with long, silky hair."

He shifted the blade, looked at her again. Three paces to the left.

"Was a quiet child," he continued without turning around. "Mother didn't tell me stories. Never cried. I had a friend, though, cried a lot. Probably why he didn't think he was too old for fairy tales. Made him cry once . . . twice, maybe. Heard his mother tell him stories. All the same: evil witch captures pretty princess, handsome prince rides to tower. The ending . . ."

He shifted the blade to his left hand. He stared at her for a moment longer in its reflection.

"It's always the same."

His arm snapped. The knife wailed. It quieted with a meaty smacking sound and her shriek of pain. He turned, smiled gently.

"There is a struggle, some brave test for the prince to conquer," he whispered as he walked over to her. "But in the end, he reaches the top of the tower—" he took the hilt jutting from her bicep, "—he kicks in the door—" he twisted the blade slightly, ignored her snarling, "—and he carries the pretty princess out."

He drew the blade out slowly, listening to it whine as it was torn from its nice, cozy tower, listening to the flesh protest. He caught his reflection in the steel, saw that his smile had disappeared.

45

"Always the same," he said. "The fairy tale is how we tell ugly children to survive. This is why the same stories are told. Through repetition, the child understands."

He lifted the blade, tapped it lightly on her nose, leaving a tiny red blot upon her purple flesh.

"And we can repeat this story forever." He slowly slid the blade over, until the tip hovered beneath her eye, a hair's width from soft, white matter. "The princess can keep going back into the tower until you tell me. Until I know where Jaga is and what you handsome princes want with it."

Now, he waited. He waited for the fear to creep up on her face. He waited for something he could use. He waited until she finally spoke.

"I have to piss."

He sighed; mistake. "Just let me—"

She wasn't making a request. The acrid smell that hit him a moment later confirmed that. He blanched, turned around; bigger mistake.

You're showing weakness.

More like disgust.

You're turning your back to her. Shall we get back into this? People counting on you and all that.

Right you are.

He turned around to face her. Tremendous mistake.

She was sitting there, grinning broadly as the liquid trickled down her chair to stain the hut's sandy floor. He showed her no disgust, though for how much longer he was hesitant to say. There was something in her grin beyond the subdued hatred, the pleasure in suffering that he had come to expect. There was something in her eyes that was beyond scorn and fury.

Something that made it seem as though she wanted him to smile back.

"What?" she asked.

"You disgust me."

"Why would a man who asks for piss and blood be surprised at getting piss and blood?"

He blinked, looked down at the stained sand. "I've known of your breed's existence for almost a month now, so if this is a riddle, I don't feel ashamed saying I don't get it."

She smiled; not grinned. "Master Sheraptus said you were stupid."

"Your master is dead."

"Master Sheraptus is never wrong," she said. She looked at him curiously, sizing him up. "But . . . you're not stupid."

"Thank you."

"But you desperately want to be."

It was generally agreed by most torturer and interrogator manuals that cryptic musing from one's victims was generally a poor reaction. He flipped the knife around in his hand, noting that there wasn't a great deal of blood on the blade.

Possibly because there wasn't a great deal of blood from her wound.

"It doesn't work that way," she grunted, smiling at his recognition. "Cut me however deep you want to. I won't bleed."

"You won't," he said, forcing his voice cold, trying to force the conversation back into his grip. "Because you're going to tell me."

46

"No."

No defiance. Only fact. She would not talk. It made him cringe to realize that he believed it as much as she did. It made him cringe again when she noticed this and smiled. Broadly.

"You're not stupid," she repeated. "There is a way it is. Everything works as it should. You call it inev . . . inva . . ." She grunted, spat onto the ground. "You give it a stupid word. Netherlings know it because we are it. From nothing to nothing. We live, we kill, we die. This is how it is."

She looked at him, searching for a reaction. He felt his skin crawl under her gaze; there was something about not being able to follow her eyes, milk white and bereft of iris or pupil, that made him shudder.

"But you want to be stupid," she said. "You want to think there is another way to do this. You want to think I'm going to break under this pain. I've had worse."

There was a sickening popping sound and he knew she was clenching her fist behind her. That he couldn't see the ruined mass of flesh and twisted bone that was her arm was a comfort that grew smaller every time she made a fist. The bone set back into place, the flesh squished as she overcame the injury out of a sheer desire to unnerve him.

It was working. It reminded him of just how much pain she had gone through. He was there when it had happened. He had seen Asper do it.

"You want to think I'm going to tell you everything you need." She smiled a jagged smile. "Because then, you can tell yourself you're as stupid as everyone else, that you just didn't know. That's why you pour reeking water down your throat. That's why you talk to invisible sky people."

He felt her smile twist in his skin.

"I bet you have a stupid word for that, too," she said.

He meant to smack his lips. His mouth was so dry all of the sudden, so numb that he didn't even feel it when the word slipped out of his mouth.

"Denial," he whispered.

"Stupid," she grunted. "As stupid as anything."

"I disagree."

She fell silent. She was listening intently. Unpleasant.

But he continued.

"If you accept that things happen a certain way, then you accept that there's no particular point in trying to change them," he said. "Thus, there's no particular point in withholding information from me. You're here. I'm here. I've got the knife. If the future is set in stone, then why are you fighting it?"

"I said you weren't stupid," she grunted. "Stop trying so hard. Things are

47

what they are, not what they should be. We are solid, nothing else is. That's what you don't understand."

"About you?"

"About you."

She leaned forward. His nostrils quivered, eyes twitched, ears trembled, full of her. Her foulness, her sweat, the heat of her blood rushing in her veins, the creak of heavy bones under heavy muscle, everything that should disgust him, that did disgust him, that he knew was in her.

"You want to think there's a way that this doesn't end with you killing me," she whispered, breath hot and hard like forged iron. "Because if I live, or if someone else kills me, you can pretend that you aren't what you are. You can tell yourself that you didn't know you'd have to kill me the moment we met."

"We didn't meet. You tried to kill me. I stabbed you."

"And that's how we do it. With metal."

Nothing primal in her smile: no hate, no rage, no hunger. Nothing refined there: no delight in his suffering, no complex thought. It was something else, something simple and stupid and immutable.

Conviction.

"But you're not stupid. You know this ends with your hands slick."

He snapped. Spine snapped. Arm snapped. Fingers snapped. The knife went hurtling out of his grip, whined sharply, continued to whine even after it had struck.

She looked to her side as it stood in the sand for only a moment longer before drooping down to lay flat and impotent upon the dirt. She looked up and he was walking out the door.

"Missed," he grunted.

"No, you didn't," she said after him.

He was gone. She was still smiling.

48 When he emerged from the cramped confines of the hut, he found the outdoors intolerable. The bright sunlight, warm winds, unbearably fresh air struck him with such force as to make his head ache.

Or that might have been his own fist as he brought it up to his temple.

"What was that?" He struck his head, trying to knock the answer loose. "What just happened?"

No idea. His conscience answered him in a jarring, disjointed train. *What was that she did? Mind trick? Brain magic? What was that? That was . . . what?*

His head hurt. The sound of wind turned into a shrill, ringing whine. The scent of sea was overpowering, scraping his nostrils dry. He felt dizzy, nauseous. It was hard to think.

Well, of course it is. You haven't had a drink in . . . in . . .

"That can't be healthy," he whispered. "Where'd I leave my drink? Back in there?"

Don't go back in there, stupid! She's still in there! You can't look at her again.

"So, what? Kill her, then?"

He looked down at his wrist, the heavy leather glove upon it. He could feel the blade, hidden and coiled upon the spring behind the thick leather. Just a twitch, he thought, and it would come singing out, a short, staccato song that ended in a red note.

Did you already forget who is in there?

The image of her smile flashed through his head. Too broad, too excited, too bereft of hatred. She was supposed to *hate*. She was supposed to *curse*. She wasn't supposed to smile and this wasn't supposed to be this hard.

Not at all this hard. She's a woman . . . well, in theory. You're good with women, right? You can't not *be good with women! You'll ruin the group dynamics! What else are you good at?*

"Killing."

NO! Women! Women are easy for you! Things don't get harder around women!

He chuckled inadvertently. "That's funny."

Yeah, I just got that. Remember that for later because—STOP TALKING TO YOURSELF.

A reasonable idea for a reasonable man, the kind of man he ought to be. A reasonable man would be able to see the problem: that the drink only soothed thoughts that he shouldn't be drinking away; that confronting those thoughts that tormented, those thoughts that returned to him when a woman smiled at him that way, when a woman confronted him as he had been confronted once before, was the only sound philosophy.

Reasonable. Denaos was a reasonable man without philosophy or drink to turn to. And so, he turned to blame.

Women, he told himself. It was the women causing his trouble.

Might be the chronic drinking, actually, his conscience replied.

No. He wasn't ready to face that.

It was that one woman, the priestess, who had nearly died. She had caused the whole thing. He had stood over her, cried over her, like he had done before. And that led to the memories, the waking nightmares, like he had had before. That led to the drink, which led to Teji, which led to netherlings, which led to Xhai, which led to her smiling with a broad smile that didn't hate him or mildly loathe him and told him he was a good man.

Like he had seen before.

Always before.

That's it, you know, his conscience whispered. *This is a sign. This is an omen from Silf.*

"No, not yet."

You're already stinking drunk. You've been drunk since this morning and you're still thinking about this.

"It is obscenely rude to be bringing this up now. I haven't had enough to—"

There won't ever be enough. Not enough to change the truth.

"Truth is subjective."

You killed her.

"Truth is—" His sentence was cut off in a hacking cough.

You opened her throat.

He tried to respond, tried to reply. The coughing tore his throat apart. The air was too clean out here, too fragrant. He needed stale, he needed stench.

You killed them all.

He fell to his knees. Why was the air so damn clean? Didn't anyone *drink* today?

You're going to hell.

He inhaled sharply, ragged knives in his throat, jagged shards in his lungs. It hurt to breathe. Hurt to think. He shut his eyes tight as he tried to regain his breath.

It was so bright out here. He belonged in a bottle, in something dank and dark that would prepare him nicely for the blackness he was going to.

And that was the truth. That was what it all came down to, what all the drinking and vomiting and crying and killing had done its best.

He was going to hell.

He killed them all.

He killed her.

And, on cue, the dead woman was there when he opened his eyes. Her feet were, at least: white with a white gown wafting just above them. The sensible choice would be to watch the feet, stare at them until this nasty bout of sobriety passed and he could stare into a puddle of his own vomit again.

Sensible plan.

Reasonable man.

So he looked up. Each sight was familiar enough to be seen in his skull before he saw it in his eyes. Ghastly white robe, ghastly white body, so thin and frail. Throat opened up in a bright red blossom, blood weeping onto her garments. Thin black hair hanging around her shoulders. The worst was yet to come: her smile, her grim and wild and hateful smile.

He looked up. The dead woman was frowning at him. The dead woman hated him.

She had never done that before. Not when she was alive. Not when he had opened her throat.

She was disappointed in him.

Somehow, *that* was the worst part.

"Get up."

A voice. A woman's voice. Not the dead woman's voice, though. Her voice was something with claws and teeth that he felt in his skin. This voice was something with air and heat, something he heard.

The boot heel that dug into his shoulder and knocked him to the earth wasn't, but he felt it all the same.

"I'd really rather not," he grunted, clambering to his knees. "A man who aspires to rise beyond his station is invariably struck down by the Gods."

"If that were true, I wouldn't be here looking down at you right now."

Asper's voice was cold. Her stare was colder. It was almost refreshing. The air was a little staler around her, possibly due to the palpable bitterness that emanated from her.

Looking into her eyes quickly quashed any sense of refreshment. Something was boiling behind her mouth, twisted into a sharp knife of a frown.

Resentment, maybe: for having arrived too late to save her the nights before, too late to have saved her from what had happened to her. Scorn, maybe: for having seen what he'd seen that he, nor anyone, was ever meant to. A face on fire, a body engulfed, an arm pulsating like a hungry thing.

Or, much more likely, hatred: for having known what had been done to her, for having known what hell she carried in her arm, and for having not so much as looked at her since it had happened.

Or maybe it was just spit?

"What have you learned?" she asked.

"About?"

She stared at him, unblinking. He sighed, rubbed his temples.

"Not a tremendous lot," he said. "It's not as though it should come as a colossal surprise, really. I'm sure the vast majority of her is bone—"

"Muscle," Asper said. "Over half."

"Whatever. The point is that getting information from her is proving . . ."

Unnerving? Slightly emasculating? A little arousing in the same way that it sort of makes you want to cry?

"Difficult," he said. "If she even knows anything, she won't tell me anything." He glanced to another nearby hut. "Dreadaeleon might be able to coerce her, or—"

"Or Bralston?" she asked, thrusting the question at him.

"Or Gariath," Denaos said. He narrowed his eyes upon the hut. "I don't like the look of the Djaalman. Too shifty."

"You're in a poor position to comment."

"And a good position to observe. The man's too . . . probey."

"Probey."

"Probish. Probesque. He's always staring at us."

"He's staring at *you*. He stares at no one *but* you." She smiled blackly. "Watch your back, lest he try to probe you more attentively." She wiggled her fingers. "Electric touch."

"Was there something else, or . . ."

She turned her stare at the hut's door, looked at it for a moment. When she turned back to Denaos, her face was a hard, iron mask. "Why not just kill her?"

"What?"

"Go in there and open her throat." She scowled at the door. "She's too dangerous to leave alive."

"Granted, but that's not for us to decide. Lenk thinks she still might have—"

"*Lenk doesn't know them*," she snarled, whirling on him. "He thinks they're savages. The only reason he hates them is that they're more longfaced than *his* little savage. *I know them*." She jabbed a thumb at her chest. "I know what they're capable of. *I* know what they do. I know how foul and utterly—"

"You think I don't?" he interjected. "You think I haven't seen what they've done?"

"I don't *think* anything about you," she said. "I know you, too. I know you're scum."

He knew why she knew, too. Just as he knew he couldn't deny it.

"And I know that *you* know *nothing* about them." She turned on him now, turned a face cold and trembling upon him. "Because *you* came too late to stop it from happening. Because *you* did nothing to stop it from happening and because you . . . you . . ."

Asper was an honest woman. Too honest to survive, he had once thought. Her face wasn't made for masks. Her face fragmented with each moment it trembled, cracking and falling off to reveal eyes that weren't as cold as she wanted them to be. There was fire there, and honest hate.

"Everything . . . everything that happened to me, what Sheraptus . . ." She winced at the name, clenched her teeth. "He *violated* me . . . and then . . . then, my arm—" Her face trembled so violently he had to fight the urge to reach out and steady her. "And with it all, after all the secrets about it and all that happened with him, I thought at least I had you, at least I had someone to . . ."

A curse would have been nice. Spitting in his eye would have been workable, too. The sigh she let out, though, was less than ideal.

"I *needed* you . . . and you shoved me away, like I was . . . like I was unclean. *Trash.* And now you won't even look at me."

And Denaos wasn't looking at her now. He was looking at her forehead, at the hut door, at the sand and the unbearable sun. Her eyes were too hard to look at, too shiny, too clear; he might see himself in them.

"You don't need me."

"You're the only one who knows this," she grabbed at her arm, "*any* of this. Do you have any idea how long I've—"

"*Yes.*" He looked at her now. "Yes, I know what it's like to wait that long. And yes, I know what happened to you and I know what's happening to you."

"Then why won't you?"

"*Because I've seen it before.*" He clutched his head. "I know why you threw yourself at me because I've seen it happen. I've seen women, children, *people* get torn apart like you did. I've seen them carry worse things and think that they have go into the arms of someone, anyone, just to tell it. But it can't be anyone, Asper, and it can't be me."

Not entirely true. There was a lot she could tell him, a lot he needed to tell her. But what, he did not know. How exactly a man went about telling a woman he had seen what women do after being violated because he had watched it happen was beyond him. He neglected to tell her that. That, he reasoned, was slightly better than lying.

"I am not a good man. I am not what you need."

She stared at him for a moment. He never saw the blow coming. It was only after she had struck him, sent him reeling, that he admitted she might be better with masks than he thought.

"No one tells me what I need," she said. "Certainly not a man hiding cowardice behind more cowardice."

She stalked off silently, swiftly, leaving him alone with his conscience.

Could have gone better.

True, he admitted.

She might hit you less if you actually talked to her, you know.

That sounds really hard.

Good point. Want a drink?

Wanted one, yes. Needed one, yes. He needed many things at that moment. The most important of which became apparent when he looked back, toward the distant huts and the figure standing amongst them.

Bralston stood out in the open, unabashed, unafraid. A Librarian did not need to hide. This Librarian, however, didn't bother to hide many things. The stare he fixed upon Denaos among them.

Denaos, too, did not bother to hide his stare. In the moment they met, the brief moment before Denaos turned and stalked into the distant forest, there was a brief trial. Accusation, confession, sentence, all handed down in the span of a blink.

And Denaos knew what he needed most, then. In the feel of heavy leather on his wrist and in the sound of feet crunching upon sand, following him into the forest, he knew.

This, at least, would be easier.

FOUR

THE DEAD MIND

She was floating, drifting upon a current that seemed to obey her without a word. Through the fish that had thinned from colorful curtains to ragged schools, over coral that was dying out and becoming barren desert underneath Lenk's feet, still stubbornly bound to the sandy floor.

But no matter how he changed his pace or tried to navigate through the coral, she remained always above him. Her shadow was colder than he had expected.

"You're not talking," he said.

A condition she was apparently not prepared to break with his stunning observation.

"If you don't talk, this all seems slightly more insane," Lenk continued, throwing up his hands. "Because now *I* have to start looking for meaning everywhere."

He swept his stare around the sea floor. The coral had vanished, leaving nothing but the most stubborn outcroppings of rock. The sole fish was a lone, ragged creature: something that vaguely looked like a bloated axe-head if bloated axe-heads were capable of eating disorders and stares that belonged to veterans, whores, and herb-addicts. Everything about the creature suggested something that had no business existing and being keenly aware of it as it slowly swam away from decent sea-going society.

Lenk blinked, staring blankly. "Okay, this one is going to take some doing." He held out his hand, as if to grasp the meaning implied by this finned degenerate. "All right . . . it looks like a . . . what? Some kind of hoe? So, it's suggesting I invest a future of farming . . . fish?" He furrowed his brow, looking thoughtful. "I guess that's not the weirdest way this could—"

"Ask me."

Her voice struck him across the cheek. A shadow stared down at him, not nearly dark enough to hide the merciless blue of her stare.

His words tasted like salt. "Ask you what?"

Her glare and the abrupt end to his heartbeat suggested they both knew the answer. It didn't start again until the words had pulled themselves from his mouth.

"Who are you?"

She shook her head. His heart moved under her gaze, trying to avoid being seen behind an immodest curtain of flesh. He wanted to say anything else. If he didn't say it, though, someone else would.

And they would speak much louder than she could.

"What do I have to do?" he asked.

"Kill."

"I don't want to."

"I wasn't talking about your friends."

"Neither was I."

She looked inside him. What she saw caused him to turn his head down. He was not lying.

"You listened," she whispered, "to the demons."

Neither was she.

He *had* listened when the demons had spoken to him. Specifically, when *the* demon spoke to him. Ulbecetonth, the Kraken Queen, Mother Deep; he could still hear her voice coming from the faint place his conscience should speak from. And like a conscience should, she begged him not to.

Not to interfere with her plans, not to embark on his errand to retrieve the tome, not to spill the blood of her faithful and her children. Not to force her to listen to the cries of her dying children as they bled out on his sword.

If he let his mind empty, in the moments between his breathing and the voices talking in his head, he could hear them, too. They cried so loud. And so often.

"Why?" she asked.

"She spared my life," Lenk said, looking at the earth as though his reasons lay in the sand. "She told me things that made me feel better." He tried to ignore her stare. "She told me I could avoid this . . . this whole thing with the tome, with them, with . . . with her."

"And so you want to kill them, anyway? But *not* the demons? Lenk, how—"

"*I AM BREATHING UNDERWATER.*" He scowled at her, heart pounding. "This is the *third* time this has happened to me. The *last* time involved a giant set of teeth in the *earth* that tried to argue with a voice in my head that's kept me from trying to kill myself while also telling me to kill a woman I really want to talk to despite the fact that she left me for dead so she could cavort with a headhunting, hideskinning, green-skinned, long-eared son of a bitch, so *forgive me if this sounds a little complicated.*"

He rubbed his temples. His head hurt. Suddenly, there was so much pressure. His mouth tasted of salt. The world, this world, began to move beneath him while he stood still. He felt uncomfortably warm as her shadow shifted off of him.

All this, though, he barely noticed.

"I don't want to do this anymore," he said. "I don't want to kill people, any people. I don't want to feel naked without my sword. I don't want to feel *right* when I'm covered in blood and I don't want to live without—"

The massive hole he only noticed when his heels went over the edge.

He scrambled away from it, falling to hands and knees as he whirled about. The coral and its colors were far behind him. The sea floor was only barely beneath him. Before him, this world had simply stopped, disappearing into a vast and endless blue.

"Where are we?" he asked.

"*Hell,*" someone replied. Was that her?

"Why?"

"*You brought us here.*"

"No." He rose to his feet, shakily. His head was spinning. His heart was thundering. His words drowned in his ears. "No more riddles. No more crypticisms. No more interpretations. *You* came to me. *You* brought me here. *You* have to tell me what to do."

"*Jaga.*"

"What of it?"

"*Duty.*"

"What duty?"

"*What we do is not our choice. We weren't born with that. We're not lucky people, Lenk.*"

"People? Do you mean you and I or . . . are there more of us?" He clutched his head, trying to dig into the flesh of his scalp and extract the memories. "There was a man . . . man in ice. I remember . . . *I* remember. It's *me*. *My* memories, *my* friends, *my* voice . . ."

"*Ours.*"

He was floating now, too. This world disappeared. His world was at the surface, far away. That world opened up beneath him. He was nowhere.

No more heart, no more head with heavy thoughts to weigh him down. In their place grew something cold.

"*Our voice.*"

His head throbbed, pounded, swelled, expanded.

"*Our duty.*"

Erupted.

He felt his eyelid twitch, then tremble, then bulge. Ice and skull cracked as a translucent, jagged spike formed where his mind had been and pushed steadily outward. Something came loose within him, with the sound of his eye socket creaking, then shattering.

He didn't even notice it until his eyeball was floating out before him, staring back at him and the jagged icicle that blossomed from its socket.

"Our death."

He felt the back of his head split apart as another frigid spike emerged like a horn. He felt his mouth fill with frost, felt the thin layer of his cheek's flesh burst in a red flower. His fingertips split apart, spine snaked out of his back, shinbones shattered as the icicles grew out of him and continued to grow until they filled the ocean and froze it.

Only when he had no voice did he think to cry out.

The frog was still twitching when he brought it to his mouth. His canines sank into its flesh and he felt the dizzying rush of raw venom on his tongue. Lately, it only took a moment for the sensation to pass.

Bones crunched behind his lips. He swallowed and a mess of pulped flesh and poison slid down his throat.

"I've had dreams."

His voice was raw with venom when he spoke.

"When I was young, anyway. I wonder if every tribesman has them. I don't think I ever asked."

His toes twitched, all six pale green digits digging into the soil. He felt connected to this earth, kin to it; poison flowed through it as it did through him.

"We didn't ask questions in the south. Maybe it's different in the Silesrian. I don't know. I once asked my uncle if he knew. He looked at me and didn't say a word. He slid a Spokesman into my hands, patted me on the head, and pointed me toward the humans.

"I had been alive for . . . fifteen years?" He scratched his chin, fingers rubbing over the inked scrawl of tattoos that ran from brow to navel. "Fourteen, maybe. Just married at that point. We did that earlier in the south. Maybe it's different in the Silesrian. My wife was the first person I ever asked. She just looked at me and shook her head.

"I stopped thinking about it, as much as I could. Time passed. I killed humans. Humans killed my uncles. Humans killed my wife." He waved a hand. "My son, too. It doesn't matter. All tribesmen die. They went to the Dark Forest and I continued fighting. We were losing, of course. It's impossible to fight humans and win . . . or it was.

"The dreams . . . didn't stop." He scratched his bald scalp. "I still had them and they didn't make sense. Maybe that was how I tried to figure it all out and get an answer. They lasted for a while."

His ears twitched. He reached up, running a long finger along each length, counting each of the six notches in them, as if to reassure himself that they were still there.

"It was when I learned why we fight that they finally ended.

"I found one of them. I couldn't tell you what nation he belonged to or what god he worshipped. All humans looked alike to me. But I found one, alone. I suppose it would have been smarter to wait for the others, maybe to interrogate him.

"But I was hungry. And I heard *it*—" he tapped his temple "—right here. And I wanted to hurt him. So I did. We fought for a bit. I struck his head with my stick. He cut me in the thigh with his sharp sword. When our weapons were lost, we fought with fists and teeth.

"And I don't know when I had come on top of him, or when I had found his throat with my hands. Everything was just moments, things that happened without me knowing how. One time, my fingers felt the hair on the back of his neck. The next, my thumbs found the hard bump in his throat. I couldn't remember either when I started to squeeze.

"I wondered if he knew the human who had killed my wife. Maybe he was. It was unlikely. There are so many humans. But this was one less. And because this was one less, there would be one more of us."

Naxiaw looked up and stared across the clearing at the young woman sitting cross-legged at its edge. She stared at him intently. There was no more fear in her green eyes anymore, no more tension in her scrawny, pale body. Her ears rose upright, each one twitching and attentive.

"And that's when I knew what it meant to be a shict."

She took a long moment before she spoke. When she did, he wasn't listening; words were something she was too good with, something she used too often. His ears twitched, listening to her other voice.

She could still speak through the Howling, the wordless language of their people, but in the same way that a child could still speak. The voice of her mind and body, spirit and anger, was a sporadic thing: snarling one moment, spitting the next, then whimpering, then weeping, then roaring.

She tried to hide it behind words. She tried to distract from it with questions she thought were insightful. But he could hear her Howling. Just barely.

He said nothing to her spoken words. He stayed silent as she rose up from the earth and offered some excuse that would mean more to a round-ear. He stared as she waved briefly, then awkwardly bowed as though it meant anything, and then turned and slipped out of the forest.

The Howling lingered behind her, shrieking and crying long after she had vanished. She was frightened, she was confused, she was barely a shict.

59

Still . . .

"You seem surprised," a voice answered his thoughts from the bushes at his back.

"Not surprised," he replied without looking behind him.

"Then what?" another voice, deeper and darker.

He had asked them to stay behind. Their presence would only have frightened her further. She wasn't ready to rejoin a people she wasn't sure she was a part of.

That will change.

"I'm not convinced it will, Naxiaw," Inqalle said, emerging from the underbrush. "She's been around humans for a long time. You agree the *kou'ru* have infected her."

"Diseases can be cured," he replied.

"We hope, at least," Avaij added, his voice sharp and smooth where his sister's was rasping and harsh. "We've all heard her Howling, though. If she can't be cured—"

"Then what, brother?" he asked. "We leave her to die? Kill her?"

"Of course not," Avaij replied.

"Maybe," Inqalle said.

"We do not kill the sick." Naxiaw rose up from the earth. "We treat the sickness, we kill the disease."

"The human," Avaij muttered. "You're convinced that the death of one round-ear will bring our wayward sister back."

"Not convinced."

"Hope is not something for the *s'na shict s'ha*," Inqalle said. "Our people *know*."

"Then you know we cannot kill her and we cannot sit back and let her suffer."

He turned and regarded his tribesmen. He wondered how the human would see them: tall and proud, limbs corded with green muscle and dotted with tattoos, black hair hacked and hewn into crested mohawks. Their weapons were sharp, their eyes were sharp, their canines were sharper still as their lips curled backward.

Humans had tales about the greenshicts, his people. They feared them, rightfully. This human might look upon them with terror in his blue stare. This human might fight back. To survive was the nature of disease.

But in these two, Naxiaw saw only brother, only sister, their Howling speaking clearly. If they doubted his methods, they did not doubt his goals. They would not let their sister suffer.

It would hurt, of course. She was attached to the silver-haired monkey, as much as she might wish they did not know. She might rave, she might rail against them, she might even mourn.

No illness was cured without pain.

Kataria drew in a long breath and released it. When the last trace of air had passed her lips, she opened her eyes.

"No," she said. "You are wrong. The answer isn't in blood. It hasn't been so far. And the answer is not in you. I offer you no apology and I ask for no forgiveness, brother. Everything I have to find out, I can't be told. I have to find it. If it means going with the humans, then so be it. Live well, Naxiaw. I will."

She nodded firmly, smiling. There it was. Everything she had been holding inside her, everything she had refused to admit to herself, much less to the *s'na shict s'ha*.

She had said it and believed it.

If Naxiaw had actually been standing before her, she would have been just fine. As it was, the pig-sized, colorful roach in front of her merely twitched its feathery antennae and made a light chittering noise; as far as personal epiphanies went, it seemed unimpressed.

"Oh, like you've heard better," she said with a sneer as she stalked past it.

Despite the insect's lack of approval, she came out of the forest light-headed. The meeting with the greenshict had gone well. Ominously well, considering she had told him it would be their last. She hoped he understood that. She hoped he *heard* that.

She could still hear the breathy, fumbled excuses in her own ears. She couldn't *understand* them, of course. But she hoped Naxiaw was a little more accepting of incoherence.

And how could he not be? She chastised herself. *What with that stirring performance of stuttering excuses and half-concocted logic, it's amazing he's not here beside you right now to give you a teary hug before he sends you to a human, the kind of breed that he's sworn to kill and you are, too.*

Were. She corrected herself. She *had* been sworn to kill humans, or so she thought. She had listened to the old logic that told the old reasons that supported the old story. The one that said humans were a disease that threatened shict and land alike, hence they must die.

And for as long as she could, she believed them.

But that time was over. The old story had never resonated with her as it should. The old reasons had never carried enough weight. The old logic had brought her nothing but a distinct pain in her belly that grew sharper every time she looked at Lenk and he looked back at her.

And they both remembered that night, when he had looked into her eyes with a blade to his throat and called out for her.

And she had turned her back on him.

But this isn't about him, she told herself as she crept into the daylight. *No, no. This is about you, and what you know is a shict and who you know you are and who you have to kill and what you have to do and how many times you have to tell yourself this before you finally believe it.*

It was getting easier, at least.

Daylight met her with the sun rising higher in the sky as dawn was left behind and a bright, angry morning took prominence. Coming from the darkness of the forest, she was nearly blinded as the sun cast a furious glare off the sand.

It wasn't enough to blind her to the flurry of activity, nor to the dread welling up inside her at the sight of work at the shoreline.

The center of the scene was dominated by the restored companion vessel they had salvaged, trying its hardest to appear seaworthy and aided ably by its scaly attendants. The lizardmen known as Gonwa worked diligently: sanding out its roughness, testing the sturdiness of its mast, securing its rudder. There was a vigor to their work, a frightening eagerness to get this vessel and its passengers to sea.

Considering said vessel was to deliver them into the maw of an island whose location was known only to the flesh-eating serpents and skull-crushing lizardmen who dwelt there, Kataria suspected she should feel a little insulted.

Not too late, you know, she thought as she began to trudge across the sand toward the worksite. *You could still kill them all and run. They'd never see it coming. Well, Lenk might . . . I mean, you* did *want to kill him only a week or so ago. But only two people know that.*

And one of them just seized her shoulder in a heavy hand with heavy claws.

Granted, given all that Gariath *could* do with his claws, she suspected she ought not to have snarled at him when he effortlessly spun her to face his vast chest. She had to look up to meet his black eyes.

And when he looked down at her, it was a harsh gaze set beneath a pair of horns that traveled down a snout brimming with sharp teeth in a bare snarl of his own.

At the best of times, Gariath didn't need a reason to kill a person, even one that approached his vague definition of "companion." Given that he had a slew of reasons, ranging from her abandoned plot to kill the only human he respected to her witnessing him talking to invisible people, she had to wonder, not for the first time, why he hadn't done it yet.

That wasn't the sort of musing one did vocally. And when he did no more than thrust an arm at her, she counted herself lucky.

"Here," the dragonman rumbled.

He let go of the long object in his hand, leaving it to teeter ominously before collapsing against her. She buckled under its weight, struggling to keep it up.

"What's this?" she asked.

"What you asked for."

She looked down at the object. A spear . . . or a harpoon? Hard to say; the amalgamation of metal long rusted and old wood left the weapon's exact purpose vague beyond being something suitable for stabbing.

Still, that *was* what she had asked for.

"I should remind you this thing has to go into a snake the size of a tree." She hefted the massive weapon; a long sliver of wood cracked and peeled off. "We want to *impale* it, not give it splinters."

"Your plan," Gariath grunted.

She stepped aside twice as he shoved his way past her: once for his immense shoulder, twice for the batlike wings folded tightly against it. She failed, however, to account for his tail, creeping out behind his kilt. It snaked up behind him, lashing at her cheek with enough force to send her snarling. Not as hard as he could have, just enough to remind her of the dangers of not giving him a wide enough berth.

"If you don't like what I found, you can go find another one."

He gestured over his shoulder with a broad hand. She didn't have to look hard to see what he gestured to.

It was staring back at her.

Considering the sheer number of the skulls littering the island, she suspected she ought to be used to their massive, empty eye sockets staring at her, their shattered jaws and fractured skulls paled in comparison. Still, one never truly became accustomed to seeing a thirty-foot-long unholy amalgamation of man and fish lying dead.

And they were just one macabre feature of the graveyard that was the beach. Fragmented ballistae dotted the landscape, their rusted spears caught between ribs whose flesh had long rotted away. Catapults lay crushed, the only remains of their ammunition within the gaping holes of the demonic skulls. Most curious were the monoliths: great statues of robed figures, holy symbols of gods carved in lieu of faces, sinking on rusted metal treads and lying in pieces on the beach.

The war in which mortalkind battled Aeons, the corrupted servants of the Gods, for supremacy. Nothing remained of that battle besides this graveyard.

That, she thought, *and the tome. Which is why you're going to Jaga in the first place. Hence the plan, hence the spear . . . the rotting, rusty spear . . .* She blinked. *You know, if you* do *kill them, the chances of this plan killing you are far lower.*

She ignored that thought. It was getting easier.

"The shict is insane."

She had been intended to hear it. Tact and volume were not qualities known to the Gonwa, or their leader.

Tall and lean, sinew and scales, Hongwe shook his head as he surveyed the vessel's progress. He scratched the beard of scales drooping from below his chin, a low hiss emanating from behind pressed lips as a long tail twitched behind him.

"Completely insane," he muttered again.

"I can hear you, you know," she said.

"Good," the Gonwa replied. He turned upon her, narrow yellow eyes staring at her from behind a blunt snout. "Better to remind you again and clear my conscience before you decide to kill yourself."

"Look, I know we've only known each other for a week now," she said, grunting as she leaned the spear against the vessel. "But trying to kill ourselves is sort of what we do."

"Sometimes each other," Gariath growled as he stalked forward to stand beside Hongwe.

"Right, sometimes." Kataria did not miss the knowing glint in his eye.

"And I tell you again," Hongwe said. "Your biggest danger is not anything with teeth or arrows." His voice was sharp, threatening. "The *shennisah-nui*, the Great Gray Wall, is a reef so sharp with stone and so thick with fog that anyone, human, Gonwa, or Owauku, doesn't even see the rock that impales him. No one passes but the Shen."

"And the Akaneeds," Kataria said. "They know the way."

"Jaga is their home. Jaga is the *home* to snakes that swallow *sharks*. Appreciate that for a moment. The *least* of your concerns are the Shen."

"Not true."

The voice was a withered one, something so used to joviality and whimsy that its mournfulness was something that stuck in flesh instead of ears. As they looked up to the nearby rocky outcropping, it was easy to see who had spoken it. Togu's body, too, had once been taller; as much as a reptile with a body like a beer keg could be, anyway.

Now the Owauku sat upon the rock, hunched over, head bowed.

Good.

A spiteful thought, Kataria knew, but a just one. That Togu lived at all was a decision of Lenk's she neither understood nor questioned. The creature, king of his people, had welcomed them to his home of Teji, delivered them from their shipwreck, only to deliver them again into the hands of the netherlings. Lenk, perhaps, only saw his betrayal as just that.

Kataria had been aboard the ship, though. Kataria had seen the creature known as Sheraptus and had seen what he had done. Kataria had heard Asper scream.

And it was only out of acknowledgment of her own betrayal that she obeyed Lenk's decision and didn't put an arrow in Togu's gullet.

"The Shen are not like us," he said. "Maybe once all green people were from the same stock. But while the Gonwa swam and the Owauku starved, the Shen killed. They killed when our peoples separated so many years ago, and they have never stopped. They come out of Jaga in their canoes, the Akaneeds swimming with them, and they kill. They kill with clubs. They kill with arrows."

He turned to stare at her. His eyes were bulbous yellow things, moving independently of one another as they both turned upon her.

"The Shen will kill you, too. All of you." He shook his head. His scaly whiskers shook with it. "I will not mourn."

"We die, you die."

It was Lenk who spoke, Lenk who came trudging through the sands. Lenk spoke in certainties these days.

"Kataria, Gariath, and I are going to Jaga," he said, fixing his gaze upon Togu, whose own eyes quickly faltered. "This ship sinks, we die, we don't come back. Denaos, Dreadaeleon, and Asper take care of you."

"There's no need for threats," Hongwe said, unflinching from Lenk's stare. "The boat will deliver you as far as you can manage it. It's solid, Gonwa craft. But you will not return. This journey is madness and the Owauku must suffer for it?"

"And Gonwa," Lenk said. "You didn't lift a finger to warn us. You could have prevented this."

Speechless, Hongwe looked to Gariath, pleading in his eyes. The dragon-man stared at him for a moment before shrugging.

"Rats die," he said. "We didn't."

"I couldn't trust you to die, then," Gonwa sighed, rubbing his eyes. "I trust you now."

"Fine," Lenk said. He looked to the vessel. A pair of Gonwa hefted the splintering spear into it. "Is it loaded?"

"With your weapons and everything else you wanted." He looked to Kataria. "Including the rope."

"And the rest?" Kataria asked.

65

Hongwe stared blankly at her, as though he desperately wished he didn't know what she was talking about. After that hope joined many others in death, however, he sighed and motioned one of his scaly workers forward.

The Gonwa nodded and, from behind the boat, produced a wooden bucket, filled to the brim with what might have been best described as the porridge of the damned. Barbed roach legs, feathery antennae, the occasional rainbow-colored wing all protruded from a thick slop of glistening insect entrails, their stench ripened by the sun to give the aroma of something not satisfied to offend only one sense.

Despite the fact that a single whiff caused tears to form in her eyes, Kataria grinned. She looked to Gariath and gestured to the bucket with her chin. The dragonman stared at her, challengingly, before grunting and holding his hand out over the slop. A claw dug into his palm and cut a thick line of blood that eagerly dripped out to splash upon the entrails.

Lenk stared at the ritual, brow lofted, until he clearly couldn't stand by any longer. He turned to the shict.

"Kataria," he said simply. "Why?"

"I've got a plan," she said.

"Should I know its details?"

"*Should* you? Absolutely." She shrugged. "Do you *want* to?"

"Outstanding." He sighed deeply, rubbing the back of his neck.

She couldn't help but grin. It was in those moments when he stared at her like he wondered what he had done to be cursed with her that she remembered what he was like before that night. In his despair, he was Lenk again, and she smiled.

She suspected she should be rather worried by that.

"Answer me this, at least," he said. "Who has to die for this plan to work?"

"Ideally?"

"Realistically."

"Well, no one *has* to die," she said, smiling broadly.

Maybe his sense of humor was just that macabre, or maybe something in him was too strong to be kept behind the impassiveness that had been across his face for the past days. Either way, he looked at her and, even if it was only slight and fleeting, he grinned.

"You don't need to know everything." She reached out, placing a hand on his shoulder. "Trust me."

And, an instant before she knew what she had said, he was gone. His grin faded, his eyes faded, he faded entirely, leaving behind a flat stare. To stand beside him was to feel a chill and she turned away.

"Where's Denaos?" Lenk asked, not bothering to look at her. "I've got something to tell him before we leave."

"Rats hide with rats," Gariath said. "He's with the crying one and the moody one."

The dragonman's recent decision to upgrade Asper and Dreadaeleon from "the tall one" and "the small one" hadn't done much to distinguish either.

"I'll find him," Lenk said, trudging off toward the forest.

Kataria watched him go. Even if he hadn't said anything, the accusation hung in the air where he had just stood, as it did whenever he looked at her.

"You're feeling guilty," Gariath noted, apparently also sharing it.

"And you're not?" she asked, turning around. "You abandoned him, same as me. We all left him to die on that ship."

"I am not," he said, hefting the bucket of guts and loading it into the vessel. "I left because I knew he wouldn't die. And if I didn't know that he would not die, I wouldn't care if he did." He turned a hard black stare upon her. "Why?"

She flinched. "Why what?"

"Why do you feel guilt?"

"It's an emotion common to those of us not reptilian," she muttered as she stalked to the other side of the boat.

"Not to shicts."

"Are you trying to intimidate me?" she snarled. "Trying to tell me I'm not a shict like you did back then? It's not going to work this time."

"When I said it that day, you ran," Gariath replied. "Now, you bare your little teeth at me. I almost killed you that day. I can do it better today."

"I'm not afraid of you."

"Shicts should be."

She opened her mouth to respond, but not a word came out. Instead, she merely furrowed her brow. "Are you being philosophical or stupid?"

"Same thing. Regardless, I never say anything that doesn't make sense." He turned to stalk away, back to some other work. "If it makes sense to *you*, I guess you can celebrate being a little less moronic today."

She almost regretted calling out to him. "Thank you," she said. "For not telling Lenk about . . . you know, about how I was going to kill him."

He waved a hand. "If you try again, so can I."

She stared down into the vessel. Like a child straining for the attention of its mother, the curve of her bow, fur-wrapped and sturdy, peeked out at her. A week ago, she had wanted this weapon to kill Lenk, to kill anyone to prove she was a shict.

She still might not know who she was, who Lenk was anymore. But she knew she had a bow. She knew she had a plan. She knew she had a goal.

That would have to be enough for now.

"No time to worry about the rest," she whispered to herself.

"What could there be to worry about?" Hongwe muttered from nearby. "Chasing an unholy book into a reef filled with—"

"You know, Hongwe," she snapped, "after a while, that kind of negativity really starts to dampen the mood."

FIVE

DRASTICISM

Wizards were elite. That word still had meaning even among men who turned breath to ice and spark to fire with a word. To Librarians, the word had definition, relentlessly branded upon scalp until it bored into skull.

To Bralston, the word had weight.

To be elite was responsibility, not privilege. To be elite was to do that which could be done by no one else. To be elite was to stand and see the heretics burned, the renegades crushed, their assets seized from wailing widows and their homes burned to set the example to those who would fall under the dominion of the Venarium and not respect its laws.

Elite, Bralston had seen many deaths, only a few of them in his home city of Cier'Djaal. Whether by fire or force or messier means, Bralston had never been fazed by death.

Not until he had seen the riots.

The Night of Hounds, some called it, the Comeuppance, the Fires; the riots had many names. It was all to describe the same thing, though: the night the Houndmistress, champion of the common people of Cier'Djaal and bane of the criminal syndicates that haunted her streets, was brutally murdered in her bed.

And the Jackals, pushed to the point of being wiped clean like the scum they were, took their vengeance. On guards, on politicians, on commoners and merchants and whores and anyone who wasn't dressed in a hood and carrying a blade, they exacted their toll upon the city that failed to expel them.

There had been fire. There had been force. There had been mess. On such a scale that the elite could but watch the city burn.

All because of one man.

The man who sat in the clearing now, head hung low and shoulders drooped as he murmured like a common drunk. That's what he was, Bralston reminded himself. Maybe he had been something more when he had wound his way into the Houndmistress's confidence and slaughtered her in the night, but no longer. He was a drunk, a thug, common.

And Bralston remained elite.

He was reminded of that word's weight as he stalked into the forest clearing. The man's head shifted.

"Asper?" the rogue asked, voice cracked and dry.

"No," Bralston answered.

"Oh," he muttered, returning to staring at the sand. "It's you."

Bralston stared at the back of his head. Maybe he couldn't see the man's face, but everything else screamed guilt: the stoop of shoulders that had been so broad when they rubbed against the Houndmistress's, the mane of reddish hair that had been dyed time and again, the voice that had plied and charmed and tongued all the right ears to earn the role of advisor to the woman who would try to save a city infested with human gangrene.

Bralston remembered him, before he had been called Denaos.

"I don't have the tongue for entertaining wizards," the man said. "Not the kind that could be matched by hearing their own voice. So, if you need something—"

"Murderer."

Denaos turned his head, just enough for Bralston to see his eyes, just enough for Bralston to know. And slowly, Denaos turned away.

"So that's it, then? Just right out with it?" Denaos chuckled. "No talent for subtlety."

"No subtlety is needed for this," Bralston said. His voice came on hot breath and beating heart, no more discipline of the elite. "It has no place amongst matters of justice."

"The only men who bring up matters of justice are those who think themselves worthy of delivering it."

"There is no worthiness, only responsibility." Bralston felt the blood rush in his veins, but held himself back. Eyes, shoulders, tongues; these were suspicions. Librarians needed logic, evidence to justify the kill, however worthy. "And it falls to any man who knows what you've done."

"And what have I done, Librarian?"

"You killed people."

"I'm an adventurer. I've killed lots of things."

"You killed *people*."

Denaos did not stir from the log he sat on. But his voice had an edge when he spoke, something crudely sharpened and dripping with rust and grime.

"The only men who tell me I've killed people," he said, "don't know how many people I've killed."

"Fourteen hundred," Bralston replied. "Fourteen hundred men, women and children with families and pets and homes that were burned to the ground the night you murdered her."

Denaos hung his head low, rubbed the back of his neck.

"More."

Bralston recoiled. He stared in disbelief, at the confession and the sheer disregard with which it had been offered, a sprinkling of sugar from delicate fingers over a plate of charred flesh.

The word became much heavier than any other. It and the sight of the man threatened to unhinge him, to force him to raise hand, to speak word and turn man to ashes on the breeze. He turned away to resist the urge. Heavy as the word was, another still had weight.

"How many?" he asked.

"Many," Denaos replied, without so much as a stutter. "Mothers, whores, businessmen, politicians." He paused. "Children. Not as many as her death caused. But these ones . . . I looked into their eyes. I had chances to stop. Many chances."

"And you did not." Bralston removed his hat, ran a hand along his bald scalp as though trying to smooth the rogue's words into something that didn't cause the mind to recoil. "How many chances?"

"I've got one left," Denaos replied. "One I've been riding for about a year now." He sighed. "The tome . . . it's all I can hope for to balance the scales."

"You think there are scales? There is *balance* for what you did?"

"I was given another chance. By the Gods."

"There are no gods."

"There must be a reason why you haven't killed me yet."

"I had to know."

He replaced his hat on his head, drew in a breath. The power, *his* power came flowing back into him. It leapt to his fingers, magic hungry and railing against all the discipline his position was supposed to carry, a magic hungry for vengeance.

"I have responsibilities," he said. "That will soon be fulfilled."

Silence.

And then laughter; not sadistic, not conceited. Humorless. A joke that wasn't funny and had been told far too many times.

"And you waited until now?" the rogue chuckled. "Well, that was silly of you."

Bralston's roar was nothing. His magic spoke for him in the crack of thunder and the shriek of lightning as he whirled about and thrust his fingers at the man. The power was reckless, a twisting serpent of electricity that leapt readily and ate hungrily, tearing up sand and splitting log and leaving scorched earth and burnt air.

And, he thought with a narrow of his eyes, *no body.*

The man was gone, but only from sight. The man would not leave, not after all he had told Bralston. The stink of liquor and guilt lingered, however subtle.

And Bralston had no talent nor need for subtlety.

In death, as in life, the netherling continued to hate.

It had hated the heated blade that dismembered its corpse, resisting each saw. It hated the fire that now ate at it, devouring purple flesh long since blackened with agonizing slowness. And Asper was sure, in whatever nothingness this thing's soul now lurked, it still hated her.

Hard to blame her, Asper thought; she knew *she* wouldn't have much in the way of understanding for someone who had dissected, chopped up, and burned her. And she was not sorry that she had done it to the longface, either.

She was a netherling. A brutish member of a brutish race that served blindly under a brutish, sinister, filthy, horrifying, grinning, always grinning, eyes on fire, teeth so sharp, and smile so broad as he slipped his fingers inside—

She shut her eyes.

She could never maintain that train of thought without returning to that night, to the creature known as Sheraptus, and what he had done to her. Every sense was defiled at the very thought of him: eyes were sealed shut for fear of seeing his broad grin, ears were clamped under hands for fear of hearing his purr, and no matter what she did, she could not avoid, ignore, or block out the sensation of his touch.

Of his two long fingers.

Nor could she ever forget screaming for help, for someone, for anyone. For Kataria, who had fled. For Denaos, who came too late. For the Gods, who did not answer.

Maybe the netherling had screamed out for something when she died, Asper wondered idly. Maybe she had called out for Sheraptus when Lenk cut her open with his sword.

She wasn't sure why she was still staring at the corpse.

When she heard footsteps, she didn't turn around. There was no man, no woman, no dragonman or lizardman she wanted to see right now. Or ever again.

"Where's Denaos?"

Lenk. Not the worst man she had expected; certainly not worth turning around to face.

"Not here," she answered stiffly.

"Obviously," Lenk replied. "I was hoping you'd know where he was."

"Gariath can sniff rats out. I can't."

"You're calling him a rat now, too," Lenk observed. "I always thought you had the more affectionate names for him."

"I called him a scum-eating vagrant who lies through teeth that should have been broken long ago."

"Still," Lenk said.

The silence that followed was awkward, but preferable, and all too brief as Lenk's eyes drifted to the burning netherling.

"What did you find out?" he asked.

"Nothing useful."

"You tear a longface open and apart and find nothing useful?"

Asper pointed to the dagger, its hilt jutting from its place wedged between the stones surrounding the fire it smoldered against. "I had to heat the damn blade to cut this one apart. They're resilient. Amazingly so. Nothing you didn't already know."

"That's it?"

She sighed. "If I had to offer any sort of advice, it would be to aim for their throat. They seemed to have the least amount of muscle there."

"Handy. Hopefully Denaos has discovered something more useful from the big one."

"Such as?"

"Where Jaga might be."

"I thought Kataria had a plan for that."

And, as a cold silence fell over them at the mention, Asper had the unique sensation that Lenk suddenly was staring intently at her throat.

"Then why," she asked with some reluctance, "do you need Denaos?"

"Kataria's plan might not work. Something could happen while we're trying it."

"Like what?"

The answer came just a moment too slow. "Something. There's no sense in going into this without doing everything we possibly can."

"I can agree with half of that sentence."

"The one that means you're going to be unbearably difficult and whiny about this?"

"You go blindly into a certain-death situation, recently wounded and not at all well, and I'm being difficult for expressing concern?" She rubbed her eyes, sighing. "This is different than before."

"Meaning?"

"Meaning I'm not just calling you insane to be charming, you stupid piece of stool." She whirled on him, blood pumping too much to keep her mouth shut any longer. "This is *not* improbable, this is not even impossible—

this is *futile*. Going completely blind into a situation where your best bets for success rely on a she-wolf who would just as soon abandon us the moment she thought our ears were too round and a cowardly, backstabbing thug who makes treachery into a hobby, searching for a stupid book to stop demons that had no interest in us until we went after the book so we could talk to a heaven that *does not exist*."

He stared, blinking. His eyes widened just half a hair's breadth, not entirely shocked. That was what made her scream.

"*WHY? WHY ANY OF IT?*"

It was not a voice familiar that replied to her. Too confident to be Lenk's, too choked to be someone else's; he spoke, he wanted to believe the words he was saying.

"Because the alternative is still death," he said.

And Asper wasn't quite sure who he was, who he was talking to or who he was trying to convince. It wasn't Lenk, not the man who spoke with certainty and didn't flinch. Not the man she had followed into this mess, not the man who had led her to that night and into those teeth. That man, for all she knew, was still back on that boat at the bottom of the ocean.

This man could only walk, and he didn't even do that well. He turned around and clutched at his shoulder, at the sutured wound beneath his shirt. This man was weak. This man made her call out after him.

"Wait," she said. She turned to a nearby rock, plucked up her medicine bag and walked to him. "At least let me make sure you won't be blaming my stitching when you die."

"You killed her."

Bralston spoke once, then again, and the tree above Denaos's head exploded. Lightning sheared the trunk apart and sent smoldering shards raining down upon him.

"You killed her," Bralston insisted.

Hardly necessary, Denaos thought; it was hard to argue with a man in the right, even if that man could make trees explode with a wave and a word.

Another word, another clap of thunder, another explosion. This one farther away. A different tree. The Librarian, at the very least, did not know where he was. Small comfort. It was a small clearing on a small island and there was only so much vegetation to hide behind.

"You killed them all."

He half expected the wizard to finish that train of thought that had been so frequent. He waited for the wizard to use his magic to open his skull up, read his mind, and tell him he was going to hell.

Well, that's just ridiculous, he told himself. *Wizards don't believe in hell. And they can't read thoughts, either. That'd be silly. Now, they might make your head explode and then read whatever's splattered on the—*

Another word came from the clearing.

Oh, right. He's still there.

And fast on the word's trail was the end of the forest. Everything to the man's right, all the browns and greens and soft earth was eaten alive in a roar of flame. It cheered in a smoldering tongue, urging Denaos to be sporting and run.

Denaos obliged, scrambling on hands and knees as the fire raked the world behind him. The sundered tree groaned, split, and crashed behind him in a spray of cinders as the fire put it out of its misery. Smoke rose up in choking gouts.

He's burning the whole damn thing down, Denaos thought. Absently, he wished he was more of a nature lover so he could fault this strategy, if only on ethical grounds.

Perhaps Bralston was more of a nature lover than he, or perhaps he *could* read minds, for in that instant, the fire stopped, sliding back into whatever orifice the wizard had spewed it from and leaving only a sky choked with smoke and an earth seared with ash.

Neither of which did anything to stifle the words Denaos could understand.

"I didn't know you well when you were posing as the Houndmistress's advisor," Bralston said, his voice sweeping the clearing. "I saw you, certainly, even met your gaze when she reached out to the Venarium for help. I didn't know what you were, then, what you would do to the city and its people."

He wants you to answer, Denaos thought as he slithered beneath a bush and peered out from the foliage. The wizard slowly scanned the forest line. *He wants you to succumb to his taunts. A little insulting that he thinks you'll fall for it, isn't it? You should go out there right now and show him what you do to—*

Oh, that is *pretty clever of him, isn't it?*

75

"But I know you now," Bralston continued, "under whatever name you pretend to have and whatever person you pretend to be. I've seen you. I know you're smart enough to know that you won't escape me. You and I both know that if you flee now I'll hunt you down and your companions will join me, once they know.

"But more importantly," he said, "I know you're a man who prays. I don't know to what gods and I won't lie to you by saying I know what they'd say. I don't know if they'll ever forgive you." He drew in a sharp breath, lowered his gaze. "But whatever you're hoping for, wherever it is you think you're going to go . . ."

His eyes rose again, drifted over Denaos. Their eyes met.

"Your best chance lies with answering for what you've done. Here. By my hand."

The wizard's eyes lingered for only a moment before passing on. He hadn't seen the rogue. Denaos wished he had.

And still, he found himself wondering if it was too late.

Reasonable men were driven by logic. The same logic that kept him alive all these years since he had opened her throat and killed the fourteen hundred and more. The same logic that stated that he could find salvation in doing good deeds, as good as adventurers could manage.

The same logic that said, eventually, he would die, and no matter how much good he did, he would face those people and her on equal footing.

Denaos was a reasonable man.

He closed his eyes and clambered to his feet. He felt the wizard's eyes upon him, the approving nod, the hand that was raised, palm open and steaming with warmth yet waiting to be released into a fire. One that purified, removed a human stain and left the earth cleaner.

Something final was in order. Good deaths had those. Final words, maybe, whispered in the hopes that they would linger on the wind and find the way. Final prayers to Silf, a last-minute bargain to get whatever lay beyond his flesh to whatever lay beyond the sky.

Something solid, he thought as he opened his eyes and heard the wizard speak a word. Something dignified, he thought as he watched the fire born in Bralston's palm.

"OH, GODS, NO!"

Not that.

But that was what came out. Of his mouth, anyway. What came out of the wizard's palm was something distinctly bigger and red.

Not that he lingered to study it in any great detail. He was already darting under it as it howled in outrage, chewing empty air and stray leaves.

Self-preservation was a strong instinct. Terror was, too. Too strong for reasonable men to ignore.

Denaos would wonder which it was that made him dart under and away from the fire, that made him charge toward the wizard. Later. Right now, he didn't care. Neither did his knife; it was an agreeable sort, leaping immediately to his hand as one eye narrowed on the wizard's tender throat and the other glanced at his dangerous, fiery hands.

Who would have even thought to look at a wizard's feet?

That no one ever would was small comfort to Denaos. Comfort that grew smaller as the wizard raised a foot and brought it down firmly upon sand that didn't remain as such for long. The moment his sole struck, the earth rolled, rising up like a shaken rug. And like a leather-clad speck of dust, Denaos was hurled into the air.

Where he lingered.

Whatever force that had shook the earth slid effortlessly through the Librarian's body, from foot to hand. One palm extended, the air rippling in a sightless line between it and Denaos, floating haplessly in the grip of it. The other clenched into a fist, withdrawing the fire that licked from it.

Only when Denaos felt the sensation of the sky turning against him, holding him suspended in insubstantial fingers, did he begin to think this was a little unfair.

"I offered you a chance," Bralston said. "Something clean and quick that you didn't deserve."

"Clean and quick?" Denaos scoffed, not quite grasping the futility of it. "What is it about fire that suggests either to you, you bald little p—"

He didn't feel bad about losing the insult. It was hard to hold onto when insubstantial fingers wrapped around his body and slammed him bodily into earth that quickly filled his mouth. The grip of unseen force tightened, raised him again. He hovered for a moment before it smashed him once more, earth coming undone beneath him, reshaping itself and crawling into every orifice.

Except the important ones, he thought, *small pleasure in that*.

Smaller still after he was smashed again and again. Each time, the earth ate the sound of screaming and of impact, rendering the sound of a man being killed into something quieter.

But the moment he thought he was going to choke on dirt, which came after the moment he thought was going to be crushed by the invisible hands, he was hauled into the sky. He stared down at an indentation of his body, noted that the nose looked a little squashed, before the wizard spoke a word.

He was twisted in the air. One hand turned into a fist . . . or maybe it was a foot all along. Hard to tell with the invisible and insubstantial. Hard to think on it when whatever invisible limb slammed into his chest and slammed him against a tree. It seized his head—a hand, then, good to know—and smashed it against the tree. He came back dizzy, winded, fragments of bark stuck in his hair . . . probably blood, too. Hard to think, hard to hear.

That must be why Bralston spoke so loud and clear as he approached to ten paces away from Denaos, holding one hand out, the air rippling before it.

"I don't enjoy it, no," the Librarian said, answering some unspoken question. "Because I can't do this without looking at your face. And every time I see it, I see when it used to be tanned and your hair was dyed black, when you pretended to be a Djaalman and you looped your arm around the Hound-mistress's and pretended you were someone she could trust."

"No," Denaos groaned, "she wasn't—"

"She was," Bralston interrupted. "Everything you think she might have been, she was. She was the one who took our city away from criminals and who didn't look at the people like commodities. She was going to end the vice dens and the gambling halls and the . . . the whorehouses. They were all going to be people again."

"Maybe we don't get to choose to be that," Denaos said, flashing a bloodied grin. "Maybe they would have found something else you hated. Maybe there's no pleasing you."

"Maybe. Maybe people are the way they are. And people who are the way you are exist."

Bralston's free hand went to his head, removed the wide-brimmed hat from it. He pressed his thumb against it, spoke a word, ran it along the steel ringing its interior. Like a hound stirred, the hat twitched. Toothy spikes grew in the wake of his digit, crinkling, growling in a way that only a man-eating hat could.

"This is going to be messy," Bralston said.

Well, obviously, Denaos thought.

"I won't apologize."

Probably smart.

"You deserve this."

Denaos looked up to heaven. *And this is who you send to tell me that? I suppose you don't mess around.*

He looked back at the Librarian, who drew his hand back. He tossed the hat lazily at Denaos. It opened wide, teeth glistening, leather and steel jaws gaping.

And the rogue's hand snapped. Before either man knew it, the dagger flew from his fingers and pierced the hat with a shriek of metal and pinned it to the earth. They looked down at the hat, writhing with whatever power animated it, and then up at each other.

And in that instant, Denaos knew the Gods loathed a heathen more than a sinner.

Maybe he would think about that later, when a knife didn't leap so readily to his hand and fly from his fingertips like an angel.

It flew straight enough to be blessed, even if it didn't strike. Bralston's word was sloppy, the wave of his hand undisciplined as it formed force from air to send the dagger spiraling away. He raised his hand, pointed two fingers forward, the electricity eagerly crackling upon their tips.

And Denaos was already there, ducking under to seize the Librarian's hand and thrust it upward. The rogue felt his arm shake as lightning flew into the sky, felt the stray current shoot down his arm as another whip of electricity shot off into nothingness. It throbbed angrily, shook muscle and bone, but he didn't let go. The Gods had sent him a message.

He was determined to fulfill it. Or defy it. Whatever.

Bralston's hand shot out, pressed against Denaos's chest. That force that had hurled him into the air and slammed him into the earth now reached inside him, those intangible fingers slipping past his skin and through his ribs. They searched for something important enough, poking and probing before they found it.

And then they squeezed.

His lungs, maybe. Or his heart. He couldn't afford to be choosy, not with the sensation of the air being wrung from him like dirty water from a rag. Bralston did not smile, did not give the slightest impression he was enjoying this.

A good man, one who should survive this fight. Wouldn't be the first one who didn't.

Denaos's right hand jerked, his grip upon Bralston's wrist shifting as the blade hidden in his glove came on spring and a bloody song. It shot through Bralston's wrist in a single red note, accompanied by the Librarian's howl.

The fingers inside Denaos retreated just enough to grip him by something more exterior and hurl him away. A ripping sound joined him as he did, like very fresh paper tearing.

Bralston was bleeding. Bralston was angry. He reached down, seized his bloodied wrist, fought to keep the blood inside him. He looked up as Denaos sprang to his feet, raised the blade over his head. Bralston narrowed his eyes upon the rogue.

And spoke a word.

Lenk felt no lighter as he peeled off his tunic, nor the shirt of mail that lay under it. When the coarse undershirt had been stripped and he sat, half-naked in the breeze, he didn't feel cold. That should be odd to any other man.

"No room for that," the voice answered his thoughts.

He didn't answer.

"For cold, for pain, for anything. We have duty. We have things to kill. First her, then them, then them."

He closed his eyes, listened to Asper's footsteps as she came up behind him and set her medicine bag on the log beside him. She gave a cursory probe to the bandage covering his shoulder, gently eased it back to inspect the sutures. He should feel that.

"It speaks. The tome. It calls. To anything that will listen. But they can't hear it. The demons can't hear it. I can. Listen closely, you can, too. It calls us to the island, it—"

What if she's right?

He hadn't meant to think it, hadn't meant for the voice to hear it, certainly hadn't meant to interrupt it. The voice remained silent.

Where is the evidence? Where is heaven? Where do the demons even come from?

The voice was not speaking. He was not speaking to the voice. But he felt its presence, something narrowing unseen eyes into a glare.

Ulbecetonth spoke of them as children. She begged me not to kill them. She wept for them. He rubbed his temple. *She offered me escape . . . to let me go in exchange for sparing her children. What kind of demon does that?*

"You're doubting."

I'm wondering.

"There is no difference."

That's the problem, isn't it? Everything seems *different since last night.*

"Last night?"

My sword feels too heavy. Everything does. Maybe it is doubt . . . but uncertainty is difference enough, isn't it?

"Nothing has changed," the voice insisted with crystalline clarity. *"Remove doubt. I will remove everything else. I will move you through pain, through fear. Your duty cannot be performed without me. I cannot fulfill my duty without you. Neither of us exist. Only we do."*

You say that, but if I don't feel pain—

"You don't."

But—

"You aren't."

He wasn't.

The netherling's knife had struck hard. The wound was not light. The suturing had been painful and the blood had been copious. He had received such wounds before. He knew it should hurt now as Asper probed, touched, eased the red and irritated flesh around his sutures.

It didn't.

"Well?" he asked, the voice matching wound in ire.

"You're healing," Asper said. "Some salve, regular poultices and keeping it covered and you'll be all right."

"Outstanding," he said, reaching for his shirt. "See you when I get back."

"Check that." She placed a hand on his unmarred shoulder and pulled him back. "You need salve, poultice, bandage, and an understanding of past and progressive tense. You're *healing*, not healed."

"Then I will continue *healing* on the way to Jaga," he growled.

"I know I've never really bothered to explain the intricacies of my craft, but medicine doesn't *quite* work that way, stupid." He heard her rustling about in her medicine bag. "You're not going to be healing when you're being eaten alive by snakes . . . or lizards."

"The Shen don't eat people." Lenk cast a glower over his back as she pressed a ripe-smelling poultice against his stitches. "We *think*, anyway. I mean, they're reptiles and all, but so is Gariath and he's never eaten someone . . . all the way, anyway."

"You're being intentionally stupid now." Her sigh was familiar, less tired and more frustrated. "Look, I don't *want* you to die. This wound was tricky to stitch up and if you go around swinging your sword, it'll eventually pop open and you'll bleed out without me to help you."

"There's no telling what's going to happen, and if the wound does open, Kataria can—"

"*No*," the voice interrupted him before Asper could. "*She cannot. We will not let her near us again.*"

"She can't," Asper said. "I don't care what she says, and I don't care what *you* say, either. You're going there to fight and, thusly, you're going to die." She cast a disparaging glance at the mail shirt lying in a heap with his other garments. "It's stupid enough that you're wearing that kind of weight, anyway."

"It's better to get used to carrying it now," he said, "so I don't get a wound like this again."

"You know, another great way to avoid getting wounds would be to go back to that one plan you had," she muttered. "The one where we *don't* go chasing after books and return to the mainland and never see each other again. I liked that one."

"That's not going to happen." The ire in Lenk's voice rose, cold and clear. "And watch your mouth. Denaos will be upset if he finds out you're trying to usurp his position as cynical worthless complainer."

She tore the poultice away suddenly. Her hand came down in a swift, firm slap against his shoulder. He felt it sting, felt himself wince, knew it should have hurt a lot more. The trembling anger in Asper's voice suggested she wholly expected it to.

"Don't you *dare* compare me to him," she whispered sharply. "*He* is a worthless, weeping coward who hides in the filth. *I* am trying to do what anyone with a conscience would, and offer you the intelligence that would save your life."

"*Coward*," the voice whispered.

"Coward," he echoed.

"We don't need her."

"Don't need anyone."

"Pain is nothing to us. We will not be stopped by pain, nor blood, nor cowards."

"We will not," he said, "be stopped."

He felt her eyes boring into the back of his skull, he felt her tremble. He felt her whisper something to herself, something that would make her hard. Something she didn't believe.

"Do whatever you want, then," she said, grabbing her medicine bag.

He felt her leave. She looked back, he was certain. She wanted to say something else.

"She won't."

"I know," he said. "She's harder these days, quieter. Like a rock."

"Only pretending to be. She's still as weak and decrepit as the rest. That is her betrayal."

"Wait . . . she betrays us because she's weak?"

"A subtle sin, no less deadly. She wishes us to fail because she wants to fail. She refuses to mend our flesh. She tries to hold us back. She tries to infect us with doubt. This is her betrayal. This is what she dies for."

"Dies . . ." His voice rang with a painful echo, like it was speaking to itself.

"For betraying us," it snarled. *"They all die for that."*

"Yes, they die," he said. "They all . . . wait, why do they die? They . . . they abandoned us, but—" He winced. "My head hurts. Like it did last night."

"You speak of it again. Last night was dreamless, dark, restful."

"No, it wasn't . . . it was . . ."

"Enough," it said fiercely. *"Ignore it. Ignore them. Listen to us. Listen to what we do. We serve our duty. We find the tome."*

"But my head . . ."

"Pain is nothing to us. Whatever happens, we will persevere. We will harden in ways that she cannot."

Lenk found his eyes drifting to the fire, to the smoldering remains of the dismembered netherling, to the hilt of the dagger jutting out from the stones surrounding it. He saw it, glowing white with heat.

"Pain is nothing," he whispered.

"Pain is nothing," the voice agreed.

"There is no pain," he said, rising up. "There will be no pain."

"I did not say that."

"And if you're not lying, if there is no pain . . ." He walked toward the fire, hand extended.

"I didn't—" For the first time, the voice stammered. *"What are you doing?"*

His fingers wrapped around the hilt, felt the heat. He pressed it to his shoulder, and felt it burn.

"STOP!"

Bralston never heard the sound of his word.

He saw it instead.

He watched his word leave his throat. He watched his voice fly out on a gurgle and a thick red splash. He watched his life spatter softly upon the earth and settle in quivering beads.

He watched the blade, never having seen it as it struck. He watched as it glistened with his life. He watched as the murderer wiped it clean, pulled it back into its hiding place in his glove.

Like it was just another murder. Common.

And the murderer stood before him, already dusting off the earth from his body, the dark blood indistinguishable upon his black leathers. He looked at Bralston, weaponless, clean, as though he had never added another body to his debt.

All that remained to speak against him was Bralston. And Bralston's voice lay in a thick puddle on the sand.

No.

He collapsed to his knees.

No, damn it.

He swayed, vision darkening.

Not like this.

He felt himself teeter forward.

Anacha, we were going to—

"Imone."

He heard the word as he felt the hands steady him. He looked up, saw the murderer's clean face, saw the murderer's dead stare. The man removed his glove, pressing it against the bright red smile in Bralston's throat. Not enough to save him, just enough for him to listen.

"Say it," the murderer said.

Bralston gurgled.

"She wasn't the Houndmistress. She had a name. Imone. *Say it.*"

"Im . . . Ihmooghnay," Bralston croaked.

The murderer stared at him. Almost insulted that a man with a cut throat should slur.

"She had a city," the murderer said. "She had a name." He stood up, let Bralston topple to the earth and splash in his own life. "One that should be spoken on the lips of dying men."

He winced, as though he only now became aware of what he had done, as he stared at the just and moral choice leaking out onto the sand. He turned away, the sight too much to bear.

"Sorry," he said.

He turned and walked into the forest, stopping only to pluck up his dagger and the hat, pitifully still, that had been pinned beneath its blade. Bralston raised his hand, trying to summon thought from a head draining, trying to summon voice from the earth. Enough for a spell, enough for a curse, enough for anything.

"You . . ." he rasped, "you . . . you . . ."

"I know," Denaos said.

The man ducked, vanishing into the underbrush. He was gone long before Bralston clutched at the spellbook at his hip. Long before Bralston cried out as he grasped at his leaking life.

Long before Bralston could see nothing but darkness.

The smell of ripe flesh cooking cloyed her nostrils.

One breath later, she heard him scream.

She whirled about. Through the smoke and the scent of char, she could see him. Bits of him.

His eyes were wide and yellow with the reflection of the heat. His face was stretched with agony, looking as though it might snap off and fly into the underbrush at any moment.

She rushed toward him, fist up and slamming against his jaw. The knife came off with pink strips of flesh curling into thin, gray wisps as it fell to the ground and sizzled into the sand.

Of all the oaths she had taken and hymns she had recited to Talanas, she was fairly certain she had, at one point or another, sworn not to do what she just did. But the Healer would have to understand, if He existed at all.

That worry would have to wait. Prayers and whatever other blows she had to complement the last, too. She made a point not to forget to deliver them, though.

Right now, her eyes were on the mass of molten flesh that bubbled like an undercooked pastry with a viscous, red-tinged filling. The sutures of gut were seared into his flesh, veining his shoulder in a tangled mass of black atop a cherry red and visibly throbbing skin. A parasite would have been a more accurate description, a fleshy tick gorged with blood that twitched as it drank deeply.

Proper metaphors were hard to come up with as he writhed in her grip and screamed in her ears.

"That hurt," he gasped. Tears fled from the corners of his eyes, seeped into the twisted contours of his grimace. He reached up to grab his shoulder, fought to rise to his feet. "That *really* hurt."

"You're kidding," she muttered. One hand came down firmly upon his bare chest, sending him to the earth and holding him there. The other wrenched his hand away from the wound. "Hold *still.*"

Closer up, it ceased to be a metaphor and she saw it for what it was: sealed up in a mass of ugly melted flesh, a seeping, weeping pustule begging for any number of infections dying to come in. The fury with which she sighed would have been better expended on cursing or punching.

"Should I even *ask*?" she snarled.

"Why didn't you stop me?" he replied, eyes shut tight. "You should have stopped me."

"What was I supposed to do?" She recoiled from the accusation, and not just because of the oddity of it all.

"You said there would be no pain." His shrieking died, consumed in an angry growl. "You said there would be *nothing.*"

"I . . . I never did!"

"Oh, you didn't expect that?" His laugh was a black thing that crawled up her spine and made itself cozy at the base of her neck. "So, you don't know everything?"

"Who are you talking to?" she pressed, her voice fervent. "What's *wrong* with you?"

"Is it not yet obvious?"

A man's voice came from behind her. Not the voice she wanted to hear. Not the man she wanted standing over her.

"He's done something amazingly stupid again," Denaos muttered. With a rather insulting lack of immediacy, he leaned over her shoulder, gingerly holding a broad-rimmed leather hat in his hands. "So, Lenk . . ." He paused, smacking his lips. "Why?"

"Not important," Lenk muttered. "Just fix it."

He glanced from the knife, thin blobs of flesh still cooking on its blade, to Lenk. "Friend, considering what you've just done, I don't think there *is* a way to fix you."

"Shut up, *shut up*," Asper growled. She frowned at the wound. "Just . . . just get me my bag. Hurry."

To his credit, Denaos did snatch up her bag with haste. It was a credit squandered, as ever, by what came out of his mouth next.

"It seems as though haste is kind of self-defeating, really," he said, holding it out to her. "I mean, he's never going to learn if you just keep fixing him up."

She couldn't spare a glare for him, nor anything more than an outstretched hand. "Charbalm."

"What's that?"

"The goopy gray stuff. I've got a little bit left."

"A little bit doesn't sound like enough," Denaos said, rooting around in the bag haphazardly.

"It won't be," she snapped. "But it doesn't matter. We're in the middle of a Gods damned jungle. It'll be a miracle if he isn't already infected."

He pulled a small wooden jar from the bag, flipping the latch on its lid and handing it to her. She poured some of the thick, syrupy liquid into her hand before snarling and hurling the jar at him.

"I said *charbalm*, moron! This is mutterbye! A digestive."

"They're not labeled!" the rogue protested, ably sidestepping the projectile.

"I said *gray* and *goopy*. How much more description do you need, you *imbecile*?" The insult was punctuated with a frustrated slap on Lenk's shoulder and, a breath later, the scream that followed and sent her wincing at him. "Sorry."

Denaos muttered something under his breath as he rooted through the jars, swabs, and vials, tossing each one upon the ground before producing something and thrusting it at her. Satisfied, she scraped out a thick paste and rubbed it upon the burn wound. Lenk eased into her arms, the salve apparently soothing some of the pain.

"Not enough," she muttered.

"Why not?" Lenk asked.

"Possibly because I used it all trying to fix another idiot's mistake weeks ago." She sighed, spreading the salve with delicate precision. "Still, assuming bedrest and coverage, I can probably keep the infection down until we reach the mainland."

"Can't you use something local?" Denaos asked. "A root? An herb?"

"Charbalm requires more refinery than I can do with a mortar and pestle. You don't find it outside of apothecaries."

"Surely, there's *something* . . ."

"If I say there isn't, then there *isn't*." Each word was spat between clenched teeth at the rogue. "You need tools to make charbalm: distillation, mincing, rare herbs and roots . . . other healy stuff."

"Healy stuff," Denaos said flatly. "You know, between that and your enlightened description of the stuff as gray and goopy, I'm not sure I feel—"

"*I don't give a winged turd what you think*," she roared at him. "I am a PRIESTESS of TALANAS, you ASS. I know what I'm doing. Now give me a Gods damned bandage and then hurl yourself off a cliff."

A man, quite possibly insane, lay burned and wounded in her arms. Another man, quite possibly dangerous, scowled at her with suspiciously dark stains on his tunic and another man's hat in his hands. It was not, in any sense, the sort of situation where she should allow herself a smug, proud smile.

But, then again, she had just rendered Denaos speechless.

"What did you learn?" Lenk asked from Asper's arms, voice rasping.

"About what?" Denaos growled, rifling through the bag, all humor vanished.

"You've had a day with the netherling. What did you find out about them? Jaga? Anything?"

"Not a lot, thanks for asking," Denaos replied. "She's as helpful as you'd expect a woman capable of reversing the positions of your head and your scrotum to be."

"You've gotten better out of worse." Lenk's voice was strained with distant agony as he shrugged off Asper and staggered to his feet.

"I've had time to do that. Time and tools."

"You've got a knife and you've had a day. What you got from Rashodd—"

"It's not that simple."

"And yet you—"

"It's *not* that *simple*." The narrow of his eye left nothing so light as a suggestion that not talking about it would be wise. A threat would be more accurate. "We won't find anything useful from her."

There had been times when Lenk's voice commanded, times when his gaze intimidated. Despite size, despite injury, Asper knew both she and Denaos looked to him for reasons beyond those. But never did his voice inspire cringe and never did his gaze cause skin to crawl than when he spoke as he did now.

"Kill her."

Denaos sighed, rubbed his eyes. "Is that necessary?"

"Well, I don't know, Denaos. When it comes to killing women who are capable of reversing the positions of your head and your scrotum, is it more necessary or practical?"

87

"What, exactly, makes this one any different from the others you've killed?" Asper asked, rising up and dusting off her robes. The gaze she fixed on Denaos was less scornful than he deserved; perhaps she simply had to know.

"It's complicated," the rogue offered, not bothering to look at either of them.

"It is not," Lenk insisted, his voice cold. "We get the tome. We kill anyone who is in our way."

"She's tied to a chair in a hut."

"She's dangerous."

"She's not going anywhere."

"Not yet. Not ever." Lenk narrowed his eyes. "No loose ends. Our duty depends on it."

When Denaos looked up into the man's stare, his own was weary. His voice dribbled out of his mouth on a sigh.

"Yeah. Fine. What's one more, right?"

He flipped the wide-brimmed hat in his fingers, tossed it to Lenk. The young man caught it, looked it over, furrowed his brow.

"This is Bralston's," he noted.

"And now it's yours." He slipped on a smile. "It's just that easy."

He turned, disappeared into the forest. Lenk stared at the hat in his hands for a moment before turning to Asper.

"Fix whatever else you need to fix with my shoulder," he said. "I leave in an hour."

"And Denaos?"

"Stays here with you and Dread. We have a better chance of slipping in with fewer people."

"That's not what I meant."

Lenk didn't seem to hear. Or care. She told herself that was rather a wise attitude to have for the rogue. The less she cared, the better. Less chance of him failing, then.

That was a wise attitude. Reasonable.

She tried to convince herself of it as she plucked up her bag and produced a bandage and swab. She looked at Lenk as he knelt down to collect his shirts and the agitated red mass upon his shoulder, glistening with too little salve.

"Why?" she asked.

"Because," his voice was gentle, "I wanted to see if it would hurt."

88

SIX

HALLOWED, HUMBLE, SOAKED IN BLOOD

He placed a foot upon salt-slick stone. Barely more than the scuff of boot on granite. The silence heard him and came out of a thousand little shadows and pools of water to greet him with resounding echoes.

A thousand footfalls greeted him in the gapingly empty hall, as though by sheer repetition the massive chamber could pretend there was life in its depths. It committed itself to the illusion with every step he took, each echo rising and waiting for him to speak and be repeated a thousand times and complete the deception.

Sheraptus was not in the habit of indulging anyone, let alone stone.

His nostrils quivered, agitated. He was not about to indulge them, either, by placing cloth to nose and masking the stench. He shut his eyes, forced down his distaste and drew in a sharp breath.

The air sat leaden in his nose, heavy with many things as he continued down the great, empty hall. Sea was first among them and with it salt, acrid and foul. Dormant ash was there, in great presence. And something else. Something familiar.

His boot struck something and he stumbled forward. Pulling the black hem of his robe away exposed a pale, hairless face staring up at him with lifeless black eyes and a stagnant aroma wafting from a mouth filled with needle teeth.

No. His crown burned upon his brow, smoldering with thought. *Not that.*

But close. The scent of death, heaviest and most pungent, was not making it particularly easy to sense out that enigmatic aroma. Understandable, he thought, given all the corpses.

He hadn't been at Irontide when it all happened, when his warriors had stormed the fortress to retrieve the tome and kill the demonic leader known as the Deepshriek. As he swept a glance about the hollow chamber, though, he absently wished he had been; *he* certainly wouldn't have left all these corpses about.

They lay where they had fallen, white and purple, frogman and netherling: gored, cut, rent, stabbed, impaled, trampled, ripped, strangled, drowned, broken, and decapitated. They swelled only barely from salt water. Gulls had not come to feed upon them, as though they were too unclean even for vermin.

He could understand why they hadn't feasted upon the frogmen, of course, demon-tainted filth that they were. He felt vaguely insulted that his warriors were similarly untouched, as though there were something wrong with *them*.

But he had not come to survey the damage; there were always more warriors. Rather, he had come seeking something else.

What it was, he wasn't entirely sure. Why he felt drawn to it, he was only barely certain. That made his ire rise.

But it was here, amidst a rotting feast uneaten.

And so he slipped across the floor, searching. In the stagnant pools of water that remained, in the flock of the crushed and beaten and drained of blood, he found something.

Not what he was looking for.

Cahulus. Male. Once, a loyal and devoted member of his inner circle, brother to the other two loyal and devoted members. Once, reckless with his *nethra*, hurling fire and spewing ice with whimsical abandon. Once, in command of the warriors sent to take this fortress.

Now, dead. The gemstone he once wore, like the three set in Sheraptus's own crown, was gone.

Dead. With eyes sunken into rotted flesh, with a dried torrent of blood staining his filthy and salt-stained robes, with his lower jaw lying eight feet away from his face.

Dead.

Like the rest of them.

Like the ones back on his ship that was now at the bottom of the ocean.

The ship from which he had escaped. The ship he had survived. And they hadn't.

"Good afternoon."

The Gray One That Grins spoke clearly, as always. His voice was soft and lilting, bass and clear; music that slid easily out between teeth as long as fingers. His voice did not echo; music that Irontide did not want to hear.

He turned to regard his companion. Thin and squatting upon long, slender limbs, the light of the sinking afternoon sun painted him black against the gaping hole that wounded Irontide's granite walls. His namesake teeth remained starkly visible.

"It is afternoon, isn't it," Sheraptus observed. "It was morning when I came here."

"Apologies. It was not my intent to keep you waiting."

"Accepted, with full gratitude, of course."

Sheraptus never had cause to cringe before. Hearing his own voice, echoed a thousand times and welcomed into the deathly halls, was certainly a poor cause to have now.

The Gray One That Grins tilted his head. "Your voice betrays discomfort. Pardon the observation."

"And your notice compounds it," Sheraptus muttered, waving a hand. "Apologies. It's this place. It reeks of death."

His associate tilted his head again, thoughtful. "I suppose it might. I really hadn't noticed."

Sheraptus glanced down at Cahulus, who looked like he found that hard to believe. Then again, it was hard to gauge the expressions of a man with half a face.

"Oh," the Gray One That Grins said. "You look and see the corpses."

"There are so many of them."

"I had thought such things would not perturb you."

"I merely see them."

"Ah. The issue is, at last, uncovered."

"Surely, you are not blind to them."

"A lack of sight, fore or current, has never been attributed to me. Rather, I see somewhere else when I look upon these halls. I see somewhere long ago, somewhere much more preferable."

He rose, suddenly no longer squat, but frighteningly tall. He became more so as he straightened his back with the sound of a dozen vertebrae cracking into place, a sickening eternity between each. Upon spindly shadows for legs, he walked down the hall.

"This was where the tapestry walked," he said. "A long and decadent thing of many names and deeds, each one exaggerated as a tapestry should be. It walked between pillars, each one carved from marble in the shape of a virgin, holding flame in hands unscarred."

Sheraptus found himself watching the space where the Gray One That Grins had just been, or where he was about to walk. Never did he look at those long, thin legs. Never did he even think about looking higher.

"That's where it ended." A long sliver of a finger pointed at the far wall. "That's where the altar lay. That's where I knelt in prayer, side by side with the woman that would come to be called Mother."

"I misunderstand or you misremember," Sheraptus said. "I was told this was a stronghold for overscum. Pirates, like the ones that allied themselves with our foe."

"It was. After that, it was a house of prayer for that Mother again. Before that, it was a house of war for those who drove her from it. Irontide is but one more meaningless name. It has existed in a cycle: worship, then slaughter, on and off since its creation."

Sheraptus looked to Cahulus. Then to the frogman beside him, the thing's ivory skin stained pink with the rotting bundle of intestines split so neatly from its belly. Then to the netherling who still held the blade, even as the fragmented cord of her spine jutted from the shredded purple of her back.

"And now, a house of charnel."

"There will be more. Possibly this one again. Such is their nature."

"Demons?"

"Demons." The Gray One That Grins's laugh was less pleasant this time. "It is not a demon's nature to destroy, but to reclaim. For them, it is a choice. The same is not said with any great conviction for humans."

"Humans?"

"Humans."

"The lack of specificity is dreadfully unhelpful."

"Specificity?"

"Just learned it."

"It is impressive."

"Thank you."

"You are welcome." The Gray One That Grins tilted his head to the side, settled down on his haunches. "As to your complaint . . . how many humans do you know?"

Sheraptus looked again to the corpses for as long as he could stand. When he looked back to his associate, seated in merciful shadow, his face wore disgust and disbelief on either side.

"They did not kill this many."

"Your warriors and demons killed each other, true. The humans did not kill *this* many." His voice dropped. "But they have killed *many*."

Many.

Sheraptus turned the word over in his head, contemplated every quantity that could bear such a title. How many had been in Irontide that were struck down by those overscum? How many had blood spilled upon the sand by their blades? How many had the humans sent to the bottom of the ocean when the ship was destroyed?

The answer was simple, and grim.

"But not me," Sheraptus whispered.

"Pardon?"

"I survived."

"You are possessed of immense power, as well as the Martyr Stones to fuel it and the confidence to wield it." The Gray One That Grins's voice dropped. "Your surprise at your own survival . . . concerns. As does your inability to deal with these humans."

"You doubt me?" Sheraptus imagined the threat might have sounded more forceful if he could bear to face the creature.

"Apologies for dancing around the issue, but . . . my associates are concerned. They have insisted upon moving forward with your assault."

"We have been gathering the forces necessary for pressing the attack. All our information suggests Jaga is not a place to be traipsed into with a few fists of warriors."

"Information?"

"Specifically, the kind of information that comes from sending thirty warriors out and finding pieces of them washing up on shore days later. We don't even know where the island lies, much less how many reptiles infest it or how well it's defended."

"Hence part of the reason for my insisting upon this meeting." The Gray One That Grins swept a glance about the ruined halls. "Your insistence on meeting here, though, comes as a surprise."

"It is difficult to explain."

"To a man that cannot see the field of corpses before him for his seeing the past behind him?"

Sheraptus clicked his tongue. "I suppose I felt . . . called here."

"Called."

His voice was darkening with each moment. Sheraptus had never felt a twinge creep up his spine at that. Then again, he considered, his associate's voice had never been anything but music before.

"It's difficult to explain."

"Attempt. I implore you."

Sheraptus turned to face Irontide's vast, corpse-strewn silence. He had not seen the battle, the knee-deep seawater that had since drained out of its wound, a fine layer of blood spilled over it with a peppering of ashes from smoldering demon flesh. Now, with stagnant pool and cinders scattered to the wind, he could still feel it.

There. In the darkness, there was something darker: a spot of blackness that might be considered for soot if it weren't just too perfectly black, too utterly insignificant not to be noticed, as though it tried to hide from him. He felt it there, too.

"A sensation." He tapped on the black iron of his crown. "Something . . . out there and in here."

93

"One hesitates to point out who just complained about a lack of specificity."

"It is like . . . a feeling, vague and fleeting," Sheraptus continued, "something that is there, but not there. Knowledge without evidence."

"You describe . . ." His associate's voice was a slow and spiteful hiss. "A sensation shared by virgins who don't bleed and men who swallow gold and excrete stool that is only brown. Do you now look to the sky and whisper quiet prayers to invisible creatures with invisible ears?"

"Gods do not exist." A casual refusal; no thought, no conviction. "This is . . . was something like sensing a power. Nothing I had sensed before the island." He furrowed his brow as he swept his stare about the gloom. "I felt it then, too. In the shadow of the statues there and when . . ."

He shut his eyes and, as happened whenever they stayed closed for more than a moment, he saw her again. Long and limber and writhing helplessly in her bonds, the scent of her tears cloying his nostrils and the sound of her shrieking drawing his lips apart. And, again, when he began to feel the swell beneath his robe, he looked into her eyes wide with fear, into a mouth jabbering nonsensical pleas to creatures that weren't there.

And he sensed it again.

"We never told you."

He turned. The Gray One That Grins was close now, too close.

"We never told you what led us to seek the tome, what led us to pry open the doors of worlds like a child pulls open closets, what led to us discovering the hole that we pulled your race out of," he hissed. "The war."

"Between mortal and Aeon," Sheraptus replied. "Your invisible gods made creatures that did not obey them and your mortals fought against them. They are returning and you wish for my degenerate race to handle them."

"I did not say 'degenerate.'"

"Feel free to refute the implication."

The Gray One That Grins chose not to. "The tome's power is in its memory. Look into its pages and you will find confirmation of any tale that emerged from the war, the horrors that demons visited upon mankind. Go further and you will find the truth that there are simply too many atrocities in any war to be held by only one side. When demon tortured mortal, when Aeon enslaved mortal, mortal struck against demon in the most vile way he knew how.

"The monoliths."

The great, gray statues that did not stand, Sheraptus remembered. Or rather, that had not always stood. They were still and calm on the beaches of Teji: robed figures with hands outstretched, arcane holy symbols in their hoods instead of faces. But they had not always been intended to be there; one did not mount iron treads upon a statue's base for that.

"They are a product, a refinement of centuries of hatred for the Aeons," the Gray One That Grins whispered. "Love dulls, awe blinds, only hatred hones. The mortals hated their oppressors, Ulbecetonth and her children, with such passion that fire and steel and poison and spit were not enough. The monoliths were."

"And what are they?" Sheraptus asked.

"Children," the Gray One That Grins said. "Some of them, anyway. Grandfathers and teachers and midwives, whatever they might have been as Aeons before they were called demons. All of them ground down by hate, mortared in hate, chiseled with hate, and sent against their parents and grandchildren and students and patients. The demons fled before them."

He flashed a long, macabre grin.

"What demon would not? What would terrify a demon, after all, beyond its companions, its children, and its lovers being forever imprisoned in statues in the shape of the Gods that had cursed them so?"

"The monoliths are . . . underscum?"

"Were. Were weapons, too. Effective ones. They terrified the demons, broke their ranks and sent their immortal minions fleeing. They gave the armies of the mortals a fighting chance, but not enough to be truly successful.

"That was when they took more from the demons they captured. They ripped something from them and put it in something more mobile, more malleable: prisons of flesh instead of stone.

"Difficult, of course. Touch the demon to the head and the vessel will not obey. Touch the demon to the heart and the vessel will die. In the end, their hatred for the demons was strong enough to refine that process, too, and they were instilled in the arm."

He held up a long, gray limb.

"The left one."

Sheraptus narrowed his eyes, focused again on the sooty spot, the spot too small and too neat not to be noticed amidst the passive carnage.

"And what happened?"

Sheraptus spoke softly, distracted. His eyes remained on the spot too dark, too deep, a black spot painted by a stiff brush in a trembling hand.

"Gods create. And as demons run anathema to Gods . . ."

A spot. Not blood. Not flesh. Not ash.

"Well," the Gray One That Grins said. "You are looking at what used to be one of your warriors."

"I see many," Sheraptus said.

"You see the one I'm talking about."

"I see no remains."

"You see all that remains."

"There is nothing left."

"You sound doubtful."

"I have never been more certain," Sheraptus said. He swept over to the spot and traced a finger over the darkness. It did not stir, did not come off on his hand. It was a scar upon matter, upon creation. "What exists is never created, never destroyed. It changes, it alters, it flows from one form to the next, but it can never be removed entirely."

"You are utterly certain?"

"There is no certainty. It implies that I may be wrong. This is law."

"You break law as a matter of sport."

He drew a long, slow circle about the spot. It did not move. It did not react. It was not affected by him, his stare, his touch at all. It used to be a living thing. One that belonged to him. And now, it was this.

The Gray One That Grins did not lie.

"Gone," he whispered reverently. "Utterly and completely gone. And this stain could have been . . ."

"It was not."

"And the only reason it wasn't . . ."

"Unimportant."

"If there is pure destruction and anathema to destruction . . ."

"*Enough.*"

He rose. He turned. The Gray One That Grins was no longer in shadow. The Gray One That Grins was standing before him.

"Your will wavers. Your doubt grows. You prepare answers to questions that began the war that we seek to end." His teeth gnashed with every word, jagged edges fitting neatly together with a firm snap. "*We,* Sheraptus. *We* pulled you out of the Nether. *We* showed you the sunlight. *We* promise you more, so much more, if you do what *we* require of you."

He turned a head without eyes toward the wound in the tower's side. Teeth too long bared in a snarl.

"We are out of time, Sheraptus. The sky has bled. The crown of storms rests upon a fevered brow." The Gray One That Grins made a vile sucking sound between his teeth. "He comes. And he comes for her."

His limbs moved like a tree's, creaking and groaning like living things dying as he raised them. Sheraptus had no idea where the object in his hand came from, from what dark shadow that clung to the Gray One That Grins's body like clothing it had been plucked from. But it was there: a single piece, a meaningless lump of granite, still and lifeless and held perfectly between two pointed gray fingers.

Sheraptus had no eyes for it, though. Nor did he have eyes for the sensation of a thin and sickly grasp about his wrist, fingers wriggling in between his fingers and prising them apart to expose a sweat-slick and vulnerable palm. He didn't dare look down at that.

The granite felt a leaden life in his palm, a thing that squirmed against its shell and writhed against his skin, seeking a way in. It beat like a living thing, shed warmth as though it had blood all its own. It was alive.

He had no heart, no will to do anything but hurl it away, let alone ask what it was. But amidst the many things the Gray One That Grins knew, he knew this.

"Salvation," he whispered through his teeth, forcing Sheraptus's fingers closed over the stone. "Not from a god."

He slipped backward, knees groaning and feet clicking upon the stones, a man who walked in and out of nightmares like a bad thought himself.

"To Jaga. To the tome. To kill, Sheraptus. Him and her. What you were created to do."

Sheraptus stared into the darkness. He might have indeed been alone, left only with the dying sun and the dead bodies and the echoes that had died at the sound of his associate's voice.

Pure destruction, he thought. *It was here. It was there on Teji. It was there on the ship. Amidst my warriors, amidst the overscum . . . inside* her. *And they are all dead.*

And I am not.

He dared not think further. He dared not dwell on the reason. He dared not contemplate what the presence of pure destruction implied.

He might not have been alone.

And so he closed his eyes and turned his thoughts outward. His crown burned, the gems set inside it smoldering on his brow as something awoke inside him. It snapped in the back of his head, awoke from an electric slumber with the faintest of crackles. It slipped from him and into the air, where it traveled on a bridge from his skull.

And sought the end.

SEVEN
RITE AND REASON

*S*o, anyway . . .

His wrist twitched. The blade came singing out of its hiding place, all sleek and shiny and puckering up its thin little steel lips.

What exactly are *you doing, anyway? You've got a throat you need to open, you know. Seems a tad rude to keep her waiting.*

He pulled its hidden latch, drew it back into its sheath. It disappeared with a disappointed scraping sound.

And I'd hate for her to think me rude. I also hated Bralston to think me a mass murderer. It seems reasonable that I should be allowed at least a day between murders.

He twitched and the Long, Slow Kiss came whistling out, eager and ready.

You've killed more in a day before, you know. Pirates, frogmen . . . you might not have the highest score, of course, but you've definitely been in the running.

He pulled it back in, silenced its scraping protest with a quiet click.

See, that's kind of the thing: they aren't points. Or they shouldn't be, at least. You shouldn't be trying to justify this. You murdered thousands, sure, but those were thousands of eyes you didn't have to look into. This is different. These ones . . . hers . . . they've seen you. They know you. Too well.

Twitch. It came out.

That's kind of what they look to you for, though, isn't it?

Pull. It went back in.

They ask too much of you. If they knew what you've done—

Twitch.

And why don't they? Oh, right. Because if you tell them, they'll always be bringing that up whenever you're in an argument. "Oh yeah?" they'll say. "Well, at least I didn't inadvertently cause the deaths of four hundred wailing children and the rapes of their mothers." And, really, what kind of retort is there for that?

Pull.

Don't be stupid. They're far more likely to kill you for it. Then you'll go to hell, where you belong, and suffer for all eternity for it.

Twitch.

Would they, though? Kataria and Gariath haven't even heard of Cier'Djaal. They wouldn't even care. Dreadaeleon is barely aware of an existence beyond himself. Lenk probably would take offense.

Pull.

Of course, Lenk also just tried to cauterize his own wound to see if it would hurt. Does his opinion really matter?

Twitch.

So that leaves . . .

He looked up. The village of Teji was quiet. The Owauku and Gonwa milled about, not paying attention to him as he sat beside the hut that held his prisoner. Not a sign of pink skin or blue robe in sight.

Huh.

Pull.

She usually comes around just as I'm thinking of her. Well, I suppose that would get a bit predictable after—

"Hey."

Ah, there we are.

He looked up, flashing disinterest at Asper as she stood over him. "Hello."

"The others have left," she said. "Just about half an hour ago."

"You didn't try to—"

"I did. Not hard. Lenk says he should be back in a few days, assuming all goes well."

"He just gave himself a rampaging infection and fell into babbling hysterics for the thousandth time," Denaos said. "How could it *not* go well with that kind of intellect in charge?"

"He was . . . under stress," she said. "I'm just glad we were there to act when we did."

"You're *glad*?"

"More than I would have been if he tried to do it on his own."

"Well, naturally. Him acting like a feebleminded toddler must appeal strongly to whatever matronly instincts have been rattling around inside your pelvis for the past ten years."

"Yes, I have a penchant for associating with men who act like children on a regular basis, apparently." She glanced to the hut's door. "Is it done, then?"

"Yes, that's why I'm sitting out here, not covered in blood and not breathing hard. Because the she-beast inside just sighed and accepted that it was her time."

"I assumed it would be quick. Cold-blooded murder tends to be, I've heard."

"You're right, I ought to just untie her. It's not like she can do a lot after you ruined her arm, right?"

She turned a glower upon him. He shrugged.

"You wanted to talk about it," he said.

"Not now," she replied sharply. "And with you, not ever." Her gaze returned to the hut. "Has she been given last rites?"

"Has the rampaging crazy woman that calls the Gods 'invisible sky-creatures' been given last rites?"

"It's likely more apparent to those with more sense than sarcasm, but last rites doesn't have to be all about the Gods," she said. "She might have last words. She might have a last request."

"She likely has both, and I guarantee that both of them consist of 'bend over,' 'sword,' and 'jam in your rectum.'" He waved at the door. "By all means, though. Go crazy. Maybe she'll repent and cover herself with the holy cloth and you two can go deliver cattle together or something."

She split her gaze between the door and the rogue, making certain neither went wanting for contempt before she finally spat on the earth at his feet.

"I don't waste my time," she said, "for any man, woman, or god."

She turned on her heel and stormed off, disappearing into the village and scattering lizardmen before her. He clicked his tongue and looked back down to his blade, feeling it twitch inside its sheath, against his wrist, trying to come out all on its own.

Lenk's not wrong, you know, he told himself. *Even if she could never lift a blade again, it's not like she doesn't have it coming. The same could be said of you, of course, and it would be an insult to ethics if you didn't cut your own throat after hers.*

He closed his eyes, drew in a deep breath.

But that's why Lenk told you to do it, isn't it? Ethics are not a problem for you.

He stood and let the blade hang from his hand as he turned to the door.

Not a lot of use in denial, is there?

He paused, ear twitching. He heard Asper coming, but didn't bother to move. She roughly shoved him aside, cursing angrily above her breath.

"Quarter of an hour," she said. "After that, come in."

Shove past her, he told himself. When that didn't happen, he insisted. *Go in there and open the longface's throat in front of her. Then confess. Then get your last rites and die.* When he stayed still, he cursed himself. *You're not making this easier by letting her delay you, you know. This is not a particularly big blessing.*

It was not. It was just enough to permit him the will to turn about and saunter toward the village, already thinking which lizardman might still have enough good will or fear of him to part with a drink. A blessing; small, ultimately meaningless and more than a little harmful.

Denial often was.

A spark. A jolt. A quick jab with a needle, just enough to jerk her out of the day-long stupor. Just enough to speak a few short words in a language only he spoke, only she understood. They flashed across her mind and then were gone.

"About time," she muttered.

Semnein Xhai rolled her neck, heard it return to life with a satisfying crack. She tugged at her bonds, felt them tight but weak. Her arm was mangled, but it was *her* arm, and its muscles twitched and creaked under her skin, hungry and angry and other words she didn't know that translated to "kill them all."

Her ears pricked up. She heard voices. Real ones, this time: the weak and airy exhales of breath of words that she hadn't felt in her head. One voice something quiet and meek and trying to pretend it wasn't; the overscum's. Another voice, something cold and hard like a piece of metal; *his.*

His voice, hard and cold and trying to convince itself it wasn't. His knives, unashamed and bold and everything he should have been. His feet, hurrying toward her. His hand, reaching through.

No, not his hand. Not him that came through. And, at the sight of what *did* come through, Xhai remembered one more word that translated to "kill."

"You."

Everything about the overscum leaked weakness. It seeped out of her eyes. It shook out of her trembling hands. Xhai knew this because she could sense the fear, the hesitation that came from those who thought there was more to them than decaying flesh and dying breath.

The overscum knew it as much as she did; that much was obvious by the fact that she sat herself down forcefully before the netherling. She moved with what she knew wasn't purpose, stared with what she knew wasn't courage.

She was lying to herself, trying to hide a weakness that she couldn't hide behind a stare she knew wasn't cold, a stare she offered everywhere but Xhai's milk-white eyes. She directed the fake sternness to a purple forehead, to a long chin, to a sharp cheekbone. Never once to the eyes; purple and pink skin alike knew the facade would shatter into tiny, useless pieces.

The overscum's bones to follow in kind.

"I am here . . ." Asper paused a hair too long between words. "To deliver you your last rites."

Xhai stared blankly at her. This one wasn't worthy of her hate.

"To permit you the opportunity," the overscum continued, "to express remorse and penitence before myself and your—" she paused, catching a word in her throat, "—self for the sins you've committed and the lives you've stolen."

Xhai blinked.

"If you've anything to say on—"

"Send in the male."

"The—" The overscum stuttered, recoiled, looked almost offended. "Who? Denaos?"

"He doesn't need a name. Send him in." She tilted her head up, offering a sneer the overscum wasn't worthy of. "*You* aren't going to be the one to kill me."

"Well, no, I'm . . . I'm here to offer you—"

"I don't need that, either."

"Well, everyone is given the chance to express remorse."

"Over lives stolen," Xhai said. "I heard you. You're not stupid because you're wrong, but you are wrong because you're stupid. Lives cannot be stolen."

At this, the overscum's eyes narrowed, forced shock into anger that drifted dangerously close to Xhai's eyes.

"So, what? They simply *gave* their lives to you?" she asked. "Did they just find your utter lack of a soul so overwhelmingly charming?"

"Lives are given the moment you come out shrieking and covered in blood. Whether or not anyone takes it is up to you."

"That's insane."

"I don't know what that word means."

"Figuratively or—" Asper rose, throwing her hands up and turning away. "No, never mind. I'm not going to listen to your poison anymore."

"Then even you think you shouldn't be here. Bring me the male."

"*NO.*"

The overscum whirled. Eyes met. Crushed against each other. The overscum's did not shatter. The weakness was still there, of course, growing weaker with each moment. It trembled and quivered and grew moist like any weak thing would, but it did not turn away.

Still, Xhai didn't really get angry until she started talking.

"I don't claim to understand him, what he does, or why he does it," Asper spoke, the quaver of her voice held down, if not smothered, by anger. "I don't claim to understand why a man like him even exists, but it's not about him. It's about the fact that *he* doesn't want to kill *you.*"

Something hot and angry formed at the base of Xhai's skull and chewed

103

its way down her spine. It gnawed. Inside her head, making her eyes narrow. Inside her heart, making it thunder. Inside her arms, making muscles twitch and crave freedom, to crave the feel of a hundred frail bones gingerly in eight purple fingers and start bending and not stop until this weak and stupid overscum could smell her own filth while it was still inside her.

It made Xhai twitch, squirm, made her turn her gaze away. An uncomfortable feeling. She was netherling: born from nothing, to return to nothing, with nothing between. She had killed before. As a matter of nature.

That she *wanted* to kill this one, that she *wanted* this one to suffer and die over words, weak and stupid and moronic and filthy *words* . . .

There was a word to describe what she was feeling, probably. Maybe there was a word for what she was going to do to the overscum as the bonds groaned behind her and threatened to break against her wrists.

"I shouldn't care," Asper said, turning away again to piece her stare together. "I *don't* care. You deserve to die. He should kill you. *I* should have killed you back on the . . . on the . . ."

She shuddered, bit it back.

"And I don't know why you're not dead. But you're not. And whoever kills you, it can't be this way. It can't just be with a sigh, like it was going to happen anyway." She drew in a deep breath, held it. "So, give me this. Give me just one reason, one lie to tell me that, at some point, it might not have happened like this."

Sunlight seeped in through the reed walls. Sand shifted under Asper's feet as she took a hesitant step in place. Xhai stared. Neither of them offered an answer. Asper released her breath, lowered her head.

"So, that's that, then. This was always how it was going to be."

"No."

Asper turned.

Xhai lamented, absently, that she only saw the overscum's stare shatter for a moment before the rest of the face followed under a purple fist. But that was an instant, when confidence and coldness broke and left only weakness to be struck to the dirt, that was enough to make her smile.

"This was going to be easy," Xhai said, rubbing the knuckles of her ruined hand. The bones creaked under the marred purple skin; maimed, but still offering cheerful, angry little pops. "This was going to mean nothing."

Wide eyes betrayed fear. Not enough to stop Asper's feet, however, as she scrambled to them and ran for the door. Xhai didn't bother to chase. There was no need.

Not when there was a perfectly good, if slightly stained, chair right behind her.

Her hand slid smoothly to it. As smoothly as it sailed through the air. It exploded against the overscum's back, sent her sprawling to the earth in a shower of splinters. She rolled, groaning, still clawing for the door; not dead.

Good. She didn't deserve it. Not this fast. Not this way.

Not when others would want her alive.

Xhai strode over to her, placed a foot between her shoulder blades and took a fistful of her hair. The overscum's shriek wasn't enough to drown out the sound of her neck creaking as she drew it back. Her neck was close to snapping, close enough to let Xhai look down upon her bloodied nose, her shattered stare, the weakness leaking out of her face.

Close.

"But this . . . this has meaning now," Xhai said. "This is something that's going to hurt. This is . . ." She narrowed her eyes, gave a stiff jerk to the overscum's hair. The ensuing shriek didn't give her any pleasure. "*He* would know."

The netherling's arm snapped, brought the woman's face against the earth. The dirt ate the scream, ate her struggle, ate everything but the overscum's breath. She lay in her grave barely dug, unmoving. But alive.

"There's a reason for this, too," Xhai muttered. She seized the overscum by her belt, hoisted her effortlessly up and over her shoulder. "And that's because Master Sheraptus wants you alive."

She pushed the leather flap aside, striding into the sunlight. Those Green Things saw her, screamed, scattered; weak things that didn't matter. Her eyes were for the distant shore, the blue seas and the dark shapes at the very edge of the horizon.

Black ships bearing kindred crew: those who had felt the same spark at the back of their head, who had heard the same call from their Master. They came for her. They came at his command.

As netherlings did, as she did, without ever asking why.

"Theory," he said softly.

Dreadaeleon held up his hands to the light, inspected them. He squinted, trying to see the blood rushing through his fingers.

An erratic, convoluted mess, the human body was. The Venarium might call it a well-made machine to make themselves sound enlightened, but no one would look at the maps of veins and slabs of sinew and call it coherent. They might say that magic came from the same machine, followed the same laws, but no one knew *exactly* how it worked.

If they did, Dreadaeleon wouldn't be dying as he spoke.

"We acknowledge that Venarie follows rules, regulations," he continued to the empty air of the village. "We acknowledge that it demands an exchange: power for power. That latter power must come from the human body, and we acknowledge that it does not come cheaply, hence the laws that govern its use.

"And acknowledging that the body and the Venarie it channels are one, we must also acknowledge that the body governs Venarie as much as Venarie governs body." He smacked his lips, his tongue felt dry. "And in our hubris, we so often forget that there is much of the body that we do *not* know. Dozens of processes flow through us, the same that govern emotional flux, can affect the channeling of Venarie.

"Is it not true that a wizard using magic in fury is misguided and reckless? Is it not true that sorrow and despair can inhibit the flow of magic? Is that not why we value discipline and control? Perhaps it is these things, these . . . these emotions that—" he blinked, his eyes stung with bitter moisture, "—excuse me, these emotional numbnesses that can cause the Decay, a stagnation of magical flow and maybe it's that . . . that same emotion that can cure or . . . or . . ."

His eyes were swimming in their sockets. His breath was wet and viscous, seeping out in tiny sobs from behind the thick lump that had lodged itself in his throat.

"I just . . . I don't want to die," he said softly. "I don't. I've got a lot of things to do here and . . . there's this girl and other stuff. And I just can't die. And I can't go back to the Venarium, either, and wait to die there. Just . . . just let me try something. Let me figure this out and . . . and . . ."

He drew in a sharp breath. He shut his eyes tight. He bowed stiffly at the waist.

"Thank you, in advance, for your consideration of this theory."

He opened his eyes. A bulbous yellow eye the size of a grapefruit looked back at him. After a moment, the Owauku's other eye rotated in its socket to give him the attention of both. Perhaps he had stopped paying attention after the first sentence and kept one eye politely on the boy while the other swiveled away to find something more interesting.

Hard to blame him, isn't it? he asked himself. *Look at him. A walking beer keg with two giant eyeballs. His day is probably bursting with excitement. This was a stupid and humiliating exercise to begin with. To continue would only be—*

"So," he interrupted himself, "what'd you think?"

"Huh?" the Owauku asked.

Yes, exactly.

"Admittedly, the ending could use some polish," he continued, forcing a smile onto his face, "what with the . . . the crying and begging and all. But ultimately, the theory is sound and the conclusion is solid. Bralston can't reject it without serious thought."

The Owauku's head bobbed heavily, not quite large enough to suit its massive eyes comfortably, nor quite small enough to convey the subtle difference between politeness and comprehension.

"So," Dreadaeleon said, "what, you think maybe present the hypothesis more quickly?"

"*Mah-ne,*" the Owauku replied crisply, "*sa-a ma? Sa-ma ah-maw-neh yo. Sakle-ah, denuht kapu-ah-ah, sim ma-ah taio mah lakaat. Nah-se-sim. Ka-ah, mah-ne.*"

Dreadaeleon nodded carefully, made a soft, humming sound.

"So," he said, looking up and sweeping his gaze about the village and the various green-skinned things milling about, "which one of you speaks human again? We can do this over."

"*NAH-AH! AH-TE MAH-NE-WAH!*"

He turned around, saw the other Owauku rampaging forward, if legs that closely resembled pulled sausages could rampage. As it was, he came closer to rolling downhill than rushing forward. Whatever urgency was not present in his stride, however, was more than made up for in his voice.

"*Ah-te mah-ne-wah siya!*" he cried out. "*SAKLEAH-AH-NAH!*"

After the Owauku serving as Dreadaeleon's audience caught the rushing one's arm, all forms of comprehension that the boy might have pretended he had quickly vanished. The two began exchanging words, gestures, rolls of their bulging eyes with tremendous frequency. And yet, as alien as the rest was, one word, repeated often and with great fear, he picked up.

"*Longface.*"

Between the direction the rest of the Owauku came fleeing from and the rather distinct sound of someone's tender something being stomped on, the rest was relatively easy for Dreadaeleon to figure out.

And he was off, heedless of his imminent death as he could be.

Which, it turned out, was not a lot.

This isn't smart, you know, he told himself as he pushed past and stepped over the fleeing Owauku. *Whatever the longface is doing, you can't handle it. You're dying already, you know. Did you forget? The Decay? That thing that breaks down your body and magic and blends them together? Bralston could handle this. You should find him. Denaos would be able to do it well, too. Hell, even Asper could—*

He didn't come to a screeching halt at the sight of the netherling, towering tall and menacing with the unconscious woman draped over her shoulder. He didn't think to express his shock with a pithy demand that she halt or a curse-laden command that she drop her captive. He didn't think about heroics or that he was going to be dead sooner than he thought or how nice it would feel for Asper to find him standing triumphant over the villain.

Dreadaeleon came to a slow, leisurely halt.

He watched the woman stalk toward the distant shore, heedless of him.

He said no words, made no gestures, felt nothing.

He simply flew.

The sand was gone beneath his feet, the power bursting from either hand and bringing the air to silent, rippling life. His left shoved against the wind and sent him flying through the air, coattails whipping like dirty wings. His right extended, palm flat, and struck with the sound of thunder.

The air twitched, an unseen wall of solid nothing erected by a tremble of palm and flick of finger. The netherling didn't see him coming, didn't see the wall that stretched before his palm. She didn't need to. The power bursting before his palm struck her as a stone strikes a river.

And she, too, flew.

She cried out, some trifling and insignificant noise against the sound of the air smashing against her and the wind carrying her and the mutter of the tree that rejected her body with a crack and a weary groan.

Asper lay upon the ground. He knelt beside bloody, broken her, earth-stained and unconscious her. She breathed, she lived. Why, he didn't know. He didn't care.

He heard the netherling rise in the creak of bones, the bare of teeth. He saw her rise before the dent she had left in the tree, a spine perforated by splinters arching as she did.

Inside his head, there were words being spewed in a language he couldn't understand, some things about logic, sense, not dying a horrible death under purple hands, that sort of thing.

Words were just noise now, same as whatever the netherling was saying to him as she stalked forward. Buzzing, annoying, worthless little words he couldn't hear over the sound of his body: fire smoldering under his skin, thunder dancing across his fingers, ice forming across his lips to the angry beat of his heart.

He was alive.

Asper was alive.

Facts the netherling had strong and decisive disagreements to as she broke into a tooth-bared, fist-curled, curse-filled charge. As her eyes burst into wild white orbs, his closed. As her roar came out on a hot breath, his drew in gentle, cool, cold, freezing.

When he could feel the earth shake beneath her stride, he opened eyes and mouth alike. His breath came out in a cloud of white, smothering her roar, consuming her flesh in tiny gnawing jaws of icicles and shards of frost. She was swallowed by the cloud, disappeared in the freezing mist. But he could hear her: voice dying as tongue was swollen, skin cracking as rime coated flesh and shattered and coated again, stride slowing, stopping, ceased.

When all sound was frozen, he shut his mouth. The cloud waned before him, a nebulous prison holding a frozen captive. An impressive feat of power, one that would leave any wizard drained, much less one diseased as he.

And you're not even sweating, his thoughts crept in, uninvited and unwanted. *You're still alive. No fatigue, no sign of Decay. This isn't right, is it?*

He tried to ignore the sensation of something scratching at the back of his skull. Thoughts weren't important. His fading life was not important. The frozen body in the cloud, the power he summoned to his hand to shatter it, only scarcely more important. The fact that Asper lay behind him, breathing, saved . . .

Because of you, old man, he thought, unable to stop. *You're the hero. You're alive. You've done it. She's going to wake up and see you standing over a bunch of shattered chunks of red ice that used to be a person and she might think that's a little weird at first, but then she'll know what happened and she'll reach up and . . . and . . .*

She's going to wake up, right?

Something twitched behind his brain, an itch that couldn't be scratched. *Maybe . . . just look . . . just check . . .*

He glanced over his shoulder. She was still there. Still breathing. Just as he knew she would be.

He furrowed his brow. *Wait . . . if you knew she would be, then why—*

A loud cracking sound interrupted his thoughts. A second one interrupted his ability to stay conscious.

The netherling came out of the cloud, her rime coating shattering into pieces, her breath a hot and angry howl as it tore from her mouth. Her fist shot out, snowflakes and shards shattering in a cloud of white and red as her fist hammered his chest.

And again, he flew.

Like an obese, wingless seagull.

Xhai took only a moment to admire the distance she sent the scrawny overscum flying. Of course, part of that might have to do with the fact that half his body weight appeared to be his coat. Still, it was hard not to smile as she watched him sail through the air, tumble across the sand, skid against the earth, and come to a halt in a pile of dirty leather.

But it got easier to resist the urge when she glanced over her shoulder and saw the dark ship bearing her passage drawing closer. Another glance at the unconscious overscum in the sand was all it took to remind her why she didn't have time to stalk over and finish off the dirty, skinny one.

There were, for once, more important things to do than kill.

She shook herself, brushing off the frost and the tiny bits of skin they spitefully took with them. She held a hand up, noting the tiny red gashes left behind. Tiny, weak wounds from tiny, weak power. "Magic," they called it. *Nethra* was different.

Nethra was power. It didn't leave tiny pinpricks. It destroyed. Master Sheraptus commanded *nethra*, she thought as she hefted the unconscious female up and hauled her to the shore. In his hands, it was pain.

The kind this scum deserved.

The ship was drawing closer to the shore. She could hear the rowing chants as the vessel crept forward like a many-legged insect upon the surface.

She stared out over the waves contemptibly as she stood in the surf. Their arms were as weak as their voices, their chants lazy and distant as they hauled their vessel closer. Weak enough that she could hear her own breathy curse, her own bones creaking inside her, sand shifting beneath a foot, a faint click.

Right behind her.

She whirled about.

And Denaos came to a stiff, sudden halt.

The Long, Slow Kiss hung, its metal lips trembling with his palm, a mere hair's breadth away from Asper's face. His breath hung in his throat, afraid to come out lest the blade move just one more hair's breadth. Likewise, he refused to move back, to relinquish any chance he might have of putting the blade in the netherling's throat.

So, he settled on his heels, steadied his hand, and looked to her face for any sign that she might move and give him the opportunity he sought. She merely smiled.

"That won't work," Xhai said, her voice grating.

"Sure it will," Denaos replied crisply. "Just move her to the left a little."

"You know what I mean."

"Do I?"

He had heard enough lunatic philosophy from the netherling to know that asking her to continue was something he would regret. And yet, a distraction was a distraction.

"You know that even if I put her down right now, she's still going to die." Xhai's voice was unnervingly cold; a rare feat for one who could rarely be described as anything particularly warm or fuzzy. "Maybe I'll stomp her head before I bleed out. Maybe she'll be swept out to sea and drown. She'll still be dead."

"You do tend to have that effect on people."

"It won't be me that killed her."

His face twitched: a momentary spasm at the edge of his mouth, involuntary and lasting only as long as it took to blink. But Xhai didn't blink. She had seen how her words had struck him.

"She came to me," Xhai continued, voice growing blacker with each breath. "She spoke of reason and fate and a lot of other words that mean 'weak.' She came to ask me if I was sorry. She said she had done it for you, to keep you from killing."

Another twitch; surprise, this time. Surprise that he hadn't wanted to kill the netherling, surprise that Asper had realized that, surprise that she thought him worth the effort.

"She wanted to know the reason for all of it," Xhai said. "The reason why you hadn't killed me. The reason why you would have to."

"For her." The words came out unexpectedly, crawling out of dry lips on a weak and dying mouth.

"*NOT FOR HER.*" Xhai didn't bother to hide the snarl, she embraced it with broad, sharp teeth. "*Never* for her. It was for *me*. For *us*. You and I, we kill because we kill. There is no reason for it beyond it being what we do, what we know has to happen."

Whatever semblance of logic the netherling thought this might possess was blatantly mad. Whatever truth she wanted to force upon him was forever marred by the fact that she was a killer, a depraved minion to a depraved master.

He could have told her any of this, if only to get her to stop talking.

"There are scars on our bodies," she said, "there is blood on our hands. We left a long line of corpses to come here. And here we are, you and me. Two more corpses left. Yours or mine . . . and hers."

His hand began to tremble, heart began to quicken.

"She lives in a lie," Xhai said. "Of invisible sky creatures and bedtime stories. She wants to think there's a way for any of this to end without killing. Stupid, even if she wasn't talking about you."

But he couldn't stop, couldn't stop her from talking, couldn't stop him- 111 self from listening.

"She can't see the bodies you've left behind you."

The woman wouldn't let him. Not the woman before him, not the woman unconscious. The woman at the corner of his eye: white skin, wide eyes and smiling, at him, telling him in words without words through that great red slit in her throat.

Telling him that the netherling was right.

Telling him that he was a murderer and Asper would die, because of him; that she already had.

Telling him to look. To look at her. To look at Imone.

He did.

And he felt his jaw explode as Xhai smashed her fist against it. Overkill, he realized as he fell to the earth; it hadn't taken much to send him there. And once he felt the sand crunch under his body, he didn't feel much like rising again.

Not with so many people looking at him with eyes open and eyes closed and eyes glazed over and dead.

"*Uyeh!*"

"*Toh!*"

Iron voices were calling out, chanting. He could see the dark shadow that was the ship coming forward, oars being drawn up as it bobbed into the surf and toward the shore.

Xhai turned, looked over her shoulder. "My Master calls."

"Your master is dead," Denaos replied.

He wasn't entirely surprised when she smiled at him like she had a very awful secret.

"Don't," he said, trying to rise to his feet.

"I do," she said. "Because he calls. Because that is what I do."

"Don't take her."

"He wants her."

"You can't know that."

She looked at him intently for a moment before raising her arm: a twisted and mangled mess, it nonetheless bowed to her will. She clenched cracked and bent fingers, forcing it into a fist. The knucklebones and wrist bones and cracked skin and visible veins conformed to the command in a series of sickening pops.

"I know she did this to me," Xhai said, voice growing hotter. "With whatever she has inside her. He will want to know."

"He doesn't," Denaos insisted, forcing himself to his knees. "He doesn't want to know. He doesn't care about what she did to you. He doesn't care about *you*. He wants *her*," he pointed to Asper, "her flesh and her screams. You know what he'll do to her. You know what he does to all of them. He doesn't deserve them."

"He is the Master," Xhai snarled. "It is his right to take. He wants *her*."

"And you *don't*," Denaos said, "and it isn't. You don't want him to have her or anyone else. You deserve him."

He wasn't sure if she had even bothered to hide the twitch, the snarl that was less than her usual display of anger and so much more than all the fury she had shown him before. He chose to focus on it, regardless, his eyes upon her mouth as he spoke.

"*You* kill," he said, "because of *him*."

Her lips trembled.

"*They* die," he said, "because of *you*."

Her teeth clenched.

"It's for you. All for you," he said. "And he wants *her*. He doesn't deserve her. You deserve him." He opened his arms in submission. "And me."

And her lips pursed shut. No snarl, no smile, no frown. Nothing she had in her limited repertoire of expressions could she offer to those words. Her eyes had never needed to show anything in their milky whites before. And so she simply stared, blankly, at him.

"Take me," he insisted. "Leave her behind, where he can't get her. It's not about her. You don't want her."

The ship pulled up alongside the beach, groaning as a great black behemoth as it drew itself through the waves. Purple faces lined up at the railing, dead-white eyes stared down at him, at her, expressionless but for the contempt that could not be contained by death.

And when he looked back at Xhai, he saw those same eyes, that same hatred, moments before she turned around.

"I want her," she said, "to suffer."

And she walked into the waves, striding effortlessly through the surf that tried vainly to push her back. Through it, he could see Asper's eyes fluttering open, hear her groaning as she rose from her stupor. Still too numb to notice Xhai hoisting her up over the railing, she flopped up into the waiting hands of the netherlings. Maybe that numbness would continue.

Maybe she wouldn't even know how he tried to save her, how he had failed so miserably, how he had sat on his knees and watched her simply be taken away. All because he never wanted Asper to look at him like Xhai had.

Maybe that would provide him a momentary comfort when he thought about what they would do to her, he thought, shortly before he turned his blade on himself for his cowardice.

He heard footsteps scurrying behind him. He heard the shrill cries of a boyish voice too angry to know it was boyish. Dreadaeleon, he thought. Dreadaeleon had seen everything.

Maybe he would kill him, Denaos thought, spare himself the trouble.

As it was, Dreadaeleon didn't even seem to see the rogue. He went running past, eyes locked firmly on the ship as it began to pull away in the surf. No cries for it to stop, no shrieks of impotence, no words at all.

Only Dreadaeleon, who came skidding to a halt just shy of the lapping surf. Only Dreadaeleon, with the blue electricity cavorting up and down his arms with crackling laughter. Only Dreadaeleon.

And the sound of thunder.

He flung his arms forward with difficulty, as though he carried a great weight upon his wrists. He flung that weight out from pointed fingers, the electricity bursting from his fingertips with its shrieking laughter. It did not sail through the air; it was at his fingers at one moment, and at the next, it was raking against the ship's hull, sending smoldering splinters sizzling into the surf as it split apart the wood.

Iron voices could express panic, too, Denaos noted. Or at least, they did when the longfaces disappeared from the railing and dove for cover. Xhai remained snarling, defiant, even as she leapt from the surf and seized the ship's railing to haul herself up and over.

Scrambling for weapons, maybe. Looking for bows and arrows. Denaos didn't know. Denaos was having a hard time paying attention to anything past the curtain of steam rising from the sea and the boy in the dirty coat who turned and scowled at him with eyes glowing red.

"Well?" Dreadaeleon asked. "Why didn't you do anything?"

"I . . ." Denaos replied. "I don't . . . I don't . . ."

"And I . . . don't . . ."

The boy shot out a hand. Vast, invisible fingers seized Denaos about the waist. The boy clenched it into a fist. The fingers wrapped, tugged at Denaos's body, pulled him across the sand.

The boy flung his hand in an overhead pitch and shouted.

"CARE!"

And Denaos flew.

He knew this was the right thing, of course, to fly to the aid of a companion and rescue her from the same fate he had failed to rescue her from just nights ago. This was a good, moral thing to do. Reasonable.

Didn't stop him from screaming, though.

He came to a stop amidst a crash of bodies, hurtling into the netherlings as they had plucked up bows to return fire upon his companion. They tumbled to the deck, a tangle of limbs and a mess of metal.

Denaos liked to think they hadn't even noticed the blade slipped into their jugulars, at least not until he rose from the heap of purple flesh and walked away on red footprints.

He caught sight of Asper first, awake and wide-eyed and silent against the jagged knife pressed to a throat laid bare. Xhai second, impassive and dead-eyed as she clenched hair in one hand and a hilt in the second. Both saw him, both spoke to him, one with words and one without.

"This isn't going to work," Xhai said.

"Sure it will," Denaos said, advancing slowly. "You hate her too much to kill her like this. You've got too good of a reason to cut her throat open."

Xhai said nothing. The hard lump that disappeared down Asper's throat, gently scraping against the blade as it did, as her eyes grew ever wider, suggested his confidence was not entirely shared. And still, Denaos advanced.

"You're not going to kill her," he said. "Not when you can do worse. Not when you need to show me there's worse."

Xhai narrowed her eyes. Asper let out a faint squeak, more than ready to lose a few locks of hair and not quite sure she wouldn't just find the blade planted in her belly later. And still, Denaos advanced, smiling.

"And because you're not going to kill her," he said, growing closer, "this is where the last corpse falls. This is where you and I die," he said, rushing forward, "this is where—"

Whatever he was going to finish that thought with, he was sure, would have sounded better if he wasn't forced to tell it to the hilt that rose up and smashed against his mouth. Asper's sudden leap to her feet and snarl of challenge, too, would have likely been more effective if Xhai had not simply jerked down hard and sent her into the deck by her hair.

And he would have felt worse about all this, of course, had his head not suddenly assumed the properties of a lead weight: dense, senseless, and utterly useless for anything but lying there.

"Not this way," Xhai growled as she hoisted him up and over her head. "Not so easily. And not because of her."

He was vaguely aware of her carrying him to the railing. He saw, vaguely, the shape of Dreadaeleon throwing his arms backward. He felt, vaguely, the sensation of air ripped apart as the sand erupted behind the boy and an unseen force sent him sailing through the air toward the ship, eyes glowing and coat-tails whipping.

"Should have killed me before," Xhai snarled. "That would have been better."

It was then that Denaos was reminded that lead weights had at least one more use.

Her arms snapped forward and he flew, tumbling senselessly through the air. He didn't hear Dreadaeleon's cry of alarm, barely even felt it when he collided with the boy and the two went crashing into the surf.

He only really rose from his stupor when he was aware that he wasn't breathing. Everything was forgotten: Dreadaeleon, Asper, Xhai, whichever one of them had sent him into the sea. He could think only of escape, only of air.

He scrambled, flailing against a shapeless, shiftless tide. It was by pure chance that he found the sky and gulped in a thick, rasping breath. It was by dumb luck and a lot of kicking that he managed to find the shore, crawling out in sopping leathers and hacking up seawater onto the sand.

After a moment, as he balanced precariously on his hands and knees, it all came back to him: breath, sense, Asper . . . and how exactly he had managed to fail so many times in one day.

It seemed as good a time as any for Dreadaeleon to rush up and kick him in the side.

"You *useless* moron," the boy snarled, delivering another sharp kick that sent him rolling onto the ground.

Denaos winced, clutching his ribs and wondering when, exactly, the boy had found time to develop any kind of muscle.

"You know," he settled for saying, "I liked you better when getting angry just made you urinate uncontrollably."

"Why didn't you do something?" the boy demanded, drawing his leg back. "Why didn't you attack her?"

"Complications."

"You just *stood* there," the boy snarled, kicking at him again.

"Hung there," Denaos said, arms shooting up to catch him by the foot, "by my throat, in the grip of a woman whose size is only rivaled by her philosophy in terms of lunatic things that should not be." He twisted the ankle, brought the boy to the ground. "What about that does not sound complicated to you?"

"Why did I use you?" Dreadaeleon muttered, kicking away and scrambling to his feet. "I could have saved her by myself. I could have stopped her."

"Why didn't you?"

"I don't know," Dreadaeleon said, rubbing his head. "There was an itch . . . on my brain, or something. Something talking in my head, I don't know."

"Next time, just say 'complications.'" Denaos pulled himself to his feet. "Makes you sound cleverer."

Dreadaeleon didn't seem to be listening. Dreadaeleon didn't seem to be doing much beyond pacing, watching the ship disappear beyond the horizon, a black dot vanishing. Denaos followed his gaze, wondering, perhaps, if he had been lucky enough to be underwater when Asper had started screaming.

After a moment, Dreadaeleon seemed to come to a decision.

"I'm going after them."

"Uh huh," Denaos said, rising to his feet.

"They can't get too far on oars alone," the boy said, turning around sharply. "Bralston has a wraithcoat, he can—"

Denaos was up, standing before him in the blink of an eye. "No, he can't."

"Yes, he can," the boy replied sharply, trying to maneuver around the rogue. "Just because you're too much of a coward to do anything doesn't mean he won't."

He had just found his way past the man's bulk when a hand shot out, clamped his shoulders, and spun him about. He stared into Denaos's stare, something harder and colder than had ever been offered to him.

"Think," the rogue said. "And think hard. Bralston is concerned with a netherling that he thinks is dead and with taking *you* away from *here*. Which of those sounds like he's going to be giddy to help you?"

Dreadaeleon's eyes narrowed with suspicion. "How did you know he—"

"You've been rehearsing speeches at the lizardmen for a day now," Denaos snapped. "Some of them *do* speak our language, you know, and they speak it to anyone who will listen."

"He'd want to go after them, regardless," Dreadaeleon said. "He'd want to track them down, to finish them off. They served a renegade, a violator of the Laws of Venarie."

"He would, yes," Denaos said. "*Without* you. *He'd* kill them. *He'd* rescue her. Do you want her to see his big ugly face when he bursts in to save her? Or do you want her to see—" he stopped shy of saying "us," "—you?"

Denaos knew his logic had been accepted, as flimsy as it was, the moment he felt the boy shrug his hands off. He turned and stalked toward the shore, staring at the point where the ship had vanished.

"Then we need a way to pursue them," he said.

"That seemed a nice trick when you flew off the beach," Denaos replied.

"That was pushing," Dreadaeleon said. "A momentary inspiration. We use magic to hurl things around all the time, turning it on an unmovable object would naturally propel us forward. But it's limited and it's strenuous."

"You didn't *look* strained."

"That's good," Dreadaeleon replied. "You just keep contradicting me and I'll sit here using my vast intellect to consider how to help Asper before she's reduced to chunks of sopping meat. This is a great plan." He rubbed his temples. "And they're out of sight now, and we don't even know where—"

"Komga."

The resonant bass of Hongwe's voice drew their attentions to the Gonwa as he stalked forward, spear in hand, with a trio of lizardmen behind him.

"Ah," Dreadaeleon said, lip curling up in a sneer. "Thank goodness the cavalry has arrived, with sticks and rocks, just in time to be of absolutely no use."

Hongwe gave a distinct snort of indifference as he stalked past the wizard and crouched down alongside the shore, staring intently at the surf as though he could track the ship through the waves.

"I came when I heard the longface escaped," he said solemnly. "When the first longface burst from the caves of Komga, she brought down six of us before we were able to put enough spears in her to kill her. When the next twenty came, we were forced to flee, to abandon our families to their mercies just to save ourselves.

"What the island is now, is not our home," he said. "It vomits smoke and fire. It is full of metal and there are no more trees. Our families are dead, even if they walk among the living, still. They are not ours anymore."

"The netherlings have a base there, then," Denaos said, raising a brow. "And you know how to get there."

"I do," Hongwe said, rising. "I have canoes to take you there, as well." He turned and began to stalk away. "On the far side of the island. They will make it there by nightfall. We will arrive by dawn. They are faster and their lead grows each moment we—"

He paused, looking over his shoulder to note that neither human had begun to follow him. He furrowed his scaly brow.

"There is a problem?"

"Well, no," Denaos said, "I mean, not really . . ."

"It's just that, usually you warn about the danger and the fact that no one has ever returned," Dreadaeleon said, shrugging. "I mean, you make a big deal out of it, usually."

He scowled at them. "This is my home that I speak of. These are my kin that I wish to avenge. This is *your* friend they have taken."

"Oh, no, I get that, really," Dreadaeleon said. "It's just, you know, surprising and all . . ."

Hongwe sighed. "Would you *like* me to offer some sort of warning?"

The two men glanced to each other. Denaos sighed, rubbed the back of his neck.

"No, I guess not," he said, hurrying to catch up, "I mean, Asper probably would hate us for it."

EIGHT

THE WORLD'S MASK

Three hours after they had left Teji, they had found the mist, and the world that Lenk knew ceased to have any meaning.

It had been dark when they arrived. The sun had slipped quickly away from them, unwilling to watch. The water was a deep onyx, the sky was indigo, and the distant trees of Teji's greenery could not have been diminished even in the dying light.

The mist did not come out of nowhere, did not coming rolling in with any flair for the dramatic. It was there, existing as it always had. It didn't shift as they came closer, didn't see a need to impress them. It had been there long before they arrived. It would be there long after they were all dead.

Lenk wasn't sure how long they had been in there. Time seemed to be another one of those things that the mist didn't see a need for.

Everything within the mist was gray, a solid, monochrome mass that hung around on all sides. Not oppressive, Lenk noted; it couldn't be bothered to be oppressive, just as it couldn't be bothered to recognize nightfall or moonlight or any sky beyond its own endless gray.

The sole exception was the sea. The mist still recognized it, as an old man acknowledges an old tree, impassive and careless for the world going on around it. And, as such, it was granted the privilege of being the only source of sound within the mist: the gentle lapping of waves as the ship bobbed about upon them, the soft hiss of foam dissipating.

The squish of blood-tinged insect innards being shoveled out over the railing in handfuls spoiled the mood slightly.

He fought down his revulsion and watched Kataria's plan in action. With her fingertip to forearm coated in glistening, sticky ichor, the shict seemed to have no such squeamishness. With a sort of unnerving mechanical monotony, she reached into the bucket and hoisted out another handful of bug guts to pour over the side and add to the long line of floating innards they had left behind them.

She nodded at the ensuing splash, brushing her hands off as though that might make a difference.

"I'll let that stew for a bit and then shovel in the next load," Kataria said, turning to him. "Hopefully there's enough here to work, otherwise we'll just start tossing anything else that's pungent and moist and see if that takes."

Lenk stared at her for a moment. "So, do you sit around thinking of precisely the right words to horrify me or do they just come to you?"

"It's been a long trip," she said. "I've had time. But that's not important." She gestured to him with her chin. "How's the shoulder?"

Well, now that you mention it, Lenk said inwardly. *It feels amazing. Despite having attempted to cauterize my own wound and opening myself up for severe infection, I feel absolutely no pain or so much as a stiff kink. As well it might, what with the voice in my head chanting "you will feel no pain," over and over.*

He blinked as she stared at him expectantly.

Probably shouldn't say that.

"*Agreed*," the voice chimed in from the back of his head.

That wasn't meant for you.

"*Tell her nothing. She does not need to know. She does not need to hear. She will die. Our duty will go on.*"

"So . . . what?" Kataria asked after the long, noisy silence. "Stupefied silence means . . . good? Bad?"

"Fine," he said.

"Good. We're going to need it for the plan." She turned to Gariath, who sat beside the rudder, claws meticulously working on something in his lap. "And that."

Despite the vow he had made to himself never to let his eyes get anywhere *near* the dragonman's lap, Lenk couldn't help but peer over. A spear, long and thick and made of unreliable-looking wood, lay upon Gariath's kilt. A knot, thick and inelegant, occupied his attentions as it trailed from the rope pooled about his feet.

He seemed neither particularly interested in the job he was doing, nor the people looking at him. That fact emboldened Lenk enough to speak, albeit in a whisper.

"I don't know how comfortable I am with a plan that puts an uncomfortable-looking piece of wood in Gariath's hands," he whispered to Kataria.

"You don't trust him?"

"The circumstances of this and the last time we were in a boat are pretty similar. You'll recall he had a spear that time, too. And that ended with us nearly drowning."

"*He tried to kill you,*" the voice whispered, "*he's done it before. He will do it again. So will she.*"

"True," Kataria replied, scratching her chin. "And yet, each of us has almost killed everyone else at some point. I guess I have a hard time holding that against them anymore."

"Point being, that's always been by accident," Lenk said.

"*Lies*," the voice countered silently.

"Or by some other weird happenstance," he continued, trying to ignore it. "Gariath is nothing if not direct. There's no telling what he might do."

She cast a sidelong glare upon him. "Men who frequently go into raving, violent fits for no reason are in a poor position to accuse others of unpredictability."

"I'd rest easier," Lenk spoke a little more firmly, "if I knew exactly why he's here."

"You told him to come."

"Like that's ever been a factor in what he does."

"Well, *you* wanted him here."

"Yes, but why—"

"Because he can pound a man's head into his stomach."

"*I wasn't finished*," he snapped. He cast a glare over his shoulder, to the dragonman that had yet to look up. "He's been fascinated with the Shen. He didn't try to stop them when they attacked us nights ago. I mean, they tried to *kill* us and he wants to . . ."

"*Kill us*," the voice whispered. "*Betray us.*"

"He's going to . . ."

"*Destroy us. Murder us.*"

"He's . . ."

"*Weak. Treacherous. Going to die. We're going to kill them.*"

"He . . ." Lenk felt his own voice dying in his throat. "Kill . . ."

A pair of hands seized him, pulled him around roughly.

Lenk had never felt entirely comfortable under Kataria's gaze; her eyes were too green, they hid too much and searched too hard. When they looked over him, seeking something he had no idea whether he even had, he felt naked.

And now that she stared at him, past him, searching for nothing, seeing all she needed to, he felt weak.

"Don't," she said, simply and sternly.

"What?"

"*Don't*," she said. "Whatever you're thinking, *no*. It's not. It never was. Don't."

"But you can't—"

"I can. I will. Don't."

"But—"

"*No.*"

He nodded, stiffly. The world was silent.

Until Kataria looked to Gariath, anyway.

"How's it look?" she asked.

The dragonman held it up, in all its jagged, rusted glory, and gave a derisive snort. "Third most useless thing on this ship." He set it to the side. "Fourth if I use that bucket of slop for holding something."

"Like what?" Lenk asked.

"Whatever's left of you, if we spend another hour out here doing nothing."

Absently, the young man thought he might have a harder time blaming Gariath for that. Thus far, Kataria's plan had yielded nothing more than a lot of time sitting in the middle of a great, gray nothingness, learning the subtle differences in aroma between the thorax and the antennae of a giant dead cockroach.

Not that the efforts aren't completely unappreciated, he thought as he peered over Gariath's horns.

Dredgespiders, dog-sized and many-legged, glided in their wake. Heedless of the mist's authority, they capered across the surface of the water, spinning great nets of silk behind them, which they used to trap the floating innards and spirit them away from hungry competitors.

"*We can kill her right now,*" the voice whispered. "*Find Jaga on our own. Easier to infiltrate, easier to navigate. Without her. Everything will be easier without her. Her plan does nothing.*"

His eye twitched. "You raise a good point."

"Hmm?"

He turned back to her. "What, exactly, *is* your plan? So far, we've been doing nothing but hoisting guts into the water and waiting."

"Oh, sorry," she replied with a snarl. "I should have asked about *your* plan for finding the mysterious island of death shrouded in a veil of mist—" she paused, pointed up at their limp sail, "—with no wind." She folded her arms challengingly. "Since we're waiting and all."

"Well, my plan was to bob in the water for eternity while contemplating the choices I had made in my life that had led me to agree to the half-cocked plan of a woman whose natural scent is somehow *improved* by the perfume of rotting, blood-tinged insect guts," he snapped back. "Of course, since I had deduced this to be an integral part of your plan, I didn't want to steal your glory."

"The plan calls for *bait*," she said. "Whether said bait is stunted, ugly, and sarcastic is not specified."

"But *this* is?" he asked, making a sweeping gesture around him. "How could *this* possibly get us any closer to Jaga?"

"The plan does not allow for senseless inquiry!"

"It's not senseless to question—"

"The plan will not be questioned!"

"Someone has to!" he all but shouted back. "I've gone this far on faith that you don't deserve! I need to know *something* for me to think that any of this is going to work! Bait? Bait for what? Why does it have to have Gariath's blood in it? What are we *waiting* for?"

His voice did not echo. The mist swallowed it whole, leaving only silence. A silence so crisp that it was impossible not to hear the sound of Gariath's nostrils twitching as he drew in a breath and a scent upon it.

The dragonman rose, gripping the spear tightly as he turned and stared out over the water. Man and shict followed, three gazes cast out upon the long trail of bobbing, glistening guts behind them and the dredgespiders that danced amongst them.

For but a single breath longer.

All at once, the insects scattered silently, scurrying into the mist and disappearing inside its gray folds. The mist seemed to close in, as though the silence had grown too uncomfortable even for it and it sought to draw in upon itself. It was dense. It was dark.

Not nearly dark enough to obscure the roiling ripples in the sea, the massive black shadow that bloomed beneath them, the great crest that jutted from the water and followed the line of bait.

Quickly. And right toward them.

"The answer to all of your questions," Kataria whispered breathlessly, "is *that.*"

It came cresting out of the waves, a wall of water rising before it. Through the mist and spray, they could see parts of it: the sharp, beak-like snout, the shadow-dark azure of its hide, and the single eye burning a bright, furious yellow through the water.

"Down!" Kataria shrieked, seizing the railing and holding on.

What else does one do when being charged by an Akaneed? Lenk thought as he followed suit.

Gariath, however, remained unmoving. He stood stoically at the rudder, baring the slightest glint of teeth in a small, deranged smile that grew broader as the great shape barreled closer toward them.

"I knew you'd come back," he growled.

"Damn it, Gariath," Lenk shouted. "I thought we were *done* with this! Grab something and get *down!*"

Apparently, lunacy was not something the dragonman was ever quite done with. He extended his broad arms to the side, a mother embracing a giant, roaring child.

"Come and get me," he said to the sea.

And the sea spoke back, in a cavernous howl from a gaping maw.

The wave struck before the beast did, a great wash of salt that swept over the vessel's deck and sent Lenk straining to keep from being washed away. Salt blinded him, froth choked him, he had barely enough sense to see if Kataria had held on, let alone for the beast rising out of the water.

The sudden shock that jolted the ship and sent him sprawling, however, was impossible to ignore.

One hand grasping desperately at the railing, the other pulled back a sopping curtain of hair to behold the sight of teeth. The rudder, the railing, the entire rear of the vessel had disappeared behind the great row of white needles, the wood loosing an anguished, splintering groan as the Akaneed's bellowing snarl sent timbers trembling in its grip.

Lenk's eyes swept the deck, soaking, choking and half-blind. Of their companion, there was no sign but the spear lying upon the deck, tangled amidst the rope.

"Where the hell is Gariath?" he bellowed over the cacophony of ship and serpent.

"How should I know?" Kataria screamed back.

"This plan is terrible!"

"THIS ISN'T PART OF THE PLAN!" she shrieked.

It wasn't until Lenk's sword was out in his hand that he took stock of the beast before him. From its thick hide, a single eye stared back at him, burning with more than enough hatred for the missing eye. That one had been put out long ago by the very dragonman that was now inconsiderately drowning somewhere overboard. They had met this Akaneed before.

His sword hadn't been much use then, either.

The beast let out a reverberating snarl, its head jerking down sharply. The boat followed it down with a wooden shriek, its deck tilting up and sending Lenk's legs out from under him and his grip slipping from the salt-slick railing.

He skidded down the deck with a cry, striking against the beast's snout and kicking wildly against its slippery hide as he scrambled for purchase. Pressed against it, he couldn't hear Kataria's cries over the heated snort of its breath and the throaty rumble of its growls. He could see her, though, one hand clinging to the railing, the other reaching down futilely for him.

He clawed desperately against the vertical deck, ignoring the pain in his fingers, ignoring the red that stained the deck as he sought to jam his blade into it and haul himself up. He had just drawn it back when the ship buckled sharply again, sending him skidding.

The last thing he saw was the beast's mouth open a little wider.

When it came crashing shut behind him, there was only a wet, pressing darkness and the stench of old fish.

He balanced precariously upon the stern of the upended vessel, the wood splintering, snapping beneath his feet as the timbers were ground between the glistening muscles of the beast's gullet. They closed in upon him, pressing his left arm to his chest, closing in upon his head, growing tighter with each shuddering breath.

Above him, a gate of teeth had shut out sky and sound. Below him, a guttural growl rose from a black hole of a throat that drew closer with each shudder of the ship. His mind flooded, panicked thoughts tearing through his skull, incomprehensible, indistinguishable.

Why isn't Kataria doing anything?

Except that one.

"She does nothing."

And that one, though it didn't really quite count as *his* thought.

"Sword."

What?

"SWORD."

The answer became as solid as the steel in his hand the moment he stopped looking up and down and stared straight ahead.

At the glistening wall that was the roof of the beast's mouth.

He had a distinct memory of drawing the blade back, plunging it into a thick knot of muscle, and wrenching it free with a vicious twist of metal. Past the great burst of blood that came washing over him, the agonized roar that accompanied it, everything was a blur. The ship crashed back into the sea, his sword clattered to the deck as it upended. He did not.

There was a floor beneath him again, but it was sticky and writhing and reeking and shifting violently beneath him as the beast pulled back. He felt himself flying on a cloud of fine red mist, chased by a wailing, anguished howl across the sky that crashed into the sea behind him.

He was aware only of the water pressing in around him, of the need to breathe. He tore through it, finding the surface. When he broke, it was with a wrenching gasp.

Around him, the mist settled. The water lapped. The foam hissed and dissipated. Gentle sounds. Poor companions to the thunder of his heart and rasping of his breath.

125

"*Lenk!*"

The voice, too, was gentle and distant.

"*Lenk!*"

A poorer match to the sight he saw as he turned in the water and found Kataria, far away upon the ship, soaked to the bone and bow in hand. Her voice was far too soft for the frantic gestures she made.

"*GET OUT OF THE WATER, MORON!*"

That was more like it. Even better when he followed her pointing finger over his head and saw the great fin sweeping out of the mist and bearing down on him.

"Hopeless" was the word that kept echoing in his head as he kicked and pulled against the water, flailing more than swimming toward the woefully distant ship. He didn't have to see the shadow in the water behind him to know his escape was futile; Kataria's arrows, flying over his head in a vain attempt to slow the beast, did that well enough.

His body went numb with the effort, the exertion too much to keep going. He was tired, far too tired to scream when the water erupted in front of him.

Gariath, for his part, didn't seem to mind. He barely even seemed to notice the young man as his massive arms and wings began to work as one, pulling him through the water toward the ship. Lenk thought to cry out after him, had he the voice to do so.

The sensation of a tail tightening as it wrapped about his ankle removed the need.

He was pulled behind the dragonman, feeling rather like a piece of bait as his companion moved swiftly through the water despite the added weight. He sporadically bobbed up and down, gulping down frantic air and misplaced salt as he rose above and fell below the surface with each stroke of the dragonman's arms. He tried to hold his breath, tried to shut his eyes.

Because every time he opened them, he could see the gaping, toothy cavern of the Akaneed's maw drawing closer, the vast column of its body lost in the depths behind it, the fire of its yellow eye burning as it bore down upon them. After the third time, he stopped trying to ignore it and simply waited to feel giant jaws sever him in half.

As it was, he heard only the sound of them snapping shut. He was hauled violently from the water, sputtering and coughing as Gariath hauled himself and his frail cargo onto the ship.

The dark shadow swept beneath them, the great wave following in its wake sending their vessel rocking violently beneath them as it vanished into the sea. Lenk strained to keep on his feet as the deck settled along with the sea, waiting for the beast to return.

After a moment of silence, he dared to speak.

"Is it gone?"

"No," Gariath replied.

"How can you be sure?"

"Because it hasn't killed me yet."

While certain it made sense to Gariath, Lenk had neither nerve nor intent to ask him to explain. Instead, he looked to Kataria, breathing heavily and pulling wet hair from her face. She turned a wary and weary gaze upon him.

"You all right?"

"Relatively," he muttered, sweeping an eye around the deck. "Did we lose anything?"

"One of the bags of supplies."

"Which one?"

"The big one."

"Oh, good. Just the one with all the food and the medicine, then." He rubbed his neck, easing out an angry kink in his spine. "I assume we don't need those. Not with your plan to guide us."

"For someone who wants to find an island no one knows the location of, you're awfully picky about how we get there," Kataria replied, glaring at him. "We've still got that." She pointed to the spear, tangled amidst the rope upon the deck. "That's all we need."

"Maybe it's the concussion affecting my reasoning, but I can't help but suspect that one needs slightly more than a rusty spear to kill a serpent the size of a tree."

"How would killing it help us?"

His face screwed up. "I'd love to answer, but I don't think I was prepared to hear anything *quite* that insane today."

"The fact that we are *not* trying to kill something is insane?"

An unsettling question, he noted, one that would be far less unsettling had it not been accompanied by her stare. Eyes like arrowheads, hers jammed into his, hard and sharp and aimed at something he could not see in his own head.

Something cold and cruel that didn't want to be seen.

"I need you to trust me."

"I can't." The answer came tumbling out on a hot breath, on his own voice and no one else's. He shook his head. "I can't do that."

"I know."

She flashed him a smile, something old and sick and full of tears. She walked toward him slowly, hands held up before her, as though she approached a frightened beast and not the man she had kissed, not the man she had betrayed.

"I'm not going to apologize for it," she said.

"I don't want apologies."

She was before him. He could feel her warmth through the chill of water. He could see her clearly through the haze of the fog. He could hear her. Only her.

"Then let me give you what you want," she whispered. "Lenk, I—"

Her voice was drowned in the crash of waves and thunderous roar as the sea split apart before them. They cowered beneath the railing, a great wave sweeping over them and sending their vessel rocking violently. Lenk looked up and beheld only the writhing blue column of the creature's body, the rest lost to the mist as he stared upward.

And, like a single star in a dead sky, a yellow eye stared back at him.

Absorbed as he might have been in the creature's stare, Kataria shared no such fascination. He could hear her bow sing a mournful tune as she let an arrow fly into the fog, aiming for the eye.

"The spear!" she screamed over her shoulder as she drew another arrow. *"The spear! Hit it! Hit it now!"*

The deck trembled with Gariath's charge, arm drawn back and splintering spear in hand as he rushed to the bow and hurled the weapon. It sailed through the air, rope whipping behind it before it bit into the beast's hide with a thick squishing sound.

Undeterred by the length of wood and rusted steel jutting from its hide, the beast began to crane toward them, the eye growing larger. A curse accompanied each wail of arrow as Kataria sent feathered shafts into the mist.

And still, the beast came. Each breath brought it closer, taking shape in the wall of gray: the great crest of its fin, the jagged shape of its skull. Within three breaths, Lenk could almost count the individual teeth as its jaws slid out of the fog and gaped wide.

He wondered almost idly, as he brought his impotent sliver of steel up before the cavernous maw, how many it would take to split him in half.

If the answer came at all to him, it was lost in a fevered shriek of an arrow flying and the keening wail of a beast in pain. The missile struck beneath the beast's eye, joining a small cluster of quivering shafts in the thin flesh of its eyelid.

"Didn't think I knew where I was shooting, did you?" Kataria shrieked, though to whom wasn't clear. *"Did you?"*

The Akaneed, at a distinct loss for replies that didn't involve high-pitched, pained screeches, chose instead to leave the question unanswered. Its body tipped, falling into the ocean where it disappeared with a resounding splash.

"See? *See?*" Kataria's laughter had never been a particularly beautiful noise, though it had never grown *quite* as close to the sound of a mule as it did at that moment. "I told you it would work! Damn thing's not going to risk its only eye just to kill *you*."

"I should have killed it," Gariath muttered, folding massive arms over massive chest. "It deserved better than you."

She sneered over her shoulder at him. "Maybe it just thought I was prettier."

"What . . ." Lenk had hoped to have something more colorful to say as he stared out over the waves, "what was *that*?"

"*That*," Kataria replied, "was the plan. To lure the thing out and then send it running. Any wounded animal will always flee to its lair." Her ears shot up triumphantly. "In this case . . ."

"Jaga," Lenk finished for her. His eyebrows rose appreciatively. "That . . . almost makes sense."

"*Almost?*" she asked, ears drooping slightly.

"Well, what was the spear for?"

A faint whistling sound brought their attention to the rope sliding across the deck.

"Oh, right." She bent down, plucking up the rope and sturdying herself against the bow. "Pick that up." She looked past Lenk to Gariath, "Mind grabbing the rudder? This is the part I didn't really think out."

Lenk plucked up the thick rope. He opened his mouth to inquire but found reason to do so lacking. Everything became clear the moment he felt the tug on the rope and felt the boat move.

Questions did tear themselves from his mouth, though: noisy ones, mostly wordless, mostly curse-filled. If any answers came back, he didn't hear them, what with all the screaming.

It was funny, he thought as he was jerked violently forward, but he had never before thought of arm sockets as a liability. As he was pulled from his feet and slammed upon the deck, though, he wondered if it might not have been easier if his arms had just been torn off and gone flying into the mist with the rest of the rope.

That thought occurred to him roughly a moment after he skidded across the slick timbers to crash against the railings and a moment before instinct shouted down rational thought.

Get up, it screamed. *Get up!*

He did so, staggeringly. And even when he found purchase, it didn't last long. Even as the vessel tore through the water, pulled along by its unwilling, bellowing beast, the deck slowly slid beneath his feet. He was dragged forward, skidding across the timbers until he came chest-to-back with Kataria.

The shict stood her ground, bracing with her legs spread and feet firmly against the bow as she leaned back and held on tight. He slid into her stance as he collided with her, the rope slipping out of his hands briefly.

She let out a sharp cry as she was jerked forward, looking as though the thing would pull her over at any moment. He snatched up the rope again, feeling it gnaw angrily at his palms as he struggled to regain his grip.

"*Hold on!*" Kataria shrieked to be heard over the roar of waves beneath them and the bellowing of the Akaneed before them.

"*I am!*" he cried back, seizing the rope and holding it tightly.

"*Hold on!*" she screamed again.

"*I said I was!*"

"*HOLD ON!*"

"*That's not as helpful as you might think!*"

"*LEFT!*"

It became clear she was talking to Gariath about the same time it became clear that they were about to die.

A great rock face, jagged and gray, came shooting out of the mist, seeming to have risen out of the very ocean just to stop them. It passed them with a breathless scream as Gariath snarled and jammed hard on the rudder, angling them out of the way and denying stony teeth a meal of more than a few splinters.

More came out of the endless gray on stony howls and wordless whispers as they sped past, until it came to resemble less a sea and more a forest, with granite trees rising up around them in great, reaching number. Kataria continued to cry out commands, Gariath continued to grunt and to strain against the rudder.

And in the shadows painted ashen against the mist, Lenk thought he could see things other than the stone faces. Great, man-shaped things that rose from the water and extended thick hands as if to ward off the mist. Thin, skeletal arms reaching out of the sea with tatters of flesh hanging from their knobby and broken fingers.

What are those? He squinted his eyes to see more clearly. *Masts? Ship masts?*

"*Down!*" Kataria shrieked as she fell to the deck.

Yes, he thought as a yardarm yawned out of the fog directly in front of him and struck him squarely against the chin, *ship masts.*

The rope tore itself from his grasp as his hands became concerned with the matter of checking to see how many pieces his jaw was in. One, fortunately, albeit one with a few splinters jutting from it.

"Up," a voice urged him through gritted teeth. "*Up!*"

He looked to Kataria straining against the rope, barely holding on. He scrambled for it, but as he rose to his feet again, something stopped him from reasserting his grip.

"*Let go,*" the voice whispered inside his head. "*Let her fly. Let her die as she let you die.*"

"Lenk!" Kataria cried, pulling hard against the rope.

"*Let her go. Turn upon the other traitor.*"

"*Lenk!*"

"*Kill.*"

He began to miss the silence.

And yet the voice was soft. His muscles were burning, his head was warm. He felt no chill. The voice didn't command. It had seen her betray him, heard him call out to her, watched her turn her back on him. In some part of him, free from the voice, he wanted to let go.

Such a flimsy thing, so weightless. It would be such a trifling matter to let go. And who could blame him?

The voice did not repeat itself. It didn't have to.

The ship buckled under a sudden pull. She hauled herself backward. He felt her crash against him, felt her muscle press against his, felt her growl course from inside her to inside him.

He felt her warmth.

"I won't let go," she snarled, perhaps to him. "Not again."

She didn't.

Neither did he.

Not that he wasn't sorely tempted to as another great rock came shrieking soundlessly out of the fog.

"*Right,*" Kataria screamed as the rock grew closer. "*RIGHT!*" She screamed as the ship drifted into its path. "*GARIATH, YOU—*"

In a wail of wood, her curse was lost. The rocky teeth bit deeply into the vessel, smashing timbers and sending shards screaming. They cowered, but did not let go, holding onto the rope only narrowly keeping them from flying off in the haze of splinters and dust.

When they cleared the rock, they had left the railing and most of the deck with it. Water began to rise up onto the deck as the boat shifted awkwardly with its new weight.

"What the hell was that, Gariath?" Lenk cried over his shoulder. "She said 'right!'"

"I know," the dragonman snarled, as he rose up and picked his way across the slippery deck. "I chose to go left."

"Why?"

"I've just been choosing which way to go on my own."

"Kataria's been calling out—"

The dragonman stopped beside him and held a hand up, the rudder's handle clutched firmly in it . . . the rest of it somewhere else. Lenk looked up, bulging eyes sweeping from the shattered rudder to the violent mess that had once been the vessel's stern. When he looked back to Gariath, the dragonman almost looked insulted.

"Oh, like I'm *not* justified in ignoring her," he snorted, tossing the useless hunk of wood overboard. His snort turned to a snarl as he reached out and seized the rope. "This was getting obnoxious, anyway."

His strength was all that allowed them to hold on as the vessel, without rudder or hope, went sweeping wildly across the sea. Rocks flew past them, some avoided, most not, each one claiming a piece of their ship.

Yardarms and masts of dead ships cropped out of the water with increasing frequency. Statues of great robed figures rose up around them, hands outstretched before them. The mist began to thin, giving sight to something in the distance.

Vast.

Dark.

Jaga, he thought. *It worked.* He could hardly believe it. *Kataria actually managed to—*

He should have known better than to think that.

Where the crop of rock had come from, he had no idea. Unlike its massive and braggart brothers, this one rose shyly out of the water, extending just its jagged brow above the surface as if to see what was going on.

As it happened, that was more than enough to completely ruin everything.

The boat all but disintegrated beneath their feet, the rope torn from their hands as they came to a sudden and angry stop. Three voices cried for it, six hands scrambled, trying to seize it, trying to seize anything but air as they went tumbling haplessly through the air alongside planks and splinters to crash into the water.

What followed was a confusion of drowning voices, sputtering commands and flailing limbs all centered around a singular, urgent need.

"*Out!*" Lenk cried. "*Out of the water!*"

His vessel bobbing haplessly around him in pieces, his attentions became fixed on the distant outcropping of rock. It rose up from a base so jagged and insignificant, it might as well not be there. But he stood a better chance on land than he did flailing in the water.

As good a chance as one typically stood against a colossal sea serpent, anyway.

He kicked his way to the great pillar rising stoically out of the sea, scrambled around its base as he searched for a place to hoist himself up amidst the jagged rocks.

And yet, he found no jagged rocks, no insubstantial footing. Slick, sturdy stone greeted his wandering grasp, a small landing, more than enough for a man to stand comfortably upon, grew out of the rock's face. It was smooth, too smooth to be natural. Someone had carved it.

He might have wondered who, if a clawed hand wrapping around his neck hadn't instantly seized his attentions. Gariath didn't seem to care, either, as he callously threw the young man out from the water and onto the landing. He hauled himself up afterward, spreading his wings and shaking his body, sending stinging droplets into Lenk's eyes.

"Watch it," Lenk muttered.

"If you said less stupid things, you'd have credibility to resent me when I called you stupid," the dragonman replied crisply, folding his wings behind him.

"Would you call me stupid less?"

"No. But I might feel a little less good about it."

Lenk opened his mouth to retort when his eyes suddenly went wide, sweeping over the sea.

"Where's Kataria?"

The first answer came with an uncaring roll of Gariath's broad shoulders.

The second, slightly more helpful answer came from the bubbles rising up beside the landing. A sopping mess of golden hair, frazzled feathers and sputtering gasps emerged moments later. With some difficulty, it made its way over to the landing and hooked an arm onto the stone. It looked up at them, the only thing visible through the mess of wet straw being an angry, canine-bared snarl.

"Help me, you idiots," Kataria snapped. "I didn't go back to get your stupid supplies so I could die for them."

She seemed less than annoyed when Gariath took her by the arms and hauled her effortlessly from the water, callously dropping her and the stuff she carried to the landing. Steel rattled upon stone, a blade sliding away from her to rest at Lenk's feet like a waiting puppy.

"You . . ." he whispered, reaching down to take it by the hilt with a slightly unnerving gentleness, "went back for my sword."

"You're useless without it," she muttered. She rose up, kicked a sopping leather satchel toward him. "And these are useless without you."

"The small bag?"

"It looked important."

"There's no food in it," he said, looking at her askew. "There's nothing in them."

Except my journal, he thought.

She stared at him intently, as though she could stare past his befuddled eyes and into his thoughts. She snorted, pulling wet hair behind her head and callously wringing it out.

"Important to someone, then," she said.

"Right," he said, voice fading on a breeze that wasn't there.

It wasn't lost on her, though; her long ears, three ragged notches to a length, twitched with an anxious fervor, swallowing his voice. Her entire body seemed to follow suit, the sinew of her arms flexing as she twisted her hair out, naked abdomen tensing, sending droplets of salt dancing down the shallow contours of her muscle to disappear in the water-slick cling of her breeches.

And amidst all the motion of her body, only her eyes remained still, fixated. On him.

Absently, he wondered if it was telling that he only seemed to notice her in such a way before or after a near death experience.

"Stairs."

He startled at the sound; Gariath's voice felt something rough and coarse on his ears. Almost as rough and coarse as his claws felt wrapped around his neck. The dragonman hoisted him up, turned him around sharply to face them: a narrow set of steps, worn by salt and storm, spiraling up around the pillar of rock.

"Right," Lenk whispered, shouldering sword and satchel alike, "stairs."

Nothing more need be said; no one needed a reason to get farther away from the water. The mist thinned as they followed it to the top, though not by much. When feet were set upon the smooth, hewn tableau of the pillar, it was still thick enough to strangle the sun, if not banish it entirely.

Perhaps the light was just enough to let them see it clearly. Perhaps there was no mist thick enough to smother it entirely from view. But in the distance, still vast, still dark, loomed an imposing shape.

"Jaga," Lenk whispered, as though speaking the name louder might draw its attention.

"It doesn't *look* like an island," Kataria said, squinting into the gloom. "Not like any I've seen, anyway." She shrugged. "Then again, I've never seen an island with a walkway leading conveniently to it."

True enough, there it was. However narrow and however precarious, a walkway of stone stretched from the end of the pillar into the mist toward the distant island.

"I've never heard of a giant rock that had such a neat and tidy top," Lenk replied, tapping his feet upon the hewn tableau. "Nor ones with naturally-occurring staircases, either. Not that it wasn't nice of them, but why would the Shen carve any of this?"

"They didn't."

There was an edge in Gariath's voice, less coarse and more jagged, as though he took offense at the insinuation. As Lenk turned about, met the dragonman's black, narrow glare, he felt considerable credence lent to the theory.

"And how do you know?" the young man asked.

"Because I do," Gariath growled.

"*He knows them,*" the voice whispered, gnawing at the back of Lenk's skull, "*because he is them. Your enemy.*"

"Well, he would know, wouldn't he?" Kataria muttered. "Ask a question of reptiles, get an answer from a reptile."

"*He betrayed you once for them.*"

Lenk shook his head, tried to ignore the voice, the growing pain at the base of his head.

"The Shen wouldn't build this," Gariath said, "because they are Shen."

"What?" Kataria asked, face screwing up.

"*He doesn't even bother to lie to you.*"

"If you don't know, then you don't need to know. They didn't build this. Do not accuse them of it."

"*He defends them.*"

"Why?" Lenk suddenly blurted out, aware of both of their stares upon him. "Why are you defending them?"

"*He is one of them.*" 135

"How do you know so much about them?" Lenk asked, taking a step toward the dragonman. "What else do you know about them?"

"*He will kill you, for them.*"

"Why did you even come?"

"You were going to die without me," Gariath replied.

"And? That's never swayed you before. But you wanted to come this time, you wanted to see the Shen. You haven't stopped talking about them, since—" The words came out of his mouth, forced and sharp, as though he were spitting blades. "Since you abandoned us to go chase them."

One didn't need to be particularly observant to note the tension rippling between them; that much would have been obvious by the clenching of Gariath's fists as he took a challenging step forward.

"Consider carefully," he said, low and threatening, "what you're accusing me of."

"Betrayal," Lenk replied.

"And that forbids someone from coming?" He cast a sidelong scowl to Kataria. "You chose poor company."

Lenk caught a glimpse out of the corner of his eye. Shock was painted across the shict's face, fear was there, too, each in such great coating as to nearly mask the expression of hurt. Nearly, but not entirely, and not nearly enough to draw attention away from the fact that she did not refute, contradict, or even insult the dragonman.

It hurt, too, when Kataria turned her gaze away from him.

"*Not about her,*" the voice whispered. "*Not yet.*"

"This isn't about her," Lenk said, turning his attentions back to the dragonman. "This is about *you* and what *you* came for. Us . . . or the Shen?"

Gariath's earfrills fanned out threateningly. His gaze narrowed sharply as he leaned forward. Lenk did not back down, did not flinch as the dragonman snorted and sent a wave of hot breath roiling across his face.

"Always," Gariath said, "it has always been for—"

The mist split apart with the sound of thunder and the gnash of jaws. Teeth came flying out of nothingness, denying man and dragonman a chance to do anything before they came down in a crash. A shock ripped through Lenk, sent him crashing to the earth, and when he found enough sense to look, Gariath was gone.

Not far, though.

Roar clashed against roar, howl ground against howl as the Akaneed pulled its great head back from the pillar and whipped its head about violently, trying to silence the writhing red body in its jaws. Gariath had no intention of doing such, no intention of a silent resignation to teeth and tongue.

And no choice in the matter.

The fight came to a sudden halt and Lenk looked up, helplessly, as Gariath squatted between the jaws. His muscles strained, arms against the roof of the beast's mouth, feet wedged between its lower teeth, body trembling with the effort as he tried to keep the creature's cavernous maw from snapping shut.

A moment, and everything went still. Gariath's body ceased to quake. The Akaneed's jaws grew solid and strong. The dragonman stared down from between rows of unmoving teeth and said something.

Then they snapped shut and he disappeared.

A single moment spared to cast a low, burbling keen down upon the two piddling creatures upon the pillar. A low groaning sound as it fell on its side, crashed into the ocean with an angry wave. A fading sound of froth hissing into nothingness upon the sea.

And Gariath was gone.

Lenk looked to Kataria. Kataria looked to Lenk. Neither had the expression, the words to fit what they had just seen.

And still, they tried.

"Do we . . ." Kataria asked, the words lingering into meaninglessness.

"How?" Lenk asked, the question hanging between them like something hard and iron.

And it continued to hang there, solid as the rock they did not move from, thick as the mist that closed in around them, unfathomable as the sea gently lapping against the stone.

NINE

SHE KEEPS HER PROMISES

The water was warm. Too warm, he thought as it lapped up against his ankles. It was too warm for the season. It should not be this warm. And at that moment, he did not care that it was warm.

He looked down at his legs, ghastly white and sickly, the faintest hint of webs between his toes, as though they had started growing and lost interest later. His eyes drifted to the legs beside him, limber and tan, healthy, all the little brown toes wriggling as they kicked gentle waves in the water.

It hurt him to think that his legs had once been so healthy, to think that they might still have been if not for the circumstances that had arisen years ago. But it hurt less to look at those healthy legs than to look into her eyes.

And it hurt more to hear her speak.

"So," Kasla said, voice too soft, "what happened?"

A question he had asked himself every breath for the past twelve hours. He had been searching for an answer for at least as long.

At first, he looked for something that would make her understand, make her realize it wasn't his fault, make her realize it was the Gods' fault. But that one rang hollow.

Then he looked for something that would take all the blame, something that would make her feel pity for him, make her realize he was a man driven to what he did, not a man accustomed to making choices. But that one tasted foul on his tongue.

Then, he just hoped to find one that would let her look him in the eyes again.

And now that she asked, he gave up on that, too.

"I didn't think anyone heard me," he said, staring down at his feet. "I called out so many times and no one ever answered. I didn't think there was any harm in just . . . doing it more." He closed his eyes, felt the warmth lap around his ankles. "I started talking . . . to no one, when I sat beside my daughter while she was sick. I started asking questions, started telling secrets, I . . . I told them I was afraid. I told them I didn't want to be alone."

Maybe Kasla said something with her eyes. He couldn't bear to look up and see.

"And then, when I said that . . . I don't know, maybe I just said so much that someone finally heard me. It was too late, then, my daughter was gone. But they answered . . . and they told me . . . and they said I didn't have to be alone anymore."

He looked up, out over the sea. It was calm.

"So I went to the shore. I started walking into the sea. And I didn't stop until I became . . ." He held out his hands, white and sickly. Not Hanth's hands. "This."

"You could have told me," she said. "I would have understood."

And then he looked up. He looked into her dark face under the bush of dark hair. It was pained, trying to figure out something and agonized that it didn't make sense.

"I wouldn't have, no," she said with a sigh. "But you should have told me."

"I should have," he agreed. "I should have done many things."

There were no stars in the sky. There were clouds. And when they shifted, a tinge of red could be seen within them. But the sky had been bled dry, of stars and of light and tears. Nothing was left.

And in the darkness, she spoke.

"Tell me why it has to be like this."

"I already told you."

"Tell me again. Please."

Hanth pulled himself to his feet. The wood of the docks felt cold and splintered underneath him, sent tingling lances up through the soles of his feet and into his calves. But he cast a smile at her, as warm as the water, as he offered a hand to her.

"Because I made a lot of mistakes," he said, gently helping her to her feet. "And the more mistakes I make, the less chances I have to make up for them." Hand in hand, they began to walk to the end of the dock, to the vessel bobbing patiently in the water. "So when they come along, I have to take them."

"I'm not a child," she said, pulling her hand from his.

He winced. "I know."

"Then don't talk to me like one."

"I can't help it."

"Because I remind you of her?"

He felt the shadow fall over them. He heard the low, guttural hiss that accompanied it. He sensed their eyes, their vast and empty stares, boring into the back of his skull. They were waiting for him, their claws twitching eagerly as they rapped upon the stone.

He did not turn around.

"Because I want you to forget this," he said. "I want to hope, somehow, that one day you'll just wake up and think everything has been a bad dream. This place, them . . . me."

"I never will."

"Maybe you can't," he said. "But I want to hope you can." He looked at her, swallowed hard. "If I can't have that—"

"You can." Her eyes were glistening, reflecting a light that wasn't there. "I'll try to forget."

He nodded, silently. To say anything else would be to give her something to hold onto. Something to cling to when she wondered about what had happened to him. Something to remember when she looked out over the ocean at night and wondered if it had ever been more than just a nightmare.

He could not give her any memories of him. He wasn't that cruel.

So he gingerly eased her into the vessel. He checked to make sure that it was laden with food, enough to see her a few days adrift in the shipping lanes. He tried not to think about what might happen to her out at sea without him.

He untied the boat.

He watched it drift out onto the sea, away from him.

He watched her, trying not to scream at her, to tell her to turn around and stop looking at him. He watched her. She watched him. And neither of them turned around.

Not until she had vanished into the night.

It wasn't enough. He could still feel her staring when he turned around to face them.

But he forced himself not to turn back around and see if he could still catch a glimpse of her. He forced himself not to look away from them as they stared down behind veils of blue light. He forced himself to look into their eyes, the black voids that hung like obsidian moons over their needle-toothed jaws wrapped around soft, feminine lips.

"You will leave her alone," he said flatly.

Alwaysalwaysalwaysalonealone.

He saw lips twitch, heard the whispers inside his head. He couldn't tell which one of the two was speaking. It didn't matter.

Apromiseisapromisepromisepromise.

MotherDeepkeepsHerpromisespromisespromises.

Youknowknowknowthisthis.

MouthMouthMouthMouth.

MouthMouthMouthMouth.

It almost sounded like a word from a language he had never heard before, the kind of direly important gibberish he had heard only in bad dreams and fever-hot ears.

Mouth.

That was his name now. That had been his name ever since he had turned around. Hanth was the bad dream now, a half-word that she would remember for a scant few breathless moments before rolling over and going back to sleep.

Hanth should stay in those bad dreams.

The waking world belonged to the Mouth.

And the Mouth belonged to Ulbecetonth, as did the city.

"Take me to them," he said.

The Sermonics turned about slowly, pressing their withered bellies to the wood and clawing their way toward the city on thin, gray nails. Their eel tails dragged behind them, their blue lantern lights bobbed before them. These were the angels that heralded his arrival, their whispers were the trumpets that announced his coming.

The Mouth of Ulbecetonth, Her will in mortal flesh, strode through the ruins of Port Yonder.

"Ruins" might have been too dramatic a word for the empty streets that greeted him, though. The buildings stood undisturbed, witnessing his procession with as much silence as they had witnessed the horrors hours ago. The cobblestones were clean of corpses, such valuable commodities having long been taken for more practical uses than decoration. The people and all their noise and fears and tears were gone and the stones weren't telling where they went.

The Mouth closed his eyes as he walked and pretended that nothing had ever happened here.

It was easy. Until a pungent, coppery perfume filled his nostrils and he felt his foot settle in a cloying pool of something sticky and thick. He winced, tugging at his foot. It came free with a long, slow slurping sound that resonated in the silence, like a thick, wet piece of paper being slowly ripped in half.

142 It followed his every step.

It followed him to the temple, and the cluster of fear and quivering flesh assembled within its shattered walls.

The people of Port Yonder were massed within the former prison. And with its captive fled, they joined between the gaping cracks, beneath the sky of shattered stone, a sea of skin and tears that roiled with every wail, rippled with every sob, heaved with every plea offered to anything. To the godless sky, to the pitiless stone, to the creatures that guarded them.

The frogmen did not seem to hear. Packed into the cracks of crumbling stone, perched upon the smashed pillars, leering out from the darkness, they paid no mind to their mass captives. They showed no fear. Even if they could feel such a thing anymore, they would have had none of it. For even if their prisoners could rise up and break free of them, there was nowhere to run.

Beyond the prison, there was water and darkness. In water, in darkness, there were things for which there were no tears.

Out of the corners of his eyes, he could see their lights. And from the corners of his skull, in whispers, he could hear them speak.

Seethemyearningbeggingpleadingwailing.

Weepinggnashingcryingscreaming.

TalktothemtellthemsoothethembethereforthemHerwordsHerwordsHerwords.

NoliesnogodsnonothingHerwordsHerwordsHerwordsonly.

He ignored them, or tried to. He didn't need to be told what was expected of him.

The whispers followed him into the temple, too loud to ignore, not nearly loud enough to drown out the sounds of the people.

The crying, the wailing, the weeping, the pleading, the cursing, and the silent people. All gathered together in a trembling pond of glassy eyes and gaping mouths, each one a little fish staring dumbly at the sky.

They didn't seem aware of him, the man that had walked amongst them as neighbor a few days ago, the man that walked amongst them now as prophet. Their eyes were fixed on the heavens or staring back up at them from bitter puddles beneath their feet.

Only one bothered to look up at him, to scowl at him. Two men who shared neither gaze nor knowledge of each other. Two men who might not ever exchange more than a single word.

"Betrayer."

And at that single word, the Mouth stopped. The Mouth turned and met the man's scowl.

He tore the blade from his belt, the jagged sliver of bone clenched in one trembling fist, the scruff of the man's tunic clenched in another. He pulled the man to his feet, tore him from the pond that wailed as though a finger had been torn from them each collectively.

143

Amidst the wailing, amidst the shrieking, amidst the many, many more words that the man shared with him, the Mouth pulled him to the edge of the pool, the liquid prison.

The waters stirred, black as pitch. And within, things blacker than pitch moved.

The Mouth shoved the man to the edge, sent him teetering upon it. The man craned his neck to turn a face, one that was just as indistinct and useless as the rest of them, upon the Mouth. And he shared one more word.

"Please."

The knife moved with mechanical precision. One thrust in, one yank out. A moment's exertion. The measure of a man, bleeding from the throat and falling, vanishing into water without a splash.

There was shrieking, there was wailing, there were hundreds of voices crying hundreds of names. None spoke louder than the Mouth's, his hands thrown out wide and his face turned to heaven.

"*SAVE HIM!*"

The oddity of the statement turned their wailing to a burbling mutter. Or perhaps they wished to save the screaming for something more astonishing.

"*Save any of us,*" he cried again to heaven.

The skies remained still, without blood and without tears. He looked around at the silence, turned around, as though checking to see if he had missed something.

"Strike down this vile betrayer," his voice lowered with his gaze, both sweeping over the crowd assembled before him. "Deliver justice to us, as we are promised. Deliver to us." He lowered his arms to his sides. "Deliver us from the betrayer."

He dropped the blade. It clattered on the floor, echoing in the silence, droplets of blood staining the floor.

"No one is answering," he said. "No one is coming. No one will save us." He smiled, bemused. "And I am the betrayer?"

They were staring now, eyes torn from the sky. Their mouths hung open, a glimpse of the emptiness within their bodies.

"I am the betrayer," he continued, "yet you placed no faith in me. I am the betrayer, yet I never claimed to be your salvation. I am the betrayer . . ." He shook his head. "And I never asked of you anything.

"And *them?*" He pointed a finger to the sky. "They, who have promised you everything, demanded everything and given you nothing? They, who claim to be salvation and enlightenment and truth? They who let that man die? Who let *you* die? They are offered deals and promises and praise if only they come down and deliver you?

"I am standing in their house. I am speaking for their foes. I am speaking to their flocks. And they do as they have done when your coin ran dry, as they have done when your family went hungry, as they have done—" he choked on something, cleared it with a cough, "when your daughters died.

"Nothing. Your temple was too small. Your sacrifices were too meager. All that you gave was not enough. And after everything you've given, in your hour of need, they are not here." He shook his head. "They were never here. No one is here but me.

"And Her."

He turned, knelt beside the pool, stared into the darkness.

"And She is there, listening. And She is there, weeping for you." He thrust his hand into the water and it rose up to meet him like a living thing, liquid tendrils rising up to caress his flesh, liquid lips suckling upon his fingers. "And She is there . . . for him, as well."

He tore the man free from the waters, cast him silent and naked upon the stones. The man lay there, limbs trembling with infantile weakness, wailing through the words of a newborn. Arched upon his back and staring up at the world through eyes made of obsidian, drawing in breath between needlelike teeth. He reached his hands up to clutch his throat, healed of the wound that had been there and colored like bone.

"Someone listened to me," the Mouth said, kneeling beside him, easing his hand away from his throat. "Someone saved him."

And his eyes turned back to the pool, to the dark shapes rising from the water. Great webbed talons reached up, dug into the stone. Their emaciated bodies were hauled up, glistening with the water that slithered and danced across their visible ribcages and over their wide, white eyes. They rose on their long legs, their jaws gaping open as they stood, unmoving but for the claws they extended, dripping with something thick, something glistening with life.

"And someone will listen to you, too."

The Mouth rose up, looked out over the sea of humanity. Their faces rippled, some twisting from fear to revulsion, some quivering with curiosity, others bubbling with awe as they looked upon the Abysmyths ringing the pool, as they looked upon the glistening substance dripping from their claws in oozing bounty.

"But this is a choice," he said. "Your life belongs to you, for now. If you choose to take it and leave, then do so. Take your life, savor it while it is yours. Savor it before it's taken from you by the armies that claim to protect you, by the priests who swear it is theirs to take, by the people who take it simply because they want it. Take up your life. Hold it in your mouths. Leave . . ."

He opened his arms wide, gestured to the beasts that stood behind him in silent, monolithic stoicism.

"Or give it to Her. To the only one that listens. Give it to Her . . . and feast."

There was an eternity before they stirred, a familiar eternity he had felt when he had been presented the same fruits. The moment in which he stood bound and free at once, beholden to no one but himself and shackled by the tremendous fear that such freedom came with.

It had taken him an age to make a decision back then. But he had made it.

And, as a single soul rose from the crowd, a single woman with no more tears to give and no face that he knew, a single woman with an empty space beside her that someone should fill, he knew what their decision was, too.

In silence, they came forward. In silence, they walked past him. In silence, they took the Abysmyths by their claws, given no resistance as they let the gelatinous substance slide into their craws.

And then, the silence was over, yielding to the sound of smacking lips and slurping tongues, to the gentle moans of unexpected delight, to the wet gagging sounds of those unprepared. The silence was gone. The Mouth had been given an answer. The Mouth heard it.

It was Hanth who lifted his hands to his ears, trembled a moment, and then let them fall at his sides.

They were there before.

When light and sound meant things. Before song was bastardized with words. Before light knew how to cast a shadow.

They saw those things taken away.

By mortals. By stone. By heaven.

They had learned to live without them.

There was no light down here; the fires of the stone city above had been snuffed out and the moon turned its eye aside. There was no sound down here; the water did not know what sound was.

But there was life down here.

They watched it from four golden eyes as they swam in slow circles about him. The faithful moved over his great skin with their hammers, driving arm-long nails into him with soundless strikes that blossomed in fleeting sparks.

He did not complain. He sat there, amidst the rocks and the sand, free at last. Yet his heart was weak, beating faint. Free he might have been, but the years in his prison had left him with pain. Pain that left him numb to the nails driven into his skin and the sparks blooming across his body.

Far away, something stirred. Far away, someone spoke in a song without words, a language without meaning. They turned their twin heads to its source.

"Can you hear it?" they asked him. He said nothing and they frowned. The pain had left him deaf. "They did this to you. Shackled you in silence, with nothing but the thunder of your own heart to listen to."

He spoke. His voice the last star falling out of the sky and leaving a black hole above the world.

"Ah," they said, smiling. "You do not care about them. Only about Her."

He demanded. His words the burbling and bubbling of the muck from which living things crawled.

"We hear Her. The faithful hear Her." Their voice brimmed with sorrow. "And you do not."

He asked a question. Somewhere, grass withered and an infant cried out in pain.

"We will wait no longer," they said, swimming around. "We will not let Her suffer longer. The faithful must hear Her clearly. The world must hear Her rise. Let it be done."

Somewhere within the mountain that was him, a light bloomed. A red light that the darkness did not understand, growing larger with each ominous beat of his heart until he was all sound, all light, everything.

"Rise," the Deepshriek whispered, "Daga-Mer."

The faithful fell off of him, their white bodies and their hammers shaken from him like snow and ash as he stirred. He rose to his feet, the rocks shattered silently beneath them. He drew in a deep breath. He opened his eyes.

And the world was bathed in light.

He walked, over reef and rock, over sand and stone, the crush and quake of earth silent against the storm that thundered within his chest. He walked, and they followed.

In shadow, in whiteness, in a sea of blue stars, they followed. The Shepherds, the Sermonics, the faithful. His sons and his daughters and his followers, betrayed by the Gods, loathed by the earth and the sky. They followed him as he followed Her.

Daga-Mer walked with his flock. To Jaga. To Mother Deep.

And earth cried out without language behind him.

ACT TWO

FORGOTTEN SKY, RISING SEA

TEN

IF MADNESS ISN'T THE ANSWER, WHY DO WE EVEN KEEP THE VOICES AROUND?

The Aeons' Gate

Reef of Dead Men (might not actually be reef name, but much more impressive sounding than whatever lizard trash they call it)

Fall . . . summer? I really can't tell anymore

I think the voice in my head might be lying to me.

And this perturbs me for a few reasons.

The big one is that I'm finding the fact that a giant red lizard who respected me enough to say my name like it wasn't a curse being eaten alive by a giant sea snake is not as joyous an occasion as I had hoped it to be.

I'm not sure how to feel about that.

Of the many profanities I would use to describe Gariath, "reliable" was never one of them. Though he might have limited his attempts to actively murder us to the single digits, he never really gave a damn about whether we lived or died. Couple in the fact that he came with us to seek out the Shen and this paints a rather bleak picture.

Summation: a lunatic dragonman who once threatened to reverse-feed me my own lungs, who abandoned me and left me to die at several occasions—most of them recent—and who sought contact with creatures possessing a vested interest in jamming pointy things into soft parts of my anatomy is gone.

And this isn't making me happy.

Maybe I just miss his conversation?

Or maybe the prospect of going into a forbidden island of doom from which no man has returned without the benefit of having a murderous reptile at my side is proving daunting. I mean, there certainly are giant, murderous reptiles out here. They just happen to be lurking in the mist.

Along with Gods know what else.

The mist goes on forever and the walkway goes with it. Or rather, walkways, since there are just a few more than way too damn many of them out here. Barely any of

them go anywhere, most of them leading to shattered bridges, pillars whose tops are lit-
tered with bones, or shrines with statues long smashed.

I should probably be more respectful. Clearly, something happened here. Clearly,
it was big. Clearly, a lot of people died and a lot of things were smashed. But I can't
help but think in terms of practicality. How are we to find anything in this? It's like
a giant web of stone built by a spider who thought it'd be much easier to simply annoy
its prey to death.

We walked until nightfall. Or what I think is probably nightfall. It might also
be morning. The mist won't tell me. It doesn't matter. I won't be sleeping tonight.

I see them in the mist. Some of them are moving, some of them are not. There are
statues there. Robed men, gods for faces, hands extended. They were on Teji, too,
mounted on treads like siege engines. Here, they're on the bows of ships. Sunken ships.
Some are crashed on the pillars, some are tossed on their sides like trash, some look like
they've been sinking into the sea for years . . . centuries, probably.

Those aren't the moving ones.

The moving ones make noise. Wailing, warbling cries in the mist, like they're
talking to each other. Not human. Not that I've heard. If they know we're here, they're
not talking to us. Or not to me, anyway. I see Kataria stop and stare out there some-
times, like she's trying to listen.

That's when those noises stop and the other ones begin.

These ones are voices. Not the usual ones, mind. They're . . . hard to hear. Like
whispers that forgot what whispers are supposed to sound like. I can't understand them,
but I can hear them. Sometimes the other way around. They are . . . calling out.

Maybe they're like us, got lost in the mist somewhere way back before language
had words and are still trying to find their way out.

Maybe I should count myself lucky that I've only been lost for a day.

Or two days? It's hard to keep track, what with no sleep, no sun, and the whole
fear of being disemboweled in my sleep . . . thing.

I should ask Kataria.

152

I should ask Kataria when she wakes up.

I should kill Kataria now.

It would be easier right now, when she can't fight back, when she can't look at me,
when she can't . . .

It's hard to think.

And I can't think of anything else.

Voices in the head will usually do that: make a man single-minded. And I can't
help but feel angry at her, like I want to hurt her, like I should. Like the voice tells me
I should.

But it doesn't tell me that. It isn't threatening me. It isn't demanding I do any-
thing. All it does is talk . . .

It talks about that night on the ship. It talks about how she looked me in the eyes and left me to die. After that, everything is me.

I've gotten close. I've raised my sword. I've seen how my hands could fit around her neck. But every time I do, I remember why it is I wanted to cry and I think . . .

. . . there must be something else. Why did she abandon me? I never asked. I tried not to think about it. She never told me why. She looked me in the eyes. She left me to die.

I remember she looked sad.

And I remember the woman in my dreams, telling me it won't stop if I kill her, telling me that I can't listen to the voice. And then the voice starts screaming. Not talking, screaming. It tells me all about her, what she did, what I must do. And I still remember the woman and I still remember Kataria and I still want to cry and die and kill and fight and drown and sleep and never have to think again.

. . . like I said, I try not to think about it. Too much.

She has to live for now. She's got the skills for tracking and the senses for getting us out of here and to Jaga and to the tome. The tome that we need to find again. The tome that the voice wants me to find again.

No.

That I want to find.

Me.

I think.

Too hard to think.

Too hard to kill Kataria.

Should have killed Asper first.

That'd have been easier.

ELEVEN

SLEEP NOW, IF NOT SOUNDLY

He had just closed his eyes when he caught the scent. It cloyed in his nostrils: silk, orchids, perfumes for wealthy women that fought and failed to quell the natural aroma of femininity. Stars. Candle wax. Violet skies.

He wanted to sleep.

His eyelids had just begun to tremble when he caught her voice.

"No, no," she whispered, a light giggle playing across her words. "Don't."

"Don't what?" he asked.

"Don't open your eyes."

"Why not?"

"Because the world is ugly," she replied. "And thought is beautiful. Whatever you're thinking of right now is infinitely more beautiful than whatever it is that awaits you when you open your eyes."

"And if I'm thinking of something ugly?"

"What are you thinking of?"

You, he thought. *How much I miss you. What kind of life I've led where I couldn't be with you. Whether I was wrong all this time and there are gods and there are souls and mine will wander forever when I finally die, far from your arms, and how much more that fact terrifies me than the other one. Always you.*

"Nothing," he replied.

"Simply nothing?"

"Nothing is simple."

"Precisely," she said. "And because nothing is simple, nothing is beautiful. There is nothing more beautiful. That's why your eyes must stay closed and you have to hold onto that."

"To what?"

"Nothing."

"That doesn't make sense."

"It doesn't have to. It's beautiful."

"I'm opening my eyes now."

And when he did, there was nothing. There was no ground. There was no sky. There were no trees and there was nothing to burn and turn to ash. There was nothing.

But her.

And her head in his lap. And her black hair streaming like night. And the ink drying upon her breasts. And her smile. And her scent. And her. Always her.

"Did I not tell you?" she asked.

"You said nothing would be as beautiful as what I was thinking."

"And?"

"It is."

"Then I was right."

"I can't admit to that."

"Why not?"

"Because then you'll be rubbing my face in it all day and night and I'll never get any sleep. Not that it matters, anyway, I've got to be going shortly."

"Where do you have to go?"

"I have to go after that man. He killed a lot of people."

"Maybe he had a good reason."

"There is never a good reason for killing that many people."

"How many have you killed?"

"I don't want to talk about this right now."

"Then you shouldn't think about it so much."

"It's my duty to think about it."

"I thought your duty was to uphold the law of the Venarium."

"It is."

"Is he wanted by the Venarium?"

"No."

"Then you can take the day off, surely. We can sit here and think about nothing until we have nothing left, and then we'll have nothing to worry about."

"He killed people."

"So have you."

"He nearly destroyed Cier'Djaal."

"Perhaps he didn't mean to."

"He could have killed you."

"You could, too, if you wanted to."

He sighed deeply, shut his eyes. "Stop this."

"Stop what?"

"Trying to get me to stay. I can't."

"You have to."

"Why?"

He opened his eyes and beheld her smile. Her teeth were painted bright red. Another thick droplet of crimson fell and splattered across her forehead, another falling upon her eye, another upon her lips, until her face was slick with blood and her scent was copper tang and sour life.

"Because," Anacha said, "you're dying."

Bralston opened his eyes with a gasp and felt the air whistling through his neck. He stared down at the earth glistening with his own blood. He pressed a hand to his throat. He felt sticky life on his palm.

Cracks in the seal, he thought. *It's not holding as well as suspected. That would explain the fainting . . . and the massive blood loss. No one ever said gaping throat wounds would be simple. Don't laugh at that. You'll bleed out. Apply another seal. Quick.*

His spellbook lay flung open at his side, several pages torn from its spine, red fingerprints smeared across those that remained. He forced his hand steady as he reached down, tore a page with two fingers. The merroskrit came out hesitantly, eventually demanding a second hand to pull it free.

It wasn't meant to come out easily. Wizards were meant to think carefully before using it, emotion never guiding the decision. Emotion caused disaster. Bralston didn't have enough blood to decide if this was ironic or merely poetic.

He pressed the page to his bloodied throat, situated it firmly over the wound, as he had done the last three. The cause would need to be dire to use even one.

Ideally, this was just dire enough.

His voice had bled out onto the sand. He had no words left to coax the fire to the hand he pressed over his throat. All he had left were screams.

And so he screamed. The fire came, bidden by anger rather than will, shaped by agony rather than discipline. With only emotion to guide it, the fire seared his throat with furious imprecision. It branded the merroskrit to his flesh, over the cracks in the seal, shutting the blood back in his throat where it belonged.

For now.

His hand came back smoking, tiny curls of flesh sizzling into plumes of gray smoke upon his palm. Running out of skin was never a problem he thought he might encounter, but here it was. Merroskrit could overcome an inanimate host easily enough and adapt to it, but it lacked the willpower to adapt to a living one. Eventually, his body would reject it.

He was going to die.

This was certainty. The seal would hold only for a while. Two days, if he was lucky.

Two days. One to plan the rest of his life. Another one to live it.

If he was an average, ignorant person who prayed to the sky, anyway. Librarians could not take an entire day to plan, even when they had more than two to spare. Librarians were meant to act.

And yet, emotion had killed him once already.

Logic and duty demanded the pursuit of the criminal Denaos. One day to track him down, one more day to make him pay for the life he failed to take. It would satisfy the emotional urge, as well. Everyone would be happy. Everyone not on fire, anyway.

And yet, some part of him that did not yet lay glistening on the sand wanted something else. A day for poems, a day for letters, a hundred pages long for a single person. Penned in ink, blood, mud, it didn't matter. Folded into a hundred paper cranes and sent on a breeze to one person in Cier'Djaal.

Back to Anacha.

Then find a nice, quiet spot, lie down, and die.

Over there, perhaps: beneath that tree. Lovely spot to rest forever. Maybe she would come visit his grave someday. That would be nice.

Maybe she would tell the Venarium what had happened to him. Maybe they would nod solemnly and come back to harvest his body and give him the honors that his duties demanded. The heretics had been slain. The law of the Venarium had been upheld. He would be harvested, turned into merroskrit, and his name would be written down in the annals of the finest Librarians to have served.

He could die a happy man.

And another man, who had murdered hundreds of people, would live.

And Bralston knew what his choice had to be.

Two more pages came out of his spellbook. Ordinary paper, nothing special but for the words he smeared upon them in crude, red lettering. One of them contained much: many names of important men, many thoughts summarizing many events. Many words.

The other contained just five.

He folded them both as delicately as he could. The cranes they became were sloppy, slovenly things, wings askew and heads insane. The words he spoke to them were gravelly and agonized, incomprehensible even in a language already incomprehensible.

But he spoke them. And they flew. They rose shakily into the air, wobbling precariously as they sailed over the treetops and disappearing with not much hope for success into the sky.

Bralston rose to his feet, drew a deep breath. It was ragged, like knives in his neck. He shut his eyes and felt his coat spread out behind him. Its tails rose, forming into leathery wings and flapping silently.

In his mind, he could sense it: a quivering, trembling power, like a flame stirred by the beating of a moth's wings. Dreadaeleon's strength, waxing and waning with the Decay that coursed through his body. He was moving farther away.

Chances were good that Denaos was with him.

Like his cranes, Bralston rose shakily into the air. The magic rushed through him like a river, crashing where it had once been flowing. It was hard to control, harder without words to guide it.

But he flew.

As he must.

TWELVE

GODS WITHOUT WATER

The statue rose from the sea.

A stone god with stone hands, its face lay in fragments about the hem of its robe, leaving nothing beneath its cowl but a mass of shattered granite. The ship that had so valiantly carried it to its fate lay crushed behind it, broken deck straining to keep it from drowning along with the rest of the vessel.

It shifted in some slight, imperceptible way. It sighed, as it had doubtlessly sighed for centuries.

It was an old god who had been crumbling as long as the mist had been here. But its hands were still strong, still whole, still stone.

It needed nothing else.

Its palm broke through the great, gray wall, parted it like a curtain and left it to crumble alongside it face. It was a testament to its strength.

Almost as strong a testament as the shattered ribcage wrapped around its wrist.

Whatever the beast had been, it had never been a god. It lay before the statue, sprawled in the parted stone curtains, skeletal claws sunk in the rock in a long-ago effort to resist the statue's stone palm. It still screamed now, from shattered ribs and out a skeletal mouth, into eternity.

And past the wall, past the bones, past the stone monolith, Jaga lay exposed.

Maybe not, Lenk thought with a sigh. *"Exposed" isn't really the word for Jaga. Nor "welcoming" or "convenient" or "not conducive to bodily injury, decapitation, and possibly castration."*

He pursed his lips, pulled them apart with a thoughtful pop.

Of course, that's not one word, is it?

But many years and many blades had taught him to consider everything, even if there *technically* wasn't any evidence that the Shen had any fondness for castration.

There was no evidence that the Shen would live on an island surrounded by a giant wall, either. There was no evidence that a race of canoe-paddling, club-swinging, loincloth-clad lizards had the time, skill, or patience for crafting such a formidable defense, let alone decorating it so elaborately.

But there it was: an eternity long, a god high, and brimming with depictions of noble men marching defiantly into the sea to be greeted with a riot of fish and coral before falling like children into the arms of a woman, vast as the wall she was carved into.

Traitor.

He cringed. They came again. Not his thoughts. Burrowing into his head.

Liar.

Murderer.

Blasphemer.

He closed his eyes, tried to breathe deeply. It was harder than it seemed.

Kill.

Destroy.

Unseat.

It never worked anyway. Talking didn't, either. But it was at least harder to hear them over the sound of his own voice.

"Kind of odd, don't you think?" he asked.

"What do *I* think?"

Kataria's breathless voice came ahead of her as she clawed her way to the top of the pillar. Her scowl burned beneath the satchel of supplies and quiver upon her back as she hauled herself up.

"I think that every time I wonder if I *might* be wrong to think you're an imbecile, you go and make such a monumental observation as noting that this whole *adventure* might contain some things that might be considered *odd*."

"I mean it's odd even for *us*," Lenk replied, gesturing at the centuries-old carnage. "Where did this wall come from? The Shen couldn't have carved it."

"Why couldn't they have?" Kataria asked as she wrung out her hair. "We don't know anything about them beyond their attitudes toward our heads being attached to our bodies."

"They couldn't have built it because there's no way a race can grasp the finer points of mass masonry projects while the concept of trousers still eludes them. And what about *this*?" He waved his hands at the monolith and the ship struggling to keep it from sinking. "What is it?"

"This is the fourth one we've seen *today*. What's odd about this one?"

"They were all over the place on Teji, mounted like siege engines. This one's a ship's ram. What are they doing here?"

"Same thing they were doing on Teji," Kataria said, shrugging. "Standing around, being ominous." She adjusted the satchel on her back. "This is the only way in and we've been following the wall for hours. You had all that time to ask stupid questions." She clapped his shoulder as she moved forward. "Now, we move."

She took the lead. And he followed.

Again.

Kataria could never be called "shy," what with the various insults and bodily emissions she had hurled at him. But she had never really seemed interested in leadership roles. Possibly because it took up time that could be spent jamming sharp things into soft things.

Yet she easily pushed past him. She looked at him expectantly before sliding down the other side of the pillar. Like he was supposed to follow.

It made sense. Her hearing was sharp, her eyes keen. If anything was going to leap out of the mist to kill them, she'd know long before he would and *might* tell him. And yet, he couldn't shake a suspicion that came from her newfound confidence.

The voice wouldn't let him.

"She does not fear you."

I don't want her to fear me. He thought the thoughts freely as he moved to follow her. It was a little refreshing to hear a more familiar madness.

"You do. And you are right to."

All right, humor me. Why?

"Because you want her to know what she did. You want her to feel pain."

I don't.

He left it at that. He tried not to give it any thoughts for the voice to respond to. Futile. He felt the cold snake from his head into chest as the voice looked from his thoughts into his heart.

"You do."

He slid down the pillar, found Kataria standing at the edge of its rocky base. A network of old carnage stretched before them: splintered wood, jagged stone, a bridge of gray and rot that led to the monolith's improvised entrance.

"Looks clear."

Lenk took a step forward. Her hand was up and pressed against his chest. Her eyes were locked intently on his.

"It looked clear right before Gariath was swallowed whole." She shrugged the satchel off, handed it to him. "I'll go first."

He wasn't quite sure what to think as she hopped nimbly from rock to rock, lumber to lumber across the gap of sea. Fortunately, he had someone who did.

"She turns her back to you."

Lenk hopped after her. *She's just confident.*

"Careless."

Protective.

"Stupid."

She's hardly stupid.

"We are no longer talking about her."

He followed her silently across the rocks, trying to keep head as silent as mouth.

Kataria nimbly skipped across the stones and wreckage ahead of him, canny as a mountain goat. But his eyes were drawn to her feet, how they slipped, just a hair's breadth, with each step. She was getting careless, distracted by something.

It would be a small effort, barely anything more than an extra hop and an outstretched hand. A gentle shove and—

Stop. He shook his head wildly. *Stop that.*

"Delusional."

What did I just *say?*

They wound their way across the precarious footing, onto the shattered hull of the ship, over the stone god's shattered face. As they squeezed through smashed ribs, Lenk paused to note just how odd it was that this was his second time doing this.

They had been everywhere on Teji. The giant fish-headed beasts littered the beach amidst the wrecked artillery and rusted weapons in numbers so vast as to paint the sand white. Their skulls had holes punched in them with boulders. Their limbs had been twisted beneath splintering shafts.

A war, the Owauku had said, between the servants of Ulbecetonth and her mortal enemies.

A war that had reached all the way to the Shen.

And, as he crawled beneath a fractured collarbone the size of a ship's plank, Lenk began to wonder which side they had been on when the walls broke.

And, as he emerged from the hole, set foot upon finely carved stone, he found that the list of mysteries surrounding the Shen grew obnoxiously long.

The highway stretched out before him, behind him, around him, wide enough for ten men to walk abreast of each other as it wound between the two great walls rising up on either side of it. The bricks of the road were smoothed to the point that they would have shined if not for the shroud of gray overhead and the black splotches staining them. Pedestals where statues had once stood marched its length, host to stone feet without bodies, stone faces amidst pulverized pebbles.

A battle had obviously raged here. What kind of battle, he had no idea. Because for all the blood, all the destruction, there were no bodies.

Only bells.

He had seen them before: abominations of metal hanging from wooden frames by spiked chains, so severely twisted that they looked like they might not even make a sound. They did, of course. He had heard it before. He still heard it as he looked at them now. It still made his head hurt.

The mist did not spare him the sight by politely obscuring it. It lingered at the edges of the wall, wispy gray fingers like those of a curious child peeking over. But it never came farther, as though out of respect. However old the mist was, the stone was older. However long it had been here, the road had been here longer.

That raised questions. He had enough of those.

Where is she?

That one, in particular.

"Lurking. Waiting. To kill you."

That answer, too, was tiresome.

If only because he had thought of it before the voice had.

"Kataria!"

She had been waiting for him to call. She never heard his voice anymore. She felt it instead, in the tremble of her ears. Far away, right beside her, it sounded the same.

Not always comforting, but familiar. Distinct. His.

Ordinarily, "revolting" would have followed on that list. She was past hating herself for coming to anticipate his voice. She knew the feel of it as she knew the feel of sweat on her skin.

She felt it now. Not as pain. Not as pleasure. But a slow, coursing ache that moved down her stomach, sliding from bead of sweat to bead of sweat, clenching muscle, pinching flesh. Not pain. Not comfort. Not anything she had felt before. But she could not let go of it.

And that was why she forced it off of her now. That was why she tuned out his voice, shut her ears and her skin to it. That was why she listened to the nothingness, felt the silence instead. This was an ache she wanted to hold onto.

And to do that, she would have to save him from her people.

She shut her eyes and reached out with her ears into the nothingness. For only in the nothingness could she hear her people. Only in silence could she feel Naxiaw.

Even if he didn't want her to.

The Howling had been weaker lately. On Teji, it had been a wild thing, roaring and raging inside her like a maddened beast. But she had been uncertain, doubtful then, yearning to feel a shict and feeling nothing instead.

But now it competed with his voice, raked at her with claws, bit at her with fangs, tried to coat sweat with blood. It might have been her choice that she felt Lenk's voice stronger, that the roar of instinct grew ever more faint.

Never faint enough to completely shut her from Naxiaw, though.

Hatred. Determination. Compassion.

Fleeting emotions. Guarded thoughts. She didn't know what they were thinking, what their instincts were saying. She didn't know where they came from. She knew only from whom they came.

Greenshicts.

They had followed her to Jaga.

And they were close.

Close enough that, when she felt a hand placed upon her shoulder, she whirled about with canines bared and a hand upon her knife.

Lenk didn't look particularly surprised at the reaction. Between the times he had tried to take some of her food and the times she had elaborately described how a scalping was performed, she supposed he had seen her teeth enough times for the shock to fade.

"Why didn't you call back?" he asked.

"Too dangerous," she didn't entirely lie.

"I suppose that makes sense." He glanced around the road, eyes slowly sweeping its stained ground. "Not too smart to go around scream . . ." His eyes drifted to the ruins of an inner wall. "Scream . . ." His eyes settled on the great gashes that split the inner wall into rubble. "Screa—"

His eyes rose up above the inner wall. And up. And up.

"That's . . . uh . . ."

"A forest," she sighed, rolling her eyes. "You've seen them before."

"That's a forest of—"

"Seaweed."

"Yeah," he said, "but where's the sea?"

166   Rising into the gray sky above, barbed leaves quivering, the kelp stood tall and swaying ponderously. That they moved without a breeze was not as unnerving as was how easily they did it. They did not quiver as a branch in the wind might. Their sway was fluid. Eerily so.

"Like they're . . . in a sea. Without water."

"It's also denser than a damn rock and it goes on forever," she said, gesturing down the road with her chin. "Stay here." She hefted her bow off her shoulder, began to stalk away. "I'll go search for an opening."

"Wait, wouldn't it make more sense for me to go, too?"

"I move more easily alone."

"Since when?"

"I always have. I'm just not humoring you anymore." She growled, already stalking away. "Stay here and guard the supplies."

She had taken only two more steps when he asked it.

"Why?"

Barely more than a whisper, the question was not for her. She should have pretended she hadn't heard it. But he would never have believed her. Not with the big, pointy ears that drooped dejectedly as she turned around.

"Why what?"

"Why are you going off alone? Why do you *keep* going off alone? Why do you turn your back to me?"

She winced; not a good answer.

She sighed; a worse one.

"Stay here."

"I need to talk to—"

"*JUST STAY HERE.*"

Sprinting away was not the best answer, either. But at least it got her far away fast enough to ignore whatever he said next. He'd have more questions and her answers were only going to get worse from there.

Like there's a right *answer*, she thought ruefully. *What are you going to tell him? "Hey, stay here while I go try to find the greenshicts I hung around with when I still kind of sort of maybe wanted to kill you. I'll bring you back a snack."*

Her belly lurched into her throat. She swallowed it back down on a wave of nausea.

Not that the truth is much better. Go on and tell him it hurts when he looks at you. Go on and see what happens when you tell him you know he wants to hurt you.

She sighed, closed her eyes.

So, that's settled. Running away was the right answer. You can't help if it's still a terrible one.

She looked up to see the wall of kelp rising taller, swaying slowly, freakishly.

167

Terrible and *useless.*

The inner wall was all but powder. Nowhere near as thick or as strong as the outer, it had crumbled to a thin line of shards that valiantly tried to hold back the kelp forest. Not that it was needed; the kelp was a wall unto itself, green and vast and utterly impregnable, marching endlessly along the road.

It was a sign, she knew. An omen sent to tell her that she should go back, talk to him, tell him that she was trying to protect him, that he made her hurt, that she wanted to hurt, that she knew he wanted to hurt her.

Riffid didn't send omens.

But Riffid was the goddess of the shicts.

Kataria was a shict . . . wasn't she?

She sighed, rubbed her eyes. This was stupid. Maybe she shouldn't go back. Maybe it would be easier to just sit here and wait for something to come along and kill her and save her the trouble.

Not likely. She cast a glower about the highway. *For the home of the Shen, you'd think there'd be more—*

Her hand shot up, thumped against her temple, trying to beat that thought out.

No! NO! Do not *finish that thought. You know* exactly *what will happen if you do.*

She settled back on her heels, drew in a sharp breath. The kelp swayed silently. The mist boiled silently. The stone watched silently. She released it.

There. That wasn't so hard, was—

Her ears twitched, then shot straight up at a sudden sound.

"Oh, come *on*—" she snarled under her breath.

Anywhere else, it might have been a murmur lost on the wind and never heard. Here in the silence, the sound of a bowstring being drawn was so loud it might as well have been using a cat as an arrow.

Hers was just as loud as she whirled around, arrow leaping to string as she aimed it upward.

The Shen squatted, bow drawn on her, high upon the wall. Not so high that she couldn't see the malicious narrow of the lizardman's yellow eyes or the glint of the jagged head at the end of a black shaft.

It stood frozen upon the wall like a green gargoyle. Its lanky body was breathless, unmoving, rigid with the anticipation of the ambush she had just ruined. Muscle coiled beneath scaly flesh banded with black tattoos. Nostrils quivered at the end of a long, reptilian snout. It did not move. As though it hoped that she might simply forget it was there if only it sat still long enough.

She wasn't sure why it hadn't shot yet. Maybe it wasn't sure if it was faster than her, had better aim than her. Or maybe it was waiting for something else.

"This isn't fair, you know," she called up to it. "I didn't even *think* your name."

The Shen's tail twitched behind it, the only sign it was even alive.

"Can you understand me?"

It said nothing.

"Look, I can admire anyone who can sneak up on me." Her ears twitched resentfully. "Even if you are all the way up there. So, one hunter to another, I'll give you this." She gestured with her chin. "Walk away. You're not who

I'm looking for and this is an ambush you don't want to waste. Come back later. I'll be distracted. You can take another shot at me then."

A low, throaty hiss slithered between its teeth. Whether it understood her words or not, the creak of a slackening bowstring, if only by a hair's breadth, suggested it recognized intent. She returned the gesture, by an even scanter hair's breadth.

It stood still.

Just a breath longer.

In another breath, it had dropped its bow and reached for something at its waist. In one more, her bow sang a one-note dirge. No more breaths came after that.

Its eyes didn't go wide, as though it wasn't particularly surprised that this had happened. It didn't grope helplessly at the quivering shaft lodged in its throat, merely grabbing it purposefully and snapping it with one hand while the other clenched whatever it was at its waist. It met her gaze for a moment and she saw in its yellow stare something determined, unfazed by death.

And then, it pitched forward.

She hurried over as it struck the stones with a muffled thump and lay still. It was most certainly dead, unless its spine had *always* bent that way and she just hadn't noticed. But in death, it still stared at her, still resentful, still clinging to that resolve.

Just as it clung to the item in its hand.

She leaned over the lizardman, reached down, prised apart its clawed fingers with no small effort. And there, curved and cylindrical, she saw it.

"A . . . horn?" she muttered.

Another question. Another complication. Things never got *less* complicated when walking lizards were involved. And now she would have to go back to Lenk and tell him all about this.

"*KATARIA!*"

Assuming he didn't come to her first.

She saw him rushing toward her. She heard him curse through fevered, rasping breath, felt his voice like a knife in her flesh. His legs pumped, his eyes were narrowed, his sword was drawn.

And bloodied.

The arrow was nocked before she even knew it was in her fingers, raised before she knew whom she was aiming at. It was so instinctual to draw on him. So easy to see him as a threat.

So easy to just let go of the arrow and—

No, she thought. *Not again.*

She lowered the weapon and sighed as he came charging toward her. She closed her eyes as he came within reach of her. She grunted as he shoved rudely past her and kept running.

She furrowed her brow, opening her mouth as if to call after him. No words came, though; she was far too confused.

"SHENKO-SA!"

Right up until she heard the warcry, anyway.

The Shen came surging up the highway in a riot of color. Lanky green muscle trembled beneath tattooed bands of red and black, weapons of bone and metal flashed in their hands, yellow eyes grew gold with fury at the sight of her.

Great webbed crests rose from their scaly crowns, displaying colorful murals tattooed on the leathery flesh. Giant fish on some, serpents on others—various peoples in various stages of dismemberment seemed a rather popular choice.

They bent at the waist, long tails risen behind them as they picked up speed, raised their weapons, and howled.

Like hounds, she thought. *Big, tattooed, ugly hounds. With weapons. Sharp ones.* She glanced up the road. *Why aren't you running, again?*

If her head couldn't form a response, her feet did. And they spoke loudly and in great favor of screaming and running away. She agreed and tore off down the highway, folding her ears over themselves to block the sound of a dozen warcries growing louder.

She saw Lenk a moment later, the young man leaning on his knees and trying desperately to catch his breath. She opened her mouth to warn him, to tell him that they were close enough behind that he had to keep moving.

"YOU SON OF A BITCH!"

That wasn't a warning, but it made him move, regardless. He sheathed his sword and took off at a sprint, falling in beside her.

"You could have *warned* me," she snarled between breaths.

"Did you *not* see me running?" he screamed back. "What, did you think I was just *that* excited to see you?"

"You had your sword drawn! I didn't know *what* was happening!"

Her ears pricked up at a faint whistle growing steadily louder. She leapt and the arrow cursed her in a spray of sparks and a whine of metal as it struck the stones where she had just stood.

"How about now?" he asked. "If you're still confused, they've got more arrows."

And in symphonic volleys, the arrows wailed. They came screaming from atop the walls, making shrill and childish demands for blood, skulking in clattering mutters when they found only stone.

The archers took only a few opportunistic shots, shouldering their bows and racing atop the wall after their fleeing pink targets as soon as they moved out of range. But there were always more archers and ever more arrows.

Precise shots, Kataria noted. Hungry shots. Little wolves of metal and wood. And like wolves, they came from all sides.

She glanced over to the side. The kelp had thinned out, giving way to another, stranger forest.

Coral formations rose out of the sand and into the gray sky. Jagged blue pillars, spheres of twisted green, great cobwebs of red thorns, and sheets of yellow blossomed like a garden of brittle, dead gemstones.

It might have been beautiful, had each formation not been host to yellow eyes lurking in their towering pillars, green feet perched upon the colorful branches, bows bent and arrows drawn.

They ducked, weaved, hid where they could, tumbled where they had to. Arrows snarled overhead, jagged tips reaching with bone-shard barbs. They darted behind one of the twisted bells to avoid a volley. The arrows struck, sent the misshapen metal wailing, screaming, weeping, laughing, grinding sound against sound in a horrifying cacophony.

Kataria clamped hands over her ears, shouted to be heard. "How far back are they?"

"I don't care!" he shouted back. "Just keep going until we can find some-place to hide!"

She glanced over her shoulder. The tide of Shen seemed a distant green ebb. They had checked their pace, pursuing with intent, not speed. They were up to something. Or maybe lizards just weren't meant to run on two legs.

"Must be the tails," she muttered. "We're bound to lose them soon. For a bunch of crafty savages, you'd think they'd have a better plan than just chasing us and—"

"*Damn it, Kat*," Lenk snarled. "Why the *hell* would you say that?"   171

She didn't have to ask. The moment she turned, she saw it, looming over-head, its gray so dark it stood out even against the cloud-shrouded sky. The monolith statue stood upon the wall, palm outstretched, a symbol of a great, unblinking eye set within its stone hood.

While it certainly didn't seem to object to the cluster of Shen around its feet trying desperately to push it over and onto the road below, Kataria picked up her speed.

"*Stop!*" Lenk rasped. "We'll never make it!"

"Yes, we will! Just go faster!"

He did go. Faster than her, even. Their breath became soundless, coming so swiftly and weakly it might as well not exist. Their legs pumped numbly beneath them, forgetting that they were supposed to have collapsed by now. They had nothing left to give but the desperate hope of passing before the statue fell.

Whatever god it was supposed to represent, though, the monolith appeared unmoved.

By their efforts, anyway.

The collective heaving of ten Shen proved to be far more persuasive.

The monolith tilted with a roar of rock and the wail of wind as it teetered and pitched over the wall, plummeting to the road below. She felt the shock of it through her numb feet, coursing up into her skull as the old stone god smashed against the rock below, sending a wave of pulverized granite dust erupting.

His legs desperately trying to remember how to stop, Lenk skidded into the great stone eye with an undignified sound. He came to a rasping, gasping halt.

Kataria did not.

With an almost unnerving casualness, she leapt, racing up his back, onto his shoulders, leaping off of him like a fleshy, wheezy stepping stone and scrambling atop the statute's stone flank. She turned, looked down at him as he scrambled to follow her, failed to even come close.

She clicked her tongue. "Okay, so I was *halfway* right."

Had he the breath to respond, he probably would have cursed her. Had he the energy to lift his sword, he probably would have thrown it at her. She didn't watch him for long, though. Her eyes were drawn down the road, toward the advancing Shen horde. Archers continued to slither out of the coral forest to join the tide, bows added to the throngs of clubs and blades raised high and hungry for blood.

But even that did not hold her attention for long.

Her ears did not prick up at the sound, for she did not hear it. She felt it, in the nothingness of the mist. Determination. Compassion. Hate. Anger.

Naxiaw.

He was out there, somewhere. Somewhere close. Watching her, even now. And his were not the only eyes upon her.

But the Shen were also close. And growing closer. Stay and chase them off, she thought, and the greenshicts would come and kill Lenk. Leave to chase off the greenshicts and the Shen would kill Lenk. Neither option was attractive.

But then he decided for her.

"I can't make it," he said, finally finding his breath. "You have to go."

"Right," she said, making a move to leave.

"*Wait!*"

"What?"

"I didn't mean it! I was trying to be noble!"

"Ah . . ." She looked at him and winced. "Well."

And Lenk was left staring at an empty space she had just occupied. Had he breath to speak, he still wouldn't have had the words to describe what he felt just then.

Someone else did, though.

"*Told you*," the voice whispered.

Don't be an asshole about this, he thought in reply.

"*More important matters, anyway.*"

The voice was right. Lenk knew that the moment he heard the hissing behind him. Breath coming heavily, sweat dripping from his brow, Lenk turned around very slowly. But he was in no hurry.

When he finally turned to face them, the Shen were waiting.

THIRTEEN

HEAVEN

"**I** have been looking for you . . . for a long time."

Sheraptus's eyes burned as he cast his stare upon the scene below. Forgepits burned, alive with the sounds of metal being twisted into blades and breastplates, audible even from his terrace. The sound of creation carried so far.

"You are not pleased to see me again," he closed his eyes, whispering to his guest behind him. "It is hard to blame you."

Another scream rose up from below as another slave, one of Those Green Things, was shattered beneath an iron sole. The cargo the slave carried fell to the ground, splashing in the red life that seeped from its many, many cuts.

"But that seems like an eternity ago. Since then I have found . . . questions. I don't like them. A netherling *knows.* We are born from nothing. We return to nothing. There is only bloodshed and fire in between. There are no questions that do not have this answer."

The sikkhuns howled with wild laughter as the dead slave was hauled by a female to their pit and tossed in. Their hunger was a thing alive itself, the gnashing of their jaws and the ripping of scaly green meat, the cycle of life to death, death to nourishment, nourishment to life.

"But there has to *be* more," he said. "It was simple in the Nether. There was nothing. But here? The slaves barely put up a fight when we came. All this green, all this blue . . ."

He swept a hand to the face of the sprawling forest, scarred by an ugly sea of stumps. Its lumber had been hauled to the surf, turned into the long, black ships bobbing in waters stained by soot and blood and scraps of flesh.

"They didn't even fight for it. Why? Is there simply more of it that they can take later? But if there is more . . . who made it?" He clenched his fist, felt the anger burn out his eyes. "Metal does not take shape without fire and flesh. Ships do not construct themselves. This? All of this, someone *had* to have made it."

He shut his eyes, felt the fires smolder beneath his lids as he drew in a deep breath and exhaled.

"That's why I asked them to find you, specifically, out of all of your small, weak race. I wanted to find *you* . . ."

He turned around to finally look at his guest. A pair of beady eyes mounted upon tiny stalks looked back. The crab scuttled across the plate, its chitinous legs rapping upon the metal. It would go one way, find its path terminating in a long fall from the pedestal, move another way, find a similar conclusion, try the other way.

It was almost as if it wasn't even *listening*, Sheraptus thought contemptibly.

He swept over to the plate, plucked the crustacean up gently in his hands. It had taken time to understand how to take something so small without crushing it. He had practiced. And upon his palm, the crab scuttled one way, felt the palm's width end, scuttled the other way.

"And you waste it all," he whispered. "You and Those Green Things and the pink-skinned overscum . . . you have *all* of this, and you simply move about. You do nothing with it." He turned his hand over gently, watched the crab flail briefly, then right itself upon the back of his hand. "Why?"

He found his ire at the crab's silence boiling. Not that he expected it to simply up and start talking, but it could at least do *something* different. He jabbed it with a finger, pushing it around on his hand.

"Do you simply not know what to do with it all?" he asked. "Does the sheer vastness of it all overwhelm you? Or do you simply choose to do nothing with it?"

It scuttled to escape his prodding finger, flailing as it found itself upon his palm again. And still, he tormented it.

"And why are you even here? What are you supposed to do? If you have no purpose, then how can you—"

He hissed as he felt a sting shoot up through his finger. The tiny pincers released him almost immediately, leaving little more than a bright red slash across the digit and a distant pain that grew to nothing in the blink of an eye.

In the next blink, his fingers had curled around the thing. He spoke a word, felt his eyes burn, felt the crown burn upon his brow. The flame coursed through his palm, licked his fingers. His nostrils quivered with the scent of cooked flesh.

When they uncurled, a tiny black husk smoldered in his palm. He turned his palm over, let it drop to the terrace floor. It shattered, splitting apart into tiny, burning slivers, quickly sputtering out into thin wisps of smoke.

"There," he said. "*There!*" He turned to the other end of the terrace, thrust a finger down at the floor. "Did you see that?"

Xhai blinked vacantly. Her brow furrowed as she looked down at what had once been the crab. With a snort, she looked up, shrugged, leaned back upon the terrace's railing, and crossed a ruined arm over a healthy one.

"So fragile," Sheraptus whispered, turning his attentions back to the black stain. "Why did they make it so fragile?"

"If it's weak, it's weak," Xhai replied. "Just the same as any other overscum or underscum. Why do they do anything they do?"

"Precisely," he murmured. "Why? Why were they made? Who made them?"

"No one did. From nothing to nothing."

"That's for netherlings, certainly . . . or is it?"

Xhai's face screwed up at the notion. He didn't bother to note the look of genuine displeasure across her face as he looked at her.

"Who's to say we weren't also made?"

"Master . . ." she said, taking a step forward.

"But this thing . . . it was made fragile. And we . . . were made strong." He tapped his chin. "The Nether made us strong."

"The Nether is nothing."

"The Nether is—"

"We are *netherlings*," she said, her voice rife with more force than had ever been used with him. "We are not called that because we were made. We are strong because we are netherlings. For no other reason."

He recoiled, feigned a look as though he had just been struck. Almost instantly, her visage softened. No, he corrected himself, Xhai was incapable of softening. Her face . . . twisted, looking as though it were trying dearly to find the muscles to look wounded.

Just as she always did whenever he looked hurt. She was so predictable, especially when it came to him. If he flinched, she was ready to kill. If he sighed, she was ready to kill. If he looked at something, she tended to assume he wanted it killed and thought it might just be easier to let him say otherwise if he wanted it alive.

The more he looked at her, the more genuine his frown became. It was a crab he saw. A crab tall, purple, and muscular, but a crab, nonetheless: without purpose but to move, to pinch when prodded, and just as fragile.

Perhaps, then, netherlings were not made. Perhaps everything came from nothing, scuttled about without purpose until they died. Perhaps this all came about for no reason.

Perhaps . . .

But then why were trees here, if not to be made into ships? Why were slaves here, if not to serve? Why was there so *much* of it? And why was he, and only he, wondering any of this?

177

"Master," Xhai whispered, edging closer. "You seem . . . well, we are to leave for Jaga soon. You said. Is your time not wasted by thinking on this?"

The invasion. To bring down Ulbecetonth. Enemy of the Gods. And the Gray One That Grins.

"Perhaps," he whispered. "Purpose is not given . . . but discovered."

"Master?"

He turned to her, smile broad, eyes bright.

"Bring me the human."

It had not once occurred to her to pray.

Not when she had awakened, bound and bruised upon the deck of the ship, her companions absent and probably dead. Not when she had been marched bodily across the great scene of fire and death that was the island's shorefront. Even when her captors had intentionally lingered near the great pits from which bestial laughter rose between sounds of bones cracking and meat slurping, not once did she look to the sky.

Not to heaven, anyway. She did look up, once, and found her gaze drawn to the terrace overlooking the blackened, blood-stained beach.

And eyes alight with fire had looked back.

Sheraptus had offered her nothing more than a stare. No jagged-toothed smiles, no wretched leers, nothing to boast about what he had done to her, of what he would do to her.

He stood. He stared. That was all he had to do to make her look at the pit and think whether it might be better to simply hurl herself into the jaws of whatever lurked inside.

But the netherlings had been upon her before she could consider it seriously, wrenching her arms behind her back, hauling her past scenes of corpses and flame and smoke and blood, into somewhere vast and dark.

After all of that, the dead bodies, the suffering so thick in the air it made it hard to breathe, the cackling laughter of those things in the pit, and *him*, she did not pray. Even as the cell door groaned and slammed shut, no light but what seeped from the cavern mouth so far away, she couldn't even think to pray.

Not until she had become aware that she was not alone in the cell.

Not until she had met Sheraptus's other victims.

After that, it was easier.

Blessed Talanas, who gave up His body that mankind might know, the old words came flooding back to her now as she strained to concentrate over the sound of sobbing in the darkness, *know this and always that I never ask You for myself, but that I might ease the pain and mend the wounds of body and soul.*

"He doesn't always come," the girl whispered. "Not always. Sometimes, he comes by and stares through the bars and I can just . . . see his eyes in the dark."

Her name was Nai. Asper had gleaned that much after a few hours in the dark. They had begun in silence, all queries as to their location or what the netherlings had in store for them were met with quiet whimpers and nothing else.

Asper did not press her. She had met victims before, wives beaten by their husbands, children who knew things of suffering that grown men did not, people for whom speech was agony. People who didn't want to be reminded that they were still people.

She had waited.

And eventually, the girl had spoke.

"And sometimes, he doesn't do anything. He'll just—" Nai continued, her voice so shaky it frequently shattered to pieces in her mouth. "He just stands there and he's watching me and he . . . then he . . . he turns around and he leaves and says nothing. Nothing. Never."

"Ah," Asper said.

Weak words, she knew, but she had nothing else to offer. She had no idea what Nai looked like in the darkness. Asper was quietly grateful for that; it meant Nai could not see her shake as the girl continued to describe her imprisonment.

She had been snatched, apparently, from a passing merchant ship. The netherlings had rowed up beside them during a calm, leapt aboard, and did what they do best. They took nothing, the carnage upon the decks seemingly wrought only for the opportunity to spit on the gutted corpses.

Nai hadn't been sure why she had been spared. Not until they dragged her to the island, past the laughing pits and the Gonwa bleeding out on the sands, not until they threw her in the darkness. And by the time she had run out of prayers, she wished she lay unmoving on the deck with the others.

Asper had listened to her. To all the torments visited upon her, to the chains affixed about her wrists, to the times she had tried to fight him, to the times that had only made his smile broader as he forced her to the floor.

179

Each word sent her bowels churning, her heart quaking. Each word told her of horrors and tortures at Sheraptus's hands she had only narrowly escaped. And with each word, Nai's voice became more distant as Asper fought the urge to shut her ears and break down.

But she withheld her tears. And she did not block out Nai's voice. And she listened. Not to know what would be visited upon her, not to try to think of a way to avoid him and his leering grin. But for the fact that Nai had nothing else but words, and Nai had to speak.

She listened.

And she prayed.

Humble do I pray and humble do I ask, she thought, mouthing the words in the darkness, *I know that I am weak and have nothing to give but give freely as You once did for us.*

"Then sometimes he just takes you," she said, voice wracked with sobs. "In the middle of the night . . . or the day. I don't know. I can't see the sun anymore. He comes and he just takes you and you fight him and . . . and you hit him and you bite him and he just . . . he just . . ."

But as You give freely, and as You have told us to give freely of our time and our love and our bodies, I beg You give unto me, she prayed, *give that I might do the will and restore that which is lost. Please, I beg—*

"He laughs. Like it's the funniest thing in the world. He takes his hands and he forces you down and—"

In the name of—

"He says things. He says words. They don't make sense. And there's a light. And you can see his teeth and he's smiling and his eyes are big and white and he's just so happy and . . . and . . ."

Please, Talanas, just . . . please give me the strength—

"He makes you scream."

Just . . . please.

That wasn't how the prayer ended. That wasn't what she thought she would ask for. She lifted her hand slowly, that Nai might not know she was moving, and wiped the moisture from her eyes.

No tears, she told both Talanas and herself. *She needs help. I asked for help. You can't give me tears. I can't give her tears.*

Words, however weak, would have to be enough.

She opened her mouth to offer them, weak and plentiful, when she was cut off. A long, inhuman wail echoed from somewhere far away, like a long, vocal hand reaching desperately out of the darkness toward daylight.

They came intermittently, sometimes many, sometimes few, sometimes one long, lonely scream from somewhere deeper and darker. Asper had asked. Nai had clasped her hands over her ears, shook her head. Asper didn't ask again.

Not about whoever those screams belonged to, anyway. She focused on the victims she could speak to.

Asper found her eyes drawn to the other girl in the cell. Or what she suspected was a girl. In the darkness, it was impossible to tell beyond the fact that Nai occasionally referred to the shaggy heap of disheveled hair and torn clothes as "she."

And "she" hadn't said a word since Asper had heard the bars slam shut behind her.

"What is her name?" Asper asked.

"I don't know, I don't know. She was here when they took me. I asked. I *asked* her. But she never told me. She just looked at me and told me that I was next and that I had to go when he came and that she couldn't do it anymore and that she was sorry and that I could never stop screaming if I wanted to live . . ."

"She" didn't move at the mention, nor at the hand that Asper gently laid on her. She didn't respond to touch, she didn't resist as Asper rolled her over. She didn't even blink as Asper stared into a pair of eyes that resembled a broken glass: shattered, glistening, and utterly empty.

"What happened to her?" Asper asked.

Nai's voice was a soft, dying whisper. "She stopped screaming."

No one in heaven or earth could blame her for wanting to break down, Asper knew. No one would blame her for weeping, for shrieking, for pleading. But as she stared at "her," this woman who drew breath and nothing more, she could do nothing but ask.

What is he?

She wasn't sure whom she asked, who would answer her. She wasn't sure why she only thought to ask now. But she had to know. She wondered who could do this. Not in the moral sense, but the physical. Who could so easily take a human being in his hands like a cup, turn her over and pour out everything inside her, then let her fall and shatter upon the floor?

What kind of creature had that power?

A god, she thought. *They treat him like a god. The netherlings tremble before him. Nai speaks of him in whispers. And she . . .* Asper looked down at the girl, who stared up at Asper, through Asper. *He took her. Everything about her.*

But there were no gods.

No one had answered her prayers.

She was still here, in the darkness, with an empty, shattered glass and a girl who had nothing but words. No one was coming. Not from heaven. Not from earth. There was no answer to her prayers.

There was only her.

There are no gods, she told herself. *And if there are no gods, there is no one who can do this. Not to me. Not to anyone again. Gods can't die.*

She looked down at her left hand, tightened it into a fist. Beneath her sleeve, beneath her skin, she could feel it. She wore the agony like a glove, the pain welling up inside her a familiar one, a welcome one. One she hoped to share quite soon.

He can.

There was movement beneath her as "she" drew in a sharp breath.

It was something so small it would go unnoticed in anyone else. In a woman that hadn't made a movement more energetic than a blink, it was enough to seize Asper's attention.

And in the span it took her to notice the sound of heavy iron boots on stone floor, the door was already flying open. She could not see the tall, muscular women as they swept into her cell. But she could feel their hands, the cold iron of their gauntlets as they jerked her to her feet, wrenched her hands behind her back and hauled her from the cell.

She might have cried out. She might have even been tempted to concentrate on the agony in her arm and summon it against them. She didn't know. It was hard to hear, harder to think with Nai's screaming.

"No, no, no, no, *no, no, no,*" the girl shrieked. Asper heard her scrambling away from them, twisting out of their grasp, raking her fingertips upon the floor as they hauled her out by her ankles. "No, please, not again, not again, not again, I've been good, I don't deserve this, please, please, please, please—"

Pleas, tears, screams. A singular, desperate sound that echoed through the cavern. It was joined by the screams from deeper inside, an endless, unrelenting cacophony marching alongside Asper as she was bodily dragged toward a distant halo of light at the end of the twisted corridor.

Within the ring of light, she saw it. A shadow standing tall, hands folded neatly behind its back.

And within the shadow, she saw them. A pair of lights, blood red and fire hot. Stars in hell.

The fear that had been bearing down upon her since she stared praying grew at the sight of him. It settled upon her shoulders. It pressed upon her neck. It ate the anger from her body, it drank the breath from her lungs.

But even beneath its weight, even through the half-formed prayers in her head and the pounding in her heart, she could still hear her curse herself.

Not now, *you idiot,* she snarled inwardly. *Not in front of Nai.* She gritted her teeth, felt her neck strain against the weight as she tried to raise it. *He's not a god. There are no gods. Not on earth. Look at him.*

It hurt to move her head, hurt to even think about it. But she forced herself to do both.

Look.

She did.

He did not.

Sheraptus stood, head bowed beneath the black iron crown upon his brow, staring intently into his palm. With one long finger, he gently pushed about tiny black fragments in his hand, attempting to piece together a charred puzzle.

It wasn't relief she felt to be denied his gaze as she was shoved past him. Her fear settled firmly upon her back and she felt extraordinarily heavy at that point. A sudden anger rose inside her, leaving no room for breath. That he could do what he did to her, to Nai, to the other girl, and not even look when his victims were paraded before him was . . . was . . .

She had no words for it. Only desires. Only a yearning to scream, a yearning to break free from her captor's iron grip and lunge at him with an arm that throbbed with a pain she wanted nothing more than to share.

Those desires left her, though, along with the air in her lungs, as the netherling twisted her about, placed a palm upon her belly and slammed her against the wall of the round, cavernous chamber. Sense left with the wind and she scarcely even noticed her arms being raised so high above her head as to pull her to the tips of her toes. It returned, however, with the eager snapping of metal as manacles were fastened about her wrists and she was left to hang against the wall like a macabre piece of art.

Her captor stepped back, met her scowl with cold eyes and tense muscles, as if challenging Asper to give her a reason to use those gauntleted fists folded over her chest. The priestess offered nothing more than a glare. The netherling, denied, snorted and left.

Nai had more to give.

"Please no, please stop, please no, please stop," she chanted the words, as though they would gain power the more she spoke them. "Please, please, please, please . . ."

The netherling holding her took no notice of her pleas as she forced the girl into a similar set of manacles on the opposite side of the chamber's door. Nai seemed to forget Asper was there entirely, shaking her head to add gesture to desperate incantation.

And no one seemed to notice the murals upon the walls.

They were almost illegible, smeared by soot from torches haphazardly jammed into the wall, scratched by scenes of struggle or boredom-induced violence. But Asper could make out a few images: men marching to war against towering black shapes, green, reptilian things marching beside them. Amidst them all strode great stone colossi, dressed in robes, hands outstretched.

She had seen these before, she realized: the great stone monoliths upon Teji, as imposing in paint as they were in person.

They marched into oblivion, crushing black shapes beneath their treads, sending white shapes fleeing before their authoritative palms. She followed them as they marched across the walls, displaying banners of many gods, holding weapons high. They descended toward the back of the chamber, the mural lost in the darkness that was held at bay by the torches, save for but a few strands of crimson paint that stretched out of the gloom.

She squinted to see them, to make them out.

Are those . . . tentacles?

The scream that burst out of the darkness shook her back to her senses. An inhuman shrieked boiled out of the back of the cavern, echoed through her skull as it did through the chamber. She turned away, shut her eyes, instinctively tried to clasp her hands over her ears even as the chains held her tight, chiding her with a rattle of links.

They faded, eventually. She opened her eyes. The breath immediately left her once more as she stared into a pair of eyes alight with crimson fire not a foot away from her.

"How did this happen?" Sheraptus asked.

He thrust the blackened pieces upon his palm at her. It had once been a living thing, she deduced by noting the charred remains of a jointed leg, even if everything else was soot and charcoal.

She looked from the remains to him. She should have cursed at him, she knew. Spat in his face, maybe. All she could form, as his mouth twisted into an expectant frown, was a single word.

"Huh?"

"Why does this thing exist?" His voice was eerily ponderous, as though he were talking to the blackened husk and not her. "It was so small that I barely had to move my fingers, barely had to think and . . ."

He turned his hand over, let the fragments fall to ashes.

"It simply turned to nothing," he whispered. "Why?"

The fire burning in his eyes could not burn nearly hot enough to obscure the glimmer in his stare, the sort of excited flashing of a boy with a new toy right before he accidentally breaks it. It unnerved her to see it, even without the malicious red glow that strained to obscure it. But she forced herself to look. She forced herself to speak.

"Because you killed it."

He frowned, the glimmer waning, as though he had hoped that wasn't the case.

"Why?" he asked.

For lack of anything else, she simply stared.

Is this it? she asked herself. *Is this the man that thinks he's a god? He doesn't even know why he kills. He's not a god. He has . . .*

"Nothing."

"What?"

She wasn't even aware that the word had slipped out until he frowned at her. After she was, though, the rest came easily.

"You killed it because you have nothing else. You killed it because that's what you do. You destroy. You hurt people." She drew in a staggering breath, but the words came flooding out, impossible to stop. "Because whatever made you, they made you with nothing else but that purpose. You don't know why, you don't know how. You know *nothing* but pain, and without pain, you are nothing."

It didn't feel good to say it. It felt necessary, as necessary as the deep breath that came after she said it. It came into her lungs clean, despite the soot, the heat, and the suffering surrounding her. *That* felt good.

It would have felt better if Sheraptus hadn't smiled broadly and spoke. *"Exactly."*

She recoiled, the very words striking her just when she thought he couldn't say anything more depraved. He didn't notice her reaction, he didn't notice she was there as he turned around and made a grand, sweeping gesture.

"Created to destroy, created to kill, *that* makes sense," he said to the cavern as he paced about its circular length. "Weapons need to be forged. *Nethra* has to be channeled. But this?" He looked down at the black, sooty smear on the floor. "What purpose is there in something so weak?"

His gaze drifted to Nai, hanging helplessly in her chains. Asper felt her bowels turn to water as though he had looked at her instead. Her feet scrabbled against the floor, the chains pulling her back, forcing her to watch helplessly as he reached out, a pair of long, probing fingers gently brushing against Nai's cheek.

"What use is there for such a thing . . ." he whispered.

The fire in his eyes smoldered, painting Nai's face crimson. She let out a soft whimper, daring not to speak, daring not to move as his fingers drifted lower, across her throat, toward her chest.

"I DON'T KNOW!"

It wasn't a lie. She didn't know the answer. She didn't know why she screamed so suddenly. And she didn't care. Sheraptus turned away from Nai, his gaze dimming to a faint glow. Asper watched long enough to see the girl go slack in her bonds again before turning to lock her gaze upon his and his upon hers.

"No one knows," she continued. "The Gods don't tell us when we're born."

"Then why?"

"Why what?"

185

"Why do anything you do?" he asked. "Why call out to gods if you can't see them, if you can't hear them and they don't talk to you?"

"They do. We have scriptures, prayers, hymnals, ritual. They tell us how to live, what to do," she paused to put emphasis on her next words, "why we shouldn't kill and—"

"Those are not gods. They do not create, they were created."

"By the Gods."

"How?"

"They told us—"

"Then why do they not tell you now? What do these rituals and things do but ask more questions? Where do you get answers?"

"They . . . they . . ." The words came slowly, like a knife being drawn out of her flesh. "They might not give us answers. The Gods might not even talk to us." She said it aloud for the first time. "They might not even exist."

It hurt more than she thought.

"They do."

Hurt turned to confusion the moment he spoke.

"Where else could all this have come from?" he asked, shaking his head. "We have no trees in the Nether, no sand, no oceans." He sighed. "No gods. But here? You have everything. And for what? What does it do for you? What is its purpose?"

"Not everything has to have a purpose," she said. "Some things are there not to kill or be killed, but simply to be . . . right? They are there to be protected, cherished." Her gaze drifted to Nai. "The Gods can't possibly watch over everything."

"But that doesn't make *sense*," Sheraptus snapped. "If trees are not created to be made into boats, then why are they here? What is metal if not to be made into swords? If something is meant to *be*, why is it so fragile?" He resumed his pacing, rubbing his crown. "All things must be created for a reason. Everything must have a purpose. What is theirs?"

He whirled about. The fires in his eyes were stoked with desperation, leaping with such intensity that they seemed to engulf his face, leaving nothing but jagged teeth twisted in a grimace. He thrust a finger at her.

"What is *yours*?"

She wanted to look away, away from those eyes that had stared at her, away from those teeth that had grinned at her, away from that finger that had—

Look at him, the thought leapt to her mind unbidden. It resounded with conviction from a place she did not know. *Look at him and know that he's not what they think he is*. It held her head high, even as it wanted to bow. *Look at him and know that he's not what* he *thinks he is.* It made her draw in a long, clean breath. *Look at him. And he won't look at her.*

"Perhaps," she whispered, "it's to tell you all this."

The fires in his eyes waned. Between shudders of crimson, flashes of white broke through. And in them, she could see something that had been stained by flame for a long, long time.

Desperation.

Fear.

A hope that somehow, some way, everything that he was thinking was utterly and terribly wrong.

"How do you know?" he asked.

She shook her head, her chains rattling softly. "It's never clear. Not without suffering."

"Suffering?"

"Only with suffering comes understanding." She closed her eyes, letting the truth of that settle upon her, atop the fear and the anger. "Great suffering."

He nodded solemnly. That which she felt within her she saw within him as his eyes smoldered, sputtered into empty whites.

"They come to you with suffering," he said, "when they are needed. That is why you called to them," he hesitated before continuing, "that night."

To stare into the white eyes of this man, as she had stared into the red eyes of the man who had violated her, should have been enough to destroy her. She should have collapsed, slumped in her chains, lost all will to raise her head again. But there was something in these eyes, something bright and vivid, that burned even more brightly than fire.

This man was no god. This man could be made to see what he had done.

She looked past him. Nai hung limply in her manacles, drawing in sharp, short breaths.

For her sake, Asper had to believe that.

"How much?" It was the edge in his voice that seized her attention, the glimmer in his eye that held it. "How much suffering before they appear?"

"I don't—" She paused, reconsidered. "Much," she replied softly. "There is much suffering, much regret, much penance."

"And one cannot begin . . . without the other."

In the instant he turned away from her, she saw it. In the corner of his eye, as though it had been hiding from her the whole time, there was a little too much of something. Perhaps it was too much of an eager glimmer in his eye, too easy a smile that came with too much knowing.

She saw it.

And in that instant, she knew that whatever had left him, it wasn't cruelty.

"No," she whispered.

Whether she had heard Asper or the sound of Sheraptus approaching, Nai looked up. What it took Asper until now to see, she found in an instant. Her face twisted up into a grimace, her hands clenched, she bit her lower lip so hard that blood gushed readily.

"No. No." Nai shook her head, fervor increasing with each word. "No, no, no, no, no." She was all but flailing as he approached her, her chains rattling wildly, her heels scraping furiously against the floor as she tried to back away. "*NO, NO, NO, NO, NO!*"

"Wait! *WAIT!*" Asper called after him. "This isn't what I meant! This isn't what you—"

"It is," Sheraptus said softly. "It makes perfect sense. Why would gods come unless called? Unless the need was great?"

"I didn't *do* anything!" Nai wailed. The cloth of her slippers wore through in a moment and soon, she was painting the floor with her blood as her feet desperately scrabbled. "I didn't. I *DIDN'T!* I've been good! I . . . I screamed! Please, no. Please, please, please, please—"

"Stop!" Asper cried out, hurling herself at him. The chains caught her, chuckled in the rattle of links as they pulled her back to the wall. "This isn't what I meant! Stop! *Stop!*"

The metal of her manacles groaned, growing weary of her futile attempts. They tugged her back to the wall, pleading in creaking metal to spare herself the torment. She spoke louder to be heard over him, screaming wildly at him with all manner of pleas, all manner of curses.

Between the chains and herself, she couldn't hear the sound of metal sizzling, of stone cracking.

Nai's wailing ceased as he came upon her, looking her over with wide, glimmering eyes. She fell still in her chains, as though if she held just still enough, stayed just silent enough, he might move on. Even then, though, she drew in wheezing breaths, sniffling tears through her nostrils with each gasp.

Sheraptus stood there, hands folded behind his back, calmly studying her. Asper held her breath, watching, waiting, praying.

Humble do I pray and humble do I ask—

Slowly, he unfolded his hands, raised them up to frame Nai's face delicately as she winced.

You who gave up Your body so that we might know—

His fingers splayed out slowly, each joint creaking as they did, like the long legs of great purple spiders, the tips gently settling upon her temples and cheeks.

I know I don't deserve it, I know I doubted You but—

"Please," Nai whispered.

Please—

Sheraptus smiled gently.

Please—

The glimmer in his eyes became a spark.

PLEASE.

And he spoke a word.

Nai's scream was lost in the violent, laughing crackle of electricity. Asper watched, eyes wide, yearning to be blinded by the flashes of electricity that leapt from his fingertips in laughing lashes, sharing some sick joke with Nai's flesh that only it found funny.

"*STOP!*" Nai screamed, struggling to hold onto language. "*STOP! PLEASE!*"

"Don't beg me," Sheraptus said gently. "*Them.* You have to ask *them* to come."

Smoke came in gray plumes, mercilessly refusing to hide the grimace of her face painted by flashes of blue, the shedding of her cloth as electric spears rent her garments. Asper could look away, to pray, to do anything.

And without thought, without prayer, without blinking, she began to walk forward.

"*HELP! PLEASE!*" Nai wailed. "*TALANAS! DAEON! GALATAUR!*"

"There we are," Sheraptus cooed encouragingly. "Just a little more now."

The flashes grew stronger, their laughter louder, their macabre jokes increasingly hilarious as they plucked at her skin. Hair smoked, stood on end. Her lips curled back to expose gums. A nipple blackened amidst a mass of twitching flesh.

The chains caught Asper, tried to pull her back. She continued to walk forward, unthinking, unfeeling. The searing of her wrist, she did not notice. The shattering of stone behind her, she did not hear.

189

"Louder, now, louder," Sheraptus coaxed. "It can't be too much longer now."

What tore out of Nai's mouth was without words, without emotion. It was the kind of raw, vocal bile offered up when there was nothing left within her. From deep in the darkness beyond the chamber, more voices lent theirs to hers, more screaming joining with hers.

They clashed like cathedral bells at first, each one striving to be heard over the other, before finding an agonized harmony, blending into a single perfect scream.

Asper didn't even hear the chains break, nor did she hear the sizzle of burning metal as the manacle fell from her left wrist, scorched and blackened.

She noticed her palm glowing with hellish red light, the bones black and visible beneath a transparent sheath of skin, only when she raised it up, extended it authoritatively, marched toward the black figure.

And wrapped it about Sheraptus's skinny neck.

Instantly, the laughter stopped, the screaming stopped, the speaking stopped. The lightning leapt back into Sheraptus's hands, which calmly lowered themselves to his sides, as though he had simply lost interest.

The only sign that anything was wrong the sickening crack resounding in the silence as his shoulder popped out of place.

"What . . . what is . . ." he gasped for a moment before there was a faint sucking sound, his windpipe collapsing.

"I don't know," Asper said, tightening her grip. "But it was sent here for you."

Something broke beneath him, a shinbone snapping, realigning awkwardly, and snapping again until his right leg possessed six different joints. He collapsed to his knees, body trembling as though it were about to come undone.

"You . . ." he rasped in great, inward breaths, "you . . . pure . . . destruction."

Asper said nothing. The hellish red light of the arm intensified, grew fat off the suffering. Sheraptus held up an arm, watched it twist and diminish, as though something sucked the sinew right out of it until there was nothing left but brittle, marrowless bones.

"Only . . . gods . . . Aeon in . . . a human," he rasped. "Gods . . . help . . ."

Snap. His knee erupted.

"Help . . ."

Snap. His arm folded in on itself.

"Gods . . ."

Creak. His neck began to—

"*MASTER!*"

She heard the cry, heard the iron boots crashing on the stone floor. She had been discovered, she knew, even without looking to see the netherling charging up the corridor, sword at the ready. Not yet, she knew; they might kill her, but not before she could kill him.

As the netherling approached, she flew her right hand out errantly, intended to catch a blow meant for her neck, to swat impotently at the netherling, anything to buy just a few more moments to finish what she had started. She expected nothing.

She certainly didn't expect her fist to find the female's ribcage.

And she didn't expect to feel it explode beneath her hand.

The netherling fell backward, wailing and clutching her side. Asper felt her own grip on Sheraptus loosen as her wide-eyed attentions turned toward her right hand. Her wonderfully normal, uselessly normal right hand.

Upon whose palm a faint, white dot of light began to glow, like a great eye opening for the first time.

It stared at her and she stared at it, unblinking. Within it, she could feel her blood flow swiftly, perfectly, in perfect harmony with the beating of her heart. And even as it slowed, she felt the throbbing pain of her left hand diminish, its hellish red glow dim, only for the white pinprick of light to grow wider, the eye broader.

She blinked. It stuttered.

And then winked out completely.

She continued to stare at her palm, once again perfectly normal. She stared right up until she heard the sound of metal boots two steps behind her.

Xhai had come without warcry or concern, letting her fist speak for her. And Asper was sent reeling, succumbing to its argument as she flew across the cavern, struck the wall, slid to the floor.

Xhai was upon her instantly, boot pressed to her throat, digging its sharp heel into the tender flesh of her neck. She gurgled, pounding at her foot with wonderful, useless, normal hands once more. Xhai narrowed her eyes, pressed a little harder.

"*STOP!*"

Sheraptus's voice was barely a voice at all. More a suppurating gasp. His hand swept with no authority, but merely flailed.

"Not kill . . . her," he rasped. "Take away . . . sent for me . . ."

Xhai frowned, looking from him to her.

"*NOW!*"

He didn't specify, Xhai didn't ask. She reached down, seized Asper by her hair, and began to drag her away. The priestess didn't care, her eyes fell to the girl hanging from the wall, whose blackened flesh still smoked, whose body still twitched.

Who still drew breath and whispered.

And through the pain and the confusion, Asper smiled as she was hauled into the darkness.

She was far away when Sheraptus made another noise, far too far to hear him chuckle to himself. Far too far to see him stare up, past the cavern roof, past the sky above, into heaven.

"Great suffering . . . still alive . . ." A contented smile came over his face. "You *do* listen."

FOURTEEN

VIRTUOUS LABOR

"*QAI ZHOTH!*"

It began with one cry, an iron voice torn from a throat, somewhere amidst the bustle and bloodshed on the beach. And at one cry, one by one, they looked up.

The shaven-headed metalshapers wiped the sweat from their brows as they looked up from the white-hot iron in their forgepits. The slave drivers held their whips at bay, giving their scaly, reptilian drudges but a moment to lower their loads and bleed quietly as their taskmistresses looked up. The females hauling yet another broken corpse to the sikkhun pits stopped, looked up, smiled broadly.

And one by one, the cry was taken up.

"*QAI ZHOTH!*"

"*AKH ZEKH LAKH!*"

"*EVISCERATE! DECAPITATE! ANNIHILATE!*"

They leapt from throat to throat, roaring over one another, accompanied by weapons thrust into the air, purple muscles flexing, howls of bloodlust. Even as the cries died down, the fervor did not. It filled the nostrils of the netherlings, drove their activities to frenzy.

The call had gone up. Bloodshed was close.

Hammers rang out nearly continuously as the shapers strained to finish just one more sword that they may start just one more sword. Whips cracked harder, forcing slaves to run instead of trudge as they hauled more and more loads. Bodies not *quite* dead—the weak, the starving, the ones that took just too long a break—were added to the corpses flung into the sikkhun pits to stoke the appetites of the beasts and drive their hunger-crazed, warbling laughter to ravenous cacophony.

The netherling war machine was a sight to behold, Yldus thought.

As it had been the first time he saw it. And the second time. After the forty-fifth, he surprised himself by realizing that one *could* grow tired of the sight of a bunch of females working themselves into a furious frenzy of snarling, spitting, and headbutting.

"Funny," he muttered to himself.

"Which part?" his companion growled behind him. "The fact that the invasion of Jaga is leaving without me? Or the fact that it's leaving without me because of *you*?"

He felt Qaine's eyes bore into the back of his skull, neither he nor she quite certain what was keeping her from planting something sharper than a scowl there instead.

Still, he couldn't help but smile as he turned to her. There was an honesty to her that he appreciated. Possibly because Qaine's particular brand of honesty allowed her to speak openly at least twice as long as any other female before resorting to grunts and bodily functions to make her point.

"Consider it a favor," Yldus replied. "This invasion is doomed."

"All the netherlings we have, being sent to an island populated by more of Those Green Things," she snorted. "There will be blood. There will be death. And I should be responsible for at *least* most of it."

"You killed plenty just a few days ago."

"And?"

"And we lost no one. Jaga is different. We've lost more than fifty warriors trying just to *find* the damn place." He cast a glower toward the cavern at the rear of the beach that served as their base. "And Sheraptus wants to send out three hundred, nearly all our sikkhuns, *and* all three males to try and find it again. I'd be insane to recommend taking one of the few Carnassials we have left when we're liable to lose at least half of them."

"That's not why you want me to stay."

He looked her over. She stood two paces away and a full head taller. Powerful arms were folded across a more powerful chest, a frowned scarred upon her long face, white hair cropped cruelly short refusing to flutter in the wind. He smiled gently at her. She snorted, spat, scowled.

An adequate summary of their relationship.

194

"Xhai is going," he said. "Xhai is violently unstable."

"And I'm *not*?" she sounded offended.

"*You* can grasp the concept of self-control. *She* can grasp the concept of killing anyone whom Sheraptus so much as looks at. Maybe Those Green Things wouldn't hurt you, but Xhai would, and she *will* if you go."

Qaine clearly wanted to protest, if the flare of her nostrils and narrow of her eyes were any indication. It was a sign of weakness for a female to admit being incapable of destroying anything short of a mountain, and even then, it would have to be a big one.

But Semnein Xhai was notably more insane than a mountain and had only been getting worse since she had returned from her brief captivity at the humans' hands. And neither Yldus nor Qaine thought she would be any more reasonable after whatever ruckus had just happened in the cavern a few moments ago; Sheraptus had forbade anyone from entering to find out.

"Fine," she grunted.

"It'll be a disaster, regardless," Yldus replied, staring down at the bustle on the beach and Vashnear standing at the center of it.

His erstwhile brother stood between the ships bobbing at sea, the red jewel about his neck glowing brighter and bloodier than the crimson robes he wore. His *nethra* sent him hovering a foot off the ground, only barely meeting the gazes of the females he presumed to command with sweeping gestures as he directed them and the cargo their scaly slaves carried aboard the boats.

"After all, Vashnear is involved."

"*Him?*" Qaine scoffed. "He trembles at puddles of piss. Will he at least grow a spine for the invasion?"

Yldus frowned as a slave broke under a particularly fearsome crack of the whip. With a throaty scream, it collapsed, a globule of blood flying from its lacerated back to splatter upon the ground.

It was bad enough that Vashnear hurled himself a good ten feet away from the bodily excretion, even *without* the cringing shriek that accompanied it.

"Unlikely." Yldus sighed, rubbing his eyes. "A male terrified of contracting a disease from the overscum is just one problem. Consider that our forces are diminished and that Sheraptus refuses to wait for more from the portal, the fact that an unstable lunatic will be leading them and . . ."

"And a male so spineless that he denies the force a much-needed Carnassial just to keep her from getting hurt?"

"Just so. Anything could be turned against us, *especially* Sheraptus. It was bad enough when he bedded the overscum females, but now he's *talking* to them . . . when he isn't talking to crabs. And *he's* supposed to be leading us."

"That's why you're not staying here," Qaine replied, as soft as a seven-foot-tall female could. "His is the right to lead. Yours is to plan."

"Indeed. My staggering intellect continues to burden as well as amaze." He sighed. "We have the First, if nothing else. They can carry the rest."

"Already, you're sounding more stupid than weak," she said, chuckling. "Glad we had this talk."

"Keep talking like that and I won't bring you back anything from Jaga."

She grunted, pulling out a small gray fragment of stone attached to a thin black chain from beneath her breastplate.

"You already gave me this, which you were stupid to do." She snorted, thrusting it at him. "Everything you could have taken from Port Yonder and you chose a pebble."

"And I gave it to you."

"Why?"

He rolled his shoulders. "It's the only thing I've ever owned. Everything else belongs to Sheraptus. It's mine to give away."

"For stupid reasons."

"Then give it back."

She pulled it away defensively, glowering at him. He half-sneered, half-smiled.

"That's what I thought."

"Shut up," she grunted, stalking down the dune. "I've got to go ready my sikkhun. If I'm going to stay behind with the high-fingered weaklings, I'll at least ride taller than them."

They descended the sandy slope, picking their way through the rocky outcroppings jutting from the dunes. Amidst them all, Yldus paused, drawing Qaine's attention as he slowly surveyed the pillars.

"What?" she asked.

"It just occurred to me," he said, beginning to walk again, "do you ever feel like it's a little stupid to talk about our strategies and weaknesses so openly like this?"

"I think talking is stupid."

Denaos peered around the stone outcropping. Risky, he knew; it was hard to hear anything over the sudden ferverous roar that rose up from the beach below, let alone the footsteps of two netherlings. But he caught only a glimpse of their purple backs as they disappeared into the activity below.

He turned, glanced to his companion expectantly.

"Did you get any of that?" he asked.

"No," Dreadaeleon replied. "How would I? I don't speak netherling."

The rogue took a cautious step out into the open. "It might have been something important."

"When have they ever said anything important?" Dreadaeleon asked, taking a less than cautious stumble after him. "I feel I should remind you that we're not here to pick up the finer points of their conversation, either."

"You don't *have* to remind me," Denaos muttered, stalking up the dune to a higher vantage point. "In fact, if you wanted to stop talking altogether, I wouldn't object."

"I'm just saying, since it's your fault and all."

"*My* fault?"

The boy rolled his shoulders helplessly, unable to deny simple fact. "You took the longface prisoner rather than just killing her, she took *Asper* prisoner, which brought us here."

"I thought she'd have valuable information about the tome."

"I refer you to my earlier point about netherlings and the relative value of their conversation. From what I was able to discern, the primary thrust of your interrogation was whether or not she could answer any question with a bodily function."

"Yeah? Well, now we know she can." The rogue snorted. "Regardless of whose fault it is, here we are."

He knelt down low upon the dune's ridge, keeping most of his body hidden behind the sand. For all of ten breaths, anyway. It quickly became insultingly clear that not a single longface was going to bother looking up.

Not that they were particularly renowned for their curiosity, but the frenzy with which they worked, their focus hammered like rivets onto the metals they forged and the slaves they whipped, was unnerving.

Not that they weren't before.

And yet, it didn't become *completely* clear until he noticed them gathering. In knots of purple flesh and polished iron armor, they clustered upon the beach. Thirty-three to a group each time, sharpening thirty-three swords, stringing thirty-three bows, coating thirty-three wedges of steel with thirty-three vials of sickly green poison.

And they continued to gather across the beach, sands stained with blood, blackened by fire.

In thirty-three groups.

"Silf's Sweet Daughters," he muttered. "They're mobilizing."

"For what?" Dreadaeleon asked, creeping up beside him. "They need *that* many to go destroy Teji?"

"To destroy Teji, they'd need a strong bowel movement and a stiff breeze. They wouldn't bring this many."

"Then . . . what? Are they attacking the mainland?"

Denaos shook his head. "I don't see any food in whatever they're loading aboard the ships."

"Do they . . . *need* food?"

"Of course they need food." Denaos paused, furrowing his brow. He looked over his shoulder at the boy. "Right? They have mouths."

"Those are used for screaming. I've never seen them eat."

"Me neither. Huh." He looked back over the dune, shrugging. "Okay, if we return to the mainland and it's been completely decimated, we'll consider the matter settled. For now, I'd say they're about to attack a much closer target."

"Jaga," Dreadaeleon muttered. "Lenk, Kataria, Gariath . . ."

"Let's focus on *one* companion in peril at a time here."

Denaos swept his gaze over the beachhead, the words slipping out through his frown. He settled on the massive spike-ringed pit in the middle, on the two netherlings hauling a twitching Gonwa to the edge and tossing it in. The spikes shook, the gruesome laughter echoing off the metal as something within stirred.

"If she's not already—"

"She isn't."

The boy's face was steeled with determination, he knew without even looking. His lips would be turned downward in a perfectly curved frown, his eyes would be acting under the impression that the more squinted they were, the more intense he looked, and he would be trying desperately to convince himself and the world that he had a jaw.

Exactly the sort of look he probably thought he should have had in this kind of situation.

If you were an honest man, Denaos told himself, *you'd tell him. You'd tell him you weren't about to suggest that she was dead. You'd tell him that you know what Sheraptus did to her, what he's probably doing to her now. You'd tell him he should look far, far worse than whatever it is he thinks he's supposed to look like.*

But Denaos was not an honest man. Not to his companions, not to his gods, and never, ever to himself.

"Yeah," he said, "you're probably right."

Trying to ignore the feeling of self-loathing that came with saying that, he returned to surveying the beachhead. The two males stood out amidst the crowd with the bright crimson glow of the gemstones around their necks as they floated about, dictating to the clusters of females, sending them rushing eagerly toward the black ships moored in the surf, trampling the Gonwa slaves who continued to haul loads.

He wondered if, at some point, she might be among those loads, bound and bundled into the ship to be taken to whatever invasion they were planning. What then? Swoop in, die horribly, be dragged to the pits along with the other Gonwa bodies to be—

Let's stop that train of thought right there, shall we? If you keep thinking of the pits filled with corpses and how she might be in there and how you'll probably wind up in there and how whatever's in there now is laughing and crunching and laughing and laughing and . . .

A cry went up from the crowd. A team of six netherlings came charging forward, a crudely-fastened ramp held between them. Denaos watched, unable to turn away, as they lowered it into the pit.

He dearly wished he could, though, long before the ramp began to tremble with the weight of something heavy climbing up it.

With a sudden howl, the creature tore itself free from the pit, scattering sand and netherlings alike as it tore the land apart to make room for its size. On thick claws, it paced in hurried circles, a great, square head sweeping back and forth across the beachhead. Muscles flexed beneath a pelt of rust-red fur, a bushy tail swishing as it loped around, netherlings scrambling to get out of its way.

It was searching for something, that much was clear to Denaos. Why it was having trouble finding it became clear the moment it turned its head toward his hiding place.

In the place of eyes were two indentations in the skull covered with thick, black fur. It couldn't have seen him, Denaos told himself over thoughts that largely consisted of "oh gods" over and over. It couldn't have seen him. It was blind.

That didn't make it any less unnerving when the thing's black, rubbery lips peeled back to reveal long, glistening rows of teeth in what was *very* clearly a smile in a *very* deliberate attempt to make him take off running, propelled by a jet of his own cowardice.

That option grew increasingly more appealing as six ears, three to each side of its head, split apart in a pair of pointed, wedge-shaped fans. The beast whirled about, canting its head to the side as its ears twitched, trembled, found something.

With a sound that was like a very sick hound laughing at a very sick joke, the thing took off at a gallop. It sent a pair of netherlings leaping out of the way before its tremendous shoulders bunched and uncoiled, sending it leaping through the air to land upon a nearby Gonwa slave that it dragged, screaming, from the line.

The feeding was gruesomely brief: a noisome tumult of flesh ripping, meat slurping, bones cracking between tremendous jaws. All punctuated with peals of gibbering laughter.

Denaos watched the grisly scene for as long as it took him to blink. He then rose up, turned around, walked away from the dune's ridge, and looked to Dreadaeleon, who raised a brow at him expectantly.

"So," the rogue said, "how set *are* you on saving Asper?"

"Why?"

"Hongwe's just down at the beach with the boat, you know. We could be back at Teji by nightfall and have a few more hours to reflect on how lucky we are not to have our genitals eaten by giant, six-eared, eyeless horrors."

"What happened?" Dreadaeleon asked. "What's down there?"

"Well, damn. There are only so many ways I can say it, Dread." He gestured over his shoulder. "Go take a look for yourself. They're fairly preoccupied down there." He cringed as a peal of wailing laughter rose up over the ridge.

"That might prove an opportune moment," Dreadaeleon said, tapping his chin. "Barring distractions, I could probably do a fair job of scrying out Asper's location."

Denaos furrowed his brow, looking a tad offended. "You could do that the entire time? You could have just used some manner of magical weirdness to *find* her and spared me the sight of whatever it is I just saw?"

"The act of seeing where one is not meant to see is a bit more than magical weirdness," Dreadaeleon replied sharply. "It requires a clear vantage, a delicate position and—"

"And what? The seed of a blasphemer? Because I'll get to work on that and be done in six breaths if that'll make this go any faster." He whirled about, gesturing wildly over the ridge. "Hell, why are we even here? Why don't you go down spitting out lightning and flying around like an underweight sparrow made of *death* like you did on Teji?"

"Because—"

"Even better, why don't you just drop your trousers right now and work up a good, flaming piss that sets them all ablaze like you did a few days ago? Why are we here, skulking about like rodents?"

"I would have *hoped* that, in our time together, you'd grasp that magic isn't so mystical that it can be just summoned up like that. There isn't an opportune moment to—"

"There is never *not* an opportune moment to shoot fire out of your prick!" Denaos snapped sharply. "What is it, then? Back on the beach, you were nearly unstoppable. Days ago, you were pissing fire." He stared intently at the wizard. "What's going on with you?"

"It's complicated," Dreadaeleon sighed, rubbing his eyes. "And I don't have time to—"

It wasn't clear what he was trying to say when the boy's body suddenly jerked, nor when his eyes bulged out, threatening to roll out of their sockets. Nothing was clearer when he snapped at the waist, leaning heavily on his knees as he loosed a torrent of vomit upon the ground to coalesce into a brackish green pool. Things were certainly disgusting, Denaos thought, and disgusting for a solid ten breaths, but whatever was happening to him didn't become any more obvious.

That didn't happen until the vomit drew itself together of its own volition, shuddered as if it were taking a deep breath and then, with a slow, leisurely confidence, began to slither off on a carpet of bile.

Denaos turned a slack jaw to Dreadaeleon, who merely wiped his mouth with the back of his hand and sneered.

"I'm dying, Denaos."

"I see . . ." the rogue replied, his tone suggesting no *real* willingness to continue with this conversation, yet compelled all the same. "Of . . . what?"

"The Decay," Dreadaeleon replied. "The barriers that separate the magic from my body are collapsing. I'll slowly lose more control over both and, eventually, my skin will catch fire, my lungs will freeze inside my chest, and my nerves will splinter and erupt out of my skin."

"Which will be on fire."

"On fire, yes."

"Well . . . that's . . ."

The wizard affixed him with a glare. "That's what?"

"I guess I just thought it would have a more impressive name?"

"What?"

"Something like 'the dragonblood,' or 'the frothening,' or 'that which explodes without mercy.'"

Dreadaeleon narrowed his eyes sharply. "I am going to *explode.* My frozen innards will fly out of my body and burst into pink and black snow and children will make snowmen with my *kidneys.*"

"I know, I know! I'm sorry! I just—"

"You just what? You're just concerned about me being out here? Thinking I can't handle it? Thinking that I'm totally powerless because my own body is rebelling against me and soon I'm going to be chopped up for spare parts and turned into a book because I'm far more useful in death than I was in life?"

"Those weren't going to be my exact words, but . . ."

There was more to that retort, he thought, and it was going to be *clever.* But he said nothing more the moment he noticed the tears welling up in Dreadaeleon's eyes, the moment he remembered the wizard was just a boy.

A scared, dying boy whose remaining fluids that had not just come out of his mouth were now dripping from his eyes in thin streams.

And he wanted something from Denaos, that much was obvious. A nod maybe, possibly a big hug and a weeping reassurance that everything was going to be fine and that they were going to rescue Asper themselves and Dreadaeleon was going to be proven a proud and powerful wizard over whom she would swoon after she told Denaos that everything he had ever done would be forgiven and he would go to heaven and he'd stop seeing the woman with the slit throat every time he stopped drinking.

But he couldn't tell Dreadaeleon that.

Lying was a sin. An awfully convenient sin, given the circumstance, but Denaos couldn't afford any more.

And what the wizard got was something different.

"I'll go gather your vomit," Denaos said with the kind of hesitation that suggested he had hoped he'd never have to say that.

What was that? Dreadaeleon asked himself as he watched the rogue stalk away. *What was that look? What was that? Pity? He pities me? A lowlife, scumsucking, barkneck like him pities me?* He sneered, felt a salty tear drip into his mouth. *Probably because you're crying like a . . . like a woman or something. No, not a woman. She wouldn't want you to say that. It's demeaning. Stop that. Stop all of it.*

He couldn't.

Weak. You disgust me. You'll disgust her. And when they hack you up, your pieces will disgust everyone else. You'll be the only wizard useless in life and in death. Look at you, unable to do anything but sit here and weep. How are you supposed to be the hero? How are they supposed to respect you? How are you supposed to save her?

"You are not, lorekeeper."

As odd as it felt to say, he knew Greenhair was standing behind him even before she spoke in her lilting tone. There was always something that preceded her arrivals: a feeling at the back of his head like cricket legs rubbing together, a sudden calm that washed over him, and the fact that she only ever seemed to show up when he felt a particular kinship with things that came out of livestock rectums.

As such, he didn't turn around to look at her. He didn't even speak to her, didn't acknowledge her existence at all.

"You have exactly until I blink to leave before I roast you alive," he muttered.

Or tried to, anyway.

"I do not wish you any distress," she said, her voice a river flowing into his ears to pool beneath his brain. "But I do not think you are in any condition to be making threats."

He half-smiled, half-sneered as he turned to face the siren. His attentions were instantly drawn to her head, framed by feathery gills wafting from her neck, a fin rising from a crop of hair the color of the sea, a pair of blank, liquid eyes staring intently at him. All the color and oddity framed a face that was expressionless. A serene, monochrome portrait: perfectly and terrifyingly empty.

"I'm always willing to make the effort," he said, "especially when it comes to deranged sea tramps that have attempted to *sell me* to the very purple-skinned longfaces I'm surrounded by right now."

Her mouth trembled into a frown. "I have never claimed to be incapable of regret, lorekeeper, nor mistake or misplaced ambition."

"And which one do I owe this visit to?" He glanced over his shoulder at the sound of a distant warcry. "Because if you're looking for another regret, just raise your voice a little."

"I have no desire to draw the attentions of the longfaces," she replied, averting her gaze guiltily. "I have . . . reconsidered my alliance with them."

"Understandable, what with their constant desire to kill things."

"It was their unique talents that drove me to seek them out," Greenhair said, a tone of accusation creeping into her voice. "The tome is too much to trust to mortals, the chance that the demons might seize it too great. I could not take that risk, for the sake of my waters and beyond."

"*QAI ZHOTH!*" a longface's roar rose over the ridge.

"If you want to ask them something, I'd do it now," Dreadaeleon replied, lowering his voice. "Before things get *weird.*"

"I was . . . mistaken. My faith in them was driven by their talent for slaughtering the demons. I did not suspect that their prowess might come from serving someone far darker."

"Darker?" Dreadaeleon asked, sarcasm replaced by curiosity. "What do you mean?"

"I . . . was at Irontide when the morning rose, seeking Sheraptus. I had hoped to reason with him, to convince him to direct his attentions toward Jaga. I overheard dealings between him and . . . something. Something old."

"The bad kind of old, I take it."

"He spoke the first words to the Aeons. He was the one that spoke on their behalf, taking their words from the servants of the Gods just as they took their masters' words. Azhu-Mahl, he was called in the darkest days. He, who was closer to heaven than any mortal, is alive and allied with the longfaces."

"They do tend to attract some odd friends, don't they?"

"*LISTEN TO ME.*" The porcelain of her face cracked, the liquid of her voice boiled in a bare-toothed snarl. "I can make no apology that would sate you, only tell you that I was wrong, in all things, and whatever sins I have wrought against you are *nothing* compared to that which is about to happen. Their allies, the old gray one, he is providing them with things that should not be."

"The stones," Dreadaeleon whispered, the realization dawning upon him instantly. "The red stones they carry. They negate the laws of magic . . ."

"And their venoms that eat through demon flesh," Greenhair said. "They have more, worse, all of which can do much, much worse and all of which require the longfaces destroying Ulbecetonth."

"How? Why?"

"I do not know yet."

"Handy."

"I know only that, to stop them and the demons both, someone is required. Someone brave, someone powerful."

"We have neither of those," Dreadaeleon said. "My greatest feat is vomit that walks, the bravest among us is off chasing it, and both of us are a little preoccupied with something right now." He turned away, looking back to the ridgeline. "Now, if you'll just . . ."

Before he felt the chill of her fingers, her hands were upon his shoulders, resting comfortably as though they had always been there. And by the time he was aware of them, he couldn't help but feel that they belonged there. They didn't, of course; she was a siren, treacherous by nature, treacherous by practice. This was a trick, obviously.

A trick that felt cool upon his skin, coaxing out the fever that had engulfed his body for the past days. A trick that came out of her lips on a lilting, lingering song, flooding into his head to douse a mind ablaze with fear, with doubt.

"I will not, lorekeeper," she spoke, words sliding into song, song sliding into thought. His thoughts. "I cannot, for I cannot do this without you."

He felt it again, the itch at the back of his skull.

She's in your head, old man. Careful. You know what she does in there. Get her out.

He should have. He would have, if her presence there didn't seem so right, so natural. Expelling her seemed like throwing out a perfectly good bottle of wine, something so sweet and fragrant that it would be a crime to do anything but drink it in, savor it.

He didn't even like wine.

"No one else can do this. Not your companions, not the longfaces," she whispered to his ears, to his mind. "I need your strength, your intellect, your power. I need *you*."

"I . . . I can't," he said. "I'm sick. I'm dying. I have no power."

"You are distracted. You are distraught. Trifling things."

"Ah . . . trifling."

"They mean nothing to you. I can ease your thoughts, give you clarity." Her fingers rose to his temples, fingers gently swirling the waters she poured into his mind. "I can give you the power to save me."

"And . . . what about Asper?"

"Leave her," she cooed, like it was just a simple thing to do so.

"She needs me."

"The world needs you. They will speak of you with tears in their eyes. They will respect you. Thousands of lives against one, all their respect against hers."

"All of them . . ." He closed his eyes, tried to imagine it. She made it easy. "They would fear me."

"They would love you."

"If I just . . ."

"Come with me." Her breath was a heady scent, filling his nostrils even as her voice filled his ears, all of her entering all of him. "To Jaga. Let me give you power. Let me give you the world."

"And she . . . she would . . ."

"She will die." It was spoken with all that fragrance, all that sweet water, all that made the siren's voice intoxicating. "She will die. She does not need you. She means nothing. But you are—"

It happened without words. It happened with barely any movement. And he wasted no thought on how he found himself with his eyes ablaze with energy, how a lock of her sea-green hair lay severed from her shocked, wide-eyed face, how his fingers still smoked and the air still crackled with the bolt of lightning he had just narrowly missed her with.

It happened. And he lowered two fingers at her, tiny blue serpents dancing across his fingertips.

"Leave," he whispered.

"Lorekeeper, I—"

"*LEAVE.*"

Her expression continued to crack, the serenity of her face shattered into fragments of anger, revulsion, and fear. She backed away from him slowly, as she might an animal, down the dune and toward the shore. Her eyes never left his, even as his fingers left her body, the electricity crackling eagerly upon his tips.

"You will never save her," Greenhair snarled. "Even if you release her from the longfaces, you can't help her. This world will be consumed, lore-keeper, in sea or in flame. You will die. She will die. And when she does . . ." The siren's lip twisted up, her sneer an ugly crack all its own. "It will be your name she curses for not doing what must be done."

He had no retort for that. He had barely any wit with which to hear her. His skull was ablaze again, her liquid words boiling inside his head and hissing out on meaningless sighs of steam. He didn't lower his fingers, didn't release the anger coursing through him until she disappeared behind a rocky outcropping.

And when he did, the power did not so much leave him as rip itself free from him, taking will and strength with it. A poignant reminder that, despite the occasional outburst, he was still dying. A reminder lost on him as he gasped, arms falling to his sides and knees buckling as he tried to stay on his feet.

He heard footsteps behind him. Denaos, maybe. Or anyone who wasn't blind, deaf, or stupid enough not to notice the bolt of lightning that had just gone howling into the sky a moment ago. It didn't matter. Anyone who wanted him dead wouldn't have had to try very hard to make it happen.

"I take it I missed something fun, then," Denaos said as the footsteps came to a halt behind him.

"Greenhair," Dreadaeleon said, breathing heavily.

"The siren, huh?" The rogue didn't sound surprised. "Where is she now?"

"Chased her off." The boy staggered to his feet, turned to face the rogue. "Have to leave. Someone was bound to have seen that lightning. Someone had to have sensed it."

"They probably would, if there was anyone left to do it."

"What?"

Denaos jerked a thumb over his shoulder. "It was faster than we expected. The ships have almost all left. Aside from a few left behind to stand guard, there are no more longfaces on the island."

"Jaga," Dreadaeleon said. "She wasn't lying."

"Huh?"

"They've left for Jaga. Going to destroy Ulbecetonth."

"That's . . . good, right?"

"When has their wanting to destroy something ever worked out well for us?"

"Point."

"Greenhair said," the boy paused, his body wracked with a sudden cough, "that they served someone darker, someone older. Even if they didn't . . ." His words devolved into a hacking fit.

"Lenk and the others are on the island," Denaos finished.

They stared at each other, the realization dawning upon them both, the choice shortly thereafter. Stay here, save Asper and possibly die? Go to Jaga, warn the others and possibly die? Of course, one of them could stay and save her while the other went to warn them and then they'd both *certainly* die.

But they saw in each other a reflection into themselves. Something in the way Denaos stared, eyes firm and searching for no way out of this. Something in the way Dreadaeleon stood, pulling himself up on trembling legs and refusing to acknowledge the pain it caused him with so much as a wince.

And in that, they both knew that they would stay. They would save her, maybe die trying. She was worth it.

To both of them, each one realized with a sudden tension, a clench of fist and a narrow of eye, toward the other. A tension they had no choice but to bite back at the moment.

"There's still longfaces down there," Denaos said. "We circle around, slide down the dune, and make our way to the cavern at the back. If she's not dead, she'll be in there."

"She's not dead," Dreadaeleon said.

"I know," Denaos replied.

"Then why'd you say it?"

No answer.

Lying was a sin, after all.

FIFTEEN

HEART OF FURY, INTESTINES OF RESENTMENT

I'm not ungrateful.

It was a resentful thought, as most of Gariath's were. Thoughts were too flexible, they could be changed at any moment, so what was the point in using them?

You have given me much.

Words were much more solid. Once words were spoken, they were there forever, hanging in the air and impossible to ignore. Like scent.

Your eye, your hatred, my life . . .

Gariath could not afford words here. Words were breath and breath was too precious to waste, where he clung precariously to slick, slippery walls by the tips of his claws. He needed it, as rare as it came, to keep clinging there, keeping himself from sliding down a vast and gaping darkness.

It's disgraceful that I don't just let go and let this be over.

Thoughts weren't enough.

But if you accepted that, you wouldn't be you.

He snarled, dug his claws in. The thick, fibrous tissue of the walls did not yield easily, but he felt liquid gush out from the scratches he carved into it, pouring over his hands. The floor shifted violently beneath him.

And if I were to do that, I wouldn't be a Rhega.

The gurgling behind him became a low rumble as something boiled up from the endless corridor behind him, sending the walls shaking, the floor writhing as he clawed his way forward.

And then, what would the point of this all be?

He tightened his grip, sinking his claws in to the skin of his fingers, stomped his feet down to secure a footing on the writhing floor. He felt liquid pour out in great, spurting gushes. He dug the claws of his toes into the floor, felt the blood pool around the soles of his feet.

The rumble behind him became something louder that shook the walls and floors and ceiling and the dark, dank air around him. And Gariath could feel by the trembling, the sound of the walls contracting around him, the great lurching shudder that shot through them, that it heralded something much, much bigger.

You have to earn *my death.*

Thoughts weren't enough.

But he trusted by the blood pouring over his hands and the great tide of bile rushing up behind him that he had made his intent clear enough.

A crack appeared in the darkness before him, quickly spreading into a great, gaping hole bordered by black, jagged spikes. In as much time as it took to blink, soft blue light poured in.

The flood of seawater came right after.

The dragonman released his grip suddenly as the seawater crashed against his chest and the bile struck against his back. For a moment, it seemed as though he might be crushed between the two liquid onslaughts. But the ocean was merely an ocean. The digestive juices boiling up behind him had an entire day's worth of hate and fury at having a clawed obstruction lodged in a tender gullet.

And expelled him like an undigested red morsel on a cloud of blood and black bile.

He went tumbling helplessly into the vastness of the sea as the Akaneed's jaws crashed shut behind him and its tremendous column of a body pressed forward. Its snout only just grazed him, but it was more than enough to send him flailing, bouncing off the beast's blue hide as it sailed beneath him.

It would have been easy to let go, to drift into the endless blue and disappear. Maybe he would survive, maybe the Akaneed would live the rest of its life with one eye happily, maybe they would kill each other later. But "maybe" was a human word indiscernible from human thought: easily twisted.

He was *Rhega.*

That was why, as the serpent's tail passed beneath him, he reached down and seized it.

A tiny red parasite on the beast's great bulk, Gariath fought to hold on against the twisting tail, against the wall of water, against his lungs tightening in his chest. Here, claws sunk into the flesh of the creature's tail, he couldn't even see where the beast's head was, the vast road of writhing blue flesh disappearing into the murk of the sea.

Such a sight would have been enough to make him consider letting go, consider the wisdom of fighting a snake the size of a ship, consider if such a thing could even *be* killed.

It would have.

If he hadn't already seen it from the inside, anyway.

The Akaneed's throaty keen echoed through the water as the beast shifted beneath him; tiny as he might have been to it, he had not gone unnoticed, his crimes against the beast had not gone unremembered. That thought gave him pride. Pride that was quickly overwhelmed by the burning need to breathe as the beast's tail swung from side to side in an attempt to dislodge him as it abruptly shifted upward.

His lungs nearly burst along with the water as the Akaneed broke the surface, out of the world of water and into the world of mist. As vast as it might have been, as much reason as it might have had to kill him, it still needed to breathe the air like him. It was still alive, like him.

And you can die, he thought, *like me.*

That thought propelled him as he hauled himself, claw over claw, across its columnous body as it tore through the waves, cleaving a path of froth and mist out of the sea. The salt stung his eyes; he didn't close them. It made his grip slip; he clung harder. The beast twisted, writhed, slapped its tail in an effort to dislodge him; he refused to let go.

You deserve to kill me, he thought. *I deserve to die.*

Pillars of stone appeared out of the mist, walkways of stone cast shadows against the gray mist overhead as the beast wound its way between them, slamming its body against the rock in an attempt to dislodge him. But stone could not stop him. Sea could not shake him. He continued to climb, to claw his way up the beast's hide, leaving bloody tracks in its hide behind him.

But I don't want to die.

And, with one more pull, he saw it. Rising high and sail-thin, tearing the sea apart, the beast's great crested fin stood. He growled, tensed . . .

And I'm not going to.

And leapt.

Not yet.

The beast roared and he felt its skull shake under him, just as it felt his claws upon its neck. His footing began to disappear beneath him, swallowed up by the sea as the serpent dove. That was fine. It was always going to be difficult. That's how their relationship worked.

And so he drew in a deep breath and took the Akaneed's fin in his claws as the world drowned around him.

Beneath the mist there was nothing but decay. Pillars of stone rose in a gray forest from the seabed. The shattered timbers of ships and their crumbled monolith statues littered the floor, leaves from the dead stone trees. The shattered hulls groaned as they passed overhead. The stone grumbled as they brushed past.

Grumbles became muted cries as the Akaneed twisted, smashing its body against the rock, hide grinding against the pillars and sending clouds of earth and foam erupting as it tried to scrape its parasite off.

Gariath shifted only as much as he needed to avoid being crushed between flesh and stone, suffering dust in his eyes and shards of rock caroming off his skull. Every movement was energy wasted and every ounce was needed.

The ancient warship came into view with astonishing swiftness, its crushed and scorched hull half-sunken into the seabed, its great stone figurehead holding its arm up as if to warn Gariath of the foolishness of what he was about to try.

But what kind of lunatic would listen to a statue?

The beast swam toward it, arching its body to scrape Gariath off on the wood like it would any other piece of tenacious, sticky filth. The dragonman seized the opportunity as surely as he seized the Akaneed's fin. He spared enough energy to growl, planted his feet, and, with the entirety of his weight and strength, pulled on the creature's fin.

Hard.

It was about the moment the beast let out a keening wail of alarm that Gariath wondered if the statue might have had a point. It was about the moment when the beast lurched headlong into the statue's outstretched arm that he was fairly sure he should have paid more attention to it.

Past that, his only thought was for hanging on.

The Akaneed smashed through the statue, its body crumbling with a resigned, stony sigh, as though it knew this had been coming. The warship itself lodged a louder complaint. Ancient timbers came cracking apart in shrieks, splintering in snarls as the beast, disoriented and furious, pulled itself through the wreck in an explosion of wood and sand.

Shards of wood came flying out of the cloud of earth that rose in the creature's wake, whizzing past Gariath, striking against his temple, bouncing off his shoulders. Each one he took stoically; to cry out, to even snarl would be breath from burning lungs that he couldn't afford to lose. Even the giant spike, brimming with rot and rust, that came flying out to sink into his shoulder with an almost affectionate embrace, he took with a grunt and nothing more.

I owe you blood, he thought.

That was easy to give, coming out in a stream of cloudy red as he pulled the spike out.

Blood is better than screaming, anyway.

It trailed behind him, filling the ocean, flying like a proud banner, boldly proclaiming his progress as he hauled himself bodily across the creature's hide.

It will let everyone know that I gave something back.

It clouded his eyes, made it hard to see. His lungs seared, threatening to burst. The serpent picked up speed, threatening to send him flying off as he clawed his way up to the creature's head.

But you gave me more. You gave me a reason to live.

And through his own blood, through the rush of salt, through it all, he looked down and saw the Akaneed. And with its sole remaining eye, it looked up and saw him.

Thank you.

He raised the spike of wood above his head.

I'm sorry.

He brought it down.

The cloud of red became a storm, the beast's thunderous agony splitting through the billowing blood. It became a bolt of lightning unto itself, arching and twisting and writhing and shrieking into contortions of blind pain as it sailed violently through the bloodstained sea.

They found the surface, bursting from the sea with a roaring wail too loud to be smothered by the mist. Gariath breathed short, quick breaths, unable to spare the effort to take more. Where he had been a parasite before, he now clung to the beast with tumorlike tenacity as the Akaneed tore wildly through the forest of pillars in a blind, bloody fury.

He was nearly thrown off with each spastic flail of the beast's tail, each time it caromed off of a pillar, each time it threw back its head and howled through its agony. Honor kept his grip strong, pride kept his claws sunken; he had taken everything from the Akaneed.

He would not waste the sacrifice by being thrown off now.

The pillars thinned out, giving way to open ocean. The Akaneed picked up speed, unable to do anything else in its agony. For a moment, Gariath wondered if he might simply ride the beast out into the middle of nowhere until it died and then, as starvation and fatigue set in, he would die with it.

But as the mist began to thin and, in the distance, a great gray wall of looming, unblemished stone arose, that particular fear was dashed. Along with his brains, he was sure, if he didn't think of something.

Options being limited as they were atop the back of a violently thrashing sea serpent swimming at full speed toward a sheer wall of stone, thinking didn't count so much as action. And his actions didn't count nearly as much as the Akaneed's.

Thus, when its back twisted and snapped like a whip, he had little choice but go flying ahead of it to land in the water with an eruption of froth. And when it came surging up behind him, jaws gaping in an agonized roar, he had little choice but to try and keep from sliding down its gullet a second time as he was washed into its open mouth.

And when he saw the wall looming ever closer to them, growing ever huger with each fervent breath, he had but one choice.

And he chose *not* to soil himself.

Of the many, *many* negatives that came with being surrounded by two dozen tattooed, scaly, bipedal lizards with clubs, arrows, machetes, and yellow, wicked stares fixated upon him, Lenk had never once thought that the worst of them would be that they didn't attack.

But then again, Lenk never once thought that he would be in this position. Not alone, anyway.

He glanced back up to the fallen monolith behind him and the empty space that Kataria had just occupied. He didn't know why she left. He didn't know why she hadn't come back. He didn't know why the Shen were apparently taking their sweet time in getting down to the dirty business of smashing his head into his stomach.

But his life had always been full of surprises. And he could do something about only one of them at that moment.

His sword was in his hand, raised as a feeble counter against the threat of the many weapons raised against him. Sturdy and red with Shen blood as it might have been, crude and jagged their weapons might have been, there was little argument his single blade could muster against their two dozen jagged, cruel-edged reasons as to why he should die.

If they were savoring that fact, they had taken an awfully long time to do so.

If they were waiting to see what he would do, they had to know by now. And so, he had to ask.

"What the hell are you waiting for?" he snarled.

Beyond a collective flash of their yellow eyes, they didn't reply. He had no idea if they even understood him. All the same, as a throaty, hissing murmur swept through them, as the crowd of tattooed scales rippled and parted, the Shen answered him.

One of them, anyway.

Their weapons lowered, just as their eyes went up to look at the newly-arrived lizardman. Towering over its brethren by a head wrapped in a headdress made of the skull of some fierce-looking beast and shoulders thick with muscle, the tremendous reptile stalked forward, unhurried.

A tail as long and thick as a constrictor snake dragged behind it. A club, big enough that it would take three hands of a human to lift and studded with jagged teeth of an animal long dead, hung easily from a clawed hand that led to a log-like arm that attached to a broad, powerful body thick with banded tattoos.

All red as blood.

One pace away from Lenk, the lizardman came to a halt. Its eyes melted like amber around two knife-thin and coal-black pupils, peering out from two black pits of its animal-skull headdress. It glanced at the tip of his sword, barely grazing its massive green-and-red barrel of a chest, only barely concerned with being a twitch away from impalement.

Lenk supposed that he might also be unconcerned were he a giant reptile wearing a jagged-toothed skull like it were his own and carrying a club as big as the tiny, gray-haired insect of a man the Shen faced.

"That's not going to work," he, for he certainly *sounded* like a man, said.

"I was, uh," Lenk spoke through a cough, "hoping that you'd admire me for trying." His blade quivered slightly as the tremendous Shen stared at him. "You know, be impressed with my valiance or something."

The tremendous Shen tilted his skull-bound head to the side. "And then?"

"I don't know. You'd all make me your king or something." Lenk raised a brow. "Do you have kings?"

The Shen shook his head, sent bones rattling. "Warwatchers."

"Fancy. You're not going to be making me one, then?"

"No."

"Really?"

"You sound surprised."

"Well, your green friends haven't attacked me yet, so . . ."

"They were waiting for Shalake."

"Who?"

The Shen tapped two fingers to his chest. Lenk sneered.

"Warwatchers get to talk about themselves in the third person?"

"I give you my name and your life, for the moment," Shalake said. "Because I want to know how you got into Jaga. We have the reef. We have the walls. We have the Akaneeds. No one gets past all three."

"If that were true, there wouldn't be a whole mess of you waiting for me once I did get past them all."

"And how did you get past them?"

The young man smiled feebly. "Luck?"

"Just luck," the Shen growled.

Lenk glanced up over his shoulder, toward an empty patch of stone atop the statue where someone had once stood. Where someone had turned away and fled from him. Again. He swallowed something back as his gaze returned to the Shen.

"Just luck," he said.

Shalake nodded with a slow, sage-like patience. His sigh was long, sent plumes of dust rising from the desiccated snout of his skull headdress. He hefted his tooth-studded club lazily.

"I see."

And then he swung.

Shalake growled. He cried out. Shen hissed in approval. All sounds were lost to Lenk's ears in a fit of panic as he flung himself to the ground. They returned in the sound of stone crunching, splintering, clattering upon his back and rolling to the highway. He looked up long enough to see Shalake pull his weapon free, a great gash left in the statue's arm.

And then all thoughts were for the sword in his hand. He took the blade in a tight grip, tensed, and thrust upward. A morbid grin creased his face as he felt the steel eat deeply of flesh until it halted, gorged. That lasted just long enough to look up and see the sword's tip hovering a finger's length away from the Shen's kidneys, a clawed green hand wrapped about the naked blade.

The weapon was ripped from him as the Shen's foot lashed out and smashed against his chest. He slammed against the statue, all thought for his missing weapon going toward desperately trying to find missing breath.

Shalake seemed in no such hurry. Ignoring the blood weeping from his fingers, he tossed the blade aside as he hefted his club with all the urgency that smashing a roach warranted.

Robbed of breath and blade, Lenk was certainly not above scurrying away not unlike a roach. Though once he scrambled to his feet, he became aware of just why the Shen could afford to be so casual. The other lizardmen stood at the ready, weapons clenched and eyes fixated upon him; whether out of respect or morbid curiosity, their reluctance to join the battle clearly only extended as far as the half-circle they had formed.

He could see it in their eyes.

Which were slowly arching up, as though looking at something—

Oh, right.

The sweeping arc would have taken off his head if he hadn't thrown himself to the side. That was small solace for the heavy, clawed foot that lashed out and drove a hard kick against his back, sending him rolling across the stone.

Small *and* fleeting, he realized as he crawled to his feet, trying to ignore the sound of his bones popping. He couldn't take another hit like that. He couldn't keep dodging. He couldn't escape.

That left two options. One would be waiting for help. He looked up to the empty air above the stone statue.

"*Foolish,*" the voice said.

Agreed, he thought in reply.

That left the other option.

He stared at Shalake as the Shen hefted his club and narrowed his eyes to slits behind his skull headdress. Lenk drew in a deep breath.

And charged.

The patience was gone from the Shen's eyes, as the laziness was gone from his swing. It sucked the very air from the sky; Lenk could feel the wind from the blow itself as he ducked low, ran beneath it, past the Shen.

The tail found him before he could find it, lashing out to strike him firmly against the chest. He embraced the pain as he embraced the tail itself, wrapping both arms around it. While Lenk wasn't quite certain as to the specific implications of grabbing a lizardman's tail, he was able to guess as soon as Shalake cast a scowl over his shoulder and roared.

"SCUM!"

He swung wildly in his attempt to dislodge the man's grip. But his tail followed him with each movement and Lenk followed the tail, evading each wild lash of claw and club with tenacious grip and desperate prayer.

After a few snarling moments, Shalake stopped and Lenk felt the tail tense in his grip as the lizardman heaved, raising the appendage up with the intent of smashing it and its silver-haired parasite upon the ground. Lenk seized the opportunity and the lizardman's loincloth at once, pulling himself up onto the creature's back.

As one might expect of any reasonable reptilian horror, Shalake's protests were loud, roaring, and interspersed with several clawing fits as he tried to reach for the man lodged squarely in the center of a back too broad for his arms to reach. With cries of alarm, several Shen rushed forward to help to be knocked aside by wild sweeps of tail and club.

While it hadn't seemed like a particularly expert idea in the first place, stuck in the middle of the reptile's massive back seemed an especially poor position to be in. Particularly once Shalake calmed enough to formulate a plan. The lizardman turned, lined his back up with the stone monolith and, with a snarl and snap of legs, backpedaled furiously toward it.

They struck with a shudder of rock, narrowly knocking Lenk from his precarious perch as he pulled himself up to the lizardman's shoulders. The folly of that, too, became all too clear at the sight of Shen bows drawn and aimed for the target that had so generously made itself clear of their leader.

Arrows shrieked. An arm wrapped about his neck and pulled back hard. His head struck stone. Shalake tore himself free. In the blur of motion, the only thing that Lenk could even be vaguely sure of was that he wasn't dead.

Even that was uncertain; he hadn't expected to see those green eyes staring down at him again anywhere outside of hell.

"Kataria," he whispered.

"Stay down," she snarled at him, drawing an arrow back.

"You . . ." he said, trying to claw his way up, "you left me . . . *again.*"

"I came back." She trained the bow upon the Shen. "And I said stay *down.*" Absently, she pressed her foot upon his chest, pinning him to the top of the statue. "Don't make yourself any easier to shoot than you already did."

He craned his neck up and saw her fire wildly down. The arrow found the thick flesh of Shalake's shoulder, another found his calf, forcing him to the ground. The third remained drawn in her bow, a thin bargaining chip aimed at Shalake's neck, reminding them what should happen to their precious warwatcher if their arrows left their bows.

And there she stood, facing down two dozen Shen and six arrows drawn upon her, with him under her boot, refusing to move, refusing to leave.

He looked at her, then to the Shen. Their fingers twitched, getting impatient around the fletchings of their arrows. *She's going to die.*

"*Good,*" the voice whispered.

No, I mean, she came back to die. She came back for me and she's about to die because of me . . .

"*There is still no discussion here. Stay down and let her die, then we escape and . . . what are you doing?*"

"What are you doing?" Kataria echoed, casting a growl out the side of her mouth. "I said stay down."

Lenk ignored her, pushing her foot aside, crawling up to join her. He stared down the Shen beside her, as bows were trained upon him, as Shalake cast his amber scowl up at him. He stood beside her, refusing to listen, refusing to leave.

"*Fool,*" the voice hissed. "*Why do we always make such progress and then you go and throw it all away?*"

Lenk didn't have an answer for that. Lenk didn't have a plan for how to avoid the arrows trained upon him and Kataria. Lenk didn't have any thought for survival, for betrayal, for anything beyond standing beside her.

Bows creaked. Angry hisses rose from the crowd. Fingers twitched. Yellow-eyed scowls were cast upward. Lenk tensed. Kataria pulled her arrow back farther. Somewhere in the distance, something let out a keening roar growing steadily louder. Lenk drew in a deep breath. Then paused.

Wait, he thought, looking toward the wall, *what was that last part?*

And then everything went terribly wrong.

With the scream of rock and the roar of sea, the wall exploded. Shield-sized shards of stone went flying on a red-tinged mist as the Akaneed tore through the wall with a great, keening wail that spat blood and froth, carried on a wave that roared alongside it, sliding it through stone, over stone, toward stone.

The impact shook the highway, sent Lenk and Kataria tumbling off the monolith, sent the Shen collapsing to the ground, sent all eyes to the great sea serpent sliding toward them. Mere paces away from the assembled pink and green skins, it came to a slow, sliding halt upon its side, the wave that had carried it onto the road slithering away and settling back, leaving its macabre delivery before them.

Understandably, all previous hostilities were forgotten as all eyes settled upon the vision of ruin before them. The Akaneed was no less majestic in death, but the awe it commanded now was one of red and black, of a skull smashed to bits so thoroughly that shards of bone jutted from the crown of its head, of teeth smashed through its lips, of two eyes dug out with wounds old and new, and of a pool of blood growing with the multitude of crimson streams pouring out of its gaping maw.

Its jaws that now twitched and moved as though they still had some life that had not yet leaked out onto the road.

Two red hands reached out, pushed back the upper jaw and then the lower jaw, as though opening a gate. Gariath crawled out of the beast's gullet, tumbling out and onto the blood-pooled ground. With a sniff, he rose to his feet, flicking his hands clean of gore even as the rest of him glistened with a cocktail coating of thick, viscous fluids.

He emerged from between the curtains of shattered teeth, gently splashing in the pool of blood beneath him as he did. He paused six paces away, suddenly aware of the crowd, stunned into silence, eyes upon him. He stared back, his black eyes expressionless. Then, he glanced over his shoulder at the dead serpent, then back to the crowd, and grunted.

"Well?"

"*Rhega* . . ."

The word echoed among the Shen, from mouth to mouth, as the lizardmen rose to their feet, their yellow eyes wide and locked upon the dragonman.

"*Rhega* . . ."

And from foot to foot, the movement followed. They began to back away, slinking into the coral forest beyond the shattered inner wall. Their bodies twisted and contorted, slipping easily into the brightly-colored, fossilized foliage.

"*Rhega* . . ."

It continued to whisper, long after they had gone. It continued to echo, long after Shalake had followed them and paused, looking over his shoulder with an expression hidden behind his headdress. It continued, long after they had left them: the man, the shict, the dragonman, and the giant, dead Akaneed.

Lenk didn't even bother for it to finish before he turned on Gariath with a furrowed brow.

"What the *hell* was that all about?" he demanded.

Gariath blinked, looked back to the Akaneed, then to Lenk. "What, is that a joke?"

"They looked at you like you were like . . . like . . ."

"Yeah," the dragonman grunted. "Because I am."

"And they *just* tried to kill us," Lenk snarled. "And you . . . and they . . ." He reached down, plucked up his fallen, blood-slick sword. "I should . . ."

Gariath folded his arms over his chest, every patch of his flesh dripping with the life of the beast he had just crawled out of. "You shouldn't."

"Look, can we do this somewhere that doesn't reek as much?" Kataria asked with a sigh. "The Shen are gone, but the smell of this thing is still here. I'd just as soon be far away from both, if that's all right."

"And *you*!" Lenk snapped, whirling upon her. "You . . . *left* me."

Her expression went blank. Her voice went soft. "I did."

He found himself stricken into a dumb silence at that, followed by an equally dumb question. "Why?"

"Because I wanted to come back to you."

"That . . . doesn't . . ."

For but a moment, he saw it. Without frown, without a crack in her voice, it happened. Her eyes glistened. With tears that might have been mythical, they were gone so quickly.

"I know," she said, shouldering her bow. "There's a break in the forest up ahead. We can get through there and plan our next move."

She stalked off. Without so much as a question, Gariath began to follow her. Lenk fell in line beside him, casting a sidelong glower.

"I still don't like it," he said.

"Okay," Gariath grunted.

"I don't like how they look at you."

"All right."

"And if it turns out you look at them the same way, you know what I'll do."

"Uh huh."

Lenk nodded grimly as he sheathed his sword on his back. He would have said nothing else if not for the involuntary curl of his nostril. He eyed the viscous coating of fluids upon Gariath's flesh.

"So, uh," he said, "do you need to . . . wash? Or something?"

"No," Gariath replied without stopping. "It was a gift."

SIXTEEN

NO EARS WHERE WE NEED THEM

He set foot upon the sand and took not a step farther.

The clouds slid across the sky in a slow-moving tide, drowning the sun. What little light made it through served only to paint the earth with shadows that waxed and waned. The world continued to move, oblivious to his eyes upon it.

And yet . . .

"I know you're there," Lenk muttered.

And the world muttered back.

As though his words had lit a candle inside his head, they came back. Fluttering like little moths on whispering wings, he felt their voices in feathery brushes against his ear.

"*Traitors*," they growled. "*Traitors everywhere.*"

"*Plotted against us*," they hissed. "*Jealous. Envious.*"

"*Didn't want this*," they whimpered. "*Never asked for this.*"

"*Seen them. Everywhere. Coming.*"

"*Want death? Give them death. All of them.*"

"*Blood. So much . . . blood . . .*"

The more he listened, the clearer they became. The clearer they became, the more he listened.

And as he did, he found his eyes drawn up to the ridge, to the naked and pale skin of a slender back that was turned to him. To long, twitching ears that couldn't hear the voices.

The voices that grew louder when he stared at her.

"*Traitors. Closing in. Kill them all.*"

"*They hate us. Fear us. Good reasons. Make them suffer.*"

"*Why do they make us hurt them? Never wanted to kill anyone. No choice.*"

He waited for them to say more. He waited for them to speak just an octave higher, to speak just a little clearer, to tell him what to do to make them go away. To make this terrible pain that grew in his chest whenever he looked at her go away.

As he looked at her now. As she didn't look at him.

And they said nothing. The light extinguished, the moths flew away on their whispers. He held his breath for fear of missing a precious word over the sound of his own exhale. Air and patience ran out as one.

"Well?" he asked.

And, in a voice that whispered into his ear with a humid breath, the wind answered.

"*It won't stop, Lenk.*" It spoke, in a voice uncomfortably familiar, uncomfortably close. "*Not with blood.*"

He blinked.

"What is *that* supposed to mean?"

"*What,*" another voice, the only one he recognized, the one with ice and hatred said, "*is what supposed to mean?*"

As one of the few moments of pride for a man who could describe schizophrenia as routine, Lenk had always consoled himself by saying he had never *truly* felt the desire to bash his own head on a rock and try to find out exactly what it was in his skull that made him think it was at all logical to hope the disembodied voices would make sense.

But he supposed everyone had bad days.

His had gotten worse once he heard that voice. That voice that had spoken to him, rather than just having spoken. That voice that spoke to him like it knew him, rather than like it could command him.

He hadn't heard it in his head or his heart. It spoke to him like he wasn't insane. In a voice so comfortable, so familiar, so warm that it hurt that he couldn't hear it anymore.

And that made him want to lie down and die quietly.

But, it wasn't the first time he had felt that way. It wasn't the first time he had tried to ignore it, either, as he shouldered his sword and trudged up the ridge to join her.

He found Kataria where he had left her, staring out over the ridge, slowly making up curses after she had long run out of real ones.

"Bloody, reeking, skunk-slathered *balls,*" she spat into the air off the ridge. "Maybe the best thing to do would be to squeeze through and come out on the other side as a pile of blood and guts."

He didn't have to ask. The small break in the forest of coral and kelp they had found had lasted as long as it took to find the small clearing. Past that, things got more complicated.

Before them, a jagged garden grew. Red thorns twisted over themselves in their eagerness to reach the companions. Jagged yellow fans twisted out of one another, rising like razor-edged suns. Pale-blue spears jutted out in clusters like the petals of flowers grown large on blood.

In those few gaps surrounding the clearing where the coral did *not* grow out with vengeful sharpness, kelp rose in walls of green, swaying impassively, unmoved by Kataria's frustration as she continued to search for a way out that didn't involve leaving behind several pounds of flesh and blood.

"It just goes on for miles," Lenk observed. "Makes you wonder what the point of having the Shen around is."

"I don't know," she spat back, "maybe so they'll make you stop asking questions."

"Oh."

"By shooting you."

"Right."

"In the head."

"Yeah," he said, "I get it."

He spoke loudly, clearly, trying to drown out the other voices.

"Want to kill us? US?"

"Make them suffer. Make them die."

"Gods will understand. Had no choice."

It wasn't working.

He opened his mouth to speak a little louder before she held up a hand to silence him, head bowing with the weight of her sigh.

"Sorry," she said. "That came out wrong."

"How . . . how else was it supposed to come out?"

"Less . . . shooty." She waved her hand at him, turned back around. "Look, just don't talk to me for a while. I need to figure it out."

"Figure what out?"

"How they got through here in the first place . . ."

She didn't emphasize the word, didn't so much as blink as she said it. All the same, his blood ran cold as he looked intently at her and asked.

"Who are 'they'?"

She wasn't listening. Not to him, anyway. Her ears did not twitch so much as turn on her head, sweeping slowly from side to side like her eyes. They would stop momentarily, fixed on some direction, and her head would follow. Whatever she heard, she wouldn't tell him.

Someone else did.

"Going to kill us. Going to try."

"Fear us. Should fear us. Will fear us."

"Make them stop . . . make them stop . . ."

He resisted the urge to shake his head as he stalked away from her, noting with only mild relief that they faded the farther away he drew.

"She waits . . ."

Most of them, anyway.

"*She will strike soon,*" the voice, *his* voice, spoke in cold clarity. "*She bides her time. She would strike you down. He would, as well.*"

"Who?"

Absorbed in his own thoughts, he only realized Gariath was standing in front of him once he collided with the dragonman's massive winged back. The young man staggered backward, snarling at his companion.

"What the hell are you doing *there?*" he demanded.

"Standing in one place, waiting patiently for someone useless to bump into me so I can hear him say something annoying," Gariath replied without turning to face Lenk. "Or maybe just resting, having just spent a day lodged in a snake's throat."

"*Or,*" Lenk spat back, "maybe you intentionally got in my way just so you could beat me about the head with what you think is witty."

Gariath cast the slightest sliver of a disinterested stare over his shoulder. "You're touchy today, as well as stupid."

"Why shouldn't I be?" Lenk said. "I'm surrounded by . . ."

"*Betrayers.*"

"*Murder.*"

"*Blood. Everywhere.*"

"Coral," he muttered.

"Probably not," Gariath muttered. He held up a hand with a fresh cut upon it. "I tried breaking it earlier. It's sharp and hard as teeth. If it is coral, it's not the kind we know."

"And we've got no way out. *That's* what's bothering me. Kataria's acting strange, too."

"So are you," Gariath grunted. "And you were both strange yesterday. How is it any different today?"

"I'm not strange."

"You can't go forty breaths without being strange."

"You're not helping things. I'm a little . . ." Lenk hesitated to finish the sentence.

"*Hate them.*"

"*Fear.*"

"*Never wanted this.*"

"Wary is all," Lenk said. "Everyone's on edge. It doesn't help when she's staring out over the coral and listening to something no one can hear."

"People who talk to something no one can see don't get to be that picky," Gariath replied.

"Some exception can be made for me," Lenk replied, forcing his voice through his teeth. "Given that my only other company is the giant ugly reptile whom the other giant ugly reptiles treat like a god."

Gariath shrugged, snorted. "Stupid."

"Stupid? Did you *see* the way they looked at you? They would have ripped off their loincloths and castrated themselves right there if you had asked them to."

Gariath grunted. "Thirty-two breaths. And it's stupid because the Shen don't have a god."

"How do you even *know* that?" Lenk demanded. "How do you know *anything* about the Shen beyond the fact that they tried to *kill* us."

"Not me."

"Not *yet*."

"Not ever."

"You can't know that. You can't know *them*. What do you know about them that makes you think they *won't*?"

"They are Shen."

"And what does *that* mean?"

"Everything."

"*Nothing*. It means *nothing* beyond the fact that they're savages. *Beasts*. It's a matter of time. You can't even see it. But they'll kill you. They'll turn on you. They all will betray you and *no one* will be around to hear you scream."

It wasn't until he saw Gariath standing tense, hands tightened into fists, eyes narrowed sharply upon him, that he realized it hadn't been his voice that had just spoken.

"They are Shen," Gariath said. "I am *Rhega*. I have nothing else."

"You have us," Lenk replied.

"I have you." Contempt strained Gariath's laughter. "Tiny, stupid weaklings so numerous that they have the privilege to look at each other with suspicion. A tiny, stupid weakling telling me his life is hard because he cannot trust a tiny, stupid weakling because she listens to things other than him."

He took a step forward, driving Lenk a step back.

"A tiny, stupid, *pathetic* weakling so obsessed with his own tiny, weak, *pathetic* problems that he thinks he can tell me I can be happy with nothing and that I cannot trust the only people I've seen in years that are even a little like myself."

He leaned down, eyes hard, teeth harder. And fully bared.

"I have you. I have *nothing*."

He turned away.

"Now, turn around and walk away before I run out of reasons not to break you in two."

Lenk did not look away. Not immediately. "How many do you have?"

"One and a half."

That did it.

Though he found little relief once he turned away from the dragonman. If anything, the voices grew stronger as he stalked down the ridge, away from Kataria and Gariath and into a small copse of thick, swaying kelp.

"*Paranoid. Fearful. Felt the same way.*"

"*No one. Trust no one.*"

"*Only wanted them to like me.*"

"I don't need this right now," Lenk muttered to himself, rubbing his eyes.

"*You do,*" the voice said. The others went mute, as if in reverence. "*You deny those who would help you, those who are with you, the only ones who are with you.*"

"There's just so many talking all at once and all saying the same thing over and over and over . . ."

"*Because you refuse to listen. Because they can help.*"

"Then how do you explain the voice that contradicted them all?" he asked. "The one that said that it wouldn't stop with her death?"

"*There was no such voice.*"

"I heard it."

"*I didn't. You were hearing things.*"

Lenk's mouth opened, hung there as he searched for an answer, somehow never having quite anticipated that the voices in his head one day may question his sanity. Finding none, he closed his mouth, drew in a sharp breath and casually went about the business of searching for a rock sharp enough to bash his head open with.

As he searched for one that looked like it would hurt a lot in the row of kelp before him, he saw it.

Out of the corner of his eye: a flicker of movement, a rustle of leaves amidst the kelp's trancelike swaying, a shadow sliding behind a veil of tuberous green, yet unaware of his presence.

His hand slowly slid to his sword. Not that he could tell exactly *what* dwelt behind the curtain of greenery, but be it Shen or worse, he had never found preemptive violence to have served him wrong before. Before the blade could even be drawn, though, the kelp shivered and the creature came out.

He tensed, ready for a Shen attack, ready for a demon to have somehow followed him here, ready for Kataria to be on the other side and ready to kill him, ready for absolutely anything but this.

But there it was.

Hanging in midair.

Like it belonged there.

A fish.

It did not fly, nor even float, so much as simply . . . be there, as if it were in water. Its translucent tail swayed back and forth, its fins wafted and wavered like elegant fans, its black-and-white striped scales glimmered as it hung, staring at Lenk with a glass-eyed expression.

As though *he* were the one with the problem.

It floated there for a moment longer, mouth opening and closing, as if waiting for Lenk to say something.

"Uh?" he grunted, squinting one eye at the creature.

Unimpressed to the point of offense, the fish swam about in a half-circle, offering a rather rude swish of its tail as it turned away from Lenk and vanished back into the kelp.

With the full knowledge that there was absolutely no way in heaven or hell he was going to ever not regret it, Lenk stepped forward. Knowing damn well that it was a bad idea, he slipped a hand through the veil of kelp and found no dense, forbidding forest beyond it. With the absolute certainty that staying back and waiting for one companion or the other to kill him was probably smarter, he drew in a deep breath.

And stepped through.

The air grew thicker, even as the kelp thinned out around him. There was no impenetrable hedge like there had been before and it was easy enough to make his way, pushing aside stalks of swaying leaves in pursuit of the fish. Nor was there any easy breath to be found here; the air didn't so much grow humid as it seemed to debate whether it should drown him or not.

And yet, he pressed on, if only because it was harder to think with the thicker air and thus harder to hear any voices. And as he did, the kelp thinned out more and more until he emerged from the towering weeds at the edge of a shallow valley.

And as he cast eyes suddenly unable to blink over it, he finally found the words.

"Well, that's alarming."

They swam.

In great, shimmering rainbows of scales painted red and black and gold and blue and green, they swam. In twisting pillars of silver mouths chasing silver tails endlessly into the sky, they swam. In slow and lazy clouds of riotous color, over each other, into each other, against each other, they swam.

In the tens of hundreds. Through the air. With no water at all.

The fish were swimming through the sky.

And amidst the curtains of brightly colored scales, other life lurked.

Rays, their fleshy fins wafting like wings, swam across the sandy floor. The shadows of sharks lurked at the edges, swimming gingerly between clouds of fish and seeking the unwary. Octopuses floated nonchalantly through the sky, colors changing as they passed in and out of the clouds of fish, as though defying the laws of reality was not worth giving even half a crap about.

The coral bloomed in all its twisted color and jagged splendor. The kelp swayed impassively in great clumps. Starfish clung to jutting rocks. Crabs scuttled across skeletal trees of hardened coral. Eels slithered in and out of dark holes.

Across the valley, an ocean without water sprawled.

And Lenk stood at its edge and watched, near breathless.

Not with awe. The sky, a shifting quilt of blues too deep to be sky and grays too thick to be clouds, roiled overhead. The air it offered was lead, weighing down his lungs as he breathed it in.

Between that and . . . *this*, whatever it was before him, he wondered if it might not be smarter to turn around, leave, and pretend it hadn't ever happened.

"What in Riffid's name . . ." someone whispered from behind him.

He turned and saw Kataria parting the kelp and emerging from the forest, Gariath close behind her. Both their eyes were fixed upon the sea of fish and sky before them as they came up beside Lenk at the edge of the valley.

She was saying something. Probably cursing. He didn't care. He couldn't hear.

He found his gaze drawn back to the valley, back to the endlessly shifting tides of scale and shimmer. What passed for a sandy floor was largely hindered by more coral, more exuberant and numerous than had been present before. Gaps of bare sand wound through the brilliant, jagged fans and reaching thorns of coral like worms through a corpse, their labyrinthine curves offering only the vaguest hint of safe passage.

His gaze continued past them, over them, drawn farther into the forest by a sense of foreboding.

It was faint. It was far away. It was at the dead center of the reef. It might not have even existed. But as he stared at it, he couldn't shake the feeling of intimacy that came with it, as though far away, something was staring back at him.

And it spoke with terrifyingly pristine clarity.

"She is going to kill you."

He shook his head and became aware that he was standing by himself on the ridge. With some indignation, he threw a glare down toward his companions, already heading toward the path to the trench.

"Hey!"

Kataria paused with an offensive dramatic sigh, looking over her shoulder. "Are you coming or not?"

"Sorry, I was just distracted," Lenk said, gesturing over the reef, "what with the giant invisible sea of flying fish that should not be, and all. Have you seen this kind of thing before or . . ."

"It was impressive to begin with, but now I've seen it," Kataria replied. "I've also seen giant snakes, lizardmen of varying sizes, giant black fish-headed priest-things, seagulls that look like old ladies, I could go on." She shrugged. "I mean, this is weird, yeah, but we've seen and *done* weirder."

"I was eaten by a giant sea serpent," Gariath offered.

"*Gariath was eaten by a giant sea serpent.*" Kataria nodded, gesturing to him. "You don't see him getting distracted." She shouldered her bow, casting a wary glance around before trudging toward the reef. "Now, come on. It's dangerous to stay out here."

It was with some hesitance that he followed her.

Not for fear of the reef. Not even for fear of her. But for the fact that the moment he set foot upon sand, it came again. Between the crunching of sand beneath his feet, it whispered to him.

"*She speaks truth,*" the voice said. "*She hurries you to your death. She will kill you. She will leave you to die.*"

Lenk forced his voice low, burying it below a whisper. "Well, which is it?"

"*You will die,*" it whispered. "*She will be the cause. You know this.*"

"How do you figure?" He kept his eyes lower than his voice, staring at the ground as he stalked between the coral.

"*Because you do not want to know.*"

"You're going to have to explain that one to me."

"*You do not know why she left. You do not know why she returned. You do not know why she goes ahead and leaves you behind. You do not know what she thinks, what she does, why.*"

His eyes were locked on her back, ten paces ahead of him, as she wound her way through the reef, ducking under low-hanging branches, sucking in her belly as she skirted alongside a jagged, reaching crest. Her eyes were locked only ahead, her ears heedless of what he whispered, upright and listening for that which he could not hear.

"*Why she will not look at you.*"

He came to a sudden halt. Above him, the coral formed a spiny canopy of thorns through which the dim sunlight came in rays impaled. Around him, a school of fish, unmoved by his plight, slowly plucked amongst the coral with their puckered lips and glassy eyes. Before him, Kataria continued to press on.

Without looking back.

"Because," his words cracked, not convinced of itself, "I don't want to."

The voice said nothing.

The voice didn't need to say anything.

He tried to walk with messier, louder steps, tried to hum a tune, tried anything that might be loud enough to drown out the sound of his own thoughts.

But he couldn't shake the thoughts from his head any more than he could shake his eyes from Kataria as she continued to wind her way through the coral. He couldn't stop wondering. Why she wouldn't look at him, why she acted the way she did, why he never even asked her once to justify herself.

Even if he knew it was because he was afraid of the answer. Death—his by her hand, hers by his—was a fear fast fading against another: the fear that he might live through it all.

The fear that the tome would be found, that he would save the world, get paid, shoulder his sword, and look, with an easy smile painted by the light of a setting sun, to his side.

And not see her there.

He didn't want to think about that. And he was terrible at humming. And so, he pressed on, and tried not to think.

He wound his way through the coral, following the distant crunch of his companions' fading footsteps. They had stopped altogether by the time he saw daylight again as the sand faded beneath his feet and gave way to thick, gray cobblestones stacked neatly upon each other.

Kataria knelt upon it, studying its surface. She glanced up at his approach and instantly tensed, eyes narrowing. He stopped in his tracks as her eyes bored into him, as her body grew taut, ears pricking upright. She rose, walked toward him. He took a step back.

It wasn't until after she had walked right past him that he realized his hand had gone to his sword.

Easing his fingers from the hilt, he turned and saw what she saw. The path behind them was completely bare of fish, of kelp and, most notably, of dragonmen.

"Where's Gariath?" she asked.

"Off doing dragonman things?" Lenk replied, shrugging.

"What are dragonman things?"

"Whatever he wants them to be, I guess." He rubbed the back of his neck. "I don't know. I said some things to him earlier. He might have taken them personally."

"If he had taken them personally, he would have twisted your legs until you could pick your teeth with your toes." She waved her hands dismissively toward the road. "We don't have time for this, anyway. It's not like he's never done this before and it's not like there's not more important things to worry about."

Lenk glanced down at the stones beneath his feet. "Right. Another highway . . ."

"Half of one," Kataria corrected.

Lenk followed her gaze and frowned. The great scar of stone, jagged and curving, frowned back.

The other half was simply . . . gone, replaced by the vast nothingness that yawned open beside it. A jagged edge of stone embraced a seeping edge of darkness like a lover, marching beside each other through the reef to disappear around a bend in the distance. The highway and the chasm, hand-in-hand, stretched into endlessness.

The reef grew up around it, over it, encroaching upon it as though it were an embarrassing blemish that it hoped to hide behind wild color. As well it might, the highway was thick with the signs of war: burnt banners on shattered standards, bloodstains painting the pavement amidst fallen weapons, and more of the twisted bells, lined up in a chorus hanging silent, some teetering over the edge.

And yet, as black and foreboding as it was, the grotesqueness of the highway only made the chasm beside it more alluring. From however far below, kelp grew, the color of a bruise the moment before it darkens. It shimmered, almost glowing as it wafted, reaching out of the chasm with swaying leafy fingers as though it sought to pull itself out to join the rest of the reef.

And against the vivid purple, the darkness of the chasm was all that much more absolute. And it was the darkness that drew Lenk's eyes, a familiar sensation, uncomfortably distinct, alarmingly close.

As he peered into the darkness, something peered back at him.

"She's going to kill you."

"What?" he whispered back.

"I didn't say anything," Kataria replied. "Though I might as well." She pointed down the highway. "We follow this as far as we can, then. It looks like it'll go on for a while."

Lenk could only barely hear her. The voices returned, clearer, bolder, and much, much louder.

"Lead us to die."

"Betrayed us. All of us."

"Should do something. Why didn't I do something?"

"Do what?" he whispered.

"Follow it," Kataria replied, blinking. "It's a road, isn't it? It has to lead to somewhere." She clicked her tongue. "And if I'm at all clever—"

She paused. He blinked.

"Something wrong?" he asked.

"No . . . I just kind of expected someone to insult me before I could finish that thought. Anyway . . ." She thrust a finger toward the horizon. "I'd guess it leads *there*."

In the distance, rising over the reef like a colossus, the mountain stood wearing a halo of clouds. But even at this distance, one could see that it was carved, lined with twisting aqueducts down which blue veins of water ran.

"If I were to hold onto a book full of weird, mysterious gibberish, I'd hold it there," she said. "And if it isn't there, we'll be in a better position to find where it might be."

"It doesn't make sense," Lenk whispered. "All this stonework and there's only Shen and fish here. Who made it?"

"Not right. Nothing right here."

"Danger. Danger all around us."

"A trap. We walked right into it."

"That's kind of beside the point, isn't . . ." Kataria's voice drifted away as her ears went upright again, sweeping from side to side, listening.

He waited for her to look back, to look at him. She did not.

"What is it?" he asked.

"Traitors. Everywhere."

"Want them to die. All of them to die."

"She's going to kill you. You're going to die."

"It's nothing." Her ears focused forward like shields, she began to walk down the road. "Stay here."

"If it's nothing, then why shouldn't I come?"

"Gariath might come back, just stay here."

"Gariath doesn't need me to wait for him."

"It could be a Shen ambush."

"We haven't seen the Shen in ages."

"Maybe a carnivorous fish or something."

"What?"

"The point is *I don't know*." She growled. She bared teeth. Her ears flattened against her head. And still, she did not look at him. "Just stay here."

The fish had scattered. The purple kelp swayed. Silence settled over the reef as she trotted off.

Thus, when Lenk shouted, she could not pretend to not hear.

"NO!"

His voice echoed. Across sky. Across sea. Across shadow. It fell into the chasm, rose up again on voices not entirely his own. Kataria didn't seem to notice that as she turned around to face him.

Not when Lenk had his sword drawn and pointed firmly at her chest.

"No more of this," he said, solid as his steel. "No more leaving. No more listening."

Her gaze did not waver from his. Her ears did not lower. Her bow did not drop from her hand.

"Let me explain," she said softly, as though she spoke to a beast she did not dare flee from.

"Lies."

"Reasons."

"Excuses."

"NO! None of that!" he screamed. "No more lies. No more silence." His blade trembled in his grasp. "I . . . I need to know, Kat."

"Traitors."

"Lied to."

"Pain. Blood."

Kataria's hands lowered to her sides, slowly. And she did not look away.

"No," she said, all trace of soothing gone, "you don't."

"Don't say that. It *said* you'd say that, so *don't. Say that.*" His eyes were quivering in his skull. "I need you to tell me. Why you abandoned me. Why you want me to die."

"I don't," Kataria replied calmly.

There was no great conviction behind the words. She did not scowl at him for the accusation. He did not apologize for saying it. Everything she was seemed to bow at once, a heaviness setting upon her with such force that it threatened to break her.

"But," she said softly, "I did."

"TRAITOR!"

"DIE!"

"BLEED!"

"Why?"

Lenk couldn't hear himself talk. The voices howled, roared, smashed off one another, off of his skull, crushing, crashing, echoing, screaming. And beneath all of them, running through his thoughts like a river, it spoke on a calm, icy whisper.

"I told you."

"I don't know," Kataria whispered.

"What?"

"I DON'T KNOW!"

Her head snapped up, teeth bared in a snarl, ears folded against her head threateningly. But these were lies, betrayed by her eyes wet with tears.

"I don't know, I don't know, I don't *know*," she said, shaking her head. "Because I couldn't hear the Howling, because I didn't know what my father would say, because I didn't feel like a shict, because you're a *human*." She thrust a finger at him. "*You're supposed to be a disease, Lenk. It's supposed to be easy to hate you.*"

Her breath staggered. Her body shuddered. Tears fell down her cheeks.

"But . . ."

A silence hung in the air. Lenk waited, shut out the voices, shut out everything, as he waited, waited for her to say something.

"But you still left me," he whispered. "But you still wanted me to die. You. *You* wanted to kill me."

"I wanted one of us to die."

"Why?"

"Why do you *think*, Lenk? Do you think the ears are the only thing that makes us different? I am a *shict*. You're a human. To look at you the way I looked at you . . . to stand over you like I did, to . . . to . . . have done what I did, it was *sick*. It was *diseased*. I was *infected*. They don't have *words* for what I feel."

"And," he spoke softly, sword lowering a hair, "what do you feel?"

She did not answer. Not with words. She looked at him. With tear-stained eyes, with grief, with pain, with anger, with something else. She looked at him.

And he knew.

And he lowered his sword.

"And now?" he whispered. "Why do you want to go away now? Why do you want to leave again?"

"Because I'm afraid."

"Of what? Of *this?*" he snarled, gesturing to himself. "Of *me?*"

"Of *you*, yes," she snarled back. "Because I hear the way you talk and I see you talking that way to people that aren't there. So *yeah*, I'm afraid of you. And whatever's wrong with you and of whatever it's going to do if I'm not there to protect you."

"I don't need protection."

"You do. If you didn't, I wouldn't be trying to do it all the time. I wouldn't be keeping one ear out, listening to you talk to whatever's inside you while I keep the other ear out for *them*."

His sword lowered farther. He stared intently at her. "Who?"

"Them," Kataria said. Her ears twitched, rose up. "The greenshicts. My people. They're close. I can hear them. I don't know how close, though, and that's why I have to—"

"TRAITOR!" he screamed, taking a step forward.

"Lenk."

Someone spoke. Outside of his head. Outside of his air. Outside of everything. Close, familiar, so much so it made him ache that he could only barely hear it over the din inside his head and heart.

"Don't."

"Tell me why I shouldn't."

The voices said nothing. None of them.

Kataria said nothing. Kataria did not look at him.

"Tell me how to make it stop."

He tried to heft his sword, found it too heavy. He tried to breathe, found his throat closing. He tried to look at her, found his vision swimming.

"Tell me."

No answers. No lies. No truths. No voices.

"Please."

Only Kataria. Only her tears. Only her stare that he could no longer bear. He turned away from her. And then, and only then, did someone speak.

"No."

It reached out of his skull, into his heart, into his blood. It clenched at him with icy fingers, twisted his muscles, sent his fingers tightening against the hilt.

"She must die."

He opened his mouth to protest, to scream, to apologize to Kataria for what was about to happen. But he had no voice outside his head.

"If you cannot . . ."

His arm rose of its own accord. His foot turned him. His eyes went wide as he felt himself, his blade, pointed at Kataria.

"I will."

Kataria did not back away, did not look away, only whispered.

"Lenk . . ."

"Kataria . . . I'm so—"

He paused, saw the shadow falling over him, growing larger.

And then he felt the stone.

It struck him from above like a boulder, smashing him to the road beneath him. He felt them: large, powerful hands pressed into his back, hopping off. He saw them: landing before him on five fingers, green as poison, walking away. And when he looked up, he saw the long, lean legs they were attached to.

From beneath a green brow, between ears long as knives and marked with six ragged notches to a lobe, two dark eyes burned holes in his forehead. From

233

down on the stone, she seemed to rise forever, body like a spear with muscles drawn tight behind bared green flesh covered only by a pair of buckskin breeches. Her mohawk crested above her shaven scalp, exposing the black tattoos on either side of her head.

"Greenshict," Lenk whispered.

"*She betrayed us! KILL THEM BOTH!*" the voice howled.

"Get up, Lenk! GET UP!" Kataria cried.

All of them were silenced. Kataria by the elbow that lashed out and caught her in the belly, driving her to her knees with a grunt. The voice by the sudden rush of fear that seized Lenk. And Lenk himself by the sight of two large, sharpened tomahawks sliding into the female's hands.

"Stay still, *kou'ru*," the greenshict said calmly. "I can make this quick."

"*So can we*," the voice growled inside him. It seized him once more, forced him to his feet, forced his blade to his hand.

The female smiled, baring canines that would look more fitting on a wolf than anything on two legs, as though she had been hoping this would be his answer. She slid smoothly into a stance, hatchets held loosely, as though she had been born with a blade in each hand.

Something inside him tensed, raised his sword, forced him into a defensive posture. Something inside him forced his eyes to search her stance for weaknesses, tender points to jam a sharp length of steel into. Something inside him smiled.

It never came to blows.

For as soon as either of them took a step forward, the road quaked beneath them. The rock shook, granite shards skittering across the pavement as something struck the stone.

Something below.

Something big.

It struck again, pounding against the road's supports. There was a crack of stone, a groan of old rock. Cracks formed beneath their feet, growing to tremendous scars in a single breath. In one more breath, Lenk looked at Kataria. She looked up, reached a hand out, said something.

He couldn't hear her over the sound of stone shattering. And in the next breath, he fell into darkness below.

"*LENK!*"

Her voice was swallowed up by the chasm, as it had swallowed him. Her reach was woefully short. And her eyes, tearful and useless, could not see him.

"*Do not look, little sister*," someone whispered, far away and far too close. "*Inqalle will handle it. Avaij will protect you. I will watch you.*"

She heard him, knew where he was immediately as she looked up to the coral. Naxiaw stood, face set in a blank, green expression, arms folded over his chest. He watched her, impassively.

She could not think to send the Howling back at him. She could not think to scream at him, to beg him to recall Inqalle, to ask him for anything. She let him watch her.

As she stood up.

As she walked to the edge of the chasm.

As she jumped in.

SEVENTEEN
THE FURNACE

Asper stared at her hand.

Twenty-seven bones, seventeen muscles, five fingernails, all spackled onto a wrap of flesh and fine hair with what she had convinced herself was a grand design stared back. She stared at it with the kind of anticipatory intensity that one awaiting a visitor might stare at a door, as though her hand would simply open up and show her what else was dwelling inside it.

Her hand was not answering.

"What," she whispered, "is wrong with you?"

No matter how many times she asked.

"Hurt."

Fortunately—in the absolute loosest sense of the word—she had more than enough to keep her occupied from such thoughts. Nai lay beside her, unmoving but for her lips.

"Hurt," she whimpered again.

Asper rushed to her side, as she had every time the girl had opened her mouth. But with no blankets, no water, not so much as a stray bandage with which to even *pretend* to be doing something useful, there was little the priestess had to offer her.

"Please," she whispered, "not now."

Except prayer.

"Just a little more," she whispered, uncertain to whom. "Not yet. Not yet." She received only one answer.

"Hurt."

"Damn it, damn it, *damn it*," Asper cursed. She forced trembling eyes to trembling hands, looking from her left to her right and back again before shaking them. "*Do* something!"

"Hurt."

Medicine was absent, Gods were lacking, cursed arms from hell were surprisingly unhelpful. Asper looked around her cell, trying to find anything that might have the barest chance. She found nothing but a pair of unmoving bodies. No help. Nothing but a single thought.

What would Denaos do?

"Hey! *HEY, UGLY!*" she screamed as she pulled herself to the cell door.

The netherling appeared from the gloom, long face staring between the bars with either incomprehension or anger; it was hard to tell with them.

"Listen, heathen, we need help," Asper said, gesturing wildly to Nai. "She's about to die. I need water, cloth . . . *something.*" The female stared back blankly. Asper snarled, pounding a fist against the bars. "You filthy purple stool-sucker, *listen* to me."

The netherling's milk white eyes drifted to Nai. "Sheraptus?" she asked. "Hurt."

"Yes, *yes*," Asper said, nodding vigorously. "Sheraptus! You know what—"

"Lucky," the netherling said, turning to leave.

"What? No, wait! Get something! *HEY!*"

The netherling wasn't listening. She simply turned around, pausing momentarily to regard the creature that had suddenly appeared before her. Tall, lanky, and possessed of a broad smile, he gently laid a gloved hand upon her shoulder.

"Hey," he said, just a breath before a loud clicking sound.

By the time she had grabbed the hilt of her blade, blood was already weeping from her neck in great gouts. She didn't make a move as he jerked his hand away, the metal spike protruding from his wrist glistening with her blood. She stared, speechless from shock. Also the hole in her throat.

And then she fell.

"Huh," Denaos noted as the netherling's blood pooled beneath her corpse. "That actually worked." He pulled the blade's hidden latch, drawing it back into his glove. "Should have said something more impressive."

"*Denaos!*" Asper cried from behind the bars.

"Hello to you, too," he replied, walking over. "Hey, if I had said 'you're working too hard,' would that—"

"Open the door! Hurry!"

"Well, *fine*," Denaos replied with a growl, kneeling over the netherling's corpse. "If you're in such a damn hurry. Just let me find the keys."

"No time! Just pick the locks!"

The rogue looked up at her with a resentful glare. "Why would you assume I can pick locks?"

"I just thought . . . well . . . you're a—"

"A man who is *not* a locksmith," Denaos said, rifling through the netherling's belt. "What's the big hurry, anyway?"

"It's—"

She suddenly realized that Nai hadn't said anything for some time. She turned and saw a pair of glassy eyes staring up at her above blackened lips that no longer drew breath. She looked from Nai's body to "her" lying nearby and saw the other prisoner also gone, as though she had simply been waiting for someone to leave with her.

Asper swallowed something foul.

"Nothing."

The lock on her door clicked, the bars creaked as it slid open. Denaos stood in it, smiling broadly as he twirled a crude iron key around his finger.

"Granted, it *would* have been a lot more impressive if I had picked the locks," he said, "but then again it would have also been more impressive if I had come riding on the back of a steed that travels by shooting fire out its . . ."

His voice drifted as he saw her, died completely when he met her eyes. She was quiet, still, barely breathing. And he saw the tremble, something held within her that seemed like it might burst if she did anything more than breathe.

So he held out his hand. She took it, stepped closer to him.

"Sorry," he whispered.

"I know," she whispered back.

"We can't stay."

"I know."

He looked over her, to the two unmoving shapes in the shadows of the cell. "But if you want to . . ."

She squeezed his hand before stepping past him. "I don't."

Denaos nodded. "Then we need to be careful. There weren't a lot of netherlings out when we snuck in here, but there's a guard force left behind."

"They've left, then," Asper muttered.

"To Jaga."

"To Lenk and the others, assuming they made it."

"Right," Denaos said, nodding. "It's a big fleet, though, and Hongwe has a small, fast boat. We can still make it before they do." He pointed down a corridor. "Now, just head that way, Dread should be standing—"

"Where? Here?"

"No, back at the . . ."

He didn't even bother once he saw the wizard come walking up the corridor. No urgency was in his step, no breathlessness, nothing to indicate anything was the matter with anything but him. Dreadaeleon's brows were knitted, his face set in a frown as he walked up to the cell.

"What is it?" Denaos hissed, reaching for a knife. "Are they coming?"

Dreadaeleon did not reply. He briefly pushed between them, peering into the cell. Without so much as a blink for the two bodies inside, he turned and walked back to the center of the room.

"Dread?" Asper asked, reaching out for him. "Are you . . ."

He warded her off, holding up a single finger for silence. Pursing his lips in thought, he cocked an ear up. In a few moments, a scream echoed out of the darkness. The boy smiled.

"Ah, there we are," he said.

And, with a rather morbid spring in his step, he took off exactly the opposite way from the exit, disappearing into the darkness. Asper looked expectantly to Denaos. The rogue looked offended.

"Well, how am *I* supposed to know?"

With little choice but to indulge this particular madness, they followed, finding him walking resolutely into the chamber ahead. Asper kept her eyes on him, trying hard not to look at the blackened wall of the chamber with a woman-shaped outline.

"Dread," she urged quietly, "we should go. I mean *really* go. You don't know what's down here."

"That's why I am down here," the boy replied, looking around as if searching for something in the round chamber. "It's not so much calling to me as just sort of sending out a thousand messages to anyone who will listen. I'm surprised you haven't heard it. Though I guess it would be difficult, what with—"

Another scream, this one frightfully close, echoed through the darkness.

"Yes, with that. Anyway, I have to find out. You understand."

He didn't wait for a confirmation before he took off running down the corridor, deeper into the darkness. Asper looked helplessly to Denaos, who sighed and pulled a dagger out, gesturing with his chin.

"Go. Get him," he said. "Be quick about it, though, I don't want to be standing here forever."

She nodded, took off after the boy. The corridor was darkness so dense she couldn't even be sure she wasn't about to collide into a wall. But she kept her pace steady, following the sound of Dreadaeleon's voice as it echoed up through the darkness between screams.

"Ah-*ha*," he said from up ahead. "That would explain it, wouldn't it?"

"*Man-eh . . . waka-ah, man-eh . . .*" another voice replied, weary and rasping.

"Hang on, let me see if . . . no. They're on there pretty tight."

"*O-tu-ah-tu-wa, man-eh. Padh, o-tu. Padh. Padh. Padh.*"

"I guess it makes sense, though I am sorry."

"*Ah-chka-kai . . . ah-te-ah-nah . . .*"

She couldn't understand the words, but she recognized the voice. It had been screaming for hours now. And she knew the desperation held within it, a breathless echo of what Nai's was.

Had been.

The thought of listening was unbearable. Though, as she rounded a corner and was washed over in a tide of bloodred light, it turned out to be infinitely more preferable to seeing it. But by then, she couldn't look away.

A sweltering gallery of skin and iron met her. They hung in haphazard exhibit, choking on chains attached to the wall, strung up on every bare patch of stone. Some wept, some gasped, only a few screamed. More simply hung, staring blankly into the bloodred haze that drowned the cavernous chamber, waiting for death.

They were Gonwa.

They once were alive.

They were not dead, though. A few were, a few were close, none were truly alive. Collars of iron were shut tight around their throats, hanging by chains hammered into the wall. The green of their skin, the yellow of their eyes, all color was swallowed whole by the hellish red light that permeated the very stone.

She felt something brush against her shoulder and whirled about. Bleary eyes stared back, a withered hand groped the air blindly. The Gonwa looked shriveled, consumed, like a waterskin with a slow leak. It was muttering something, in no language she could understand.

She stepped closer. The Gonwa continued to grope the air, even as she stepped past it, unaware of her presence, barely aware of his. Her eyes were drawn to the collar, to the brief flash of color in the iron circle. A red stone, glowing brightly, positively brimming with crimson life.

"It's how they did it, for the record."

Dreadaeleon's eyes were on the collar of another Gonwa, barely alive, a sac of flesh resembling a wet frock drying more than anything that ever walked or talked. He tapped the red stone, which chirped to light brightly.

"The stones, the netherlings wore them, the males," he said. "It alters their magic somehow. Usually, there's a price to pay, something in the body that has to be burned. They didn't pay it. Thought it was the stones. Had it wrong. Doesn't negate the cost."

He reached into his pocket and fished out another stone on a thin black chain. It twinkled, growing brighter the closer it got to the stone on the collar, the two glowing like a pair of soft, bleeding stars. The Gonwa let out a groan. Dreadaeleon frowned.

"The price is still paid," he said, "just by someone else."

Behind her, a scream erupted. A Gonwa writhed, hanging limply from its collar, only enough energy left to let out an ear-piercing wail. The rest of it went somewhere else, wherever Sheraptus and his stones were. What was left was something that was a few drops of blood, a few shallow breaths, and a lot of useless flesh.

"Open their collars," Asper said. "Open those up. I'll . . . I'll get water and . . . and . . ."

Dreadaeleon looked up. "And?"

"And I have to do *something*," Asper shot back. "They're alive. We *know* Gonwa. We have to help."

"How? The collars are welded shut," Dreadaeleon replied. "And there's not a creature here left that I would call a Gonwa. There's barely enough material to make two whole ones out of what's left."

"They aren't material, they're—"

"Still, doesn't make sense." He scratched his chin. "These are all advanced decays: muscle consumed, blood drained." He pinched at a stray fold of flesh where a bicep should have been. "Burnt up, like kindling. For them to be this far advanced, they would have had to been casting spells all day and all night for months. But they haven't been. They're reckless, but not that reckless. These are being repurposed for something else."

"*Stop it.*"

He glanced over to Asper, looking utterly confused at her horrified expression.

"Stop *talking* like that," she said. "Like they're things, like they're . . . materials. They're *people. Living* people, Dread."

He looked from her to the creature before him, back to her and shook his head.

"Not anymore."

Callousness on the battlefield was something she was used to. Emotions could easily get someone killed, as could sympathy. She had hardened herself to that long ago, told herself it was necessary that her companions act that way, that they step over bodies and calmly ram their weapons into the chests of the enemies who still lived.

But to see *this*, to see someone so cold, so callous, so blatantly *not* moved by the sight of dozens of creatures being eaten alive before his eyes . . .

Asper had no words. Asper didn't want words. And Dreadaeleon stood, humming thoughtfully, as oblivious to her horror as he was to everything else.

He snapped his fingers. "Oh, *obviously.*"

Almost everything, anyway.

Before she could say a word she didn't have, he was off, disappearing into another shadow at the far side of the room. She hadn't even noticed it amidst the red light, only barely felt the urge to follow him. But he was still Dread, still the boy she knew.

And so, as dozens of bleary, blind eyes stared blankly at her, she walked past the gallery of sagging flesh and drained blood. Trying to ignore it. Trying not to hate herself for doing so.

The walls of the cavern grew rougher the farther back she went, in crude contrast to the smooth and worn walls of the previous chambers, like they had been gnawed away instead of carved by anything natural. They were bigger, cruder, and much, much darker.

"Dread?" she called out. "Where are you?"

He didn't answer. Not her, anyway.

"Amazing."

A faint whisper. A faint word. One she had a distinctly uneasy feeling following.

But she did, and as she did, a light grew at the end of the tunnel. It did not beckon, though; it glowed far too dim, far too harsh, far too purple for that. Rather, it warned, threatened, told her to take her friend standing before it and go. But whatever it said to her, it did not say to Dreadaeleon.

He stood at the center of it, a shadow within a shadow, staring up into darkness. What exactly "it" was, though, she wasn't entirely sure.

It stretched out like a bruise upon creation, an ugly patch of purple and black that expanded in ways that made her eyes hurt: too high, too wide, too malformed. It was as though someone had simply jammed a jagged knife into the air and started twisting it and this was what bled out from existence.

It twitched like a living thing set in the vast iron frame that surrounded it. From the twisted metal rods boxing it in, hooks extended, piercing the vast nebulousness that it was, drawn taut in its chains, holding it wide and open, like a portrait on display.

No, not a portrait, she thought.

Portraits didn't move.

In the bruise, the blood, she could see them. Images flashed with schizophrenic sporadicism inside it, as though it tried to see everything all at once. Here, it showed a forest with great, black columns for trees rising against a sunless sky. There, it showed long, quadrupedal creatures capering through shadow, laughing in the darkness. Here, fire and forges and the shattering of metal. There, the barking and howling of warcries and chants.

And everywhere, in every vision, in every space there was not darkness, were the netherlings. Thousands of them.

It was no portrait.

It was a gate.

"This is it, you know."

Asper didn't ask, didn't even look at him. She could not bear to hear the answer, she could not tear her eyes away from the sight.

"It answers nearly everything about them, the longfaces," Dreadaeleon continued. "Why no one's seen them before we found them, why they don't look like anything we've ever seen, why they have all those Gonwa back there." He clicked his tongue. "And what they're doing here. They were the first, the expedition."

The vision in the gate sharpened, intensified, swept across a vast, plant-less field beneath thousands of iron boots, over a sea of long, purple faces gathered in a cluster, up to thousands of blades held in gauntleted hands, thousands of eyes white as milk, thousands of jagged-tooth mouths open in silent, shrieking war cries.

"This," Dreadaeleon said, "is the army that will follow."

"Why . . . why didn't they bring it with them?" Asper asked, breathless.

"Obviously, this . . . gate, however it works, it doesn't have enough of whatever it needs to let more in. The Gonwa can keep it open, but not enough to let the rest of them out." He hummed, scratching his chin. "Still doesn't explain how they got here in the first place, though, without any sacrifices . . . unless, of course, Greenhair was right."

"Greenhair?"

"Someone else had to have found them," he continued, ignoring her, "someone else had to have let them in. And in exchange, they . . ." He sighed. "Ah. Demons. Undying. More fuel, obviously, to let the rest of them in. It's brilliant."

"It's . . . horrifying."

"It's revolutionary. There are all sorts of theories out there about how the same power that lets us bend light to create illusions could be used to hide entirely different worlds. But they were wrong. The priests had it right all along. Heaven, hell . . . and something else, entirely." He chuckled. "It's amazing."

"It uses *people* to work."

For the first time, he looked at her. And even that was just a sidelong, dismissive glance.

"You just don't understand."

"Of *course* I don't understand," she snapped. "Not this . . . thing. I don't care about that. I don't understand how you can look at it and not think of the Gonwa, of the suffering, like . . . like you're *impressed* with it."

"It's a *gateway*. An opening into another *world*. How can you *not* be impressed?"

"It's not just that. The stones, the Gonwa, *everything*. People are dying and all you can think about is the stones!"

"Because they *transfer* everything! The physical cost! The toll! All the prices of magic! With it, I can—"

"It's *you!* I don't understand *you*."

"Convenient," Dreadaeleon said with a sneer. "Do you not care about me, either?"

"How the hell would you draw *that* conclusion?"

"Process of elimination, numbers," he replied, voice as fevered as his eyes were as he thrust both upon her. "Lenk and Kataria. And for the past few days, you've positively *fawned* over Denaos like . . . like he's . . ."

Asper held her fist at her side, held her gaze level, held her voice cold and hard. "If you try to guess, I will *break your jaw*."

"And what? I don't get to know? But *he* does?" He gestured wildly back down the cavern. "*I'm* the one with the power, *I'm* the one with the intellect and you'd rather share your secrets with some thuggish, scummy *thug*?"

"I don't . . ." Asper stammered for a reply. "I didn't . . ."

"You *did*. Because that's how it works! Lenk and Kataria. You and Denaos. And what does that leave me? With *Gariath*?"

"It doesn't work that way."

"*THEN TELL ME HOW IT DOES*," he screamed back. "Tell me how I'm supposed to figure this out when no one tells me *anything* and I have to figure it out on my own! Tell me what I'm supposed to do to . . . to . . ."

She watched him, spoke softly. "Go on."

"No."

"Dread—"

"*NO*." He held up a hand, rubbed his eyes with the other. "Forget it. Forget everything. Look . . ." When he looked back, she saw a weariness that he had kept hidden from her, a dullness in the eyes growing worse. "You want to help the Gonwa."

"So should you."

"I want to . . . find out about this and keep however many netherlings from coming forth and killing us all, so yeah, similar goals." He pointed down the cavern. "We can't free them all. Not without the stones. The netherlings are heading to Jaga, to get more fuel or to kill something or . . . what. We can agree that stopping them from doing . . . this again is a good thing, I assume?"

"Right."

"Then our best bet is to go there. To find Sheraptus and stop him."

"Him," she whispered.

"All of them," Dreadaeleon said, turning to leave.

They walked out in silence and suddenly, Asper found herself more aware of the boy. Or rather, more aware of what he once was. He seemed diminished, as though more had left him than just air with the last outburst. He walked slower, paused to catch his breath more often.

But every time she would look behind, every time she would open her mouth to say something, he would look at her. The weariness would be replaced with something else, a quiet loathing, and she would say nothing.

The thought never left her, though. And so she didn't even notice the netherling corpse until she tripped over it.

Don't remember it being there, she thought. *Denaos could have moved it somewhere a little more—*

She tripped again. Another corpse stared up at her from the ground, a dagger jammed in her throat.

There definitely hadn't been two of them.

"Hey."

She looked up. Denaos definitely hadn't been clutching a bleeding arm when they left. The rogue snorted, spat out a glob of red onto the floor.

"We should go."

EIGHTEEN

FOR BLOOD, EVERYTHING

*S*hould've punched him.

Gariath looked down at his claws, made fists out of them. Big hands. Strong hands. Probably would have left a good-sized dent if he had swung and meant it.

Yeah, he thought. *Probably would have taken . . . what? Eight teeth? Maybe twelve. How many do humans have? Could've taken at least half.* He snorted, unclenched his fists. *Definitely should've punched him.*

He'd have deserved it, of course, for reasons other than being weak and stupid. Gariath might not have been Shen, Gariath might not have known much about Shen, Gariath might not have even considered himself all that scaly. But the insinuation that the Shen were beasts made him feel something.

Something that didn't immediately make him want to punch someone.

Though the acknowledgement of *that* feeling *did* make him want to punch something, though the urge came far too late.

In the end, though, simply breaking off when neither human was looking and leaving had been the better decision. Not as satisfying as a punch, of course, but there would be no questions, no queer looks, no one wondering what might have been bothering him.

When a creature can kill something twenty times his size, he does not admit to having his feelings hurt.

Not without immediately eviscerating whoever heard such a confession, anyway. Leaving and skulking off into the coral, unnoticed and unquestioned, just seemed a little easier.

Still, he noted, it probably wasn't too late to go back and break the human's leg just on principle. Maybe break the pointy-eared human's leg, too, to make it fair.

He thrust his snout into the air, took a few deep breaths. Salt. Fish. Blood. Quite a bit of blood, actually. But none of it blood that he knew. Nor flesh, nor bone, nor fear, nor hypocrisy. No humans nearby at all.

But something was.

Something not human.

As good as any scent to follow, he reasoned, and if it would get him out of the coral, so much the better. And so he followed it, winding through the jagged coral, between the schools of fish passing amongst the skeletal forest, tearing through the kelp in his way.

The forest opened up around him, coral diminishing, sand vanishing and giving way to stone beneath his feet. A road stretched out behind him. Somewhere, on air that wasn't there, he caught a vague scent. One that was almost familiar, but far too fleeting. He snorted; scenting anything was difficult here. The air was too thick for odors to pass through.

Not that that mattered.

The road stretched both ways. And what opened up before him was far more interesting.

Netherlings.

Dead ones.

They lined the highway like banners, rising up into the heavens on either side, held only by the tethers about their wrists, swaying with a sense of lurid tranquility violently contradicted by the state of their bodies.

Each one boasted an impressive collection of wounds: arrow holes, gaping cuts, bruises so dark as to stain even their purple flesh, and a collection of skulls flattened, pulverized, and a few that could only be described as artistically tenderized. The expressions they wore in death were unreadable, what with their faces smashed in and all, but none suggested that they had gone without a fight.

Shen work.

Granted, he didn't know much of the Shen. Not nearly enough to know their handiwork, anyway. But there were few options as to who would go to the trouble of stringing up dead netherlings. Besides, to admit that he didn't know the Shen would have been to admit that Lenk was at least partially right.

That thought made him sick where corpses could not.

Some were old, desiccated, flesh torn off to expose bone. Some were newer, littered with fresh bruises and scabbing wounds. And some, he noticed as a flash of red and black caught his eye, were even fresher.

Their blood poured not in streams, but in a cloud that blossomed at the top of the tether holding her swaying in the air like a red dandelion. Fish darted in and out of the cloud of red, dark shapes on dark fins, glassy eyes reflecting nothing as they seized pieces of purple meat in their jaws, shook fiercely and swallowed them whole before swimming back for another bite. At least a dozen sharks, heedless of biting iron, flesh, or bone, feasted.

Being made of the kind of meat that probably wouldn't go down as gently as the dead kind, the sharks had as much interest in Gariath as he had in them. He glanced down the road, toward the distant mountain. If the Shen were anywhere, they would be there. Why else would they bother to string up so many meaty warnings?

But he didn't take another step forward.

He couldn't very well with someone following him.

"Let's get this over with," he said with a sigh. "I can smell you. I've smelled you since I got here. I smelled you back on Teji."

His eyes swept the horizon, the jagged coral canopies and wafting kelp reaches revealed nothing but thick air and empty sky.

"I don't know *exactly* where you are. The air's too thick to smell that. But you might as well come out."

He threw out his hands to either side, gesturing to the vast road cutting a smooth stone path through the coral.

"It's too open for an ambush. You can't sneak up on me. So just find whatever courage you have and—"

He stopped suddenly. Somehow, having one's head smashed from behind made talking harder.

He staggered forward, straining not to collapse as his eyes rolled in his sockets and his brains rattled in his skull. He flailed blindly, trying to ward off his attacker, wherever it might have been. His vision still swimming, he found footing enough to whirl about and face his foe.

And his foe, all seven green feet of him, stared back.

Another pointy-eared human, he recognized. A pointy-eared green human. A pointy-eared green human with hands for feet and what appeared to be a cock's crest for hair.

There had to be a shorter word for it. What had the other pointy-eared human called it? Greenshict? She had carried their scent, too.

This one was taller, tense, ready to spill blood instead of teary emotions. The greenshict's bones were long, muscles tight beneath green skin, dark eyes positively weeping scorn as he narrowed them upon Gariath.

He liked this one better already.

At least until he looked down to his foe's hand and saw, clenched in slender fingers, a short, stout piece of wood.

"A stick?" The fury choked his voice like phlegm. "You came to kill me with a *stick*?"

The shict snarled, baring four sharp teeth. Gariath roared, baring two dozen of his own. The stones quaked beneath his feet, the sky shivered at his howl as he charged.

He lashed out, claws seeking green flesh and finding nothing as the greenshict took a long, fluid step backward. He flipped the stick effortlessly from one hand to the other, brought it up over his head, brought it down upon Gariath's.

It cracked against his skull, shook brain against bone. But this was no cowardly blow from behind. This was honest pain. Gariath could bite back honest pain. He grunted, snapped his neck and caught the stick between his horns to tear it from the greenshict's grasp.

The stick flew in one direction, his fist in the other. It sought, caught, crushed a green face beneath red knuckles in a dark crimson eruption. Bones popped, sinuses erupted, blood spattered. A body flew, crashed, skidded across the stones, leaving a dark smear upon the road.

Therapeutic, Gariath thought, even as the blood sizzled against his flesh. It hurt. But he couldn't very well let the greenshict know that.

"I AM RHEGA*!"*

Yelling hurt, too. Possibly because his teeth still rattled in their gums. A trail of blood wept from his brow, spilling into his eye. The greenshict had drawn blood—with a stick.

Impressive, he thought. *Also annoying.* He snorted; that hurt. *Just annoying.*

The greenshict did not so much leap as flow from his back to his feet like a liquid. He ebbed, shifting into a stance—hands up, ears perked, waist bent—with such ease as to suggest that he had simply sprung from the womb ready to fight.

Suggestions weren't enough for Gariath. He needed more tangible things: stone beneath his feet, blood on his hands, horns in the air, and a roar in his maw as he fell to all fours and charged.

And again, the greenshict flowed. He broke like water on a rock, slithering over Gariath, sparing only a touch for the dragonman as he leapt delicately over him and landed behind him. Gariath skidded to a halt, whirled about and found his opponent standing.

And just standing.

He didn't scramble for his stick. He didn't move to attack. He just stood there.

"Hit back," Gariath snarled as he rushed the greenshict once more. "Then I hit you. Then you fall down and I splash around in your entrails." His claw followed his voice, twice as bloodthirsty. *"Don't you know how this works?"*

The greenshict had no respect for Gariath's instruction or his blows, leaping away, ducking under, stepping away from each blow. He never struck back, never made a noise, never did anything but move.

Slowly, steadily, to the floating corpses.

The next blow came and the greenshict flew instead of flowed. He leapt away and up, hands and feet finding a tether and scrambling up. Hand over foot over foot over hand, he leapt to the fresh netherling corpse and entangled himself amongst its limbs, staring down at Gariath.

Impassively.

Mocking him.

"Good," he grunted, reaching out and seizing the tether. "Fine." He jerked down on it. "I'll come to *you*."

Hand over hand, claw over claw, he pulled, drawing his prey and the corpse he perched upon ever closer.

One more hard pull brought him within reach and Gariath seized the opportunity. His claws were hungry and lashed out, seeking green flesh. That green flesh flew again, however, leaping from the corpse. The flesh his claws found was purple and wrapped around a thick jugular.

That promptly exploded in a soft cloud of blood.

Engulfed in the crimson haze, he roared. His mouth filled with a foul coppery taste. His nostrils flared, drank in the stench of stale life. No sign of the greenshict, no scent of the greenshict. Annoying.

But merely annoying.

At least, until the shark.

He saw the teeth only a moment before he felt them as they sank into the flesh of his bicep. He had seen worse: steel, glass, wood. That was small comfort when this particular foe was hungry, persistent. Its slender gray body jerked violently, trying to tear off a stubborn chunk.

Gariath snarled, struck it with a fist, raked at it with a claw. The beast tightened its grip, snarled silently as it shredded skin, growing ever more insistent with each attempt to dislodge it.

It was only when he felt the stick lash out and rap against his skull that he remembered there was a reason for trying to fight off a shark on dry land.   251

He staggered out of the cloud, his writhing parasite coming with him, his suddenly bold foe right behind him. The corpse went flying into the sky and the rest of the sharks flew for the easy meal. Not his. He *would* have to get the only shark with principles.

The greenshict leapt, stick lashing out like a fang. It struck against wrist, skull, leg, shoulder, anywhere that wasn't a flailing claw or a twisting fish. The pain was intense, but it wasn't as bad as the insult of being beaten with a stick. Gariath fought between the two, dividing his attention between the shark and the shict and failing at fending off either.

A choice had to be made.

And the shark was only acting out of hunger.

When the stick came again, Gariath's hand shot out to catch it. He found a wrist instead and, with a sharp twist, made it not a wrist. The greenshict's limb came apart with a satisfying snap, not as satisfying as the shriek that followed.

Gariath held onto that sound, clutched it like an infant clutches his mother. He used it to block out the pain as teeth sawed through his flesh. He used it to ignore the sensation of being tasted. He used it to find enough strength to tighten his grip, twist his body, and fling.

A discus in flight, the greenshict flew through the corpses, twisting violently through the air before crashing onto the road and skipping like a stone, each impact punctuated with a cracking sound. He skidded to a halt slowly—bleeding, broken, but breathing.

He didn't flow to his feet. He rose and staggered like an earth-bound thing. His body protested with popping sounds, bones setting themselves aright as he swayed on his feet. Gasping, he sought his stick and found it nearby. With the taste of his own toxic blood in his mouth, he turned to find his foe.

The shark's glassy eyes and gaping mouth greeted him.

A gray hide kissed a green cheek. The fish's razored flesh ripped apart the tender skin of the greenshict as Gariath swung the beast like a club, smashing it against his foe. The dragonman's hands bled, the writhing tail causing denticled skin to rub his palms raw.

Small price.

One hundred pounds of writhing, coarse hide struck at the greenshict. Countless saw-teeth ripped at his flesh in a blind panic. Fins slapped, jaws gnashed, blood wept, bones snapped, and the screaming lasted only so long as the shict still had breath.

Gariath did not stop once he ran out. He did not stop until his foe fell to his knees, then to his belly, then to his face. Gariath gave him a few more thumps with the fish on principle before he stared down at a mess of red cuts and battered green skin, the creature hanging limp in his hands, a flaccid spine encased in so much useless meat.

Gariath released the beast from his grasp. It never even struck the ground, but lazily drifted into the thick air above, another course for its former brothers' grim feast.

The dragonman was bleeding, breathing hard. Every step brought back echoes of the greenshict's stick, his bones still rattling inside him. But that was more than could be said for the long-eared thing. He knelt beside his green foe, reached down to seize a fistful of blood-smeared hair and twisted it up to face him.

What looked back at him was only half a face. One eye was lost in a thick mass of bruising, the other held only the faintest glimmer of life. The greenshict's nose had become a flute: a mess of holes through which breath whistled faintly. All these paled next to the creature's grin, though, as he smiled at Gariath with only half his teeth, the other half either scattered on the ground or embedded in the shark's hide.

"Good fight," the greenshict rasped.

"I won, so yeah," Gariath replied.

"You didn't."

Gariath glanced over the unmoving mass of red, purple and green that was the greenshict's body. "I don't know. By anyone's standards, the fighter that looks like a half-digested turd at the end is the one who lost."

"That is fine. Whether you live or die is irrelevant to the victory." He smiled a little broader. "*Your* death is not our concern."

Gariath narrowed his eyes, growling. "Whose is, then?"

"One of our own's."

"The pointy-eared one? You wanted to kill her?"

"We saved her. We cured her. By killing the other one."

"And how do you intend to kill Lenk when I'm about to force you to kiss the stones?"

"There are more of us. I keep you away. Inqalle will have killed him by now. Naxiaw will have cured her by now. She will be safe."

Gariath said nothing as he stared through the greenshict, into nothingness. When he spoke, it was soft. "Why are you telling me this?"

"To remind myself," the greenshict rasped, breath harsh and bleeding, "why I am dead."

"For her? All this, for her?"

He stared into Gariath's eyes, even as the last flicker of life left his.

"For family," he replied, "everything."

Gariath released him. His head fell unceremoniously to the stone where it lay. Where he lay. Unmoving.

Instantly, the dragonman regretted not having smashed his face into the pavement. He wondered if he still could, just out of spite. Not that it would matter, the shict had still spoken and Gariath could still hear those words.

And they irritated him, like an itch at the very center of his back.

His stare drifted away from the corpse and farther down the road as his thoughts drifted to the human. To Lenk.

And the words still bothered him.

"He is not floating, I see."

Only rarely did Gariath ever take offense at being sneaked up on. Only

253

rarely did anyone ever do it without the consequence of being crushed into a pulp. When he whirled, he caught a pair of yellow eyes peering out from beneath a bone headdress.

Shalake glanced down at the greenshict's corpse.

"The sea is picky as to who it takes up to the clouds. Perhaps this one would not have fed the sharks as well as the purple things."

"We are far from the sea," Gariath pointed out.

"Sky, sea . . ." Shalake shrugged. "The difference is pointless on Jaga. Enough blood has been shed here that the island took it as its own, used it to find its own life."

"Whose blood?" Gariath asked.

"Everyone's. Demon's, Shen's, human's . . . *Rhega's.*"

Another word that bothered Gariath. "You speak the name like you've been saying it for a long time."

"We have stories of the *Rhega*," Shalake replied, head turning down a bit. "And only stories. You are the first we have seen since the war."

"A war . . ."

Gariath remembered. The bells, the monoliths, the destruction on Jaga. The bones, the corpses, the decaying weaponry on Teji. The spirits. The ghosts. The *Rhega*.

Grandfather . . .

"What kind of war?" he asked. "Who did the *Rhega* fight? How did they die?"

"I am the warwatcher. I lead the battles. I swing my *shenko*. Mahalar holds the stories." He eyed Gariath's injuries. "Also, the medicine." He turned about, began to stalk down the road. "Come, *Rhega*. We will tell you."

"Tell me what?"

"Everything we can."

He watched Shalake a moment longer. Then, a stray scent caught his nostrils. The familiar odor of fear and lust and pain and anger that always came with humans. It hung in his nostrils for a single desperate moment, almost overpowering as it cut through the thick air before disappearing.

Back down the road.

"You have something else you need to attend to, *Rhega*?"

Gariath looked down the road for a moment before turning.

"I have nothing."

NINETEEN

DEATH LANTERNS

Beneath the world, between earth and hell, the differences between life and death seemed more trivial.

The chasm stretched out into a vast trench beneath the highway, a great and cavernous maw into which the sun was swallowed and promptly digested in a stomach of stone and sand.

Here, the signs of battle hung like afterthoughts, a bad dream that could never really be forgotten: corpses entangled amidst the phosphorescent kelp, bones layering the earth, weapons shattered into shards, and the bells, hanging from cliffs, half-buried in sand, swaying delicately and precariously from nooses of kelp and coral.

In the stillness, silence. In the darkness, death.

And still, there was light.

The luminescent violet glow of the kelp and coral was made all the more vivid by the lack of sunlight, painting the sands the color of a dying sky, giving the skeletons an insubstantial flesh, casting a thousand different hues in the reflections of a thousand shattered weapons.

And still, there was life.

Or supposed life, anyway.

They hung; like lanterns, like mirrors, or perhaps like stars that had fallen too far and had forgotten how to get back home. But they hung, in quivering and undulating blobs, thick as jellies, weightless as feathers, their tendrils hanging from viscous bells to brush against the sea floor and caress the hollow cheekbones of the dead.

A beautiful sight, Lenk would have thought as he darted between their reaching tentacles, had he not been struggling to keep footing and breath alike. He would have to make a note to come back and reflect on the beauty when he wasn't running for his life.

Somehow, the interesting things only ever seemed to crop up when someone was trying to kill him.

And this time he had not the sense to notice the life around him. Because this time he had not the sense to think beyond a single word.

Run, run, run, run, run, run, run, run, run . . .

"Turn around, fool," the voice hissed in reply, trying to wrest control from him with an icy, unseen grasp. *"Turn and fight."*

No sword, no sword, no sword, could be anywhere, anywhere, can't see her, can't hear her, run, run, run, run, run—

"There is nowhere to run."

Before him, a world the color of a bruise stretched into infinity: great wreaths of violet kelp swaying upon a carpet of sand and bone. Behind him, a world of refuse ran with no end in sight: skeletons of many creatures spread on every spike of coral and swath of kelp with artistic abandon.

Around him, nothing but darkness, offering no escape. In which anything could hide. Including him.

He ran toward a crop of kelp, weaving himself into the folds of it, trying to disappear amidst the violet plantlife.

"This cannot save you," the voice whispered. *"Not hiding. Not running."*

"Kill them. Kill them all."

"Hate them. Want them to die."

"They want us to hurt. We can't. Not anymore."

"There is only one way out," the voice spoke: louder, colder, clearer than the others.

They scratched at his skull, it gouged deep furrows in his eardrums. Theirs were a thousand gnats buzzing in his ear, it was a cricket chirping on the surface of his brain. They growled, hissed, whimpered. It commanded.

"Kill. Kill them both."

"Shut up, *shut up.*" He only barely spoke, his voice forced in slivers between his teeth. "She'll hear you."

He stared into the chasm, from shadow to shadow, darkness to deeper darkness. The sunlight was forgotten, only the narrowest sliver slipping through. The violet glow of the kelp was no honest light. It revealed nothing, only served as another source of shadows, to make the darkness deeper, an absolute blackness in which she hid.

256   Watching.

Waiting.

The air stirred above him. A shadow fell over him. He whirled about, choking on a shriek, and saw nothing. His eyes drifted up to the creatures circling in a shadowy halo overhead.

The rays slid calmly through the air, as unperturbed by the darkness as they were by the terror bursting out of him. Their tails swayed like the kelp they wound through, their fins rippled like wings too dignified to flap. They flew. Artistically. Hypnotically. Not vultures presiding over a pit of death, but doves, too elegant to be moved by the corpses staring up at them with envious, hollow eyes.

It would have been nice to fly away at that moment, Lenk thought, up out of the chasm and into the sky until he couldn't see the land anymore.

But he was down here. Somewhere beneath the land. With her.

The air stirred.

Beside him.

He had a moment to see her face, a mask carved out of green, hard lines and all points. He stared at her, mouth scrambling for a word, eyes searching for a way out. She stared at him without a snarl, a growl, so much as a blink.

She almost seemed to smile, like she was thinking of a pleasant summer day, as she casually brought a sharp-edged tomahawk over her head and aimed for his skull.

"*MOVE.*"

One of them had yelled it. He didn't care. He threw himself to the side, a bright spurt of red bursting as the tomahawk gave his arm an envious caress, the metal whining spitefully as he pulled himself to his feet.

"*FIGHT.*"

"*KILL.*"

"*HATE.*"

"*DIE.*"

They shrieked, pounded at his skull, clawed at the bone, trying to dig their way out. His head swam, mind pounded to ground meat by the screaming. He couldn't hear, couldn't think, could barely see. There was too much noise, too much cold.

Perhaps it was because of it, the madness, the pain, that he could feel a brief touch of warmth, hear a voice too close, too kind to be down here. Perhaps that was why he listened.

"*Run.*"

Panic propelled him. He flew across the sand as the rays flew overhead, bones crunching beneath his boots, kelp shuddering at his passing, light appearing, reappearing, disappearing as he rushed through the chasm, trying not to think of the greenshict behind him.

He didn't.

She wasn't behind him anymore.

He caught glimpses of her out of the corner of his eye. Her muscles shimmered in the flashes of light as she swung, leapt, tumbled through the air, hand over foot, kelp to coral. She flew, effortlessly leaping alongside him, over him, between the light and into the shadows, in the air, on the ground, running across the sands before him, slipping behind him as he stumbled through the darkness.

She was everywhere, every movement blending together. Every shadow held her, every twitch of movement was her as she stalked him, chased him, laughed at him without words.

He tried to track her, tried to watch her, tried to tell which shadow was hers and which was his. The kelp shook violently around him, its glowing fronds a riot of light. He lost himself in the darkness, unsure where he had been running, which way she had gone.

Then she came out and made it all abundantly clear.

Leaping from the darkness, her shadow sailed over him. He felt her feet wrap around his throat, their thumbs crushing down on his windpipe as she tumbled, landing on her hands and snapping powerful legs up and over to send him hurtling breathlessly through the shadows.

He left that breath in her grip, his blood on the sand, didn't bother to pick up either as he pulled to his feet and continued running, trying not to let her impassive stare look deeper into him than it already did. His body fought him every step, fear fighting the cold in his blood, each one trying to hold him.

"*Fight*," the voice urged. "*Turn and FIGHT.*"

Can't, he thought back. *No sword. Can't kill her. Can't fight. Kataria betrayed me. Left me. Can't fight. No point. Run. Run.*

"*We don't need her. We don't need* any *of them. We can do this. With or without a sword.*"

How?

A pain lanced his arms, shooting down into his wrists, draining the warmth from his palms and freezing the blood in his fingers. He looked at them, watched the fleshy hue of his hands slowly be replaced by something cold, something dark, something gray.

"*I can save you.*"

The color drained from his extremities, the gray crawled up his arms. His breath grew frantic and came out on cold, freezing puffs of air.

"*I can make everything stop hurting.*"

Icy talons sank into his skull, numbed thought, numbed action.

"*Just . . . stop . . . fighting.*"

He screamed. For the cold seeping through his body. For the voice snarling in his head as he shook it violently. Mostly, though, for the sound of feet-with-thumbs padding up behind him.

Panic was as good a remedy as denial; the voice slipped from his thoughts, if not from his body, as he continued to rush through the chasm. The sound of the greenshict behind him faded, but that meant nothing. She could be any-where, in the kelp, in the coral, in the shadows, even right in front of him.

Actually, he thought as he skidded to a halt, *probably not in front of me.*

Another forest stretched out before him. A forest of pale, thin tendrils, hanging like unknotted nooses from the darkness high above. The jellylike creatures hovered serenely overhead, either oblivious or uncaring to the eerie curtains they had laid down beneath them.

Lenk happened to catch a hint of movement: a stray fish, something that had lost its way and found something much worse, hanging limply in the grasp of one of the tendrils. It coiled about the body and dragged it up into the shadows to be consumed, preserved in the creature's bell-like body like a frog in a jar.

A crunch of sand behind him was all it took to break his hesitation and send him flying into the mess of tendrils. He was bigger than a fish, including them, he thought, and whatever they could do couldn't be worse than what she could.

He thought that right up until he felt his flesh on fire.

They stung, bit, did *something* to him that he couldn't see. But as he weaved his way frantically through the tendrils, he could feel the agony of tiny cuts nicking his arms, tiny venomous burns sizzling on his flesh. They conspired, grouped to attempt to overwhelm him.

Fear turned out to be a pretty good solution for that, as well.

The pain lingered, but only lingered. No fresh agonies visited him and when he looked up from his mad rush, he saw the tendrils behind him. And only the tendrils. They swayed with the same gentle impassiveness, as though he had never even run through them. Certainly, she hadn't followed him.

Had she?

He squinted into the shadows, trying to see his pursuer. She hadn't. She hadn't even come to the edge of the tendril curtain. There was no kelp for her to climb, no way through except the way he had come.

Did she just give up?

Perhaps her ears were long enough to hear thoughts, for her retort came in the whine of steel and the shriek of air as a tomahawk came hurtling through the darkness straight at his head.

Fortunately, he felt the air erupt from his lungs before he could feel his head cloven from his shoulders as someone tackled him to the earth. Unfortunately, he didn't have the sense not to look at his rescuer.

"*You*," he hissed.

"Yeah," Kataria replied. "Nice to see you, too." She took quick stock of his wounds and stings. "What's left of you, anyway," she said, reaching out to touch his face.

"Don't," he said, batting her hand away. "Contact with shicts isn't exactly working out for me today."

"You can't blame a shict for *these*. What did you expect you'd get, running through a bunch of jellyfish?

"Jelly . . . fish?"

"The sailors back on the *Riptide* said their touch is dangerous and needs immediate treatment." Her hands went for her belt. "Hold still a moment."

His eyes went wide with alarm. "Wait, what are you doing?"

"The sailors also told me what the treatment was. Stop squirming."

"No, *you* stop whatever you're about to—"

"Look, I'm not going to—"

"There is absolutely no way I'm going to let you—"

"*Damn it*, Lenk, I am *trying* to help you, so would you just hold still so I can piss on you?"

"*Get off, get off, get off, get off, get off!*"

"Fine," she said, hopping off before he could hurl her off and holding out a hand to him. "We shouldn't stay here long, anyway. I don't know why Inqalle isn't following you, but it won't last for long."

Ignoring her hand, Lenk clambered to his feet. "You know her name?"

"All their names," Kataria replied. "They're shicts."

"So are you."

She affixed a glare upon him. "Don't."

"I won't. I shouldn't have. Any of it." He glowered at her, saw the hilt in her grasp. "You have my sword?"

"I found it earlier. I've been trying to track you down since." She held it out to him, snatching it back as he lashed out a hand for it. "What do you plan to do with it?"

"I don't know. I was intending to kill the thing that's trying to kill me, but I suppose I could just turn it on myself before you can say anything more stupid."

She stepped back. "That won't be necessary."

"Like that," Lenk grunted, reaching for the weapon again.

"It doesn't need to be like that. They're . . . I can talk to them. I can reason with them. They think they're protecting me, saving me from you. I just need to tell them that—"

"*Liar. She consorts with them. Kill her.*"

"No," Lenk growled.

"I don't know, maybe I can just say . . ." Kataria said, searching for an answer in the darkness.

"*Strike her down. Kill her now. Remove one less threat.*"

"*No.*"

"It's a misunderstanding. I can make them see. No one has to die here today—"

"*KILL HER.*"

"*NO!*"

He clutched his head, scratched at his skull, tried to pry out the icicles digging into his brain. His scream was violent, his howl wretched, the tears in his eyes frozen upon his cheeks.

"*Traitor!*" he screamed. "*You left me to die! You led her to me!*" Shrieking turned to snarling. "*No, can't do this. Not yet. Run. Hide. Don't want to do this.*" He choked on the voice coming out of his throat. "*I can't . . . I can't . . . I can't . . .*"

She did not move. She took no step forward, reached out with no gentle hand as he cowered beneath something she couldn't see, covering his head from a gaze that wasn't there. Nor did she run, resisting every instinct and shred of common sense that told her to.

She stared. She held back tears of her own.

"I didn't betray you," she said softly.

"You didn't choose me, either," he said.

"I couldn't. I can't."

"Neither can I," he said. "Any of it."

"Then . . ."

He rose. He turned to face her. Halos of frost ringed his eyes, but he was impassive. His skin looked drained, colorless, as though all the life had seeped out of his body and into his eyes. And they, bright and vivid and full of something cold, held her captive as he approached her.

He reached out. The fine hairs on her belly rose as his fingers brushed against her midriff, disappearing to encircle around her waist. They returned with a sword held firmly in hand. She could feel the chill from his lips, cold as the steel in his hands, as he spoke.

"Then don't."

It hurt to walk away from her. His body rebelled, unseen frozen digits trying to wrench his muscles into their control. And accompanying each twist and jerk, the voice screeched.

"*Kill.*"

He had no voice to retort with, no words to refuse. Every ounce of his being was focused on holding back what was inside him.

"*Don't turn your back on her!*"

He sighed, dragging his sword in the sand as he pressed on, trying to ignore the voice.

"*Either of them.*"

"*LOOK OUT!*" Kataria screamed.

He turned and his blade turned with him. The steel saw his foe before he himself did. It whirled up, caught the tomahawk crashing down in a spray of sparks.

The greenshict trembled, holding the weapon in both hands as she tried to drive it down, to break the deadlock and finish it. But her eyes were calm, her lips were still even as the rest of her trembled; she took no pride in this.

He glanced over her shoulder and saw her opposite in Kataria's face. She glanced from him to her and back to him, eyes wild and confused, hands fumbling between her bow and nothing.

"She can't help you," the voice snarled. *"She never could."*

It ate the color in his hands, turned his flesh gray. The greenshict's eyes widened at the sight of it, at the sensation of him pushing back. His blood ran cold in his veins, wouldn't allow him to feel the strain of the deadlock.

"I can."

His body twitched.

"I will."

The blade snapped forward.

"We will survive."

The metal embrace parted with a shriek as he lashed out a sloppy blow, not entirely sure who was driving it. The blade itself went wide of flesh as the greenshict twisted out of its way, but he snapped it back, caught her on the chin with the hilt. She reeled and he struck again, snarling as he drove the pommel of his blade against her face.

Bone snapped. Teeth fragmented and fell like snowflakes. A mouth filled with blood. A body struck the earth.

The assault was broken as an arrow flew wide over his head. He looked up and saw Kataria holding an empty bow and full eyes. He wasn't sure which of them she had been shooting at, or how she expected such a sloppy shot to hit anything. And from the looks of it, neither was she. Someone was, though.

"Kill her. KILL HER NOW."

Not a request. Not even a command. It was a statement of fact, one that turned his eyes upon her, one that moved his feet forward, one that raised his sword above his head.

That which was in Kataria's eyes was something he could not describe. Despair and fear were evident in her tears, anger and impotence in the clench of her teeth. But there was something else there, in the long, deep breath. Relief? Lament? Regret?

Whatever it was, it consumed all that they both had. She stood, unable to move. His blade held, unable to fall. The voice was screaming at him in words he could not understand.

But it could not move him.

A flash of color out the corner of his eye caught his attention. First green, then, as the female inhaled and spat, red. Thick, viscous red for a moment. And then, nothing but bright, searing pain.

He screamed through burning lips, raked fingers blistering across a face that burned beneath the spatter of venomous blood. It clung to him spitefully, coming free from his face with great effort and greater agony. Through half-blind eyes he could see flashes of movement: a struggle, a limb raised and ending in a glistening tomahawk blade, stilled and trembling as two arms so pale and puny as to look like straws of wheat trying to hold back a tree wrapped around it.

Kataria cast a desperate stare over the greenshict's shoulder and screamed something to someone, unclear to him.

The greenshict understood and made her disagreement known as she reached up, seized Kataria by her hair and pried her from her shoulder like a pasty tick. With a look between contempt and apology, she hurled the smaller shict to the earth and scowled up at the fast-fading form of Lenk as he fled.

He was limping. His vision was swimming. His body was breaking down. And the voice was still screaming. Screaming to be heard over his pain, over his fear, over the other voices in his head.

But he had nothing left to give them, any of them. No more blood to spill, no more thoughts to consume, no more will to keep going. Behind him, Kataria was still there. She would always be there, always with eyes full of despair and uncertainty. Before him was darkness, emptiness, a long empty road he would simply walk until he could die.

All around him was death. Bones littered the floor. His sword hung from his hand weakly, fell to the earth. Above him, caught in the kelp, a bell hung precariously, swaying along with the purple weeds that suspended it. A cathedral, he thought, singing sermons to skinless people who had seen the same emptiness he had seen and chose to stay here.

Perhaps, he thought as he collapsed into a nearby copse of kelp, they had a point.

She came a moment later, walking calmly into the clearing, unfazed by her elusive quarry or the ruin that had been her face. As though it was just an inconvenience to be missing teeth and weeping blood onto the earth. She slowly swept the clearing for him, searching.

Perhaps the pain distracted her more than she let on. Or maybe she knew what he knew, knew that he had nothing left in him, and was waiting for the inevitable discovery. He didn't at all doubt she could hear his thoughts with those ears of hers.

Those big . . . pointy . . . ears.

His eyes drifted up to the ceiling of the cathedral of sand and kelp and bone, to the bell hanging above.

And he burst out of his hiding.

If he died, he died. That would be it. But for now, he was running without knowing why. For now, he was leaping to the kelp and trying to haul himself up. For now, he was giving more than he had, for a reason he didn't know, trying to accomplish he wasn't sure what.

For the thousandth time in his life.

She was upon him, loping after him silently as he ran, leaping after him as he climbed. Her tomahawk slashed, always catching the heels of his boots as he scrambled up into the kelp, hand over hand, coral over weed. With a snarl, the only she had spared for him thus far, she reached out, caught his foot.

He winced, swung his sword.

Not at her.

His steel struck the bell. Or grazed it, anyway. It was a glancing, sloppy blow. But the bell shook as though it had been waiting for such a touch for centuries. The kelp tore, the bell shifted and swung.

And sang.

It reverberated off itself, metal upon metal, keening a long, lonely wail. Its metal screeched, howled, whimpered, cackled, gibbered, sang an off-key song like it feared it would never sing again, a thousand iron emotions it had been keeping inside it unleashed in a horrible cacophony that hurt Lenk's ears to hear.

Though not nearly as bad as it hurt his foe.

She fell like a stone, hands free of tomahawk and kelp and pressed fiercely over her ears. Her ruined mouth gaped in a long, shrieking scream as she collapsed to the earth, her skull a bell unto itself, the sound pounding against ears, bones, brains, sending her vision spinning and her body writhing upon the sand.

She looked up through eyes rolling in their sockets. For a moment, she saw him. And then she saw his blade, growing closer.

He fell upon her, sheer luck being all that he could attribute to the blade being pointed downward as he did. It was gravity that struck and drove the steel into her chest. It was his weight, leaning upon the pommel, that jammed it deeper. It was his exhaustion, his agony, his pain that made him stare into her eyes, that made him hear her as she whispered on a dying breath.

"Worth it. For her."

"Yeah."

It was Lenk who said that.

Whether it was Lenk who fell backward off of a corpse and staggered to his feet, whether it was Lenk who shambled farther into the darkness and didn't dare look behind, even he wasn't sure.

She found him after combing amongst the dead.

After stepping over the body of she who was supposed to be her sister, after picking between the skeletons, after following the blood and weariness and dead voices in the darkness, she found him. Standing amongst the dead as though he belonged there.

Talking to the dead.

"I can hear you," he whispered. "I can hear you, but I'm just so tired and you really don't seem to be listening to me. What's that? I'm saying, you couldn't do it. When the time came, you couldn't make me do it. That's my entire point. You aren't as strong as you think you are."

She didn't turn away from him. Didn't so much as blink. This was a choice she had made the moment she'd had the opportunity to shoot him and let it go, as she had so many times before.

"They're not going to answer, you know," she said.

He didn't look at her. "I know."

"You don't have to keep talking to them."

"They keep talking to me, though. I've asked them to be quiet so many times."

"Then stop asking them."

"Please—"

"Stop begging them."

"I can't—"

"I know," she said. "I know you can't."

His shoulders slouched, his head bowed. When he spoke again, it was a voice that was cold. "More trickery. Can't tell us what to do anymore. Betray us eventually."

He was tensing, fighting something inside him, losing. She did not run.

"I know, I know," he whimpered. "And that's why we have to kill. Always kill. The others spoke of traitors, betrayal, they know. That's why they scream."

"You want to kill me."

He said nothing.

"Then go ahead." She threw her bow aside. "I won't fight you."

He spasmed, as though he had just swallowed a knife. He clutched at his head, trying to dig out whatever was going through it right now. The scream that burst from his lungs was something beyond his, beyond whatever voice he had spoken with before.

And when he turned to face her, his eyes were bereft of pupil, of white, of anything but a blue that froze over with fury.

"*KILL!*"

He hurled himself at her without purpose, nothing but hateful screaming and frenzied flailings. She looked into the eyes in his face, saw hate, vengeance.

265

And she did not run.

She merely stepped to the side.

He almost flew past her, would have if she hadn't caught him by the throat. Her forearm wrapped around his neck, pressed against his windpipe as she jerked back with a snarl.

He flailed, clawed at her arm, kicked wildly. He collapsed to his knees, drawing in sharp, rasping breaths that grew steadily weaker. But even so, the fury inside him didn't relent. Neither did she.

"Liar," he choked, "lied to me, said wouldn't fight."

"I won't fight *you*," she replied. Her forearm tightened around his windpipe, drew his head close against her in an intimate hatred. "But this isn't you. This is something else."

She pulled harder. He grew weaker, his body limper. The fight left him along with his breath.

"And if you can't fight it, Lenk," she said, "then I will."

When he hung limp in her arms, helpless and lifeless, she released him, easing him onto the sand. She turned him over gently and looked into his face. His face. Slack as it may be, it was his face with mouth hanging open, his eyes that were shut tight.

Him.

No one else.

Her ears pricked up at the sound of padding feet. Naxiaw emerged from the shadows, eyes steady, face calm. He looked at her, searching for something inside her. She looked back, offering nothing. Whatever he found, though, he nodded.

"That must have been difficult, sister," he said.

She looked down at Lenk. "He isn't dead. Not yet."

"I saw. You used the lion killer on him."

"It was supposed to be painless," she said, skulking over to collect her bow. "Maybe mercy is more respected in your tribe. The *s'na shict s'ha* have no use for it. We left it in our homes when we went to go cure the land of this disease."

"Uh huh."

He stared down at Lenk's unconscious body, studying it. "The way he fought, his eyes . . . I suppose it is the nature of the disease to mutate. Find an antidote for it, the disease becomes more resilient, virulent. This one . . . he is something I have not seen."

"He was a rare case."

"Was." Naxiaw slid his Spokesman stick into his hand. He raised it high above his head. "Turn away, sister. I wish you no more pain."

"Me either."

The air whistled. The sand crunched softly as the stick fell from his hands. It took a moment for him to realize what had happened. He still didn't understand when he saw the arrow shaft quivering in his leg. Not even when he looked up and saw her drawing another one, aiming it at him and releasing.

It struck him in the shoulder. Now he bled. Now he knew.

And he screamed.

"*INFECTED!*" he roared, clutching the arrow in his shoulder. "You're further gone than I thought, sister. Put the bow down before your cure becomes even more—"

"There is no cure, Naxiaw. Not for what happened to me." She spoke without a quaver in her voice as she calmly nocked another arrow. "And there's no such thing as no more pain. For anyone."

"So you intend to kill me," Naxiaw snarled, gesturing down at Lenk. "For *this*? For the thing that killed Inqalle? Your *sister*?"

"She wasn't mine," Kataria replied, drawing the arrow back. "I'm sorry she died for me. I'm sorry you bleed for me." She took aim. "I'm sorry, Naxiaw. You don't have to believe me. But I do."

"Think of what you're doing, sister. Think of what your tribesmen would say."

"What they've always said. What I never understood."

"They will hate you. They will *hunt* you."

"I know."

"They will *kill* you."

"That, too."

"Stop being so damn *calm* about it, then."

"I can't be angry. Not about this, no more than I can be angry about the dirt and the sky and the dead. This, what's happening here, is not something I can help. It simply is."

He snarled. "Do it, then. Kill me, as he killed Inqalle, as *you* kill Inqalle's memory."

"I don't want to. And I won't. Because you're going to leave."

"Leave?" He backed away, hunched over like a wounded animal. "Leave this unavenged? Leave my sister's body here?"

"No. You can take her body. You can come back and kill me someday. You can kill every human in the world and however many tulwar, couthi and other people it takes to make you happy."

She stepped over Lenk.

"But this one belongs to me."

267

What passed between them, as their eyes met and narrowed upon each other, was not the Howling. But it was something. Something that made him realize, made her stronger. And for the first moment since they had met, they understood one another.

He turned and stalked away, into the darkness. "Your father would hate you for this."

She lowered the arrow as he retreated. "And my mother?"

He did not answer. He was no longer there. He was somewhere far away, where shicts were. And she was not.

"Naxiaw?" she called into the darkness.

And it did not answer back.

TWENTY

GIBBERING, GIGGLING MESS

For a long time, Dreadaeleon did not look at either one of them. Denaos bore a scowl so fierce that the boy didn't dare risk having it turn on him. Asper's despair was so deep that he felt it might swallow him up if he even looked sideways at her. Fortunately, both their agonies were directed at the sight on the beach before them.

Still, it seemed like someone should say something.

"So, uh," he said, "that's bad, right?"

"In the grand scale of things?" Denaos asked, shaking his head. "Not so much."

"And in the immediate?"

"Yes, idiot, it's bad."

Like calling me names is going to help, Dreadaeleon thought resentfully. But he supposed there was little that would.

Their boat sat, snugly ensconced between two rocks, the sand beneath its rudder and its tail end only just brushing the water that had, this morning, been keeping it afloat. Like it was testing the water before it was ready to go and get them the hell out of here, Dreadaeleon thought.

Either way, there it was. Stuck in the rocks. And the water was *there*. Receded from the shoreline. There was little to do about it.

"Gods *damn* it!"

Except that.

"Hongwe, you scaly, slithering *idiot*."

And that.

"Why the hell wouldn't you *tell* us the tide was going out?" Denaos demanded of the lizardman standing beside them.

"You go to an island full of longfaces to rescue a friend that was probably dead. I thought you had enough to worry 'bout." He inclined his crested head to Asper. "Good that you're alive, though."

"Uh . . . thanks?" Asper replied.

"Then why wouldn't you move the boat?" Denaos asked, tone growing sharper.

"I *did*," Hongwe protested. "I moved it behind these rocks when I saw longfaces on the beach. The tide left before they did. It's not *my* fault." He thrust a scaly finger at Denaos. "*You* weren't supposed to take this long. 'In and out' you said, 'very quickly' you said."

"*I was trying to sound like I knew what I was doing*," he snarled. "I didn't actually *know* how we were going to do any of that."

"Then I'm not sure why you're upset that things aren't going as you didn't plan."

"I . . . but . . ." With words failing him, he turned to his second most tried-and-true method of conflict resolution. "You!" he barked, shoving Dreadaeleon fiercely. "*Fix it!*"

"How?" the boy asked.

"Magic it out. I don't know."

"I could try shoving it out, yes, but that would rip up the boat."

"Can you *lift* it out or something?" Asper asked.

Yes, absolutely, he thought. *I mean, it'll speed up the Decay in my body, make me die quickly, and I'll probably come spurting out of two or more orifices as I do, but at least it'll be more humane than sacrificing a stupid lizard for a magical gem of untold power and wonder that could actually, you know,* cure *me.*

"No," he said.

"Why not?"

He blinked and said with a straight face, "The flow of magic is just a hair too whimsical today."

She stared at him for a moment before sighing ruefully and looking away.

She believed that? I can't believe she's that dumb. Or does she just think that whimsy is something that would be a problem for you? Maybe she— He stopped himself, rubbing his temples. *Keep it together, old man. Netherlings all over the place. Now's not the time. You can still come out on top.*

How? he demanded to himself. *How can you possibly do something about this? You're drained. You're dying. And she's . . . she doesn't think anything of you. But him . . . him she thinks is just so . . . so . . .*

His temper flared inside him and he instantly felt wearier. Even thinking an outburst drained him. He rubbed his eyes and sighed.

The netherlings had to be halfway to Jaga by now, he reasoned. Little choice, then, he reasoned. He had to do something to get them off the island. There was a way, he knew, not a good one, but there were no good ways out of it. And so he chose the one that wouldn't end with him soiling himself.

Look, he thought, not to himself, *I know I called you some bad names and I said that about you earlier, but . . . if you're listening to this, I could use you right about now.*

He heard steel sliding out of a sheath. He heard Asper curse. He heard Hongwe mutter something reverent in his own language.

Greenhair had come faster than he expected.

He looked up and saw the siren rising out of the sea, striding out of the surf, the salt and her silk clinging to her pale body like a second skin. She wore a knowing look on her face as though she had been waiting for him all this time.

Like she knew *you were going to mess everything up, given enough time.*

"Do not chastise yourself unduly, lorekeeper," the siren replied liltingly.

Ah, right, she reads thoughts . . . or just mine?

"No."

"Then you probably know that you shouldn't come any closer," Dreadaeleon said, eyeing the dagger flashing in Denaos's hand, "at least until I can explain why you're here."

"Explain the presence of the woman who betrayed us and sold us to a bunch of longfaces who would eagerly finish the job if they knew we were fifty feet away from them?" Denaos flipped the blade in his hand, drew his arm back to hurl it. "Let me save you some time."

"*Wait!*" Dreadaeleon cried out.

He jumped up and wrapped his own scrawny arms about Denaos's, hanging from it with all his weight. Lamentably, he wondered if that would do any good.

"You can't kill her!" he cried out.

"I assure you I can," Denaos grunted in reply as he shook his arm and tried to dislodge the boy, "and with amazing efficiency and minimal mess, once you let go."

"She can help us!"

"Hold on," Asper said to Denaos before looking at Dreadaeleon. "All right, Dread, we're listening . . . how can she help us?"

"I . . . don't actually *know.*"

Asper nodded considerately. Then she looked to Denaos. "Just use your other hand."

"Lovely," the rogue quipped, flipping the blade to his free hand.

"The lorekeeper does not speak false," Greenhair replied, apparently not at all concerned about the fuss, or the knife, directed at her. "You are in need of much that I can grant."

"Such as something fleshy to sink this steel into?" Denaos asked. "I quite agree."

"Look," Dreadaeleon attempted to protest, "ordinarily, I'd agree, but we're on an island full of longfaces with a stuck boat and a bunch of *other* longfaces marching—"

"They're on boats."

"—sailing—"

"Oars."

"—*oaring* to kill our friends. Point being, options are limited."

"Options are never so limited that we have to deal with the monster that sold us to other monsters." The coldness of Asper's voice betrayed just how much fury she was trying to contain.

"Look, I know she—"

"No, Dread," she continued with a tempestuous calm, "you don't know. You can never know and I hope to whatever god watches over you that you don't ever have to know what she did to m—" She caught herself, bit her lower lip. "All you *need* to know is that she did something terrible, to all of us, and that if you try to stop Denaos, I'll try harder to stop you."

His reply was a gaping mouth and an expression both hurt and befuddled; somehow, he suspected that might not be enough to persuade either of them.

"You are unwise to make yourself deaf to the lorekeeper," Greenhair spoke from the surf. "You are not so out of options that you cannot yet avoid bargaining with me. But every moment you waste, the longfaces draw closer to that which they seek, the earth groans as something claws at it from below and the sea goes silent . . ."

She turned her distant gaze out to the waves, her voice a whisper that merged with the hiss of the surf. "It fears to speak, lest it interrupt. You cannot hear it, and I am grateful for that, but someone out there is singing a song that once filled blasphemous chorals. Someone out there is calling. And many, *many* are answering.

"Distrust me. Loathe me. Fill your head with images of my entrails on your hands. I do not blame you." She turned to them again and her face was cold porcelain. "But you won't forsake your companions. Not when fates rush to crush them. I have looked into your thoughts. I know it to be so."

The glares didn't dissipate. The tension didn't, either. But the knife slipped back in its sheath and Asper turned her cold stare away. Denaos muttered and shoved the boy off of him.

"Well, so long as you already *know* all of that, we can skip the part where we pretend not to need your help." He cast a sneer at her. "But, given that you can read thoughts, have a good look at this."

He narrowed his eyes on her, bit his lower lip, assumed a look of such concentration that it appeared he might pull something. She stared back, blinked, and then recoiled, aghast. He offered an ugly smile in reply.

"*Yeah*," he said with a black chuckle. "Just remember *that*."

"So, how exactly do you plan to get us out?" Asper asked.

"The tide is stubborn, set in its ways. I can coax it back, but only for a short moment. Not nearly long enough to let your vessel slide out naturally."

"So all our sliding will fall to the *unnatural*," Denaos said. He reached out, clapped Dreadaeleon on the shoulder. "You're up, boy."

Dreadaeleon felt something shift inside him and his cheeks filled. Trying to hold back the look of disgust, he swallowed the bile back down.

"Right," he gasped afterward, "just . . . just let me . . . you know."

"What? *Now?*" Denaos asked, incredulous.

"Now what?" Asper asked, slightly less so.

"*Nothing*," Dreadaeleon insisted.

"She might as well know," Denaos said. "I mean, she's *going* to."

"Know what?" Asper asked.

"That he's—"

"Did I not just stop you from killing the only woman that's going to get us off this island?" the boy snarled, cutting him off. "Have I *not* proved my vast, vast, *vast* intelligence by stopping you from doing something exceedingly stupid yet again? Do you think you can find enough comfort in my almost terrifyingly expanded mind to trust me when I say it's *nothing?*"

"Uh . . . I suppose . . . yes?" Denaos answered sheepishly.

"Fantastic. I'll be back in a moment."

A graceless exit, he knew as he tried to keep himself from bursting into a full sprint up the dune and behind a large rock. Yet it wasn't half as graceless as spewing out a pile of vomit that may or may not start moving of its own accord once it hit the ground. And his hasty retreat would bring about far fewer difficult-to-answer questions, anyway.

Such as why so much as a hard slap could make him feel like his body was crumbling beneath itself.

He fought to keep himself from collapsing, bent at the waist, hands on his knees, heaving into the dirt.

273

One good push, old man, that's all it'll take. Just a quick heave, a splash of bile, wave goodbye as it goes off to find its destiny, then you're fine. Well, you're dying, *yeah, but you're still fine in the immediate sense. And it's the right thing to do. Now the lizardmen are all nice and safe and you're dying and you should have told her, oh my Gods, you should have said something, should have used them, but she was so . . . so . . .*

Calm down. He smacked his lips, threw his esophagus into his throat. *Just go with it. Out with the bad, worry about the rest later. Just so long as you don't have to puke in front of two women at once. Once more now. Make it good.*

He tried again, heaving and heaving, forcing himself to retch. Nothing came of it but a lot of hot air and a thick, panting sound.

A *very* thick panting sound. One that persisted long after he held his breath.

One that steadily grew louder.

With the instinctive knowledge that he was being watched, he looked up slowly. No eyes stared back at him. But if tongues could stare, the big, pink thing quivering between two rows of giant, sharp teeth certainly would be.

To look at it, the thing's jaws seemed so terrifyingly huge as to have left no room for anything else, let alone eyes. A blunted, vaguely wolflike head squatted atop powerful shoulders from which long, muscular legs ending in curving claws dug into the sand. A long body ended in equally powerful haunches, a bushy tail slapping at the sand behind it as it stared at Dreadaeleon.

With its tongue.

The longface female, clad in black armor, her sword hefted up over her shoulder and staring at the boy with a morbid grin framed by white hair cropped cruelly short seemed almost a redundancy.

He took a step backward. The sand shifted under his feet.

The creature's mouth closed, head tilted curiously to the side. Six knife-shaped ears, three to either side of its great, eyeless skull, snapped open like a twitching, furry fan. Its blind gaze followed him as he continued to backpedal, as he stumbled once, as he turned around and ran.

"*ZAN QAI YUSH!*"

The first thing he heard was the netherling barking a command.

The second thing he heard was the crunch of sand beneath giant claws.

After that, all that remained was the beast as its jaws gaped and it loosed loud, long peals of laughter.

He came flying over the dune and down the sands a moment later—tumbling, really, like a bird whose leather, boneless wings couldn't lift it from the ground. Sputtering through sand and sick, he tried to shout a warning to his companions below as they cast confused stares up at him.

That didn't matter, for a moment later, his panic came rampaging over the ridge.

The sikkhun was not any more graceful than the wizard had been as it came crashing onto the slope of the dune and sliding down in a frenzied, gibbering mess. Of course, Dreadaeleon thought as he reached his companions, grace probably didn't count for a tremendous lot when nature compensated with teeth the size of fingers.

"Gods damn it," Denaos spat, "why the hell couldn't you have just *held* it?"

"I'm sorry! I didn't know!"

"How could you *not*?"

"Shut up and *move!*" Asper shouted.

The sikkhun came barreling forward with great, shrieking laughter as the companions scattered in every direction. Its head swung back and forth, ears wide and twitching as it tried to pick one, its grin as wide and toothsome as a child in a sweetshop, all but heedless of its rider jabbing her spurred boots into its flanks.

Only a swift, metal-handed blow to the back of the beast's head caused it to settle on a target. Its ears curved like a bell, its head swiveled, and amongst the many cries of alarm, it picked out the loudest. With a giggle and a flurry of sand, it took off.

After Asper's shrieking form.

The earth trembled under its great weight, the sand spat every which way as it tore itself across the beach after her, tongue lolling, rubbery lips peeled back in an excited smile. Only a moment before they snapped shut with a resounding clack of disappointment did Asper hurl herself out of its path. The rider cursed, her tremendous blade spitefully swinging and narrowly missing Asper's head as the priestess scrambled to her feet and tore off in the other direction.

All right, old man, this is it, Dreadaeleon told himself. *You almost let it out. It's do or die now. She might see you vomit, she might see you expel fire from your urethra, but she's in trouble. You've got to do something . . . as soon as you can get up, anyway.*

It was a bigger difficulty than it seemed. When he had hurled himself out of the beast's path, it felt like he left both his guts and his dignity behind. Breathing was a challenge, standing an ordeal. Being actually useful seemed an impossibility.

And yet as the beast circled about, gave another cackle as though this were a particularly fun game, and took off after Asper again, he knew he had to do *something.*

A minor spell, then, he told himself. *Something that won't seem beneficial, but will ultimately change the course of the battle. Yeah, then she'll think you're just so clever. That's it. Just think of something to confuse it . . . to baffle it. Like an illusion. That'll work . . . despite the fact it has no eyes son of a bitch, you're useless.*

"Will one of you morons *do something?*" Asper screeched as the beast closed in on her.

Damn it, old man, later. LATER. For now, something . . . anything! Think . . . the magic might kill you, but if you don't . . . He thumped his head. *Damn it, damn it,* damn it. *What would Denaos do?*

He got his answer as the rogue came running up to the beast's flank.

Oh.

He threw himself across the creature's back, nimbly scrambled up to take a seat behind the rider and wasted no time in bringing a dagger up to her throat. The rider interrupted the impromptu assassination with a quick jerk of her neck, smashing her skull into Denaos's face and sending him nearly toppling.

The dagger fell from his hand as he flailed to keep aright, grasping wildly at the female's neck before a firm elbow dislodged him and sent him rolling into the sundered wake of the sikkhun.

Ah, well there you go, that wouldn't have worked, anyway.

A small consolation that grew smaller as the beast closed in on Asper. She suddenly skidded to a halt, whirled around and extended her left hand out, as though she expected the beast to halt immediately . . . or explode at the sight of her palm?

Whatever it was she expected, it didn't happen. She thrust her right hand out, shaking it wildly at the creature. When it didn't bother to stop at that, either, she threw herself out of the way.

"*What the hell was that?*" Denaos screamed at her.

"*I don't know! It worked last time!*" she shrieked back, hopping to her feet and resuming to run.

The priestess turned sharply, wildly, trying to throw it off, but lost a little more distance each time.

And he watched on, helpless.

No, no, he thought. *NOT helpless. You can do something. Up. Get up! You can do this. You can do this, old man. You just need to think . . . thinking is hard with all this noise.* He rubbed his ears. *What is that? Is someone singing?*

Someone was.

Greenhair's lips barely moved, but a song too pure to be tainted by language flowed from her mouth into his ears. He instinctively reached up to clap his hands over them, remembering how such a song had put him under once. But this song flooded his skull like water, sent his brain bobbing gently. Thoughts flowed, coursed without pain. His bowels steadied themselves, strength returned to his legs and he found standing a less daunting task.

Lovely, he thought as the song filled his mind, his ears.

He blinked.

Ears.

He sighed.

You really are stupid, aren't you?

Asper turned sharply again, veering toward him. Calmly, he stepped in as she sped past him, walking directly into the beast's path. Its ears pricked up at the sound of his footsteps. Its mouth gaped with an excited cackle. It picked up speed, spurred on by its rider's snarling command.

He spoke a word. The electricity came painlessly, leaping to his fingers and dancing from tip to tip. He raised his hands to either side as the beast drew closer, ears brazen and fanned and quivering. It drew close enough that the sound of its laughter hurt his ears.

And then, as he brought his hands together in a clap, he returned the favor.

Electricity sparked, cobalt flashed, and the sound of his hands clapping became the sound of skies crashing with thunder. It echoed across the beach, drowning out song, screams, and laughter alike. The beast's wailing laughter dissipated into simple, feral wailing as scarlet plumes erupted from the creature's ears. They folded in on themselves and it began to swing its head wildly, the thunder lodged in its ears like a parasite it couldn't get rid of.

Dreadaeleon smiled broadly, closed his eyes and waited for Asper's cries of adoration and Denaos's begrudging admiration to reach him.

"*MOVE, IDIOT!*" the rogue cried out.

He didn't really care about the admiration, anyway.

"*DREAD, IT'S NOT STOPPING!*" Asper screamed.

He opened his eyes.

Not that it did him a lot of good. The world erupted in a bright light as something hard struck him in the belly. When he regained breath and sight, the world was moving sporadically beneath him as the sikkhun snarled and shook its head, trying to shake off a new, obnoxious passenger.

Its longfaced rider seemed to share its sentiments. Her snarl was twice as fierce as she pulled back her blade and swung it wildly, missing only due to the beast's own shifting, swiveling skull as they charged across the beach.

Dreadaeleon would have been alarmed. Dreadaeleon would have been terrified. He might even have been screaming if he hadn't found his mouth suddenly and unexpectedly full.

And then empty.

Vomit spilled out of his mouth and into the air like a glistening yellow-green kite. It splattered across the beast's shoulders, onto the rider's hands, into the rider's face. There was no disgust, only annoyance, and only for a moment.

After that, just pain.

The bile began to sizzle, steam, hiss angrily. Whatever it was that the Decay did to him it did to his humors and now did to them, turning acidic in a brief moment.

The sikkhun let out a shriek of agony and bucked hard, sending rider and wizard flying into the air. No sooner had Dreadaeleon struck the earth than he found hands on his arms, hauling him up and flinging him over a shoulder. Half-blind from pain, the siren's song left him, he groaned.

"Who? Denaos?"

"No," Asper replied as she hefted him like a particularly sickly sack of potatoes. "Sorry, but he's trying to move the boat."

"I saved you, you know."

"With vomit. I saw. Very impressive."

"You weren't supposed to see that part. Sorry."

"It's fine."

"I was supposed to be the—"

"Can you just shut up for now?" she asked. "Please?"

Just as well, he thought. The next word in that sentence was going to have been something he had digested earlier. That didn't make the indignity of being hoisted and shoved into the boat any more bearable, though. Denaos and Hongwe stood at the helm, oars in hand, shoving at the rocks, trying to dislodge them.

Greenhair's song lilted, the water rising about her ankles, coaxing the water to flow up to the boat as she had coaxed clarity through Dreadaeleon's mind.

She makes water move, he thought. *In the blood, in the mind, in the loins. That's how she does what she does. Good trick. I should ask her about that.* He glanced up at the beach. *Assuming that isn't what it looks like.*

It was.

The netherling was up, on her feet, at the side of her flailing mount. Its thrashing lasted only as long as it took her to bring her fist against the side of its head. A crack of bone, a shake of its jowls and it was smiling broadly as she hauled herself up onto its back.

Netherlings, in his brief experiences with them, were not renowned for possessing a vast panoply of emotional expression.

It all tended to be variations on rage, as was on her face now. But those had been natural rages, something they simply did. The fury twisting her face into a mass of scars and lines was something personal.

It spurred her, just as she spurred the beast forward into a headlong charge. And it came, in a shrieking, warbling, cackling ball of bone and blood and fur.

"She looks angry," he said.

"They all look angry," Denaos said between grunts.

"I mean *really* angry." It was at that moment he noticed something wrapped around the rogue's hand: a chunk of stone hanging from a chain. "What's that?"

"I grabbed it when she threw me off," he replied.

"Well, give it back!"

"*It doesn't work that way!*"

"Will you just push harder?" Asper demanded, huddling defensively behind the rails of the boat. "She's getting closer!"

"Why is it all on me?" Denaos snarled, shoving violently. "Why can't your sea-tramp sing harder?"

The earth exploded under the sikkhun's feet, the sun refused to shine off the massive blade held high above the netherling's head. Teeth, claws, and a tremendous wedge of metal grew ever closer.

And yet, that seemed not quite so important to Dreadaeleon anymore.

His head hurt.

Or at least, it started as just a hurt. Pain became searing in but a few moments, blinding in another few. Too much pain to be from any cause within him, even as strong as the Decay was. It was magic.

A lot of it.

Coming very close.

Very quickly.

Just like the shadow that had appeared over the netherling and was growing immense.

Just moments before the entire beach exploded in fire.

Something struck the earth hard, scorched the sand into smoldering, blackened clumps as the impact sent it flying through the air like offal from a volcano's craw. The impact sent the boat flying from the rocks and into the sea amidst a hail of black and red, between curtains of steam as the fiery debris crashed into the water.

Through the veils of rising vapor, over the sides of the vessel, Dreadaeleon peered. He saw the corpses first. One of them was the netherling, the other was the sikkhun. Both had been splintered and blackened beyond recognition and lay smoldering amidst the fields of fire that stained the beach.

Against the carnage, the figure was scarcely noticeable: a scarecrow of a shadow rising against the flames, looking as though he might be consumed by them at any moment. But as Dreadaeleon stared at him, at the rounded head, at the familiar coat, at the red, burning eyes, he felt the pang of familiarity.

"Bralston?"

Followed shortly by the pang of terror.

The blood painting the man's face and neck were unmistakable, even blackened and steaming as they were. The crimson power burning through his eyes was as bright and vivid as the fires burning around him. The electricity dancing at his fingertips, the thrust of his fingers, the gape of his mouth—

"*GET DOWN!*" he screamed.

It was hard to tell which was worse: the thunderous cackle of the lightning bolt shearing overhead as they hit the deck of the boat or the cry of rage that tore itself from Bralston's throat that guided it. Dreadaeleon was more inclined to think the former, given that it twisted and lashed the boat, cracking off shards and tearing out splinters as it wildly thrashed about like a living thing.

It dissipated after a long time, too long for it to have been normal. The air smelled torched and the latent electric chuckles in the sky stung at the boy as he peered up. Bralston stared back, murder in his eyes, and soon to be on his lips and springing from his hands.

"What the hell was that?" Denaos demanded. "Even for a wizard, that was insane!"

"There's no words," Dreadaeleon muttered. "No gestures. He's just screaming. His Venarie isn't being guided at all, it's just sort of . . ." He made an all-encompassing gesture. *"This."*

"Meaning?"

"Meaning row until you *puke*, idiot, he's about to cast again!"

The rogue and lizardman began to paddle furiously, shoving their tiny vessel farther and farther away. They hadn't even come to vomiting when Bralston opened his mouth once more and screamed.

His voice came with ice, a deluge of frost that lay over the sea like a blanket and froze the water beneath it. A serpentine trail writhed across the surface of the sea, chasing the pitifully slow vessel. That itself wasn't much concern, Dreadaeleon noted.

The fact that Bralston was raising his foot over it, was.

It came down with a crash of thunder and the ice shattered. The sheets of frost broke and clashed against each other, great white spikes bursting up, following the bridge of frost that was now forming beneath the vessel itself.

The gesture was instinctive, the word seemed perfectly natural. Dreadaeleon thrust his fingers at a downward angle and spoke aloud. The cobalt electricity sprang to life and danced from digits to water. A tiny blue worm against the great serpent of frost, it charged across the water, bursting to crackling life as it struck the impending wall of jagged ice and splitting it in twain.

The pain that followed was not natural, collapsing to his rear end was not instinctive, but he couldn't help either. Asper caught him, eased him down, though neither her eyes nor his ever left the smoldering shore.

"Faster, faster," Dreadaeleon urged, "oar faster."

Bralston's bloodied mouth gaped. His eyes went ablaze. But in the instant he turned about and noticed them, so did Dreadaeleon.

"AKH ZEKH LAKH!"

Their war cries were audible even so far from the shore. Black against the fire, the longfaces came barreling through, undeterred by flame or fear. Blades aloft, they rushed the lone figure on the shore standing over the charred corpse of their companion, without fear, without hesitation.

And, very soon after, without skin. Bralston's fire leapt from his hands, raked those closest to him. He twisted, turned the jets of flame pouring from his palms as he turned his feral yell upon them. They continued to come, they continued to die, he continued to howl.

That would stall him for a time.

Hopefully long enough to prepare for a future as ashes and spit.

"What was he doing?" Asper asked. "He was on *our* side yesterday."

"He didn't look well. And he certainly wasn't acting well," Dreadaeleon replied. "He was using power like it was nothing. He'll burn himself up before the day's out if he keeps doing that."

"Something must have happened to him to make him do that, right?"

"Whatever it was that made him bleed like that, yeah."

As if by suspicion, or perhaps instinct, eyes turned slowly to Denaos. The rogue was already staring at them, as though expecting such silent accusations. And, just as easily, he pointed a finger at them.

"Racists."

"Racist against whom?" Asper asked.

"What did you do back there?" Dreadaeleon pressed, suspect. "Back on Teji?"

"What makes you think *I* did anything?" Denaos demanded, offended. "Are there really not enough things trying to kill people that you automatically think *I* did something?"

Asper looked somewhat disappointed. "He has a point."

"Besides, you're missing the important bit," Denaos said. "I'm coming to appreciate just how unique a problem this is to *us*, but we've got bigger concerns than the screaming lunatic wizard who sets the earth on fire."

"*He speaks true,*" a voice lilted from the water. Somewhere, within the current, Greenhair spoke. Somewhere, beneath them, she began to guide their vessel forward. "*The longfaces go to Jaga, just as Jaga begins to stir. Your friends are poised to be crushed between fates.*"

She's saying that just to get them to believe her, Dreadaeleon thought. *She's not concerned about us . . . oh, damn, thought-reading. Uh . . . uh . . . bat guano!*

If the errant thought fazed Greenhair, she didn't say anything. The water moved like a living thing, a sea of blue and white hands that slowly tossed their vessel from grip to grip. Denaos and Hongwe released the oars, unable to resist the artificial tide.

"Sheraptus . . ." Asper whispered. "He's gone to Jaga, too?"

"It'd be a safe bet," Denaos said. He fixed eyes on Asper, his fingers twitched. "Look, there might be another—"

"There isn't," the priestess replied. "Lenk and the others are there. We have to try to warn them, at least."

"'Try' is a good word for it," Hongwe muttered. "The Shen rule Jaga. They aren't going to care about what you want to do. If you can even find it, they'll bury you there."

"*Water heeds no rule,*" Greenhair burbled from below, "*there are other ways in.*"

Note that she didn't say anything about the burying part, Dreadaeleon thought. *Or anything about that whole 'Jaga begins to stir' thing. She's not telling us something . . . and that something is probably going to kill us.*

It was hard to panic at that thought. Between that something in it, the invading longface army sailing to it, and the bloodthirsty lizardmen already on it, Jaga was looking like a pleasing prospect.

The chances of him dying before the Decay could get him were increasing.

Small comfort.

Growing smaller.

TWENTY-ONE

STARLIGHT AND SHADOW

He called it a man.

There might have been better words for what he stared at, but they were words that he didn't know or that had not been created yet. But while he called the thing that sat in the darkness across from him with crossed legs and palms upon his knees a man, it was more than that.

His eyes were nebulous and fluid, a river of blue that flowed through like a living thing, drowning pupil, drowning white. It was the only movement from the man. He did not breathe.

There was much wrong with him, Lenk thought, enough that he shouldn't be called a man. And yet, Lenk had to call him a man. For, save the eyes, he looked exactly like Lenk did.

And Lenk knew his name.

"You," he said.

The man did not speak.

"I think I've finally figured out how you work." He cleared his throat. "To a point, anyway."

The man listened.

Lenk made a gesture like he was about to strangle whatever he was about to say. "See, I *think* you're just one big hallucination . . . or something. You're something in my head, that much is obvious, and you twist things so I see them as you do."

The man stared.

"So, these things that you tell me don't *really* happen. I make them happen because *you* make me make them. You take my emotions and . . . twist them, somehow, into something worse than they are. You made me think Kataria would try to kill me. You are a lie."

The man spoke.

"*No.*"

"Then what are you?"

"*Important.*"

Lenk rubbed his eyes, sighed into the darkness. "I can't do this anymore."

"*What?*"

"The threats, the commands, the cryptic mutterings . . . I can't. I don't want to." He met the man's stare. He did not blink. "I'm not going to. Not anymore."

The man blinked. Behind him, a horror of fire was born in the darkness. Images of burning farmhouses and corpses falling beneath wandering shadows flickered like shadows cast by a candle. They shifted to dark chambers, dark waters, and six golden eyes peering out from bloodstained liquid voids. They shifted to a distant figure staring with forlorn green eyes before fading behind a veil of fire.

All moments he should have died.

All moments he was saved thanks to the man in front of him.

"*You would be dead without me. I saved you, I preserved you, I kept you from falling into the shadow.*"

"And at what cost?"

"*Do not pretend to be confused. You call cryptic that which is obvious, you deny that which is inevitable. You know that without me, you will die. Your hand, her hand, someone else's hand; it does not matter. You will die. I cannot allow that. There is no choice.*"

"You say that, but . . ."

Lenk faltered a moment as the man's eyes intensified. A cold fire smoldered behind his stare, too bright to be drowned. It burned through the darkness, brighter than even the flames roaring silently behind him. It forced itself upon Lenk, sought to bow his head, to break him.

It did not.

He did not.

"You couldn't make me do it."

"*What?*"

"I heard you. I heard every word you said. I had the sword in my hand, above her head." He tried to feel the weight of it in the darkness. "She wasn't moving. You were screaming at me, along with the other voices, and I could . . . I could understand it, but . . ."

He looked up at the man. He looked into his burning, flowing, bright-blue eyes. He smiled as though he were pleased.

"With everything, all of what I felt and all of what you told me, you couldn't make me kill her."

The man's eyes widened. They grew wide enough to see further, to see into the future, to see the words that would fall from Lenk's lips only a moment later on a breathless sigh that had been held in for years.

"You can't control me."

"*Don't.*"

"You have no power."

"*You need me.*"

"You can't do anything."

"*She will kill you.*"

"To her."

"*They will kill you.*"

"To me."

"*You can't just—*"

"To anyone."

"*WE STILL HAVE TO—*"

"No."

"*LISTEN—*"

"No more."

There was darkness.

There were better words for what it was, that profound emptiness that is left behind when something great and terrible is gone. There may never be such a word created for what he felt when he stared at the space where the man had sat before the flames and the shadow. But he called it darkness.

And he fell into it.

A shadow.

Light.

And then another.

First one, and then the other, in an endless, silent tide. They circled beneath the light, chasing each other with no particular hurry. Their wings were water, black flesh that rippled with silver light as they wove their way between the stars peering through a hole in the world.

Somewhere in the chasm, the earth had opened up overhead. It had let just a hair too much light in for the kelp and coral to be comfortable and they shied from it, lurking in the shadows, while the stars overhead peered through, watching what he watched, watching the two rays circle each other overhead with no particular care for what he did or if he ever rose from the sandy grave upon which he lay.

For some time, neither did he.

And so he lay there, as he had lain there since he had awoken. It wasn't that he couldn't rise. He felt light, unbearably so, as though he might be carried away with whatever tide wasn't there that carried the rays so effortlessly through the starshine.

But standing seemed a daunting prospect.

"You can get up now."

Daunting as it was, though, he looked up from the sand, stared past his chest, past his stomach, between his feet. She sat not far away, beneath the stare of the stars, beneath the envy of a frond of wafting, purple kelp.

Light and shadow painted her. The naked skin of her shoulders glowed silver against the light, twisting against the black bands encircling her, spitefully chasing the starlight away as the starlight chased it, in turn.

Like the rays.

He could see her eyes. They were bright and green, like a thing that shouldn't be growing down here in the dark. They weren't looking at him. She stared at the sand. Her ears twitched, she pointed to them.

"It's how I know," she said. "You breathe differently when you sleep and when you're awake. I can hear it." She smiled sadly. "I know that about you."

He came to his feet. It was hard. The earth kept moving beneath him and the sky was going the opposite way overhead. He stood between them, trying to keep his balance, trying not to get dizzy as he stared at her and her shadows and her light.

"Is that you in there?" She tapped her temple.

"Yeah," he said. His words felt too light on his lips, like he knew he would need the breath he was giving away for them.

She nodded.

"Are you afraid?" he asked.

She nodded.

"Do you believe me?"

She looked at him now. Her eyes flashed, stared past him, through him, around him. The color was too much, too bright, too vivid, too full of . . . something. It threw him, upset the balance of light and black. He swayed, did not fall.

He stared back.

Did not blink.

"I shot my brother," she said. "I stepped over my sister's body." She turned back to the sand.

"For me?"

"*Not* for you. Not entirely. They were something I wasn't. You were when I realized it."

"Why?" He felt a pain in his neck, the question hurt to speak.

She shook her head.

"You're all I have left."

The pain grew sharper, twisted in his throat at the question he dreaded to ask, the answer he was terrified to hear.

"What if that's a mistake?"

She looked at him. Her eyes were no less bright as they hardened.

She rose. She stood before him. The stars painted shifting stripes across her face, turned it into a mask of silver and black. Her hair drifted in a breeze that wasn't there, licking against the lobes of her ears, sending them twitching.

Her belly rose and fell with each breath. The shadows moved with her, tracing the contours of her muscle, drawing a circle of perfect pitch about her navel. The finer hairs of her body shone translucent beneath the silver, alight where the shadow's hands did not slide across her belly as it rose, gently; fell, gently.

She breathed. She lived. Her body moved as the earth moved and the sky moved and the world moved and everything moved around him.

Except her eyes.

So he stared into them. And he clung to them to keep from falling.

"Then I'll keep beating you unconscious until it isn't," she said.

She stood there. Her body trembled. Her eyes did not. She waited for him to do something. For him to fall dead at her feet. For him to kill her instead. For him to turn away and leave and fade into something else entirely.

The silence hurt his ears. There was something in his mind, something he had trouble hearing. It had no words. It had no language.

He stepped forward, just to hear the sand crunch beneath his feet. And at that moment, the world moved a little too much one way, the sky too much the other. He fell.

And he felt her as she caught him. He felt the shudder of her breath against his chest. He felt the chill of her shadows slithering over him.

"I'm tired," he whispered. "I am . . . very tired."

And she could feel it. She felt the groan of muscles that struggled to keep him on his feet. She felt the murmur of a heart in his chest flowing warm and weary in his chest.

"You need to rest," she whispered.

"I need . . ."

She could hear his voice. She could hear a quaver that wasn't there anymore. She could hear a sigh that was on every breath.

"I need . . ."

She could hear his body. She heard the slide of flesh as his arm wrapped around her. She heard the desperation in his grip as his hand pressed against the naked small of her back. She heard the crunch of cloth as he pressed her belly against his.

"I . . ."

No more voices.

No more language.

He leaned into her to keep from falling, pressed his lips against hers to keep from being carried away.

Nothing was left to hear.

She felt him now.

She could taste the desperation in his lips, the urgency that dripped off his tongue and onto hers. She could feel him, every part of him, everything that was left of him. In the grasp of his hand around her wrist, in the tension of muscle and the coarseness of his tunic against her belly, in the low, urgent growl that slid from his mouth into hers.

And as he poured everything he had left into her, he fell. His knees gave way beneath him and he clung to her as he slid to the sands, arms wrapped about her waist, face pressed against her skin. He clung as though there was not enough of him left to keep him on the dirt and keep him from drifting away on a tidal sky.

She said something. Something to herself, something to him, something hateful, something teary. Maybe. Maybe she said nothing. Maybe he should say something. If he had a voice anymore, he might have. If she had one, she might have.

All her language now was in her body. The protest of fine hairs standing on end in the wake of his tongue, the whisper of muscle in her stomach as it yielded to his lips, the howl in her fingers as he felt them tangle into his hair and pull.

She had no voice to make a sound. No more words. No more curses. Not so much as a moan. The slightest escape of air between lips barely parted. The world above was too far away to hear. The world below was silent as the darkness it held. There was no sound. There were no voices.

Lenk liked that.

His fingers found themselves trembling over her belt buckle. It was too complex for him now. He pulled on it, tore it free, let the leather hang limply about her waist. His fingers found the space between her skin and breeches and he pulled.

She slid out of them, watched them pool about her ankles. Maybe it was them that caused her to fall, to feel the grit of sand upon the skin of her buttocks. Maybe it was him. No use for words. She had none left.

He pulled himself on top of her, felt her hands at his belt, felt his trousers sliding from his legs. He felt her beneath his hips. He felt her thighs pressing against his. He felt her nails sinking past his tunic, into the skin of his shoulders.

He made not a sound.

She barely even breathed.

No words.

No voices.

No people.

Nothing but a shifting of shadow and stars above as he leaned into her.

She felt the breath inside her, the sudden rush of air as her mouth fell open. She saw the flash of her teeth in his eyes as he stared at her. She felt her ears flatten themselves against her head, bury themselves in the locks of her hair, pressing so hard, trembling so fiercely they hurt.

He felt the shudder of her body against his hips, the hairs on her skin stand up and reach out to the ones on his. He felt the clench of his jaw as he strove to keep back a word that had no place down here. He felt himself close his eyes and felt the shadows washing over him.

She felt the blood blossom beneath her nails.

He felt the sand rub beneath her buttocks.

She felt the agony inside him, the muscle of his abdomen contracting so hard it hurt to have it pressed against her.

He felt the scream inside her, the snarl broiling behind her lips as she leaned up and caught his in her teeth, the blood beneath her canines.

She felt the hardness of his stare as he opened his eyes and met hers.

He felt the ferocity of her embrace as she pulled him closer onto her, wrapped her thighs about him, pressed the soft flesh of her neck into the sloping curve of his shoulder.

Her gasp.

His breath.

Her hair.

His blood.

Everything they had.

With no more voices.

With no more people.

There was only shadow.

And the world moving beneath them.

ACT THREE

TEARS UPON THE PROUD, DEAD EARTH

TWENTY-TWO

THE DEAD TALK
TO THE DEAD

"**A**re you asleep?"

"Yes," Lenk replied.

"Are you dreaming?"

"Mm."

"About what?"

"Nothing," he said through a yawn. "Nothing at all."

"That doesn't sound very good."

"No, it's nice. I can't see any fire. I can't hear any voices."

"Should I let you sleep, then?"

"I think I'd prefer being awake."

"No, you wouldn't."

He opened his eyes at that. Kataria lay next to him, her arm coiled protectively around his neck. Her eyes were closed, her body rose and fell with quiet breaths, growling in a dream as he moved beneath her. Unstirring. Unwaking.

The starlight was gone. The dim glow of the kelp had become dimmer, leaving only a vague imagination of what light was supposed to be like. Lenk stared into the shadows of the chasm. Out of the corner of his eye, something slithered away, retreating into the darkness.

"Go back to sleep," something whispered, somewhere down there.

He blinked. Tears stung at his eyes. The air was thick and lay across his bare chest like a blanket. Even if he could convince himself that this was simply part of a dream, the sensation of gritty sand clawing its way between the flesh of his buttocks was distinctly waking.

For a moment, he wondered if he ought not to just go back to sleep. He wondered if he should lay there, with her body pressed against him, with her scent still cloying his nostrils, and cling to it as though it were a dream.

He was still wondering that as he rose to his feet, but only until he found his trousers. After that moment, even though he wondered why exactly he felt compelled to follow the voice into the darkness, he knew that he would feel better if he went into the unknown wearing pants.

Shadows consumed everything as he descended. Sound went first, so that even the crunching of his feet on the sand was inaudible. Light was next, the purple glow eaten alive. And then he, too, felt as though he were disappearing into the darkness as it ate everything.

Or almost everything.

Somewhere, incredibly distant and far too close, there was the noise of something sliding across the sand. In glimpses, he caught the reflections of light that wasn't there against something slick and glistening.

Something was down here with him.

He wondered if that weren't a good enough reason to turn around.

He didn't. He had to keep going. To protect Kataria, to find a way out of the chasm. He had a whole slew of reasons he didn't believe. Perhaps it was just primitive, mothlike stupidity that drew him toward the light.

That light. That tiny little blue pinprick at the very end of his vision that grew steadily brighter as he approached it. He felt compelled to follow it.

After all, it was talking to him.

"I didn't mean to wake you," it said from somewhere far away.

"It's fine."

"It's harder to hear you. You were loud before, but now . . . sorry. Could you hear me? Up there?"

It was no more than a whisper, faint like a fish's breath. And because it was so faint, he knew it. He had heard it before. The light grew bigger, not brighter, as he drew closer.

"Yeah," he said. "Clearly. You tried to warn me."

"You seemed afraid. I thought I should try to warn you. Did she kill you? Are you dead right now?"

"I'm talking to you, aren't I?"

"That doesn't tell me anything. We always talk, even when we're dead. And when we're dead, we do nothing but talk."

"Oh," he replied. "Then, no. I'm alive."

"That's good."

A great fragment of rock was all that stood between him and the light, something immense and jagged that had been of something even more immense and less jagged. The glow spilled out around it, a blue light that bloomed expectantly.

He had occasionally had cause to doubt the interest of the Gods in the affairs of men before. Here was proof, this single opportunity that Khetashe gave him to turn around from the disembodied voice in the darkness and return to a warm, naked body in the sand.

He had only himself to blame, he knew, as he rounded the stone and beheld the girl.

A girl.

A very young girl.

Despite the gray of her hair and the sword in her hand, she couldn't have been more than fifteen years. At least not past the age where people stop being a mess of angles and acne and crooked grins that they think look good and start being humans. She had such a grin, a big, bright one full of teeth situated directly between big, blue eyes and a big, black line opening up her throat.

It was the grin that unnerved him. More than the spear jutting through her chest and pinning her to the black shape behind her, more than the sheet of ice that encased her like a luminescent coffin, the fact that she was still smiling as though she might ask him to go pick flowers at any moment made him want to look away.

He still wasn't sure why he didn't.

"Don't stare," she chided. "It's rude."

"Sorry," he said.

Her smile didn't diminish. Her eyes didn't waver, the blue glow from them remained steady. She didn't even look at him. Yet there was something, a crackle in the ice, a strain at the edge of her grin, that made him turn away.

"Do you have a name?" he asked.

"No."

"Oh. Well, I'm—"

"I know."

He was aware that he was staring again. As it happened, *not* staring at a talking dead girl was somewhat more difficult than he anticipated. He cleared his throat, forcing his eyes away again.

"Sorry, I just thought you'd be older."

"I am very old," she replied.

"Less dead, then."

Though, there was little reason why he *should* expect her to be that. The last one he met was even more dead than this one.

The image flashed into his mind. A man encased in ice in a cold, dark place, corpses entombed with him, arrows jutting from his body, eyes wide, mouth open and screaming. He thought of it for only a moment, the thought too unnerving for anything more.

"I remember him," the girl said before he could.

He cringed. Not that it was all that surprising that she could see what was happening in his head, but having people in his mind was something he

295

had vowed to never get used to. She noticed this . . . or he assumed she did. It was hard to tell with her face frozen in that grin.

"He talks to me," she said.

"The man in the ice?"

"Him, too. We all talk to each other, through him. We could hear you through him, but faintly. You keep yelling at him. He doesn't like that."

He didn't ask. He didn't want to. But he knew all the same. The voice was gone, the chill that came with it was gone, but their absence left a place dark and cold inside him. He could feel her voice in there, and between the echoes, he could hear—

He tried not to think about it. Tried not to think at all. It was harder than it sounded with all the silence.

"Ask me."

Her voice jarred him from his internal stupor. He stared up into her broad grin. She stared through him.

"Ask me," she repeated.

"I don't want to," he said.

"I know. Ask me, anyway."

A voice telling him what to do would have been simpler, he thought. He could just say he had no choice, had to do what it said. But it was him that stared at her, the dead girl that talked, him that sighed, him that spoke.

"What are you?"

"No."

"What?"

"That's the wrong question. Ask the right one," she urged.

"What do you want?"

She looked unsettled at that. He wasn't quite sure how he could tell that, what with her grin unchanging and eyes unblinking. But the silence was too deep, lasted too long.

"I wanted you to come visit me," she said softly. "I wanted you to survive."

"And that's why you've been screaming in my head? All of you?" Ire crept into his voice. "You were screaming so loud I wanted to smash my head open."

"I know. I heard that part."

"Then why didn't you *stop*?"

"We . . . it's hard to hear down here. Everything is muffled. It's so dark. There's nothing but dark down here and I . . ." There was pain in her voice, pain older than she was. "We can't hear each other. We can speak, but we can't hear. But you . . . I could . . . we could hear you. We wanted you to be safe. We wanted to talk to you."

"So you've been slowly driving me insane with whispering so we could have a conversation? That's insane!"

"*NO!*"

Her voice cracked the ice, sent veins of white webbing across the face of her tomb. Her grin remained frozen, but the voice echoing from inside her mouth didn't belong in a human being, let alone a girl.

But she was neither.

"*Don't call us that! Don't say that!*" she howled in a voice not her own. "*They looked at us that way! They called us that for being what we are! Better than they are!* BETTER! *They betrayed us! We fought back and they called us insane and they* killed *us for it! We never wanted this!* NEVER!"

He hadn't ever said the words, not those words, not as she had spoken them. But they were known to him. The anger behind them was his, the hurt bleeding from them was his, the fury, the hatred, the cold . . .

That voice had spoken in him. It had coursed through his mind as surely as it coursed through her mouth, with all its cold anger.

He didn't have to ask what she was now. He knew by that voice. She was like him, like the man in the ice had been, like the voices in his head. He knew. He didn't want to know.

It had been the wrong question.

The cracks in the ice receded suddenly, solidifying into a solid, translucent coffin once more. Her grin was unchanged.

"Sorry," she whimpered. "He gets loud sometimes. I can't stop him from doing . . . that."

"Neither could I. It's all right."

"It's not all right. He's angry with you. He's worried about you. He thinks you're going to kill yourself."

"I'm not."

"You are. I know why you're here. I know what you're after. He told me. We came here to find her, just like you did."

"Her?"

The girl's eyes widened a hair's breadth. The light beaming from her stare grew, chasing away the darkness and bathing the chasm in a soft blue illumination. Lenk's eyes widened, too, without light, without glow, without anything beyond horror dawning on his face.

The walls of the chasm were glistening.

The walls were moving.

The walls were alive.

They writhed, twisting over each other, bunching up as if shy and recoiling from him before deigning to twist about and display an under-

297

side covered in quivering, circular suckers blowing mucus-slick kisses at him.

Tentacles. In many different sizes. Dozens of them, reaching around the wall and coiling about each other like some slick, rubbery bouquet of flowers. They reached, they groped, they searched, they sought.

Not for him. They seemed to take no notice of him at all, slithering blindly about the stone, slapping the sand, some as big as trees. Something caught his eye, a flash of pale ivory amidst the coils. Stupid as he knew it to be, he leaned forward, squinting, trying to make out what he thought to be a tiny spot of something pale, white, soft . . .

Flesh?

He raised a hand out of instinct, not at all intending to actually touch it. But as his fingers drifted just a bit closer, the tentacles shifted, split apart and with a slick sucking sound, something lashed out and seized him by the wrist.

It came with such gentleness that the thought to pull back didn't even occur to him. Pale fingers groped blindly down his wrist to find his fingers. An arm, perfectly pale, perfectly slender, blossomed from the tentacles, reaching for him with tender desperation.

It sought him, searched his flesh, taking each of his digits between two slender fingers and feeling each of his knucklebones in turn, sliding up and down between white fingertips. It was as though this was something it had never felt before, this touch of a human.

"She is reaching out," the girl said from behind him. "Her children are calling to her. She claws against that dark place where we put her, trying to escape. But she can't escape, not yet. She can't see. She can only barely hear. So she reaches, and she searches for something to touch."

He knew. Not by touch, but by the warmth behind her fingertips. The warmth he felt on his brow, in his mind, in his body. The warmth that had engulfed him, told him that he deserved happiness, that gave him his life.

He knew her touch.

He knew Ulbecetonth.

And she knew him. How, he wasn't sure, but her hand tightened. Her nails dug into the skin of his wrist, clenched him as though she sought to pull him into whatever moist hell she reached from.

As the shadow fell over him, he realized her goal wasn't to pull him in, but merely to hold him. All the better for the giant tentacle swaying overhead to crush him.

He leapt backward, leaving his skin and blood staining her nails. The tentacle came smashing down, shaking the walls and sending its fellows writhing angrily. More reached out, wrapped around his ankles, tried to pull him back. He beat wildly at them, seizing a sharp fragment of coral and jamming it into the soft flesh of the tentacle. It didn't so much as quiver. Only with great pain did he pull his leg free and scramble away from the tentacle.

He stalked back toward the girl, rubbing his wrist as Ulbecetonth's slender arm slipped back between the mass of flesh, disappearing.

"And why . . . is she here?" he asked.

"Right question," the girl said. "This is not an island. This is a prison."

His eyes grew wide. Jaga held Ulbecetonth. And somewhere on the island, the Shen held the key to her cell. But for what? To release her? Did they even *know* what they had?

"She's . . . coming closer." He turned back to the girl. "You called me down here to warn me."

The girl grinned.

"To warn you, to talk to you, to beg you," she said.

"What for?"

"Not to die."

"That's kind of out of my hands."

"It is not. Ulbecetonth is coming. The walls between her world and ours are weakened, she's scratched them so thin. She is coming. And she knows you are here. She hates you. She will kill you. You can survive." Her voice grew soft, fearful of itself. "If you let him back in."

"No."

"He can save you."

"It's not a *he.* It's an *it.* An it that tried to make me kill my friends, filled my head with . . . with something horrifying."

"To protect you. He only wants you to live. Your flesh is too weak."

"It's been strong enough so far."

"It has not. You didn't hurt the tentacle, did you? You couldn't hurt her."

"That's not—"

"And you never could. *He* hurt the demons. *He* killed the Abysmyths, through you. Without him, you will die. And not by her hand."

"What do you mean?"

"Look at your shoulder."

He did. Even the unearthly blue light was not enough to mask the sickly coloration of glistening pink and blackening flesh from where he had attempted to cauterize his own wound. An infection, thriving.

"It was . . . it was fine earlier!" he said. "I didn't even feel it."

"He mended it. He kept you whole." Her voice quaked, something else seeping in. "But you sent him away. You may not even survive long enough for Ulbecetonth to have a chance to kill you."

"Then I'll find the tome first, keep it from happening. They need that to summon her, right?"

The girl said nothing.

"Or . . . if worst comes to worst, I'll just . . . *leave*. I'll go somewhere else."

"You had the chance to do that. You had a dozen chances to do that. You could do that right now, but you won't."

"*He* doesn't command me! Neither do you!"

"No," the girl said. "Neither of us. But you're still here. You know what Ulbecetonth will do when she returns. You've seen what her children do without her. You could leave, you could leave it all, you could watch everything drown."

He said nothing.

"But you won't," she said. "And you won't survive without him."

"I don't believe in fate."

"Fate and inevitability are not the same things."

"I don't believe in that, either."

"Very hard to lie to someone who can look into your head." Her sigh sent a cloud of fog across the face of her tomb. "Go, Lenk. The chasm ends soon, rises up to the place you need to be if you follow it. But you know you won't get far without him."

He stared at her. She stared through him. He glared. She grinned. He sighed, turned on his heel. He had taken two steps before he paused and asked without looking back.

"Who is he?"

She said nothing for a moment. When she spoke, her voice trembled.

"If you really want to know . . . ask me again. And I'll tell you."

He did not ask.

He walked away.

Trying to ignore the pain in his shoulder and the light that chased him.

TWENTY-THREE

THE FADING LIGHT
OF DAY

"**W**ill you just wait up?" Kataria called after him from far away.

He wouldn't, so he didn't bother to call back "no" this time. He kept going, jogging through the chasm. Admittedly, he should be nicer to her given that her scent was still all over him, but he trusted she would understand why he wanted to leave a dark, brooding chasm in which he had nearly died and then spoken to a dead girl.

Of course, he hadn't told her that last part.

So she hadn't understood when she awoke and found him hurriedly dressing, taking a quick swig of water, finishing up the remains of a fish they had managed to catch, and telling her to come with him. Nor did she seem to understand now as they leapt over rock and coral, over skeletal hand and rusted sword, hurrying farther into the darkness with no end in sight.

He would explain later, he told himself, when they got out of the chasm.

Explain the dead girl living in a block of ice in a room filled with tentacles as she spoke of how a demon queen from beyond hell was bursting out from her prison and the only way to stop her was to bring back the voice in his head that apparently had a gender and other people he occasionally took up residences in so that his shoulder didn't rot off and kill him first.

Or maybe he'd just tell her he needed some fresh air.

That would be good, too.

Of course, before any of that could happen, he had to find the way out. The girl had said to follow the chasm and that's what he had done.

He came to a halt, casting a stare up and down the chasm.

But which way had he been following it?

All right, he thought. *Let's think about this a moment. You passed the skeleton, the purple coral, the purple kelp, then the other skeleton . . . in that order? Or did you pass the . . .* He scratched his head. *So this is why people draw maps in their books. Okay, there was a dead shict somewhere and that was back the way you came and you didn't pass that dead shict . . . unless someone moved the body. Or ate it. Do shicts eat their dead? Is that true or did we just make that up?*

He cast a long, curious look at Kataria as she came jogging up, breathing heavily. She shot him a glare.

"What are you looking at me like that for?" she asked.

"Do you eat—"

Don't ask her, *stupid!*

"Nevermind." He looked up at the jagged rent in the earth. "How much farther do you think it goes?"

"Oh, is *that* what we're trying to find?" Kataria snarled. "Maybe if you had *told* me instead of running off, I could have figured something out."

"Can you figure something out now? I'm kind of getting tired of this."

"Well, so long as *you're* getting tired of it." She sighed, followed his gaze up to the sky. "No, I have no idea how and I have no idea why you think following this thing will lead us anywhere, anyway."

He frowned, stared down into the emptiness of the chasm and muttered under his breath.

"I can't believe she would lie to me."

"Who?"

"The dead girl."

"*Who?*"

What was that? You don't have *voices in your head anymore! You should be saying* fewer *weird things!*

He opened his mouth to explain and some jumble of words that sounded vaguely like an excuse tumbled out. It was with some relief that he saw her looking over his head, clearly not listening. Relief that quickly turned to fear as he saw her reach for her bow.

His sword was in his hand by the time he turned around and stared into the yellow eyes staring back at him. It was those eyes—and only those eyes—that betrayed the creature as a Shen. The rest of it, bent back, dirty robes, drooping cowl from which ancient smoke and dust emanated, were so impossibly decrepit they might as well have been lifted from the dead.

It stood there for a moment, watching them. It made no other movement, said nothing, did not blink. And they, in turn, made no move to release arrow or tighten grip on sword. For the moment, anyway.

"Should I shoot it?" Kataria asked.

"It hasn't attacked us," Lenk replied.

"Ah." The bowstring groaned a little. "So . . . do I shoot it?"

"Give it a moment. It might know a way out."

"And why would it tell us that as opposed to, say, splitting our heads open . . . you know, like all the other ones try to do?"

"Because it's retreating."

"Slowly shuffling away" might have been a better choice of words for what the creature was doing, even if it didn't carry the same disdain for how brazenly it turned about and slipped into the darkness, tail dragging behind it.

"After it!" Lenk barked. "It could lead us out of here."

"Should we give it a longer head start?" Kataria asked. "The thing wasn't exactly in a hurry."

Yet even as they hurried after it, the creature seemed ever in the distance. Even as they charged, even as it shuffled, it seemed to draw farther and farther ahead of them, moving from shadow to shadow as a man moves through doors. By the time they were out of breath, the creature was still yards away, disappearing into the shadows once more.

"Not fair," Kataria exclaimed through heavy breath. "They're not supposed to be able to do that. How are they doing that?"

"It's just the one. This one is different."

"Could have shot him."

"How would that have helped?"

"How is *this* helping?"

His only answer was to run. He continued on, her at his side, hurrying after the creature that had vanished from sight completely. Shadows engulfed them as the chasm began to close overhead and become a tunnel. The earth grew damp beneath their feet, the sand squishing instead of crunching.

Soon, before they knew it, the earth was gone entirely, swallowed up by still, stagnant water that rose to their ankles. And still, he pressed on, despite a rather strong argument.

"Do you seriously not see what's happening here?" Kataria called after him. "It's leading us into water so we can *drown*, because it thinks we're stupid enough not to turn back."

Probably not an unjustified thought, given the idiocy of following it in the first place. Lenk did not think about that. Instead, he focused on a flash of light ahead. A golden ray punched through the roof of the wall, illuminating a vast, pale face staring directly at him.

A stone face of a woman he had seen before, adorning the walls of Jaga. A woman with a broad smile, wide eyes, and a neck shattered into pieces as her head lay atop the fragments of her broken stone body.

The statue lay in a heap, half-drowned in the water, her head a crown atop a haphazard burial mound scraping a hole in the ceiling, the last trace of light in the void. A chance at escape, the only thing left in the darkness.

That was reason enough to climb. Without a sound save for the occasional grunt of effort as they helped one another up the rubble, over the rubble, and over each other. It was only when they stood perched upon the statue's nose that they shared a look.

"Could be an ambush," Lenk said.

"It could've been an ambush when you first started chasing the thing. Better opportunities back there, too." She looked up to the hole in the earth, the pit through which the stone lady had fallen. Her ears trembled. "I don't hear anything up there."

"What if they're just . . . quiet?"

"Well, goodness, I guess if my enemies have learned how to be quiet I'm just a little screwed, aren't I?"

"Fine," he snarled. "I'll go up first."

"Why you?"

"Well, if you give me a bit, I can come up with something about feelings, heartache, you having protected me and me wanting to return the favor and it'll probably involve the words 'my personal autumn.'"

She clicked her tongue. "Go on, then."

He hurled his sword through the opening, pulling himself up after it. The daylight was not particularly bright, filtered through a hue of gray, but after the darkness of the chasm it was more than enough to send him shielding his eyes as he crawled out onto the sand.

And there was plenty of sand. Stretching out like an ocean all its own, bereft of coral, kelp, or bone, it ran flat and featureless for what seemed like miles in a vast ring. Circling it, a low stone wall segregated the small desert from the kelp forests beyond. Stray fish would fly over it, around it, above it as they passed from one copse of kelp to another.

Never through it.

The light that had seemed so bright beneath the world was all but vanished. Much of it was smothered behind the endless swirling halo of clouds that swam overhead, but most of it was muted to a dull, dim gray by the shadow. The mountain stood impassive at the far end of the ring, stoically ignoring the rivers that wept down its craggy face to collect upon a long, stone staircase that ran from its rocky brow down to the sands of the ring.

That would have drawn more attention from him had he not found himself transfixed by dozens of stares upon him.

Cold stares. Stone stares.

She was everywhere. Surrounding the vast, valley-like ring of sand that stretched for at least a mile in all directions, she stood above the coral and kelp swaying in an endless forest surrounding the ring. Tall, proud, clad in stone silks, raising stone arms, stone smile broad, stone hair scraping the sky, the statues surrounded the great ring of sand.

Tall.

Proud.

Broken.

By chain, by boulder, by chisel and grit and a sheer determination to see her fall, she stood in varying forms of decay about the great ring. Here, her head lay in fragments. There, she stood smiling with her limbs torn off. Behind him, she was nothing more than feet, the rest of her collapsed into the pit from which he had climbed.

Even in stone, he knew her. He knew the smile. He tried to look away, but everywhere he turned, even where she was headless, she was there. Looking back at him.

Ulbecetonth. Proud and broken.

Transfixed by her gaze, he stared at the omnipresent smile. Straight stone teeth in cold stone lips. And yet somehow, he swore he could almost see them moving. Somehow, he swore he could almost hear her.

"I took pity on you. I gave you a chance. Never again. You come here to die."

"How the hell did he get all the way over there?"

When he looked at Kataria, she was standing beside him and staring out toward the far end of the valley. And there the creature sat, on the bottom-most step of the long staircase climbing the mountain's face, beneath a halo of stormclouds slowly circling a hidden peak.

Half a mile away, its yellow eyes were all but pinpricks beneath its cowl. And yet, he could still feel the creature's stare, as he could feel dust settling upon his skin. It unnerved him.

Not enough to hold him back, though. He shouldered his sword and began to walk toward the creature. Kataria was by his side, though her bow remained in her hands with arrow drawn.

"This is a bad idea," she whispered to him.

"He's not running," Lenk replied. "He has answers."

"You can't be sure of that."

"It was your idea to come here. You said the tome would be here. We don't have a lot of other leads."

"It could be an ambush."

"There's no reason to think that."

"Right." She kept her voice low. The sound of a bestial hiss carried clearly to his ears from behind. "Except for the ambush."

He glanced over his shoulder into half a dozen yellow eyes. And then a dozen, then two dozen. And more and more as they came from the kelp forest. Seeming to melt off the swaying fronds like water from ice, the Shen came, warpaint bright as blood, eyes sharp and fixed upon the two, weapons decidedly more so.

He didn't draw his sword; it would have seemed rather pathetic to offer it against the machetes and hatchets drawn on him. Kataria apparently disagreed, as evidenced by the groan of her bowstring.

"I can put one down," Kataria whispered. "The others might back off for a moment."

"There are thirty of them. What do we do after that?"

"I'll shoot you, then myself. We'll deny them the pleasure."

"That's insane."

"At least I'm contributing."

Enough bows were trained on them that they'd both be perforated before she could even twiddle her fingers. Enough machetes were drawn to suggest that whatever happened to them next would probably involve the words "fine stew." And yet, the arrows remained in their strings. The machetes remained in their claws. The Shen remained well away.

"They're not attacking," he noted.

"They're not retreating, either," Kataria said.

"Then we keep moving."

More came, emerging from the forest. More arrows were drawn, more machetes slid from their sheaths. More yellow eyes were fixed upon them, more guttural hisses, mutterings in a thick-tongued language followed them.

And nothing else. As they continued to move toward the creature, the arrows did not fly and the hisses did not turn to war cries. They were merely being herded for the moment. Lenk remained tense; herd led to slaughter, eventually.

The creature at the foot of the stairs continued to stare, heedless of the Shen behind them or the Shen appearing around it. Against its fellows, this one, in its dirty cloak and hood, looked positively puny, something old and bony that would probably be made into some piece of tribal decoration. It didn't seem to mind, didn't seem to care, didn't seem to blink.

It continued to stare.

Its gaze, duller, darker, like petrified amber, drew Lenk's attention. So much so that he narrowly missed the figure moving forward to stand before him. It was more than a little difficult to miss the giant, tooth-studded club that flashed into view.

He took a step back as Shalake moved to impose himself between the ancient creature and Lenk, his sword leaping to his hand and raised before him. Shalake made no move to respond, his massive club resting easily in his hand, staring from his skull headdress. Slowly, his free claw went to the ornament of bone, prying it free to reveal a face scarred by black warpaint and old injuries.

Lenk held himself, but the sheer contempt that radiated from the lizardman was more palpable than any he had felt before.

Almost any, anyway.

A red hand reached down and took his wrist in its grip. He looked up to the tremendous creature standing beside him, taken aback only for as long as it took him to recall that the black eyes staring down at him were ones he knew.

"Gariath," he gasped. "We thought you . . ."

The dragonman snorted. "Thought I what?"

"I was going to accuse you of something, but lately I'm never quite sure what the hell you're doing."

"At the moment," Shalake rumbled, hefting his club, "he is stopping you from killing yourselves."

"Merely slowing us down," Kataria snapped back. "We'll kill ourselves when we damn well feel like it and there's nothing you can do about it." She raised her bow, aiming the arrow between Shalake's eyes. "You can come with us, if you want."

Another bowstring creaked as a Shen, slighter and lankier than the rest, moved protectively beside Shalake, bow in hand. A single yellow eye burned hatefully upon Kataria, the other one, a ruined hole of black flesh in his skull, merely smoldered.

"Yaike remembers you," Shalake noted with a glance toward the creature. "He says you took his eye."

She smiled broadly, taking care to show each and every tooth.

"What I did to his eye goes a little beyond 'taking.'"

She snapped her teeth together, the sound of her canines clacking short and vicious. Yaike snarled, the bowstring tensing even further.

"If we wanted to kill you," Shalake said, "we would have done it back in the coral forest."

"Or in the chasm," Gariath grunted.

"Or when you were crawling out of the chasm," Shalake said, nodding. "That would have been a good time."

"If it would spare me this posturing, I'd welcome it," Lenk said, rubbing his eyes. "But somehow, I find myself surrounded by lizardmen who are suddenly not so eager to kill me." He turned to Gariath. "And *you're* with them, apparently not killing them." He looked back, over the island. "And I'm here following a gorge full of tentacles and dead girls to a desert ringed by big, dead, stone demon queens looking for a book to keep said demon queen from being less dead and less stone and less spilling me open and eating my insides like she said she was going to the last time she started talking to me inside my head."

He paused for breath. It was long and slow. When he looked back up, every eye—black, green, and yellow—was fixed upon him in varying degrees of confusion.

"It has been a long, confusing, *stupid* day." He threw his arms out wide, turned around to face the lizardmen surrounding him. "So, will someone either kill me right now or tell me what the hell is going on?"

No arrow through the chest, no blade hacking his head off. No one was going to kill him. So much for things being easy.

Instead, they parted. Shalake stepped aside. Yaike retreated. The Shen moved away. Even Kataria took a step back as the creature, nearly forgotten, stood up.

Bones groaned with the sound of stone cracking. An ancient layer of dust fell from the creature's shoulders as it rose. There was a symphony of sickening snapping, cracking, popping sounds as it stepped from the stone staircase and came to stand before Lenk, staring up at the young man.

He caught a flash of what lurked beneath the creature's cowl. A glimpse of skin veined by wrinkles that had grown so deep as to become rents in faded green flesh. A flash of white bone where skin had fallen away above brow and beneath jaw. A hint of teeth rotted to black, gums rotted to blacker, tongue a dead thing rolling about inside a mouth full of dust.

Just a glimpse.

More than enough.

"You," the creature said with a voice of old stone and old dirt, "have been looking for me."

"I assure you, I haven't," Lenk replied, unable to look on any part of the creature's face for long and yet unable to look away.

"You came to Jaga," he said, a cloud of dust with each word, "looking for something. You came to Jaga because you were called. You came to Jaga because you are needed here."

"Well, which is it?" Lenk asked.

"You will tell me, soon," the creature said. A hand slipped into the folds of his robes. It emerged carrying something so old and tarnished it looked like it belonged on . . . something like the creature that held it. "But first, I must tell you." He held the object up. "You know this symbol?"

He did. It had been a while, but he recognized it. A gauntlet clenching thirteen black arrows.

"I suppose I have been looking for you, then," Lenk said, "Mister . . ."

"Mahalar," the creature finished for him. "Warden of Ulbecetonth. Protector of Jaga. Member of the House of the Vanquishing Trinity."

TWENTY-FOUR

FAR BEYOND MORTALITY

Elsewhere and far away.

Somewhere far beneath his feet and behind his brow, burning like a fever.

In the tremble of his hands upon his lap, in the tremble of his eyes as he closed them, in the sharpness of the air as he drew in a breath and held it in his throat.

He could feel it.

They were out there.

And they were speaking. They were speaking to him.

"You are listening to me, aren't you?" someone asked from behind.

He narrowed his eyes. Not *them*. They weren't important.

"Your silence does nothing to bolster my confidence," Yldus said, sighing. "Nor does your . . . change of wardrobe."

Sheraptus held up a hand with some difficulty. The withered limb beneath the sleeve, its muscle and bone eaten away by that . . . that *woman's* touch, he had taken care to hide behind a new robe. Something as bright as this world's sun-kissed skies to stand out against the darkness surrounding him.

Those who walked upon the clouds beside the sun would look down and see him glorious on the stain of this world. They would know him. They would tell him everything.

"If you refuse to consult with us on our strategy, I must once again voice my opposition to this."

If other people would just *stop* talking . . .

"We can find our way through the mist well enough, but beyond that, we know nothing. No warriors have ever returned from this island. A dedicated scouting force supported by a male and a few Carnassials could—"

"Could return with infection, disease, anything but information," Vash-near interrupted. His sneer was audible. Such an ugly thing, so typical of a *netherling*. "Better to come with all our power and destroy them in one fell swoop that we may take our leisure and precaution in exploring their filthy holds. That would give us more ample time to locate the demons and—"

"It means nothing if we wander into a trap. For all we know, the demons might already be there," Yldus insisted.

Sheraptus did not chuckle. His voice was something harsh and raspy since that *woman* had collapsed his throat to a narrow hole. Not that his former fellow's voice didn't deserve it. He knew the demons were not there. Because he knew he still had to kill them.

Much had become clear to him in the events following her. His theory was correct: in pain, the sky-people, these . . . gods, had come to him. He merely had failed to surmise whose pain was necessary to contact them.

He had not cursed them. It was a weakness of the pink skin and feeble mind that pleaded for them and asked them where they had been. He could tell that they had not cursed him with that *woman*, with her wicked touch, with the withered and broken body she had given him.

They had given him this as a warning. *They* had implored *him*. They spoke to him in his withered arm and his crushed throat and his crumbled knee. They told him to go to Jaga. They told him to eradicate their enemies there.

He smiled as he clenched his good hand, felt the smoothness of the gray pebble rubbing against his palm. The gift of the Gray One That Grins. It was warm. It was alive.

The Gray One That Grins had always been his ally, but now Sheraptus could see he had been sent there to help him. Everything in his life: the discovery of the world beyond their own, the opening of the portal, that *woman* . . . it had all been the sky-people reaching out to him, telling him to come to them, telling him to reduce their foes, these demons, to ash.

His victory would be theirs. Their reward would be his. They would promise this land to him, in all its greenery and blue skies and white sun. He would have it. He would be beyond all netherlings.

It all made sense now.

310

It was all so perfect.

"Sheraptus."

Or it *would* be. Soon.

"*Look* at us, Sheraptus."

Feet trampled across the deck. Yldus advanced.

"Damn it, you will *not*—"

Two great feet stomped upon the wood. Yldus's advance came to a sudden halt as something stood between him and Sheraptus.

"You will do whatever Master Sheraptus says you will do," Semnein Xhai growled. "If he tells you nothing, then you need to know nothing else." He could hear the grate of her teeth in her voice. "*Leave.*"

Only at the sound of their retreat did Sheraptus look over his shoulder. The two males cast indignant scowls over their backs as they strode down the middle of the deck, between the females silently oaring. With words of power, flashes of crimson about their throats, the males leapt, propelled by *nethra* to their own ships as their fleet advanced slowly across the ocean, oar over oar, rumbles of discontent rising from their decks.

They could complain. That was fine. They did not know what he knew, any of them.

"Master . . ."

Especially *her.*

"The females that have spoken against you have been silenced, as well as . . . those two, but you won't tell us what you're thinking. You won't lead us. If you would just talk to us . . ."

He could feel her drawing closer.

"To me . . ."

He could hear the clatter of her gauntlet as she reached out a hand. Her horrible, maimed hand. The result of the touch of that overscum woman: a gift from the gods that Xhai simply could not recognize in her netherling futility.

He rose up to his feet and felt her draw back, a child wary of a parent rising from interrupted slumber. His good leg took the brunt of his weight; the other was far too cracked and useless to stand on its own. That was fine. He didn't need it.

He didn't need the withered arm that couldn't keep his robes secured as they fell from him. He didn't need the females that looked upon his shattered body with grimaces. He didn't need the female that whirled a furious gaze over her shoulder and sent their gazes low.

He had everything he needed in his palm.

And at his feet.

He spoke a word, made the gesture, felt the pain that normally came with *nethra.* He had so little of himself to give, but the magic always demanded. But he wanted to remind himself of it again before he returned the crown to his brow. He wanted to remember who had the power to take this away.

And who could give him more.

The air quivered beneath his fingers. An invisible hand reached down, plucked the black box from his feet and delivered it into his hands. It had taken all the cunning of his indelicate warriors to create something worthy of housing the weapon that would strike down the demons, the weapon they had brought back from the overscum city. He opened the lid, stared at the spear.

311

Bones stared back at him without eyes. They were not impressive bones. No thicker than any other he had seen come from a human. Not particularly sturdy-looking. The jagged head of obsidian that sat amongst them only barely resembled a spear's. But his warriors had brought them to him. His warriors had found them where they were supposed to be found.

It would become a mighty weapon. Sheraptus could see the grooves where the bones locked together to create the spear. It would be driven into the heart of Ulbecetonth. It would slay all that stood before it. It would fulfill the desires of the people in the sky.

Or so the Gray One That Grins had said.

Sheraptus trusted in these bones, in the creature they had come from, in the hands that would wield them.

He turned around and saw her hands resting on her knees as she sat before him. One was in a gauntlet, wrapped in steel. The other was a ruined, twisted thing, a pale imitation of the powerful purple fist it had been before. But it was a capable hand.

He knew this from her eyes, those pale, empty things that looked up to him only, that softened for him only. He knew this from her pleading gaze, the desperation she would show only him. He knew this from the words that trembled upon her lips, that she simply did not have the language to speak.

She loved him. That was it. The netherlings had no word for such a thing. He barely knew what it was himself before he looked to the sky and knew someone looked back to him. But he knew now, the desperation, the beautiful futility of doing something with the hope that it would someday beget reward.

And yet, he wondered what had happened in her, who she had spoken to, that let her show such desperation, that made her try to form the word she didn't know.

It didn't matter. Her love mattered. And with her love, she would carry these bones. She would kill in his name. In *their* name.

She did not cringe from his withered hand, thin and stretched like a child's, as he rested it upon her brow. She did not cringe as he held out his other hand and looked at the small gray stone in his palm. She said nothing as he clenched it, as he squeezed the tiny life ensconced within it.

And into him.

He could feel it, that warmth that coursed inside it. A living thing, something unseen and significant that had been wrapped into a single stone pebble. It had disgusted him at first, repulsed him. The Gray One That Grins had, too, once upon a time. But that was before he knew what his true purpose was. And now that he knew, now that he had the life of this stone in his hands, he knew what it was sent to him for.

And he welcomed it.

With agony, it came. The life flowed from the lump of stone into his body with an exhalating scream of freedom that poured into his hand and out of his mouth. He threw back his head, felt his throat being restored, opened to allow the shriek to leave him. He tensed his arm as its muscle and shape returned to it and filled it. He stomped his foot in agony as the bones were mended and set themselves alight. He roared with laughter, with a voice he shared with someone else, into the sky to show the things that walked up there that he was worthy.

And when laughter died, when the night air hung still, he stood upon the deck.

Sheraptus in body. Restored and whole and unbroken.

His warriors stopped midrow, looking up at the creature brimming with life. They watched him with awe as he stepped over Xhai, walked between his warriors to the prow of the ship.

He stared out over the black shapes of his fleet cutting through the waves, at the warriors he commanded. All for the death of the demons. All for the glory of what walked in the sky.

All for him.

"Go," he commanded. "We go to Jaga. We go for glory and for death. The demons await us."

He knew this.

Because he had to kill them.

And because whatever had left the stone, whatever was inside him, knew it.

And wanted to help.

TWENTY-FIVE

THE LOVES AND HATES OF STONE

It was a rare and unfortunate occasion, Lenk thought, that he could not enjoy food. It always seemed like it had been some time since he had eaten, let alone anything freshly-cooked. But he chewed the skewered fish, plucked from the sky like fruit from a tree, without much joy.

It was, after all, difficult to enjoy a meal that had been handed to him by a gang of bipedal reptiles that had been eager to kill him just moments ago. Even if said reptiles now clustered in small campfires about the base of the stone stairs, even if they had offered him food, they continued to stare at him warily, their weapons never far from their hands.

Their leader was no less unnerving and twice as frustrating. Shortly after revealing his affiliation with the organization that had, over the course of weeks, led him to this very island, Mahalar had disappeared without a word. His green-skinned brethren had simply shrugged and said "Mahalar knows," as though this were all perfectly normal. Perhaps it was for half-rotted lizardmen who spat dust with each word.

But Lenk could have gotten beyond all that. Lenk could have enjoyed his fish. Lenk could have celebrated a warm meal, the fact that he was no longer in immediate danger of decapitation, and the memory of scents of sweat and sand from the chasm.

And he would have.

If not for the statues.

He couldn't explain it, the feeling he got as he looked across the shattered and broken women. They were but stone, ancient and decrepit and crumbling. But they hated him. They loathed him with a fury clenched in that smile, hidden behind those eyes, held within those outstretched, benevolent palms. The fish knew. That was why they gave her a wide berth when they swam.

He had just begun to turn, content to follow their example, when he heard the sound of grinding. He looked up and saw stone eyes rolling in stone sockets. From high above, and in the rubble where her head lay fragmented, she turned her eyes upon him.

The grinding became a groan, ancient granite dust falling from her shoulders as her many heads turned toward him. And the groaning became cracking, and the cracking became thunder as her many stone mouths opened and spoke in one old, hateful stone voice.

"I gave you a chance. I let you run. Not this time."

He blinked.

The statues were once again mere stone. No moving eyes, no moving lips, no voices. He held up the half-eaten fish and scrutinized it carefully.

"It is not poisoned."

The words came with the stench of burning dust. He turned, saw the creature wrapped in the dirty cloak standing before him.

"What you saw was not a hallucination."

Mahalar inclined his head. Amber eyes, dull and glassy, stared out from the shadows of his cowl.

"She remembers you."

Lenk nearly choked on his fish.

"You saw . . ."

Mahalar's eyes drifted up toward one of the statues of Ulbecetonth. A cloud of dust came out with his sigh. Beneath him, tiny fingers of sand rose up to seize the motes of dust leaving on his breath, to take them down into the sand of the ring like precious things.

"I have lived a long time," he said, noting Lenk's gaze drifting to the ground. "The earth and I have bled together and it no longer remembers a time without me. Or her. We have both been here.

"Live with someone a long time," he muttered, "and you begin to notice things. The wrinkles that appear when she smiles, the way her laugh is slightly annoying. I have lived with the Kraken Queen a very long time. I have heard her screaming. I have felt her scratching at the roof of hell. I hear her weeping. I know her laughter. I cannot stop from hearing when she cries out for her children.

"These days, she screams more often." He turned back to Lenk. "Two days ago, she started screaming. She hasn't stopped." He sighed deeply. "But you know that, don't you? You can't hear it, but you've seen it. You know what's happening in the chasm." His eyes flashed. "You know she's coming back, as do I. You remember her."

There was a flash of movement, motes of dust in the dying light. Mahalar stood mere hairs' breadths away from Lenk, eyes boring into the young man.

"And I remember you."

Lenk met his stare for as long as he could bear. While the creature was old, older than the dust that came from his mouth on each breath, old enough to have his skin flaking into powder, somehow his gaze was older, more unpleasant to look at than even his rotting body. His eyes had seen too much, knew too much, and even the tiniest scrap of what they shared in the instant they met Lenk's eyes was too much.

There was recognition there. Not for Lenk, but for what Lenk was. Beyond whatever Kataria had seen, beyond whatever he had seen in himself, Mahalar saw. Every drop of blood that had stained him, every hateful thought that had ever been muttered inside his head, every chill that had coursed through his body, Mahalar saw.

Mahalar knew.

And Lenk couldn't bear to look at him anymore. He turned on his heel, suddenly preferring the living, screaming statues.

"Think before you walk away from me," Mahalar said, toneless. "Think of the weight you'll walk with. Think of how many chances you'll have to ask."

He paused. He thought. He sighed.

"If I *do* ask," Lenk replied, "you have to promise me something."

"That being?"

"You have to tell me, straightforward, without any cryptic, riddle-speaking, I'm-old-and-oh-so-mysterious-so-I-get-to-not-make-sense garbage." He glanced over his shoulder. "Do we have a deal?"

Mahalar stared straight ahead, as if in deep thought as to whether he was willing to give up that rare joy. In the end, he bowed his head in acquiescence.

"And . . ." Lenk began.

He glanced over Mahalar, to the distant firepits, to the sole flash of pale skin amidst a sea of green. Kataria sat amidst the Shen as though she had always belonged there, laughing at some joke they obviously didn't share, looking up and flashing a broad, bare-canined smile at him.

"This stays between us," the young man finished, "whatever it is you tell me, you tell no one else."

"And what is it you wish to know?"

"You said you remembered me."

"I did."

"Does that mean you know . . ." He choked on the words, eventually coughed them up. "What I am?"

"I do."

He stared at the elder Shen for a moment. "Well?"

Mahalar slowly turned his gaze upward. He raised a hand, stretched out a finger to a relatively intact statue of Ulbecetonth. The digit straightened with a sickening popping sound, a noticeable chunk of flesh sloughing off. It tumbled from his fingers, hit the ground, and became dust upon dust.

"It all began," he said, "with her."

"Gods damn it, what did I *just* say?"

Mahalar continued as though he had said nothing, either then or now. "It was all hers to begin with. This." He stomped the earth with a foot. "This." He tapped his own chest with a hand. "And we were whole back then. Jaga, Teji, Komga . . . Gonwa, Owauku, and Shen. One land. One people. We lived under her. We breathed at her mercy. I was born here."

"I gather most Shen were."

"I was born *here*," Mahalar replied, pointing to the earth beneath his feet. "Here, under her eyes, beneath her court. My very first vision upon opening my eyes was of this statue as my father was carving it."

Lenk fixed him with a confused glare. "How old are you?"

"Would you consider 'old as the song of heaven and the depth of hell' to be cryptic?"

"I would."

"Old as balls, then."

"Ah."

"I grew up under her gaze. I labored under her gaze. I watched my father and mother die under her gaze. All for her and her children." He sighed a dusty sigh. "They were not so wretched then. They possessed fins, flowing green hair, pale skin. They were not called 'demon' back then."

"What did you call them?"

"'Master.' On us, they built a place for themselves. She did anything for them: fed them whatever flesh they desired, provided them whatever amusement they wanted, tended to their every weeping wail. Her children flourished and those who suckled at her teats never wanted.

"And for this, for her love of her children that eclipsed everything else, she was punished. The Gods accused her of loving herself and her children more than her duty. The mortals she was sent to serve, she neglected and enslaved. For this, they twisted her."

He fingered the pendant of the gauntlet clenching the arrows hanging around his neck.

"You did not flinch when I showed you this," Mahalar said. "You know it."

"I know enough to know what you're telling me. The Gods cursed the Aeons for trying to usurp heaven, the war with the House of the Vanquishing Trinity put them to rest."

"You know some, but not all. It was not heaven they tried to usurp, but heaven they tried to create. It was not the House that sent them to hell, but us." His tone grew cold. "The war did not start until they came back.

"When the Gods struck back at Ulbecetonth and cursed her, we rose up.

We drowned her children. We defiled her temples. We screeched and beat our chests and hailed freedom. Whether it was her love or their hate, no one knew. But her children came back. Vast and terrible and with souls as black as their skin. The House came to our aid. The House marched on Ulbecetonth. With their great moving statues, with their spears and banners and holy words . . . and with you."

Lenk cast a wary glance to make sure Kataria was still far away before turning back to the elder Shen.

"The war went poorly, at first. For as strong as we were, as hungry for freedom as we were, the war was still between the mortal and the immortal. We faltered. We failed. We died, in great numbers. Even when the *Rhega* stood alongside us, fought alongside us, there were more of us dead than they.

"But then, they came from god. Not one we knew, not one they would speak of. But their hair was that of the old men and women. Their eyes were cold and hateful. And they spoke with the voice of that god they came from. They could cut the demons. They could hurt the demons. They fought. They won. And with them, we cast Ulbecetonth and her children back into hell.

"Not without cost, of course. You've seen the bones. The worst of it happened on Teji and our brothers there suffered for it and became the Owauku. But even here, on Jaga, from which she reigned, we spilled blood. Much of it spilled into the chasm when the road was shattered. Much of it was spilled here beneath our feet.

"But it did end. She was driven back into that dark place the Gods made for her. The House appointed us her wardens. And we have guarded her ever since. Shalake and the others know only the story and the duty it carries. Only I know what happened. Only I remember how we nearly lost everything, if not for the House . . . and for *them*."

The word echoed against nothing.

"Who were they? The ones who came?" Lenk asked.

"We didn't give them names. They didn't give us any, either."

"What happened to them?"

"Apparently," Mahalar said, looking back to Lenk. "They came back."

Lenk had been stared at many times. As a monster, as a curiosity, as something else entirely. But the way Mahalar stared at him now, eyes heavy with knowing, was the same stare one might use to appraise a weapon.

Lenk had never before felt the kind of shudder he felt now.

"Whatever you think I am," he said, "whatever you think I can do, I can't. I left it behind in the chasm with the bones."

"Maybe." Mahalar rolled his shoulders. "Maybe what I felt wasn't you. Maybe it was someone wearing your skin, your soul. But my feet have never left Jaga in all the time I've been alive. I knew your presence when you set foot on my island, as I knew theirs. And I knew why you had come."

"The tome."

"To kill," Mahalar said, "to end. Ulbecetonth is coming. I can feel it. You can, too. You were driven here. If you say it's for the tome, that's fine. It is a key to open a door. But you came here to kill what's on the other side."

"I came to stop her."

"Many ways to do that."

Lenk held his stare for a moment before turning away. "I . . . maybe. Before things stopped making sense . . . or started."

"It seems a little hypocritical for you to start talking in riddles, yourself."

"I'm entitled to sound a little insane," Lenk snapped back. "I came here to kill her, but it wasn't my idea. She was inside my head once. She sounded . . . hurt, panicked, worried for her children. She let me go, telling me not to hurt them again and I . . . I really didn't want to."

"But you're here now."

"Because something *told* me to come here."

"Then clearly, it knew what it was talking about."

"It told me to kill my—" He waved his hands about, frustrated. "We're not going to argue this. I came here to kill her, but I stayed here for a different . . . are you even listening to me?"

Mahalar was not. Mahalar was turning. Mahalar was moving, five feet away. Then ten feet. In the blink of each eye, he moved impossibly quick, impossibly slow, and growing farther all the while as he moved closer to a sudden bustle of movement at the staircase.

"This, for the record," Lenk shouted after him, "counts as 'cryptic.'"

Lenk came hurrying up to find the Shen assembling around the foot of the stairs once more, Mahalar seated upon the stone once more. He forced his way through a gap in their ranks, found Gariath and Kataria standing nearby, Shalake hovering protectively over the elder.

"And *this* is why I said 'no cryptic gibberish,'" Lenk snarled. "Because somehow, it always ends up with me, rushing up to some smelly creature I'd rather not be around, demanding what the hell is supposed to happen now."

"Now?"

Mahalar smiled broadly, dust seeping out through his teeth, amber eyes shining dully. He drew back his cloak and there it sat upon his knee, like a baby made of leather black as night, sitting smugly in Mahalar's hands.

The book.

The Tome of the Undergates.

He remembered the book. He remembered paper smiles, paper eyes, dusty mutterings and writings that made sense only to him. He remembered reading it and hearing voices going quiet, replaced by voices that grew darker in his head.

But he didn't remember this.

The tome upon Mahalar's knee was *the* tome, to be certain. But it was just *a* tome. Something leather and paper. No smiles. No eyes. A book.

Perhaps he had left more in the chasm than he thought.

Not his senses, though. He still knew something insane when he heard it.

"Now," Mahalar said bluntly, "you kill Ulbecetonth."

"What?" Kataria turned a scowl upon Lenk. "You were gone for a quarter of an hour. How the hell did you come to this conclusion?"

"We didn't!" Lenk protested, turning on Mahalar. "And I'm not! We came here for the tome. The Tome of the Undergates. The thing that's going to get us paid so I can move away from islands full of freaky dust-lizards and go live on a patch of dirt somewhere. Remember?" He turned to Gariath. "*Remember?*"

"Barely," Gariath grunted.

"And you didn't think to mention this to them, what with all the time you've been spending with them?"

"I didn't come here for that," the dragonman replied. "I came here for them." He gestured to Shalake. "They stood with the *Rhega* against the demons. They know the *Rhega.* They have told me stories."

"Great, fine, good," Lenk grumbled. "Stay here with them, then. Scratch each others' scales, play tug-the-tail or whatever it is people with more than four appendages do. *I* came for the tome." He swept a hand out over the assembled Shen. "*You're* obviously not too fond of me. Just give me the stupid book and we'll leave."

"We killed thousands to see our duty done," Shalake snarled, stepping forward. "We will kill one more to do it."

"We cannot give you the tome," Mahalar said, nodding. "It was too precious to be penned in the first place. It has knowledge that no one should have. It was designed only for woe." He fixed those scrutinizing eyes upon Lenk. "But it can be used for good."

"No," Lenk said.

"You have the power," Mahalar insisted.

"No."

"There are stories," Shalake said, "stories of those who came and cut the demons down."

"*No.*"

"Listen to them, Lenk," Gariath said, "I've heard them, too. People with hair like yours, eyes like yours, who cut like you can. You're the only one who's been able to hurt the demons."

"*NO.*"

"We can kill her," Mahalar said, "before she breaks out. We can summon her, on our terms, with an army of Shen to assist you." His eyes lit like the barest flicker of a candle. "Forgive me for my selfishness, but *think* of it. My people can be free, Lenk. Our duty can be fulfilled. We will no longer have to live with the burden, the agony, the *screaming*, if only you can—"

"He can't."

The voice came from Kataria. Not with great volume, or great joy. But everyone turned and looked to her, all the same. She did not look up to meet their stares.

"He can't do that anymore."

When she did look up, she looked only at Lenk.

"I followed you earlier. I overheard you. Talking to the dead girl. You didn't want me to know, so I pretended I hadn't. But . . ." She swallowed something back, then looked to Mahalar. "Whatever was in him is gone now. He sent it away. He can't kill her. He can't do anything for you."

She hadn't spoken loudly. Somehow, everyone heard. The same despair settled over every scaly face present. Lenk looked to her, an apology carved across his face in his frown.

"I really didn't want you to know," he said.

"Yeah," she replied. "Well."

He smiled sadly. "If you were dumber, we wouldn't have this problem."

"I sincerely hope you don't think you were particularly clever about it," Kataria snapped. "I knew something was wrong with you from the day I met you. It's just now I know exactly *what* is wrong with you."

He laughed. No one else did.

Mahalar merely settled back and breathed a cloud of dust.

322   "That," he said, "is a problem."

"One that gets worse, Mahalar," someone said.

He—or at least, it looked and sounded like a "he," it was hard to tell with lizardmen . . . or lizardwomen—came stalking out of the forest, tall and scaly and bearing a long, carved bow on his back. Many more emerged behind him, Shen armed and glowering as they slithered out of the coral and onto the great sandy field.

"Leaving a warwatcher's post is a grave offense, Jenaji," Shalake said in a gravel-voiced snarl.

"There are few things you don't consider grave offenses, Shalake," the tall and lanky newcomer replied, his voice smooth and heavy like a polished stone. "And there are fewer things I consider worth answering to you over." He turned his eyes, bright and sharp as the arrows in his quiver, to Mahalar. "We have an issue, Mahalar."

"*An* issue?" Lenk muttered. "Just one?"

"We have many problems, Jenaji," Mahalar replied. "Or have you not been listening?"

"I have only just arrived," Jenaji said. "And I did not come alone."

The Shen parted to expose pink, familiar shapes amidst their greenery, trudging wearily up to join the congregation. There were no smiles on their faces as they approached, no relief at seeing their companions again. Only weariness, wariness and, in Denaos's case, just a pinch of resentment.

Lenk looked them over. Dreadaeleon's clothes were soiled with soot and worse. Asper's eyes betrayed a drained weariness that went beyond the flesh. Denaos stood bandaged, bloodied, battered.

"What happened to you?" he asked.

"Longfaces," Denaos replied. "You?"

"Shen, shicts, snakes," Lenk said.

The rogue sniffed. "It's not a contest."

"It is bold of you to bring outsiders here," Shalake said, narrowing his eyes. "These ones at least fought their way here."

"Ah, so you are more honorable because you failed to stop them?" Jenaji said with a sneer. "I didn't come to compare tails. They have cause to be here."

"They say that?"

"They do not." Jenaji stepped aside. "She does."

Weapons immediately were drawn by the companions at the sight of Greenhair standing amidst them, like a pale white flower amidst endless green stalks. Hatchets and machetes came out in response as the Shen closed in protectively about the siren. Lenk flashed an accusatory glare at Denaos as the rogue stood with his daggers hanging at his belt.

Denaos merely shrugged. "Yeah, I was like that at first, too. But she helped us and she has something to say."

"Something you need to hear, Mahalar," the siren spoke in her liquid voice. "I bring dark words to you. I bring doom. I bring disaster."

Mahalar looked up. Mahalar smiled a dusty smile.

"*Maka-wa*," he said, "we have plenty to share with you, too."

Doom, as it turned out, needed only half an hour to summarize.

The companions, Shen, and siren exchanged their stories, their experiences, all—or at least all that was pertinent and didn't involve parts without pants, Lenk noted—that had happened since they had set out.

They spoke of netherling armies fueled by the dying Gonwa. They spoke of demons stirring beneath the earth. They spoke of Mahalar's plan to draw out Ulbecetonth, to use Lenk to kill her, and its subsequent and tragic failure.

And there they had fallen silent. An hour after death had been summarized, they sat on the edge of disaster, waiting for someone to put it to words and dreading it, too.

If Mahalar held that dread, though, it showed in neither gleam of eye nor sigh of voice.

"How many?"

Would that everyone could boast such calmness at the question; as it was, every face went to wincing.

"Many," Greenhair replied. "Three males, with all their power. Boats full of females, with all their swords. Great, savage beasts, teeth brimming with—"

"Did anyone bother to *count*?" Kataria piped up impatiently.

"They clustered in groups of thirty-three," Dreadaeleon said. "Each one to a boat. There were at least ten boats." He scratched his head. "Maybe more."

Whether or not the Shen excelled at math, they could grasp the severity of the statement. Most of them, anyway.

"The longfaces have attacked before," Shalake snarled. "We have killed them before. Stalk them, hunt them, and then," he hefted his club, patted it into his palm, "*shenko-sa.*"

"Are you willfully stupid or does it just come easily to you?" Lenk snapped. "Do you not grasp the numbers here? *Ten* boatloads. *Thirty-three* each. There are . . . how many of you?"

"Not that many," Jenaji muttered.

"We strike swiftly, from the forests," Shalake replied. "Hunt them like animals, as we have done before. We cut them down and feed them to the sharks."

"They'll burn the forests down," Dreadaeleon said. "They have the power, the fire. Their magic is infinite."

"So you say," Shalake said, suspicious. "But this is much to ask us to accept from people we would have killed a moment ago, had *maka-wa* not vouched for you." He glanced over them, sought a stooped, green figure amongst the masses. "Hongwe, did you see this?"

The Gonwa lifted his head reluctantly, said nothing. His eyes seemed heavy enough to roll out of his head, his frown deep enough to slide off and follow. He had worn the expression ever since the fate of his kinsmen had been revealed to him. He had said not a word since. Whatever bonds still linked the Gonwa and the Shen, they were enough to keep Shalake's voice stilled.

"And they come for the tome," Mahalar muttered.

"The tome is inconsequential," Dreadaeleon said. "They come for fuel. Whatever it is they're coming through, it can't be powered by the Gonwa. They succumb too easily. A demon, however . . ."

Mahalar loosed a low groan. "They fight one another, and whoever wins . . ." He didn't bother to finish the sentence. "We stand and fight, against that many, against that much metal and fire, and . . ."

He didn't need to finish that one.

"Not that it's entirely unexpected that I suggest this," Denaos began softly, "but has anyone considered running?"

"The Shen don't run," Gariath growled. "Neither do I."

"Well, good, no one invited you, anyway. The rest of us can just hop in Lenk's boat and—"

"Ours got destroyed," Lenk interrupted. "What happened to yours?"

"These damn lizards sank it before we could get close enough to tell them not to," Denaos said, rubbing his eyes. "So, did you commit any crimes against nature before I got here? Some horrid blasphemy to make the Gods hate us as much as they do?"

Lenk exchanged a quick glance with Kataria. "Define 'crime.'"

"It does not matter," Mahalar said wearily. "The longfaces have found their way through the reef before. They can do so again. The way out would put you in their path. They come. And they come with many."

In the deathly silence that followed, in the bow of heads and the swallowing of doubts, the sound of grains of sand shifting atop one another could be heard as clear as a bell.

Asper's voice could be heard only if one strained.

"There is a way," she whispered.

The eyes that turned upon her were so intent it seemed as though they might pierce her flesh. But she did not flinch or shy away, even if she did not look up to meet them.

"They don't act on their own. They follow one man."

"Sheraptus," Dreadaeleon muttered the name like a riddle.

"He controls them, the females. They obey him totally." She cleared her throat, swallowed something back. "If you can kill him, their numbers won't mean anything."

"If." Dreadaeleon spared a black laugh. "If you can kill someone with an entire furnace of blood and flesh feeding him fire and frost and lightning and whatever else the hell he feels like throwing at us."

"She's right, though. I've seen it," Kataria said. "They bark like dogs at his command."

"It's worth a try," Denaos said hesitantly, as though he himself hadn't expected to say it.

"No, trying to jump over a wall to get into a farm is worth a try, you bark-necked dimwit," Dreadaeleon said snidely. "What you are proposing is the equivalent of trying to beat down the wall with a twig and the wall is sixty feet high, made of metal and when you hit it, it electrocutes your genitals and makes your head explode." He took a breath, then snorted. "It is *impossible*, in other words."

"I've killed plenty of longfaces," Gariath grunted.

"And yet, none of us have even been able to *scratch* this one. Even Bralston couldn't hurt him," Dreadaeleon said. "I'd say it could be done, but I also said that magic had limits and he went and disproved me there. We don't even know if he can be hurt, much less—"

"He can."

Asper only barely whispered, but she commanded their attention nonetheless.

"I hurt him."

"How?" Lenk asked.

"He came to me and he did . . ." She swallowed a breath. "And I hurt him."

"If anyone was to kill him, it would be me," Gariath grunted. "You expect me to believe that you could do anything to him?"

"Take a step back, reptile," Denaos said, stepping protectively in front of her. "And then continue going that way until you fall off a cliff. If she says she hurt him—"

"Humans lie. Humans are weak. Humans are stupid." Shalake stepped beside Gariath, hefting his club. "Which is why they threaten a *Rhega* in front of the Shen."

"And everyone fears the Shen." Kataria stepped in front of Denaos. "My arrows feared them, too. Must be why they tried to hide . . . in Shen gullets."

"Look around you, pink thing," Yaike growled, narrowing his good eye on her. "Look what surrounds you."

"Yeah? Why? Is it harder for you to see with only one eye?" She clacked her teeth together.

"*ENOUGH.*"

Mahalar's voice was a hungry thing, eating all other voices, all other sounds, even its own echo. Muscles relaxed, weapons were lowered. He turned his stare to Asper.

"What did you do?"

She looked at him intently. She spoke resolutely.

"I hurt him."

Mahalar was silent.

Without looking up, he raised two fingers and waved them at Shalake. The immense lizardman grunted, reached to his hip and pulled free an immense warhorn. He trudged heavily up the stone stairs. Then raised the horn to his lips and blew.

The noise was no shrill, shrieking warcry. It was something deep, heavy and inevitable. It blew across the island, through the forests, through the coral, scattering fish and sending eels slithering back into their holes. It ate the sound, as the clouds overhead ate the light. And all was silent.

For a moment.

Then, the other horns came. One, two, three, blowing from the forest and shores and walls in response.

Shalake came back down, belting the horn at his hip. He nodded at Mahalar, who merely grunted back. Lenk blinked, glancing to the ancient lizardman.

"What?" he asked. "What just happened?"

"The watchers are summoned. They will come. We will fight. We will bleed."

"That's it?"

"That is not enough?"

"I mean, just like that? One horn and that's that? Everyone comes to fight?"

"We took the oaths, human," Mahalar said. "Every Shen is born dead, knowing that they walk with hell under them and that they will kill . . . and die to do so."

His sigh was older than even he was. No dust came from his mouth. The light behind his dull ambers dimmed and he closed his eyes with such heaviness that he didn't seem to see much point in opening them again. He said softly, he said sadly.

"That is duty."

327

TWENTY-SIX

AS THE STARS

The last footfall came heavily, crunching upon the sand as Gariath reached the other end of the ring. He stared at his feet, sunk slightly into the moist earth, before looking back over his shoulder.

Fires burned at the foot of the stairs. The coral burned brighter than wood; he hadn't thought it would, but he supposed that was the least weird thing about Jaga. In ever-increasing numbers, more warbands of Shen continued to emerge from the forest. From here, they seemed like tiny lights, fallen stars burning out on the earth.

He didn't know how many paces he had taken, how far he had come. He was sure he had started counting, but after a while, as the sand went on and on, he stopped thinking about how long it was he walked and instead wondered about this earth.

And how much blood it had drank.

He had heard the stories.

This is where it happened, the Shen had uttered. They uttered everything. They never laughed or whispered or wept. *Here, in this ring. This was where she held court. This was where she fell. She was driven back, into the mountain to be sealed away forever.*

The Rhega, they had uttered, not said, *were there, too. They fought. They died. Their blood spilled in oceans. When they lay, they lay with Shen. Where they lay, so lay a thousand corpses that went with them. Why they lay . . .*

He had never heard the end of that story. They had never finished.

Rhega was a word they uttered with the reverence reserved for spirits, as though they—he—weren't actually real. And when they uttered, there was an envy to their voice, a nostalgic resentment for those who had died and left them behind.

On the day it had happened, there was said to have been carnage. The Shen said that. Uttered it. He had asked Mahalar; the elder Shen had said nothing. He had asked Shalake; the warwatcher had simply smiled. He had no one else to ask. There were no ghosts here.

And so he stared out over the ring and tried to imagine it.

He saw fragments of a vision: the bells of Ulbecetonth's chosen shattered and mingled into heaps of scrap along with siege engines and statues of mortal armies, titanic corpses of demons forming a soil of flesh watered by blood for the rest of the mortal flowers to wither and die in. He could see red.

So much red. So many unmoving bodies.

It was a vast field. It had taken him a long time to cross it. There must have been a lot of them. They must have lain screaming, cursing, howling to mothers and reaching out to brothers lying beside them and fathers bleeding out and refusing to die.

He could see that.

But he could smell nothing.

Ktamgi had reeked of memory. Teji stank of regret. And Jaga smelled like nothing. No death. No laments. Not even a faded aroma of a long-ago tear, shed into the earth and waiting for him to find it.

There was no smell of memory here.

There were no ghosts here.

There were no *Rhega* here.

Except for him. And the ones in the stories the Shen uttered.

And could he trust them? Could he bring himself to believe them? To see the *Rhega* walking here, living here, fighting alongside the Shen, alongside humans, as countless as the stars?

He looked to the night sky for reference and snorted. The analogy might have been easier to grasp had he stars to which he could actually compare. There were lights up there, to be certain: purple ones, yellow ones, even the occasional pale blue glow that *might* have been mistaken for a star.

But then they shifted. The fish carrying the lights in their bellies and brows twisted and swam from one another, countless and impossible to keep track of.

"We have no stars here."

To see Shalake standing nearby was no particular surprise. The lizardman had been by Gariath's side since he had arrived, always the one to tell the stories, always the one to utter. He now stood by Gariath's side again and stared up into the sky.

"The sky and sea are one here. There's no room for anything else." He traced a slow-moving, blue-glowing fish with his claw as it swam across the sky. "And these fish only emerge in the shadow of the mountain."

Their gazes shifted to the vast stone monument standing stolidly at the other end of the ring. Haloed by storm clouds, the blue rivers veining it bright and glistening against the many firelights below, it stood with an earthen weariness. It had seen much in its time: many deaths, many bodies.

The blood spilled before its stone eyes tomorrow would be nothing particularly worth noting.

"It's a mistake," Shalake grunted. "We shouldn't be fighting here. The Shen way is to strike quickly from the sea and from the shadows. We should be back there."

He gestured behind them. The kelp forest rose in great masses of twisting, writhing stalks, cleaved neatly down the middle by the stone road leading into the ring.

"Our best chance of success comes from fighting in the forest."

"Scared?" Gariath asked, unsmiling.

"Intelligent," Shalake answered him. "There's no way for the longfaces to move a force as big as the humans claim they have, but for the road. We fight them there at dawn, we paint the sun red with their blood and ours. Their dead are fed to the sharks, ours are sent back to the sea."

Gariath stared at the kelp forest and wondered if it was that simple. Had he ever spoken so casually of throwing himself to his death? Did he ever have the same sliver of an excited whine that crept into Shalake's voice when he said the word "blood"?

Perhaps he wondered too loudly. When he looked back, Shalake had an intent gaze fixed upon him.

"Do you agree?" Shalake asked.

"The humans . . . think a lot," Gariath said. "Especially the little one. They spend a lot of time in their heads talking to themselves and wondering how they can stay alive. If they think it's better to fight here . . ."

"You trust them?"

The dragonman hesitated before speaking. "The longfaces are strong. I've fought them. I've killed them."

"Then they can die."

"They have no concept of 'death.' They look at blood spilling out of their bodies and don't blink. They see their others lying cold on the ground and walk on top of their bodies. They die only when you convince them that they can die."

The smile that creased Shalake's face was morbid enough without the amorous gleam in his eye.

331

"And there will be many," he whispered in a shuddering voice.

Gariath furrowed his eyeridges at the lizardman. "Yeah. A lot."

"The fight will be a story unto itself."

"It might not come to that. As strong as they are, it's the males that are the real danger. The little ones control the others and tell them what to do. If one of them dies, this whole thing becomes simpler."

"The pointy-eared thing's plan." The wistful joy in Shalake's voice dropped back into a growl. "I don't trust it, her or the ones that think it's a good idea."

"Mahalar did."

"Mahalar is our elder. Even if we must respect his decisions, I am the warwatcher. *I* say there should be more warriors in the forest. We can't entrust it to a stupid, pink-skinned thing like her."

"Some of her plans are stupid," Gariath said, nodding.

"The last one almost got you eaten by an Akaneed, you said."

"Almost," Gariath replied. "And it brought me to where the *Rhega* lived."

"And died," Shalake was quick to respond. He swept his hands out across the ring. "Atop the demons, atop the humans, atop the steel and the blood and even the Shen. They fought and they died and they bled until the dead were as countless as the stars."

Gariath looked out over the ring and repeated to himself.

"As countless as the stars."

He tried to imagine it.

He found he couldn't.

"And we may join them." Shalake's voice grew excited. "In a way that only we know how, in a glory that only *we* know. The humans, they will scream and weep and beg. But we will know what it is that meets us on the other side."

"I already know what it is," Gariath muttered. He had talked to enough ghosts to know.

"Because you are *Rhega*," Shalake said. "And we are Shen. We are the same, you and I. To the humans, it will always be a mystery, something to be feared. As will you. Have they never looked at you as we have? Have they never stood here with you and spoke to you like a true creature?"

Gariath tried to remember the last time they had spoken like that, without fear or terror in their voices.

"No," Shalake said. "They are weak things, *Rhega.* You are amongst the Shen now. All we have is each other. And our glorious death."

While not quite certain how lizardman anatomy worked, Gariath dreaded to think what was going on beneath Shalake's loincloth, given the excited quaver in his voice.

The lizardman positively beamed from beneath his scales. His eyes were alight with glorious stories. His heart thundered with memory. His smile glistened with bloodlust reflected in every tooth.

And none of it was his.

That story was someone's else. That memory died on the battlefield. That bloodlust belonged somewhere far away and long ago.

That face Shalake wore, *his* face, belonged to someone who had earned it, not someone who had dug it out of an earth glutted on stories and blood.

It belonged to a *Rhega.*

"I'm leaving," he grunted.

"Rest well. Eat well," Shalake said. "Tomorrow, we die well and see our ancestors."

"Yeah."

Gariath trudged across the sands, head bowed, feet heavy.

He didn't bother to count the steps.

Dreadaeleon chewed absently on the blackened fish, not sure whether his mouth was open or not. He downed a swig of water from a skin, heedless of the belch that followed. He wasn't even aware that he seemed to have stopped blinking. The entirety of his attention was focused on his dinner companions.

And the Shen shared his sentiment. Seven yellow eyes, bright against the fire between them, stared back at him. Two of them, the ones whose lids drooped just slightly and were angled down at the boy, belonged to the towering Shen called Jenaji. Four more belonged to the two Shen flanking him, each of them bearing more black stripes than red as warpaint—something Dreadaeleon began to suspect indicated a role of leadership, based on the way they sat apart from the rest.

The seventh belonged to the lanky thing called Yaike, a Shen who never seemed to leave his bow behind and never seemed to stop glaring. Admittedly, it was difficult to glare with only one eye, but damn if Yaike wasn't trying his hardest to.

Slowly, as though unaware that they were staring back, Dreadaeleon leaned over to the woman beside him and, in what he thought was a whisper, asked.

"Is this as incredibly weird as it feels, or is it just me?"

Asper made a pointed note of keeping her attentions focused only on the fish skewer in her hands. Dreadaeleon acted like he didn't notice her discomfort.

"I mean, waiting to die, sitting next to a bunch of lizards that were ready to help us along with that up until a gang of netherlings decided to come and now they're sitting here with us, *also* waiting to die and—"

"We speak your language, you know," Jenaji suddenly interjected.

"Oh," Dreadaeleon said, blinking. "Well, you hadn't said anything all night, so I assumed only a few—"

"All warwatchers learn your tongue. It is part of our duty." Jenaji leaned back. "I was using the silence to think."

"About what?"

"The battle."

"What about it?"

"Does that really need to be answered?"

Dreadaeleon took another bite of fish and nodded.

"About all my brothers, all my sisters, all the Shen I've lived with," Jenaji replied with a sigh, "all for this battle. It takes silence to try and think why we do what we do in the name of duty."

"What about the others?"

Jenaji glanced at the Shen seated around him and shrugged. "Maybe they just don't like you."

"*Shiat-ay*," Yaike grunted.

"Sorry. Yaike wants it to be known that he *definitely* doesn't like you."

"Why didn't he tell me himself? Can't he speak the tongue?"

"He can. He just doesn't like to."

"*Na-ah*," Yaike suddenly interjected. "*Atta-wah, siat-nai, no-wah-ah tanna Shen.*"

"What was that?" Asper asked, finally curious enough to look up.

"He said it's a Shen's duty to speak the Shen's language," Jenaji replied, plucking another fish skewer from the fire and taking a bite of it. "That's not what we were told, but Yaike is the kind of Shen who likes to do a lot of things that aren't necessary."

"Well, he's got a point, doesn't he?" Asper suggested. "You . . . warwatchers, is it? You're the leaders of your . . ." She frowned, searching for the words. "Tribes? Clan?"

"Shen."

"Leaders of the Shen, right," she said. "Shouldn't it fall to you to protect your people's heritage? Your culture? I mean, you speak for your people, don't you?"

"The Shen have not spoken in some time," Jenaji replied. "We have only a few words to say a few things. We use your tongue only to ask questions of you before we kill you. A warwatcher does not lead through words or through life."

"I'm not sure I understand."

Jenaji reached up and patted the bow on his back.

"My heritage."

He traced the warpaint on his body, a line for each life he had taken.

"My culture."

He stomped a foot on the earth, old and dead.

"My people."

"So, everything about you revolves around death," Asper said, voice souring.

"All the important things."

"No medicine? No arts? No traditions?"

"We have those. To fight longer, to celebrate the kill, to remember the dead."

"How can a society live on those?"

"When the mortal armies freed us from Ulbecetonth, we took our oaths. The lives of our fathers, our brothers, our sons; all were offered up to guard Ulbecetonth. We do not live. We serve the oaths."

"But what about your children? What about your trade? What about villages, religion, stories?"

"Our children are born dead. Our trade is death. Our villages are graveyards, we worship there and we pluck our stories from the cold, dead earth."

"So . . . what? You just sit here, killing people until you die yourself?"

The Shen, save for Jenaji, nodded firmly in response.

"Huh," Dreadaeleon chimed in. "That's stupid."

Only Jenaji nodded.

Asper elbowed Dread firmly, adding a scolding glare to accompany it. Dreadaeleon shot her one back, save with a little more confusion, as he rubbed his side.

"Well, it *is*," he protested.

Yaike leaned forward, muttered something to the Shen in their own tongue, and they rose in reply.

"Shalake calls," Jenaji said curtly. "We go."

"Is there a plan, then?" Asper called after him as he and the other Shen stalked away. "Do we know what we're going to do?"

"We know what *we're* going to do," Jenaji said. "Do what humans do and try to survive."

"But why?" she demanded, rising to her feet. "We can do more together than we can apart, surely." The Shen said nothing as they turned and stalked away. She looked around for support. "Right?"

Dreadaeleon shrugged, took another bite of fish. Asper watched Jenaji as he disappeared into the crowd of Shen.

In silence.

There was something to it, though. It was not a serene silence of meditation, nor a tense, fearful silence. It was a heavy, weary silence, like there were words to say, words that had been rehearsed and repeated so many times no one saw much of a point in reiterating them.

She wasn't sure what they were. They probably didn't involve the words "goodbye," "love," or "forever." "Kill," "die," and "through the rectum," maybe.

She surveyed the assembled Shen and frowned.

"How many could there possibly be?"

"A hundred," Dreadaeleon replied. "Probably about a hundred and a half by now."

"A third of the longfaces' numbers." Asper's frown deepened with every word muttered. "That explains it."

"Explains what?"

"Have you honestly not been paying attention?" she asked, frustrated. "To how they're all walking around, acting like it's their last day alive?"

"It probably is." Dreadaeleon's cavalier attitude was not at all diminished through a mouthful of fish. "I mean, they're going up against twice their number in berserker warrior women led by weird, magic-spewing males, with rocks and sticks." He belched. "Sharp rocks and sticks, admittedly, but still."

"We've gone up against the same and survived."

"Not this many. And the times we've fought Sheraptus have not gone well for us."

She wondered, idly, if she would ever stop shuddering at the mention of that name.

"Kataria's plan . . ." she began hesitantly.

"If it works, glorious," Dreadaeleon replied sharply. "If not—and I have several solid reasons why it should not—then the Shen seem a little wiser." He stared into the fire for a moment. "Personally, I admire their certainty."

"So you're saying they're right to act like we're all going to die?" she snapped. "We should all lie down and wait for the longfaces to come and—"

"I'm saying that some outcomes are more likely than others. Some things, no matter how . . ." He caught himself, swallowing something. "No matter how much we might want them, just aren't likely to occur." His face twitched. "And sometimes, death is a more comforting thought than the alternative."

And with that, the boy assumed the same silence as the Shen, as deep, as dark, as lamentable. To stare at him caused her to ache. Whatever words she might offer him he had rehearsed, repeated a thousand times to himself and found them not worth bothering with once again.

And so he sat.

And so she stared.

"Well, this looks a tad uncomfortable," a voice said from nearby.

Denaos stood at the edge of the fire, a rucksack slung over one shoulder and a rather pained expression painted across his face.

"Where've you been?" Asper asked.

"Are you quite sure you want to ask me that? I'd really hate to get in the middle of you nurturing your philosophical erections."

She looked and spoke flatly at him. "So, can you just not answer questions normally or . . ."

"Fine, if you're going to be *that* way," Denaos muttered, hefting off the rucksack and emptying it onto the sand. "At my insistence, our scaly friends have seen fit to allow us to look at their stockpiles to see if there's anything we can use."

"They have stockpiles?" Dreadaeleon asked, looking surprised. "But not pants?"

"Well, the reef catches a lot of boats, some lost, some searching for the island," Denaos said, sifting through the contents. "The Shen come, pick off the survivors, loot them for metal, food, that sort of thing."

"Anything they can use to kill more people and sink other ships," Asper said, voice souring.

Denaos plucked up a stout, curved blade from the stockpile. "Just so."

"What's this?" she asked.

"A sword, moron."

He tossed the blade to Asper, who caught it with only miminal stumbling and bleeding. She winced at the cut, sucking her finger as she inspected the weapon. A short, ugly little thing, thin and curved like a cleaver instead of a proper sword.

"Why?"

"Look, if you keep asking stupid questions, you can't really blame me for my answers," Denaos said with a sigh. "Clearly, tomorrow, what with being fraught with danger and death—" he paused and cast a look at Dreadaeleon, "—certain death, anyway, you'll need something to defend yourself."

"Yeah, I get that, but—"

"That's a handy one, see." Denaos gestured as he spoke. "It's short, meant for getting in close. You use it to strike at soft parts." He pointed two fingers, pressed them beneath his chin. "Thrust that thing into their neck, like so, it's near instant."

"And this is supposed to help against . . . what, three-hundred-odd females?"

"And males."

The intent of his voice met with the intensity of his stare and she knew what he meant.

In his eyes was a dreadful promise that, if they should fall tomorrow, if the Shen should collapse and the netherlings overrun them, if they should come to her with chains and the intent of delivering her to their Master . . .

The blade, indeed, would save her.

She understood. She swallowed that knowledge in a dry, queasy breath and nodded at him, understanding. A frown creased his face, like he had hoped she might not have.

"Is that . . . a jar?" Dreadaeleon asked, leaning forward.

The rogue plucked up the small glass container. "Kataria wanted it. Had to dig through a mountain of crap to find it."

"So her master plan to save us . . . involves a jar," Dreadaeleon said, rubbing his temples. "Why do we keep listening to her?"

"Because Lenk does," Denaos replied. "For obvious reasons."

"What reasons?"

"Obvious ones."

"Which ones?"

The rogue quirked a brow. "You didn't catch it?"

"Catch what?"

"The tension in her stomach? The bead of sweat running down his temple? The faint but unmistakable odor of fear, shame, and day-old fish?"

The boy shook his head, slack-jawed. Asper blanched. The rogue shrugged.

"I'll tell you when you're older."

"What? *What?*" The boy leaned forward. "What is it you're getting at? What did they do? What—" Though it seemed as though to stop that line of questioning would break his neck, something else caught his attention. "Where did you get that?"

"That" turned out to be something out of place with the rest of the equipment: a single stone, fragmented and decayed, attached to a black iron necklace. Dreadaeleon let it dangle before him, inspecting it carefully.

"I took it from that netherling riding the . . . thing."

"Sikkhun."

"Whatever." Denaos reached out a hand to the boy. "Give it back."

"Why do you want it?" Asper asked.

"Because throughout this whole damn episode, I haven't gotten a *single* pretty thing. I took it, it's mine."

Dreadaeleon, without looking at him, tucked it away into a pocket of his coat. The rogue shot him a look of offense and shoved his various contents back into the rucksack.

"Fine, then. But if we find some kind of stupid book or something *you* want, I'm taking it." He hefted it over his shoulder and sneered at the boy. "And I'm going to wipe with it." He trudged away, pausing to lean obscenely close to the boy. "In *front* of you."

The rogue left, presumably to dispense the rest of his deliveries. Asper cast a glance at him before turning to follow.

"I need to . . . talk to him about something."

"Of course," Dreadaeleon muttered as she hurried away.

When he was certain she wouldn't notice him, he turned and scowled at her.

He watched her as she walked away without looking back at him, so brazenly strutting up to Denaos, laying a hand upon his shoulder. He could see her silhouetted by the firelight, drawing closer to the tall man, looking up at him. Her eyes were flashing in the light, bright and wet and—

They're doing it, you know.

The thought came suddenly and unpleasantly unbidden. And like an itch that grew into a rash that grew in leprosy, it festered there.

Right in front of you, like they don't even care you're here—because of you, I might add. You *saved them—again—from the netherlings, from Bralston. You're the one who knows magic and they haven't even* thought *to ask your advice. No, instead they ask the* shict *because she smells like fish or something. That moron Denaos didn't even* think *he might have something here.*

He pulled the stone from his pocket and studied it. To all appearances, it seemed to be just a chunk of rock on a chain.

But is it? Did *Denaos have something here?*

Well, possibly not. It looks like just a piece of rock. But there's no sense in being stupid about this. Rocks on chains are not something I trust netherlings with, considering what we've seen.

The stones, yes?

The red ones, right.

The ones that could achieve limitless power by avoiding the price—

Transferring. Transferring the price.

Apologies. The ones that could take your illness away from you. The ones that could make you the strongest, the most powerful, the most—

One moment . . . am I talking to myself or is there someone else there?

He shook his head violently, throwing the thoughts from his head like gnats. He turned, teeth clenched and scowling at the pale figure standing behind him. Greenhair stared back impassively, glistening against the fire, a slight smile upon her lips.

"Damn it, stop *doing* that!" the boy demanded angrily.

"Apologies, lorekeeper."

"Oh, good. At least you're sorry." He rolled his eyes. "What need have I for things like sanctity of thoughts when I have the apologies of sea-tramps?"

"I merely intended to—"

"Ah, good, because for a moment there I thought all I was going to get from you was apologies, invasion of thoughts, and convenient betrayals that sell me and my friends to perversile longfaced lunatics. But so long as I get *intentions*, I'm fine."

"There's no need to be—"

"There is *every* need." Dreadaeleon held up a single finger. "You helped

339

us once. *Just* once in a series of mishaps that have led us to nearly being killed and, in those moments when we're not, you're in my head, telling me things I don't want to hear. You may have helped us out at Komga, you may have kept the Shen from killing us, but that's no reason to trust you."

"Reason and trust are squabbling siblings, often disagreeing," the siren replied as calmly as though she hadn't had a litany of accusations leveled against her. "That which demands trust needs no reason, that which possesses reason does not always require trust."

Riddle-speak and cryptic gibberings. Dreadaeleon drew a sigh inward. *But the logic is at least a little sound.*

Thank you.

"I said stop that," Dreadaeleon snapped. "I suspect you had a point in coming to me beyond making me hate my own tremendous brain."

"A point, an offer, a promise." Her eyebrows raised a hair's breadth. "You are going to die tomorrow."

"And is that a point or a promise?"

"Both, if a plan is not formulated."

"Kataria has one."

"I have doubts in her abilities. As do you. As does everyone. The thought echoes inside their heads, loud and screeching, begging for someone to draw upon a vaster intellect, a stronger knowledge."

Watch yourself, old man, he cautioned himself mentally. *The flattery is only slightly less subtle than that step she's taking toward you . . . that thigh sliding out of her silk . . . that glistening, porcelain thigh . . .* He shook his head, forced his eyes back upon hers. *You should protest, tell her she's not going to get to you like that.*

His eyes flickered downward. The silk rode dangerously upon her hip, as though just one more movement might send it slithering down her body completely.

Then again, maybe it's enough that you know and that you don't *act on it, right?*

"The Shen are strong, it is true, but the longfaces are stronger, more numerous, their powers unlimited." Her smile was slight, suggestive, edged with just a hint of greed. "As yours could be."

While he had been rendered speechless by many things ranging from a well-placed barb from Denaos to that one time Asper bent over a bit too far, rarely had Dreadaeleon been rendered thoughtless. And while he could certainly guess at what the siren was suggesting, he couldn't quite bring himself to think of the specifics, of the implications.

Of the cost.

"No," was the sole word he could manage.

"I have seen him, lorekeeper. I have watched him. He presumes the world, and all in it, bows to him as his warriors do. That is why your friend's plan will fail. He cannot comprehend of a world that allows him to die."

"No."

"But the crown . . . he covets it. He wears it constantly. He fears its loss. I have seen him remove it. I know it can be taken from him—"

"*No.*"

"—and given to another—"

"*NO.*"

"—that they might wield what he does."

"*ENOUGH!*"

His roar, shrill as it was, drew attention from the encircling Shen who, at a glare from the siren, returned to the business of sharpening weapons and fletching arrows.

"Do you *hear* yourself?" Dreadaeleon demanded. "Do you *know* what you're suggesting?"

"I know the crown gives power."

"And do you know where it comes from?"

She nodded, solemnly.

"And do you know that it's heresy in the eyes of the Venarium?"

"I know it's necessary in the eyes of the Sea Mother and the world," Greenhair replied firmly. "A world that breaks beneath our feet as Ulbece-tonth begins to claw her way free from that dark place she was sent."

"And I'm to stop it with the lives of . . ." He laughed, slightly incredulous. "I didn't even count how many were in that furnace, how many more there might be, how many they spent like kindling to keep their powers running far beyond the point they ever should."

"As powerful as they are, you are more so. You have the vision, the drive. If only your limits were as removed as theirs are."

341

"The stones transfer limitations. The price is still paid, but by someone else."

"And with that burden no longer yours to bear, you could—"

"*LOOK AT THEM.*" He swept an arm out over the Shen. "Do you *see* how they look at you? With reverence? With awe? And you say I should sacrifice their kinsmen? Living beings who speak your name like it's to be respected, people who don't know that you're saying I should eat them alive to commit heresy."

"I say you should sacrifice some," Greenhair said, voice raising a quaver.

"And when some isn't enough? When we need *more*?"

"It will not come to that."

"You can't know that. It's too high a price to pay to save just a few."

"To save *everyone*," she all but snarled. "Are you deluded with the idea that Ulbecetonth's threat is contained to this island? The demons are returning. If Ulbecetonth breaks free, she will drown the world, return people to oblivion for the sake of making her children more comfortable. If the longfaces prevail tomorrow, they will deliver this world to darker hands still. *You* could stop them both if only you lacked—"

"A conscience?"

"*Limits.*"

For the first time, the porcelain of her face cracked, the melody of her voice broke. She became a creature of desperate stares, bared teeth, sweat-slick temples and urgent, pleading whispers. A greedy, hungry, weeping mortal thing.

"I *know* you. I know your thoughts. I know what you want, I know what you would do to get it and I know the dark places you don't dare to tread and they simply *do not exist.* Your only fear is that they won't respect you, that you won't be strong enough to make a difference, that you can't do what you need to to save *her.*"

Dreadaeleon felt his eyelid tremble. Somehow the word "her" on the siren's lips sounded a vulgar thing.

"But you can," Greenhair said, nodding vigorously. "And I can make it happen. I can give you the power to save her, to save yourself, to save the *world.* You will die tomorrow, lorekeeper, and she and all of them with you unless you take this power when I offer it to you."

Dreadaeleon stared at her a moment. That thoughtlessness that had possessed him earlier vanished for but a single moment. And for a single moment, she saw something inside his head, something big and bright and beautiful.

And it made her smile.

And it made him feel sick.

"If, indeed, we're all going to die tomorrow," Dreadaeleon said calmly, "then I won't give everyone the added problem of knowing you've suggested what you have. But if it's over and you and I are both still alive, I will eagerly endeavor to remedy that."

He turned.

"We are done," he said.

He walked.

"Your thoughts suggest differently," she called after him.

He did not stop.

More than anything, it was how horribly candid she was being that irritated Lenk.

She dipped another two fingers into the mixture of ash, water, and dye ground into an ugly, dark-red paste. She drew two lines upon her left cheek, complimenting the ones upon her right and the solid bar of red across her eyes. It matched the stripes encircling her arms, the tiny slashes running along the tops of her ears, the curving barbs running down the sides of her midriff.

She leaned over the edge of the stone bridge that ran over the vast, circular pool below. She stared at her own reflection, checking the application of her paint. Satisfied, she rose back up, dipped another two fingers in, and resumed her work.

As though preparing to go die was a perfectly normal thing.

"For the record," Lenk said from the other edge of the bridge, "I think this is completely stupid and you're completely stupid for doing it."

"Your objection has been noted," she replied as she drew a single red line from her lower lip to her chin. "And once I'm done here, I will be more than happy to reassure you that it is, in fact, *you* who are stupid." She dabbed her fingers again. "And then kick you in the groin."

"You don't see the idiocy in this? Painting yourself to be as inconspicuous as a bipedal, wounded raccoon and calling it camouflage?"

"Ordinarily, this *would* be a poor choice of camouflage," she said, checking herself in the pool once again. "And, if you can tell me that there's anything at all ordinary about a forest made out of coral through which fish fly like birds, I'll gladly stay behind."

"I misspoke," Lenk said. "What's idiotic is the fact that you're going out there to try and shoot a man who can stop arrows with his *brain.*"

"Mind," Kataria corrected. "If he stops arrows with his mind, that's a problem. If he stops them with his brain, that solves my problem."

"But—"

"I have an idea." Kataria whirled on him, narrowing her eyes and baring her teeth. "Let's you and I just pretend for a moment that I'm actually smarter than a monkey and have already thought about how dangerous this is and how scared I am of doing it and that I'm trying very, very hard *not* to think about what Sheraptus does to people and what he did to Asper and what he might do to me and then let's pretend you stop sitting there and telling me how dangerous this is before I pretend to put an arrow through your eye socket just so I can have a moment to tell myself this needs to be done so no one else has to die. *How about we do that?*"

When she had finished talking she was breathing hard through her nostrils, her lips pressed together to keep from trembling as much as her eyes were as she locked them onto him.

And he was silent.

343

"It's not like we have a lot of options," Kataria said, returning to painting herself. "It has to be this way."

"I liked Shalake's idea of attacking Sheraptus through the forest."

"And then when he realizes something's up, about the time the arrows start flying, he starts shooting fire. A forest on fire is a death trap, Lenk, one that will waste warriors we need here." She drew in a long, slow breath. "No. One warrior, one shot is all that's needed. Right in his neck. Before he knows it. Then I run." She nodded to herself. "One shot. In his neck. Before he knows it. Then I run."

She repeated each word, enunciating each syllable carefully until it became mantra, repeating the mantra until it became a deal with some god listening from far, far away.

She was fragile, if only at that moment, if only unwilling to admit it to herself or to him. And so, instead of speaking what he was thinking, he kept it in his head.

There has to be another way, he thought. *I mean, Shalake knows the forests. He can find a place that . . . doesn't burn . . . in a forest. Okay, maybe she has a point. But there's got to be another way. There's clearly no way to win this, right?*

It took a moment for him to remember that no one would be answering him this time.

There's always retreat, he conceded to himself.

"You ever notice how easily we run away?"

It wasn't the first time he had suspected her ears might just be big enough to hear what he was thinking. She stared into her own reflection, a solemn look upon her face.

"I mean, it's not like we're cowards or anything . . . or not all the time, anyway. We run when it's practical, when we're outmatched or in danger or something." She looked out from the top of the stairs, out over Jaga and to its distant shores. "We could probably figure a way out of this, if we wanted to; a way to run away and let the Shen fight it out and hope that everything works out all right."

She glanced at him.

"You've probably thought out a few."

Kill a Shen and steal their boat, kill Hongwe and steal his boat, kill enough Shen and possibly Hongwe to strap them together to make a boat out of flesh and then flee using a sail made out of their skin.

"It hasn't been on my mind," he said simply.

"Either way, I like that you haven't brought it up."

"And why is that?"

"A couple reasons," she said, shrugging. "I guess there are some things you can't run from. I tried." She looked back at her reflection, her face covered in a red deep enough to be blood. "I tried hard."

"And was it worth it?"

She looked at him. And did nothing else but look.

"This seems like the sort of thing we can't run from," she said. "The sort of thing we shouldn't try to run from." She held out a hand. "Demons rising from below. Netherlings coming out to get *them*. Neither one of them has a problem with us dying. We don't stop them both, a lot more people die."

"We've seen a lot of people die," Lenk said. "Killed a lot of them ourselves."

"There's got to be a reason for it," she said. "Beyond money and survival. There's got to be a good reason for doing what we did here, even if we haven't done it yet. Because if it is all about the money . . ."

She didn't finish the thought with words. Her frown did it well enough for her.

It was hard to see her hurt. So he looked away. It was harder to look at the other end of the bridge, opposite the top of the stairs, and the stone door ensconced in the mountain's face.

A simple slab set impassably within a frame hewn of granite stood seven feet within the face of the mountain. The image of Ulbecetonth was carved as a mantle atop it, hands extended from the mountain's face in benevolence. The rivers that wept from the mountain's crown turned to thin trickles here, a thousand tiny tears shed every moment to empty into the pool below.

This. This rock. This rock within a rock, and all its tiny, weepy tears, was what they were going to fight for tomorrow.

What people would die for.

"Death hasn't bothered you before."

"Well, maybe it does, now. I know it does, you."

"I was actually feeling pretty okay with just getting on my skin-ship and leaving."

345

"Your skin . . ." She stopped herself from pursuing a line of conversation too stupid to bear. "If you didn't care, you wouldn't have come here in the first place. We had a hundred chances to leave, to take an easier job with better pay, but you chose to follow the tome all this way."

"I didn't, no. Something else made me come. Something in my head. It wasn't bothered by however many people could die. I think it got a little giddy at the prospect, in fact. But I didn't come here for them. I came here for it."

"And you could have resisted it, like you have before. But you're here, with me."

"And the demons. And the netherlings. And the Shen."

"And me," she repeated. "But if you still want to run away, this is your last chance." She clicked her tongue, looked up at the shifting stars overhead. "But if, just once, you want to do something that might be worth not running from . . . well, I guess this is also your last chance."

He turned from her gaze, sighing as he leaned onto his knees.

"I'm just having a hard time seeing the point in it all. We kill the netherlings, then what? Ulbecetonth is still under there."

"Then we kill her, too." She sneered. "I said we can't solve this by running away. Violence is still a good answer."

"How do we kill her, then? Whatever was in me, *it* killed demons. *It* kept me alive. Without it, I'm—"

"Not crazy," she interrupted, edging over to him. "Not insane. Not listening to anyone but you. Everything else you've done has been for some voice in your head, some dream that haunted you. But now . . ."

She lay a hand upon his shoulder, gave it a gentle squeeze, and smiled.

"Now, whatever you do tomorrow, you do for yourself."

He returned the smile, hoping she would think the tears forming at the corners of his eyes were the result of overwhelming emotion and not because she was currently squeezing a hunk of decaying, pus-weeping flesh that was his shoulder.

She rose to her feet. He took a moment to swallow a scream and followed her. They walked to the edge of the stairs together and were caught between stars. Beneath them, the fires of the Shen continued to burn as the lizardmen continued to work in silence. Above them, the fish brimming with the lights of their bodies continued to dance and sway in the shadow of the mountain.

"There." Kataria pointed out over the distance, where the road slipped from the vast circle of sand and disappeared into the coral forest. "That's where I'll do it."

"You sound awfully confident."

"Why wouldn't I be?" she asked, her grin gleaming with her canines. "I'm *me*."

"It might take more than fancy new arrows to kill him, you know."

"Ah, yes." She plucked her weapons up, stringing them across her shoulder. She took a single arrow from the quiver, a long, black-shafted thing with a nasty-looking barbed head. "Ravensdown fletching, barbed heads that can't be pulled out without causing excessive bleeding." She batted her eyelashes at him mockingly. "How *did* you know?"

"I just saw it in the Shen stockpile and thought of you," he replied with a shrug and a smile. "You like them, I take it."

He wasn't sure if she was trying to appear amorous, seductive, or maybe a little hungry, but her gaze was hard, unwavering, and more than a little predatory as it ran up and down him.

"If we had more time, I'd convince you." She slipped the arrow back in the quiver. "But I've got to go get my jar and get into position."

He chose not to ask about the jar.

"I suppose I should tell you something deep and profound before you leave, shouldn't I?" he asked.

She looked him over and gestured with her chin. "Go ahead, then."

He drew in a sharp breath and nodded. "Ever since I was young—"

He made it about that far before she seized him by his collar, pulling him closer to her. Fragile as anything else about her was, the firmness of her body as she drew him up against her and pressed her lips to his was not. His arms found her tense, taut, trembling beneath him.

He felt as though he held a precarious grip on a tall mountain with nothing but emptiness beneath him. And when it ended, when she pulled away, he felt as though he fell.

"It was going to be boring, anyway," she said, smiling as she wiped a bit of warpaint from his lips and reapplied it to hers. "Stay alive."

"You, too," he said, watching her as she traipsed away and down the stairs. After a moment, he called out after her. "If you don't return, I just want you to—"

"Gods, I *get it*, Lenk!" she snarled back. "Riffid, if I knew you were going to get like this, I would have just let Inqalle kill us both."

He glanced to the bridge, saw one of the many stone fragments broken from its edges. He resisted the urge to wing one of them at her head as she trotted down the stairs, if only because his shoulder was currently in agony.

Agony became searing pain in a matter of a few short breaths and one decidedly unmasculine squeal. He could feel his skin breaking, dying beneath his tunic, he could feel the blood and disease weeping from it. He peeled out of the garment before more than a few spatters of red could stain it.

He threw himself to the edge of the bridge, only narrowly keeping himself from tumbling into the water as he strained to scoop up a precious handful. He had only a moment to notice how it tingled unpleasantly upon his skin. When he splashed it onto his shoulder, though, he had more time to appreciate just how painful it was to feel the cold chill of the water upon the blackening rot of his wound.

And more than enough time to try not to cry like a little girl.

He could see his face contorted in the rippling reflections below, the screwed-up agony distorted into something even worse as he swallowed his screams, let his tears fall into the pool and lie on top of it, like they weren't good enough to simply blend in with the rest of the water.

He shook, brushed, clawed the water from his wound. It fell upon the stones, gathered together, slid off the bridge to smother his tears and rejoin the pool.

"The water will not soothe you."

Had he not been close to crying, he might have had the wit to ask how Mahalar had appeared at the end of the bridge and what he was doing there. But the elder Shen's comings and goings and the very intent way with which he stared at Lenk from behind his hood were, at that moment, not the weirdest thing about him.

"It does not remember you."

The Shen rose to his feet, shambled to edge of the bridge and leaned over, casually letting a hand dangle several fingers' lengths above the water.

And, like a cat pleased to see its master, the water rose to the Shen. In liquid tendrils, it reached out from the pool to caress his fingers, running water over the rotted skin and exposed carpals of his hand.

Lenk cringed; this seemed like the sort of thing he would regret asking. Still . . .

"How?"

"It was there. Ages ago. And so was I." He pointed a bony finger to the storm clouds encircling the mountain. "From there."

"Rain doesn't do . . . *that*," Lenk pointed out.

"Rain touches the earth, is drank, is gone." Mahalar bobbed his head. "Some of this water touches the earth. It flows beneath the mountain. You saw it in the chasm."

Lenk nodded. He recalled the vast tunnel from which he and Kataria had emerged, brimming with inky black water, stretching into a dark void.

"Those dark places run beneath the mountain. The water there remembers nothing but darkness . . . and her. It drowns. It kills. This water . . ." He stroked the liquid tendrils, which caressed his hand adoringly. "This water touches no ground. It stays between heaven and earth."

He drew in a breath and let it out in a cloud of dust that settled upon the water. The liquid shrank from it, wary of something earthen.

"The blood of the Sea Mother," Mahalar said. "Too pure for mortals."

"So, that makes you . . . what?" Lenk asked.

"Very, very old."

A sneer came over Mahalar's face. He clenched his fist so hard the exposed bones cracked with the effort. The water trembled as though scolded and slid away from his hand.

"She chose this as her seat, to defy the Sea Mother. And we chose it as her prison for the same reason. This water remembers her. It remembers what she did."

He extended his fingers to the water once more. They obliged, warily, reaching up to touch the exposed bone claws of his worn tips.

"They called us slaves from this water. Us, the children of the Sea Mother. And when we no longer called them masters, we sent them back to it. It remembers them, when they did not look like the demons they are now. It remembers them when they were beautiful and wicked. It remembers the stones we tied to their feet when we hurled them in and sent them into the water."

He sighed wearily, closing his dull, amber eyes.

"It remembers when they rose up again."

"As the Abysmyths," Lenk muttered.

"We called them 'enemy.' As did the mortal armies. And we fought them together."

"I've heard it said that memory is all that really kills a demon."

"Memory shapes everything. The sky and sea of Jaga no longer remember what it means to be separate." He swept a hand to the fish swimming through the night sky overhead. "The land no longer remembers my name, I have been around so long. But water remembers everything . . ."

He tapped a slender bone claw against the surface. A ripple echoed across the water, tearing the reflections of themselves and of the dancing stars into pieces and swallowing them whole.

When all light was gone, all that remained was something vast and black, something deep and dreadful.

A hole.

A hole stretching into infinite void beneath the water.

"How . . ." he began, staring down over the edge, "how deep does it go?"

"All the way to hell," Mahalar replied casually.

It was difficult to tell if the elder Shen was being cryptic or literal. Lenk decided he didn't want to know.

The young man leaned over farther, as if to see if there were something that would tell him. Some trace of light not yet swallowed, some fragment of reflection to tell him that this was still water. He found nothing.

Or rather, he *saw* nothing.

From the void, from the water, smothered by void, muffled by liquid, he could hear it. It was something soft, something trembling, something too quiet and too pure and too old to know what language was or what words were or anything beyond a simple, mournful melody.

A song. Just for him.

It pained him to hear it. He could feel it, in his skull and in his blood and seeping into his shoulder. He winced, touching a hand to the throbbing mess of flesh.

"Ask it to help you."

Lenk turned to the elder Shen who stared at him with the same patient intent one watches a corpse to see if they're really dead.

"Call out to it," the lizardman said.

"I don't know—"

"You do," Mahalar insisted. "I've seen it. Back when they walked with us, against the demons. They talked to it in the darkness, they cried out to it when the blood was so thick they could barely speak for fear of choking on it."

The elder Shen lowered his gaze, unblinking.

"And it answered them. Always."

"It," Lenk said quietly, "is not that simple."

"Can you call it?"

"Do you know what it feels like?"

"I asked—"

"And so did I," Lenk said. "Do you know what it feels like?"

"I do not."

"I guess you wouldn't. Do you want to know?"

"I do not."

Lenk stared at him for a moment before looking back into the water. "It's like . . . an itch." He shook his head. "No, that's stupid. Not like an itch. It's like . . ." He chuckled a little, incredulous of himself. "Not like anything, actually. It just . . . *is.* You know?"

He looked to the elder Shen and nodded. The elder Shen did not nod back.

"And what it is, is constant. It's . . . always there. Always. Even when it's silent, it's there. It's watching you. It's listening to you. It's tensing. It's getting ready. When it first started happening, I guess I just felt it was . . . stress, I don't know. Whatever it is that goes on inside people that makes them hate themselves."

"But?"

"But then it . . . started saying things. It starts talking, even when it isn't talking. It wants things, it needs things, and if you ignore it, it . . ." He drew in a sharp breath, held it. "It doesn't like that. And it keeps talking. And it keeps saying things. It wants you to do things and it wants you to kill things and it wants you to . . . to *hurt.*

"So you start talking back, just so you think you aren't insane for a few moments. And then it keeps insisting and you bargain with it and you beg it and you agree with it and it keeps talking until you just can't . . ." He bit his lower lip until it bled. "You need it to stop. You need it to be quiet. So you do what it wants."

His entire body shook as he released his breath, as he sputtered a few droplets of blood onto his stomach. A tension he wasn't sure was even there released itself. A cold hand took itself off his shoulder.

"You kill for it."

He eased himself onto his elbows, onto his back and lay there, trying too hard to forget he could still remember what the voice still sounded like.

"And then?" Mahalar asked.

"And then what?"

"How does it feel?"

"For a moment, it feels right."

"And then?"

"And then . . . it starts talking again."

Once the words had all been spoken and spent, Lenk was a little surprised at how easily they had come. He imagined it would all be more painful. He had always feared that, upon hearing him speak so candidly about murder and bloodshed and voices in his head, he would be met with horror.

Somehow, Mahalar's stare, alight with eager curiosity, was worse.

"If you called to it—" the elder Shen began.

"You're not listening," Lenk interrupted.

"I am. I hear you now as I heard them then. I heard them weep and I heard them cry out. But they still killed the demons like nothing else could. Their suffering still prevented more from happening. The netherlings come to free Ulbecetonth and use her for their own purposes. They aren't the first. They won't be the last unless you call out to it and kill her."

"So what? Why can't we leave Ulbecetonth in wherever you left her?"

"Because then *we* still have to guard her. *We* still have to tell the stories. *We* have to hand our children hatchets as soon as they can walk and teach them how to kill before they can speak."

"So it's all for your people," Lenk chuckled. "And here I thought you were some benevolent, wise old fart who just wanted to make the world a better place."

"I don't care about the world. I've been on it long enough to have grown bored with the novelty of it, human," Mahalar growled, dust exuding from his mouth. "I care about my people. That's why I want to save them."

"If you wanted that, you wouldn't be standing by and sending them to go die tomorrow."

"Die? No, human. We are born dead. Every Shen child is raised to know that his life belongs to the oaths we swore. We escaped slavery under Ulbecetonth to be made slaves again through generations. The oaths became hymn. The Shen below have been waiting for tomorrow all their lives, the time they can kill and die and be free of this . . . all of this.

"I would have them live. I would have them have an island that was a home and not a battleground waiting to happen. I would have them find uses for things other than weapons. And that cannot happen unless you—"

"I'm not going to," Lenk said. "I can't."

He staggered to his feet, plucked up his shirt, and eased it back over his head. When his vision was cleared of the cloth, Mahalar stood at the edge of the stairs, staring over his shoulder at the young man.

"I am well aware of what you can't do, human," Mahalar said. "I know you can't survive without it. That wound in your shoulder is not the only thing that pains you, is it? All the agony it has spared you from is coming back."

"This isn't doing a lot to convince me," Lenk replied.

"I suspect it might not. If you can't see that you will die without the voice, then you cannot be convinced. But I was in the chasm, too. I saw you. And you know that Ulbecetonth will break free one day. And you know she will come for you, the murderer of her children."

The elder Shen turned and began to shamble down the stairs.

"But maybe you'll get lucky and die tomorrow. That way, you won't have to see what happens when she *does* break free."

Lenk watched him go. He watched the fire pits go dark as the Shen extinguished them and hefted their weapons. He watched the fish flee from the sky as the first light of dawn began to creep over the horizon. He watched the forest and wondered where Kataria might be in that tangle of kelp and coral.

And he tried to ignore the pains creeping through his body.

TWENTY-SEVEN
THE IDEAL TIME

Dawn came timidly over Jaga, unwilling to challenge the mist that slid through the forest. And the mist, sensing weakness, did everything it could to smother the light. The result was something that crept over the island like a slow-moving tide, washing out colors in a foggy gray.

Those ambitious fish that emerged early to peck at the coral and the sands, and those opportunistic fish that emerged earlier to prey upon the former, moved like motes of dust in light. They were bright and vivid against the gray, living grafitti on something perfectly bland and respectable.

The island was perfectly devoid of sound.

The island was drained of color.

The island was a gloomy hell of serenity with absolutely nothing to do but sit quietly in a perch of sturdy red coral and wait for something to happen.

Summarily, Kataria thought, it was the perfect time to put an arrow in someone's gullet.

Or it would be once he decided to come by. She sat nestled amidst the coral, perched upon the perfect spot. Just enough twisted red branches to conceal her with a fair amount of space to offer a clear view—and a clearer shot—of the highway before her and a fair amount of space to wriggle out when everything went to hell.

Not that everything is going to go to hell, she cautioned herself. *Goodness no. It's all quite simple. He's arrogant, unaware, uncautious. He'll never see you and he won't know what's happened until you're gone. All that could go wrong is the extremely unlikely event of him . . . looking up. Then you're dead. Or worse, alive and at his mercy and* then *you're—*

Stop, stop, STOP!

She clutched her ears, trying futilely to block out her own thoughts. There was a time and a place for self-doubt and it most certainly wasn't when one was about to try to kill a sexual sadist who spewed fire and lightning like a chubby child spews cake crumbs.

Especially when that chubby child was composed of hundreds of berserker, sharp-toothed warrior women brimming with jagged metal and bloodlust and quite possibly—

Stop it again, she urged herself. *What did you usually do in times like these? Shoot something? Right, right, that's coming. What else? Ask your friends? Gariath would tell you to shoot something. Asper would tell you to pray. That works for her, doesn't it? Right. Good. Start praying.*

She opened her mouth for a moment. When no words came out, the thought occurred to her.

Pray to . . . who, exactly?

Riffid was the obvious answer. Riffid would have been helpful. Riffid gave shicts nothing but the skill and the will to get things done. She sent no boons and offered no miracles. Riffid would have let her shoot and be done with it.

But Riffid was a goddess for shicts.

Riffid was down in the chasm, where Kataria had watched Inqalle die, where Kataria had spilled Naxiaw's blood, where Kataria had chosen to protect a human. Riffid was taking Inqalle to the Dark Forest. Riffid was hearing Naxiaw ask for the strength to kill the traitor who shot him.

Riffid would not listen to her.

And when—and if—she walked away from this, she was not sure who would.

For a long time, she tried not to think.

A long time turned into a longer time. While her mind was content to remain silent, her body was slightly more vocal. She could persuade herself not to think about all that had happened, but his scent lingered in her nostrils, she could still feel the tension of his muscle as she dug her nails into him, she could taste his sweat, his blood, his skin against her skin as he—

This isn't helping, she grunted inwardly. Thoughts of him were as distracting as thoughts of the others and one invariably led to the other. So, as she felt the need, she attempted to empty thought and body at once.

Pulling her pants down and positioning the jar, wouldn't have been easy for anyone else but a shict. But it was a common practice amongst hunters to keep their waste, liquid and otherwise, off the ground to avoid upsetting the prey's delicate sense of scent and alerting them.

Admittedly, she had no idea if netherlings even *had* a sense of smell or if their noses were just there to be broken, but by her third filling of the jar she thought she might as well keep going. And once the tinkle of liquid stopped, she hiked her breeches back up, sealed the jar, and let it hang from the straps she had used to secure it to her belt.

Well, then, she thought, *if only shicts do that, you've still got . . . something.*

She forced her head silent.

And in that silence, she heard it. Her ears pricked up, full of the sound of iron upon stone, alien curses upon lips. It began softly at first, distant clanking and distant roaring. And then the kelp quivered and the coral rattled with the tromping of boots. The fish scattered, fleeing into folds of forest and shadowed holes. The mist slithered away into the trees.

And she saw them.

They came one by one at first, a few females in ratty armor wielding crude spears. They snarled amongst each other as they used their weapons to pry stones and debris from the ancient highway, kicking them into the forest as they cleared the path for the purple tide that came boiling up the road.

Rattling, clanking black armor grinding against armor as shoulder brushed against shoulder. Spikes masquerading as swords held hungrily in gauntleted hands. Shields with jagged edges clanged in eagerness. Long faces curled up in jagged-toothed snarls as the female netherlings marched forth, their impatient, foreign-tongued curses blending seamlessly with the sound of grinding iron.

In teeming numbers, rows of black-haired heads, columns of twitching purple muscle, masses of iron and spit and snarls, the netherlings came in a slow-moving wave of flesh and metal, their thunder barely contained.

And yet, contained it was. For all the very palpable hatred and anger they spewed into the air with every breath until it was choking, they did not fight, did not blink, did not even look anywhere but forward. Their milk-white eyes were thrust straight and sharp as the swords they carried, purposefully and violently pressed forward as though they expected their scowls to kill just as effectively as a blade.

And they weren't looking up.

They were focused, Kataria noted, too intent on their distant battle to bear much ill will toward each other beyond the occasional growl. Something drew them together, united them, drove them forward as one, as only one thing could.

That was bad, for obvious reasons.

But at least she knew Sheraptus strode amongst them.

Which was also bad, for obvious reasons.

She tried not to think about those as the line moved on. They marched in order, of a sort. Thirty-three to a unit, as Dreadaeleon had said. Thirty-three angry, spewing, iron-clad creatures wholly intent on wholesale slaughter.

Thirty-three angry, spewing, iron-clad creatures driven by just one will.

Kataria slid an arrow from her quiver and strung it. No sense in drawing it in preparation; it would only make her arm tired, her aim shaky. She needed both strong for the sole shot she would get at this.

They continued to march. The warriors with their swords led the archers, that followed a trail of derision and scorn spat their way from those in the lead. The numbers were intimidating. She stopped keeping track of them by the time they passed the Shen's number, which took an alarmingly short time.

By that moment, though, something else seized her attention.

Behind the archers' grumbles and the warriors' snarls, another unit came marching up in perfect, silent harmony. Clad in armor as black and shiny as a beetle's carapace and covering them so that not a single trace of purple flesh could be seen behind the walls of glistening metal, they came. Their shields were tall, hammered to crescent shapes. Their spears were topped with cruel barbs.

As distressing as the sight was, the sound—or lack of it—was worse. They never said a word, never shared a single snarl of their less-clad companions. Their visored helmets betrayed no eye, no mouth, no sign of even a face as they marched in perfect, terrible synchronization.

Netherlings with discipline.

Worrisome.

Not half as worrisome as what followed.

Its groaning metal, creaking wood, and shrieking, roaring wheels could be heard for an eternity away. But it was only when the metal machination came rolling up, pushed by several grunting warriors, that she could appreciate the terror that came with the metallic cacophony.

A ballista, she had heard it called. A big bow mounted on wheels. Where the netherlings had found one, she didn't actually know. She wasn't even sure if it *was* a ballista. It had the bow part, but everything else was slathered in spikes and metal parts that had been punched on. Two giant arms of flexible wood were tied back at the sides of the engine, each one ending in a strange claw that clenched a jagged, twisted star of sharpened, unpolished metal.

356 She wasn't quite sure if it would actually work or whether it was just there to look intimidating. It did, of course, but only because she knew netherlings had a talent for making anything into a weapon and making anything that already *was* a weapon into something . . . like *that*.

And if it did work, the Shen would have to know. She studied it as it rolled past and up the highway, trying to figure out how it worked and where it could be struck. Once she was done here, she would have to hurry back and tell them. Maybe they could get to it before—

Her ears perked up. Her eyes widened. Her heart slowed a beat.

She couldn't explain what it was about him: a sound too faint to be real, an aroma that couldn't be smelled, a threat that was never spoken. But she heard him, felt him, knew he was coming.

And she nocked her bow.

They came in a knot: white-haired females dressed in gleaming, polished armor, carrying titanic slabs of sharpened metal half-heartedly pretending to be swords on their shoulders. They were bigger, stronger, more laden with scars than any other warrior that walked amongst them.

Carnassials.

And Sheraptus rode at their center.

Two other males flanked him, short and slender with white hair and red and purple robes, wearing arrogant scorn upon their long faces. Xhai rode ahead of him, looking twice as vicious as the great beast she rode. For all their fury and their hatred and their bare-toothed savagery, they paled in comparison to the specter that rode between them.

He was wearing white robes, shrouded in them like they could keep in whatever he was, seated so comfortably in them with a small smile on his face as though he belonged in something that was worn by holy men. It was a poor farce, a poor disguise.

Even if it wasn't for the black crown upon his brow burning with three fiery stones, even if he rode something other than a creature of muscle and claws and jaws and six twitching ears the color of coal, nothing he wore could hide what he was. His cruelty stained the cloth. His viciousness seeped through it.

And he was right there.

Waiting to be killed.

Her fingers tensed around the fletching of her arrow when the cry came down the line, an iron-voiced howl that was echoed from unit to unit until it reached Sheraptus's. The entire column came to a grinding, groaning halt. Curses were exchanged in alien tongues, inquiries made with what Kataria was certain were threats following. Xhai smashed her fist against the nearest white-haired longface and barked an order, they complied with a growled reply. The Carnassial sneered and reined her beast around, trotting over to Sheraptus.

"Something in the way ahead," she grunted. "The low-fingers need more muscle to move it."

"No hurry," Sheraptus replied, his smile twitching.

Kataria hadn't seen anything in the road on her way here. She didn't care. The line had stopped. And he was right in front of her, stopped and smiling and waiting for an arrow in his gullet.

The purple of his flesh was vivid in the muted light. His jugular gyrated with each breath he took. And with each breath he took, it became bigger, a big, fat boil just waiting to be lanced.

She held her own breath as she raised her bow, drew her arrow back. The coral trembled slightly. The bowstring moaned in quiet anticipation.

On the road, the beast that served as Sheraptus's mount twitched. Six ears fanned out like a dish as it swept an eyeless gaze about the road. She held her shot. Surely it couldn't have heard her . . . could it?

No time to wonder. The nervous wariness from Sheraptus's mount spread to the others. And like a fire it spread to the netherlings. Xhai looked down as her mount's ears extended and it emitted low, excited whines.

"*QAI AHN!*" she roared, drawing her massive blade from over her shoulder. The warriors around her followed suit, seizing their weapons and raising them before them as they huddled together warily.

Kataria held her aim. She held her breath back despite the overwhelming urge to panic and run. She kept her calm.

Right up until the moment she saw a flash of green out of the corner of her eye.

Something was down in the coral, moving. Something with weapons. Something with bright, yellow—

Shalake, she had time to think, *you stupid son of a bitch.*

"*SHENKO-SA!*"

The Shen came leaping out of the foliage, machetes in their hands, warcries in their throats, arrows chasing them like faithful puppies. The missiles struck first, sinking into netherling throats and exposed purple flesh. The longfaces fell with gurgles and cries of surprise, stepping stools of metal and skin as the Shen came leaping through the lines, waving their weapons.

One of them made a lunge for Sheraptus, machete held high with the intent of smashing it into his black-crowned skull. He loosed a cry, leapt from a fallen longface high into the air and, like a bird beneath a metal hawk, was snatched from the sky.

Xhai's blade screamed not as loud, moved not as elegantly as the lizardman, but its howl was metal and unyielding and its edge was vicious as it clove the lizardman from his leap and sent him to tumble and bounce upon the earth.

In two pieces.

Kataria quickly scanned the fight. The arrows still flew, but those netherlings they struck did not fall. They snarled, as if it were mosquitoes biting them instead of arrows stuck in their arms and legs, and swung their gigantic blades unhindered by blood loss or pain.

The metal ate of scaly flesh, separated limbs, shattered spines, clove skulls. No blow was clean. No blow finished them. The Shen fell to the ground, their flesh sizzling and burning as the venom coating the swords ate them alive. They writhed, they wailed, they screamed for as long as it took the nearest netherling to bring a spiked metal boot upon their skull and stamp them out like wet ashes.

And Sheraptus watched it all with a serene smile.

Whole and complete, he sat upon his beast's back, unharmed. What had Asper done to him? Had she been lying? He looked completely fit, even more full of arrogant cruelty than she remembered. Perhaps this was not worth it. Perhaps retreat was the wiser—

No, no, NO.

Kataria swallowed her shock, bit back her scream and took aim. *Now or never*, she told herself. *One shot. In his neck. Before he knows it. Then I run.*

She drew the string to her cheek, released it.

One shot.

It wailed as it flew.

To his neck.

He looked up.

And before either of them knew it, the arrow had found a mark.

It lodged itself into flesh with the sound of meat being tenderized and breath being stolen. It quivered eagerly beneath a purple collarbone, pleased with itself. A purple hand, too twisted to fit into a gauntlet, reached up to seize it and snap it off at the shaft.

Xhai, looming before Sheraptus like a wall of metal and iron, scowled up at Kataria. She snorted, broke the remains of the arrow with a twitch of her ruined fingers.

Kataria stared for a moment, slack-jawed and unblinking. Sheraptus merely raised an eyebrow at the shattered arrow falling to the stones. He looked back up to Kataria. And, as he held out his hands in what almost looked like it could be a gesture of benediction if not for the blossoms of fire blooming upon his palms, she wasn't quite sure what to do next.

Until someone told her.

Now you run.

Her head knew, but her legs didn't. She fell backward, tumbling from her perch, just as the sky exploded.

Fire washed over the coral as a tide, blackening her perch and shattering it. It flooded the forest, turning coral into pyres, kelp into sheets of flame. Kataria could see the Shen now from their hiding places. She could see Yaike as he looked up at her, as unaware that she had been there as she had been of him. She could see him yell something, she could see his eye reflect the fire, she could see his mouth twist and distort as his face became scaly green melting wax as the fire rose up around him in a titanic sheet.

Warriors were fleeing. Fish were swimming. Fire was racing to catch them both and winning, engulfing the forest and eating it alive. Kataria hauled herself to her legs and told them to go. They remembered now, they remembered how to run and how to not stop and how to tell her lungs that they couldn't stop breathing even as smoke rose up in plumes around her and she couldn't stop running ever as the fire closed in around her, behind her.

And then in front of her.

The wall of kelp went up in a glorious burst. The coral collapsed around her and in her path, forming a ring of blackening spikes and fire around her. It ate everything, all color, all light, all sound. The screams of the Shen dying were engulfed in the laughter of the fire. The greenery of the forest was bathed in red. The fish fell from the sky, their colors painted black with soot.

Kataria could feel the sweat mingle with her warpaint, streak down her body in long tears of red. She could feel her heart beat as it struggled to free itself from her chest. She could feel the breath beginning to leave her.

She closed her eyes.

She gritted her teeth.

And she prayed. To someone.

From far away, the forest screamed. Its voice was fervent and choked with ash. Its blood was painted in a cloud of black and red upon the gray dawn sky. It wailed through a shudder of kelp and a groan of blackened coral before it finally fell to a broken sigh of ash and embers and then fell silent.

Lenk wasn't quite sure how long it spoke. Lenk wasn't at all certain how long he stared at its black blood pooling in the sky, bright embers dancing in it. Lenk didn't know what to say when he finally found the words to speak.

But they came, anyway.

"Kat?"

As though she might pop up behind him, wrap her arms about his middle and say *"just kidding."*

He whirled about on the stone staircase, casting a furious scowl at the creature one step above him.

"What the hell just happened?" he demanded.

Shalake looked down, yellow eyes narrowed through the sockets of his skull headdress. He made no answer. Not as Denaos and Asper both turned irate and suspicious scowls up the stairs. Not as Dreadaeleon looked agog from the devastation to him. Not as Gariath shot him a sidelong glance.

Only when Mahalar cleared his throat from one more step above did Shalake speak.

"They failed," the hulking Shen said simply.

"Who? Who is they?" Lenk demanded, ascending a step.

"The brave warriors who gave their lives in the ambush," Shalake replied. "They will be remembered."

From beside Shalake, Jenaji, nearly as tall and half as tattooed, seized the Shen's arm.

"How many?"

"Twenty," Shalake replied, shrugging Jenaji's grip off. "Twenty who will be honored at sunset."

"Honored as charred husks of overcooked meat along with Kataria because you are a stupid, scaly piece of *shit* who can't follow an order!" Lenk all but screamed.

"I am the *warwatcher*," Shalake roared back, looking down at Lenk and taking an aggressive step forward. "I do not take orders from *you* and I do not trust pointy-eared weaklings to do the duty of the Shen."

"Whatever just went wrong happened because *your* warriors couldn't be trusted not to send everything to hell!" Lenk roared.

The hulking Shen glowered as he removed his tremendous warclub from his back, the tooth-studded weapon roughly half the size of Lenk sliding easily into his hands like it had been waiting for this for days. Lenk responded, pulling his sword free and hoping no one saw his hands tremble with the effort.

On the steps below, the green crowd trailing into the sand of the ring, close to two hundred Shen warriors looked up in anticipation of the brawl—or decapitation—about to happen.

Mahalar cleared his throat.

Shalake's glare did not dissipate, but softened considerably as he turned it toward the elder Shen.

"He challenges me," Shalake snarled. "He accuses me. I have the right to—"

"Of course. Later." Mahalar gestured with his chin. "After that."

"Holy . . ." Asper began. The rest of her words were lost in the sight that came from the forest, with a herald of smoke and fire.

Like children called to supper, the netherlings came racing eagerly from the forests in a stream of purple skin and glistening black iron. A stream became a tide as they poured into the ring, tearing the earth beneath their boots.

Legion after legion, long face after long face, they came. With shields on their arms, bows on their backs, swords slung over their shoulders, they came. In numbers vast and with bodies blackened by soot and flame, they came. They filled the ring, rushing until they came exactly halfway between the Shen and the forest and assembling into lines.

And there they stopped.

From the top of the steps, no sand could be seen. The ring had become a sea of purple skin, lit by the white of hundreds of empty eyes and hundreds of jagged-toothed smiles.

"*KENKI-AI!*"

The call boomed from Shalake's mouth like a drum, echoing down the line. The Shen assembled on the steps drew arrows from quivers, nocked them into great bows of wood and bone. The Shen on the sands below seized their clubs in both hands, banged machetes against shields made from turtle shells and dried leather as they hunkered behind barricades brimming with sharp coral spines.

Lenk felt his attentions drawn to the center of the line, an insignificant white speck of froth amidst the purple sea. From this distance, he could pick the figure out. From this distance, he could see Sheraptus sitting there, smoke still trailing from his fingers and leading to the bleeding sky behind him.

And from a place tenderly close, Lenk could feel a scratching at the back of his skull.

"Kill him," he hissed. "Kill him now. He's right there. Shoot him."

"Not close enough," Jenaji muttered.

"Then rush out there and *kill* him."

"Any chance we have relies on them coming to us," Mahalar muttered. "We wait."

Lenk knew the wisdom in that. He could see the line of shields and swords stretching out before him. He could see the arrows being drawn back by netherling bows. Any charge would be brief, futile, and end in him lying in a puddle of his own fluids. At the very best, he would die with his sword in a netherling's chest. Probably not Sheraptus's. It was a very messy suicide.

But something inside him dearly wanted just that.

"Roughly what we expected," Yldus commented, "a small number in a fortified position. No other choice for them, really. The ring winds down at the other side, meaning we can only put so many of our warriors there before they start trampling each other." He gestured to the brightly-colored coral fortifications. "And they set up those . . . things to try and funnel us further. Smarter than we'd given lizards credit for."

"Not a problem, I assume," Sheraptus muttered, though only half paying attention. His attentions were turned outward, over the heads of his warriors, over the spiraling coral thorns, out to the distant sea. Something out there drew his eye as an itch draws a scratching hand.

"It was nothing we weren't prepared for," Yldus replied. "We can rip through those defenses with the . . ." He paused and glanced at the monstrosity of metal and spiked machinery that stood at the center of their line. "What did you call this thing again?"

A female loading a star-shaped blade into the thing's flexible, side-mounted arms looked up and shrugged. "I don't know. It shoots stuff."

"Of course." Yldus sighed. "At any rate, the blades are thick enough to shred those barricades. Given time—"

"How much time?"

"A few hours or so. We'll need to put the low-fingers and their bows up ahead so that—"

"And how quickly can you get this done?" Sheraptus asked, turning to the side.

Vashnear looked at him, then turned a stare out to the Shen assembled at the other end of the ring. He sniffed.

"Quickly," he answered.

Sheraptus swung his gaze over to Xhai. The female grunted and turned to her nearest subordinate, another Carnassial clad in the storm gray armor of her rank. The Carnassial snorted in response, looking up through the thin slits of a skull-hugging helmet rife with spikes and jagged edges.

"Three fists," Xhai grunted. "Three Carnassials. Whoever can get to the front first." She spurred her cohort with an iron boot to the flank. "*Go.*"

The Carnassial snarled a response, barked an order to the rest of the netherlings. The hungriest ones fought their way to the front, leaving the weaker ones to clean up the soon-to-be mess.

Sheraptus wasn't sure how they decided who got to charge. Amongst males, it was generally considered wisdom not to try to understand the finer intricacies of the females' hierarchies. Sheraptus didn't care, either way. His concerns were beyond the sea.

And drawing ever closer.

"Quickly, Vashnear?" he asked.

"Quickly, Sheraptus," Vashnear said, spurring his sikkhun forward to take his place at the center of the assembling netherlings. "And with a great deal of mess."

"What's that they're doing?"

"They're moving . . . fighting? Yes, fighting. No, now just moving again . . . faster . . . closer. Oh. Oh dear."

"They're grouping up, are they—"

"*Attala-ah-kah, Jenaji. Attala-ah-kah.*"

"They're definitely—"

"*KENKI-SHA! ATTALA! ATALLA JAGA!*"

"Oh sweet Silf, they're coming to—"

"*QAI ZHOTH!*"

They were all talking at once. The mass of green and yellow blending together around Lenk, the great wave of purple washing across the sands toward them, the blobs of pink and blue and black that reached and grabbed at him as he pushed his way down the gray slope.

It was hard to hear them. It was hard to see them. There were too many of them all and he only cared about one of them. And he was far away, seated atop a pitch-black beast and dressed like an angel from hell with a halo of fire and shadow.

And between them came the purple, countless bodies intertwining, countless mouths howling, countless swords in the air. There might have been a lot, there might have been a few.

He had to hurt them. He had to make them bleed. He couldn't care about numbers or jagged-toothed smiles or the great metal birds flying overhead.

Arms caught him about the waist, a pair of bodies brought him low as the air was cut apart in a metallic wail. Flesh and bone exploded in a bouquet of red and white flowers as the great, jagged star tore through the Shen behind them, carrying through bodies and screams to impale itself in the stone stairs.

"Down! Down! Keep him down!" Denaos cried.

"There's more coming, Lenk! Stop *moving*, you idiot!" Asper shrieked, trying to hold him down.

"*JAHU! ATTAI WOH!*" Shalake howled.

Shields went up around them, a poor defense against the jagged stars descending from the air. In the distance, between the scaly green legs, Lenk could see them hurled from great wooden arms on the netherlings' ballista. He could see them fly into the air, whirring violently before falling like falcons, ripping through coral, shields, flesh, bones, sand, stones.

And still, the screams were drowned out. And still, the blood spattering the earth around him was nothing. Nothing compared to the rush of purple flesh and black metal charging toward them.

"*ATTAI-AH! ATTAI-AH!*" Jenaji screamed from the steps. "*ATTALA JAGA! SHENKO-SA!*"

His warcry was echoed in the hum of bowstrings, a choral dirge that sent arrows singing through the sky. Fletched with feathery fins and tipped with jagged coral, they rose and fell in harmony, their song turning to battle cry as they tipped and descended upon the charging netherlings.

They sought. They found flesh, digging into necks, thighs, wriggling between armor plates and jutting out of throats. Some fell, some stumbled, some tripped and were trampled by their fellow warriors. But one still stood.

A great hulk of a female, armor stark gray like an angel wrought of iron, swinging a massive slab of metal over a helmet flanged with spikes and edges. She embraced the arrows like lovers as they found a bare bicep, a flash of thigh, a scant spot of skin just beneath the collarbone.

She laughed. She bled. She lowered her head.

And she did not stop.

The Carnassial did not meet her foes. She exploded into them. A coral barricade was smashed into fragments, many of them embedded in her flesh to join the arrows as she met the cluster of Shen warriors full on. For a moment, their warcries died in their throats and their numbers were meaningless.

She swung her slab of a sword, cleaving shields in two, swords from wrists, heads from shoulders in one fell swoop. She stepped forward with each blow, driving the warriors back as more netherlings rushed into the gap she had cloven into the barricade. Those Shen that fell screamed, steamed like cooked meat as sheens of sickly green liquid gnawed at their wounds.

She threw her bloodied sword up. She presented a body wrapped in metal and kissed in blood and shards. She roared.

"AKH ZEKH LA—"

The fist struck her and rang her like a cathedral bell. The sword clattered to the ground next to the jagged teeth she spat out beside it. She blinked. She looked up.

Gariath's black eyes met her first.

His fist came after.

He pounded her relentlessly, hammering blows into her face, into her body. His fists were cut upon her armor and his blood joined hers upon her flesh. And still she would not fall. And still she looked at him with a mouth shattered and a body bleeding and roared.

And his reply was the ringing of metal.

He clapped his hands against either side of her helmet, ignoring the spikes biting into his palms, ignoring her blows hammering his body, ignoring everything but the feeling of squeezing an old coconut between his hands. His earfrills were shut. He could not hear anything. Not the defiant roar, not the groaning of metal, not the sickening splitting sound that came before a thin line of blood spurted out from a much narrower visor and she hung limply between his palms.

She fell.

His wings flew open. His jaws flew open. His head flew back.

365

His roar was long, loud, and it spread like the fire on the sky.

The Shen took up his howl, bastardizing it with words and neutering it with order. Gariath's anger was pure. It drove his fists into netherling jaws, thrust his claws into netherling flanks, brought his jaws to netherling throats. The Shen followed his example, machetes and clubs held high to push their aggressors back as arrows from the stairs picked off those unfortunate enough to get clear enough of the action.

"There you go, then," Denaos muttered. "There are no problems that can't be solved by letting Gariath do whatever the hell he wants to. Stay down and everything will be fine."

Absently, Lenk wondered if he couldn't begin to predict disasters by Denaos's assurances that everything would be fine. For at that moment, a wounded sky was ripped further by the cobalt bolt of electricity that lanced over the heads of the warriors to strike at the staircase. An explosion of dust and stone fragments erupted, sending Shen archers flying from the staircase, their screams lost in the thunder.

Through the press of bodies and the spines of barricades, the male was visible. Far from the melee, seated atop his sikkhun, his burning red eyes were visible through the veil of smoke wafting from his fingers. The words he spoke were unheard, the gesture he made insignificant, the bolt of lightning that sprang from his fingers was neither.

It shot across the sky to rake at the stairs once more. No explosion came this time, no screams or flying bodies. Only a grunt of effort and the flapping of a dirty leather coat from a figure positively tiny against the cluster of Shen. Dreadaeleon extended two fingers and like a rod, the electricity snaked to them, entering his body with a cobalt crackle and a sizzle. The boy panted with the effort, his body shaking with the absorbed power, tiny sparks flew from his mouth.

He wouldn't last to take another.

That, some small, bitter part of Lenk reasoned, was good enough to do what he did.

"Someone tell the archers to—" Denaos's words were cut short by a cry of alarm as the young man slipped from his grasp. "Hey! Wait! *WAIT!*"

That would have been good advice, the more sensible part of Lenk realized as he leapt over a barricade, ducking stray blows and snarls as he charged past the melee. But that part wasn't speaking loudly enough.

The part that had watched the fire in the sky, that had wanted to kill Shalake, that saw the forest burn with Kataria inside it was roaring now, laughing with a strength that dulled sense and reason and any part of him that told him this was suicidal stupidity.

He didn't even feel his legs beneath him. He didn't feel the sword in his hand. He didn't feel how cold he was. There were netherlings coming toward him, those few who had stayed behind to guard the male. He could barely see them. He didn't need to.

His sword knew where they were, his sword spoke in the ringing of steel and the splitting of flesh and told him he wasn't needed here. It lashed out with mechanical precision, unaware of him as he was of it as he ran past them. It cleaved hand from wrist, opened belly from navel to sternum, found a throat and cut it.

No pause to avoid the stray blows of iron and fist that caught him. No need to. He wasn't in control now. Something else was.

And in the back of his mind it cried out with a breathless shriek of joy the way it did in his nightmares.

And he didn't care that the netherling male atop his beast turned a bloodred stare upon him and smiled broadly as he shouted something.

Not a word of power. No, this red-robed male was feeling bold. His words were for the beast beneath him and its six ears unfurling like sails. The creature's gibbering cackle matched its master's as it was spurred forward, claws rending the ground beneath it as it rushed toward Lenk, tongue lolling out from gaping jaws.

The motion was seamless, driven by numb muscles. He didn't feel himself falling into a slide across the rent earth and under the beast, he didn't feel the wind break as jaws snapped shut over his face. Every bit of awareness in him was for the steel in his hands and the great, furry underbelly above him.

Without a word, he twisted the blade up.

And thrust.

A wailing shriek poured out of the beast's mouth as something warm and thick fell from its underbelly in black curtains. It reared back, taking Lenk's blade with it. From beneath a shower of gore, he twisted as the thing bucked and stamped, ripping up stained sand and tossing its master from its back.

The male tumbled to the ground, cursing as its beast scratched and shrieked, trying futilely to dislodge the weapon from its gut. But neither he nor Lenk were concerned about it any longer. Lenk's attentions were on the male's neck, the male's on Lenk's hands wrapping around it.

"Don't touch . . ." the male tried to gasp. "Diseased, unclean . . ."

No words for the male. No breath to speak them. No chance to wave fingers or spit ice or fire or anything else. There was no magic here. Only flesh. Only the purity of choking the life out of a monster.

And it was pure, Lenk thought. His hands fit so easily around the male's neck. His windpipe felt big as a column to his fingers. He could see his own eyes in the male's horrified stare, his own pupilless stare. He could feel his fingers turning gray, the color draining from his arms, his face. He could feel his body going numb, the warmth leaving him and the bitter, comforting cold that began to blanket him.

And he could feel that part of him, that small and angry part, growing large inside him. And it felt good to feel this way again.

"He dies."

This numbing cold.

"He is weak."

This bitter voice.

"And we cannot stop."

This death in his mouth.

"You ever notice how easily we run away?"

Another voice. That one was smaller. That voice was another part of him that spoke weakly inside him. But it was insistent. It kept talking.

"You're supposed to be doing things for yourself now."

It was something that made him uncomfortable to hear.

"If you still want to run away, you can keep holding on."

It wouldn't shut up.

"But if she could see you now . . ."

She would scream.

He let go.

Without knowing why, he released the male from his grip. Without knowing how, he fell breathless to his rear and felt a fever-sharp warmth grip him. And without even knowing who he was facing anymore, he watched the male hack and scramble to his feet, eyes burning brightly as he held out a palm and spoke a word.

The fire in his hand lived and died in an instant, sputtering to smoke as an arrow bit him in the shoulder. No Shen arrow. This one had black fletchings. This one sang an angry song and ate deeply of the male's shoulders. This one was joined from the side of the ring.

Lenk was barely aware of her as she came rushing out from the forest, bow in her hands, arrows heralding her with angry songs. She was a creature of black ash and bloodied skin and red warpaint, overlarge canines big and white against the mask of darkness and crimson that obscured every patch of bare skin on her.

Maybe Kataria was alive. Maybe Kataria's angry ghost had returned just to save him. Or maybe to take him back to hell with her.

But first, she would deal with the male.

Her arrows flew at him, begging in windy wails for a soft piece of purple skin to sink into. The male spoke word after word, throwing his hands up, twisting the shimmering air into invisible walls to repel her strikes. But she would not relent, and his breath had not returned. One would get through, eventually.

Unless she reached into her quiver and found nothing there.

The male found his breath in a single, wrathful word. He thrust two fingers at her. The electricity sprang to him, racing down his arm and into his tips. She pulled something from her belt and hurled it at him. Something shiny. Something golden.

He twisted his arm at the last moment as the thing tumbled through the sky toward him. The lightning left his fingers in a crack of thunder and a shock of blue. Glass erupted in the sky, fell like stars upon the ground.

The liquid that followed in a thin, yellow, foul-smelling rain, was decidedly less elegant.

For a moment, the entire ring seemed to fall silent. The battle seemed too distant to be heard. The world seemed to hold its breath. The male's mouth was opened a hair's breadth. His eyes were wide, white, and unblinking as rivulets of waste trickled down his brow and onto his crimson-clad shoulders.

And then he began to scream.

Over and over, breath spent and drawn and spent again every moment in utter, wailing horror. He stood frozen, ignoring everything else but the reeking liquid coating him. He stood screaming about contamination and filth and infection in every language he knew.

He didn't stop until Kataria tackled him about the waist, pulled him to the ground and jammed her knife in his throat. His screams continued to escape in bubbling, silent gouts. She no longer seemed to care.

The sigh she offered as she rose to her feet seemed not weary enough to match the creature that had emerged from the forest. She was a creature painted gray and black by ash and soot, her eyes and teeth white through the dark mask painted across her face. Her body was likewise stained, the darkness broken only by scars of bright-red blood. Cuts criss-crossed her arms, swathed her midriff, tore her tunic and her breeches. Her hair was thick with dust and the netherling's blood painted a long stain from her chest to her belly.

All that remained of the shict that had gone into the forest were the feathers in her hair and the dust-tinged sigh that left her.

"Hey," she said.

"Hey," he replied, staggering to his feet. "You're alive."

"Yeah." She sniffed. "Plan didn't work."

"I know."

"Kind of want to kill Shalake."

"Yeah, me, too." He glanced over his shoulder. The battle at the barricades had ended, the netherlings pressed back. "We should go back."

"We should." She swayed slightly. "You mind?"

He shook his head and turned around. He felt her collapse into him, no more strength in her to walk. Hooking his arms under her legs, he hefted her onto his back and began to trudge back, stepping over bodies and gore-stained sand.

He made a note to remember to go back for his sword once she was clear.

"So . . ." he said, "that was what the jar was for?"

"Uh huh."

"So . . . uh, why did you bring it back?"

"What was I supposed to do? Just *leave* my piss behind where anyone could get it?"

TWENTY-EIGHT

HIM

It might have been well-cooked leather that Asper wiped the cloth against, maybe the tenderer part of an alligator in heat, she wasn't sure. Something bright red was underneath, not pale and pink. She drew back the cloth and saw not a white spot left. It wasn't a cloth anymore. It was all black and red now, rust peeled off a sword.

She sighed, dropped it with the others onto the stairs.

"You could at least help me," Asper muttered, plucking up a small jar from the stone. "You know, so I don't feel quite like a mother cat bathing a cub."

Kataria didn't bother to look up as she took a long swig of water from the skin. "If you used your tongue, you'd talk less."

"And then I'd choke on smoke and blood and paint and . . . and . . ." Her eyes were drawn to the heap of cloths. "Should I ask what the other smell was?"

"I've never lied to you before," Kataria said, shaking her head.

"Right." Asper rolled her eyes as she dipped a pair of fingers into the thick, goopy balm and rubbed it onto the woman's shoulder.

It was the last inch of exposed skin not touched by a bandage or char-balm. Beneath the soot and the ash and the blood, Kataria had been red and raw. She had been spared the fire, though the heat had kissed her lightly, but sloppily, leaving a lot of black-stained spit behind. Even beneath all the soot and paint, she had been cut. Red lines ran down her arms, her abdomen, the palms of her gloves. Her right ear continually flicked, perpetually perturbed by the bright gash across its length.

The priestess looked up over the sky and the fonts of smoke still pouring out of the forest.

"How?" she asked.

"Climbed," Kataria replied, not following her gaze. "With great fervor, with great speed. Had to circle around, got back just in time."

"To . . ."

"Yeah. To see it."

Asper wouldn't have asked even if Kataria's tone *hadn't* suggested that doing so would result in severe bodily harm. They had all seen it.

Him, Asper corrected herself. *We saw him. Lenk. He's a him. Not an "it." He's still . . . he's still . . .*

She wasn't sure how to finish that. She wasn't sure what he was. What sort of creature moved like he had? What sort of creature's skin went gray as stone in the blink of an eye?

He was Lenk.

And only now she started to wonder what Lenk was.

It was a question she wasn't prepared to ask herself, let alone the green-eyed black-and-red hellbeast he had carried back with him. And yet, the shict's body shuddered with a sigh beneath her fingers.

"Whatever happened," Kataria whispered, "whatever did or didn't . . . or barely didn't . . . he's all I have left."

Not technically true, Asper noted as she looked up from the stairs down to the barricade and the battlefield. She also had a corpse wallowing in various liquids lying in the sand next to a large and hairy corpse of a sikkhun, whose blood still seemed to be leaking out of it hours later.

But that was only one corpse. There were more at the barricade. And most of those belonged to Gariath. They had been stacked in heaps of flesh and iron, walls of flesh to shore up those spots where the coral had been shattered. In heaps of limbs, pools of blood, and shattered skulls they lay, struck down by machete, club, or overzealous fellow netherlings who had tried to push past them.

The Shen dead had been removed, taken farther up the stairs by fellows with eyes too envious for Asper to feel very confident in them. Even if they had lost far less than the netherlings, they were still far fewer than their foes, who were showing remarkable restraint as they lingered at the center of the ring.

Occasionally, a stray knot of longfaces would grow too excited to heed whatever commands the Carnassials would shout at them and charge forward. Regular hails of arrows from the Shen archers above kept them at bay, littering the field with their bodies.

The Shen below screamed at them to stop shooting, howled at them to let the warriors come, to give them the fight they deserved. Even the occasional star-shaped blade that came crashing through their barricades did little to diminish their bloodlust. They would have sounded just like the netherlings, Asper thought, if not for one thing.

The voices of the Shen were glutted, fat and slow with whatever confidence Gariath and Lenk and Kataria had given them. Theirs were cries of leisure, simply asking for seconds. The netherlings were hungry in their shrieks, starving in their swords. They needed more.

They were netherlings. They would have more.

Because he would give it to them.

She stared out into the crowd, so far and still so vast. The tangles of purple flesh and black iron were so dense, yet she searched and she stared and she feared the moment her eyes would catch him and—

"Stop it."

Kataria's growl was low, threatening. Her glower was sharp and cast over her shoulder like a spear as she thrust it at Asper.

"Stop what?"

"Looking for him. You know he's down there."

Kataria held her gaze for a long, painful moment. And the moment stretched, long enough for her to realize the pain was not from Kataria's eyes, but from the quake of her jaw as she fought to keep it fused shut.

"You were supposed to kill him," she whispered through her teeth. "You said you would."

"I didn't."

"You were *supposed* to—"

"I *didn't*." Kataria snarled. "And I can't right now. I don't know if I can *ever*." She gestured to the blade tucked into the priestess's sash. "And that's not going to be as useful as you think it is."

"I'm not going to use it on him," Asper said.

"I know what you think you're going to use it for." The shict's ears folded against her head. "Whatever it is that kills him or you . . . it's not going to be me *or* that blade."

"Then what?"

Kataria took another long swig of water. She looked at Asper and offered no words. She looked out over the field and said nothing. No poignancy in the silence, no meaning. No answer.

Asper's fingers scraped an empty bowl. The last of the charbalm lay glistening upon Kataria's pinkened skin. She set it back inside her satchel, hiked it up over her shoulder.

"I should go down to the barricade," she said. "There might be wounded down there."

The priestess left without another word exchanged between them.

Kataria had no objections leaving it at that. She could have easily pointed out that there were never any "wounded" amongst the Shen, merely the dead and the envious living. She could have stayed and talked her through whatever she felt after Sheraptus's return, told her that he was whole and whatever the priestess had done to him wasn't enough. She might have even felt better about her own failure to kill him.

But her ears were upright and rigid with the sound of dust settling upon stone. Her burned skin tingled with the sensation of being watched. And her teeth ground behind her lips as she rose and turned upon the withered, decaying creature standing a few steps above her.

"You are alive," Mahalar observed. Not with any great relief.

"Yaike isn't," she replied. Not with any great sympathy.

"Their loss weighs on me heavily."

"Then why did you send them out there to die?" At his raised eyeridge, she chuckled, an edge of hysteria to it. "You told Shalake to let me go attack Sheraptus alone. Shalake agreed to it. I've seen the way he looks at you. He wouldn't send them out against your wishes." She pointed a finger at him. "So you changed your wishes."

"It was no wish. I asked Yaike if he would save us all. He took his warriors to do just that."

"By what? Ruining an ambush? Ruining all our chances for survival? I had him in my sights. I would have *killed* Sheraptus and we'd be facing a rabble of disorganized, leaderless animals instead of . . ." She swept a hand out over the battlefield. "*That.*"

"Whatever is ruined is made so by you." There was no anger to his voice. He spoke in a cool, dusty observation. "You weren't supposed to survive."

"There's a reason killing your own isn't really a viable military strategy, you know. Mostly because it's completely stupid and makes your own come back to beat the stuffing out of you."

Mahalar did not so much ignore her as make her transparent. His dull, amber eyes stared through her. He shambled down the steps and walked through her, in front of her in one moment, behind her in the next. When she turned, his back was brazenly turned to her, his eyes down upon the barricades.

Lenk sat there, a silver pimple on a green backside, amidst the Shen that pointedly did not look at him. His sword lay in his lap, blood stained his hands, his eyes were somewhere far away.

"Did you hear it?" Mahalar asked.

"Hear what?"

"Him."

"I saw him."

"Then you saw what we all saw. You saw him cleave them apart, stain the sands with them, rip them open. You saw him bring down that monster, nearly kill the male. All on his own."

"I saw what happened to him. I saw the way people looked at him when he came back."

"But you didn't hear him." The wistfulness in his voice bordered on the obscene. "No one did, of course. If they had, they would try to kill him, as they killed the girl in the chasm, the rest of them. The voice has that effect on people who do not understand it.

"I do, though. I heard it. I heard it screaming in his head, clawing against his skull. It begged for more, cried out with joy, wept and wailed as he ripped them apart. It was just like I heard it the last time, when they all spoke out in unison, when their voices were as one and their swords slew demons."

He exuded the kind of morbidly nostalgic sigh the rest of his scaly brethren did. It trailed from his lips on a cloud of dust.

"I didn't understand what they were, anymore than you understand what he is. But I watched him since he came to Jaga. I knew that your death would enable him to kill. Kill the netherlings, kill Ulbecetonth, kill everything if we merely stepped out of his way."

He shook his head. "I don't blame you for surviving, no more than I blame myself for placing our survival above yours. But in doing so, you've ruined us, shict." He twisted his gaze out to sea, to the dark storm clouds gathering over the waves. "But I suppose you can't hear that, either."

"I hear everything, lizard." Her ears folded flat against her head. "And all I hear out of you are a bunch of reasons that fail to convince me that I shouldn't kill you."

"And yet . . ."

"And yet, I'm still aware of where we are: wedged up the collective rectums of a hundred reptiles who would be left leaderless against a horde of longfaces and who would probably eat me alive if I laid a hand on you."

"Wisdom."

"Patience," Kataria corrected. "I can wait, until we're all alive or you and I are almost dead. And then, despite the fact that I have no idea what it is that's been leaking out of you all this time or if it's edible, I'm going to pummel it out of you and *eat* it."

Mahalar blinked. She cleared her throat.

"In front of you."

The elder Shen frowned.

"While you're still—"

"I understand," Mahalar interrupted. "You are as obsessed with death as any of my people. If we come out of this, if my death will still soothe you, it is yours. But hold your . . ."

His voice trailed off into nothingness, as did his stare. Just as well, Kataria wasn't listening anymore. Her eyes were drawn to the battlefield below. The horde of netherlings had begun to stir. Shouts of command, audible even from so far away, went up in a raucuous cacophony.

They were preparing for something.

She took off, shoving past the elder Shen and hurrying down the stairs to rejoin the barricade.

He stumbled, fell to his knees, didn't bother to get up. He didn't feel her shoulder bumping into him, couldn't feel the stone beneath him. But he felt the island, he felt Jaga, the land he was forever bound to. He felt the breath of thousands of living things upon it go still. He felt the forests shuddering in a wind that wasn't there. He felt the land itself tense, as though readying itself to be struck.

And at that moment, in a fleeting instance, he felt feet upon Jaga. Two. Then ten. Then hundreds. It was the pain of an old scar, the awareness of the space left by a lost limb, the feel of blood drying on his skin.

He knew this pain.

He knew these feet.

And in the sweep of his amber gaze to the sea, in the storm that had come from the sea to the shore, in the dusty and breathless gaze that emerged from his lips, he knew what was happening.

"He comes."

"Is this really wise?" Yldus shouted to be heard over the rattle of metal and the roar of females. "Our last charge lost Vashnear. While I lament the loss of a male, I can't help but feel . . ."

Undoubtedly, he had taken the hint that Sheraptus's distant glare and hundreds of roaring females had strived so hard to convey. The male's gaze was locked hard upon the warriors knotted around him as they howled with ecstasy for the impending command. The order had been given moments ago, its mere mention like the scent of blood to them, inspiring a frenzy they had no choice but to unleash.

His eyes found Xhai's sikkhun as it panted heavily, its grin as broad and toothsome as the warriors surrounding it. The Carnassial herself glanced to him, an eyebrow cocked.

"This is what you command?" she grunted, the iron grate of her voice more than adequate to carry over the excited din.

A fever burned behind his eyes as he spurred his beast around and swept his gaze to the distant shore. A great mass of gray clouds came roiling over the horizon like a living thing, slithering across the sky to chase away wind and smoke alike. In the distance, a roll of thunder could be heard.

And in it, a voice.

His palm itched, burned where he had clenched the stone that had restored him. He could feel it as keenly as he heard the voice in the clouds, the scream on the wind.

Unbeckoned, the Gray One That Grins's words returned to him.

"We are out of time," Sheraptus muttered. "He comes."

"Who?" Yldus asked.

"The weapon." Sheraptus asked, turning a glower to Xhai. "You have it?"

She patted her back. An obsidian spearhead loomed over her shoulder, stark and black against the gray of the sky. Sheraptus nodded grimly, forced a hiss between his teeth.

"End this."

Xhai offered a stiff nod before turning and sending a roar down the line. *"BRING UP THE FIRST!"*

Her howl was echoed amongst the warriors, rattling through the crowd, twisting amongst the iron voices until it was without word or language, a mindless, bloodthirsty howl of anticipation. For the First was brought up for one reason and one reason only.

A reason that became clear, Sheraptus noted, in the sound that followed. Boots, thirty-three of them, marching with such rigid unison as to grind the howls and the bloodlust beneath their heels, heralded the arrival of the pride of Arkklan Kaharn.

They came with armor, thick black plates bound so tightly that the purple of their flesh was obscured completely. They came with helmets, crested and barbed and polished like the carapace of beetles. They came with spears and shields, jagged heads held high, crescents of metal clenched tightly against their bodies.

They came, as one. The only netherlings capable of following orders more complex than "stab this."

The crowd of warriors parted like a tide to let them through. Even Xhai reined her beast aside to make way. They came to a sudden and disciplined halt, long enough to turn their visored gazes to Sheraptus in compulsory acknowledgment, before turning back to the field.

"QAI QA LOTH," one of them at the head barked the order. She lowered her spear, thrust it out to the distant barricade. *"KEQH QAI YUSH!"*

And with the thunder of their boots, they marched out, spreading into a long line of black plate and speartips. Sheraptus had no smiles of pride for the sight that had won him many battles back in the Nether. He had no time.

A mutter of thunder caught his attention. Overhead, the storm clouds swept in, darker than even the halo of gray that encircled the mountain. The voice in the thunder was audible. The anger in its odor stung his nostrils.

The crown of storms had come. And its bearer came with them.

"We move," Sheraptus snarled to Yldus and Xhai. "Be ready."

"This isn't fair, you know," Denaos muttered as he peered over the barricade. "They've got giant, no-eyed beasts, ballistas that shoot metal stars, *hundreds* of crazy ladies that feel no pain and *now* they've got big, black bipedal bugs."

He whirled around and glared at the assembled Shen.

"*We're* supposed to have the unholy amalgamations between men and animals. They're *cheating.*"

"They're doing something," Asper said from beside him, a hint of panic creeping into her voice. "They're coming closer. Marching. They're not charging. They charge, don't they?"

"Sheraptus is moving with them," Dreadaeleon whispered. "The other male, too. I can't see them, but I can sense them."

"So they're making a push," Lenk said as he pushed his way through the Shen to rejoin his companions, Kataria close behind. "Couldn't expect them to be content with sending out warriors to get shot one by one forever."

"That system was working perfectly fine," Denaos griped.

"What do we do now, then?" Asper asked. "They're coming closer. He's going . . . *they're* going to be on top of us in a moment. What's the plan?"

"Plan?"

Shalake's voice boomed with contempt as he strode to the front. His smile was so broad as to be visible even from beneath his skull headdress. He held his club up, flicking free a few lingering chunks of viscera that had been wedged between its teeth.

"Kill them all, of course."

"Look, it's not that I *object* to the conclusion," Lenk said, rubbing his eyes, "just the logic behind it."

"And the crazy, murderous lizardman that tried to kill us posing it," Kataria added.

"Right, and the crazy, murderous lizardman that tried to kill us."

"Death needs no logic. Death needs nothing but us," Shalake replied coolly.

Lenk blinked. He turned to the Shen surrounding their leader. "So, do you guys just never tell him what he sounds like or . . ."

"Enough of plans and cowering behind coral like *fish*," Shalake spat. He held his club high above his head, the stray chunks of meat and bone spattering down upon his headdress. "We will charge. We will meet them upon the field. We will make them *bleed* and we will show our ancestors that we are worthy of the sacrifices they made!"

The cheer that went up at his words was enthusiastic, if muted. Sensing this, Shalake turned to seek Gariath out in the crowd. One could rarely accuse the dragonman of trying to avoid detection, and one rarely did without detecting the dragonman's fist in their face a moment later. But Gariath looked as though he attempted to shrink into the crowd, which would be impossible even if he weren't tremendous and the color of blood. Shalake gestured to him with his club.

"And with the *Rhega* leading us," he crowed, "the first to spill blood, the last to die, we will honor *all* the dead! *Attala Jaga! Attala Rhega! Shenko-sa!*"

"*SHENKO-SA!*" the Shen howled, vigorous and full of life they were desperate to spill.

Gariath was silent.

While it was difficult to read the face of a man who happened to have a snout instead of a nose and largely didn't bother to convey emotions beyond rage, Lenk had known Gariath for some time. Lenk could see the shine in his eyes grow dull, the frown tug at the corners of his mouth, the tightness with which his earfrills were held.

"Gariath," Lenk said hesitantly, "do you . . . want that?"

He looked at the young man, straight into his eyes. Possibly for the first time, Lenk thought. Because for the first time, in his brutish companion's eyes, he could see the same doubt he had seen in Kataria's eyes, the same doubt he felt in his own, the doubt he had thought Gariath simply didn't feel.

"I am . . ." Gariath began to speak.

"Dead."

Not that it was entirely unwarranted, but everyone turned up to see Mahalar, hunched and stooped and breathing heavily amidst the lizardmen. There was a direness to his stare that burned straight through his cowl.

"We are all dead."

"Well, not *yet*," Lenk said, glancing over his shoulder. "They're moving kind of slow and—"

"And you have killed us." He leveled a finger, half-sheathed in flesh, at Lenk. "You could have ended this. You could have saved us. You could have done something if only you had listened to me."

"I don't—"

"You *didn't*," Mahalar spat. "You didn't and now it's too late." He pointed the finger at his temple. "Have you not heard it? Have you not felt it? She's been calling to them this entire time." The finger shifted overhead. "And now, he has come to answer."

They looked, as one, to the darkness broiling overhead. No longer stormclouds, they were ink stains oozing out upon a pure gray sky. Thunder groaned overhead. The clouds split open. A single drop fell from above.

It plummeted to earth and splattered across Lenk's face. Warm. Sticky. Red.

"Blood?" he whispered.

"Daga-Mer," Mahalar said. "The consort comes to free his queen."

The world was a riot of sound and color. The dawn had fled at the first sign of trouble and taken its gray draining with it. Now remained the broken purple and green flesh, the bloodstained coral, the howls from the netherlings and the roars sent up to meet them.

And through that, all the cacophonies and all the dizzying miasma, they could hear it in the echo of Mahalar's words.

Somewhere, not far away enough: a single heartbeat. Slow. Steady. Inevitable.

"We must go," Mahalar muttered, turning around to shuffle back up the stairs, "take the tome and—"

They didn't even hear the arrow flying before it caught Mahalar in the shoulder. The elder collapsed to his knees with a hiss as a trail of earthen substance began to leak from the wound.

They turned and saw the line of netherlings bold and black and drawing closer. The crescents of their shields locked together defensively, the jagged heads of their spears pointed out like the legs of a great, shiny beetle.

"*TOH! TOH! TOH!*" they chanted with every careful step, not a crack in their great, black carapace showing.

Without breaking their march, two shields would occasionally pull apart. An archer would appear in the gap, fire off an arrow that flew noiselessly to send another Shen to the stones. The gap would slam shut as Shen arrows flew in retaliation.

Shen archers assembled as warriors with shields fell back to protect them. Lenk ducked one such missile, hearing it curse his name as it sped past his ear.

"Gods damn it, whose job was it to watch those things?"

"Nevermind that," Mahalar snarled, swatting away the aid of a nearby Shen as he staggered to his feet. "They are coming."

"They are *here*, you moron," Kataria snarled, stringing an arrow.

"Not them, not them," Mahalar gasped, shambling up the stairs. "They are coming. *He* is coming." He made a fervent gesture. "Quickly. We must take the tome away. You must protect it. Follow me."

"Follow you?" Lenk asked. "Up the mountain to the dead end? We stand a better chance here."

"Even if we *did* trust you," Kataria added.

"There's more room to escape here," Denaos said, nodding. "It doesn't make sense to—"

"Doesn't make sense?" Mahalar whirled on them, his eyes bright with anger. "*Doesn't make sense?* The sky is raining *blood!* There is a heartbeat in the storm! Are you so stupid as to think that the person with the *least* idea of what's going on is the lizardman that bleeds earth?"

The companions fell silent, exchanged brief, nervous looks.

"I mean," Lenk said, rubbing the back of his neck, "I *think* that's a good point?"

Another arrow hummed past, narrowly clipping Denaos's shoulder. The rogue shrieked, clutched the grazing blow. "I'm for it."

"They're here!" Asper cried out. "Go. *Go!*"

They stole glimpses over their shoulders as they hurried up the stairs, the Shen closing in defensively behind them as Mahalar barked commands in their language. They could see the netherling line grinding to a halt. They could see one of the males suddenly break off and rush to the edge of the ring. It was the flash of red flesh that caught their eyes collectively, though.

"Gariath!" Lenk cried. "Come on!"

The dragonman looked up over his shoulder. A forlorn gleam flashed in his eyes before it died, replaced by a dull, black acceptance.

"His place is with us," Shalake called back. "He dies with us as we died with him!"

"Oh dear," Denaos said, rolling his eyes. "The Shen are insane and Gariath's decided to stay behind and be insane with them in an attempt to kill himself. This is so unexpected. Oh dear, oh no, oh Gods, oh well."

He took another ten steps before he was aware that his footsteps were the only ones he heard. He flashed an incredulous grimace at the companions standing stock-still upon the steps.

"Oh, for the love of . . ." He sighed, seized Dreadaeleon by the shoulder and shoved him down the steps. "Go get him."

After the boy had staggered several steps, paused to cough violently, he glowered up at Denaos. "Why me?"

"You're the one that has the connection with him."

"Since when?"

"Look, now's not the time to argue. Just go get him."

Resentfully, Dreadaeleon wormed his way between the Shen down to Gariath at the barricade. A glance over green shoulders and he could see the netherling line halted. Their shields held fast, barely quivering under the hail of arrows sent from the Shen.

Sheraptus was still there, somewhere behind the wall of shields. He could feel it in the burning of his brow, the chill in his veins, the great pressure bearing down on him. The mere hint of the longfaced male's presence was enough to make him feel ill, enough to send the power in him spiking in response, a moth twitching around a burning flame.

He tried to swallow the vomit roiling in his throat. He tried to ignore the fever burning behind his eyes. Wouldn't do to break down now, start pissing fire and vomiting acid in front of the Shen and lose all this hard-earned respect he didn't have.

"Look, Gariath—"

That was as far as he got, a meek whimper lost amidst the shriek of arrows and guttural howls. Gariath said something in response, something about this being the only way, about having nothing left. Dreadaeleon didn't hear. His brow suddenly began to burn, the vomit clawed its way to his throat and he got the very distinct feeling that things were about to go very, very wrong.

"*NAK-AH! SHIE-EH-AH!*"

He couldn't understand the Shen's warning. He didn't have to. He knew what was happening even before the magic started.

At the far end of the ring, the other male spoke a word. Lightning flew from his hands, leaping out to gnaw angrily at the stone ankles of one of Ulbecetonth's towering statues. It increased with each breath, its electric teeth pulverizing the granite and sending out clouds of powder. Stone snapped. The Kraken Queen let out a moan as she toppled forward.

Another word, the air rippled, the statue was suspended above the male, smaller, less grand than Sheraptus. He visibly tensed, grunted as the invisible force from his hands kept it aloft. Dreadaeleon could sense the strain, the weight. But only for a moment. After that, another surge of power from somewhere distant coursed through him, sent bile spilling out his mouth and onto the stone.

"Sheraptus," he choked through vomit.

This lesser male grunted, threw his hands and the statue. It flew through the air, was caught, hovered there. A great monolith the size of a spire hovering over the netherlings like a crown.

It didn't take an incredible amount of intelligence to know what was happening.

"Shoot," Dreadaeleon gasped. He pointed a trembling finger. "Shoot! He's there! In there! *SHOOT HIM!*

"Shoot!" Gariath roared to Shalake. "*SHOOT HIM!*"

"*KENKI-SHA! KENKI-SHA!*"

The command was carried on the scream of arrows, flying one after the other until there was not a space of bare air in the sky. Desperation in every shot, the arrows flew, shattering against the statue, shattering against the shields. The rare netherling went down, the others shuffled to fill in the bare space. In those moments, Dreadaeleon could see the white robes, the broad smile, the eyes burning bright and red.

A gap in the firing. The arrows slowed for a moment. The netherlings seized their chance.

They split apart, revealing him. His hands extended to either side in lazy benevolence, as though he were delivering some great truth instead of holding several tons of stone over his head with the burning heresy upon his brow. His smile was soft and easy, his eyes relaxed and calm despite the fire leaking out of them.

His word was gentle.

As he raised his hands and threw.

The statue went flying through the air, rising up black against the storm clouds brewing overhead. It seemed to hang there for a moment.

"Can you move that?" Gariath asked, looking up.

"No," Dreadaeleon said, wiping his mouth.

"Huh. We should probably move, then."

"SCATTER! SCATTER!"

"SHIGA-AH! ATTEKI MO-KI!"

"NO! NOT LIKE THIS! NOT LIKE—"

The statue fell.

Their screams were eaten alive. Their wails disappeared into clouds of dust. The frantic struggle to escape, the clawing over each other, the desperate prayers to someone else, all had ended.

Their bodies lay, as broken as the fragments of stone that rained from the sky.

TWENTY-NINE

THEM

The world and he choked together. Blood and dust rose up around him in great curtains of red and black. It throttled vision, smothered sound, strangled him from within as he crawled across the earth. The shattered barricade lay amidst the bodies, cutting hands and feet of those who still ran in panicked confusion. He could hear the screaming only in hairs' breadths, their voices lasting as long as they lingered near him.

The sound of metal, however, he could have heard for miles.

Without a noise beyond the rattle of their boots and the whisper of their spears sliding into flesh, the netherlings moved through the dust, their shadows black. Mechanically, they sought the survivors scrambling to flee, spared a killing thrust, and moved on.

Maybe he was just too insignificant, crawling breathlessly on his hands and knees, for them to notice. Perhaps they were so focused on their goal, as they charged past him and toward the stairs—or where he thought he remembered the stairs were, it was hard to tell—that they simply couldn't be bothered with him.

Or maybe they see a guy in a dirty coat with a mouth stained with puke crawling around and trying not to piss himself and they just don't have the heart to finish you off.

Do not question good fortunes, lorekeeper.

A cricket chirped in the back of his skull.

Greenhair! Where the hell have you been?

Watching, lorekeeper.

Ah, was it a good show, then? Saw what just happened? Are all the broken and mangled corpses quite a sight?

What horrors that man has wrought are nothing to what is coming, lorekeeper.

Oh, good. I was getting really bored with the godlike, limitlessly powerful wizard hurling giant statues around.

Cease *your weeping, lorekeeper.* That thought came with a surge of agony, like someone screeching at him. *I require a wizard, not a sarcastic worm. I need a hero.*

He had no thoughts for that. None that came with words, anyway. She didn't seem to need them. Whatever it was that surged inside him, she sensed.

Come to me.

No words that he could hear in his ears. A song without language beckoned him, drew him to her. Weaving his way between the iron legs and the bodies falling around him, he followed the song.

The curtains of dust thinned as he crawled out and clambered to his feet. Still more of the black-clad warriors brushed past him, charging into the fray. The screams of the dead and the wounded were fainter here, smothered beneath the gigantic statue of Ulbecetonth that lay, her smile spattered with crimson, upon the stone steps surrounded by sheets of dust and screaming.

The bulk of the netherling force was still midring, as though waiting. Sheraptus was ambling back to them atop his sikkhun, back casually turned to the slaughter, as though it weren't even remotely the most interesting mayhem he had seen.

Of Greenhair, there was no sign. Nor thought.

Or there might have been. It was hard to hear himself with all the thunder. The clouds were roiling, roaring, groaning. And amidst them, all he could hear was the slow and steady sound of something.

A heartbeat?

No, too fast. Footsteps. Feet? Many feet.

Coming his way.

The gibbering alerted him first, the slathering cackle that turned him about and then sent him lunging to the ground. The sikkhun came roaring past a moment later, its claws tearing up the earth and its wailing laughter cutting the air as it rushed past him.

He looked up, met Xhai's hateful glare for a moment. And a glare was all he got, spared the great blade in one of her hands and the thin, pale spear in her other. Those were weapons meant for a nastier job than whatever it would take to finish him off. And that job lay in the dust cloud as she charged after the black-clad warriors.

386

And his job?

Return to the fray?

He glanced back at the dust and slaughter and quickly discounted that.

Run away?

He glanced at the surrounding kelp, netherlings, and aforementioned slaughter.

Find Greenhair? No, she'll just tell me to stop Sheraptus or something. Not that that wouldn't be a bad thing to do.

But with what, he wondered? He was weary, breathless, armed only with an apparently beneficial insignificance and a rather ominous inkling that he was about to explode out of one orifice.

That might work. Position it just right and—no, no, no. Look, you've got some-thing that can work here, right? You had one of their stones, didn't you? If you could use that . . . no, it's heresy.

His fist found itself in his pocket, regardless. His body, apparently, was done waiting for his brain to decide if it was ready to live. He fished around, wrapped fingers around something firm and cold. The stone. The stone that would cure him, that would give him enough power to—

Ah, wait, no, he thought as he pulled it from his pocket. *That's not the right one, is it?*

This was the meager granite chunk from a black necklace that Denaos had found. Thick and raw and thoroughly useless.

"Where did you get that?"

It was his head, he was certain, all the noise and the dust was getting into his head. *That's* how people kept sneaking up on him. Or maybe he really *was* so stupid as to be able to miss the great sikkhun approaching. It remained there, panting as its rider stared down at Dreadaeleon.

The other male, tall and thin and sporting a white goatee. His face was more expressive than the others, full of shock and horror at the sight of the boy. Probably not for the good reasons.

"That stone, I gave it . . ." He held out a hand, as if to grasp it. "You took it. Qaine, she . . ."

"Uh . . ." Dreadaeleon began to back away, hoping he wasn't necessary in this conversation.

"Qaine. *Qaine.*" The male reiterated.

His lip trembled for a moment, eyes quivered for as long as it took him to draw in a breath. He held it there, shut his eyes tight. When they opened again, they burned red with energy.

"I need you," he whispered, "to die."

Gariath was still alive.

He had never been aware of his failure to die without a sigh of disap-pointment and resentment. He felt a dizzying rush as blood and breath fought to reassert themselves over his body. He swayed as he staggered to his feet, feeling strangely empty, as though his head hadn't quite realized he was still alive and his spirit had already taken off for the afterlife.

Slowly, it returned, as if rejected and skulking back dejectedly.

There were hundreds more in line before him.

Something brushed his foot. A long, green limb groped blindly across stones slick with a pool of sticky red and black. Five fingers. An elbow joint. Skin. Claws.

All that remained of the Shen, buried beneath the stone. It dragged its claws against the stone until they snapped, tried to pull itself out until the flesh of its fingers shredded.

The emptiness of his head filled with the screams and the blood and the explosion and the twitching limbs and the statue flying through the sky and the scent of death everywhere, rising up on curtains of dust, the resigned sigh of an earth that had seen too much blood already.

Blood and broken bodies and glistening pink matter that had burst out of mouths and spilled upon stones. This was what remained. Of the Shen, nothing else.

But what about the others? Where were the humans? The little one had just been standing here, hadn't he? Was he somewhere in this broken heap under the statue? Was he one of the shadows rushing about, screaming into the dust?

Was that him there, Gariath wondered? That stark black shape growing closer? He leaned forward, peered into the dust.

The jagged head of a spear shot out silently, found the muscle of his side and bit with iron teeth. His roar was eaten by dust. He reached down, seized the spear's haft in his claws.

The warrior emerged from the dirt. No face, no eyes, untouched by the dust and the agony. Gariath saw his twisted grimace reflected in the carapace of her helmet as she approached, twisting the spear. He could feel it taste him, express the hatred and fury that the netherling's faceless stare couldn't.

This would have been a good death, he reflected briefly. At the end of a long fight, by a worthy foe. It would have, if he was ready to die.

But that time was passed. He saw no reason to reward latecomers.

His fist shot out, caught the female's chin with the clang of metal. Her grip loosened enough for him to smash his fist again onto the haft of the spear, snapping it in two. He tore its splintered remains from her with one hand, reached out and slammed the butt of the other's palm against her chin. Her neck twisted back as she lashed out with fist and shield, bending so far back it seemed it might snap at any moment.

That, too, would have been a good death.

Less messy, too. But again, latecomers.

He flipped the splintered haft in his palm, jammed it forward. It punched through her exposed purple throat to burst out the other side. She bled, she staggered, she collapsed and disappeared beneath the swirling dust and sand.

Too much dust, he thought. Too much sand. It wasn't natural that sand should be this irritated, should linger in the air like a cloud of insects. There were lots of problems with this particular situation, the biggest one being the spearhead embedded in his side. He reached down to tear it out, braced himself for the scream to follow.

Wait. He forced himself to stop. *Pull it out, the blood comes gushing, you're dead in a few breaths. That's what the human said, right? That sounds right. Leaving a giant wedge of metal embedded in your skin sounds right . . .*

He blinked. Nothing about this made sense. He had to get away from it. He had to get higher.

He clawed his way up her stone body, over her hand, slipping on a patch of blood, trying to ignore the feeling that he could feel their screams in the palms of his hands. He emerged atop the statue.

He was not alone.

"*Rhega.*" Shalake did not turn around. His eyes were out over the sandy field. His club hung limp in his hands. "You are alive."

"Shalake," Gariath grunted, "are you . . ."

"No, *Rhega.* I am not." He slowly turned around. His skull headdress was gone but for a single shard lodged into his right eye. "I am dead."

"You aren't," Gariath replied, stalking forward. "You're wounded. The rest of the Shen are scattered. The longfaces are moving up the stairs. You need to—"

"I can't. I can't hear my people. I can't see my ancestors. I am somewhere else, *Rhega.* My body is down there, in the blood and dirt. My soul is here, talking to you." He blinked. His eyelid trembled, flickering over the bone shard. "Are you dead, too?"

"No."

Gariath's fist shot out, caught Shalake across the chin. The Shen staggered, spat out blood.

"Neither are you," the dragonman grunted. "Now, get down there. Rally the warriors. We have to—"

"We can't, *Rhega.*"

389

"We can, we just have to—"

"We can't."

Shalake raised a claw to the coral-splintered horizon and the crown of storms swirling atop it. Thunder crashed, banished the war cries and the screams and the rattle of iron and left the ring in an echoing silence. A great flash of lightning lit the sky and cast in shadow a mountain. A mountain that bled red in great weeping streaks across its body. A mountain that grew steadily bigger.

A mountain that walked.

"They're already here."

From the forest, out of the silence, a voice emerged. A distant wail, a bestial gurgle, the echoing reveberation of a bell, a hush of whispers and the flutter of wings and over it all, blending it into a single sound, the beating of a heart.

A cry went out from the netherlings, only barely heard, even echoed amongst the warriors. Their line began to move as they shifted to change their face toward the edge of the ring and the creature emerging from it.

The sheets of kelp parted, trembling as it came forth, a tall and skeletal shadow. On long, thin limbs wrapped in glistening ebon flesh, it strode onto the sand. Through great white eyes, empty as the void between its gaping, fishlike jaws, it surveyed the carnage. Thunder muttered overhead. A drop of crimson rain fell from the sky to splash and leave a weeping red streak across the white of its eye.

Its ribcage buckled. Its webbed claws tightened into fists. The Abysmyth threw its head back and howled to heaven and hell.

And the world exploded behind it.

They came streaming over the horizon in sheets and tides. The Omens flocked in great, sweeping streams, their withered faces alight with an echoing chorus. The frogmen surged out from the forest in a sea of pale flesh and glistening spears, flooding onto the battlefield and rushing toward the center of the ring. The Abysmyths strode amidst the hairless flood, leisurely strolling toward the impending slaughter.

The netherlings were not so patient.

"*QAI ZHOTH!*" they roared in their iron voices, challenging the storm and its demonic chorus.

"*ULBECETONTH!*" the tide shrieked back.

"*AKH ZEKH LAKH!*"

"*THE KRAKEN QUEEN!*"

"*ZAN QAI—*"

"*ULBEC—*"

All of it lost in a crash of metal and flesh as they collided in the middle of the ring in a great spattering, screaming agony.

Gariath's breath was lost somewhere in it all. He had seen carnage. He had caused carnage. But this was . . .

"The end, *Rhega*."

Shalake had a rather good way of putting it. The Shen held his hands out helplessly, the club hanging limp and impotent from his claws.

"This is everything we fought for. The chance to watch it all end and go with our ancestors."

"I'm not ready," Gariath snarled.

The Shen's good eye flickered, dispelling a fog that settled over his pupil. "No, not ready. We can't go . . . we . . . we need to help the others."

"They're down there somewhere," Gariath muttered. "Dreadaeleon is . . . somewhere. I have to find him."

"Him? No, no. *Them.* The Shen. There are survivors, lead them to . . . to . . ." He stared at Gariath. The shard lodged in his eye wept a thick substance. "We can't go looking for—"

"There is no 'we,'" Gariath snarled suddenly. "I am not Shen. I am not ready to die. I am *Rhega.* I am the *only Rhega.* I will do what I have always done." He reached out and tore the club from Shalake's grasp. "And I need this."

It wasn't until he launched himself off the statue and into the ring that he bothered to wonder what he needed the club for exactly. It wasn't just a fight that was raging, it was a massacre undiscerning.

The frogmen continued to stream out, the netherlings did not give a single footstep before drowning it in the frogmen's blood. The Abysmyths swung their great limbs, seizing warriors, strangling them as the Carnassials and their great blades rushed forward, heedless of their breathless comrades as they brought their metal to bear.

Against that, he wondered what good a hunk of wood full of sharp teeth was going to do.

"*QAI ZHOTH!*"

She came leaping over a drift of corpses, pulling free from the great spreading stain of flesh and blood of the melee. Her sword was above her head, her shield was hanging off her arm. Blood covered her purple flesh as she charged toward him. The netherling's mouth opened in a roar, jagged teeth bared.

Without realizing it, he swung.

A satisfactory crunch. Enough that he could barely feel the agony of his wound. The netherling's teeth lay on the ground. The club lodged somewhere between her jaw and her left temple. Her eyes stared with a thick chunk of wood between them.

Ah, right, he thought, watching a bit of gray porridge slide down the wood. *That* is good.

His earfrills twitched with the sound. Not screaming. They *were* screaming, of course, but all that was drowned out in the sound of embers crackling and smoke belching. The frogmen fled as bipedal pyres, scattering like cinders on the wind before the gouts of flame pouring from the netherling's hands. Not the netherling everyone was worried about; this one was smaller, weaker.

As weak as anything spewing fire from its palms could be, anyway.

But neither the netherling nor the creatures scattering before him were Gariath's concern. Just one of them.

Dreadaeleon stumbled, scrambling on whatever limbs happened to be on the ground at the time in an effort to get away from the male and the great, laughing beast he spurred after the boy. The male seemed in no hurry. He possessed a burning serenity, leisurely sweeping great reins of fire through the crowds to sear blackened roads across the sand to leisurely follow after his quarry.

Gariath drew in a deep breath. The air was full of blood and dust and smoke. And for the first time in a long time, it tasted sweet. The scent was full of life, fading fast. It was a scent he wanted to cling to.

He didn't want to die.

Which made it hard to justify what he was doing.

Running. Charging. Roaring. Swinging. A hairless head split apart, black eyes drowned in a spray of red. It fell, was replaced by another, purple one. Iron lashed out, his arm bled, a jaw splintered apart. More came, one after the other, blends of purple and white and red. It was hard to tell them apart. Color didn't matter. Sight didn't matter. The scent of life was growing stronger as it painted his face and stained his hands. The club hung to him. It belonged in his hands.

The longface with her head split apart didn't really *belong* there, but he found her body in his hands all the same. He drove the body forward with a roar, a limp, leaking ram that smashed through the knots of combatants across the field, taking spears and swords and arrows meant for him as he bowled over frogmen and longfaces alike.

It was a disjointed and ligamented mess that he tossed aside when he emerged. The scent of life brimmed, in plumes of smoke from the scorched sand and in the hot breath of the sikkhun beast. The beast's ears were fanned out, its rubbery lips peeled back in an eager smile as it advanced upon Dreadaeleon, stumbled and scrambling backward as the male rider looked on with contemptuous eagerness for the impending evisceration.

Gariath was slightly more enthusiastic.

The beast's ears quivered at his roar, turning its sightless gaze upon him. It matched his howl with an eerie cackle as it turned about to face this new, more interesting quarry. Gariath matched it, tooth for tooth, noise for noise, as he closed the distance and raised his club above his head.

Roughly about the time he felt an invisible force tighten around his throat did he remember the male.

He felt his feet leave the sand as he was lifted helplessly into the air, snarling and clawing wildly at an unseen grip. That became slightly harder when he felt the sand meet his face as the male brought an arm down swiftly, slamming him into the earth and pinning him breathlessly beneath the magic. He swept his burning scowl between the dragonman and the boy.

"And you," the male said, "were you there, too? Which one of you was the scum that killed her?"

Gariath grunted, looked to Dreadaeleon and mouthed *"who?"* The boy offered a hapless shrug before the air about his throat rippled. They were lifted as one, a hand outstretched to either of them as the male's eyes burned like fire. The sikkhun beneath him giggled, pawing at the ground in anticipation of fresh meat.

"I wanted to spare ourselves this."

The words came slowly, the concentration needed to hold onto the spell an endeavor even as the red stone burned brightly at the male's throat. Gariath could feel something groaning, threatening to break as the trembling air closed around him like a vise.

"And look where that got us," he hissed. "Sheraptus was right. Sheraptus *always* has to be right. That's fine. That's entirely fine. We can end this—"

A sound filled the air.

Something long, something loud, something from a very deep hole filling up with stale water from a storm that had gone on for centuries. It rendered the din of iron and death in the ring a pitiful background noise, something easily ignored. It had to be such a sound that made the male's concentration snap and sent the boy and dragonman tumbling to the earth. It had to be such a sound that made eyes look up to the thundering skies above in awe and fear and joy and panic.

In thick, sticky drops, red tears fell from the sky. A shadow of a mountain with a white peak appeared at the edge of the ring. A roar rose from it, the sound of existence groaning under a great weight.

"Tremble, heathens."

A man from atop the mountain spoke. A tiny, pale figure made significant, a voice made loud by virtue of from where it spoke.

"The long march of the inevitable has led us here."

"Daga-Mer . . . Daga-Mer . . ." a chant began to rise from the crowd of onlookers.

"The sky bleeds for him. The storms are his crown!"

"Daga-Mer! Daga-Mer!"

"The faithless are crushed beneath him! The blasphemers tremble before him!"

"DAGA-MER! DAGA-MER! DAGA-MER!"

"FATHER!" an Abysmyth howled from below, echoed by many more. The mountain stirred at the word, rose as a living thing.

"HE COMES!"

Life came to the mountain in an eruption of hellish red light. It veined the limbs that spread out from it, it pulsed with the beat of a heart that thundered in time with the storm, it burst from a pair of eyes, sweeping out over the penitent and the damned assembled in the ring.

The earth trembled as Daga-Mer raised a colossal foot and stepped onto the field.

Before the sound of him, there could be no words. Before the sight of him, there could be no blinking. He stood as an Abysmyth, tall and thin. But his head scraped the bleeding skies above, his thin hands were bigger than even his demonic children, and his jaws gaped open, void seeping out from between jagged teeth. Crude, rusted plates of metal had been hammered into his black flesh, a horned helmet to his skull from which the pale man spoke, rays of red light seeping out from between thin slits carved in the metal.

He said nothing. He made no movement. Circles of light cast from his stare swept slowly over the battle below and not a soul moved, none wishing to draw his attention.

The frightened whine of the sikkhun could have been heard for miles.

Gariath, however, was left with no miles. The sikkhun's squeak, the shuffling of its claws as it backpedaled, the panicked whispers of its rider as he tried to calm the beast were agonizingly loud.

As was the sudden sound of his heart stopping as a halo of red light fell upon them.

A crack of lightning above illuminated Daga-Mer's hand rising into the sky. The plates on his body ground and groaned against each other as his hand clenched into a fist. The sky, the earth and hundreds of small, insignficant bodies screamed in unison as it came down.

A sharp, terrified whine, the name "Qaine" screamed out, bones snapping, skin exploding, the earth breaking beneath a fist the size of a boulder. Everything was lost in the eruption that sent the earth rising up and sending Gariath flying, carried on a wave of dust and gore.

He landed somewhere, he didn't know where. Cries rose up around him, fear and panic and calls to arms. He was without Shen, without humans, without anything but the colossus of light and shadow that rose above the dust and insects.

As Daga-Mer threw back his head.

And roared.

Denaos looked up and over his shoulder, back toward the ring.

"That's funny," he said, "I could have sworn I just heard the sound of us about to be horribly murdered."

"What was that?" Asper craned to see over the heads of the Shen warriors who had accompanied them to the top of the stairs. "What *is* that?"

"We should go back," Kataria grunted, arrow drawn and at the ready. "We left Gariath and Dread behind to die."

"There is nothing back there *but* death," Mahalar growled. His attentions were focused on the great slab of stone at the end of the walkway running over the pond, his skeletal hands searching its smooth face. "Shalake failed. You failed. We all failed and now—"

Somewhere below, a roar shook the stones and the sky.

"*That*," the elder Shen muttered. "We have no other options now. We go forward or we die."

"We go forward and Gariath and Dread die," Kataria said. "The rest of us will follow a little later."

"Not 'we,'" Mahalar snapped. "*We.* You. Me. Jaga. *Everything.* Can't you hear it? Can't you hear *her?*" He stomped his feet upon the bridge. "She's stirring. Her beloved is close. Her children are close. She is coming."

Kataria narrowed her eyes at the Shen before turning to Lenk. "We can't just leave them, Lenk."

Lenk grunted in reply. Lenk was listening to something else. Lenk could hear it. Lenk could hear *her.*

Somewhere deep. Somewhere far. In the chasm. In the earth. In the utter darkness. Something scratched against the floor of the world. Something pounded against the door. Someone heard the screaming in the ring. Someone screamed back.

And in the dark place of his head, something awoke.

He shook his head, tried to ignore it, tried to dismiss it as anxiety and paranoia. That was what it was, he told himself. He left that part of himself back in the darkness, back in the chasm. He touched his shoulder, it seared. He felt flesh as liquid beneath it.

He was still dying.

Good.

Wait, no.

And yet, as he tried to fight it, tried to ignore it, the voice came to him anyway, came out of his mouth.

"She comes."

"Not yet," Mahalar said. "She's close, she's trying hard, but she can't come unless called." His fingers found a piece of slate, thin and barely recognizable from the rest of the stone. He pulled it back, revealing a jagged indentation in the rock. "We take that away from her, from the longfaces, from everything."

"By doing what?" Denaos asked. "There's nowhere to go but back down." He glanced over the edges of the walkway. "Or, you know, in there. I mean, either way it's going to be messy."

"There is another way."

Mahalar pulled from his shabby robe the sigil of the House of the Vanquishing Trinity, the gauntlet clenching arrows. Tearing it from its chain, he pressed it into the indentation and slid the slate back over. Something shifted within the stone, it began to rumble. It began to rise.

Albeit painfully slowly.

Lenk looked down as a sudden, familiar weight was thrust against him. The tome whispered to him, muttered a voice onto another voice, beckoning, begging, whispering, whining. Mahalar's eyes were dire, his voice darker.

"Take it there. Take it below. Keep it out of their hands and we can plan. Flee now. Save us now."

Lenk glanced at Kataria. She shot him an urgent look. He sighed, turning to Mahalar and nodding.

"*Why?*" she demanded.

"It's what Gariath and Dread would want," he said. "For us to not run away."

"Gariath, maybe," Denaos replied. "Dread, I think, would have a problem with us leaving him to be eaten alive . . . or stabbed . . . or otherwise dying horribly."

"Well, we don't have a lot of choice, do we?" Asper asked hotly, backing up as she reached for her sword.

"Oh, what? Because if we don't, the world is doomed?"

"Because of *that*, you idiot!" she replied, thrusting the blade at the top of the stairs.

And *that* came barreling up the steps. Cresting up over the stairs, atop the back of her sikkhun, eyes wide and white and mouth full of a roar, Semnein Xhai came.

"*QAI ZHOTH!*"

"Stop her! Hold her back!" Mahalar howled to the Shen. "The door isn't open yet!" He thrust a finger at Lenk. "You stay here! We can't let the book get away!"

The door was rising too slowly. And Xhai was not deterred.

She hacked wildly into the cluster of Shen that rose up to stop her. The great wedge of metal split turtle shell shields, cleaved through spears, ate of green flesh and drank of red blood. Those warriors that strayed too close to the sikkhun were snatched up in its jaws, shaken wildly like toys.

"We should do something," Asper said. "They're dying."

"Right, do something," Denaos said, edging behind her. "Maybe we can throw ourselves at the monster and hope it chokes on us."

"Or maybe we can let Kataria do everything *again*," the shict snarled.

She drew an arrow back and let it fly. Its song was short and ended in a meaty thunk as it bit into the netherling's leg. The longface looked up, spared a glare for Kataria, as though she were simply being obnoxious. It wasn't until she looked over the shict and caught sight of Denaos that her face twisted up like a fist.

"*YOU!*" she roared. She clove through a Shen in a single blow, sent two parts of him flying into the water.

"What did you do?" Asper asked, backing away breathlessly. "*What did you do?*"

"Yes, blame *me*," Denaos said, backing even farther. A small gap, barely larger than a child, had appeared beneath the door. "What the hell is taking so long?"

"The earth moves slowly, human," Mahalar muttered, "it feels nothing for mortal—"

"*No, Gods damn it!* You had plenty of time to be poetic down there! Now we need *results*!"

"Then it's just old as hell! I don't even know if it will open all the way," Mahalar snarled. "As soon as there's enough space, *move*!"

There was not enough space to move yet. More concerningly, there was not *nearly* enough space between Xhai and the companions. Lenk watched as the last three Shen hurled themselves at her. Lenk watched as the last three of them fell in pieces.

Black shadows crested up behind her. The black-armored warriors, spears shining, came marching up to join a battle already finished. Lenk wasn't concerned with them. Xhai wasn't, either. The longface's eyes caught a glimpse of the black book in Lenk's hands. She snarled, spurred her beast forward. It cackled wildly, bits of flesh bursting from its mouth as it scrabbled across the stones and charged.

A snap behind him. A sharp shriek of metal. The arrow flew, caught the beast in its nostril. Its cackle became a shrieking whine. Its charge ended as it flew onto its hind legs, scratching wildly at its snout with its claws. Lenk blinked, felt an arm seize him.

"Move, idiot!" Kataria snarled, shoving him toward the door.

Denaos's boots were just disappearing beneath the stone slab, Asper already gone in. Kataria tossed her bow under and slithered on her belly after them.

"Come on, come on!" she barked at Lenk.

"Mahalar! We're moving!" he cried as he threw himself to the ground.

The elder Shen nodded, turned to hobble after them as Lenk tumbled beneath the gap. He could see that the stone was just a cover to a wooden door, a series of groaning gears and chains slowly raising it.

"It's just going to keep opening!" Asper shouted in the darkness beyond the stone. "Find a switch or something!"

"What makes you think there's a switch?" Denaos asked.

"I don't know, just *find something*!"

Lenk watched the desperation in Mahalar's eyes, watched the dust fly from his mouth like spittle. He watched the Shen drag his body across the stones. He watched a brief smile flit across his face at the thought of his plan coming to fruition.

He watched the obsidian spearhead burst out the Shen's chest.

Xhai appeared from behind, hoisting the weapon by a pale, ivory-colored shaft. She looked at the impaled Shen contemptuously, irritated that she hadn't used it on something a little more impressive. Contempt turned to a wicked delight in an instant, though, as the spear's head glowed an ominous blue.

The Shen's flesh blackened as he writhed helplessly upon the shaft. The moisture and warmth left him, sucked into the spear by a great inhale. Even the dust left him as the spear swallowed it all.

He watched Xhai shake the weapon and dislodge a blackened, frozen husk from the shaft.

He watched Mahalar fall to the ground.

He watched Mahalar's lightless, dark eyes stare back at him.

"Here! Here's something!" Denaos called. "Quick, help me pull it!"

A clicking sound. The stone groaned as more black-clad warriors came up on the stairs, carrying something thick and heavy between them. The door slid shut as Xhai shouldered the spear and walked back to her mount.

And Lenk was left staring at the darkness.

THIRTY

FIRE

"S<small>o . . . what now?"</small>

Lenk could hear Denaos clearly in the darkness. Just like he heard him the last six times. There was surprisingly little to do in a pitch-black room full of warm, stale air and the reek of decaying moisture.

They had spread out, searching blindly for another switch, for anything that might lead them out. The crude metal lever that had shut the door had been found nearly by accident and had promptly snapped in half shortly after. They couldn't go back even if they wanted to.

"*Uyeh!*" a distant voice cried through stone.

"*Toh!*" five others sounded in reply.

The stone door shook as something smashed against it.

They most certainly didn't want to go back and see what that was. Nor did they want it to come through. Not that such a thing seemed all that feasible. The door did nothing more than tremble. It was a comforting fact, Lenk thought, right up until he remembered it meant the sole route of escape was quite closed off.

Then it was back to groping.

He found nothing but cold stone. Still, cold stone was preferable to any number of options. One of which bumped rather harshly against him.

"Sorry," Kataria muttered.

"It's fine," Lenk replied.

"Oh, it's you." She bumped again. This time with fists.

"Gods damn it, will you *stop* that?" he hissed.

"I should do worse," she said. "Gariath would want me to do worse." She struck him again. "How could you leave them like that?"

"Because we can't run anymore," he said.

He could feel her glare. "We ran in *here.*"

"In that case, because I wanted to die in one piece," he snapped back. "Look, I know we should have gone back. I know we shouldn't have even come up here. *I* wanted to sail away on a ship made out of skin but *you*—"

"*Weak. Traitor. Betrayed us.*"

"Never wanted them here. Killed them. Too dark."

He shook his head. Whispers. Memories of whispers, no less. Easily ignored. He believed maybe one-quarter of that.

"We don't have a lot of options left," he said. "The tome can't fall into the netherlings' hands."

"Not like there's a lot of choice," Asper replied from the other side of the room. "They'll break through, eventually."

"Not if the demons kill them first," Denaos chimed in. "If you pray hard enough, maybe the Gods will take pity on us. The demons will kill the long-faces and be left without a way in and we'll have the privilege of starving to— *oh, good GODS.*"

His curse came with the shuffle of stone as the rogue fell backward.

"Something . . . something . . ." he stammered. "I just touched . . . *something!*"

"Something?" Kataria asked. "Is it big and black?"

"No."

"I don't see it, then."

A soft light bloomed in the darkness. It grew, painting a slender, writhing body, vacant, glassy eyes, faint dots of green light that grew brighter with each breath. The fish twisted, slithered in midair, upward.

Toward a dozen more lights that blossomed in sympathy. Fishes swirled about the ceiling of a large, circular chamber carved into the mountain, illuminating the darkness in a soft nausea of blue and green. Carved upon the walls were images of tall, powerful women with hands extended in benevolence and faces scarred out by fire and sword. *"Death to heathens," "Glory to Gods," "Kill all Demons"* and other more colorful phrases were smeared across the walls in dark, soot-stained graffiti.

"In many different languages," Kataria noted.

"Huh?"

"That one's in shictish," she said, pointing to a line of writing upon the wall. "That one in something else."

"The mortal armies," Lenk muttered. "All peoples bound together to fight Ulbecetonth."

"Well, so long as every culture got the chance to write something dirty," Denaos said, walking past them. "But unless one of them has a curse you haven't heard yet, I suggest you come look at this instead."

"*Uyeh!*"

"*Toh!*"

Another tremor shook the stone door. It was all the persuasion anyone needed to follow Denaos to the other side of the cavern. A great archway rose up, flanked by two statues posing as pillars. Both depicted strong, young men with long, flowing hair and fins on the sides of their heads, tridents held in webbed hands.

Their stone skin was worn, however, by the intricate web of chains that wrapped around and between them to meet at a focal point at the center of the archway.

Another statue, shorter though far more imposing, stood there: a hooded man with a tremendous stone eye for a face, left palm outstretched in a warding motion, like the others Lenk had seen on Teji and Jaga. The chains bound it to the pillars and, hanging from every third link, a scrap of paper with barely legible script was woven to the metal.

"Do they say anything?" he asked, peering at the slips of paper.

"'Turn back, ye who wanders,'" Denaos read off a slip, "'the way ahead is shut to all but the dead. Enter, ye who seeks their joining.'"

"Really?"

"No, not really. I just thought that sounded ominous enough to make you stop thinking about it for a while." He tried to pull a pair of chains apart to make a gap large enough to pass through. "Give me a hand with these."

"Right." The young man stepped up and took the links. "Kat, watch our back. Asper—"

He certainly hadn't meant to finish that sentence with a scream that was usually reserved for people with hot pokers in the eyes. But the moment he had tried to pry the chains apart, he felt something inside him tear. His shoulder became damp, sticky. He could smell something pungent.

"The hell's wrong with you?" Denaos asked, cocking a brow.

"Uh . . ."

Any chance he might have had of coming up with something more clever than that ended as Asper pulled the collar of this tunic away, exposing the glistening infection in his shoulder.

"I told you," she snarled. "Didn't I tell you? *Didn't I?*"

"Tell him what?" Kataria asked, wide-eyed. "What's wrong with him?"

"I'm fine," Lenk said.

"I can't tell if you're trying to be stoic, clever, or stupid," Asper said, pointing at his shoulder. "But *this* sort of precludes two of those." She studied the wound, wincing. "It looks bad."

"How bad?" Kataria asked.

"Not bad enough to stop," Lenk muttered, pushing one leg through the gap in the chains.

"*Very* bad. He shouldn't be up and around, let alone doing . . . well, any of this," Asper said, reaching for the bag at her hip. "But if we can spare a moment or two, I might be able to—"

"UYEH!"

"TOH!"

The word came with a shattering sound. A great stone hand came smashing through the door. Ulbecetonth's arm, fingers cracking and crumbling to powder, carved a hole, fragments of timber and stone clattering to the floor as it withdrew, pulled by black-plated hands.

"UYEH!"

"TOH!"

Another blow splintered it totally. The arm fell, making way for what came shrieking out of a cloud of dust.

"Move! *MOVE!*"

Lenk's scream, and the subsequent cries of alarm, were lost in the sikkhun's gibbering laughter as it charged into the chamber. They scrambled to get out of the way as it rampaged across the floor, tongue lolling, smile wide with excitement. Denaos released the chains, letting them pull tight over Lenk's leg as he darted away.

"*Denaos!*" Lenk screamed at him. "*You son of a bitch!*"

"*You said to move!*" the rogue screamed back, already far away.

The young man tried desperately to pull his leg free. The pain in his shoulder and his thigh weren't easy to ignore. The sound of a gibbering mass of muscle and fur thundering toward him, even less so.

He pulled himself free with a wrenched scream, falling to the floor. Kataria was there in a moment, seizing him by his ankles and dragging him ignobly away as the sikkhun threw itself wildly forward.

The statue buckled as its skull collided with it, its robes cracking, chains clinking. The pillars groaned, swaying as the chains pulled them from their roots. That might have been more alarming, Lenk thought as he rose to his feet, if not for the sikkhun scrambling to its feet. It shook a cloud of granite dust from its fur, loosed a delirious giggle as it turned and began to stalk toward the companions.

That, too, wasn't the worst thing at that moment.

"*QAI ZHOTH!*"

They came charging through the sundered door, spears alive, metal rattling. Lenk was already running to the archway, even before he heard a violent crack and scream behind him. The chains slackened as the pillars swayed. The others had already picked up on this idea. Kataria was alongside him, Asper right behind him, Denaos . . .

Even farther behind him, on the floor with a metal boot digging into his back. Xhai stood over him, blade raised above her head, a joyless smile on her face as her sikkhun came padding up, grinning broadly.

"Oh, Gods *damn it*," Asper snarled.

By the time he had discerned what that meant, Lenk and Kataria were already through the chains. The priestess had whirled about, charging past the netherlings to tackle Xhai at the waist and knock her aside. The longfaces didn't seem to notice her, intent on what was clear to everyone.

The pillars were collapsing.

"Come on, come on!" Kataria cried, pulling on Lenk's arm.

There was no choice but to run as the netherlings filed in after them, as the pillars groaned and toppled over, as darkness swallowed them whole.

Are you well, lorekeeper?

Am I dead?

You are not.

Are you sure?

I am certain.

He tried to rise. Something inside him suggested that such an action and keeping all his organs inside him were mutually exclusive concepts.

Oh, you lying little harlot.

Lie still, lorekeeper. Her thoughts came into his head on lilting notes, a spoon stirring whatever soup his brain had become. *Let me soothe you with—*

Stop. Stop thinking at me.

"We can use words, if you wish," she sang.

No, no. I don't think I have lips anymore.

"Open your eyes, lorekeeper."

That seems like a bad idea.

He did it anyway.

It was.

The battle raged across the ring still. The netherlings seemed to have a stable hand, if not an upper one. Each warrior stood knee-deep in bodies as frogmen hurled themselves at them. Abysmyths waded in tides of flesh, reaching down to pluck netherlings from the sea of combatants and twist an offending body into a purple knot before absently tossing them over their shoulders. They were heedless of blades sinking into their ribcages, arrows finding their gullets. It wasn't until a Carnassial, wild with fury, would tear herself free from the combat and bring an envenomed blade to hack off a demonic limb that they noticed there was a battle going on.

Their father seemed even more heedless than that.

Daga-Mer and the storm strode as one. Each time the titan's foot set down, it did so with the sound of thunder that crushed the screams of the frogmen and netherlings beneath it. Each time the hellfire in his eyes swept across the field and found a target, lightning danced joyously for the impending doom. Each time his great fist came down, red tears filled a shallow grave across the sand.

Dreadaeleon went unnoticed because he was currently heaped amidst a small pile of bodies. He was fine with that. He was more than fine with being absent from this mayhem.

Which made it difficult to justify why he was rising up, albeit shakily.

"Lorekeeper!" He felt Greenhair's hand on his shoulder, steadying him. "You cannot be feeling well enough to do what you're thinking of."

Perhaps she had known what he was planning even before he had the thoughts to put it into name. Maybe he really was that obvious. After all, for what reason could a skinny little ill boy in a dirty coat get up and begin staggering toward a vile melee like this?

What could he hope to accomplish?

Go in there, find Sheraptus, or his corpse, locate the crown, use it to save his friends who were . . . somewhere else? Or go in there, hope that he'd been wrong all his life, discover that Gods were real and would smile on him enough to let him end all this? Or maybe just go and die and feel anything but the disease running through him?

All terrible plans, of course. The more he thought about them, the more stupid they seemed.

A good enough reason, then, to stop thinking about them. Actions, theoretically, were better.

Doing what he could to stop Sheraptus. Doing what he had to to help the others, wherever they were. Doing what he had to, to prove he still wasn't as weak and useless as everyone—

He bit back a shriek. A hand thrust against his head as a sudden spike of agony lanced his skull. Fever and chill swirled about him, an immense pressure came down on his skull. He fought to hold onto consciousness, then to breath, then to thought.

Magic. An immense amount.

That made finding Sheraptus easy enough, even if the longface didn't look wildly out of place amongst the carnage.

The boy caught sight of him not far away, standing at the center of a ring of charred sand and smoldering bodies, pristine in his white robes, fingers still steaming as he folded his hands behind him. He was casually observing a small crew of netherlings loading their spiky siege engine with a tremendous ballista bolt, a trio of Carnassials standing beside him, wary of the carnage he was seemingly oblivious to.

Dreadaeleon's eyes drifted down to the twisted, blackened husks that ringed the longface.

more than a flinch from the beast as he reached into the melee and scooped out a longface.

A surge of power sent pain creasing across Dreadaeleon's mind. Sheraptus raised his hands to the chain. The stones burned on his brow, his eyes erupted with red light. Electricity danced from his fingers onto the chain, link to link and flesh to flesh.

Daga-Mer convulsed as the electricity raced across his colossal body. His shrieks tore apart the sky, his hellish red light turned to a vivid blue pouring out of his mouth and painted against the storm with his scream. When it ended, the titan collapsed to one knee. Earth trembled, smoke bloomed in a gray forest.

Sheraptus smiled, flicking sparks from his fingers and making a vague gesture toward the demon.

"Finish it," he said. The Carnassials obeyed, rushing off across the battlefield. He turned to Dreadaeleon with a smile on his face, almost seeking approval. "You see?"

Dreadaeleon was having a hard time seeing anything. The surge of power persisted, pressing down on his skull. He breathed heavily, trying to listen for Greenhair's song, just for a moment of reprieve.

"You presume they're there to give you things," Sheraptus continued, waving a hand to the sky. "But they're not. They're there to make you *prove* you deserve it. They called me here. They sent the demons here. Everything that came before, all the killing, being surrounded by these *females* and doing nothing but what we thought we were meant to do. It all had a reason!"

Just a flinch. A fleeting twitch of a purple lip.

"Right?"

"I can't think," Dreadaeleon said, holding a hand to his temple. It burned to the touch. "There's too much power surging about. How are you producing so much without casting any spells?"

"Ah, you feel it, too?" Sheraptus looked genuinely perplexed. "I thought that was you. A symptom of your condition."

The two wizards looked at each other for a moment. Their gazes slowly turned upward.

"Oh, dear," Sheraptus whispered.

They went scrambling for cover, boy and netherling alike. The ballista crew drew their swords, looking up and uncertain of what they were seeing. It became clear as soon as they heard the screaming. But by that point, the sky was already ablaze.

Bralston struck the ground in an explosion. Bodies, living and dead, were as wheat around him, bending into coils of blackened matter. They were

Seemingly.

But more, his eyes were drawn to the crown. Burning bright as fires, alive with energy. He tried his best not to remember where the energies came from.

He had to try harder not to remember what he could do with it.

He forced his attentions on what would have to come first. He raised his hand, focused on the crown, called the magic to mind.

"I can smell your wings burning, little moth," Sheraptus said suddenly. "Finish that spell and you might very well burn to ash." He turned to Dreadaeleon and smiled. "Only one of you?"

He couldn't hear Greenhair's song in his head. Had she fled? She was getting more efficient with her betrayals, if nothing else.

"The rest are busy trying to stop what you're interfering with. They're demons. Unnatural. You can't use them like you used the Gonwa."

"Use them? For what?"

"The . . . the red stones. Fuel."

"The martyr stones?" Sheraptus grinned. "That *would* have been a good idea, wouldn't it?"

The boy furrowed his brow. "Why did you come here, then?"

"I dislike that word. It's only three letters, yet it's been annoying me greatly. We have no equivalent in our tongue. We do not ask, we simply do. I have found this to be effective, thus far."

"Ulbecetonth is rising, Sheraptus! That means certain death for us all!"

"If that were certain, we'd already be dead. The fact that I'm still here must, therefore, mean that my victory is certain." The longface pointed a finger upward. "They have shown me this."

"Has that crown finally burned a hole through your brain? Do you not hear yourself?"

The Carnassials hefted their blades, began to stalk toward the boy. Sheraptus held them back with an upraised hand.

405

"I don't blame you for your faithlessness. It took me quite a while to realize the error of it myself and I'm so much more than you." He turned and nodded to the ballista crew. "That is why I am about to do their will and end this."

Creation shook with a howl. Daga-Mer challenged heaven and earth alike, throwing his titanic arms back as he roared to the sky.

Sheraptus answered softly.

"Let it fly."

The ballista bolt went shrieking over the heads of the combatants, a great chain snaking behind it. It sank into the titan's midsection, inciting barely ignored. The carnage raging around him went unheeded. He could see none of it. His eyes were alight, his vision burning out. All that was left of him was reserved for one sight.

A heretic.

The heretic. Bright red in Bralston's vision, burning like the sun. No sign of the weak concomitant. No sign of his murderous ally. That was what he had come here for, yes? To avenge Cier'Djaal and the Houndmistress?

Hard to think. His mind seared, boiling under his own power. Everything in him leaked out of his eyes. He had come here for something. That was not important.

Duty was everything.

The heretic must die.

Bralston threw out his hands and screamed a word.

There was only the fire burning him alive, sending the wings of his wraithcoat flapping, hurling him toward the longface wizard. He could see the magic forming in the netherling's hands, erecting walls of force. That, too, meant nothing.

Bralston struck it with a scream, hands outstretched like a battering ram. Their air crashed against each other, sent the longface skidding on his heels. He was burning too bright, spending too much power trying to hold back Bralston. Bralston screamed louder. Bralston pressed harder.

The netherling flew, tumbling over scorched sand and through bodies. Bralston pursued. The walking wheat that came at him, he could not see. They fell before his screams, the fire in his step, the frost pouring from his mouth. He walked among them, burning brightly, the longfaces and hairless things and towering beasts charred and shattered and sent flying.

They kept coming. That did not matter. The heretic mattered. Duty mattered. He had to keep going, he had to keep burning, he could not stop burning until the heretic was dead.

The heretic burned less bright in his gaze. He rose to his feet, diminished. He was weakening. He was stumbling backward, waving his hands wildly, sputtering words that meant nothing.

Bralston screamed, threw his hands forward and let the sheets of flame roil toward the heretic. He fled. The longface was burning dim, fading against the flames, flickering out of existence, blackening.

No, that was his own vision. Bralston's vision. Darkening at the edges. Burning black. Burning out. Flickering. Dying. So tired. He needed sleep. He needed beds. He needed silk and her and perfume and her and poetry.

And her.

Duty. Duty first. Duty always.

He pressed on, following the heretic. Monsters rushed, were burned. Longfaces charged, were flung aside. It was hard to see the heretic, a fast-fading light. He had to keep going, he had to keep burning.

Someone seized him. He turned. A weak fire, waning, flickering candle snuffed by moth's wings. Dreadaeleon. He was talking, saying words that weren't magic. Pointless. Senseless. He needed to keep burning.

"—*bleeding!*"

Words.

"—*dying, not going to*—"

Fading.

"—*the* crown*! The crown will*—"

Burning.

He had to keep burning. The concomitant would not let go. The concomitant. Friends with the murderer. Killed hundreds. Where was the murderer? The concomitant would not let go. He had to find the heretic. The murderer. He had to scream. He had to keep burning. The concomitant would not let go.

Bralston raised a hand. Bralston screamed.

Lightning flashed. A single bolt. The concomitant had let go. Flesh burned. Bralston was still silent.

Bralston was bleeding.

From the throat. From the chest. He looked down. He was burning. His chest was black. He was burning out. He was not breathing. His vision was blackening.

He fell forward.

Soft hands caught him.

He could smell the candle wax, the silks, the orchids, the night sky, the perfumes that real women didn't wear. He could feel the softness of her legs as he lay his head upon her knees. He could feel the warmth of his own breath, the gooseflesh rising upon her thighs, how very heavy his eyes were.

"No, no," she said. "Don't open your eyes."

"I have to," he said. "There is a heretic out there. There are murderers out there. I have to open my eyes."

"I'm in here. Don't open your eyes, Bralston."

"All right."

He felt her hand running across his scalp. He felt her hand sliding down across his chest.

"Don't," he said. "I'm hurt."

"No, you're not, Bralston. You're here with me."

"Where?"

"In a very long and very wide rice field. The mud is thick and it reeks of dung. The sun is very hot."

"I only smell silk and perfume. I don't feel warm at all. Anacha?"

"Mm?"

"Are you happy here?"

"We are happy here, Bralston."

"I'm so tired, Anacha. I've missed you."

"I've missed you, too. Sleep now, Bralston."

"I love you, Anacha."

"Sleep, Bralston."

"I love you."

"Sleep."

"I . . . I . . ."

"Yes? You what?" Sheraptus asked, peering down at the dark-skinned human. "Sorry, you'll have to speak up. I think you're dead."

"I . . . I . . . I . . ."

The human was still going. Sheraptus would be impressed if he wasn't so annoyed. He had run. *He*, a male, had fled from this babbling thing. In front of all the females. In front of the people in the sky.

But he had had no choice. This overscum had knocked the crown loose, sent him reeling. The words hurt to speak. The price for *nethra* had burned him after so much time of not paying it. He could barely muster enough skill to cast the lightning that had slain the human.

No matter, he could find the crown now. He could finish this. This dark-skinned overscum had killed an impressive number. Only Daga-Mer and the most resilient of demons remained. Of course, only a few of his own warriors remained. That didn't matter, either, once he had—

"The crown."

He saw it there, lying like some forgotten thing. He scrambled toward it on his hands and knees in the gore-soaked dirt, careful not to be seen by anyone. He grew quicker as he approached, limbs flailing in desperation to reach it. He lunged for it.

It was in the air.

In pale, pink hands.

On a dirty, sweaty brow.

Dreadaeleon closed his eyes. He drew in a long, strong breath. When he opened them again, he was ablaze.

THIRTY-ONE

BLOOD OF MOUNTAINS

His shoulder hurt. He was bleeding. Darkness pressed in all around him. Bloodthirsty women were somewhere behind him.

"Two more we left behind."

Kataria wasn't helping.

"We had no choice," he said.

"I know," she said, sighing. "I know. But we left them behind with her. With Xhai."

"And that means we're not here with Xhai," Lenk said. "That's something."

"Is it? I can't even see my hand in front of my face. Can you?"

He collided with the heel of her palm and recoiled with a snarl.

"You're hilarious."

"I'm angry. I also have no idea where we're going and I have no idea why it is you think we shouldn't stop and try to figure it out. And of course, you're not going to tell me. Because that would just be *too* sane, wouldn't it?"

He was pleased she couldn't see him wince at that. After all that had happened, he had thought sanity and accusations surrounding it wouldn't be such a touchy subject. That had been before they had fled into the tunnels, though, before they had run through the winding darkness to escape the netherlings.

Before someone, somewhere, down there in the dark wet stone, started muttering his name.

"We lost the netherlings, didn't we?" he said. "We're still alive. The tome is still in the least dangerous hands possible. We . . . we did good."

"We left them behind."

"What the hell did you *think* was going to happen?" His voice did not echo in the darkness. "Why the hell did you think I *wanted* to run? I had everything I wanted back there. You, no voices in my head . . . but you said we shouldn't run and I thought you were right."

"I was right then and I'm right now," she snarled back. "I'm right *all the Gods damned time* and we should go back."

"Through a bunch of netherlings to dig ourselves out of a heap of rocks?

We might emerge in time to see Xhai strangling Asper with Denaos's intestines. We go forward."

"At the very least, we should stop and check your shoulder."

"We go *forward.*"

"Lenk."

He said nothing.

"Never should have come here."

She hadn't said that.

The wall became cold beneath his hand, a kind of urgent cold that reached out with stony fingers to intertwine with his. He felt a pulse through his palm, an airless breath drawn in. And when it released, the light came.

"But you did," the man in the ice said. The light in his eyes filtered through the tomb of frost, staring past Lenk and into nothing. *"And you brought it back here."*

He was strong. And he was dead. His beard was white and his lips moved mechanically. Cords of flesh pulled him against a pillar of rock and crushed his body into macabre angles beneath the tomb of glassy frost, blackened and frozen in ancient rigor. His eyes beamed with blue light. His voice was hollow.

"You should not have returned, brother."

Kataria was shivering, hovering around Lenk, uncertain whether to hide behind him or stand before him. She tried to make her chattering teeth seem a bare-toothed snarl. Lenk stared into the man's eyes. He felt cold. It didn't bother him.

"What the hell are you supposed to be?" she demanded of the man in the ice.

"I am the one who stayed behind, to watch my brothers, to see the end of this war. I am the one betrayed, the slayer who waited for the world to betray us as he said it would."

"So . . . is that *whole* thing your name or do you have a regular one?"

"I once did."

"And . . . what are you?"

The answer came, no matter how badly he wished it hadn't.

"He's me," Lenk said. "They all are."

"Who?"

In answer, the glow from the ice grew brighter, enough to illuminate the tunnel into a cavern. They stood upon a high ledge above a chasm yawning into nothingness. And below, a dozen other blue lights bloomed like dead flowers, reflecting off a dozen other tombs of frost.

They marched into the darkness, with their swords high and their black cloaks flying and their eyes alight with a cold fury that death could not diminish. In scenes of battle and of death, with arrows and blades and wounds decorating their flesh, they were frozen. They endured, constant as the death in the air and the dead beneath their feet. Demons, humans, wearing the images of Ulbecetonth and of the House of the Vanquishing Trinity, skeletons all, long gone from the battle the people in the ice still fought.

"Riffid," Kataria gasped breathlessly, staring out over the pit.

"*That name is memory,*" the man in the ice said. "*They cried out to many gods in that war. For nothing. We are too far gone from the sun. No god can hear us down here.*"

"What happened?" Lenk asked.

"*This is where we ended it. All of it,*" the man said. "*The mortal armies were failing. The demons were endless, the Aeons were all-powerful, the Gods were deaf. All was lost for the mortals and their House. Until he decided to intervene.*"

"Who?" Kataria asked. Neither man answered. She looked to Lenk. "*Who?*"

A desperate incredulity was lit upon her face. A demand, a plea, something that pained him to see. He didn't want to admit it any more than she wanted to know.

"Him," Lenk repeated. "Mahalar spoke of you, the ones who killed the demons. But you only carried the swords, didn't you? It was him who gave you the power, him who speaks through you. It was him who killed the demons and drove back Ulbecetonth."

"What?" Kataria asked.

"*God of Gods,*" the man in the ice answered. "*He had no name. Like us. He had no need for them. He decided there would be no demons, no gods, no rulers of mortality. The terrible burden of their existence was theirs to bear. Ours to deliver.*"

"You talk like you aren't one of them, aren't mortal."

"*I am no god. My flesh rots beneath this ice. My bones snap under her grasp. But I am not like them. They hated him for his declaration. They hated us for delivering it. Men and the gods they served. They turned on us here, in this cavern, in this battle as we fought to make it to the drowned throne of the Kraken Queen. A pitiful jest. Without us, they could not kill her. They could only lock her behind doors of meaning.*"

He sighed centuries out into the darkness.

"*And you returned her key, brother.*"

Lenk looked to his satchel. Even in the darkness, even obscured by the pouch, the barest glimpse of the tome's cover revealed a blackness that refused to be obscured. If anything, it grew darker, heavier, more significant. An eager child perking up when it knew someone was talking about it.

"The tome . . . you wrote it?"

"*Long ago. He knew that the gods would need to be challenged one day, as the demons were, that tyrants could never be traded for tyrants. And he told us to write the book, with all the knowledge of the demons and mortalkind and all that it meant to fear and hope. It was intended to stay in our hands.*"

He laughed the sounds of ice breaking.

"And he was right. Yours are the only hands left, brother."

"What is it you think I'm going to do with it?"

"There is no thinking, brother, for there is no question. There is only certainty and his will. You will use the tome as you are meant to, as he wills you to."

"And if I refuse?"

"Reiteration is a poor defense against inevitability, brother. All that he speaks shall pass. He, the God of Gods, told us our duty, so we carried it out. He told us to kill, and we did. He said we would be betrayed, we were, as you knew you would be."

He did not look behind him. It did not help. He could feel the hurt in Kataria's stare as keenly as any metal.

"That was a fear. The same as any man of flesh and bone would have."

"It was a certainty."

"If it was certain, then I would have accepted it."

"Denial is a poor shield, brother."

"And a great weapon. You swing it hard enough, it breaks just about anything. Especially certainty."

"We heard you when you came to this land. We heard your fears through him and they spoke loudly."

"And what do you hear now?"

The man was silent.

"I sent him away," Lenk said. "I rejected him. I rejected everything he offered me, every price he asked. I'm free of him." He felt the pain in his shoulder. He did not reach for it. "I'm free of that ruler."

"He does not rule. He speaks. He blesses us, tells us what must be done and gives us the strength to do it."

"Sounds like any other tyrant masquerading as benevolent."

"Perhaps. Or perhaps he knew that it was the price we had to pay for the rest of mankind. It's a great power, brother. It came at a price we paid willingly."

"Not me."

"Then you will die."

"I haven't yet."

"You haven't accepted it yet."

"You talk about leaving gods and rulers behind and in the same breath tell me about inevitability and fate."

"They are not the same thing. He does not come to us and tell us this is how it must be. We felt the same that you did, the same fears, the same urges, the same knowledge that those around us loathed us and hated us and feared us. He does not come to us, brother. We call out to him, whether we know it or not."

Lenk looked to Kataria. Instinctively. Shamefully. He looked to her and tried to convince himself that it was the voice inside his head that had said all those things about her and told him she would kill him. He looked to her and mouthed, noiselessly, "it was not me."

She looked back. He could not bear her stare.

"I came here to get the book away," Lenk said, turning back to the man in the ice. "Is there a way out of here or not?"

"Walk amongst your brothers. Down there in the darkness and the cold. Water carved these tunnels. It will lead you."

"Where?"

"There is only one way."

In the distance, he could hear something. Echoes of war cries carried on the gloom. The rattle of armor. Growing louder.

Whether the corpse was being intentionally cryptic or not, he was right. There was only one way.

They made their way down into the pit, amongst the many frozen bodies and the dead. And still the man in the ice spoke, his voice as clear and close as it had been a moment ago.

"He still calls to you, brother. He scratches at the back of your head. He tells me this. He can heal you. He can make you strong. If only you let him back in."

He almost turned to look back at them and answer. He would have, if Kataria were not right there, seizing his neck, forcing his eyes down and his feet forward.

"You're not them," she snarled.

"Down there, brother, you will find him," the voice called after him. *"Or you will find her."*

And his voice echoed in the darkness. And his lights lingered in the darkness. As they walked farther, following the sound of rushing water.

I'm doing it.

The hope came, despite the blood trickling into her eye.

I'm stronger than her.

Despite the muscles in her arm breaking beneath her skin.

I can do this.

All ten of her fingers wrapped around Xhai's fist, keeping it and the massive blade it clenched trembling over their heads. Xhai's boots scraped against the rock. Her cursing stained the chamber's still air. She pushed against the priestess and found the woman unyielding.

I can do it. I am doing *it. I'm going to beat her and I'm going to survive and I'm going to save Denaos.*

The thought came with a sudden waver.

Denaos.

She tossed the scantest glance over her shoulder, trying to catch the barest glimpse of the rogue.

It wasn't clear how much of a mistake that was until she felt the netherling's boot. It slammed into her belly, shattering her grasp and hurling her away. Somehow, though, she summoned just enough to curse him.

"Even—" she paused to gasp, collapsing to a knee, "—when I think about the bastard . . ."

"I don't appreciate that kind of negativity."

His hands were on her arms, hoisting her roughly to her feet, heedless of her glower. "Doesn't make it less true." She tried to find her breath. "She's strong."

"I really hadn't figured that out when she beat me hard enough to make piss come out my nose."

"But she's not invincible," Asper said. "If one of us can occupy her while the other one . . ." Asper paused, watching him run past her. "Where the hell are you going?"

He didn't have to answer. The loud cackle that came from behind her did that well enough.

Scantest glance, barest glimpse. Sharp teeth in a wide, black-lipped smile. And she was running, too.

Breathless, staggering, struggling to stay on her feet. The sikkhun trotted after her, clacking claws and giggling wildly. It could have taken her in one pounce, but chased her with all the urgency of a child skipping through a field of dandelions.

There was, apparently, no aspect of netherling society that wasn't, in some way, completely messed up.

"Thakh qai yush!" Xhai's voice carried across the chamber. The sikkhun broke off suddenly, galloping toward her.

Asper came to a halt at the shattered doorway of the chamber where Denaos was trying to catch his breath and leaned against it, doing the same. She glanced at the beast as the Carnassial leapt atop its back.

"That thing could have killed me," she gasped. "But it didn't." She looked at Denaos. "*You* should be dead by now."

"Dead by the sikkhun or some other reason?" The rogue spat. "Not that I disagree."

"Why didn't it kill you while I was fighting her?"

"It's complicated."

"You don't say," she muttered.

"She doesn't want me to die unless she can do it herself. And she's not going to kill me unless she can take her time with it."

"How do you know that?"

"Did I not just tell you it's complicated? Look, I know her, so I know how to get out of this."

"Listening."

"Well, I don't know it *now*. Give me time to think. Keep her busy."

"Why do *I* have to keep her busy?"

"Because she wants to kill you first."

"AKH ZEKH LAKH!"

Like *that* wasn't obvious. The ground shook with the sikkhun. It was focused now, jaws wide and laughing as it charged toward them. Xhai spurred it on, sword over her head, snarl painted on her face.

They split, Denaos running one way, Asper the other. True to his word and Xhai's fury, the Carnassial whirled her beast upon the priestess. It squealed in delight, rampaging after her.

She twisted and turned, forcing it to follow her erratic movement with its clumsily eager bulk. But each time she darted away, the beast had a smaller gap to close.

"Do something!" she screamed.

In answer, a stray rock came flying. It struck the Carnassial upon the brow. She grunted, rubbed her head. The sikkhun did not stop.

"What the hell was that?" Asper shrieked.

"I said give me time! That was fifteen breaths, tops!" the rogue cried back.

It might have been worth it, she thought, to try to strangle Denaos before the sikkhun killed her. That might be more satisfying. But before she could catch sight of him, she saw something else.

The statue with the outstretched hand, lying amidst the rubble in the archway. Cracked, but not broken like the pillars. Sturdy stuff, that particular stone. Sturdy enough to give her a single, desperate idea.

She ran toward it. She felt its breath on her heels. She felt its laughter in her spine. She felt its jaws widening.

She leapt to the side.

The sikkhun's giggle twisted into a shriek. Stone screamed and she could feel it, through the cold earth and in her stomach.

Asper picked herself up and turned about.

The sikkhun lay before the pile of rubble, whining pitifully, trying to scrabble to its feet with a brain that couldn't remember how feet worked. Shards of granite jutted from its face in thick points from brow to snout. Its ears folded against its head as it whimpered, staggering away, drooling a thick black liquid.

Not dead.

It wasn't half as gruesome as what had happened to Xhai. Asper looked up and saw the dark red streak painted upon the wall. The netherling slid down the stone on a thick trail, limp as a slug, to settle upon the rubble. The Carnassial groaned.

Not dead.

She should be worried about that.

She should be looking for Denaos, she should be reaching for the sword in her belt and going to finish Xhai off, she should be doing anything but staring at the pile of rubble and the body upon it.

But she couldn't do anything but stare at the shattered rock.

And the two black eyes staring back at her.

The statue lay in pieces, divided neatly down the middle. The extended left arm lay upon the ground. The head lay atop the rubble.

And between them, a body lay.

A man made out of paper. Long and skinny, ragged around the edges, cut out of a parchment with a sticky pair of scissors. It did not lie upon the rubble. It unfurled. Its limbs had been folded to fit in the statue and now its limbs spread out, twitching, like a wadded-up piece of paper uncurling itself.

Its only solid pieces were its eyes. Black. Glossy. Alive. And blinking.

And it was looking at her.

And she felt its gaze in her, in her arms, the pain searing, the blood boiling, the skin tightening. As though something inside her was looking back at it. As though something inside her was desperately trying to get out of a statue made of flesh.

It moved. All that it had left, everything in it, pooled in the tip of a long left finger that twitched exactly one-half of the length of a hair from a man about to die, to point briefly at her.

And she felt herself erupt from within.

The stone beneath her. The blood weeping from her temple. His arms around her as she fell. She could feel none of it. The world swept into her, all the feeling drawing into her blood, beneath her skin, setting her on fire.

It knew her. The thing in the statue knew her. It knew she hated the taste of alcohol. It knew she slept with a candle burning for fourteen years of her life. It knew she once held hands with a girl named Taire. And it reached into her with a voice without words and said with a smile without a mouth.

How are you, my friend?

She was screaming. She was screaming and she couldn't hear anything else above it as she lay back into his arms.

Denaos wasn't talking. Maybe there was something in his eyes, some question he wanted to ask, some fear he wanted to voice. But she couldn't tell. He was wearing a mask now, pretending to understand, pretending that she needed nothing more than his arms around her, pretending that he was the kind of man that could pretend hard enough and everyone else would believe it.

And maybe it worked. A little.

She found her breath. She held it inside her. She tried not to feel. She tried not to hear.

"Get away from her."

A voice from the rubble, broken and dead and pretending it wasn't. Xhai came staggering out. Her neck bent to one side. Her face was a mess of blood. But she held a sword so tightly the bones of her ruined hand were set aright. And through her broken teeth, she still snarled.

"That's not how it ends," she growled. "That's not how I die."

Denaos looked down at Asper for a moment. There was something else there. Something that told her that it hurt him to ease her down to the floor, to let her go and to rise up alone.

"It's something you get to choose?" Denaos asked, turning to the Carnassial.

"You chose. When you hurt me."

"I've hurt a lot of people."

"You chose to."

He hesitated. A mask dropped. "Yeah."

She continued to stagger toward him like a dead thing pretending to be alive. When she shook her head, there was a cracking noise.

"You think you chose to. But there isn't a choice for you and me. Even if we didn't have masters, it would end this way. I knew how I would die when I met you."

"How do you die?"

"After I kill you."

"I could fight." Denaos was walking, leading her away from Asper, who was clutching her arm, holding herself from eruption. "I've got knives." **419**

"You couldn't kill me before."

"I tried my damnedest."

"If you had, I'd be dead. No. You knew I'd kill you. Because you've known for a while now that you deserve to die. Not clean. Not peacefully. You knew I should be the one to do it."

Denaos was silent. When she smiled, the skin around her mouth tore.

"Because I was going to make it hurt."

Maybe there was something in him that knew she was right. Maybe he weighed the odds of escaping alive. Maybe he had figured a way out of it and maybe he hadn't.

But he stood there. He held his arms out wide. Challenging her. Welcoming her. It was all the same. The netherling smiled, lowered the spear.

"*QAI ZHOTH!*" the scream was ecstasy, the scream was agony. She charged. "*AKH ZEKH LAKH!*" Boots thundered. Voice thundered. "*ZAHN QAI YUSH!*" She charged.

The spear found air.

He fell.

The spear found flesh. And a scream to go with it.

The sikkhun had been reflecting its mistress. It had charged with her, from behind. It hadn't the strength to laugh. She hadn't the discipline to stop. The spear was lodged in its gaping mouth, its tongue flailing, voice warbling as it squirmed and tried to dislodge the ivory shaft. It shrieked, clawing at the spear as it reared back and tore it from her grasp.

It shrieked as its skin turned black and shrank around its skull. It shrieked as the spear ate the warmth, ate the voice, ate the life from it. And when it collapsed, it was silent, still and cold.

And so was Xhai.

"I killed that sikkhun's mother to get him when he was weak," she said to the silence. "I fed it the first thing I ever killed. I raised it on blood. It was . . . *mine.*"

"Maybe you shouldn't have killed it, then," Denaos said, picking himself up and dusting himself off.

His hand brushed his vest, a dagger all but leapt to his fingers. He whirled, the blade angling for the Carnassial's flesh. It found metal, a gauntlet clenching his wrist. His eyes found hers, white and rimmed with the blood seeping from the cuts upon her face.

"No."

She hauled him from his feet, into the air.

"No more."

Her fist trembled as she tightened it around his wrist.

"We are done with this."

Bone snapped. His wrist bent, his voice was torn from his throat in a shriek. She silenced him, drawing her fist back and ramming it forward. Her fist sang a droning rhythm, an iron harmony as she struck him again and again in a song that spoke of a broken nose, a split lip, a swollen eye.

And when it ended, she held no killer in her hand, no creature that had once harmed her. And it was a broken thing she tossed aside to land beside Asper.

The pain that wracked her was echoed in his stare. In a single, squinted eye rimmed with blood that wept from the gashes upon his face. A single eye. Dark. Glistening. Alive.

Barely.

"I can't move, Denaos," Asper whispered.

His voice escaped on a red groan. "I know."

"It'll see me. It knows me. It hurts. I can't."

He pressed his good hand against the floor, began to push himself up. "I know."

"You can't, either. She'll kill you."

He coughed. Blood wept from his mouth. "I know."

"Denaos, don't."

He rose to his feet, staggering. "I have to."

"Why?"

"Because I can't."

A dead man who didn't know it. He got up, tucking his broken wrist beneath his good arm. He turned to face Xhai, who wore a disappointed frown, as though she had hoped he would do something else.

"Stop," Xhai said.

"I can't," he replied, limping toward her.

"It isn't supposed to end this way. You can't die for her."

"Well, I can't die for myself."

"You're supposed to die for me," Xhai said. "You're supposed to die trying to kill *me*. That's what we do. We kill until we are killed."

"Not for me. I always should have died for her."

"For her."

"Yeah."

Her ruined face twitched for a moment, trying to remember what it was supposed to look like. But it could find no snarls. Despite her torn mouth and her broken teeth, despite the blood painting her purple skin and her ruined arm, Semnein Xhai, Carnassial and killer, looked hurt.

He staggered toward her. She struck him to the earth and he did not rise. There was no enthusiasm in her boot as she pressed it between his shoulder blades.

He didn't even bother to scream. He didn't fight. His mask lay somewhere else, between a pool of his own blood and the dead sikkhun. What stared at Asper as he lay on the ground was him.

A man. Broken. Whose mouth could only twitch with a word he desperately wished he had breath to speak.

Sorry.

Asper found herself rising to her feet. Only the barest part of it was her. Only a faint desire felt through the agony to rise up and go to him. The rest, that which forced her to her feet, that which propelled her forward, came from elsewhere. Came from the paper creature on the rubble. Came from the thing inside her that it recognized. That thing remembered Xhai.

That thing wanted to see her again.

Her left arm rose up. Xhai didn't look up. Not until Asper felt her fingers against the Carnassial's throat. Not to strangle, not to harm, just to touch. The thing inside her remembered that skin, that strength beneath it. Xhai felt it, too. Xhai remembered. Xhai looked up.

"No," she whispered as she looked at Asper. *"No."*

Sorry.

Asper pretended to say that. Her voice was on fire. Her limb was alive. The hellish light erupted from her palm, swept over her flesh and painted her bones black. It raced up her arm, onto her shoulder, splitting cloth and flesh and baring the black skeleton beneath.

Her grip was death. Xhai swept her arm up to shove her off. Her fist bent, arm snapped and folded in half, fingers curled over so that their tips brushed the hairs on the back of her hand. She clenched her jaw so hard that the jagged shards of teeth punctured her gums.

"No. *NOT AGAIN.*"

Sorry.

She could only pretend. The thing inside her reached out, leapt into Xhai's own flesh. She could feel it keener than she ever had. It was searching. It was digging holes in the Carnassial. It was looking for something else.

It had a voice.

Where is it, where are they, where are the rest of them, what are these bones, oh, they break so easily, what is this skin, why does it split apart, what is an arm, a leg, a rib, they all snap and break, and there is nothing in her anymore but bone and blood and I need more and I never find it and I can't find anyone else like me and where is he, I heard him emerge, I heard him scream, I thought he was there in those people, in that creature, in that girl, in Taire, I remember Taire, I keep hearing Taire, but he wasn't there, I need them, I need to talk to them, I need to see them, let me out, let me out, let me—

"*SAVE ME—*"

Xhai was still alive. Xhai was bending. Xhai was breaking. And she was screaming.

Screaming his name.

"No, no, no, no, *NO!*"

It was Asper screaming now. Asper hurling herself to the ground. The fire retreated, dissipating back into her flesh, leaving bare and steaming skin. The muscle beneath was ablaze. The blood boiled. The voice inside her was a jumble of wordless babble. It was still there. It wanted out. It wanted the paper creature.

It wanted something like it.

And now that it was so close, so close to the familiar, it was talking. It was within her. Alive.

She heard footsteps. Heard breathing. Above all of it, after all of it, Xhai was still standing, still walking. The Carnassial came to a halt over the priestess. Asper didn't look up. She knew what she looked like.

"It talked to me." Asper whispered softly. "It was in me. It was awake. I could feel it, all this time, feel it screaming. But . . ." She shook her head. "It's like . . . that thing in the statue. That's in me. That's . . ." She inhaled, felt the tears forcing their way out the corners of her eyes. "I stopped it. I couldn't let it. I couldn't give it anything."

"Why."

Xhai's voice was a croaking thing, a voice that belonged to something without a throat. Not a question. Not one that she thought had an answer.

"Because you cried out his name," she said. "Like you . . . I don't know. But you're down here because of him, we're fighting because of him, he acts like he knows you better than anyone, you kill, you're dying, I hurt you . . . and you still called out to him like . . ." It ached to say it. "Like he was going to save you."

"Why."

"I guess . . . I didn't want that. For you."

"Why."

"I don't know. I can't—"

"Why."

A fist against the back of Asper's head. She fell to the ground.

"Why."

A boot to her side. She reeled.

"Why."

Again. Again. Striking with what were once limbs, twisted beyond recognition. Again. Again. Snarling in a voice that wasn't hers.

423

"Why. Why. Why. *Why. Why. Why.*" Xhai, snarling and striking and flailing as Asper quivered on the floor, trying to protect herself. "Why do you do that? Why do you not act like you're supposed to? Why aren't you *dead*?"

She looked up and saw Xhai. Saw one eye wide, the other a thick crunch of flesh and shards of bones where the eye socket had folded upon itself. She saw her mouth flapping, the jaw separated at the chin. She saw blood seeping out between jagged teeth.

She saw a woman who shouldn't be alive.

She felt the broken woman's twisted arm and bent legs hammering her into the ground.

She left Asper there as she collected her sword, dragging it behind her on a withered arm. She hauled it, hefted it over the woman who had not died, who tried to kill her, who *hurt* her worse than even *he* had.

"Wait."

No urgency. No desperation. Denaos pulled himself wearily to his feet, pausing to spit out a glob of blood on the dusty ground. He didn't hurry.

"Don't kill her," he said.

"I have to."

"No, you don't."

"This is the way it has to be."

"Why," he asked. Not a question.

"Because there's no other way. There is killing and there is dying and the more you do it, the more it makes sense."

"And then the more you do it, the more you keep waiting for it to make sense," he said. "You want to kill her because she hurt you, because you think that doesn't happen, because people like us . . . we aren't supposed to get hurt. But people like us," he gestured between them, "it's not a necessity. We just don't know anything else."

Xhai looked down at Asper.

"There's another way."

She looked to Denaos through her good eye. The rogue approached her, held her gaze despite one eye swollen shut.

"Take me instead," he said.

"You mean kill you."

"I mean take me," he insisted. "So long as you never choose anything else, you'll never have anything but death."

"I don't need anything—"

"Liar. If that were true, you wouldn't look at Sheraptus like your sikkhun looked at you. You want something else. You can have something else."

He came to a stop. Two paces away from her.

424

"So choose."

Xhai looked at her blade, hanging from her hand, like it shouldn't be doing that. She grimaced at it, at the withered stump of a hand with only three working fingers holding it. She frowned at her reflection, so distorted in the iron that it almost looked like a living thing.

And then she looked back up at him. Staring at her through one good eye. Blood weeping from his face. Broken, battered, alive. Choosing her.

Over *her*.

"Come to me," Xhai said.

He did.

Limping forward, broken and battered and pretending he wasn't, he came to her. Hers, something of her own. Something that didn't belong to Sheraptus. Something that she didn't kill to earn. The little pink female could live. Who cared.

She had something.

She had him.

And he was sliding his arm around her, drawing her close. And she found the touch painful, but impossible to turn away from. She slid closer to him, pressing her ruined body to his. She closed her good eye as she felt his hand slide around her shoulder. She smiled a torn mouth as she felt the heel of his hand slip so easily into the crook of her neck.

She was still smiling when she heard the click and the blade entered her throat.

When he pulled away, when her blood spurted out to splash upon the floor, she looked at him.

"You lied," she said, uncertain of what that word meant.

"It's what I do," he replied.

She looked at him for a moment. Her arm moved before either of them knew. The blade sank into his side, biting through flesh all the way to something soft and dark. He shuddered. He grimaced. He looked surprised.

When he fell, he did not rise.

When she fell, she was last.

And they lay. Broken.

THIRTY-TWO

GREAT, DEAD, OLD ONES

Once, it had been great.

It had begun as something old and vast, the empty spot where the mountain's blood had carved out the cavern. The stalactites still hung overhead, teeth in a stone mouth that stretched in a great echoing chamber.

They had made it greater. They had carved the great stone steps into the sides of the cavern, the long stone walkway that circled its center, the tremendous statues of Ulbecetonth that rose up on all sides, womanly shoulders holding up the cavern roof in a testament to her strength and beauty.

The heart of the mountain. Once, it had been her throne.

War had unmade it. War had brought the banners of the House of the Vanquishing Trinity hanging over the walls, draped around the necks of Ulbecetonth's statues like nooses. War had brought the great flood that drowned the middle of the chamber in dark water.

The heart of the mountain, Lenk thought as he stepped out of the archway into the tremendous chamber, was dead.

"He lied to us," Lenk muttered. "Why the hell do I keep trusting dead people in ice?"

"Probably because having to interact with dead people in ice is a problem for you," Kataria replied, following him out. Her bow was nocked with an arrow drawn. She scanned the room. "Look, there are other archways all along the wall here. We can try to follow one of those out."

"Who knows how far they go," Lenk said. "And what are we going to find on the other side?" He shook his head. "The man . . . he said to follow the sound of running water. I know I heard it."

The water here was not running. The water here was barely even water. It was liquid shadow, a great teeming lake stretching from the stone walkway to the back of the cavern. It had been choked with so much blood and suffering and hate that it had become a living thing itself, a great hungry blackness that ate the green light burning from braziers hanging high in the toothy ceiling overhead.

And yet, as dark as it was, he thought he could almost see something beneath the surface. Something darker still, something staring at him from beneath the darkness with a hateful familiarity.

And then, whatever it was blinked.

"Let's go," he said, turning around.

"Which way?" Kataria asked as he pushed past her and started toward a random archway.

"It doesn't matter. We have to go. We never should have come here." He broke out into a jog, moving faster with each step. It was looking at him, whatever it was, watching him go, glaring at him. He could feel it. He could hear it. "Hurry the hell—"

He had no more mouth to speak. As he approached the darkness of the archway, a shadow fell over his face. An emaciated, webbed claw seized him by the throat, lifted him up and off his feet. The ensuing struggle was meaningless, the limbs flailing against the fist and reaching for his sword ignored as his captor strode out of the shadows.

The Abysmyth's vacant stare took on a kind of serenity as it swiveled empty white eyes upon Lenk. Its voice gurgled from its gaping jaws with a throaty clarity.

"You turn from light, fearing blindness," it said. "You fight fate, fearing oblivion." It drew Lenk up in its grasp, closer to its jaws. "What great gifts have you missed in the name of your fleeting terrors?"

It only barely quivered when the arrow entered its eye. Instead, it swept its gaze toward Kataria, unhurried. Its head didn't even wobble as another arrow lodged itself in the beast's mouth. The shict strung another arrow and let it fly, planting another one in the beast's eye, face, mouth.

"Does it not ache, child?" it spoke, shafts splintering between its teeth. "The desperation? The futility? Can you not feel the change beneath your feet?"

"Shut up and drop him," Kataria snarled, drawing another arrow. "Unless you like the feel—"

Not another word could pierce the webbed hand that clasped over her mouth. She could not struggle from the other hands seizing her arms, forcing the bow from her grasp, the arms wrapping around her torso, the weight of hairless bodies forcing her to the ground. She snarled, she bit, she fought and spat. The frogmen pinning her took it with stoic silence, holding her steady even as she struggled to get free.

Lenk cried out to her and felt the Abysmyth's talons press against his throat. Even then, he struggled, flailing until another titanic claw caught his arm. It was only then that he noticed another frogman come scampering from the black water, searching over him with webbed hands until they found what they sought in his satchel.

With trembling reverence, the frogman pulled free the perfect black square of leather that was the tome. Eyes, demonic and frogman alike, turned toward it with breathless adoration as the creature slowly slid back to the water.

The man in the ice, Lenk could only think, *he led me here. He wanted me to come here to die.*

Or to kill.

"Is it cold?"

Risen from the surface of the blackness like a stone, two golden eyes peered over the water at Kataria. Strands of auburn hair floated atop the water like kelp, eerily delicate.

"The earth," the voice came from the darkness. "The stone. Is it cold?" The eyes narrowed sharply. "It always felt such, even when we had legs, even when we walked upon it. She made it bearable, of course, but now it's . . . cold. It's hard."

The shadow clung to its skin as it rose out of the darkness, rising with needy tendrils as a human face, milk-pale, glass-boned, rose on a thick stalk of gray flesh. The woman's lips pulled into a frown.

"We were Her most trusted, Her most ardent. We turned to Her when our families turned us away, when our lovers turned us to whores, when the earth turned us to bodies. And She welcomed us."

"And She loved us." Another head rose from the water, hair ebon black, eyes narrowed angrily. "And took us from cold earth. And when the mortal armies and your wicked people came for Her, we leapt into the darkness after Her. And we came back. For this."

The Deepshriek turned both heads to the frogman with the tome and nodded. The creature dove beneath the water, disappearing into shadow.

"Don't—" Lenk managed to speak before the demon's claw tightened around his throat. He struggled with one arm, grasping and beating on the demon's hand, hoping the other wouldn't be noticed as it crept closer to the hilt of his sword.

"Are you so selfish, creature?" The Deepshriek spat the words. "Did you not see the suffering your breed caused? Did you not look at the faces of the hollow children and the dead? Do you think that your own twisted nature is enough to deny the world Her warmth?" Fangs bared, a hiss burst forth. "I heard you speak to that cold thing in the darkness."

"I am nothing like—"

"You are. You are everything like it. She has been in your head. She has seen your thoughts. Murder. Treachery. Hatred. All that grows in your mind is born of the same murderous seed. You came here to kill Her, She who only wishes to be reunited with Her children."

Its eyes steadied. Its lips closed. It smiled.

"That's why She wants you be alive to see this."

The heads disappeared beneath the water. Lenk reached after them, as though he could still stop them. The Abysmyth held fast, not even bothering to remove the arrows from its eye.

And soon, the darkness was alive. Words burbled up, too powerful to be contained by the gloom, too powerful to be spoken by mortal lips. Red light flashed in great spurts beneath, illuminating them in flashes: Abysmyths and frogmen swimming in a dark halo. The Deepshriek's heads bent over a book as its shark body swam around it, the epicenter of the endless circles. A great shape, a vast circle of light that painted the darkness in brief flashes, ever longer, ever wider.

The Aeons' Gate.

Opening.

And from the light, something greater emerged, something painted dark against the crimson, a stain of ink spreading into a pool of blood. Great tentacles emerging, golden stars winking into life, a pair of bright jaws opening.

"No, no, *no*!" Lenk screamed.

His blade was in his hand, drawn free. He swung it, struck the Abysmyth's arm. It dropped him, though with no great roar of agony, no blood. His blade could no longer hurt the thing. He had left that power behind, in the chasm. His shoulder hurt. He was tired. He was terrified.

He didn't care.

He ran toward Kataria. His blade could still cut the frogmen. She lashed out a leg, striking one in the groin. It gurgled, loosed its grip on her. The others tried to seize her arm as she reached up and began to claw at their eyes.

"Kataria!" he screamed. "Kataria, hurry! We have to—"

430

In the roar of water being split, he could not be heard. In the wake of the shadow that fell over him, he could not be seen. And as the tentacle, red flesh quivering, suckers trembling, swept down and wrapped about his ankle, he could no longer stand.

"*Come to me.*"

A voice, somewhere down in the dark, spoke to him.

"*Come to me.*"

The tentacle pulled, dragging him as he raked at the stone floor wildly.

"*Come.*"

He reached out.

"*Come.*"

He shouted out to Kataria.

"*Come.*"

He fell into darkness.

"Stop."

His voice was parched and weak.

"Wait."

He grasped only their shadows as they ran past.

"I need help."

The Shen couldn't see or hear him. They were running, screaming, trying to dig their companions out from beneath the statue, carrying off the wounded into the forest.

And he was bleeding.

And his friends were somewhere out there, in the great melee, amongst the dead. Or behind him somewhere, where the longfaces had charged up, along with the she-beast on the regular beast. His friends were gone. The Shen were running.

He was bleeding.

He walked through the dust that would not settle, the blood pouring from the sky. He walked over the bodies heaped on the ground and past the women who were alive only in their swords. He walked to the giant mountain, kneeling upon the field of death, breathing heavily as smoke poured from his flesh. The longface had done something, sent lightning into his body. He had to stop that thing before it killed the others. He had to keep going. He had to fight . . .

A hand went to his side, he felt traces of life slipping past the spearhead embedded in his side, out between his fingers. Slowly. It was a courteous wound, in no hurry to kill him and more than willing to let someone else take a crack at it first.

And she came. A Carnassial, tall and ragged and painted in blood. She approached him with eyes that belonged in the heads of dead people, eyes that forgot why they were doing what they did. She hefted her sword, loosed a ragged howl on a ragged breath and took exactly two steps forward.

When her foot hit the ground, the Abysmyth's foot hit her.

The great demon had arisen from the sheets of dust and blood, emerging from such carnage that a beast of such horror would scarcely stand out. It stomped its great webbed foot upon the Carnassial, grinding her into the sand. Its flesh was carved with wounds, bits of iron jutting from its skin. In place of a left arm, a stump, sickly green with poison, hung from a bony shoulder.

431

"They don't call out when they die," the Abysmyth gurgled, "to god or man. They simply . . . scream. It is a strange thing to see." At that moment, the beast seemed to notice Gariath. "When you die, who will you call out to?"

Gariath wasn't sure why he answered honestly; perhaps because he had thought upon the question for so long it merely slipped out.

"My family."

"Do they live?"

"No."

"What infinite mercy do I grant you, lamb." The Abysmyth's foot rose with a squishing sound. "What terrors do I spare you, child." Its single arm reached out, almost invitingly. "What glories do I send you to. Come to me."

A green arm appeared around the beast's neck. The demon scarcely seemed to notice the added weight on its back. Truly, Gariath himself only barely noticed the bright yellow eyes appearing from behind it. And only when the creature had climbed up to the beast's shoulders and held the waterskin high above his head did Gariath recognize Hongwe.

"*Shenko-sa!*" the Gonwa cried out, a fleeting and insignificant noise against the din of war. He thrust the waterskin into the beast's mouth.

The skin punctured only barely upon its teeth, but the water came flooding out like a wolf free from a cage. It swept over the beast's mouth, through its teeth, over its jaws. It engulfed the creature's jaw, eyes, neck, throat, shoulders. The Abysmyth was aware of it, of the pain it caused the creature, as it clawed at the liquid with its free hand. Those droplets that were torn free and fell upon the ground quickly reformed, sped back to the demon and leapt upon it until its black skin was replaced with a liquid flesh.

The creature flailed, a raindrop falling from heaven, before it splashed to the earth. The water fell from it, was drank by the glutted earth. What remained was a gaping, skinless skull staring up at Gariath.

"You are alive."

Even against the Abysmyth's skeleton, Hongwe looked tiny. Too clean to belong on this field. He stood with only a few cuts, another pair of waterskins hanging from his waist.

"I am," Gariath replied. "So are you."

"I was in the battle. Lost. But I am alive. And . . . and . . ." His gaze drifted to Gariath's midriff.

"And?"

"And you've got a spear in you."

"There's a little spear in all of us."

"I don't think that's—"

"Look, I have lost a *lot* of blood, so if you could speed this up a little."

"The Shen have been trying to recover their people, salvage the dead and the wounded. I do what I can to keep the demons and longfaces away."

Gariath looked down at the skeletal Abysmyth. "You do a good job of it."

"The water comes from the mountain," Hongwe said. "My father swore the oaths. My father remembered the stories. My father told me. Everything."

"It's not enough."

Hongwe looked over the carnage raging and frowned. "It is not."

"Why, then? They are not your people."

Hongwe sniffed. "Close enough."

Gariath stared for a long moment. He drew in a long breath and inhaled only the scent of blood and fear. He could hear no screams through the thunder and the pain. No ghosts. No humans. No Shen.

Only a voice.

"Come to me."

From the earth.

"Come to me."

From the water.

"Come to me."

For a single moment, the battle died on one side. Abysmyths looked up from tearing their longfaced victims apart. Frogmen stood stock-still, heads turned upward even as netherlings lopped them off in messy blows. The great beast Daga-Mer stirred upon the field, the smoke dissipating from his form as he cast his great red gaze up, over the heads of his children and his foes and the bodies.

Toward the voice.

Toward the mountain.

"She calls to us!" the pale man atop Daga-Mer's skull cried out. "Mother Deep cries to the faithful!"

"On the cries of the Mother do we march," the Omens shrieked in choral ecstasy as they flocked overhead, writhing and twisting in the bloody wind, "on the faithful's feet, we march to the mountain."

The mountain.

Where the humans had gone, where the Shen still were. And one by one, they began to move.

Gariath reached out instinctively, tore the waterskins from the Gonwa's waist. Without thinking, he began at a light jog, trying not to think about the spear in his flank, about the blood that still wept, about the fact that he was charging into a wall of advancing demons.

This plan required him not to think. If he did, he might start wondering exactly how he planned to use a pair of waterskins filled with freaky magic liquid to stop clashing armies of longfaces and demons. He might start thinking how stupid the only plan he had to stop them was. He might start noticing how idiotic it was to do this for them. For the humans, for the Shen, for the things that weren't *Rhega*.

He had abandoned the former, the latter had abandoned him, he had found not so much as a ghost of a *Rhega* here, and he was charging toward a walking mountain of flesh and blood through the waves of demons and netherlings with a pair of waterskins.

Not a good plan.

But close enough.

Arrows flew, swords shot out to catch him, some scored against his flesh. More of the longfaces, though, either chased the frogmen and demons who broke off from the fight to begin a march toward the mountain or found themselves collapsing, exhausted or dead, without a foe to fight.

That didn't matter. The humans were the ones who fought the little things. Gariath had always sought the biggest and strongest, the ones most capable of giving him the death he had craved. The only difference between then and now was that he was no longer seeking his own death.

That and this thing was much bigger than anything he had ever fought before.

"*Come.*"

Daga-Mer stirred to life with the noise. The smoldering black flesh began to grow bright red, his blood illuminated as it spread from the beating of his heart, into his veins, into his eyes. He rose from the earth, the corpses of those that had been beneath him when he fell peeling off like grains of sand as he turned toward the mountain.

Gariath leapt, found the titan's ankle a mountain unto itself. Each knob of flesh, each ancient scar, each slab of metal grafted to the creature's skin gave footing. Hand over hand, foot over foot, Gariath began to climb.

Daga-Mer seemed to take no notice of the red parasite climbing up his leg, of the ballista bolt and chain still sunk in his chest, of the demons, frogmen, and netherlings he crushed underfoot with each great stride. And the demons did not look up themselves as he marched across the blood-soaked ring. They were crushed into pulp without a sound, those bodies that still twitched trying to catch up in his wake.

And Gariath climbed, over knee, onto thigh, up bony hip. Ignoring the pain in his side, ignoring that he had next to no idea what his plan was and no idea whatsoever if it would work.

Over metal, over flesh, over lightning-charred scars.

Ignoring the blood that dripped from him, the blood that dripped from the sky, the puddles of blood and bodies on the ground that might be the humans.

Rib over rib, clinging to the beast's flank, watching the titanic arm swing like a pendulum with each step.

Ignoring everything. Everything for this. For them.

He drew in a breath. It hurt. He leapt for Daga-Mer's arm. He caught the beast's wrist, wrapped his arms around a forearm the size of a tree and looked up. The great head, hell-light pouring out of its eyes, looked as far away as a mountain itself. He snarled, he bit back pain, he raised an arm to climb.

He never even saw the fist coming until it had connected with his jaw.

On the other side of the forearm, blade slung across her back, the Carnassial took exception to Gariath having the same idea as she had. He couldn't say when she had jumped, when she had started climbing, nor did he care. For when she snarled at him and bared her teeth, he showed her his.

Up close.

He caught the hand as she moved to strike him and, with a swift jerk, hauled her from her precarious footing and into his jaws. Between helmet and armor, his teeth found the flesh of her throat. And with one more jerk, he tore free a purple chunk, spitting it out after her as she fell, her scream painted on the wind in red.

And he climbed, still, not thinking about how much it hurt, how he could still feel pain, how his grip felt slippery the farther he got up. How, if he fell, he would be the last *Rhega* to fall here and disappear forever and leave nothing behind.

Only flesh. Only climbing. Up the forearm. Onto the bicep. Over the rusted plates grafted onto the blackened skin. Climbing. Bleeding. No more feeling. No more thinking.

"*Lastonelastonelastone . . .*"

Whispers in his head, the closer he got.

"*Dieherediehereherehere . . . nomorenomorenomore . . .*"

Irritating.

"*Nomorefatherssonssweepingchildrencryinginthesandohpoorbeastgobacktotheearth-andwaittodrown . . .*"

A light atop the shoulder. A face appeared over the blackened flesh. A withered hag's head, bulbous and sagging, dominated by black void eyes and a lantern light on a gray stalk from the middle of its head. It smiled with two mouths at him and spoke in whispers.

"*Shecomesshecomesshecomes . . . theyalldiediediedie . . . likeyoulikeyoulike—*"

Interrupted. A thick red claw around a twig of a neck would do that.

"No more thinking," he growled. A quick pull.

Whatever a demon plummeting to the earth sounded like, he didn't care. It hurt to hear, but pain required feeling. He was done with all that. The spear shifted inside him, the wound grew bigger. That would be a problem for creatures weighed down by thought, by fear, by pain.

He was *Rhega.* He was the last. He died here, atop the last of the demons. All for humans.

If he was still a creature burdened by thought, that one might trouble him.

He hauled himself onto Daga-Mer's helmet. The world moved slowly beneath him, he could feel the tremors from each stride reverberating up into the creature's skull. He could see the red-tinged mist of the beast's breath, hear the thunder of the heart.

"You shouldn't be here."

The pale thing. Skin scarred by lightning. Eyes wide and white. Not a frogman. Still alive. The Mouth. Looking at Gariath.

"This is for the faithful," the Mouth said, clinging to the twisted horns jutting from the helmet. "This place, this is where I belong. You should leave. So should I. But Mother Deep, She spoke and I . . . I . . ." He looked up at Gariath solemnly. "If I could see her once more, my daughter, I would—"

He stopped talking. A head cloven from shoulders would do that.

The body plummeted to the earth. The Carnassial watched the body bounce off Daga-Mer's knee and fall into a pool of blood below. She sniffed, looked to Gariath, who settled a scowl upon her.

"Oh, like you were interested," she said, snorting.

They advanced on each other, snarling, and were sent grasping for the helmet's horns as the beast's head shifted beneath them. Daga-Mer groaned. The beast had finally taken notice of them.

No time to deal with the Carnassial, Gariath thought. He had to finish this quickly. He took the waterskins in hand, tried to angle himself over the helmet. Daga-Mer's lower jaw was considerable. One good swing, he thought, and he could send both—

A boot struck him hard against his head.

That's what he got for thinking.

"We're in the middle of a fight here," the Carnassial snarled. "Don't you look away from *me.*"

Her boot shot out again. He shifted his body to absorb the blow. That might have been a good idea if she hadn't instead found the spearhead. It tore into him, through him, the tip jutting out the other side of his flank. He bled. Profusely. He felt pain.

A hand shot to his side. The waterskins fell from his grasp, plummeted below to splatter in useless silver stains on the earth.

The Carnassial grinned, hefted her massive blade with a free hand as breath, blood, and vomit leaked from his mouth. It shone dull gray against the sky for but a brief moment. Then, all was black.

A tremendous webbed claw fell from overhead, like a tree falling. It lazily came over the helmet, scratched the Carnassial like an itch, and tore her body, snarling and shrieking, from the rusted metal. The blade slipped from her grasp, clattered upon the helmet and slid down to Gariath's waiting claw.

He heard her cursing. He heard her screaming. He heard her bones breaking as Daga-Mer's hand closed upon her. And then, he heard the sound of a pimple bursting.

He could think only of the sword in his hand, the metal under his body as he slid down Daga-Mer's helmet. One hand was upon the horn, slipping. One foot sought purchase in the eye slit of the helmet. He kicked, the rusted metal bent beneath his foot. He snarled, releasing the horn and catching the eye slit. He bled, his muscles straining as he pried the slit open and clutched the sword.

The hell-light blinded him. The beat of Daga-Mer's heart was in his ears as he stared into a bright-red eye. For one fleeting moment, he saw a red pupil contract, the light abating long enough for him to see his own reflection.

When he looked at himself, he was smiling.

As he raised the sword.

And thrust.

The demon that was a mountain was neither in that moment. The titanic abomination, the immovable creature of flesh and bone was lost in a spurt of blood and the sizzle of an envenomed blade. The blood that burst from its eye was lost in a great stain of steam on the sky.

In the scream that followed, in the scream that echoed across creation, Daga-Mer was something loud and wounded and agonizingly mortal.

The demon's head snapped back. Gariath was sent flying through the sky. His wings flapped wildly, trying to regain purchase against the wind. In the end, all they could do was guide him into a patch of kelp that took him and rejected him in a bend of leaves, tossing his bleeding body back into the ring.

He staggered to his feet, breathing heavily. He reached for his wound, gasping. He began to head toward the mountain, limping. And trying his damnedest not to smile at what was going on.

Daga-Mer's scream split the sky apart. His feet tore the earth into pulp. His body was a twisting wind of light and flesh, flailing wildly as he groped at his wounded eye, thundering across the sand as he fought to keep on his feet.

Beneath him, demons were crushed, frogmen were sent flying, netherlings were ground into the earth. Faith and fury were forgotten, everything giving way to Daga-Mer's pain. Longfaces who had never spoken the word suddenly screamed for the retreat. Frogmen screamed pleas to a titan too tall to hear them. Abysmyths raised their hands to him, as if to soothe him with whatever words they could utter before being crushed underfoot.

And Daga-Mer continued to stomp, continued to scream. He groped at his helmet, claws digging under it, pulling. It came free with the squeak of bolts and shriek of metal, the grafted rust torn free with scathes of flesh hanging from it. He tossed it aside, pawed haplessly at his eye to no avail.

It was gone.

And in its place was a gaping void from which a bright light poured like blood from an open wound. A great hole that swept across the battlefield.

And settled upon Gariath.

The dragonman stopped smiling.

The dragonman started running.

As Daga-Mer's mouth gaped open, as Gariath's legs pumped, and the demon and the sand screamed in harmony.

THIRTY-THREE

THE KRAKEN QUEEN

Before he even knew he was alive, Lenk could feel her inside his head.
"Look at me."

He didn't have much choice. Down here, his will was not his own. He could breathe under the water. His steel floated beside him. He could not blink.

None of this boded particularly well.

Brief flashes of red lit up the darkness. In each flash, he could see the stain that was Ulbecetonth blooming like a flower out of the gate, growing bigger. A mass of tentacles and flesh and eyes. So many bright, yellow eyes, winking into existence like stars giving birth. But he only knew these as fleeting things, he could not take his attention from the great jaws in front of him. Pristine white teeth, jagged sharp, a mile long, twisted into a great white smile.

"I would have let you go." Down here, her voice was clear, crystalline shards thrust neatly into his ears. "Knowing everything—the kind of creature you were, the children you killed, the murderous thoughts in your head—after all of that, I would have let you go."

He could not speak down here. She didn't will it.

"But you defied me. You hated me too much. You came here, to a land that wanted you dead, just to stop my children from coming to me." The jaws cracked as they twisted into a frown. "Did you delude yourself with lies that it was all for someone else? To save the world?"

Another flash of red light, like lightning. He could see the great bowl that this place had been: the drowned ring of seats, the banners floating like kelp. It had been an assembly once, where they had gathered to worship her, to feel the warmth of her presence. But now it was cold but for the light flashing from the Aeons' Gate.

"From what? From feeling the same devotion, the same peace my children did before *you* came into their lives?"

He could see the holes broken in the seating. The tunnels, the same one he had come through Jaga in. That's how they had gotten in here. They had been waiting for him. The man in the ice knew. He had sent Lenk here.

"The truth is, you wanted them all to hurt like you hurt. To feel afraid, betrayed, alone like you do with your deaf gods and uncaring world. I looked into your head, Lenk. Whatever voices you think are controlling you are not. They do not put thoughts in your head. They merely agree with what you're thinking."

Something shifted in the water.

"And that voice that told you to kill . . ."

He felt his throat close.

"That voice that said they had to die . . ."

The water turned unbearably warm.

"That voice that wanted her to bleed . . . it was merely agreeing with you."

No more air. No more sound. No more light. She willed him to stop breathing.

"For my children, for the people you would have killed . . . I do this for them, Lenk. Die."

Her jaws gaped open. Teeth ringed a throat that stretched into hell. The water shifted, he felt himself being sucked into her maw. He could not fight back, he didn't want to. Her voice was in his head, the water was seeping into every orifice, and on each droplet was the unbearable truth.

He wanted it. He wanted Kataria to die. He wanted her to hurt. He wanted everyone to hurt. He deserved this. He deserved death. The man in the ice knew. Everyone knew.

Except that tiny voice in the back of his head. The one he left behind. The one pounding at his skull and whispering.

"Not here. Not this way."

The water shifted. The light flashed. Around him, a dozen shapes began floating toward the surface. The jaws snapped shut. The yellow eyes, the dozens of staring yellow orbs, grew wide.

"No. No. *NO*."

The water quaked like earth, a distant rumble boiling out of the Aeons' Gate, growing louder.

"Leave them *alone*!"

The Kraken Queen was shrieking at someone. The yellow eyes turned toward the surface. Something like a great black limb reached up and out. And Lenk felt something inside him cry out.

"Swim."

That small act of obedience was all it took. His blood was cold as he swam for the surface, sparing only a moment to seize his sword. The whispering in the back of his head grew louder. That was a worry. But that was a worry for people whose lungs *weren't* about to explode.

He burst out of the surface with a gasp and the sound of agony. He treaded water, looking through bleary eyes toward the walkway upon which the carnage rang.

They moved like shadows. The longfaces clad in black armor darted into combat, their spears lancing out and into frogmen, shields deflecting crude knives and the reaching grasps of Abysmyths. When the opportunity presented itself, one leapt upon a towering demon, jamming her spear deep into the creature's mouth before producing a green vial from her belt and hurling it into the open wound. The ensuing mess of steam, screams, and flailing sent her flying back.

Still, they came. Frogmen and Abysmyths pulled themselves out of the black water to assist their brethren. Longfaces continued to charge in from the archways, following the sound of carnage.

Kataria stood at the edge, backing away farther. Her captors lay at her feet in varying stages of torn-the-hell-apart and she stood, wielding one of their crude bone knives, letting the blood on her hands suggest just how easy a target she might be.

"What the hell is *this*?" Lenk demanded, swimming up to her.

When Kataria whirled on him, her eyes were mirrors reflecting the blood painting her mouth. She stared at him just long enough to know he wasn't anything to kill before turning her attentions back to the carnage.

"I don't know," she grunted. "They just showed up after you got dragged under, and started fighting. I've killed about four so far."

"What," Lenk gasped as he tossed his sword onto the stone and pulled himself up after it, "and you didn't think to come back after me?"

"No, Lenk, I didn't jump into a bottomless pit of shadow teeming with demons rather than fight off the frogmen trying to kill me." She bared bloodied teeth. "Why the *hell* do I have to be the one that saves you all the damned time? I killed a longface for you. I shot my *brother* for you!"

"So you admit there's precedent."

441

"You stupid son of a—"

Her ears pricked up, her body tensed. By the time he heard the high-pitched whine, by the time he saw the air tense as she did, by the time he thought to look behind him, it was too late.

He saw the Deepshriek's gaping jaws a moment before he felt the air erupt. The creature's wail cut through the air, flayed moss from stone, cast frogmen into the shadows, slammed netherlings from their feet, and struck him squarely in the chest. He felt the earth leave his feet, the wind leave his lungs, the stone meet his back as he was smashed against the wall.

An airless, echoing silence followed, all voice and terror rendered mute by the distant ringing in his ears. And in that silence, he could hear her. So closely.

"I am close to you, my children." It came from the deep, rising like a bubble. *"So close. I can hear your sorrow. I can feel your pain. Let me see you. Let me hold you."*

At the center of the great pool, between the two pillars, he could see the shadows boiling. A shape stirred beneath the water, rising. Pale, thin fingers reached out from the darkness. They would have been delicate, had they not been the size of spears, each joint topped with a cluster of barnacles and coral. They wrapped around a pillar rising from the darkness, a slender arm, monstrous and beautiful, tensed as it pulled the shape closer.

"She comes."

In the echo of the Deepshriek's fury, in the resonance of Ulbecetonth's whisper, he could hear it. Louder. Clearer. Reaching into him.

"But she is weak, still. She is not all the way through. Strike her now. Kill her now."

"Kataria," Lenk muttered, pulling himself to feet that felt like someone else's. He swayed, no breath or thought to guide him. "I need to find her."

"You need to save her."

"I can't see her." His vision was darkening at the edges. His skeleton shook inside his body. The world blurred into dimming colors and bleeding lights. "I can't see . . . anything."

The question came without breath.

"Am I dying?"

And the answer came in the drip of blood down his back and in the scent of decay and rot weeping from his shoulder.

"I can't die." He drew in a breath and found none. "I have to save everyone." He took a step forward and fell. "I have to save Kat." He looked to the ceiling and saw only darkness. "I wanted to run." He tasted blood in his mouth. "I don't want to die."

And in the darkness, in the absence of breath, in the weakness of his body, the answer came on a cold voice.

"Then let me in."

A moment's lapse in concentration, a reflex, a thought about what would happen if he bled out on the floor here and all hell came to pass. Whatever it was, he didn't know. Because when his vision returned, the world was painted in cold, muted color.

He couldn't feel the blood weeping from his shoulder. He couldn't feel the decay in his skin. He couldn't feel the sword in his hand or the stone under his feet. He couldn't feel anything.

Not even fear for what he was doing.

He surrendered to the familiarity. To the feel of nothing. To the steel in his hands and the air under his feet as he rushed toward the edge of the walkway and leapt.

The Deepshriek's auburn-haired head swept toward him and opened its mouth moments before he landed upon the gray fish's hide. He fought to keep his footing as his hand shot out and caught the fleshy stalk of the beast's throat, choking its scream. Its mouth gaped open, its head flailed wildly in silent screaming as he hefted his sword and aimed for the thickest part.

He couldn't feel the agony of his shoulder. Not even when the Deepshriek's other head swept down and sank its teeth into his skin.

He was aware of it, of course. Of the fangs clenching in his flesh, of the pus bursting in its mouth, of the violent thrashing of its stalk as it pulled something from his shoulder. He was aware that the creature's smile was curling up over something wet and sopping in its mouth. He was aware of the blood and the fact that he should be screaming.

But screaming was for men with voices to call their own. He was a man with a sword and a voice in his head that told him how to use it.

And he listened.

He swung without a word. It clove through the beast's neck before it could even drop his shoulder. The creature's head went flying, his flesh still lodged in its mouth. Blood wept from his shoulder.

"Not much time," the voice said. *"We have to strike soon."*

"Before there's no blood left," Lenk replied as he hefted his sword.

The Deepshriek was flailing, face twisted up in rage as it tried to find breath to curse him. Its scream welled up in a bulge beneath his grip, threatening to burst. He swung, the head flew, his grip faltered. And the Deepshriek's fury was voiced in a wordless, quavering wail on a shower of black blood. The gray stalk flailed wildly for a moment, spraying the blood across the water, before going limp.

The shark beneath his feet ceased to struggle, ceased even to move. It bobbed lazily in the water, responding not even to the sword Lenk jabbed into it to keep his balance.

"Good," the voice said. *"We are free to strike now. She is coming."*

He looked to the pillars. Another arm snaked out, caught the other pillar and began to pull. A great mass of hair, tangled like kelp, wretched little fish and eels weaving between the massive strands, rose from the depths. Lenk caught a single glimpse of an eye, bright and yellow and beaming with hatred as it looked upon him, bathed in the blood of the Deepshriek.

"Through the eye. A solid blow, before she can pull herself out of the gate. It will end her."

"She will die."

"*Our duty will be fulfilled.*"

"And everyone will be all right . . ."

The voice said nothing.

Not until he looked over his shoulder.

"*NO!*"

He was aware of her voice, aware of her backing away, her bloody hands and bone knife a poor match for the netherling's jagged spear and the bodies left in her wake.

"*No, no, NO. Remember your duty. Remember, this is to save her. Turn away now and she dies, regardless, and so do you.*"

He was aware of the chill in his body subsiding, of the pain returning. But still, he stared and watched as Kataria made a desperate lunge at the longface. Her knife found the gap in the female's armor, bit deeply. The long-face accepted it, like a fact of life, and lashed back with her shield, knocking Kataria to the earth.

"*Listen to me. LISTEN. Reject me now and you will never again know me. You'll die without me! The world dies without you! Without us! We will stop her, together.*"

A black boot went to Kataria's belly, pinning her to the earth.

"*We can save the world.*"

A spear was raised and aimed over her chest.

"*We can save her if you—*"

He was aware of the darkness.

And then, he could feel everything.

The wound in his shoulder, the blood, the pain, the cold of the water, the fear, the wailing inside his head, the great emptiness beneath him slowly filling as something reached up from the darkness to seize him.

These were problems for men with perspective, men with nobler causes, men who had gone so far into the light they couldn't see the filth they stepped in anymore.

Lenk had simpler problems. And a sword.

It wasn't reflex. It wasn't natural. It wasn't easy to pull himself from the water and rush toward the netherling. It was bloody. It was painful.

He struck the netherling with his good shoulder. It still hurt. They tumbled to the ground in an unpleasant mess of metal. His sword found her armor, grinded against the metal. The tip found something softer and bit. Then, he pushed until they were both bleeding and lying upon the floor.

Only one of them moved. And then only with Kataria's help.

"I came back for you," he groaned.

"You want a kiss or something?" she all but spat at him as she tore her belt free.

444

"Well . . ."

"No."

"Oh." He winced as she tightened her belt around his shoulder as a makeshift tourniquete. "I don't think that's going to help."

"Better ideas?"

"No, it's a good one. But I was talking about—"

"*AKH ZEKH LAKH!*"

The longface came charging toward them, leaping over the body of a venom-doused Abysmyth. Her feet never struck the floor. A tentacle the size of a tree trunk swept out of the darkness, snatching her into the air and twisting her warcry to a desperate scream as it dragged her beneath the waves.

From the shadows the tentacles came, snatching the longfaces from the stone. Dragging them screaming into the air, crushing them in fleshy grips, pulling them from darkness to darker.

And all pain was drowned, all agonies rendered moot as the water erupted and Ulbecetonth rose.

"Yeah, that," Lenk grunted.

A child torn from the womb of hell, she came into the world pale and screaming. The shadows slid off her body in tears, as vast and cold as any of her statues, reluctant to leave her as she loomed over the waves. Barnacles and shells grew in clusters upon skin so pale as to be translucent. Coral sprouted in pristine, rainbow-colored rashes across her body. Creatures of many legs and many eyes crawled across her, into the shadow of her navel, across the slope of her breast, into and out of a mouth gaping wide and lined with bone-white sawblades.

Lenk felt his eyes fleeting across her in unblinking flashes, unable to look at any part of her for long, unable to turn away. His gaze was fixed upon the bright gold of a single eye not by his own choice. It burned with such hatred that it commanded his attention, demanded he look at it until he could see how he was going to die reflected in its gaze.

Her mouth grew wide, her shriek the sound of a thousand drowning maidens that sent the tears of shadow and the many skittering fiends falling from her body.

And Lenk felt himself moving.

"Come on, *come on.*" Kataria had both arms around him, equal parts propping him up and hauling him away. "We have to go."

"We can't." Reflex. His voice, even if it shouldn't have been. "We can't run from this."

"I said it and I meant it," she snarled, "but I thought we were going to get the tome before it happened. Now we run."

"We can't. She's limitless," Lenk said. "Down in the chasm, I saw her. She's under the island. She's the blood of the land. We can't outrun her." He looked into Kataria's eyes. "Not both of us."

"That's not what we're going to do," she said, pointing to a nearby archway. "We're going to run to that. We're going to keep running. We're going to go somewhere else and hide there until we can figure out something else."

"We can't do that," he said. "Neither of us makes it out unless . . ."

"Don't use that word if you're going to do something stupid."

"Too damn late for that."

He tore free from her grasp, took off running before she could grab him again, threw himself into the water and disappeared beneath the darkness before she could scream at him and make him think just what the hell it was he was doing.

He had no room for thought, though. That was not what duty was about.

Because he certainly had no idea. Not beyond giving Ulbecetonth something to focus on, something she couldn't resist attacking. How effective that would be with just a sword on his back was another problem best left to men who weren't incredibly stupid.

Men with simpler problems had simpler goals. Both of his were bobbing in the water. The severed heads of the Deepshriek floated, brushing against each other as though they couldn't bear to be separated in death.

He could feel the great emptiness below him again, the vast yawn of space and silence that came before the moment of calamity. His shoulder seared with the agony. The water boiled with Ulbecetonth's anger. He made a single desperate grab and caught the auburn and ebon hair of the two heads a mere moment before the water erupted and something seized him.

He struggled to keep ahold of sword and heads alike as the tentacle wrenched him from the water and pulled him into the air. The world spun around him as he hauled up to face a coral-scarred visage and a single burning eye.

"You came back," Ulbecetonth murmured, voices echoing off of each other. "You hateful, vile little thing. You came back."

Her voice robbed him of any sort of reply he might have had. It drank the breath from his throat.

"I could have given you anything, I would have given you anything, just to leave my children alone."

"Can't," he replied, straining as the tentacle tightened around him.

"I wanted to believe."

The world shifted, the tentacle raised him. The ceiling loomed closer, the mossy stalactites shimmering against the green firelight. For a moment, he thought he might be crushed against the tremendous stone teeth. The Kraken Queen didn't like him nearly enough to be that gentle with him, though.

He looked down. In the shadows of the waves, he saw the thousand eyes staring up at him like a thousand hateful stars. Her mouth gaped open beneath him, baring row upon row of jagged saw-teeth that stretched down her gullet. And from the darkness of her mouth, eyes stared back at him.

They came lashing out of her gullet, eels snapping and screeching and smiling wildly as they reached out to snatch and chew and wail for his blood. His sword slashed wildly, beating back each eager maw, each wild eye. Heads were bloodied, the eels fell back, but rose again and again. His arm seared, his shoulder bled and Ulbecetonth's teeth loomed ever closer as the tentacle lowered him like a writhing worm.

Tactics that did not range from stupid to desperate had never been plentiful. Now seemed a poor time to shun them. He hurled his blade and watched it lodge in Ulbecetonth's cheek, the demon not even flinching.

Right, he thought. *That'll do it for stupid.* He hefted the twin heads, aimed them as best he could. *Now for desperate.*

"Scream."

They obliged as their sister had. The sharp whine amplified to a wail as they opened their mouths and made the air quake. They erupted, swallowing both his screams and Ulbecetonth's as the great demon was sent reeling. Her tentacle flailed, weakening, as it shot up toward the ceiling.

Lenk seized the moss purely by chance, slammed against the stalactite as the tentacle tossed him, the screams of the Deepshriek having left him barely any wit to know what was happening. He held on purely by grit, clinging to the moss as he watched Ulbecetonth trying to shake the shrieks loose from her skull. She turned her scowl upward and, slowly, every tentacle joined in purpose as they slithered up from the deep and reached toward his precarious perch.

Desperate, stupid, everything.

He tied the heads to his belt, pried a patch of the moss from the stalactite, jammed it into his ears.

Sorry, Kataria. Sorry I couldn't do it the right way.

He felt a tentacle brush against his boot, straining to reach him.

But it's you I'm going to think of when I die. With my own thoughts, no one else's.

He tore the heads free, lifed them, aimed them toward a sizable stalactite hanging overhead.

Hope that's enough.

"Scream."

They did.

The air and earth shook, their wails joining the Deepshriek's agonized harmony. The air was flensed, the stone was cracked, Lenk felt blood pooling behind the moss in his ears. His shoulder bled. His arm felt too dead to hold the heads.

But the stone cracked. The stalactite quivered at its ancient root. Lesser spears broke, fell to dig into Ulbecetonth's arms, face, ignored by the demon. The great old stone groaned ominously, its pain rivaling even that of the Deepshriek. Lenk felt something coil around his ankle, tug appraisingly. He could feel Ulbecetonth's mouth yawning beneath him. He could feel her whisper to him from the dark.

"It was always going to end this way."

And then, nothing. No more sound. Everything went silent as the stone cracked, quaked, broke.

And fell.

A spear sent from above, it plunged into her, making her two as it drove down into her chest. It split her squarely down the middle, dividing her, spilling darkness into darkness. Her scream matched the stone's, the air's, the water's, sending the waves trembling and the rocks falling from above.

And still she reached. Still she pulled.

"*I SHOWED YOU MERCY!*" she howled. "*I GAVE YOU THE CHANCE TO RUN! WHY? WHY DO YOU HATE ME SO MUCH?*"

In every part of him, every drop of blood, every dying limb, every thought that was his own, there was no answer to that question.

The earth met her scream with another of its own. The ceiling cracked, the great wound left by the stalactite's plummet widening. They came at first as small drops of silver, splattering upon her flesh to blacken the translucence. Then, they came as rivulets, seeping into her eyes.

Then, it came as a flood.

A great column of water descending from on high, drowning her in silver and steam and shrieks, with no end in sight.

The blood of the mountain.

The water that carried her to hell.

She remembered it.

The ceiling cracked further. His own perch twitched, quaked, collapsed. He plummeted into the water below. In the darkness, he drifted and watched her die. Her teeth gnashed down there, screaming out in water that wouldn't obey her anymore. And Lenk watched her, breathlessly and bloodlessly, as her countless eyes winked out, one by one, until only one remained.

And it remained, fixed not upon him, but on the vast, dark emptiness surrounding it. Until it, too, disappeared.

Lenk closed his eyes and told himself he did the right thing. Ulbecetonth was dead. He was content to follow her.

Someone else, apparently, was not.

He felt himself dragged awkwardly through the water, Kataria's violent thrashing pulling him away from the walkway vanishing beneath a rising tide and through a veil of steam.

Ulbecetonth's skin crunched beneath him as he was dragged up onto her back. He stared up at the silvery water raining from above, falling through clouds of steam rising on sighs glutted by suffering.

Pretty, he thought. *Kind of like clouds, right?*

No one answered.

Never seen something so pretty.

A face, dark and stained by blood, appeared over him a moment later.

That's more like it.

"You were supposed to run," he said, voice weak.

"Where?" she asked.

"Somewhere else."

"There is nowhere else."

He heard the ceiling cracking overhead. All around, more and more scars appeared in the earth as more stalactites fell and more columns of silver plummeted into the water. The water drank the stone, the walkway, the statues, the archways disappearing as it rose upon tides of black and silver. Lenk felt himself rising as Ulbecetonth rose. And fell.

She was breathing.

She was still alive.

"I should not blame you." Her voice rumbled beneath him. Lenk turned and saw a single eye staring at him, wide and white with a gold iris from skin blackened. "You did as you were supposed to, as your kind did back then, too, listening to a father of your own."

Water, neither silver nor black, rimmed her stare.

"Perhaps you wanted to protect those you loved. Perhaps you wanted to prove me wrong. Perhaps you will, still. I should not hate you."

Her voice rasped on plumes of steam.

"My children have no mother. I have no children. I hope you live your life well, Lenk. And I hope that whatever hell you go to when you die, I will be waiting for you."

The water carried her up on the rising tide, closer to the dying earth. Lenk lay still upon her body, felt her breathe no more. Despite the steam, despite the blood, he felt cold.

"Mother?" A voice, weak and trembling. "Mother."

He looked and saw the Abysmyth, wading up to Ulbecetonth's body. It laid claws upon her, tried to shake her colossal form.

"Mother," it said, its voice a whisper. The silver water splashed on its skin, sent it steaming and charring like its mother's. It took no notice. "Mother, wake up."

"Please, Mother, please wake up." It was joined by more demons, more hands upon her, more voices pleading to the dead. "Mother, please don't leave me."

"Mother, it hurts, please don't—"

"—Mother, I don't want to feel it, anymore, please—"

"—we succeeded, Mother, we got the book, you can—"

"—Father is outside, Mother, please, just—"

"—Mother—"

"—please—"

"—I'm scared—"

"—Mother—"

Their flesh turned to steam, their claws to bone, their voices to ash. As, stain by stain, piece by piece, the water unmade them, their fears, their whispers, until only bones remained. They rested their skulls upon her body. They lay still and peaceful.

"I killed them," Lenk whispered. "All of them. And her."

"Yeah," Kataria said. She wrapped her arms around him, pulled him to her body. He felt his own life painted upon her skin. "You did."

He reached up, wrapped his fingers around her hand. "You're still alive."

"Yeah." Her grip tightened. He steadied the tremble of her hand, she found the life left in his arm. "I am."

He felt her breath upon him. He felt her heartbeat through her hands. He felt her hair brushing against the blood on his face. He felt warm.

"Wish I had something better to say," he said.

"Don't worry about it."

They looked up toward the ceiling. The earth was gone. Only the great clouds of steam, all that was left of Ulbecetonth and her brood. Only the water, falling in sheets and tears.

"Pretty, though," Kataria said, pulling him closer to her.

"Yeah."

And they rose. To the closest thing to heaven they would ever see.

Carried on endless blue.

THIRTY-FOUR
THE REMNANT

It was funny, she thought, but he weighed less than she thought he would. She had seen him unclothed. He had always seemed a strong man, then, a man of weight. But she could feel his ribs through his vest, hear his breath come so weakly, see his eyes glazed over like a sick man's.

And still he smiled. All that was left of him was the mask. A face that belonged to a man at peace.

"How's it look?" His voice was a hollow, fading thing.

"Shut up," Asper said. He knew damn well how it looked. She had stolen only a glimpse under his tunic, saw the pink organs, the copious blood. She knew what it meant. "You're going to be . . ." She looked around. "I just need my bag . . ."

"If you did, you would have gotten it," he said.

"I said shut up. You're not helping anything by talking."

"But you didn't. You're here. Holding me like I deserve it."

"Denaos, please, just—"

"Because you can't give me anything else."

And she offered nothing but silence. The kind of weak, painful quiet that came when only three words could be written on a long, blank piece of paper.

She could have contented herself saying there was nothing else she could have done. She could have watched him die. She could have lived with that quiet.

But then he spoke.

"Last rites."

"No."

"Come on."

"*No.*"

"I don't have anything left, Asper. Nothing but a dead girl and a lot of sin. I can't take that with me."

"Denaos, don't ask me to do that. I can't do that. You're supposed to die long after we've parted ways, grinning as someone sticks a knife in you."

"What, you've thought it out?"

"A little."

"Well, it hasn't worked out that way. Just listen to me while I've got the blood to speak, okay?" He forced a smile, red at the edges. "Look, I'll even grin while I do it."

What else could she do but nod?

"Riots in Cier'Djaal. You heard of them, right?"

She had. She had been amongst the few to work the injured who were sailed day and night to Muraska, propelled by the Venarium when Cier'Djaal's own healers were overworked.

"There were . . . a lot of people dead," she said. "A lot. We saved . . . three. Three out of the hundreds that came to us."

"You know how it happened?"

She said nothing.

"Please, Asper, it saves me from having to say it—"

"She was murdered." Asper said, choking on something. "The Hound-mistress. She challenged the Jackals, drove them back, and they . . . someone killed her and that started the riots."

"And people died."

"Yeah. Fourteen hundred."

"More."

She looked down at him. He looked up at her. Past her. Into heaven.

"How many," she asked, "did you kill, Denaos?"

His smile faded. His mask broke.

"One." He coughed. "All of them."

"Which is it?"

"Both."

Had she not been so numb, had the feeling of her body not been welled up inside her throat, she would have dropped him. Had she worshipped any other god, she would have risen and walked away.

What could she do but whisper?

"Talanas . . ."

"He wasn't there when it happened."

"Denaos, you . . ."

"Yeah. I did."

"How? Why were you there? What were you doing with her? Were you some . . . some kind of assassin? Some thug? Did you know? Didn't you *realize* what you would do?"

"I was in the palace. I was around her a lot in those days. I was near her. I knew what she was doing and I knew how to . . . how . . ." His eyelids flut-tered. He drew in a rasping breath.

She was squeezing him. She wanted him to hurt. By her hand.

"You killed her."

"Yeah."

"You killed all of them."

"Kind of, yeah."

She could not blink, could barely breathe. "What the hell do you expect me to do about that, then? Absolve you? Tell you it's going to be okay?"

A glint in his glazed eyes. Fading. "Can't do that, I'm guessing?"

She simply stared.

"Then just listen."

"I can't. Whatever rites I could give, I was going to give to Denaos. You're not him. I don't know who you are."

"That's fine."

"You're a murderer."

"Yeah."

"You killed them all."

"Yeah."

"You killed her. You killed the Houndmistress. You killed them *all.*"

"She wasn't the Houndmistress." He looked at her now. Not at heaven. Not at ghosts. "Her name was Imone." He smiled, briefly. "She was my wife."

His smile began to fade, leaving nothing behind. No peace was on his lips as they went slack, no contentment in his eyes as they dimmed. All the sin he carried, he carried with him as he, too, faded.

But not completely.

He drew a shallow breath, held the faintest light in his eye. Wherever he was, it was neither heaven nor hell nor earth, but some place between them all.

Slowly, she found her left hand reaching for his neck. Her fingers trembled as she did so, wary to unleash the power behind them. It seemed not so much a mercy. Those who had felt her touch before had felt the pain as she had, as whatever was in her arm had destroyed them. But he wouldn't last that long. One moment of pain, then she would send him on his way. Maybe it was a mercy. Maybe it was agony.

But he deserved it. One confession and everything was all right? As though he had never done it? No. Some part of her, the part that watched only three people walk out of her temple and leave hundreds left to be buried, wanted this. Some part of her wanted him to suffer for his crimes. And that part of her brushed the tips of her fingers against his throat.

"He can not be sal va tion."

The sound that paper makes when it burns. Ashes unmoved by wind. Dust falling in thin beams of light. She looked over shoulder. The paper man was staring at her with its black eyes. All too alive.

"Feel noth ing in your arm, lit tle crea ture?"

453

And speaking, sounding almost amused.

She shook her head.

"*He can not do it.*"

"Who?"

"*He has no name. He was nev er giv en one bef ore he went there.*"

"Where?"

"*Un der the skin. In the bone. He spoke to me when he sensed me. Such a hap py voice. So ea ger to talk to some one who could hear him.*" The creature's voice came slowly, on each exhale and inhale. "*There, he is blind. Here, you are deaf. He can on ly hear you. He can not speak to you.*"

"He's . . . like you? The thing in my arm?"

"*But he was close. I could hear him. And he was young. He knew noth ing of the war. Been trapped in the flesh for so long. Re fresh ing. Wan ted to know me, wan ted to know ab out the sta tue, wan ted to know my name.*"

"It was . . . looking for something. Earlier. I could hear it."

"*For me. Could hear him. But could not speak to him. Deaf in there. On ly knows you, your voice, your fears, your pains. Gets scared in there, tries to es cape.*"

"Then why isn't it doing it now? Why won't it kill him?" she asked, holding Denaos up.

"*Be cause you do not want him dead.*"

She looked down at Denaos, emptying like a vessel.

"He deserves it."

"*When you dream, do you see a world where ev er y one gets what they de serve?*"

She looked from the paper man to Denaos again. The rogue drew in a short breath. It did not come out again.

"What . . . do I do?"

"*You speak. He will li sten. He can not hear an y thing else.*"

Somewhere far away, there was a crashing sound in the darkness beyond the rubble. Then a moment of the hollow quiet, the long, blank page waiting for the words. She pressed her left hand to Denaos's face.

"*Not like that. He does not be lieve you.*"

Her right hand trembled. She closed her eyes, let it fall upon his body, slide down beneath his tunic to the great wound beneath.

"*Ask him a gain.*"

She spoke a whispered word.

"Please."

And she could feel him dying. She could feel the blood drying, skin blackening, organs failing. Pain. Agony. Her fingers drank it like water, all the suffering in the blood. Her arm grew heavy, glutted with the agony. She felt it course into her, into her arm and from death into life.

She could feel a life lived in reverse, pulled out of the darkness and into a burning light, the sensation of skin kissing steel, the sound of air dying before a body hit the floor, the first breath a woman takes when her husband plans to kill her, the wail of a mother when she gives birth to a murderer.

She was screaming. Her arm was ablaze. Skin was bathed in something bright white, something hideous and hungry that drank his pain and left behind black bone as it grew brighter with each drop drank. She was screaming. And through it, she could hear him. In her arm, she could hear the demon.

What is this, don't like it, it hurts, can feel it, why does it hurt, why can't I find anything here, I can fix this, I can make this work, I can make it work, I can fix everything, I will, do not be worried, do not fear.

It was a sensation she had felt before, in Sheraptus's clutches, as she watched a young woman die. It had craved her pain, then, craved to fix it as Asper had wanted to. She opened her eyes long enough to look down at her arm. No skin remained. No cloth remained. Only the bright white light. Only the black, black bone. Only the blood growing wet, the skin pulling itself together, the organs waking up from their slumber.

Only the light.

Over her own agony, she could not hear the crash in the distance growing louder. Against the light, she could not see the stream of water racing across the floor. As she felt Denaos's body grow warm, as she felt the pain inside her own arm, she could not feel the earth shake beneath her.

A moment before the wall of water came to swallow her up. A moment between when she drew breath and when the thing in her arm went silent and the water had just begun to burst beyond the archway. A perfect silence, the moment of the quill pressed to parchment.

And she heard Denaos breathe as the silver glow enveloped them both completely.

Gariath came to the crest of the staircase after he had left a good deal of his life on the stone steps below. He looked up at the face of the mountain and saw the carving of Ulbecetonth, arms stretched out and smile wide with benevolence. He looked over his shoulder to see what the hell she was so damn happy about.

Bodies. Some of them his friends. Blood. Some of it his own. The battle in the ring raged, as it would always rage until they all fell. But they hadn't all fallen. The netherlings that did not know the words "lie down and die" swung at the demons that spoke to them with gurgling voices and reaching claws. As they would, always.

Perhaps that was just how life for the *Rhega* was, to drift from battle to battle. To stand over corpses and say, *"This is what we fought for."* He had done just that, or intended to. He had intended to stand over the corpse of Daga-Mer, to look at his friends and say, *"This is what I fought for. These humans. Not my family. Not even close. The Shen were close. And I left them. For these humans."*

Maybe it would have sounded better if he had been standing on the corpse of a titanic demon.

But he was going to die here alone, at the top of these stairs, surrounded by the water and with only one corpse to share it all with.

Mahalar. Blackened and split apart, lying there like ashes from a fire. His eyes were still dull, still yellow, still staring as Gariath approached him. The dragonman reached down, plucked the elder Shen up in his arms. Funny, he thought; his eyes still looked alive, as though he were expecting something from Gariath. Words of encouragement? A report?

Why the hell not.

"The fight isn't going well," the dragonman said. "Your people, they fled. They left their oaths behind and ran. Some are alive. Some are not." He sniffed. "I thought you should know."

Maybe not the best words to end on. Maybe not something the elder wanted to hear in the afterlife. But for a moment, the Shen's eyes looked like they grew darker, slipping away from whatever they clung to.

But that might have been from the vast shadow falling over them.

Gariath turned and saw him. Daga-Mer's light was a dim, steady, bloodred throb as he loomed over the dragonman at the top of the staircase. His great webbed claws clutched the bridge. Stale wind tinged with red burst from his jaws with every long, ragged breath. Deep within a hollow eye socket, a red fire burned upon Gariath.

The dragonman took a step back and felt something beneath his foot. He looked down and saw a trickle of water weeping out from the doorway behind
456   him. Daga-Mer clawed forward, reaching out to haul his tremendous body forth with a great quaking sound as he settled upon the stone. His hand rose, clenched into a fist and prepared to bring it down upon the tiny red parasite on the stone before him. There was silence. All of creation held its breath for fear of being noticed.

Almost all, anyway.

Gariath's earfrills fanned out with the sound. A distant rumbling, growing louder. The stream beneath his feet grew swifter, sweeping over the bridge, beneath Daga-Mer's fingers. He watched the black flesh of the titan's skin sizzle and steam. The great beast did not seem to notice.

Gariath did.

Gariath slung Mahalar's body over his shoulder and leapt, scrambling up over a pile of rubble and into the arms of Ulbecetonth over the doorway.

And the water came in a great roar of froth and liquid, dragon's breath from an old, rocky beast. It washed over Daga-Mer, striking him like a fist and bathing him in a silver glow. The titan howled with agony as it raced over him like a living thing, setting his black skin afire with steam.

He roared, he thrashed, he held out his titanic hands as if to hold it back. But the water kept coming. The water was pitiless. The water devoured him.

Gariath watched as Daga-Mer disappeared beneath a colossal wave and a cloud of steam. He rose again with a howl, his white bones left bare as the black skin of his body shrank like puddles under the sun. He fell beneath the water and rose again, soundless, stretching out a skeletal hand as if to grab Gariath with whatever hatred kept those bones alive just long enough to swing out with a skeletal claw and sink back beneath the water.

He did not rise again.

Gariath watched the water rush endlessly out, sweeping down the stairs and onto the battlefield below. His eyeridges furrowed. Theoretically, this would be a good time to say something pithy.

But at that moment, he caught a glimpse of them. The humans, the tall ones, carried out over the water and down it. Alive? Dead? Irrelevant. He had only one course of action and, thus, only one thing to say.

He turned to Mahalar and grunted.

"Hold your breath."

Voices without words. Screams without substance. Agony unending. He could hear them as though they were drops of liquid dripping into his skull from the tiny gouges the crown's spikes dug into the tender skin of his brow. He could hear pleas, wails, individual terrors blended into a swampy soup of pain that could not be shaken.

The Gonwa. Screaming. As their lives fed into his skull, down his throat, into his body.

He looked at his hands and saw them tensed and strong. He could feel the disease burning away, the weakness sweeping into the stones upon the crown and being carried to someone else.

Dreadaeleon felt strong. Impossibly strong.

And this would have come with such impossible relief had he been able to disregard the screaming.

"They won't stop, will they?"

Sheraptus was still smiling when Dreadaeleon turned upon him. Despite the fact that his eyes were a pale white and his body was fragile and weak, the longface was still beaming as though nothing had changed.

"It was difficult for me to get used to, at first, too," Sheraptus said as he picked himself up off the earth. "Eventually, you learn to block them out."

Dreadaeleon found that hard to believe with how long and loud they screamed, with how clear and crystalline their pain was. He would have torn it from his head and cast it upon the ground if not for . . .

Damn it, old man, he cursed himself. *Not this way. You're not supposed to feel this. It's heresy. It's treason. It's against every oath you took and every lesson you knew. It's . . . it's . . .*

"It's power," Greenhair chimed, coming up alongside him. "The power to end all of it." She swept her arm over the battlefield. "The power to do what no one else could do."

"In all fairness, I *tried* to do it," Sheraptus replied. "But the people in the sky had a different plan for me."

"Starting with *him*," Greenhair hissed, pointing a webbed finger at Sheraptus as she laid a hand on Dreadaeleon's shoulder. "He tried to kill you. He defied the Sea Mother. He served darker masters than even the Kraken Queen."

"Shut up," Dreadaeleon replied, rubbing his eyes. "Just . . . let me think."

It was hard to do so. The sound of the Gonwa's pain did not fade. Every ounce of their life that flooded into him, burning away his sickness, filling his body with life, came accompanied by a scream to a god, a cry to a mother, a wail to a brother to save them.

"I wouldn't take too long," Sheraptus replied. "She might grow tired of you and arrange for someone else to kill you, as she did me."

"Don't listen to him," Greenhair said.

"Yes, *don't* listen to me, little moth. Don't listen to the only one here who's had dealings with that creature. Don't listen to the man who knows what she's about. She proclaims to want peace, bliss, for the Sea Mother or whatever. But all she's interested in is the power. Same as any sensible creature, really. I can't fault her."

"Lorekeeper," the siren said, pulling on his shoulder. "Ignore him. All that I have done has been to save this world, to preserve it from Ulbecetonth, to serve the will of the Gods."

"Ah, that's where you're wrong." Sheraptus held up a finger. "Of course, you claim to serve the Gods. You get others to do it for you, naturally, to use their power to serve them on your behalf, but it's a false power you wield. A liar's power. One I hadn't really appreciated until everything was made clear to me by them."

He pointed upward, to the bloodstained sky, and smiled. He drew in a breath, let it out as a cold cloud of frost.

"And so, I do name you a pretender to their power and their servitude, and so honor their distaste."

Dreadaeleon saw it. The gesture of the hand, the twitch of the lips that heralded the spell. He saw the ice crystals form in the cloud of frost and become a jagged icicle. He saw it fly past him. He felt the warmth of her life spatter upon his face as it struck her squarely in the sternum and carried her to the ground, pinning her there. He saw it, before it had even happened, as it happened, after it happened.

And he did nothing.

Greenhair lay upon the sand, eyes wide and reflecting the cold blue chill of the icy spear pinning her to the earth. She reached out a hand to him, as if to beg him to pull her up, as if there *weren't* a jagged chunk of ice in her chest. She gasped for air through a mouth dripping red.

"Why?" she gasped. "Why didn't you stop him?"

"She has a point."

When Dreadaeleon whirled on him, his smile had faded. The longface simply looked at Dreadaeleon, all the boy's wide-eyed, jaw-clenched shock, and blinked.

"What?"

"You killed her," Dreadaeleon said.

"Sorry, have you not been paying attention? I kill lots of things."

"She . . . she helped you, though. She was your ally. You treated with her and you killed her like . . ."

"So? She helped you and you watched her die. You have the crown, you could have stopped me."

"I was confused, the screams, they're just . . ."

"Just more screams. No different than any you have heard before. You could have stopped me. You could have saved her."

And Dreadaeleon was left with nothing more than a silence and Greenhair's blood crackling as it froze upon the ice.

"You're ashamed," Sheraptus observed. "Afraid, perhaps. I felt the same way." Now a grin began to creep across his face, as though whatever he were about to say he had been dying to say for ages. "The awareness of it all, how insignificant it all is, and then you realize it's not insignificant by design, but by perspective. It is looking down upon the crab and marveling at how tiny it is without realizing just how very tall you are next to it.

"To summate: she died because you no longer felt it worthwhile to save her. Not with what else you could do with that crown."

459

"Magic wasn't meant to be used that way." He cringed as another chorus of screams echoed through his skull. "*This* way."

"This is where you fail to understand. Power, magic, *nethra:* all the same. It's there to be used. As a concept, it's worthless. Gods are the same way. They do not sit there and wait to be assailed with the whining of weaklings. They wait for worthiness. They wait for me, little moth. I am alive because I use their strength and the chances they gave me."

Dreadaeleon hadn't even noticed the lightning crackling on the long-face's fingers until they were raised and thrust in his face.

"Just as that power is not yours to wield."

By the time the longface spoke the word and sent the forked lightning from his fingers, all Dreadaeleon could muster was a feeble hand raised in defense. But in the flash that it took, he needed nothing more. He could feel the electricity enter his skin as though it belonged there, snaking into his body and disappearing into his fingertips with a few stray sparks. It crackled inside him, settling into his body like a new home.

And the two shared a look of shock, neither having expected that. But neither had the opportunity to dwell upon it.

The distant rumble grew to a roar. They turned and saw the wall of water rushing down from the staircase, becoming a colossal wave unto itself. It swept away the living and the dead, the screaming and the silent, the faithful and the faithless alike in a pitiless rush.

"Ah." Sheraptus sighed. "I see." He clicked his tongue. "They really are fickle, aren't they? It seems a little unfair."

With that, the longface folded his hands behind his back and walked. Slowly. Toward the water.

"What are you doing?" Dreadaeleon demanded. "You can't—"

"Enough with the limitations, little moth," Sheraptus said, waving a hand over his shoulder. "They saw fit to give you the crown and give me . . . this. I suspect you'll find that limitations mean nothing to those willing to recognize their insignificance."

"But where are you going?"

The water rushed up to meet him. Sheraptus had but enough time to look over his shoulder and smile.

"I suspect we'll find out."

And he disappeared beneath the flood.

Dreadaeleon should have dwelt on just how psychotic that was. Or on how he could have saved Greenhair. Or on the fate of his friends. But desperation lent clarity to thought. He drew in a breath, spoke the words, and released.

The wall of force formed nearly instantaneously. Nothing more than a flick of his wrist, a wave of his hand, and the air became rippling, solid, parting the colossal flood as easily as he would fold paper. And in brief, fleeting moments of clarity, he could but marvel at how effortless it all was. How easily the power flowed from him, how he felt nothing burning or breaking inside him to do it, how swiftly the water carried the blood and the bodies and the skeletons around him.

But only in brief, fleeting moments.

The rest of him was dedicated to trying not to listen to the screaming as he heard the Gonwa's voices rise to shattering and fall silent, one by one, until their agony was a candle flame flickering in the wind.

THIRTY-FIVE

AWASH IN GLORY

Waist-deep in water, Dreadaeleon waded among them, and the dead would not stop looking at him.

Bobbing in the water, their long faces still screwed up in a battle they had not stopped fighting, the netherlings scowled at him. Hollow and empty as they had been in life, the skeletons of the Abysmyths stared at him from fleshless eye sockets as they lay submerged beneath the crystalline water. The Shen . . .

The Shen floated upon the lake that had been the ring. Face down. Motionless.

He paused and looked to the mountain. The clouds swirled overhead. Perhaps unable to bear giving the rest of the sky a look at what happened on the earth below. The water still vomited from the mountain's face, though in a slow, steady stream that twisted down the shattered stone stairs and beneath the ribs of Daga-Mer's colossal skeleton.

The fleshless titan froze in death, reaching out to the mountain with a bleached-white hand, as though still, in some small way, alive. As though, if he could but try a little harder, he could reach what he sought.

All in your mind, old man, he told himself. *There's no one left here but you.*

He looked over the ring. The entirety of it was submerged, the bones and bodies bobbing along its surface like lilies of purple and white.

Somewhere in his mind, someone whimpered.

They're still alive, he thought. *Some of them, anyway. After all that. After all you did to them . . .* He paused, shook his head. *Stop that. You didn't know. And by the time you did, there was no choice. The power was there, you happened to have it, so you had to use it and . . .*

He paused and wondered if the Gonwa could hear him as he could hear them. He paused and wondered if they had heard this before from someone else.

Off to the side, he could hear the sound of splashing. He whirled about, hand extended, power leaping to his fingertips. The Gonwa could but groan.

Gariath didn't even bother to look at him as he trudged through the waters. The dragonman moved slowly, limping. Stray bits of cloth and leather had been tied tightly around his middle, staunching a red stain. Over each shoulder and under one arm, he carried a body.

He paused as he came to Dreadaeleon and grunted. "Alive?"

The boy nodded; considering everything, it didn't seem a stupid question. "You?" After Gariath nodded, he looked to the bodies. "And what about—" His eyes widened. "Is that Asper?"

"Yes and yes," Gariath replied. "Alive. Not sure how." He shook Denaos's prone body under his arm. "This one either."

Dreadaeleon looked to the limp, blackened figure of Mahalar and frowned. "And . . ."

"You don't need to ask and you know you don't. Give me something to put them down on."

A dull whimper in his mind as he breathed over the surface of the water and formed a small floe of ice from his breath. Gariath slumped the bodies upon it. Sure enough, Asper and Denaos drew in short, shallow breath.

"Anyone else?"

Dreadaeleon looked around the ring. The waters chopped gently.

"What of Lenk and the pointy-eared human?" Gariath grunted. "Did they—"

"I don't . . ." The boy's eyes widened. "But maybe . . ." He tapped his cheek. "Greenhair."

"What?"

Dreadaeleon ran to where he saw her last and found her there. The icicle that had pinned her to the earth was but a sliver. Her body was torn and twisted where the waves had sought to take her and the frost had sought to keep her. Dreadaeleon reached down and plucked her from the water.

She seemed a fluid thing, then, head lolling in his arms and hair streaming down into the water. Without substance. Without weight. The gaping hole in her body was clean, as though the water had taken her blood with it when it cleaned this cursed place.

"Lorekeeper."

She spoke. No melody. No song. Words. Crude and painful to hear.

"Lorekeeper," she gasped.

"I'm here," he said.

"The Kraken Queen . . . dead."

"I know."

"I . . . did it. For the Sea Mother. Duty fulfilled. I . . ." She could not lift her head to look at him. Her arm could only brush against his cheek.

And her arm went limp. And she faded. And she dissolved. Flesh into water, hair into water. She spilled through his grasp, down into the water to disappear into the endless blue.

"She's dead." When he finally said it, after so many times he wondered how he might, he was surprised at how easy it was. "Just like that."

"You were expecting her to live?"

"No . . ." He looked away, then back to the water. "But . . ."

Gariath didn't ask. He didn't have to. Dreadaeleon's fingers began to weave, knitting into complex, painful-looking gestures. He coaxed the waters to rise in a column and with delicate brushes of his hands, he sheared the liquid away until it resembled something more shapely, something human.

"Sheraptus was right . . . in a way, of course, but not the correct way. Magic isn't meant to be used this way—recklessly, that is—but what *are* limitations, anyway? We recognize the function of the power as it pertains to our bodies, but what of our minds? He negated the costs of magic—"

Dreadaeleon winced sharply, rubbing at his temple.

"That was a law that could not be circumnavigated. Not until he figured out a way. And if one law can be made pointless, what of others? What else could we possibly do with it? What else can be made insignificant?"

He stepped back. The water hung in the air, no longer a column, no longer even human. She was blue, of course, and liquid, but everything else about her—the flow of her hair, the fins upon her head, the crystalline hum she made when Dreadaeleon flicked her liquid body—was her.

"The siren," Gariath muttered. "You . . . just—"

"I did," Dreadaeleon said, beaming. "I can. Lenk, Kataria, anyone else, maybe even all the Shen lost today, if we can recover their bodies. If power can be transferred, if a being can be broken down into energy, then surely it can be reconstructed. Surely, with the proper motivations and more thorough thought than Sheraptus, I could . . ."

His smile was wide when he turned to Gariath.

"Gods, do you realize what this—"

His smile disappeared when Gariath punched him.

"Yeah." The dragonman grunted as he caught the boy and tore the crown from his head before letting him drop into the water, the liquid Greenhair splashing into nothingness after him. "I do."

For as much trouble as it had caused, it was like paper in Gariath's hands, its iron bending in soft, whimpering creaks as he wadded it up into a mangled, blackened mess.

"What are you doing?" Dreadaeleon sputtered, flailing to his feet. "*What the hell are you doing, you moron? STOP!* That may be the only chance we have to—"

"There's nothing you can say that will make me stop," Gariath grunted, continuing to mangle the crown. "And only a handful of things you can say that won't make me punch you again."

He turned and threw it. It tumbled out of sight, disappearing somewhere beyond the line of kelp. Dreadaeleon itched at his scalp, his mind suddenly seeming a very empty, constrictive place.

"*WHY?*" he demanded.

"It was a cursed, evil thing."

"Can you tell me *why* it was a cursed, evil thing? Because you can't understand it? Because you don't know how anything works if you can't hit it real hard and make it do something?"

"Yeah," Gariath growled, "because I don't understand it. And because I don't understand how someone thinks you can pull a dead body up, put something in it, and call it alive again. And I don't understand how you can think anyone having that kind of power is a good thing." He snorted. "So, in the absence of understanding, I turned to violence. It worked out pretty well for me."

Dreadaeleon opened his mouth to retort, found himself silent as his eyes were drawn to the edge of the ring. The kelp forest parted as they came emerging from the shadows. In numbers too small for the leaves to even notice their passing.

At their head trudged a creature with a bent back and a long shard of bone wedged in his eye. Behind came the others, holding the prone bodies of a man with silver hair and a bloodied woman, both unmoving. They came until there were but a few.

Shalake said nothing as he looked past Gariath and Dreadaeleon to the ice floe and the blackened body of Mahalar. He said nothing as he looked to his few brothers, who stepped forward and deposited Lenk and Kataria upon the ice. And he said nothing as he bent low and began to pull a body of one of his fellows from the water.

And they said nothing, as one, as the Shen who knew they were dead were collected and heaped upon the ice by those who had yet to admit it.

THIRTY-SIX

FAREWELL TO
THE DEAD

It was enough smoke to choke a god. But then again, it was a lot of fire. Because there were a lot of bodies.

Still.

Three days after.

On the beaches below, they worked as one. The Gonwa and Owauku had come from Teji, summoned by Shen that had once threatened them. They carried the bodies, they built the pyres from coral and wood, they bore the torches. They filed between the fire and the pile of dead, green flesh in a slow march, as they had since dawn, as they did at sunset, until they moved with such certainty between deaths that it was impossible to tell the difference between them.

"We do not burn our dead."

Lenk looked up. Jenaji stood at the edge of the cliff, staring down over the beach. The sole patch of sand that was not walled away from the world.

"When my father died," he said, "it was by a human sword. We were raiding a ship that wandered too close. Shalake called him a hero. We left him his club, his shield, and let the tide rise and take him."

He looked down at the bodies below. "We had ways of doing things. Ways that we had done things when we were one people. The years came. The Gonwa grew lazy, the Owauku grew stunted. Their suffering changed them. We loathed them for it. We made them swear oaths that our ancestors took when we were still one."

Lenk looked to the center of the beach, the largest pyre, the brightest fire. Mahalar. They had set him ablaze first. Three days later, he was still burning.

"It took us this," Jenaji said, gesturing to the scene below, "to see what they had seen. All that you see below is all that remains of us. All of us. We found only bodies and embers on Komga. We came to Teji on bended knee. We begged the Owauku, the weakest of us, to come and bring wood for . . ."

He sighed. "Less than one hundred. Three islands, each one of them a graveyard. And all that we had, the best of us, flies on the wind."

Lenk looked down at the fire and smoke. He rubbed the secured poultice on his shoulder. He coughed.

"So, yeah, I'm fine," he said, "like I was saying. Just . . . uh . . ." He coughed again. "Thought you'd want to know."

Jenaji looked at him. He smiled weakly.

"I mean, thank you, for your help," he said. "When we came down from the mountain, I probably would have died if you hadn't helped us. Kataria collapsed, probably from carrying me all the way down—thanks for not mentioning that, by the way—but, uh . . . thanks."

Jenaji held his stare for a long while before turning back and grunting.

"It's fine." He rubbed his eyes. "You did us a service. The Shen would be proud to die for this. We did our duty. We died well."

Jenaji paused, shook his head.

"No. I still don't believe it."

Lenk glanced to his sword at his side. It would seem a little petty to thank them for fishing it out when the waterways beneath Jaga emptied out, he thought. And his request was going to be awkward enough already.

"So, this might be a bad time what with the whole . . . mass death and such," Lenk said, "but . . ."

Jenaji didn't wait for him to finish his thought. He took the satchel from his waist, held it up before him.

"Look at that. It weighs nothing. Toss it in a fire, it would burn like any other book. And for this . . ." He looked out over the fires and sighed, tossing it into Lenk's lap. "Take it. Whatever reason we had to care about it is gone now."

"We'll be gone in a day or two," Lenk said. "Are you sure you can spare a vessel?"

"And food," Jenaji said. "And a sea chart we seized from one of the ships. It will take you back to your lands." He looked at the tome for a moment. "Had we just given that tome to you, perhaps none of this would have ever happened. Irony?"

"Poetry," Lenk replied. "But I guess, all things considered, we're kind of lucky."

"Luck is why you are alive and my brothers are dead." Jenaji shook his head and sighed. "If we were lucky, I would never have met you."

Lenk looked at Jenaji as the lizardman turned and stalked down the ridge.

"Where are you going?" he asked.

"Away."

"I mean, where will you go? You and your people?"

"Same answer."

He watched him go to join the procession heaping bodies onto the fire. He looked down at the satchel in his lap. He didn't open it. He didn't need to. No voice called to him, he felt no great desire to open it. Whatever inside him that had spoken the book's language was now silent.

Now, the Tome of the Undergates was just a book.

And he was just a man sitting on top an island made of corpses.

"That's it?"

He looked over his shoulder. Kataria stood at the edge of the kelp forest, arms folded over her chest, bandaged about the limb and midriff.

"Yeah," he said, holding up the satchel. "It's over. Everything is over. We can go back and get paid now."

"And you're all right?" she asked.

"Mostly," he said, rubbing his shoulder. "Asper stitched me up, did her business and such. I was in and out for a lot of it and I think she said something about sneezing killing me or something, but—"

She was turning and walking. He called after her, her ears were folding over themselves. She disappeared into the forests.

And Lenk and the tome were left upon the cliff.

"Patron's coin," Denaos cursed, "you're supposed to be *lighter* without armor." He grunted as he pulled the corpse to the pyre. "But you won't lend a hand, will you? You don't even care." He wiped sweat from his brow as he looked down disdainfully at the burden. "What with being dead and all."

He had shut her eyes. Once more when they had somehow opened themselves. He had considered blindfolding her, but he didn't think it would help. Even in a cold, blind death, he could feel Xhai hating him.

"Not like you deserve this, anyway," he growled. "You tried to kill me. A lot of people have done that before and gotten away with burials much less pretty than this." He looked down at her, shrouded in the leather wrapping, and frowned. "I don't have to do this, you know."

He dropped her a few feet away from the crude pyre he had assembled at one of the few remaining dry spots at the edge of the ring. A meager thing, cobbled together out of whatever he thought might burn. She could knock it down, smash the pieces and jam the sharp bits somewhere tender without ever breaking a sweat.

Could have, he corrected himself. *Probably would have, too, if not for . . . well, you know.*

Now, it seemed as though a pile of driftwood and sticks would be something to defy her. She was heavy. He was tired.

She stirred. For a moment, just a fleeting moment that had saved his life before, he wondered if, after all that, she could still be alive. But he saw Asper's hands around Xhai's ankles. The priestess did not look up at him.

"On three," she grunted, "one . . . two . . ."

They placed her upon the pyre awkwardly; she looked more like she had been smashed to rest than laid. The flint would not start and the spark would not catch at first; it was afraid to come out. When it caught and she was engulfed in flames, they watched her burn; as mangled as her face was, after all she had been through, she still looked pissed as hell.

No one said a thing.

It was a fitting funeral for Semnein Xhai, first of the Carnassials.

And then Denaos had to go and ruin it.

"Should you say something?" he asked without looking at Asper.

"She didn't believe in my god, or any god. What would I say?"

He looked to the fire. "I guess you're right."

She looked to him for only a fleeting moment. It was enough for him to feel it, like a brief slap. Embers rose with her sigh.

"I don't know who she was. I don't know anything about her beyond the men she was drawn to. Maybe if we knew each other in another time, if they didn't exist, we wouldn't have hurt each other like we did."

Denaos observed a moment of silence.

"Probably not," he said.

"Yeah." She sighed. "Probably not."

Another silence followed. Not nearly long enough before she asked.

"Would you have given a funeral for Bralston, too?"

"I would."

"He wanted to kill you, too, didn't he?"

"He did."

"But you—"

"Yeah. I did."

"Why do you mourn for them, Denaos?"

He rolled his tongue over in his mouth a moment. He stared intently at a stray ember burning out on the ground.

"I learned to read when I was eight. First thing I did was visit every temple to every God that had a holy scripture and ask to see it. They all talked about redemption, but there was never any list to it. You just did good and went to be at the side of your God when you died. And they all contradicted each other."

He sniffed. The ember danced slightly on the breeze, growing bright.

"I killed my first person when I was five. Little boy in Cier'Djaal. He took a liking to me immediately. I wasn't from Cier'Djaal, so everyone was fascinated by the little pale northerner. The boy's father was rich. There was a celebration for his son's fifth birthday. The little pale boy was invited. I remember a big, silver platter with honeytreats. I asked the little boy if he wanted to play a game. A couple of moments later, I showed the little boy's father his son's four biggest fingers in one hand and the bloody knife in the other. Took a note to the Jackals and by the end of the night, I was eating honeytreats before I cleaned the blood off my hands."

The ember rested upon the sand again and dimmed.

"There were a lot more before Imone. I had a talent for killing. I could do it pretty easily, too. Put on a mask and I could be a lover, a supporter, a genuine friend. Knife them in the dark or get them to do what the Jackals wanted them to. 'Friendly murders,' they called them back then."

The ember sizzled to a dull, dark splotch on the ground.

"I guess it was when Imone die—" He paused, caught himself. "When I . . . I killed her, two years after our wedding night, that I started really reading. I went to every scripture, every book, of every god and kept re-reading them, hoping I missed something. Maybe there was some kind of passage marked 'for those of you who have especially fucked everything to the point that you are almost totally definitely going to burn when you die, please read on.'"

He sniffed again.

"There wasn't. So I packed up and I went and I just kept going until I met you and Lenk and the others. I needed to do something good, but I was only good at killing. So I suppose I just do what I can to show the Gods that I at least *mean* good. Like giving killers funerals, sending them to whatever god will have them. You've got to figure that you do what you can, when you can, as often as you can, eventually someone up there will tell you you're okay and you're coming to heaven with everyone else, you know?"

He finally looked at her. She was still staring at the fire.

"Right?"

When she looked at him finally, he cringed. For the same reasons he cringed when he entered a temple. Because there was no judgment in her eye, no pondering, no hope. Just sadness.

471

"You talk like it's a checklist," she said. "Like you can just keep doing it and someone's keeping score and you can always come back. Maybe it is like that." She held her hand out, watched the way the sunlight made the edges of her fingers pink. "I think I thought it was like that, too, at one point.

"But then, if it's all about numbers, how high can you count? How many good deeds equal a life wrongfully stolen? How many people do you get to kill before you lose count?"

He touched his side. The flesh there felt alien, new, someone else's. "You saved me, though. You and your arm. I got another chance. That means something, doesn't it?"

"It means I didn't want you dead. And whatever's inside me thought that was enough to save you."

"So . . . you forgive me?"

She smiled sadly. "Fourteen hundred, Denaos. I don't think it matters what I say."

In all the times he had been cut, she didn't think she had ever seen so much pain etched across his face.

"A waste."

Dreadaeleon's footsteps heralded his arrival before his grumbling did. The boy looked surprisingly healthy. His color had returned, his eyes were clear, he hadn't so much as looked at his crotch for days. And yet, everywhere he went, he staggered, stumbled fitfully. As he did now as he approached the pyre and swept a disdainful glare over it.

"You managed to find *this* thing in all that mess?" He snorted. "One broken, twisted husk of something vaguely pretending to be a woman out of hundreds. Meanwhile, I search for a corpse positively *bursting* with magical power and I find *nothing.*"

"You didn't find Sheraptus's body?" The tension in Asper's voice was palpable. "Does that mean—"

"It means I didn't find his body." He rubbed his eyes. "Or Bralston's. Thus, I walk away from this with *nothing.*"

"You've got your health," Denaos observed with a grin. "And with all the water that came, I bet you no one could even *tell* if you soiled yourself. Small blessings and all that."

And instantly, Asper saw the mask come back on. All the pain from his face was gone, hastily buried in whatever shallow grave he kept all those secrets and the terrified, pale little boy. Once again, he was smiling and beaming with no cares beyond what he could be drinking and who he could be groping.

Maybe this was the real him. Maybe what she had just seen was an act.

But she had saved him, whoever he was. With whatever she had.

No, she told herself. *No more whatevers. You know exactly what it is.* She stared at her hand. *You heard him speak to you. And he can hear you, the paper man said.* She paused, turned her thought upon herself like a knife. *Hello? Are you there?*

She reached out to him, the thing inside her. As she had reached out to Talanas before, as she had reached out to Taire. And there was silence, but not as she had heard before. No empty silence of a god gone deaf. A tense silence. A moment before a cat pounces upon a mouse. An instant between an awkward laugh and a long, slow kiss. A silence of someone there.

Listening.

And Asper quietly wondered if she would ever miss the days when she thought she was alone.

"Nothing but smoke and ashes."

She caught Dreadaeleon's mutter as the boy folded his hands behind his back and watched Xhai burn.

"You can break something like a living being down so thoroughly with only fire. When they're gone, they're nothing more than smoke and ashes. And yet, for some reason, the creature you loathed and that loathed you is made a pitiable and honorable thing when they're reduced so thoroughly." He snorted. "And by the envy of savages and bark-necks, our knowledge of life and death goes no further than that. A bunch of soot and dust is all we'll ever know."

"Look, if you were going to be all dour and depressing, why'd you even *come* to a funeral?" Denaos snapped.

"It's not as though I had anything better to do. Gariath is off being hailed as a hero for slaying that colossal fish. Lenk and Kataria are being hailed as slayers of demons. People with no knowledge beyond how to swing a heavy piece of metal are heroes and I . . ." He narrowed his eyes. "I am here."

"You can't be serious," Asper said. "We stop a threat to the mortal world, kill a beast that wasn't even supposed to *exist*, somehow come out of it alive and you're upset that no one paid enough attention to you?"

"It just seems a little unfair is all."

"Well, it's not like you didn't get anything out of it," Denaos chimed in.

"Didn't I? I couldn't find Bralston's body, either. The only person remotely worthy of a graceful disposal of his corpse and he's washed away on the tide. The Venarium will not be pleased."

"The Venarium will be one item on a formalized list of guests warmly invited to suck the hairiest parts of my anatomy," Denaos said, folding his hands above his head as he turned back to the pyre. "We're alive, miracu- 473 lously." He shot a sideways glance to Asper, who looked away. "And we're here. The only three humans in a world filled with talking lizards and dead fish-things."

"Three?" Asper lofted a brow. "What about Lenk?"

"If everything Lenk says is true, it's beyond a miracle that he's alive. It's suspicious. And if everything we saw him do in the battle, what with the turning gray thing and speaking in tongues, then . . ."

A frown creased his face.

"Whatever he is, he's not one of us."

They said nothing more. The fire filled the silence with solemn chatter, crackling and hissing as it slowly carried Xhai away and into the sky on a cloud of smoke and ashes.

"Right here."

Shalake put his foot down on the earth. It was damp and moist under his scales, the water having reached this far into the forest.

"It was going to have happened right here." He pointed to either side of the clearing. "See, it's not a far journey from the wall or the ring. But that's not the important part." He pointed up, to the moonlight shining through the crack in the coral canopy. "The moon shines through here just so."

He walked to one of the openings. "In my mind, it's always on the walls. I'm repelling some great invasion force. I'm full of arrows. But I've left far more dead behind me and my brothers lived because of me." He took long, trudging steps toward the center of the clearing. "I limp here and stagger." He demonstrated, leaning on his tooth-studded club. "I can go no farther. All the years of service and bloodshed have taken their toll. I look up to heaven."

He did so. The shadows of the coral branches blended with the black stripes of his warpaint to paint him almost pitch-black.

"And I whisper my last words." He sighed, kneeling upon the earth, letting his club fall. "And then, I die. Right here on the ground. One with Jaga forever."

Gariath watched impassively, crouched on his haunches atop a large stone. Shalake's one good eye glimmered with mist. His other was wrapped tightly behind a bandage.

"The thing is, I never knew what my last words were going to be. To my father, to Mahalar . . . maybe the oaths I swore when I became a warwatcher. Just one more time." He stared at his footprint in the damp earth. "And when I finally had the chance to utter them . . . I said nothing. I did nothing. My brothers were all dead and I couldn't remember what the oaths were."

He looked to Gariath.

"Isn't that strange?"

Gariath rose up. The wounds he had taken just three days ago were already looking old, the foundation for good scars. His eyes were older, darker than a week-long night, as they looked down at Shalake.

"It wasn't your death."

"What?"

"The oaths you took were not yours. The words you spoke were someone else's. When the time came for your last words, you had none of your own to give."

"What do you mean?"

Gariath's voice became a growl. "You wanted to die like a *Rhega*. But you're not a *Rhega*." He held out his hands. "You can no more die someone else's death than you can live his life."

"I don't understand."

"*WHY THE HELL NOT?*" The roar tore itself out from somewhere deep in his chest. "Why can't you understand? Why is it every time I try to explain this, no one seems to be able to figure it out? Everyone always just says 'what' or 'huh' or 'wow, Gariath, what the hell does a *Rhega* even do?' And then *I* have to say that a *Rhega* charges onto a giant fish-thing on the off-chance it might save some *humans* while the green-skinned cowards that were *supposed* to be like him skulk and cry and weep about not dying gloriously."

Shalake's lip curled backward in a sneer. He mustered as much indignation as he could with one eye. "You dare call us cowards?"

"You fled."

"*We were wiped out!*"

"You were given death. Was it not as glorious as you hoped it would be?"

"Ah, how wonderful for the glorious *Rhega* to honor me not in battle, but in lecture." Shalake spat. "You intend to try to tell *me* the weight of death? My brothers and friends are dead. My leader is dead."

"And all you can think about is how you could say nothing for it. No goodbyes, no great monologues, no answers from ancestors or ghosts to tell you you did good. No words. That's true death."

"*True* death? And you claim *I* give it too much glory? I saw death today, *Rhega*. I saw two hundred corpses and they all looked exactly the same." He thrust a finger at Gariath. "*You* carry death on your shoulders like it was your son. *You* ran off into battle without a second thought for us. Those who knew you, your people."

"You knew only songs." Gariath snarled. "You knew legends." His eyes narrowed. "And until I came here, I realize that's all I knew, too. I came here expecting to find a ghost, a scent of memory, an answer from death. But I can smell only water and death now. Do you know why?"

"Possibly because of all the water and death."

Gariath glared at him before leaning down to the earth. "There's no blood here. There's no scent here. There are no ghosts here. The *Rhega* who were here took everything they needed when they left to the afterlife. They had no need to stay behind. In their deaths, they did all that they needed to.

"I thought that was impossible. How could anyone die without having regrets? How could anyone die without sorrow for the sons he lost?" He drew in a breath, found it sweet and coppery on the back of his tongue. He blinked moisture from his eyes. "Maybe some never do. And maybe some just turn their sorrow into rage. But there are others who do what they need to when they need to. And when they die doing it, they don't linger.

"Not all deaths are the same," Gariath said. "Some of them last forever."

Shalake's good eye reflected a pain not present even when the other had a shard of bone stuck in it.

"And that's who you would die for? Not us, who know your songs. Not the closest thing to a *Rhega* you will ever see. But humans. Weak, stupid humans who stand for nothing but gold."

"Yeah."

The moment he said it, some unconscious part of Gariath wanted to punch himself squarely in the face.

"Yeah. For them."

Shalake opened his mouth to ask for justification. Gariath's glare silenced him. Fortunate, the dragonman thought. It was difficult to justify that which was barely understood, much less what was painful to say.

But between the two creatures that shared scaly skin, between their clawed hands that clenched into scarred fists, in the barest space between the point where their easy scowls and easier rage clashed in the air, the knowledge was there.

The knowledge that, when the bodies lay dying, Gariath had made his choice.

Shalake raised his weapon. Through it all, it had lost only a few teeth. The club's wood was strong and uncracked, despite the skulls that couldn't claim the same. He held it out in front of him and dropped it in the sand.

"Where we go from here," he said simply, "we will need no more old and dead things."

Gariath watched him go. Gariath looked up at the moonlight pouring down from the sky. A storm cloud, perhaps very late to the party that had raged days ago, rolled over, obscuring the light.

And Gariath stood in the darkness, alone.

THIRTY-SEVEN
EMPTY AND BEREFT

The beach was warm under his feet. The sun was shining. He smiled for a moment, savoring it all, save the feeling of sand crawling insistently up his rear end. He yawned, stretching his arms over his head. He paused.

It didn't hurt.

He looked to his arm and saw it whole, unscarred. He looked down the rest of his naked body, saw no wounds or blood. He laid his head back on the sand and cursed.

"Oh, come *on!*"

"What's wrong?"

He rose, turned around and saw her there. Clad all in black, despite the shining sun. A sword at her hip, long and white like her hair. Eyes as blue as the sky overhead and concern etched across her hard-lined face.

"This was supposed to be over."

"What?"

"This," he said, flailing out over the beach. "These weird dreams that only a crazy person would have."

She looked around the beach. "Plenty of people dream of warm shores and sunshine. What's so weird about it?"

"Aside from the fact that I'm talking to a woman I've only heard in my dreams, who is standing wearing pure black on a beach I wasn't standing on an hour ago, but upon which I now stand, hale and hearty, despite having wounds that threatened to kill me?" He shook his head. "I'm naked."

"What, you've never dreamed of yourself naked before?"

"Not when I'm alone."

"But I'm here."

"Which brings me back to my original point. Why are you here? I thought these dreams were from the voice and that's gone, right?"

She pointedly looked at her feet.

"*Right?*"

She cleared her throat and looked up with a sheepish smile.

"Kind of," she replied.

"Oh, son of a—" He slapped a hand over his face, dragging it down. "I can't even lie quietly with the threat of soiling myself from agony without something psychotic happening. I abandoned the voice."

"But then you brought it back."

"*But then I got rid of it again,*" he snarled. "I threw it away and I haven't heard from it for a week . . . or . . . like, two weeks. It's hard to keep track at sea." He pointed affirmatively to the ground. "Point being, *this* crap is supposed to be over."

"Oh, look at you," she said, smirking, "all upset that a crazy voice in your head that tells you to kill demons isn't making sense." She sighed. "The reason you're dreaming of me is the same reason you were able to call upon it. Him, rather. He never really leaves."

"What? Never?"

"He's a part of you. As much as you are of him. He invested his power in you and can't be separated that easily."

"I never wanted that."

"Well, no shit you didn't want that. None of us did. But he chose us, regardless. And we do what he wants us to."

"But . . ." Lenk rubbed his head. "I heard other voices. The people in the ice, telling me things. But there was one that told me not to hurt Kataria, that it wouldn't—" His eyes widened upon her. "You. You told me that."

"I did."

"But you said we did—"

"He only wanted you to kill her because you were getting distracted from what he wanted. You fought him over her. Naturally, he wanted her gone. But you denied him, again and again."

"And now he's . . . what? Sleeping?"

"To be honest, I have no idea. No one's ever really *done* that to him. He might be gone, he might be away, he might be trying to figure out how to control you to pull your own testicles out through your nose."

"So, what, you came here just to tell me that?"

"I came here because I was worried about you. I wanted you to be safe and happy. Because there really aren't that many of us left and the ones who are tend not to live long. We're either cast out and killed by people or murdered by demons when we're old enough to fight them."

"What, there are other demons?"

"Obviously. They've been around for ages, privately plotting against each other, striving to be the one to come in and assume total power over mortality. Now, there's one fewer." She chuckled. "Of course, that means the others just have one more obstacle removed and are that much closer to enslaving us all, but don't let that bring you down."

Lenk blinked and looked down at his feet. "So . . . what happens now?"

"It isn't really something I can tell you. You don't have anyone telling you what to do anymore." She turned around and shrugged. "I suppose your will and your fate are your own." She frowned. "I envy you a little."

"Why a little?"

"Because you might die from your wounds and he won't be around to help you."

"Oh." He stared at the ground as she walked away, down the shore. Then, a thought struck him. "Wait. I could hear you . . . and I could hear the dead people in the ice. I can't hear them anymore, but—"

She smiled impishly over her shoulder. "I guess I must not be dead, then." She looked up, as though she could read something in the cloudless sky. "You're going to want to wake up now."

"But I've still got—"

"Trust me on this one."

And she continued walking, fading into nothingess in the span of three breaths against a sun growing brighter.

He awoke with a start, though only by habit. He simply couldn't remember how people usually woke up. Maybe that was something he would have to learn again.

Unless he died from his wounds. Which still hurt as he rose onto his elbows. He thought briefly about rousing Asper to check his stitches, salve and bandage regimen. But a quick look at her, curled up in sleep with her back to Denaos and Dreadaeleon wedged in rather rigidly nervous sleep between them, discouraged him. Gariath hunched over at the rudder, quietly dozing above the satchels of fruits, fish, and water the Shen had sent them on their way with.

They slept a tired, dreamless slumber for the weary and the wounded.

Most of them, anyway.

479

At the prow of the boat, she lay, arms over the railing, head tilted backward staring aimlessly up at the sky. Only the rise of breath in her belly and the twitching of her ears suggested that she was alive.

She was not a beautiful sight, not ethereal or mysterious. Her skin did not glisten in the moonlight, though the beads of sweat upon her body shimmered. Her hair hung in dirty, messy strands about eyes lined with weariness. Her muscles were tense, her body hard and unyielding, those parts not covered in bandages or filthy leathers. Her ears were scarred with ugly notches. Her curves were small and hostile. Her skin, bandaged and not, was coated in grime and sweat.

She was Kataria. And every part of her was bloody, dirty, and beautiful. And she hadn't spoken to him in a week.

He hadn't pressed her. Most of his time had been spent getting treated by Asper, arguing with Denaos over the sea chart, or trying to break up fights over who had to look which way when it was someone's turn to make water.

In all that time, she hadn't so much as looked at him.

But the woman in his dreams had told him to wake up. He was awake now. And she was there.

He edged over to her, trying not to wince with the effort. He hesitated when he drew close to her, then he opened his mouth to speak. Her hand shot up.

"Not yet," she whispered. "You should hear this."

He waited. She didn't say anything. He looked around as her ears went erect.

"Hear . . . what?"

"Wait until she comes close." She pointed over the edge. "There."

A great shadow of some old fish, vast and with a horizontal tail like an axe blade, slid beneath the surface. And so close, Lenk thought he could hear it. A low, keening wail. A long, lonely dirge.

"She's singing," Kataria said. "She's the only sound down there. I don't think there's any fish left in these waters." She frowned. "Maybe that's why she sounds sad."

"Because there's nothing left for her?"

And then, she looked at him with two eyes. In one, there was the way she had always looked at him, with the fondness, with the laughter, with the curiosity. And in the other, there was the way she had looked through him, with the fear, with the anger, with the cold appraisal of a predator sizing up prey.

Between them, there was something else entirely that she looked at him with. And he stared straight at it.

"Because something happened," he said, "and whatever was supposed to happen, didn't, and now everything's changed. And she's not sure what happens now."

She looked down at the deck and drew her knees up to her chest.

"Yeah. Something like that."

A long silence passed. The waters chopped at the boat's side.

"What do you think you'll do when we get back to the mainland?" she asked.

"My original plan was to get paid, take the money, and go hack dirt somewhere until I die," he replied. "Maybe that won't happen again. But I want to find somewhere to hang up my sword."

"Liar."

"What makes you say that?"

"You've lost that sword a hundred times and it keeps finding you," she said. "If you hang it up, it'll just come back. You keep calling to it."

He looked at it, sitting in its sheath next to the tome. "Maybe I'll put it to better use."

"Than what? Killing? What else is it going to do?"

"I don't know. Guard duty or something. Something good."

"There are only a few good things you can do with a sword," she said, frowning. "And none of them involve what you do with it." Slowly, her eyes became one, full of doubt, full of fear. "Do you want to kill forever?"

He found himself hesitating before answering. Of course, he didn't want to kill forever. But could he? Even without the voice, she was right. The sword returned to him. And he never hesitated to call it.

"Say no," she said.

"No."

"Liar."

"It's the truth."

"No, because you can't answer it truthfully. You don't want to kill, but you're not going to have a lot of choice. What you are . . ." Her voice drifted off, she struggled to find the words, much less speak them. "You're . . . I don't know. All this and I still don't know anything about you except one thing."

He didn't ask. Not with his mouth.

"I . . ." The words came slow and painful. "I feel . . . *things.*"

He blinked.

"Things."

"And they make me scared. And they made me scared in the chasm when I shot Naxiaw to save you. And they made me scared when you touched me. And they make me scared now that I'm talking to you, because I'm not sure what they are and I don't know what they make me and I don't know what I'm going to do because I have them."

He didn't have an answer. No answer he could voice, anyway. Because everything he could say would only convince himself of the obvious: that she was a shict, that he was a human, that there were differences that went beyond ears and that he had almost killed her over them.

Because whatever the voice had told him, he had listened. Whatever the voice had asked him, he had agreed. Whatever part of him that had wanted to hurt her . . . was part of him. Not a voice.

She would be safer without him. She could go back to her tribe, tell them she had made a mistake.

"You should go," he said. "Go back."

"No."

"It's for the—"

"Sorry, but are you of the impression I don't mean what I say when I say it?" She snarled, baring canines. "I'm not going back. And if you bring it up again, I'll eat your eyes."

"Oh. Okay, then."

"Sorry, it's just . . . I can't go back. Because of these things. Not all of them are about you. I . . . maybe I am a shict. I've got the ears and I'm good with a bow. But there's some part of me that isn't. And if I go there, I'll feel . . ."

She sighed, rubbed her eyes.

"But if I stay, we'll never stop killing. Shicts, humans, whatever else. They're still my family. They're still people. I can kill them, sure, but after this . . . whole thing with the tome." She looked up at the sky. "There was just so much blood."

There was nothing he could say to that. Everything he could say would just be confirmation. Everything he might suggest would end in "you can't stay." And every whisper he could make would be desperate and end in "please don't go."

Strong men would say "leave."

Good men would say "watch, I'll throw my sword overboard for you."

Wise men would say nothing at all.

"I . . . you . . . it's hard."

Lenk said this.

"Because everything about you is hard. The way you look at me, the way you talk to me, the way I am . . ." He rubbed the back of his neck. "It's all hard. It was hard when I met you. It's never not going to be hard and even when it's not, it's going to be painful."

"So why do it?"

"Because I don't have anything else. I'm not talking about family or something like that, either. I just don't . . . know what else to do besides fight and kill. Even when I say I'm going to go to a farm, it all sounds fake, like something I'm never going to ever see and I can just keep talking about it like that makes me better for wanting it."

She was looking at him now. Hard. Her stare was unbearable. But he couldn't look away from her. Her eyes, even in the darkness, seemed huge. And the more he looked at them, the larger they seemed. They grew to take him in and they became everything, her eyes.

"But then you look at me. And then I touch you. And then I smell you. And there's something else there, besides killing and fighting. And I want that more than ever. And I'll do whatever it takes to hold onto it."

He reached out and took her hand. He pulled her to him. She slid onto her belly, against his body, her back curving and her body sliding into the slope of his as though she always belonged there from the very beginning. He could feel the breath in her stomach, the scent on her hair, the fear in her eyes.

And it hurt.

"So . . . just tell me what that is. I'll figure out the rest."

There was nothing they could have said. Nothing he could say to allay their fears. Nothing she could say to convince him this was a good idea. Nothing that came on words that were too full of things that would make them be afraid.

And so he drew her closer to him.

And she leaned into him.

And he felt her breath fill him and she felt the callouses on his hands against her back and they felt themselves slide into each other as though they had always been supposed to do that.

And he closed his eyes.

And she closed hers.

And she laid her head upon his chest.

And he held her.

And they said nothing.

THIRTY-EIGHT

I MISSED YOU, TOILETS

"They were not good people. They were not moral people. They were not of particular fiber but for the sinew that fueled their often-misguided deeds." Knight-Serrant Quillian Guisarne-Garrett Yanates lowered her head, placing a bronze gauntlet to her breastplate. "But they were, indeed, children of the Gods. And at least one of them was definitely a priestess, questionable though her choices might be, so that should at least earn them a little favor. So . . . you know . . . have fun in hell."

She turned and flashed a smile beneath a tattoo under her right eye. The dark-skinned man with the bald head and the well-made clothes seemed less than impressed.

"It loses something toward the end," Argaol said.

"Like what?"

"Like any semblance of sanity or dignity."

"They're lucky they're getting this much from me," Quillian replied with a sneer. "I doubt there are two people in the world that would give an elegy for a group of unsanitary adventurers, let alone practice it."

"For there to be a funeral, there need to be bodies."

"Several weeks missing? In that tiny boat? No word from Sebast or anyone we've sent after them? In the absence of a body, I opt for logic." She glanced at the shorter man in the even-better-made clothes next to Argaol. "From what I understand, we have little choice."

The harbormaster of Port Destiny glared at her. "I'm simply saying, as I was before you went off and did . . . *that*, that you have no bodies so you can have no funerals, so your request to stay in port without extra charge has been denied."

"And as I was telling *you*," Argaol replied, "it's out of my hands. The charter doesn't want to leave yet, so we don't leave."

"And where is the charter? This . . ." The harbormaster flipped through a ledge. "Miron Evenhands."

"*Lord Emissary* Miron Evenhands," Quillian corrected. "You speak of a member of good standing of the Church of Talanas and would do well to remember that."

"And said character is somewhere . . . out there."

Argaol swept a hand out toward the distant city, its spires rising from the blue sands of the island and sprawling well past its boundaries into the ocean, a city standing on rocks and pillars carved by someone that no one cared to remember or honor.

"He went there a week ago and hasn't come out of the city since. We checked the temples, the inns. He's got some kind of sense that lets him know when people he owes money are coming, I don't know."

"The charter you signed made it perfectly clear that you couldn't keep a vessel like *this*," the harbormaster said, gesturing to the great three-masted vessel moored next to them, "without the fees."

"Yeah, whatever," Argaol grunted. "You can take it up with his bodyguard."

"It's been *well* past the date we agreed to meet up with the adventurers," Quillian replied with a shrug. "The Lord Emissary insists on waiting longer out of compassion, but he is a reasonable man. Within a few days' time, he'll come to terms with the fate of the heathens and we'll be on our way."

"Then you'll pay for those days and however many more it takes for you to wait," the harbormaster insisted. "The concerns of Talanas or his emissaries are not mine and—"

"And?" Quillian punctuated the question with the gentle clink of a bronzed gauntlet resting on the pommel of a longsword.

The harbormaster eyed her blade carefully for a moment. "I'm a civil servant, Serrant. There is little you can do to me that life already hasn't."

"There will be no need for any of that."

Austere and pure as a specter, Miron Evenhands glided across the dock. Tall and stately, he walked through a press of dockhands and sailors toting loads to their ships without so much as brushing against them. His white robes remained bright and untarnished by salt, water, or more unsavory substances around the dock. His smile was soft and benevolent, as though he were meeting his granddaughter instead of interrupting impending violence.

"Will there be a need for getting answers? Because I might like that," the harbormaster said as Miron walked between them.

"All shall be answered in time," the Lord Emissary replied, his gaze cast out over the harbor waters.

"And in the time it takes, there's the matter of the coin—"

"In much more humble terms, I must concur with the heathen, Lord Emissary," Quillian interrupted. "The adventurers are long dead and their mission doubtlessly failed. Our time would be better served formulating a secondary strategy for the procurement of the tome."

"I didn't mind them so much, but this is costing me some money, Even-hands," Argaol chimed in. "And she's probably right. They're probably dead. Eaten. Whatever. It's just not practical to wait any longer."

"Faith often contradicts practicality," Miron replied. "And for this, the faithful are rewarded."

"With coin, I hope," the harbormaster grumbled.

"Something much better," Miron replied.

The smile upon his face grew broader. He took a slow, deliberate step to the side to reveal the shape. A small, black dot on the horizon growing closer until it took shape. A boat, six bodies aboard, rowing tirelessly toward the harbor.

"The knowledge that the Gods do, occasionally, listen. Even if it takes a few weeks of praying."

"That and the opportunity to look as smug as a bloody—" the harbor-master grunted as Quillian delivered a stiff elbow to him.

The vessel rowed its way forward, a reeking cloud of stench heralding the arrival like several cherubs possessed of indigestion. It was fitting for the rabble that clawed its way off the ship with a few weapons, clothes stained white with salt, hair stiff from dried sweat, bodies in various stages of disre-pair and all eyes sunken.

Lenk was alive in name only. But that was enough for him to stand before Miron as he held up the satchel.

"Here."

His voice came on a very soft breath. "Is that . . ."

"Uh huh. Doom of the world, key to heaven, all that good stuff."

Miron accepted it with eyes wide. "I must admit, in some part of me, I doubted you could actually retrieve it." His whispers were reverent, eerily so. "I prayed, of course. But how could a man pray to Gods to retrieve an item they so loathed? How could a man ask for that which could unmake their cre-ation? How could—"

"Hey." Lenk cleared his throat. "I haven't bathed in a couple of weeks now." 487

Miron looked at him blankly.

"Just . . . thought you should know," Lenk said, "before you got going there. So . . . we're going to go remember why outhouses are made with only enough room for one person, if you know what I mean."

"I do not."

"Well, think about it for a while. I don't really have the time and you don't have the stomach for me to paint a picture," the young man said, pushing past. "Just point us to wherever you're staying and we'll catch up real soon. You know, after everyone's bathed and eaten things that don't taste like insoles."

"Wouldn't have had that problem if you had just heard me out," Denaos said, tossing a sack out of the vessel and climbing onto the dock. "It's not like it was a bad idea."

"Cannibalism is not typically noted as a traditional second resort after the meat runs out," Dreadaeleon replied as a spell carried him up and over the rogue's head and onto the dock.

"We could have had a more thorough discussion of it if we hadn't all argued who'd be eating who."

"Who'd be eating *whom*."

"And that's why everyone decided we'd eat you first," the rogue muttered. He glanced to Lenk. "Did he tell you where we're bedding down or what? Some of us need baths."

"Some of us desperately so," Asper replied, glaring over her shoulder as she crawled onto the dock.

Kataria came bounding up after her, teeth bared in a snarl. "If you were intimidated by a shict's natural odor, you should have thought of that before you decided to stay in a boat for weeks with one."

"I didn't have a choice *or* an issue with your aroma . . ." Asper cringed at the memory. "Not until you started . . . *rubbing* yourself on things."

"Well, how do *you* let people know what's yours, if you're so damn smart?" The shict snorted, sneering at her. "Kept you from touching my share of the food, at least."

"And mine," Asper muttered.

"Should've said something. Or rubbed something." Kataria snarled. "Can we feed little miss 'can't-eat-something-that-someone-else-touched,' then?"

"We will as soon as Miron tells us," Lenk snapped. "Which would help if everyone could just stop being the center of attention for a moment and let the man speak."

They looked expectantly to the Lord Emissary, who in turn nodded to the harbormaster. "We will be at sea within the hour, sir. You have my thanks for your generosity."

"Wait . . . what?"

"Yes, if you wouldn't mind adjourning to the *Riptide*, I'll be happy to fill you in," Miron said, looking to Argaol. "Would you kindly rally your crew, captain?"

"This isn't funny," Lenk said.

"Unfortunately, the only thing keeping us here was your absence," Miron replied. "With your timely arrival, we may finally depart."

"I just spent . . . *weeks* at sea, Miron. I put *things* that came out of me into the ocean."

"And now you'll at least have larger accommodations."

Lenk held up a hand to silence the unrest fomenting behind him. "Fine. We'll do this. We'll go back aboard the ship. But out of protest, we're not bathing for another day."

Denaos leaned over to the young man. "Did . . . that sound like a better threat in your head?"

"Shut up and come on," Lenk sighed, trudging off toward the ship with his companions in tow.

"One moment!" The harbormaster cried after them, flailing at the tiny vessel. "You can't leave something like this docked here! Not without signing, not without a fee!"

"Gariath will handle it."

The dragonman hauled himself onto the dock before the harbormaster could ask. Wordlessly, he pushed past the assembled to the far end of the dock and returned dragging a freshly-polished anchor behind him. With a heft, a grunt, and a snarl, he tossed it onto the deck of their vessel. There was a loud crack, then a sputtering sound.

"Handled," Gariath growled, turning to stalk toward the ship with the others.

"It won't be poor accommodations," Miron said, walking alongside Lenk. "Goodness knows you've been through enough. We'll arrange for private cabins . . . or one, at least. And food. You've done us a great service, Lenk, and are to be rewarded justly."

"As I recall, the reward is just about one thousand coins," Lenk said. "Gold. *Un*sealed. No kings or gods or birds or crap on them. I want to be able to spend them in any nation I happen to feel the need to get drunk in."

"And you shall have the full amount," Miron said, voice dipping, "in time."

Lenk came to a halt. "What?"

The Lord Emissary's smile turned sheepish. "There were expenses, I'm afraid, that had to come from somewhere. And Port Destiny is largely Zamanthran. Rest assured, when we return to the mainland and to a proper temple of Talanas, we'll be able to—"

"How much?"

"Pardon?"

"How much can you give me now?"

Miron smiled. "Well . . ."

489

"Thirty."

Denaos stared at him for a long moment from across the table. "Sorry, I couldn't hear you. I think I had a *if you think I'm going to take that crap I will gut you like a fish* in my ear."

"The deal was for one thousand," Asper said, wincing. "Granted, I wasn't keen on taking money from the church and I was planning on giving it all back, anyway, but to make the gesture would have been nice."

"Well, *I* had plans," Kataria muttered. "Plans that involved me replacing a bow I lost while I was out nearly *dying* for the pious moron who was supposed to pay us."

"This does seem like duplicity," Dreadaeleon said. "My share was going to go toward research, fees for the Venarium, that sort of thing. How am I to get anything done with *five* coins to my name?"

"Four, actually," Lenk said. He tapped the bottle at the center of the table. "This stuff is actually supposed to be pretty good, according to the smelly gentleman I bought it from."

"And is it?"

"I haven't tasted it yet."

"You spent five coins on a bottle of whiskey," Kataria said, "without knowing what it tastes like."

"He was *very* smelly. I assumed he was a drunk. So, I figured he probably knew what was good enough to smuggle out of Argaol's hold."

Denaos blinked, struggling to find words. "I mean . . . that's *kind of* logical, but—"

"*And* I wanted to celebrate," Lenk said. "I mean . . . we're alive, right? We succeeded in what we set out to do. We retrieved the Tome of the Undergates, stopped a demonic incursion—"

"We set out to get paid, technically," Dreadaeleon corrected him. "Adventurers, and all."

"So, we *procedurally* succeeded, shut up," Lenk spat. "And we owe ourselves a drink for it." He all but tore the cork from the bottle and downed a long, slow swig. When he set the bottle back down, they were staring at him curiously. "What?"

"I feel you're acting like we've accomplished more than we have," Asper said. "No matter what happens next, whether we all stay together or go our separate ways, we're still adventurers, still not exactly a respectable trade."

"Which might affect the glory of this whole thing," Dreadaeleon said. "Not a single one of the sailors believed me when I told them what happened. Nor would I fault them for doing so."

"We left behind a lot of dead bodies and a couple of races previously unknown by most cultures that join those same cultures in hating us," Kataria said, slumping in her seat. "We . . . did things on those islands."

"So, when you get down to it," Denaos added, "we went out to the middle of nowhere, nearly killed ourselves, came back with terrible injuries that will probably last us a lifetime, somehow managed to earn the wrath of *several* races through the actions of six people, all for the sum of thirty—"

"Twenty-five."

"*Twenty-five* gold coins and to possibly spare a world that loathed us a gigantic demon eating them alive, which they wouldn't believe we did, anyway." He looked around the table. "Have I got that right?"

"Roughly," Asper said.

"Yeah," Kataria grunted.

"More or less," Dreadaeleon sighed.

"So, why should we be celebrating?"

Lenk had no answer. He looked at himself, wounded and hurting. He looked at his sword, resting in the corner of the cabin and ready to be called back. He looked back in his mind and saw the Abysmyths latching onto their mother and calling to her.

And he wondered if he had done anything more than kill a mother trying to reunite with her children because someone in a robe told him to.

He had no answer.

Someone else did. That someone rousted himself from his cot and with slow, lumbering steps, came to the tiny table of their tiny cabin and sat down in a chair that was tiny for him. Gariath leaned on it, the wood groaning beneath his weight. He stared at the bottle for a moment, as though he expected it to come alive at any moment and give him a profound answer.

When nothing came, he reached over as if to strangle it and took it by its neck. He looked at each of them, in turn.

"Because this," he said, "is all that we have. And it is something solid."

He threw his head back and poured the liquid down his gullet. His nostrils flared. His earfrills fanned out. He snorted, passed it to Lenk.

"This tastes like shit."

THE GRAY MAN AND HIS LONG TEETH

The Aeons' Gate
The Sea of Buradan

To my most esteemed colleague,

It may grieve you to hear of the loss of Sheraptus and his warriors. It most certainly may grieve you to know that the vast majority of his knowledge on the manipulation of portals went to the grave with him. You undoubtedly know by now that our agents were unable to retrieve anything from his operations on Komga but bodies and a flimsy gate he used to enter.

Comparatively, the loss of the martyr stones he loved so well may seem a trifle.

Still, I must urge you to look at this as a gain for us. Ulbecetonth is dead. This is certain. And her brood and consort and prophet followed her back into hell. I can sense no more of her taint in this world. It is of little consequence that Sheraptus's hand was not the one that struck the final blow, as was intended.

It may even be to our boon that it was not. I know you were originally skeptical of my decision to send adventurers as insurance should Sheraptus fail—and for this, I will expect more deliberate thought given to my ideas in the future—but I presume you take no issue with the results of their handiwork, admittedly sloppy.

Regardless, the item is once again in my possession. I make for Cier'Djaal at once and shall rejoin you in ample time.

I anticipate the guise may have to be left behind, unfortunately. While Toha is far enough removed from civil society that the nation of the House of the Vanquishing Trinity is easy enough to believe, it will be harder to masquerade as a Lord Emissary of a nonexistent organization in a more populous area.

You will have questions, undoubtedly. I will provide answers. With one more obstacle removed, our goals are that much closer. I can speak only for myself, as I ever do, but I view any loss as acceptable so long as it brings us closer to our goal of awakening these mortals to the reality of their situation and the blindness of their gods.

Yours,
A.M.

493

When he was done, Miron set aside his quill and inkwell. He neatly folded his letter into thirds and placed it in an envelope. He dripped a bit of wax upon it and let it dry before holding it to his lips and muttering something in the old words from the old speakers.

And then he turned to his window.

The creature perched there looked at him without eyes. A woman's face, gentle and curved, rested on her hands. Behind her, a bulbous abdomen quivered beneath a pair of moth wings. Those wings rose, the eye spots upon them blinked. She spoke through teeth contorted into a permanent smile.

"It goes?"

"It goes," Miron replied, handing the letter to the creature. "Far away and you know where."

"I cannot forget. Ever." Its eyes drifted to the book, the flat black square upon the table. "This goes?"

"This stays. You go."

"I go."

And with that, the creature took the envelope and fluttered away into the night. Miron did not bother to watch it go. He had watched it go many times and always had it found its way. The Laments had their way of going unnoticed.

That was no worry for him, either. He had more pressing concerns.

The book. The tome. The key to everything. Despite everything else he had ever spoken of, he had been earnest when he said he doubted the adventurers. Even knowing Lenk to be what he was, he had doubted the man's ability to deliver.

Maybe it had been that inside him that had delivered it. Maybe it was something else, something mortal.

Little problems for little men.

He had a vision.

And now, he had the means to realize it. He slid his hands over the tome. The change came almost instinctually, reaching out to the words in the book as they reached out to him. His skin slid off of his hands, his fingers suddenly too large for it. Gray flesh shone stark like stone in the firelight. He felt his lips peel over themselves, his teeth too large for his mouth.

He felt his hands tighten around the book as it whispered to him. As it told him all the great things he may accomplish, all that he was doing was good.

It spoke to him.

And Azhu-Mahl answered.

ABOUT THE AUTHOR

S AM SYKES is an author. You probably already figured that out, since you've just read his book, though. Unless you skipped right to the end? Shame on you. Or did you skip right to the About the Author page? That's weird. I'm not sure why you would do that. Nobody reads these things.

And since nobody reads these things, I can say pretty much anything I want to back here. And you know something? I really don't care for manatees *at all*.

Sam Sykes is 28. He lives in Arizona. He can eat most animals alive.